For my parents.

This is your fault.

WINDBORN

ALEX S. BRADSHAW

CHAPTER ONE
A GLUT OF PLUNDER

THE LONGSHIP WAS TOO SMALL.

Men and women, stained from our raid, dripped sweat and worse onto the wet sand. They shouted and pointed, trying to be the first to load their spoils.

The taste of blood still bothered me and I turned back to the small waves clawing at my feet. As I crouched down to wash the blood from my face, the taste of salt seeped past my lips to mix with the iron. I spat a glob of blood and seawater onto the sand. Up and down the shoreline others did the same. We stained the sea red.

"Edda."

I splashed another handful of water on my face before I stood and faced Atli.

"What is it?" I snapped. This was our first rest in what felt like forever and we were about to be stuck together on a sea voyage for five days, if we were lucky, longer if we weren't. Ask any raider and they will tell you their last moments of solitude are precious.

"Go and get Bjolfur," he said and pinched the bridge of his nose.

I pushed myself to my feet and stormed over to the longship. It was beached in a sheltered cove near to the temple we had raided. The temple was too large for us to raid alone, but we had joined forces with other longships who had beached themselves further along the shore. Each of them would be hauling their plunder onto their ships and making ready to leave before nightfall.

The argument had grown more heated, and the air was

1

heavy with a tension that suggested bloodshed was a single misstep away. I sighed as I heard my husband in the middle of it, his voice the loudest, and saw him jab a finger at the raid leader.

"—need to get home. We took the hostages to put them to work. We shouldn't wait to see if anyone comes to ransom them back. We need to sail."

A chorus of agreement from the fighters behind him.

Malka, our raid leader, raised a hand to try and placate the crowd. "We should give them a few days to pay the bounties, Bjolfur. Gold is easier to carry across the sea. If they come for the captives by then, we should still be back with plenty of time for you to do your work on the farm."

Some of the others looked unsure. Whatever Bjolfur had told them, he likely hadn't told them the whole truth.

"I took my hostage to help me with the farm. What good is gold when I need to get the flock in for the winter?"

Malka balled her fists and looked around. She saw me and relief washed over her face.

"Can you talk to him?"

Bjolfur spun around but his anger faltered when he saw me. He looked ready to continue the argument regardless, but my arrival provided enough of a disruption and most of the onlookers had started to move away to collect their shields for the return journey. Bjolfur came over to me as he grumbled to himself. I took his hand and dragged him to the sea.

"She wants me to leave the hostage behind," he said as I bent and soaked a strip of cloth in the water.

"Do we really need an extra pair of hands on the farm?"

Bjolfur huffed. "You can never have too many hands."

"Maybe," I conceded and passed him the wet rag. "But we've managed fine so far. And if Malka takes the gold and silver instead of hostages then we'll be able to hire help. If we get enough gold we might even have enough to start our own farm."

He stopped washing his face and frowned at me. "We need help more than we need gold."

We looked at each other. His face shone with half-washed blood and dirt and there was a blunt tiredness in his eyes. It had been a long raiding trip and Bjolfur always worried about the farm, even if we were only away overnight.

I sighed and went to him. His arms fell around my waist and he rested his head on my chest. I leaned down and kissed the top of his head.

"If you keep arguing with her, Malka will never let us leave." I tugged softly on his braided beard. "And then it won't matter if we have extra help or not. We'll be stuck here, watching the winter storms. What'll happen to Scratcher or the rest of the chickens? To the sheep?"

Bjolfur scowled then kissed me. The taste of iron and salt pressed against my lips again.

"She wants to keep us waiting here, anyway. What do you suggest, wise wife of mine?"

I shoved him playfully. "Let's see if we can convince Malka to leave tomorrow. If they don't come to get their loved ones by then they probably never will, and if we leave any later then we risk winter storms."

Bjolfur looked unconvinced. He scrubbed his hands over the stubble on his head that had grown in the weeks we'd been raiding.

"Look, one day's delay won't matter and the longer we talk about this, the less likely we can set sail today anyway."

He stopped scrubbing his head and stared at the horizon through the gap in the cove's cliff walls.

Gulls laughed above us. People shouted to one another as they gathered supplies and weapons. At the other end of the cove, a larger longship slithered into the sea. Compared to our band of fighters their crew moved with a slick precision that they had mirrored on the battlefield.

"Fine," Bjolfur said, then slapped my hand. "Stop picking your scabs. They'll scar."

"I like my scars," I said. "They remind me of things. You see this one? I got this three years ago the last time we came raiding in Ertland."

"I remember," Bjolfur muttered. "Some fucker stuck you with a knife and was about to finish you off."

"And you leapt out of nowhere and killed him." I ran my thumb over the puckered skin with exaggerated affection. "It reminds me that you love me."

"Atli's wife is content with jewellery," Bjolfur said, shaking his head. "He gave her a gold ring last raiding season."

"I might lose a ring. Come on, let's talk to Malka."

After I had taken Bjolfur away, the dissidents dispersed to tend to their equipment. Malka and Atli were the only two people on board, moving sacks around to pack as much as they could into the small vessel. The line of twenty-seven bound captives huddled in the longship's shadow ducked their heads as we approached. Too many to fit comfortably on our longship, but they were hard-won and could fetch a pretty price.

"Malka!"

Bjolfur's voice echoed through the cove. Everyone glanced up like feasting crows from their carcass. For a little man, my husband can make a lot of noise. Two heads appeared above the shields hung over the side of the longship. Malka squinted against the setting sun, then rolled her eyes when she realised who it was.

"You were supposed to talk some sense into him, Edda," she called out and leapt down onto the sand.

Bjolfur bristled. I put a hand on his shoulder.

"I tried, but I think you need to reconsider what he's been saying."

Malka narrowed her eyes. "Edda, we took those hostages to be ransomed back. We have no room on the ship, and no room at home for them."

"Here we go again." Bjolfur threw his hands in the air. "You and Dagnur don't have room for them, maybe, but there's plenty of us who'd appreciate the help over winter. Try thinking for yourself instead of thinking like that gold-hungry bastard."

Malka took a step forward, putting Bjolfur into the shade of her bulk. "There'll be none of that talk, Bjolfur. This is Dagnur's ship and I'm his representative out here. You speak ill of him, you speak ill of me."

"Malka," I said, stepping between her and Bjolfur. "We've been out here for weeks. Dagnur wouldn't want us to get back so late we miss the harvest, or can't get our animals in, would he? All for a little extra gold?"

4

Malka bit her lip. She played absently with the ring of woven copper on her arm, the ring Dagnur had given her to show the oath sworn and loyalty owed. "We wait another three days for them to pay, one day for each of the sacred trees. Then we leave."

I could almost feel the heat behind me as Bjolfur's anger rose again.

"It's taken us longer than that to drag them back here," I said.

She looked at me. I saw the tension in her jaw loosen. We'd been on enough raids together to know that the longer you held hostages, the less likely it was their ransom was paid. She was wavering, and I was about to try and push her over the edge when a couple of rocks tumbled down from the nearby cliffs. Something about the stillness that followed made the hairs on the back of my neck stand on end. Malka felt it too. She straightened and looked away.

The beach was silent.

No one packed or spoke. Not even the gulls made a sound. Atli threw us our shields, then jumped from the longship and picked up a spear. We looked around, trying to find the source of our unease. All I could hear was the wind swirling in the cove and the rhythm of the waves, but years of raiding had taught me to trust my instincts and my fellow raiders. We gathered our weapons.

Something snapped. A tiny sound nearly lost under the quiet hiss of the sea. It came from the rocky path leading out of the cove. The path that led back to the temple.

We moved together without a word. Malka, Bjolfur, and I layered our round shields to make a shield wall as Atli moved behind us, ready to stab his spear over our shields at whoever came too close.

A bush beside the path twitched.

"Form up," Malka shouted out over the beach. "Shield wall."

Raiders all over the beach grabbed their weapons and scrambled toward us. A shout echoed out from the cove and caught the attention of the crews of the distant longships, though they were too far to tell what was happening.

Ahead of us, a warrior leapt from the bushes.

"For Edwyn," he cried and drew his sword.

As he ran forward more figures emerged from the shadows of the cliff path and joined the charge. Chain shirts and half helms glinted in the dim afternoon sun.

"Where were these fuckers when we attacked the temple?" Bjolfur muttered.

"They must have gone for help," I replied and slipped the knife from my belt.

More and more fighters spewed from the cliffs like a tide of steel and vengeance. Ertland had rallied its defenders, though some clutched woodcutting axes and wore no armour. There were so many, they threatened to overwhelm us with numbers alone.

"Shield wall!" Malka shouted, voice strained with urgency.

A few fellow raiders caught up to us and slammed into our shield wall. It wouldn't be enough.

The rest of our raiders sprinted across the sand. They wouldn't reach us in time. We had dragged the longship too far up the beach, our crew had gone too far in their need for solitude, and we would pay the price. The charging Ertlanders enveloped us like a sea serpent's jaws.

"Brace," Malka called.

We set our feet in the sand and they hit us.

The first charging warrior bounced off Bjolfur's shield. Atli stabbed at him, but the spear scraped off their chain shirt.

Someone rammed into my shield. The force of it pushed me back in the sand. I held firm.

A woman's face, mad with grief and rage, appeared above my shield. She reached over to bludgeon me with a hammer. I shoved her back and sank my iron knife into her gut as she fell. She screamed and crawled away.

Two more fighters battered my shield. Axes swung down at me. I ducked and their shafts bounced off my shield's rim.

"There's too many," Malka said. "Fall back to the longship."

As we tried to retreat the Ertlanders charged around the edges of our shield wall and cut us off from the longship. They slashed and stabbed at us from all sides. Atli cried out and went to a knee as an axe found his leg. He speared his attacker through the rib but another warrior took their place. We were stones in a river and the Ertlanders washed over us with murder in their hearts.

More raiders joined the fray. Too late to help the shield wall, but they evened the fight. The sounds of battle became mixed with cries of anger and pain as we sank iron teeth into our enemies.

Bjolfur and I pressed our backs together. Our shields swung wildly to try and deflect the mad horde's attacks. A knife slashed and I blocked. An axe hacked at Bjolfur and I twisted to save him.

Something clawed across my back, ripping easily through my shirt, tearing deep into my flesh. I yelled and spun to face my opponent. The man wore a light tunic and trousers, no armour. One of his arms hung bloody and limp at his side and in his good hand he held a small knife. He slashed at me. It was clumsy and I ducked to one side before my own knife tore out his throat. He put his good hand to his neck as though to keep the blood in, but it was too late. He was already dead.

People shoved at me as they rushed past to get to the hostages. I tried to stop them with knife slices and shield bashes, but there were too many.

The once quiet cove echoed with the cries of the dying and the laughter of gulls above us, waiting for the dead.

A hostage sprinted away from the longship. Rope still dangled from his wrists and ankles. He tried to leap through the gap between Bjolfur and me, but Bjolfur turned and caught him with his shield. The man scrambled up and jumped onto Bjolfur's shield. He clawed at Bjolfur's head and gouged bloody tracks across it.

I lunged and stuck my knife into his back. He yelled as I stabbed him again and again. Then, he screamed and dropped to the ground.

Before I could check on my husband, the man grabbed my shield and yanked. The force of it took me by surprise and I was pulled down to one knee.

I let go of my shield and slashed at him. The knife caught his chest, bouncing off his ribs before slicing into his jaw. He went down.

"Are you—" Bjolfur's question was cut off as another

opponent found us.

This man had a woodcutter's axe gripped with both hands and swung it at Bjolfur with all his might. The axe stuck in the shield and the force sent Bjolfur stumbling backwards. The Ertlander let go of the axe and, without pausing for breath, pulled a knife and came for me.

I tried to regain my shield but he was driven by righteous fury and I had no time. He thrust the knife at my neck.

A spear burst through his chest. The man's eyes went wide. His relentless fury carried him forward and I was forced to dodge out of the way of the gore-soaked spearhead jutting from him. The Ertlander stopped himself and looked down at the wooden shaft coated with his insides. His eyes fluttered and he collapsed.

I looked past him to see who had saved me, but I saw no one, only the distant silhouette of a woman running into the cove. The spear quivered and ripped itself out of the corpse, though no one held it, and floated above my head. Bjolfur moved to stand next to me and grunted as he pulled the axe from his shield.

A shadow passed over us and we looked up to see a man's silhouette cut through the clouds like a falcon. I felt the tension ease in my chest.

Bjolfur turned to me and grinned. "The Windborn are here."

The floating spear twisted in the air to point at another would-be rescuer, then flew off as quick as an arrow. An anguished cry told me it found its target.

The rage in the air distilled into fear as the two Windborn took to the field. The Ertlanders spun to face their new foes. Perhaps they wanted to try and slow the Windborn, to give the rescued hostages time to run. The fools. There weren't many stories about the Windborn on this side of the sea, but they had to know that each of those resurrected warriors was worth five strong fighters. Or ten Ertlanders.

I looked back down the beach and saw several Ertlanders converging on the woman with crow black hair. Dalla Thyrisdottir. The Windborn who could move objects with a thought. She walked with predatory grace. Knives and axes, picked up from nearby corpses, floated in the air around her. Whenever anyone stepped too close she flicked her fingers and a blade sundered flesh. With every few steps she took, she found another spear and threw it at an Ertlander.

As I watched her pick her way purposefully through the battlefield, two burly warriors wearing chain shirts charged at her from either side, trying to catch her in a pincer movement. Dalla raised open palms and they were lifted off the ground. They kicked and clawed at their necks as though they hung from a noose. Dalla closed her fists and the warriors' necks twisted with a crunch. They fell limp to the ground.

The fighters ahead of Dalla began to retreat.

"Have mercy."

"They have brought demons to our shores. Demons!"

"Gods save us."

She smiled and walked forward. An axe lifted from the ground and, with a twitch of her fingers, Dalla sent it spinning through the air before it sank deep into someone's chest. More screams filled the air.

It was too much for the Ertlanders to watch their friends killed without a weapon being touched.

They broke.

Any fighters that escaped Dalla's deadly projectiles met Finnr Gellirson; the Sky Treader.

Finnr struck like an eagle snatching rabbits. He brushed the clouds in slow circles then swooped down towards the fleeing warriors. He swung a massive piece of driftwood like a club and cracked open skulls as easily as I would crush a dry leaf.

A few of them tried to stand and fight Finnr. They hunched low to the ground and jabbed up at him with spears. Before the spear-fangs could sink into the Windborn, he twisted in the air and launched the driftwood at them. Spears snapped and Finnr slammed down into the fighters and lay about his enemies with Windborn fists. Shields cracked and skulls crumpled.

We had all stopped, mesmerised by the show of supernatural force. As Finnr crushed an Ertlander's chest with a well-placed kick, another Ertlander, the last one standing, stabbed their shattered spear into Finnr's shoulder. The Windborn snarled and whipped his hand out to grip the

Ertlander's throat. The man clawed at Finnr's iron-strong fingers as the Windborn lifted him off the bloody sand then began to float above the ground.

I marvelled at his speed, his power to lift himself up off the ground as easily as I could walk. Finnr raised his captive into the air, higher than our longship's mast, and then let him fall. I shuddered as the man flailed before he hit the ground. I prayed I would never have to face a Windborn myself.

After a few more heartbeats of pained yells and wet crunches, it was over.

*

The bodies stained the sands crimson. Most were Ertlanders, but several raiders lay with unseeing stares. We stripped the valuables from the Ertlanders, adding whatever we could to our hoard of plunder, and gathered our own dead to give them their due. We left the Ertlanders for the gulls.

The Windborn made their way back to their camps, content that the killing was done and the threat to the longships was over. Despite the death they had trailed across the beach, neither were out of breath. Dalla picked at something under her fingernails as she rounded the beach and moved out of sight. Finnr floated by, several feet above our heads, and offered a nod as he passed. Gore still dripped from his fists.

Malka helped Atli to limp over to the longship. His wounded knee leaked down his leg and he left bloody footprints in his wake.

I looked over to Bjolfr, slumped down in the sand, and went to join him.

"Are you hurt?" he asked.

"No. How's your head?"

He put his hand to the four bloody lines across his scalp.

"Fine," he said, though he winced as his fingers brushed the wounds. "Those fuckers were out of their minds, attacking us like that. Did they really think they had a chance?"

"Maybe." I shrugged. "There were enough of them. If the Windborn hadn't turned up we might not have made it. Come on, let's see if Malka will let us use some freshwater to clean this up."

I took Bjolfur's hand and wound a trail between the bodies to the longship.

Atli sat on a barrel with his wounded leg extended out in front of him. Malka was bent over the wound. They had removed Atli's trousers so she could get a better look.

"How are you doing?" Bjolfur asked as we got close.

"I've been better," Atli replied with a weak smile. He grimaced as Malka did something. "Be careful, would you?"

"You want an infection? Then shut up and let me get on with this."

We watched Malka soak two rags with freshwater and pass one to Bjolfur before she used the other to clean Atli's leg. The gaunt man hissed as she wiped away the half-clotted blood, but he did not complain again.

Bjolfur and I walked a little way before he sat down and let me see to his head. The lines were deeper than I anticipated, rage and fear having lent strength to the Ertlander who had carved furrows in my husband. As I mopped Bjolfur's brow I looked out across the cove. The still bodies, which cast fat shadows onto the beach as the sun started to set, reminded me of a group of seals. I wondered if the tides would rise enough to carry them away.

"You wanted someone to come for the hostages," I said.

Bjolfur started to look around, but I forced his head back down and slapped the rag on his stubble-covered scalp.

"With gold in their hands," he huffed. "Not axes and spears."

"Some of them didn't even have those."

"Aye. Now there's no one left to help us when we get back."

He was right. The hostages had either been killed whilst they were tied up, or had been freed and injured as they tried to flee. Injured hostages were no good to us.

"We've got a larger share of plunder now, though."

"A few extra helms and axes," Bjolfur scoffed. "Not really enough to buy our freedom."

I glared at him and scrubbed a little harder at his head than I needed to.

"Ow, come on, easy."

I shot him a mischievous grin. Bjolfur tried to scowl, but it quickly broke into a reflection of my smile. I kissed him to offer some recompense.

"Give me that," he said and swiped the wet rag from my hand. He dabbed at his head with it, though there was little left to do. The wound was clean and it wouldn't get any cleaner using that rag. I let him get on with it, sometimes no matter how good a job I did, Bjolfur would take over and try to do it better.

"What's the plan, Malka?" I called over.

She looked up from Atli's leg and frowned at me.

"What?"

"We got our answer about the hostages. They weren't of a mind to pay the ransom. When do you want to leave?"

Malka grunted and examined the bodies all around her before glancing over at the other raiders nursing their wounds.

"We took the brunt of that attack. Tonight we rest, then we leave at first light."

I nodded and Malka went back to Atli's leg.

"See," I said. "We'll be home with plenty of time to see to the farm before winter."

Bjolfur looked unconvinced.

*

The other longships had left. We were the last raiders on this side of the sea. Our campfires sprouted across the beach like weeds. Not everyone wanted their own fire, but enough of us wanted our own space that we had spread out across the whole cove. This was our final chance to be alone before we crammed ourselves into our longship for the five or six days it would take to journey home.

I walked over to Malka's fire and sat down next to Bjolfur. Atli and Bjolfur had scored a grid into the sand and managed to find enough pebbles to play a game of Little Soldiers whilst Malka tended to some meat spitted over the flames. Alti scowled as Bjolfur hopped one of his pebbles over three of Atli's in quick succession and finished up at the far end of the grid.

"My first king," Bjolfur said with a smirk and stuck the pebble upright in the sand to upgrade the piece.

Atli grumbled and made his move.

Malka caught my attention and gestured to the steaming meat twisting above the fire.

"Gull," she said in response to my raised eyebrow.

"No, thank you," I said with a grimace.

"Suit yourself."

I leaned against the longship as Malka began to serve up the gull. I let the evening noise wash over me. The uneven crackle of the fire, pebbles clacking together as Atli gathered them up to start another game, the rip and crunch of overcooked meat. After days mixed with extended silence and moments of thunderous battle, these mundane sounds cleaned away the tension in my muscles like waves on sand.

Bjolfur won the first game with Atli but lost the next two.

"You got lucky." He pushed himself up and dragged his foot through the marked lines. "I'm going for a walk."

"Come on," Atli said as he gestured to the scuffed sand. "No need for that."

Bjolfur grunted and waved a hand at Atli as he wandered away from the camp.

The rest of us sat around the fire in companionable quiet. Atli muttered to himself as he collected the scattered pebbles, but neither I nor Malka wanted to play a game with him so he started to pick at the bandages tied around his leg. Malka lay back and closed her eyes and I traced runes into the sands by my feet.

He sighed and poked at the fire with a piece of driftwood.

"It's a good night for a story," he said at last.

"Depends on the story," Malka said without opening her eyes. "You're not going to tell us about the time you cracked three eggs in a row that had double yolks?"

"No." Atli scowled at Malka. "How about one of Solveig's stories?"

"As long as it's not the one about her drowning," I said.

"What's wrong with that story?"

I shot him a look that said there was plenty wrong with it. "We're about to cross an ocean, Atli. I don't want to spend my last night on land hearing about some idiot who capsized her boat."

13

"Really?" He frowned. "Sure, Solveig died, but the story's a comfort, isn't it? She became the first of the Blessed Drowned. Even if we drown, they can cast a rune-stone into the ocean for us and we'll make our way to palaces of the Sea Giants."

"She still drowned," I said.

"What do you think, Malka?" Atli pointed his driftwood poker at her. "I want to tell the story. Edda doesn't want to hear it. What about you?"

"I don't care, Atli, I'm going to sleep. Do what you want."

"That's good enough for me," Atli said with a grin.

"Fine," I groaned. "If you're going to tell the story I'm going to leave."

I grabbed a blanket and walked away, following Bjolfur's footprints. They disappeared as they wove through the thin patches of grass at the end of the beach, but they pointed to a narrow pathway that lead to the clifftop and eventually I found him. He sat against a boulder, looking across the island to the west and out to sea.

"That's not the way home," I said as I sat down next to him and threw the blanket over both of us.

"I thought I'd take a last look at this place and the western horizon. There're more lands out west, you know, if you go far enough and set the right course."

"Who says that?" I asked, chuckling. "You'll find land anywhere if you go the right way."

"I suppose."

Away from the campfire smoke, the cliffs around us were illuminated with gentle starlight, the waves twinkled, and the world felt gentle again.

"I'm still not sure we have enough gold," Bjolfur muttered.

"We should. It was a good raid."

I put my head against Bjolfur's shoulder and ran a finger down his arm, following the contours of muscle and tracing the splinters of scars across his skin.

"Once the snows start to melt we should be able to get enough help," I said. "You're sure that we'll be able to have the land once we've cleared it?"

"Yes," he sighed. This was an old conversation, but I couldn't help asking. "My cousin has done the same thing. I helped him clear the land for his farm and he says that Queen Vigdis is happy to have new farmers. As long as they pay her something, she'll protect them."

"That doesn't sound too different to our situation now," I muttered.

"Right now, we're struggling, Edda." His muscles tensed and he took a few breaths before he went on. "Dagnur takes almost everything. We don't even own the house we live in. When we've cleared the land, we'll have our own home and Vigdis will take maybe a tenth of what we make. Unless the ice somehow descends and swallows us, we'll be fine. Better than fine."

I wrapped my arms around Bjolfur's and leaned against him. "I don't trust Dagnur. He won't just let us leave."

"It's not up to him. He'll be pissed off, but the fjord that my cousin told me about is on the other side of the Broken Mountain. He won't chase us that far. It'll be easier and cheaper for him to find another tenant for his farm. He won't waste his time on us."

I murmured a wordless half-agreement.

"Edda." He turned my head and stared into me. "We will be fine."

I looked into his storm-grey eyes and found nothing but assured confidence and something softer he seemed to reserve just for me in our quiet moments. His mouth quirked into a smile and I felt my mouth do the same. I leaned toward him. His lips found mine, then his hands found the rest of me, and we lost ourselves in each other.

*

We lay tangled together, safe under the folds of the blanket, wrapped in the heat of each other, and watched the night. The crisp stars shimmered as a line of green light appeared before them. Another line of light snaked across the sky, and then another until the night was full of dancing lights. It looked like the sky had cracked, spilling green and purple fire from another world.

15

I held my breath. The gentle sounds of the shore and the shiver of dry grass that had been reassuring moments ago now felt too loud. I worried they would scare away the precious burning sky.

"Have you ever seen the Winds so clear?" I whispered.

Bjolfur shook his head but stayed silent. He found my hand with his and squeezed.

The lines of light forked and danced above us and we watched them for what felt like hours. As we lay beneath the long lines of green and purple light stretching from horizon to horizon, I understood why the gods destroyed the Giants' bodies and trapped their souls as the Winds. Traders, ignorant of the Winds' true nature, called them the northern lights and Ertlanders thought them demons and called them the dancing sky fire. Whatever you called them, their power was obvious. I shuddered to think how strong they must have been with their bodies intact.

"Maybe they are hunting," Bjolfur whispered. "Windborn are made on nights like this. Perhaps the Winds are searching for their next vessel."

"Vessel? I wouldn't call Finnr or Dalla a vessel."

"What else would you call them? They've got the power of the Winds running in their veins. Finnr flew right over us, and remember how quick he was when we attacked the monastery? He's a vessel for the Winds' power. His soul's all mixed together with the Winds. How can you tell it's still him or something working him like a puppet? It doesn't sit right with me."

I rolled my eyes.

"You've been spending too much time with that fear-monger, Halli. He's always complaining about the Windborn for no good reason. Finnr's not doing the Winds' bidding, is he? He's not trying to free the Winds or anything. Finnr swore an oath to his king and Finnr serves him. He might have a few extra tricks, but he's no different to any other sworn warrior."

Bjolfur slipped his hand out of mine and put his hands behind his head. "If they're not making Windborn to set themselves free, why do you think they do it?" he asked. "How come they only give their powers to the warriors they resurrect?"

"I don't know. Maybe they get bored up there. It must be cold. Wouldn't it be more exciting to come down and give someone another chance? Maybe they can see us from up there and it's a more interesting world with Windborn in it."

"You think they can watch us?" Bjolfur's eyebrows raised, a playful glint in his eyes. "Is that why they only came out once we started fucking?"

"Maybe," I said and pressed myself against him. "Let's give them something else to watch, shall we?"

I kissed him and our hands found each other again. He kissed me and I pulled him on top of me. I forgot about the Winds. I forgot about the raid. For a little while, everything was us.

Afterwards, we fell into a happy, weary silence. We watched the Winds dance and counted the stars beyond them. I fell asleep couched in the gentle sounds of the world and nestled against Bjolfur.

*

The beach was a hive of activity.

Bjolfur and I collected the plunder in the shadow of the longship. We swept sand-covered coins into sacks along with golden cups, jewelled religious icons, and shining helms. We filled one sack after another and I couldn't help but shoot Bjolfur gleeful glances as we reached our sixth full sack.

Around us, people hauled supplies onto the longship while others gathered their possessions from their camps. A few optimistic raiders walked between the dead one last time, hoping to find some hidden trinket that no one else had claimed. The gulls cried out in irritation at anyone who disturbed their feast.

"Look at all this," I said and nodded towards the bulging bags beside us. "I didn't know we'd gotten so much. We'll surely have enough once we add our share to everything we've already saved up."

Bjolfur looked from me to the sacks as they were passed up into the longship.

"Maybe," he said. He tried to keep his expression solemn but

17

a smile crept out of the corner of his mouth and his eyes twinkled. He tugged on his beard to try and stop himself from smiling.

Once everything was loaded we combed the cove one final time to squeeze as much plunder as we could from Ertland. We found none. There was nothing left on the beach but bodies and feasting gulls.

We had what we came for.

It was time to go home.

"Okay, everyone," Malka shouted. "Let's get this thing in the water. You know how this works. Edda, Halli, Katla, Varin. You're with me at the back. Everyone else, once the keel starts moving you get your arse on a bench and get ready to row."

We took up our positions around the longship and I fell to the stern along with the others that Malka had selected. Everyone strained against the longship and it creaked as it ground along the sand. A few people cheered as the keel shifted and jokes bounced between the raiders.

"Come on, Varin, put your back into it. You're not even touching the boat!"

"Fuck off, Steinar. All you've done is eat and shit this whole raid."

The jokes died away as the waves clawed at our legs and dragged hungrily at the longship. After a moment it slid easily along in the water and the rowers clambered up to find their benches.

I stayed with the others and kept the longship moving until the sea came up to our waists and the smooth-hulled ship stopped scraping the sands. One by one we climbed up the rope trailing the longship as though we clutched at the tail of a fleeing sea serpent.

I stumbled across the deck and sat behind Bjolfur. I leaned forward to give my husband a final kiss before the start of our hard journey home, then set myself to my oar. Bjolfur turned his head and smiled at me. I smirked back and then offered a final prayer to the gods that our voyage would be swift and safe.

Malka pulled herself onto the deck and shouted for us to get moving. We bent to our task and the oars clawed through the water. I watched my husband's muscles strain against his oar and I smiled. My heart felt lifted by the sea winds that would soon carry us to familiar shores.

We were going home, and now we would finally have a place to call our own.

*

The gods tested us as we crossed the sea.

The storm was fury and wrath.

The longship was too small.

Dark clouds moved over us like wolves as large as the horizon. Savage lightning stabbed through the air and for a moment I thought the sky would crack and fall to crush us. Our oars snapped as hungry waves threw themselves against us. We dropped the sail, but the gales still threatened to tear the mast free. Waves rose like writhing sea serpents and tossed us between their surging backs.

Our world became rising waves, pelting rain, and furious lightning.

We screamed and fought and clung to each other, but it was no use.

The longship crashed down into another wave. A plume of foam-streaked water exploded up on either side of us.

A wave hit the side of the longship and swept across the deck like a sea serpent's tail. Supplies and plunder slid from the deck as the ship tipped until the sail dipped low enough to brush the waves. Anyone who didn't have hold of something was ripped away from us as the water crashed over the longship. We threw all our weight to the other side of the ship and managed to right ourselves, but danger was still thick around us.

The storm pushed us until we had nothing more to give and then shoved us over the edge.

Another wave surged over us and carried Bjolfur to the edge of the longship. I shouted prayers and begged the gods for help as I leapt to him and caught his arm. I had hold of him and hooked my leg under the nearest bench. I could not let him go. We had done it. We had enough plunder for our own farm.

This was our last raid. This was too cruel a time to die.

I screamed for help and Atli rushed over. He grabbed Bjolfur's tunic and yanked, pulling my husband half-way back onto the ship.

As I took hold of Bjolfur's other hand and began to pull, another wave slammed in us. The force of it threw Bjolfur back. He caught himself on the edge of the longship and I clutched his hand to keep him from going overboard.

Bjolfur looked at me. There was fear in his eyes. Fear, gratitude, and that soft something he reserved for me.

He tensed against me, using my weight to pull himself back to safety.

Another wave swept the deck.

My legs were knocked from under me and I felt the surge of water threaten to shove me out of the longship and into the ocean. Someone grabbed my legs, keeping me from falling into the ravenous waves.

The water still seethed over Bjolfur and his fingers, slick with sea and storm, slipped through mine.

We stared at each other as he was carried overboard. There was terror in his eyes, and something soft. His lips moved, but the sound of the words were lost under the howling wind and the shape of them was lost in the rain and tears. He burst through the surface of the water once. I screamed and made to leap off the longship, but Atli caught me and dragged me back to safety.

When I looked back there was only the storm.

CHAPTER TWO
AN EMPTY HOME

THE MOUNTAINS OF HOME ROSE INTO VIEW three days later. It was the end of the raiding season, but we had made it back in time. Barely.

No one cheered when we saw the god-stones; the monoliths that guard our homeland. Several enormous runes were carved into each of them, and each shone with ghostly light that cut through the morning mists to guide us home.

Our longship carved through calm waters that were either mourning with us or mocking our grief. Half of the oars had snapped in the storm and we had just enough crew left to use what remained. Somehow, the shields remained tied to the sides of the longship like battered barrow stones bravely raised against nothing at all.

We followed the curve of the coastline for a few more hours before turning into a fjord and sailing in-land until we saw the harbour.

A crowd waited; their faces were full of laughter and they held their children high to watch our glorious return. Cheers swelled as we slid into place in the harbour, but the crowd's shouts died away when they saw the broken oars, the shredded sail.

As we drifted into our berth the strip of water between our longship and that happy shore felt like a cliff-edge. The longship towered over the fishing boats moored next to us. It was strange how the perspective changed in a few short days. The storm had batted us around as though we were no bigger than a fly, but here the mast stood tall and proud and looked, for all the world, like nothing could break it.

"Welcome home, travellers," a voice boomed out and echoed around the fjord.

Dagnur. The chief of our little settlement, and the last person I wanted to see.

The fat old man stepped to the edge of the jetty and held out a hand for the rope to fasten the longship in place. He fumbled the catch and had to move quickly before the rope fell into the water.

"How was the raid?"

Malka leapt onto the jetty. "It was thrice-blessed. The gods graced us with an easy journey to Ertland. When we met our enemies the gods favoured us in battle. And the gods blessed us to allow us home again."

It was the proper response to give. The same that any returning raid captain would give, regardless of their success. Malka's monotone words and tired eyes told a different story.

Now that the tattered longship was next to the crowd, the cheers had turned to confused whispers. People craned their heads to try and find whomever they had come to greet. Some faces broke into a relieved smile when they saw them, but not everyone had that luxury.

One by one the survivors clambered off the ship. Each was met with a tight embrace and loving words. Children shouted and screamed at their returned parents as though they had never thought to see them again.

I hadn't moved from my seat.

My gaze was fixed on the carved figurehead at the ship's prow. I let myself pretend that he was waiting in the crowd. Somewhere out on the jetty, Bjolfur was waiting for me, his mouth twisted into a grin, ready to pull me into an embrace once I got off the boat.

Soon the sounds died away. Dagnur led the crowd to the meeting square where there would be food and drink waiting.

"Edda," a voice called.

My head snapped around, but it was only Atli. His expression softened when he saw me.

"Come on," he said, gently. "It's time to go. Let's go get some food and drink while there's some left, eh?"

He held his hand out for me.

Water slapped against the longship's still hull like echoes of the storm. A lone crow's cackle joined with the raucous gull calls.

After a deep breath, I took Atli's hand and let him pull me up. My heart splintered when I saw Bjolfur's empty bench. Nothing remained to prove Bjolfur had been there, not a rune idly carved into the wood or even a dry patch where his body had stopped the sea spray.

We had been so close to a better life together.

Somewhere, the gods were laughing.

I tried to tell Atli to go on without me, to let me have another moment with an unmarked bench, but it felt like black feathers clogged my throat and all I could manage was a strangled sob. Atli guided me off the ship, despite his injured leg, and we followed the crowd celebrating the triumphant return of their families.

I had no family left. I had no triumph in me. All I had was a crow named grief clutching my heart.

*

By the time we arrived at the celebrations, most people were several drinks in. All over the square, people showed off their plunder, gathered to hear stories of their time apart, or danced together. Dagnur and Malka hunched together in muttered conversation and wore grim expressions. Atli took me past an open barrel and drew two cups of mead. I downed mine in one gulp and Atli passed me his cup. When Dagnur saw us arrive, he waved Malka away and slathered on a smile as he turned to face the crowd.

The old man raised his hands to catch the attention of the crowd and then shouted out over the noise. "My friends."

He let the conversations die as he walked over to the raised platform normally reserved for legal announcements or poetry if a skald passed through. As he stepped up onto it, silence fell.

"Today, we welcome back our brave fighters from their daring journey across the sea."

Excited murmurs rippled across the square as Dagnur gestured to the pockets of raiders within the crowd.

"The westerners fill their temples with treasures and pray to their gods for protection. They pray and hide behind stone walls and think that it will be enough, but their gods are sheep and we are wolves! Our triumphant raiders have stormed their walls and have sailed back to us with a longship heavy with gold, silver, and jewels."

The crowd cheered and stamped their feet, even smothered in grief I felt the surge of pride and triumph flutter in my chest.

"We thank the gods that our friends, our family, have returned safely to us before the end of the raiding season. Though perhaps next time the gods could help them get home a little faster."

Dagnur said the last part in a conspiratorial whisper and a few people chuckled. I scowled. Most people might think his words teased us for how long we had been away, but Dagnur had gouged enough from us over the years that I knew better. He always had one eye on his profits. If we had not come back before the end of the raiding season, before winter truly started, then his farms would struggle to get their stock or harvest ready to sell before the end of the year. That meant less gold for Dagnur's hoard. Last year Bjolfur and I had been forced to pay for a sheep that had lamed itself on the hills. A sure sale we had sabotaged, he had said.

"But we must not forget," he continued in a voice dripping with solemnity, "those that did not make it back. May the gods be merciful and the sea cradle their souls."

Dagnur bowed his head and let the sentiment hang in the air. The quiet stretched out and I felt the weight of the people around me. It was the soft, insistent weight of families reunited and I stood alone within it. When the silence had gone on for long enough he raised a cup high above his head.

"To the dead."

"To the dead," the crowd echoed back.

Everyone finished their mead and held the empty cups high as though for the gods' inspection.

Dagnur hopped down from the podium and the low rumble of conversation returned to the square. Everyone's attention fell to the sacks behind the podium. Excitement simmered through the crowd and the conversations grew louder. The spoils.

This was what most people had come for. They wanted to know what that distant bloodshed had paid for.

Someone tugged at my shirt.

I turned to see Loi, the young man we had asked to look after our farm whilst we were raiding. He panted with exertion and his face shone with sweat.

"The farm's all safe, Edda. All the animals are healthy. I was chopping some wood for you when I heard the longship was coming in."

He must have run all the way here.

"Good."

He looked away and started searching the crowd, likely for his father who had been on the raid with us.

"Where's Bjolfur?" Loi asked, absently.

The crow in my chest stretched and pecked at my insides. Its black feathers surged up my throat, but I swallowed them down.

"Go find your father."

He ran off without looking back.

A loose ring had formed around the platform so that everyone could watch the ceremonious plunder-sharing. I moved away to lean against a rack of dried fish between two houses. Jealousy thrashed under my ribs as I saw reunited lovers leaning into each other. I closed my eyes to stop the tears, and sucked down deep breaths, hoping the cold air would freeze my grief.

Dagnur called out to the raiders and one by one they accepted their spoils. The crowd cheered as they held their plunder high. Men and women I had fought with, protected, and killed for, came forward. Part of me hated it. I knew they'd earned the gold and silver now gripped tight in their hands, but each excited conversation between them and their family was a twisted knife in my crow-soaked heart.

"Edda Gretasdottir," Dagnur shouted. He twisted his head as he tried to find me in the crowd.

I pushed my way through the throng and stepped out into open space.

"For a fierce warrior." Dagnur handed me a fist-sized stag made of gold, one of the religious symbols we had taken from the Ertlander's temple.

I hefted the weight of it. It was a beautiful piece, swirling lines curved over its flanks, but it was too small. It did not balance out the blood and loss.

"Go on," Dagnur growled, ever a man to hate a wasted moment. "Hold it up and let me get on with this."

I held the stag up to him. Confusion flickered across his face for a moment before the mask of generous host reasserted itself.

"You're not giving it back, are you?" he said, loud enough to carry to the closest spectators who chuckled dutifully.

"Where is the rest?"

His brow furrowed as the confusion returned, thicker this time. "What do you mean?"

"I fought for you," I said. "I killed for you. I've got fresh scars for you."

"And you have your reward." Dagnur's voice had lost its warmth. The act he put on for the crowd was gone. "Accept your lot and step away."

I held out my other, empty hand.

"Bjolfur fought for you. He killed for you. He bled on foreign shores for you. A widow is due her husband's share."

The crowd was silent.

Dagnur's eyes searched mine, but if he wanted to find some hint of doubt in me, he would be disappointed. He found only grief and fury.

"Ingvar," Dagnur called over his shoulder without looking away.

Ingvar moved up to stand beside us. He served as the law-keeper, a position made clear by the polished silver arm-ring that gripped his left arm, it was his duty to know all laws and pass judgement wherever necessary.

"Yes, my lord?"

"What does the law say that a fallen raider's wife is owed?"

"A fallen raider's wife, or rather their widow," Ingvar's voice quavered. He cleared his throat then continued more clearly. "The spouse of a fighter lost on a raid may claim that fighter's share of the spoils."

I bared my teeth in a sharp grin, but Dagnur's sickly smile

stretched across his lips.

"And what share does the law dictate for those lost at sea?"

Ingvar's eyes went wide and he looked from Dagnur to me with his mouth open, unwilling to answer.

"Come on, law-keeper, what share?"

"The law does not specify any share to be given, but it is customary to—"

"Nothing." Dagnur cut across Ingvar with a slice of his hand. "The law says your drowned husband is owed nothing."

"You can't be serious?" My voice echoed around the now silent square.

"Only a brave death entitles the family to the warrior's plunder," Dagnur said. "If a raider is lost at sea, they get nothing."

Dagnur dragged out the last three words. Each of them hit me like a spear thrust to the gut.

Someone in the crowd gasped and angry muttering sprang up in its wake. After the raid's patron was given their share it should have been divided equally between all of its participants. The word of the law spoke of brave deaths, a relic from the days when the only law was the gods' law, but it was unheard of that any death on a raid would not be brave. Dagnur had always hoarded as much gold as he could wrap his sweaty hands around, but to deny raid plunder to a widow was a step too far. I let my hand grip the knife at my belt.

"Are you calling my husband a coward?" My voice cracked like a breaking glacier.

Images flashed through my mind of our final, storm-drenched moments together. His white-knuckle grip on the side of the ship. Slick fingers slipping through my hands. The stuttering flash of lightning that showed me his struggle against the waves, then, only waves.

"How dare you," I growled and took a step closer. Behind Dagnur his warriors put hands to weapons. "Bjolfur fought bravely right until the end. Do you know what he did for you out on that raid? This plunder lies before you because of him.

"What enemy could be greater than the sea? You dare to say that he died a coward's death when he fought the oceans themselves? Where were you when we fought the Ertlanders to bring you gold? What help were you when he strained against the storm to keep the longship on course? What enemy did you face as the gods tried to drown every one of us?"

Dagnur smiled, his uneven grin a reflection of my bared teeth. "Don't worry," he said. "I'll put his share to good use."

He straightened and looked away from me to the rest of the gathered crowd.

"We will raise a runestone in honour of all those we lost on the raid," Dagnur called out to the crowd. Some seemed mollified by his words, but others kept their stormy expressions. Then, Dagnur pitched his voice low so only I would hear. "Whether they died bravely or not."

My knife was in my hand. The warriors behind Dagnur rushed forward, but Ingvar got there first. He shoved me, throwing me off balance, and I stumbled.

"Ask about the blood-debt," Ingvar whispered. "He may pay it to safe face."

I looked up at the law-keeper and saw an instant of concern on his face before it faded into schooled disinterest. Dagnur's lip curled up in a sneer, but I cut across whatever insult he was about to throw at me.

"Then I request a blood-debt."

Dagnur laughed. "From who? Ingvar, who usually pays a blood-debt?"

"The murderer or his representative," the law-keeper said. His voice was monotonous, but I noticed the bunched muscles in his jaw.

"And you want me to what?" Dagnur sneered.

"Take it from Bjolfur's share of the—"

"Put the sea on trial?" he shouted over me. "Demand your blood money from the ocean? Pan for gold until the water pays you your due? Don't be absurd, Edda. Take your share of the plunder and stop embarrassing yourself."

He turned away. I felt as though the ground was falling away beneath me. Any hope I had to get away from Dagnur, start my own farm in Bjolfur's memory was getting swept away. Grief's black wings stretched inside me. My vision blurred.

"But—"

"Your tenants can be paid a blood-debt in the event that one of their family dies," Ingvar whispered to Dagnur. "To make sure that there are enough hands to do the work so that the farm's profit does not suffer."

I saw Dagnur falter. Ingvar had touched on Dagnur's weakness. Money. For an instant, I saw the war in his eyes and hoped I would get Bjolfur's due. It might be enough to flee from Dagnur. I could pay people to clear land for a farm of my own. Just like Bjolfur and I planned.

Dagnur's gaze swept over me and then locked on the pile of plunder. Avarice flashed in his eyes and his scowl deepened.

"She swore an oath, Ingvar," Dagnur snapped. "Everyone did."

Dagnur stalked towards me, his fur cloak hissed as it dragged along the ground.

"You swore to me that you would take no more than your lawful portion of the plunder. You remember that, don't you, Edda?"

I met his gaze for a moment, then dropped my eyes.

"Yes."

Swearing an oath to Dagnur had tasted sour when I'd said it, and now the memory felt rotten against my tongue.

"Then get out of my sight."

Dagnur kicked the gold stag over to me. His lip curled into another sneer, but he swallowed whatever final insult squirmed against his teeth.

Grief turned to fury. Bjolfur's sweat and blood had earned the plunder I was being denied and now Dagnur twisted the law to make sure I got almost nothing. I snatched up my sorry plunder and brandished it at the chief.

"Fuck you, Dagnar."

I spun and stormed away. Embarrassment burned on my cheeks and my sorrow threatened to pull me down with every step. I paused before I reached the edge of the square and turned to find someone in the crowd.

I saw her a few paces away.

"You're going to let him do this, raid leader Malka Eylasdottir?"

She looked at me with tear-filled eyes.

"What can I do? What could I have done?"

"You could have lied," I hissed and stepped in front of her. "What did you gain in telling him that Bjolfur drowned? Did he not fight bravely enough? Did he not die bravely enough?"

"I swore an oath that I wouldn't lie about what happened on the raid, Edda." She looked down at the jewelled cup in her hand. "Here."

I looked between her face and her plunder. Scabs covered her knuckles like red coins. Each one earned during the raid and each one paid for her plunder. Malka deserved that plunder as much as Bjolfur did. I couldn't take it from her. I couldn't do to her what Dagnur had done to me.

"Keep it, brave raid leader."

Malka's mouth opened, but I left before she could say anything else.

I went back to the harbour before I started the long walk home. I might be denied Bjolfur's plunder but there was something else that would not be taken from me. Once I was away from pity-filled eyes, my embarrassment stilled and the anger in my chest died away to a smoulder in the face of the cold sea spray.

The longship that I had hoped to never see again bobbed on the water. A shiver ran through me at the sight of the quiet waves out beyond the jetty. I looked up and down at the shields still tied to the side until I found Bjolfur's. I played my fingers over the scars in the wood, trying to remember what had caused them. It seemed that hundreds of cuts and scores decorated the painted wood. I unpicked the leather ties holding it in place and hauled it free. I considered taking some of the weapons still lying in the longship, but they were Dagnur's. The price I would pay for the theft would be much worse than the weapons' worth.

With the shield over one shoulder and my possessions clutched in my hand, I made my way home.

*

Grief almost brought me to my knees on the long walk home, but it would not let me stop. It felt like a riptide dragging me down and unceasingly onward without mercy.

The distance from our farmstead to the fishing village was bittersweet as the silence misted around me and left me with nothing but myself. I tried to focus on the steady thump of my footsteps, but black-feathered thoughts unfurled in my mind.

I thought back to the last true conversation I'd had with Bjolfur. I almost felt the sand in my hands again. Those plans we'd made to get away from this, away from Dagnur, all gone like a bridge ripped away leaving behind nothing but churning waters.

Grief stabbed its sharp beak against my heart until I felt like it would tear out of my chest.

Eventually, familiar sounds washed over me as I stepped onto the crest of the hill and our... my farm came into view. It looked the same. Wooden walls held up a sharply angled roof covered with grass that quivered in the breeze. Woven willow fences staked out each of the animals' territories as they wandered in and out of their sheds and coops. I heard the bleating of the goats and the rising clucks of the chickens. Everything should have been the same, but it wasn't.

I started to call out for Loi, but I remembered that he had already rushed off to welcome the raiders home.

I was alone.

The thought was a numb comfort, like a deathbed.

As I approached the house I let Bjolfur's shield fall from my shoulders and into the mud at my feet. The house looked darker than I remembered, every shadow a crow's feather as though the creature inside me had flown ahead to mark its territory. I stood for a time, unwilling to move, until the sun dipped below the treeline and I shivered in the early evening shadows. With a shuddering sigh, I forced myself go inside.

Without the strained light of the winter sun the cold reality of my losses stared back at me. Our life was built here and scattered across the house in myriad signs that I had never noticed before. There, a scratch on a roof beam from a chicken. I had brought it into the house to frighten Bjolfur, but the chicken had escaped and it took the whole afternoon to coax it down from the ceiling. And there, a stain on the floor from when Bjolfur had tripped and dropped a lamb steak. He had been trying to surprise me with my favourite meal and when I got home all I found was him trying to clean the dust and dirt from the meat.

I smiled and sat down next to the fire pit then dragged the sack from the raid between my feet. I rummaged in the bag and pulled out my plunder.

Away from the crowd and the burning injustice of what had happened, I barely had the strength to hold it. The gold tugged my hand down and banged against my leg. This was my reward. A shining trinket in the shadows of my loss.

The stag looked so small. I needed to feel that it was worth something, even if only as a weapon, so I threw it as hard as I could at the wall. It flew across the room and slammed into the wood. I watched the gold come to rest on the floor. The stag glittered in the dying light from the open door, and the shadows retreated a little. How many times had I told Bjolfur not to let his anger get the better of him? How many reminders that it only ended up with something broken?

What did that matter now? I was already broken.

I strode across the room and picked up my plunder. One of the antlers was bent. Not a good weapon, then.

I pulled up a loose floorboard to reveal a collection of sacks and other treasures underneath. Before I shoved the golden stag in with the rest of our hoard, I felt around for the old plunder, trying to calculate its worth.

The pile of coins and offcuts of gold and silver looked large against my hands, but it wasn't enough for the farm we wanted. It needed to be enough. I couldn't stay here after what Dagnur had done. What other laws would he twist to give him exactly what he wanted? I stared at our hoard and realised that the farm we had wanted would be too large for me alone. I only needed enough land for myself now.

That thought broke down whatever was left of my defences and exhaustion swept over me. I rolled into bed and felt the weight of the emptiness press against me.

The bed was too big, too cold, too empty.

*

A knock at the door woke me. I looked around, bleary-eyed, and saw that I had forgotten to close it. A familiar silhouette stood in the doorway.

My heart leapt.

"Bjolfur?" I slurred.

He'd swum to shore and found his way home. I scrambled out of bed.

"Edda?"

A woman's voice.

My heart broke as reality came crashing back and sent me to my knees.

Fjola, my shield-sister, stepped into the house and knelt next to me. We had been a force to be reckoned with when we went raiding together, but she'd lost an eye to an Ertlander's knife and decided the risk was greater than the reward.

"I'm sorry I didn't come and meet you," she said. She lifted my chin and looked into my eyes with her own worry-soaked eye. "One of our chickens—"

"He's gone, Fjola," I stuttered. "He's gone."

My voice broke and I fell, sobbing, into her open arms.

Old oaths bound us together. When we were shield-maidens, we had sworn to protect each other. When we had each gained a farm, we swore to help whenever it was needed, and when Fjola had given birth, I swore to treat her children as though they were my own.

With Fjola I didn't need to, I couldn't, pretend. I let my grief flow out of me. Next to her, I felt like shards and splinters compared to solid stone rubbed smooth by a stream. Slowly, the sight of her calmed the fidgeting, fighting crow under my ribs. The weight of her next to me anchored me and my breathing eased.

I pulled away, flinching from the wet stains dotted across Fjola's tunic, and met her gaze. She didn't look away, just met the raw pain in my eyes with soft, unflinching empathy and support.

"I'm so sorry." She whispered the words as though anything louder would break the dam of tears again.

The raw outline of worry in her solitary turned to simple compassion and she wiped away one of my tears with her thumb.

"Why don't you go and wash the dirt off your face? You look like you just rolled straight into bed when you got in."

She turned her head to take in the state of the house. Bits and pieces from the raid supplies were scattered all over the floor where they'd rolled out from the dropped bag. My hoard was scattered around the hole in the floor where I had pulled the floorboard loose.

"I'll go to the stream." I pushed myself to my feet. "I don't know how long that bucket of water has been there. Probably since before we left."

Fjola nodded and showed me a small smile. "I'll be right here until you come back."

I wanted to return the smile, but I couldn't. My soul was too heavy. Instead, I squeezed her hand as I stood.

The winter sun set me blinking as I stepped outside, but it felt warm enough after a night in my shadow-soaked home so I decided not to get a cloak. It was early enough that my boots crunched through the frost-coated grass. The animals were calling out, in need of food and water most likely, but they could wait. I trudged into the forest that encroached the edge of my farmstead and after a short while the cries of chickens and goats were replaced with the gentle burble of water.

The stream looked as clear and pure as ever, and in that moment I hated it. After all that had been lost, all the new cracks in my heart, the stream showed no signs of mourning. No streaks of dark mud evaporating to show respect for the dead. No broken sticks caught in rocks to try and stop the water from flowing out to sea and burying my beloved under more waves. Even as those thoughts came to me, I heard how ridiculous they sounded and a sullen smile tugged at my lips.

I knelt, closed my eyes, and listened to the hushed flow of the stream.

When I opened my eyes it felt like some of the colour had come back into the world. The dirt caked onto my cheeks and the salt crusted into my hair felt wrong for the first time in weeks, no longer a mark of hard work during a raid, but a sign of apathy and grief.

As I scrubbed my face and washed my hair the stream blossomed with black spots of dirt, but with each dirty bloom that disappeared downstream, my heart weighed a little less. I rinsed my hair until it was back to its usual blonde, and scrubbed my cheeks and arms.

I knelt for a while longer to let the thin warmth of the sun dry my pale skin and damp hair. The trees around me whispered amongst themselves and the stream continued to flow. Soon there was nothing left of the muck I had been covered with, and for a moment the world was still and peaceful. Perhaps this was the world's way of grieving, not by accompanying my mourning with black omens, but with gentle, respectful silence.

Fjola smiled at me when I arrived back at the house. The animals were quiet now and Fjola carried a bucket half full of feed.

"You didn't have to do that," I said.

"Try telling the animals that."

She put down the bucket by the door and we went inside. The clutter from my outburst and Loi's haphazard stewardship had been cleared away. It looked like someone's home. Without Bjolfur, it didn't feel like mine.

Fjola pulled me towards the bench by the fire pit and we sat together.

"Tell me what happened."

Her voice was so gentle that it took me a moment to realise what she meant. I flinched as the crow in my chest exploded to life and stabbed its nail-beak into my heart.

I looked away and counted the knots in the seat next to me to calm myself down.

"The longship was too small," I whispered without looking up. "There was a storm like nothing I've ever seen before. The lightning was so bright I thought the sky had cracked, that the Winds were coming back."

The crow was trying to escape, pressing itself against my ribs and pushing, pushing. Fjola put her hand on mine.

"It felt like the end of the world."

Fjola squeezed my hand.

"I'm sorry, Edda."

She opened her mouth but closed it again. I squeezed her hand back. We both knew that words couldn't be enough now,

35

no matter how much we might want them to be.

"We were so close, Fjola. We were on the way home." I let my hand slip out of Fjola's and stared at the dirt between my feet. "He went overboard and there was nothing I could do." I swallowed and looked up and met Fjola's gaze as if I might find an answer there. "That's the worst part. Surely I could have done something to save the man that I love?"

"Hush," Fjola said and pulled me into her arms. "Nothing good comes from a question like that."

After a moment I gently pulled away and wiped at the wet streaks on my cheeks.

"I know, but—"

"No," she said in a firm, gentle voice.

We sat like that for a little longer. I leaned against her again and let myself breathe in time with her rising chest. Fjola stroked my hair and started to tell me about what had happened whilst we had been away. She told me about her children, Nona and Bersi, who caused as much mischief as the Trickster god himself. The stories about them soon stopped my tears, and I found myself chuckling along with Fjola as she told me about Bersi hiding one of their chickens in his father's bed.

"Will you come to the festival tomorrow?" she asked.

"What?" I sat up. "I thought we were too late for the Summer's End festival. The raiding season's already over, isn't it?"

"Yes, but Dagnur pushed the festival back a week. He said the gods wouldn't mind if we waited for the raid to return. He even got Sif to ask the gods. Everyone was happy to wait, except for Hilde, but you know what that old crow's like. She just wants something to complain about."

I nodded absently, but my mind raced.

"Yes, yes, I'll be there."

Fjola stood and kissed the top of my head. "Good. You come straight over if you need anything, okay?"

I said I would, and hugged her goodbye at the door.

As soon as she was out of sight I ran over to where I had dropped Bjolfur's shield. The metal rim was cold to the touch. I wiped the dew and mud from its face as I walked back to the house and propped it up against the door.

I undid all of Fjola's work in a moment as I scattered cups

and plates from the tables to try and find a sturdy knife. My twinge of guilt was quickly drowned by exaltation when I found one.

Outside, I sat on a tree stump and laid the shield across my knees. I let my eyes wander over its surface. The paint, once the colour of fresh oak leaves and now stained with blood and salt, was chipped and gouged from the killing blows it had saved my husband from. I ran my fingers along its surface, starting at the metal boss in the centre and spiralling out to the iron-clad rim. Each tear and nick in the wood brought back a memory of thumping hearts and beating shields. It felt like I was touching his scars one last time. They took me back to those moments when we lived on the edge of an axe and I was happy.

A cloud passed over the sun and the wind's chill snapped me out of my reverie. I gripped the knife in my hand and set to my task, wincing as I made fresh gouges in the painted wood.

CHAPTER THREE
THE CLIFF EDGE

THE SQUARE SWARMED WITH TWICE THE NUMBER of people than had welcomed us home. I pushed through the tightly packed bodies with Bjolfur's newly carved shield hanging over one shoulder. As I walked by, people offered me their sympathies. Varin told me how much she would miss skipping stones in the fjord with him. Steinar mumbled something about the tragic loss of a good man. Others squeezed my shoulder or offered vague sympathies as I walked by. Every comment, squeeze, and smile was a worm guzzled by the grieving crow clutching my heart. Each one a writhing reminder that this sorrow wasn't something that I could enjoy alone. Even now I had to share my husband.

I stopped near the edge of the crowd. Everyone around me had their shields, with intricate sagas carved into them, slung over their backs.

A longship rested in the open space beyond the crowd. It looked real enough, but it wouldn't float if you took it out. The longship was built from wood too poor to craft a real vessel and was stuffed full of kindling and straw. Hooks ran along its edge. Soon they would be loaded with the shields of everyone around me. It lay ready and waiting like a beached driftwood whale.

Dagnur stood on the other side of the ceremonial longship surrounded by lackeys, laughing at his own crude jokes.

"Edda, what are you doing up here?" someone hissed at me.

It was Fjola. Her auburn hair hung in a single, thick braid down her back and she wore a tunic threaded with bright patterns. I ran a finger through the tangled mess of my own

39

hair and realised I hadn't changed my clothes.

"I thought you'd come and find me when—" She stopped as her eye flicked to the shield over my shoulder. "I didn't realise you'd be doing the ceremony today."

"I didn't think about doing this until after you left."

"Is that your shield?" She ran her fingers along the spiral of crudely carved images. "I don't remember you doing some of these things."

"No, it's Bjolfur's."

Fjola frowned and cast a furtive look around as though trying to see if anyone had heard me.

"Can you do that?"

"I don't know," I said with a shrug. "We were going to burn our shields this year, Fjola, this was it for us. I'm going to do it for him."

"Okay." The frown deepened. "Just come and find me when you're done, okay?"

I smiled back at her and told her I would as soon as the shield was on the ship. She grabbed my hand and squeezed before moving back into the crowd to find her family.

The conversations around me started to die away. Dagnur had stepped up to his podium. He raised his hands for silence.

"My friends, we are here to finally celebrate the end of summer. Some of you have raised concerns that we will fall out of the gods' favour for having the Summer's End festival almost a week too late, so let me allay those fears once and for all."

He stepped down and an older woman came forward. The remnants of whispers that had slithered through the crowd during Dagnur's speech all stilled.

The woman, God-Speaker Sif, seemed to loom over each person in the crowd from where she stood. She was built like a spear; slim and straight, with a sharpness in her eyes that could wound you. When Dagnur spoke he had leaned forward to invite your attention, but Sif stood tall and demanded it. She raked her gaze slowly across the crowd then raised a hand for a silence that was already there.

"I can feel the fear in your hearts, friends," she began. "I felt that same fear myself. I wondered if the gods would look down on us with disappointment, with anger, if we did not celebrate the Summer's End festival on time. It is the gods' law that no raiding shall take place in winter, but our raiders had not yet returned and the end of summer loomed. Without performing the rituals of Summer's End will the gods think we have forsaken them?"

Some in the crowd began to shift and fidget. It seemed that Sif's proclamation rang close to the truth.

"I raised these concerns to Dagnur, as some of you did to me, when he asked me if there was any way to delay the ceremony. Everyone should be present, he said, we should begin the winter as a community, as a family, but he did not want to anger the gods. I thought on this and could not see a clear answer, so I went to the sacred grove and gave the gods a sacrifice on the roots of the oak tree. I asked the gods to send me a sign if we could delay the festival, a sign that to do so would not incur their wrath.

"As I waited for an answer, the goat's blood soaked into my clothes. I thought that this was a sign of our error, that we would soon be drenched in blood. Then, three ravens flew into the grove. They settled on the low branches of the oak and laughed at me."

Sif sucked in a deep breath and raked another stern expression across the crowd. She had always had a flair for the melodramatic.

"They dropped three leaves before me." Sif held up a hand showing the leaves. "One of oak, one of elm, and one of ash. One for each tree planted to mark the end of the god-war. Once I had gathered the leaves, the ravens hopped onto the goat carcass and began to feed. The gods accepted the sacrifice.

"We should not fear that we are celebrating the Summer's End festival too late. We have always been good and faithful to the gods' laws in our actions and the gods know this."

A collective sigh of relief swept through the crowd and an excited murmur soon followed as Sif stepped down from the platform.

Dagnur stepped back and took her place. He looked over the crowd with a smile too wide to be genuine. The crowd's noise died down again as he started the ceremony.

"The gods have seen fit to bless us with a bountiful season," he said, he pushed his voice deeper as he tried to infuse proper authority into it, "both at home and across the sea, but now it must come to a close. The season has ended already, but it would not do to celebrate without all of our friends and family with us."

He waited for the gentle cheer to die away and then gestured to the crowd around me.

"Brave warriors, you have fought long and hard for your families, for me, and for your gods. If your sword arm is tired and it is your desire to lay down your weapons and serve the gods from your homes, then step forward now. Bring your saga-carved shields, show us your stories, and let us celebrate your victories."

A louder cheer went up as he finished. All around me, the shield-bearers shifted and muttered to one another. Most of the people carrying shields had years on me. They were too old to go on a raid and expect to come back, but there were a couple of others my age. Kare had lost his brother on the raid and was needed to help with the farm. I saw Revna as well who, rumour had it, had a child on the way and refused to risk her life over the sea any longer.

An older man stepped out into the space between the crowd and the longship. He was taller than anyone else there and built like an oak tree. He swung his shield from his shoulder and held it high above his head to show the carved saga to the crowd.

"Leif Vorson offers his shields to the gods."

The cheer that exploded from the crowd shook the ground. Leif had been raiding since he had been old enough to hold a knife, though he had not been out on the ships in a couple of years. Everyone there had fought by his side and he had saved my life more than once. In order to fit all of his exploits onto his shield, he had been forced to carve his saga in a finger-thin spiral.

Someone in the crowd started chanting his name and soon everyone was calling out to him.

"Leif. Leif. Leif. Leif."

The chant quickened and exploded into cheers and stamping feet as he hooked the shield onto the longship. Leif raised his hands, accepting the adulation of his friends, and then knelt in front of Sif. The god-speaker muttered a prayer and smeared a line of ash across Leif's forehead with her thumb.

"The gods accept your offering," she called out. "You fought in their name, offered blood and plunder in their name. Now, rest."

More cheering accompanied Leif as he walked to the crowd opposite the shield-bearers. Someone passed him a horn of mead and those around him offered congratulations.

The crowd fell silent as another shield-bearer stepped forward and showed her shield, just as Leif did.

"Runa Berasdottir offers her shield to the gods."

This time the cheer was muted by surprise. Runa was a vicious fighter and had only been raiding for a few seasons. We all thought she would get a taste for it and go out on the ships for many years yet.

Her shield carving was not as long as Leif's, but the exploits carved into it were no less impressive. At the start, a woman leapt from a longship into a wall of spears. A grim smile tugged at my lips. I had been on that longship. It had been Runa's first raid, she was barely more than a child, and we were ambushed as our longship crept up a river. Runa had been off the ship and killing before the rest of us had laid down our oars.

She turned and placed her shield on the longship. Sif marked her forehead and said the words and we cheered.

One by one the shield-bearers around me stepped out and put their shields on the longship. The crowd cheered. The gods accepted their offerings. The air around us became hot with anticipation and laced with an underlying hum of power as the ritual began to take hold.

Only I was left. I took a deep breath, felt the familiar black-feathered flutter in my chest, and stepped forward.

As I lifted the shield above my head and turned it to face the crowd, I saw a few people nod. As far as they were concerned it was only right that a widow lay down her shield.

"Bjolfur Hugison offers his shield to the gods."

Expressions of shock, disbelief, and confusion looked back at me. A few cheers broke through, but most people muttered amongst themselves. Dagnur's eyes burned with fury. He took a step forward, but Sif got to me first.

"You can't do that, Edda," she said. Her voice was gentle and her eyes full of sympathy.

"W—" The black feathers pushed their way up my throat and caught my voice as I tried to speak. "Why not? Doesn't he deserve this?"

Sif put a hand on my forearm and gently forced me to lower the shield. There was a soothing warmth to her touch that seeped into me. It was the strange heat of the gods' magic, the kind that was only gifted to a god-speaker.

"Of course, but what we deserve and what the gods give us aren't always the same thing."

"He died a brave death," I whispered.

"I know, and I am sorry that I cannot allow this. For someone to make the offering it must be their saga carved on the shield."

Sif pulled me around to face her, but her eyes were filled with such raw sorrow and genuine regret that I couldn't meet them. Instead, I looked at the runes tattooed across her cheekbones.

"He might not be here to make this offering, Edda," she said in that same, soft tone, "but we can help the gods to find his soul, wherever he is. Come on, let's—"

Dagnur's rough hands slapped down on our shoulders. I bared my teeth at him, but he was already talking.

"We can't blame you for this mistake, Edda." He leaned forward as though we three were in a private conversation, but his words dripped with forced sympathy and they were loud enough to carry. "Grief has broken the heart and will of many a fine warrior."

Sif's strong grip on my wrist stopped me from pulling my knife and showing Dagnur exactly how fine a warrior I was. He shook his head and then flicked his hand at someone behind me. I turned just as one of Dagnur's guards stepped up behind us.

"He deserves this, Dagnur," I said through gritted teeth. "Will you tell him you refused when you meet him in the afterlife?"

"He doesn't deserve anything," Dagnur hissed. Fury flashed in his eyes, but the sympathetic smile never left his face. "He was just a tenant, like you. Don't you forget that. What do you have if I throw you out? You've got nothing but what I give you."

He turned to face the assembled crowd.

"Edda asks for your forgiveness. A broken heart can make for an unclear mind. Sif, let us finish the ceremony."

The guard gripped my arm and tried to drag me out of the way. I ripped my arm free and looked at the guard's face. Green eyes shone with apprehension in the shadows of his helm.

"If you touch me again, Njal Leifson, I'll break your fucking arm."

I brought the shield around in front of me. I wanted him to try. I wanted to break something, to show Dagnur that he didn't control me.

"Come on, Edda," he mumbled. "I don't want to fight you. Just let them get on with it, yeah?"

Sif came up to us. She shot a reproachful look at Njal and pressed a pebble into my hands.

"You can do something for him, Edda, if—"

"Sif," Dagnur called. "Will you honour us by completing the ceremony so that we can start the festivities?"

She scowled at him.

"Make him one of the Blessed Drowned, Edda."

Sif dropped my hands, then walked to the burning torch next to the longship. She held it high and showed it to the crowd.

This is what everyone had come for. They had come to watch the longship burn and usher in the winter. People stared at Sif and the flames. Excitement flashed in their eyes and my spectacle was forgotten.

"The gods have accepted these offerings. May each warrior know that they have an honoured place with the gods."

The magic tension grew all around us like the air before a thunderstorm and the hairs on the back of my arm stood on end. Sif threw the torch in a long overhand arc to land in the straw surrounding the mast. Cloaks and tunics rippled as some force escaped from the longship and shields. Flames engulfed

45

the longship in moments and a weight settled on the air. The weight of a god's gaze, but which god, I couldn't say. Everyone cheered and at the front of the crowd Leif whistled.

"As this longship burns, let the gods take this as our promise to follow their laws and lay down our weapons. It is the season for hospitality, co-operation, and peace. Summer has ended and we welcome winter in its place."

The festival had begun. The longship would burn all through the night, much longer than any bonfire naturally would, and as the ash fell the magic would change it to snow. This ritual was our first glimpse of winter. It had always been a joy to watch, but not this time.

I tried to shrug off the heavy air, to throw off the sight of whatever god had come, but it was inescapable. I looked up, hoping I might see a sky-sized pair of eyes looking down on us. Then I would know where to direct my fury and demand to know why they would come for this ritual, but had not bothered to save my husband. There was only smoke, ash, and sky.

Someone grabbed my hand, Fjola, and pulled me away from the throng.

"Edda, why wouldn't they let you do it? Was it—" She trailed off when she saw my expression. "Are you okay?"

Bitter disappointment warred with something new in my chest. The pebble in my hands had sparked an ember of hope inside me. I stared at the dark stone as it lay in my palm, its cool weight was reassuring after the hot flush of my earlier embarrassment.

"Sif told me it has to be your shield. You can't offer someone else's. But, why shouldn't I offer his shield to the gods, Fjola? Doesn't he deserve that much?"

I met her gaze. Her worry and sorrow mirrored my own.

"Of course he does, Edda, but if Sif says it can't be done then it can't be done. She doesn't refuse anything without good reason." She took a step forward and took my hand in hers. The pebble pressed against my fingers. "I'm sorry."

I sighed, my breath as heavy as a black feather. "I need to make him one of the Blessed Drowned. I can't just let his soul wander the ocean floor forever."

"Of course not, but it's too dark to do that tonight. Let's just be thankful that you're home safe. Come on," she said, gently, and led me away from the crowd. "Let's get you a drink."

She took me to her family at the edge of the square. Her husband ran around a couple of barrels trying to catch their children. When the children noticed me they broke off their barrel-circuits to leap onto me.

"Edda!" they screamed.

"Hello, you two."

I wrapped my arms around them and spun them around. They laughed, then squirmed free and ran off to play another game.

"Edda, it is good to see you," Ulfur rumbled and pulled me into a rib-creaking hug.

Fjola's husband was a head taller than me and looked as though the gods had stretched him. He had plaited his beard and someone had smeared blue paint in random patterns across his face.

"The children wanted to make me look pretty for the festival," he said, with a sheepish grin.

Fjola pressed a full cup of mead into my hand. "Here. This is supposed to be a celebration. Let's celebrate Bjolfur tonight, okay?"

I gave Fjola a small smile then raised my drink. "To Bjolfur."

"To Bjolfur," they echoed and we drank.

There was something different about the mead. When I asked about it, Fjola delighted in telling me that she had put ginger in it. She went on to tell me how she had strong-armed the merchant into selling the ginger for half the price he asked for. I shook my head at the ferocious glee in her eyes as she relayed the height of her argument with the vendor.

"And when I gave him my best offer I thought his eyes would pop right out of his head. He even called out for the guards. Said I was robbing him! They weren't happy with his little show and he sold it to me just to get the guards to go away."

A booming laugh echoed over the crowd and cut through our conversation.

I turned to see Malka surrounded by a gaggle of onlookers waiting to hear about the raid.

As Ulfur refilled our cups he looked around to see what I was looking at and his expression softened.

"Forget her, Edda," he said. "She's just trying to impress those idiots."

"Bjolfur saved her life out on the raid, you know. She wanted to be first into the temple, but a priest hid behind the door. He looked scared shitless and wouldn't have been a problem if she'd been paying attention. He jumped out with a spear he'd gotten from gods know where, but Bjolfur was there and killed him before he stuck Malka.

"Even after that she still told Dagnur that he drowned. Not a brave death. Bjolfur was brave enough to save her life though, wasn't he?"

My voice was just a growl when I finished speaking. I wiped the beginnings of tears from my eyes. Out in the crowd, Malka started to act out her story, lifting an arm as though she held a shield, and used the other to bat away an imaginary spear thrust.

I took half a step forward, but Ulfur had his hands on my shoulder and pulled me back.

"We're done with blades and blood this year. Ignore her."

He tried to push a full cup into my hands, but I turned away. My nails dug into my palms as I balled my fists to keep them from shaking. The pebble tapped my hip from within my pocket and I thought of Solveig, the first of the Blessed Drowned. Fighting with Malka now would be more trouble than she was worth.

"You're right," I said. "Now isn't the time, but I can't stand here and listen to her laugh like nothing's changed. I'm going home."

I shoved my way through the crowd. After one or two cries of indignation people parted before me like the sea to a longship. Everyone avoided my gaze. Fury mixed with grief in my chest like hot ashes clinging to my lungs.

*

The sky was dark and the farm was quiet by the time I got home. I looked around for Scratcher, my favourite chicken, in the hopes that her colourful feathers would cheer me up and give me some reminder of the world that was, but she had already gone to roost for the night.

The long evening walk hadn't improved my mood and now I was being ignored by a chicken.

I yelled to vent my frustration and threw Bjolfur's shield into the soft mud in front of the house. It slid along the ground and came to rest at a low, slanted angle. The carved side stared at me as though to accuse me of failing Bjolfur again. I couldn't save him and now I couldn't burn his shield. I found a wood-axe and raised it over the shield ready to smash it to pieces.

Clouds moved above me and I stood, rooted with indecision. It felt like the gods had swept the clouds aside to watch my misery. My arms tensed. My anger and embarrassment at being turned away from the ritual evaporated as I imagined the sound of the splintering wood, the shards flying from the axe-head as it bit into the shield. What would I have left of Bjolfur then? He deserved better than a crudely carved shield destroyed in a fit of shame. He deserved fury and retribution and remembrance.

I dropped the axe and fell to my knees. I picked up the shield and ran muddy hands over the rough images.

The black-feathered grip on my heart eased as I remembered our time together. Finally, I could breathe without the weight of grief pushing down on me. My fingers smeared dirt across the spiral saga as they followed its path, highlighting the carved wood in bleak, earthen shades.

The story I had carved started the day we met, showing the two of us drinking from horns full of mead. Bjolfur had come to our town as one of the neighbouring chieftain's retainers. They had come to trade and Dagnur's predecessor had put on a feast for the occasion. Bjolfur and I found each other during the festivities and tried to drink each other under the table. In the end, it was a draw as Bjolfur passed out when he went for a piss and I threw up while he was gone. I smiled as I remembered stumbling out to find him slumped with his face against the side of a longhouse.

The carved saga swept through the raids and the adventures we had shared. The last picture of us on the spiral, near the edge of the shield, showed us climbing aboard a longship. The rest was waves.

That final image, the roughly chiselled waters, churned at my soul. There was so much given over to the waves. The black wings wrapped themselves around me again, but this time they were hot and furious instead of smothered in frigid grief. We could have had so many more memories. My fingers tightened on the rim of the shield.

"You could have saved him," I screamed at the sky. "He could have come home."

The goat brayed at me for disturbing his sleep and some of the chickens clucked from their beds.

The gods said nothing.

As I rubbed my thumb over the rough wooden waves, the story of Solveig, the first of the Blessed Drowned, resurfaced in my mind. I knew what I needed to do with the stone Sif had given me. Solveig's children had been terrified that their mother's body would be dredged up and forced to fight at the end of the world along with all of the dread monsters that lived at the bottom of the ocean. They had carved runes into a stone and thrown it into the sea to anchor Solveig's soul in the hopes it would save her. Soon after, the Sea Giants had found her and, moved by the love and compassion shown by her kin, offered her soul sanctuary in their deep palaces. From then on, if ever anyone was lost at sea, the Sea Giants would offer their soul sanctuary if someone threw a runestone into the ocean for them.

I scrambled back over to the house and rescued the carving knife from within the graveyard of woodchips I'd chiselled from the shield.

Before I began carving, I turned the stone over in my hands. It was perfectly round and the colour of midnight. It reminded me of a summer evening the year before. Bjolfur had just returned from an unsuccessful attempt to find another farm tenancy. I walked out to meet him on his way back and we camped by a lake. As we waited for our fish to cook over the fire we skipped rocks across the water. His longest throw was sixteen skips, beating mine by two. I stood on the beach skipping stones long after he had given up, but couldn't match him. Bjolfur presented me with a pebble he later told me was veined with a lightning streak of metal, but I'd been so intent on beating his record I skipped it across the lake without thinking.

I choked on a laugh as I remembered the shock on his face, his splashing sprint as he tried to retrieve it.

Turning my focus back to the stone I held, I saw tears had covered its surface as I relived the memory. I wiped my eyes with the back of my palm and gripped the knife. If nothing else, I could give Bjolfur this. I put the knife to stone and scratched through my tears.

The noises from the animals dwindled until only the scratch of the knife against stone penetrated the night.

*

I went to bed as soon as I finished the runestone, intent on throwing it into the ocean at sunrise, but the weight of it next to me anchored me to consciousness.

Bjolfur's soul was still drowning. I could go without sleep.

I wrapped myself in fur-lined clothes to protect against the cold, and made for the sea. I followed the forest stream behind our home until the trees thinned. Midnight was well and truly gone by the time I reached the sharp cliffs and the stream had become a shallow river that flowed through a deep chasm and out into the sea.

I took the runestone out of my pocket for the fifth time and turned it over to make sure that I had inscribed both sides of the stone, though I knew I had.

The runes glinted in the starlight. On one side, I had managed to scratch Bjolfur's initials. On the other side, I had inscribed a single rune. Peace. An instruction, a plea, and a fervent hope.

I looked to the clear sky. The stars looked like the eyes of gods as they speared the night, but the moon was uninterested, with only half of her face turned to shine down on me. As I watched, the stars were joined by blurred streaks of green and purple. The lights began to dance. They flexed and stretched as though trying to test the limits of their sky-prison.

The Winds.

My stomach churned when I realised that the gods had not saved Bjolfur, but instead their imprisoned enemies would watch me cast the runestone. For a moment, I wished that Sif was with me to interpret that portent even as much as I wanted this moment to be mine alone.

I dragged my eyes off of the dancing lights and down to the sea.

My breath caught in my throat.

This was the first time I had truly looked at the churning water since we had returned. In the depths of night, it seemed alive. The waves were endless, ravenous. They moved together, against each other, constantly throwing their formless black weight against the cliff. The taste of salt filled the air as though marking the ocean's territory, and the scrape of the sea spray against my cheeks felt like eager talons trying to drag me into the water's unending jaws.

The Winds watched from above and the waves hungered below.

I stepped up to the edge of the cliff and tried to ignore the constriction in my chest as the ocean snapped and hissed. I took a deep breath and forced my attention on the pebble clutched in my hand.

The runestone seemed to glow in the light of the dancing Winds. I squeezed it tight, closed my eyes, and muttered a prayer to all of the Sea Giants I could remember. I hoped it would be enough for them to find Bjolfur.

As I prepared to throw the runestone, something flashed at the edge of my vision and for a mad heartbeat I thought the gods had returned my husband. I ran to the shallow river-chasm and peered over the edge to see two empty boats knocking against the rock. Someone moved in the deep shadows. They seemed to be tying the boats together.

I knew that fishing crews sometimes got blown off course and were forced to take shelter in an unknown cove overnight, but gut instinct stopped me from calling out to them. I pocketed the runestone and crept back onto the sloping ground. I cursed myself for leaving my weapons behind. All I had was the carving knife.

Shadows further up the cliffs perked up their heads. Three figures, moving quiet enough for the sea to drown out any sound they might make. Moonlight glinted against something. A spear.

"What was that?" one of them hissed.

"What?" said another.

"There's someone out here, Soren."

"I didn't hear anything. Go and help Ragnar."

I slid onto the ground, hoping the meagre light would hide me even though it showed me their spear. I cursed under my breath as the shadowed strangers moved between me and my way home. More weapons glinted in the pale light from the moon and the Winds. Raiders, then, and mine and Fjola's farms were the closest targets. Again, I cursed myself for leaving my weapons behind. My best chance was to let them pass me, then get home ahead of them and fetch my weapons.

"There. What's that moving?"

The shadow-figures stood straight and the glinting spear pointed straight at me.

I leapt up and sprinted away.

"Fuck!"

"Get them!"

One of them lunged for me as I passed them, but I ducked through his outstretched arms. They cried out to each other as I ran.

"Don't catch her, kill her!"

Something hit me in the shoulder. The force of it, and the lancing pain, knocked me off balance and I tumbled forward. I tried to push myself up. My shoulder gave out and I fell face down onto the floor.

A rough hand wrapped around my foot and dragged me back. I kicked out with my other foot, felt a crunch, and heard a yell.

I scrambled upright and ran. I took a few steps then someone grabbed my tunic sleeve.

I spun to face them.

My knife flashed.

A spurt of blood and a pained scream.

The blood looked alive in the eerie Wind-light as it soaked

into the ground. As my attacker reeled away from me, clutching their wounded arm, I leapt at them. Sharp iron punched into their belly, chest, neck. They went down.

"Shit! Ada!"

Two others moved towards me, cautious now. They stepped forward and I stepped back. They blocked me and I felt the sea spray caress my neck. I had nowhere to go.

Anger burned in the eyes of the one wielding a knife and axe. The other, clutching a spear, kept glancing from me to the writhing body at my feet.

"What are you doing here?" I said, to try and distract them as I tried inched away from the cliff's edge.

"Killing you," said axe-wielder.

They spread out, cutting off my escape, but I refused to step back. Their arms and faces were covered in paint. Blue, green, purple streaks twisted in strange patterns painted across their skin.

"Wind-hunters," I growled.

Wind-hunters believed the Winds only resurrected the strongest, fiercest fighters. They stalked the nights when the Winds danced and killed as many people as they could before they were slaughtered in turn. Becoming a Wind-hunter was punishable by outlawry and execution. They took the risk so they could become Windborn. Either way, they wouldn't stop until their last heartbeat.

Axe-wielder grinned, a white slash through the dark paint. "We'll kill you first, then go and give a proper offering to the Winds."

"Your friend thought I'd go down easy too."

They glanced at the body. The writhing stopped. They started closing in. I prayed the body at my feet would make them nervous and clumsy.

"It's not going to work," I said. I tried to edge around the spear-wielder, but she jabbed at me until I retreated. "Your friend is dead and the Winds haven't brought her back. What makes you think you'll be any different?"

Axe-wielder's smile sharpened. "We haven't made a good offering yet."

He swung the axe. I dodged it, but a spear-thrust from the

other Wind-hunter scored my leg. I cried out and went down onto one knee.

Spear-wielder let out a whoop of victory and jumped towards me, pulling her spear back to strike again.

Quick as lightning I grabbed the spear's shaft and pulled. The force jerked the Wind-hunter off balance and she fell forward as I pulled myself to my feet. Our bodies crashed together in a tangle of limbs.

We struggled for a moment, but fear lent me strength and I got behind her. I took hold of the spear and tried to use it to crush her windpipe. As she pushed against me, straining so hard veins bulged on her painted arms, I managed to pivot us so her body was between me and the axe-wielder.

"Soren, do something!" she rasped through her half-crushed throat.

Soren, the axe-wielder, growled and circled us, but couldn't get to me without hacking apart his companion.

I grunted with effort as my captive tried to pull away. My hand slid up the wooden shaft and the spearhead sliced into my palm. Blood wept down the spear and my hand slipped.

The Wind-hunter bucked hard against me.

The blood-slick spear slipped from my grip and I fumbled for my knife.

We stumbled away from each other. She stooped to regain the spear and I leaned forward to stop her. My fingers brushed her sweat-soaked hair but did not snare enough to pull her away.

Soren seized on the broken stalemate and swung his axe. Before I could move the freezing iron clawed at my side, skipping over my ribs to slice my belly. Agony blossomed. I screamed. Cold night air snatched at my exposed ribs as hot blood splattered on the ground.

I twisted towards Soren and jabbed at him, but the movement was feeble and I fell to my knees.

A blood-dark puddle pooled around me. It reflected my shocked expression and the writhing Winds. Something crashed into the back of my head and I collapsed onto the blood-puddle. The warm, sticky liquid spread around me as though it wanted to find its way back inside me.

"Shit," a distant voice said. "Are you okay?"

"Yeah," growled Soren. "Where the fuck were you? How long does it take to take down a fucking sail?"

"Same time it always takes. How the fuck was I supposed to know you'd be fighting off some mad bitch?"

Someone kicked me over. I stared up at the dancing Winds. The distant lights twisted in the space between the sky and the stars. They pulsed from blue to green to purple and back again. Some far away voice whispered to me in words I didn't understand.

Soren's face appeared and blocked the Winds from view. Braided red hair hung limp and his moustache bunched together as he pursed his lips.

"What was she doing out here?"

"Who cares?"

"Come on, it's cold, let's go burn some houses."

"Leave her. Let's go."

The voices flowed together. I couldn't tell who was talking.

"What are we going to tell Hraki? We can't tell him some bitch took out Gellir before we even reached the village."

My village. My house. My friends.

"Hraki doesn't give a shit as long as he gets his Windborn. You know the deal: he gave us weapons and we give him Windborn."

I needed to tell Fjola what was coming. My body screamed as I tried to move. My hand groped for a hold to drag myself away. My fingers slipped on the bloody rocks. I tried to leap up and run away, but I only twitched.

Pain ran through me like wildfire, but underneath it, I felt something fall out of my pocket and onto my leg. The crow in my chest, which deflated as my life poured out of me onto the clifftop, laughed and told me what it was.

The runestone.

I had not thrown the runestone.

"No. Someone cast the runestone. I'm begging you. Just throw this stone into the ocean. Please."

I screamed the words with as much force as I could, but all emerged was a desperate, gurgling wheeze.

"Can someone get rid of her? That noise is creeping me

out."

"No. Just throw the runestone. Say the words." Blood bubbled at the corners of my mouth.

Footsteps. A silhouette against the Winds. The sounds of the ocean grew hungrier, as though eager for the gift of carrion.

"The first offering of the night," someone mumbled.

They dragged me across the cold ground. My knife slipped from my numb fingers and the runestone fell away from me.

They shoved me off the cliff.

There was a heartbeat of weightless calm. Then the ocean roared in my ears and the cold spray reached me. Lightning strikes of pain pummelled me as sharp rocks stabbed and tore my limbs, but my mind was focused on the small stone abandoned on the clifftop. I prayed that the rocks didn't kill me. Please, by the Trickster's black heart, let the ocean make the final blow.

Under the roaring waves, I thought I heard Bjolfur calling to me. It was good that I hadn't cast the runestone, that he wasn't one of the Blessed Drowned. Now our souls would wander the ocean floor together.

I smiled as the waves devoured me.

CHAPTER FOUR
THE GODS' PITY

COLD ALL AROUND ME. WET.

My body was heavy under the weight of water and exhaustion. Above me, the waves roiled, slow and furious as they sought a new meal.

No.

Not waves.

Storm clouds.

I wretched as the realisation hit me then twisted and vomited something dark. It pooled out next to me on the beach. Blood and seawater. Iron and salt.

Weak daylight broke through the pregnant clouds and illuminated the cove I had washed into. I lay on a thin beach surrounded by rough cliffs that curved out into the ocean as though trying to claim part of it for themselves.

Small waves lapped at my feet. I looked down to watch the foaming surf gum at my sodden shoes. All the fury of the ocean replaced with an insatiable, unending caress.

I tried to pull myself up, but pain beat me back down. Instead, I rolled over and dragged myself away from the water. I crawled, scraping sand under my fingernails until I could lean against the bottom of the cliffs.

"Why wouldn't you take me?" I croaked. My throat ached, but I sucked in a breath and screamed out to the ocean, "Why not me?"

The sea hissed. Waves peaked in the distance like shrugging shoulders.

I inspected my sliced palm and scored leg. The sea had washed away the blood from each and left only a pallid slit in the skin. I pressed my hand against the wound in my side. The wound that had almost killed me. That should have killed me. Instead of soft, parted flesh, I found something hard and cold. Maybe it wasn't as bad as I thought. Perhaps Soren's axe only carved away the flesh and exposed the bone.

As I cursed whatever god or Sea Giant had saved me from my ocean grave, images from the night before sparked in my mind.

The Wind-hunters.

I pulled myself up and tried to run but stumbled and scraped my palm on the sharp cliffside. My injured leg was weak and trembled as I put weight on it, but did not give way.

I found a path out of the cove and got my bearings. The gentle hiss was replaced by a ravenous roar. Churning waves leapt up against the cliff like sea wolves hungry for another taste of me. My head started spinning as I watched the ocean's endless gnashing mouth. I fell to my knees and shut my eyes tight. I couldn't face the sea again. Not now.

After a few deep breaths, I opened my eyes and made my way inland without looking back.

I soon saw the tips of trees swaying east of me and realised I was not far from where they had kicked me into the ocean.

As I walked, my cold-saturated tunic peeled itself from my skin. I knew I couldn't keep these clothes. I had seen enough warriors win bloody victories only to lose the slow fight against the cold. Reluctantly, I turned away from the forest and limped along the cliffs until I saw a shape huddled on the ground. The dead Wind-hunter. I stripped out of my soaked outfit and dressed in the Wind-hunter's. My clothes were a deep, ocean cold but these were only as cold as death.

Without the heavy, wet clothes draining my energy, my strength returned with every uneven, limped step. My mind, too, cleared a little more and I realised this would be where I had lost the runestone.

For a moment I froze. The runestone could save Bjolfur's soul.

I circled the stripped corpse and searched desperately for the runestone in the rocks and mud. Churned patterns showed where the fight had been and a furrow in the ground marked my journey to the cliff-edge. I sifted through the wet soil and rocks until my arms were caked with mud, but I could not find my precious stone.

Fjola's face flashed in my mind. Had the Wind-hunters found her? I couldn't stay and risk losing her too. I bunched my fists until my fingernails cut into my palms and cursed the gods and their fates.

"Could you not give me this?" I screamed. My voice sounded small against the clap and hush of the waves at the base of the cliff. "Will you leave me nothing?"

I needed to go. I hobbled away from the cliff and broke into a limping run as soon as the ground was even enough.

It seemed like I stumbled through the forest and along the stream for hours. By the time I burst from the trees behind my farmstead my breath was a conflagration in my chest, each gasp like a bellows fuelling my pain, but after battling through brambles and low branches the last hundred paces felt easy.

My feet knew this ground.

I was home.

Or where home had been.

I fell to my knees when I saw what was left.

Blackened wood jutted from a scorched patch of earth and the smell of burnt hair and flesh wafted on the breeze. Charred pillars plotted the corners of the house and between them, my home had been reduced to ash clumped together like snowdrifts.

A sob escaped me, then another, and I wept.

My home. The memories I had made there. All of the things I had to remember my husband by. Destroyed.

Something shifted in the wreckage and one of the immolated pillars collapsed. There was an axe at the edge of the woods behind me, surrounded by half-chopped logs. I picked it up and stalked forwards.

Someone stepped out from behind one of the ash-drifts. A familiar face framed with wild red hair turned to me and her single eye went wide. I dropped the axe.

"Edda!"

Fjola rushed over and wrapped me in her arms. I tried to take her weight but was still too weak, and we fell back onto the ground.

"Oh Edda, I thought you were in there. Where have you been? I thought they'd killed you!"

She squeezed me so close it was hard to breathe, but I held her just as tightly. She was an anchor against the storm of grief and loss the gods thrust on me and I couldn't let go, otherwise I too would be lost.

We pulled apart and knelt side by side in the dew-clogged grass. I watched the smoke and steam rise from the wreckage and dissipate into the blue sky.

"I couldn't sleep," I said. "I needed to give Bjolfur a runestone, but they found me before I could finish. I got one of them, but the others got past me. I'm so sorry."

"Oh, Edda, no. You don't say sorry. I'm just glad you're alive." She took my hands in hers. Dried blood crusted her fingertips and her forearms were covered in scrapes and slashes. "Gods, Edda, your hands feel frozen. Even your hair's got ice in it. Here, have my cloak."

"What happened?" I asked as she wrapped me in the warm fur.

Fjola glanced at the remains of the farm and shook her head.

"We didn't notice them right away. Ulfur was putting the animals to bed and he saw the burning. I sent the children to fetch help and then we all rushed over here."

"Did they hurt anyone?"

"No," Fjola said. She stared at the wreckage. "There were only three of them and six of us. They were easy to put down."

Fjola had always been the most tenacious of the raiders. She never stepped back, never dropped her weapons, no matter how many enemies she faced. It was how she'd lost her eye. It had taken the strength of her love for her husband and their children to keep her from raiding.

We sat and stared at my home. The crow in my chest grew restless at the sight of it and spread its grief-coloured wings until it felt like my ribs would crack.

Something glinted in the ashes. Probably a knife. If a knife could survive, then could my plunder have made it through? If it had and I could get a blood-debt from the Wind-hunters, then I would have enough money to get away from Dagnur.

"Where are the raiders now?"

"They're dead, I think." She turned back to face me. "Hildr and Sten have taken them back to Dagnur's hall."

I nodded, but inwardly cursed. You couldn't claim gold from a dead man. My renewed hope cracked like a frozen stream, exposing a flowing river of raw sorrow and regrets.

"What were you doing here, then?" I asked. "Shouldn't you be back at the farm?"

She looked at the house and then back to me. Tears shone in the corner of her eye. "I wanted to see if the house was cool enough to look through, to see if you were in there."

Her voice cracked and she threw her arms around me again. It was a swift embrace filled with relief.

We turned to watch the smoking timbers. I looked past the broken shape of my home and saw myriad intimate moments that were built into its bones. I thought of the time Bjolfur hit his head on the door frame and I'd laughed so hard I'd fallen off my bench. I remembered the rune Bjolfur carved into the wooden beam above my head to keep my dreams happy. There were so many tiny scars in that house that made it a home. Now it was ashes and charcoal.

Fjola put the back of her hand against my forehead, bringing me back to the present. She shook her head.

"You feel frozen," she said. "Come on, let's get you warm."

*

When I walked into the house, Ulfur swept me into an embrace so tight I thought my ribs would crack.

"By the First Wolf's furry tits, Edda, we thought you were dead," he said when he finally put me down.

"So did I."

He raised an eyebrow at me, but Fjola ushered him off to warm some mead.

Once I had removed the blood and mud-splattered clothes Fjola threw them into a corner and gave me some of hers. They were snug on me as Fjola was slim where I was broad, but the gesture warmed me for the first time since I had fallen into the sea.

Soon we sat around the fire in the middle of their longhouse with a blanket draped around my shoulders, and hot, spiced mead in everyone's hands. Their home was covered in the debris of living with children. Carved animals and small clothes were scattered everywhere. I took a sip of mead, but for some reason, the warmth of it didn't reach me.

"What happened out there?" Ulfur asked. He gestured to the blood covering the Wind-hunter's clothes with a horn cup.

"Ulfur!"

"What?" The big man looked at his wife with incredulous indignation. "We fought off the first raid in winter I've ever seen, then Edda shows up in clothes covered in blood and looking like she decided to go for a midnight swim. Don't you want to know what happened to her?"

Fjola looked like she was about to throw something at her husband. "She's clearly been through—"

"It's okay," I said.

I finished my drink and took a deep breath. The children, supposedly taking care of the animals, could be heard screaming at each other through the walls.

I quickly told them what had happened. Fjola's eye went wide then she reached out to me before putting her hand to her mouth when my story reached the cliff edge. Ulfur's brows furrowed with concern and he stayed stone-still. When I was done he shook his head and put his hand on my shoulder.

"You did well to survive against three of them," he said. "The gods must have been watching."

I scoffed at that. "If they were watching, they didn't try to help. There were four of them, though. I got one, then they overwhelmed me and kicked me into the ocean."

With those words, the memory of the surging, ravenous waters swelled inside my chest and I thought I would vomit. I closed my eyes, but then I was back under the waves and sinking and I snapped them back open. I watched the dry, bright cookfire until my breathing returned to normal.

Ulfur laughed, a booming sound that bounced around the house. "Listen to her. The way you tell it, Edda, surviving against four insane fighters is a punishment."

"Isn't it?" I whispered.

They didn't answer.

Ulfur refilled our drinks. I watched the flames. Last night, whilst my home burned, how tall had the fire been? It must have dwarfed the forest if Ulfur and Fjola saw it. Would there be anything to salvage from the ashes? We had carved a life into those beams only to have it fuel my grief.

"Did someone fish you out of the water?" Fjola asked.

I looked up to see her gaze soaked with concern.

"No, I don't think so. I woke up on the beach and came straight home." I took a swig of mead and sat up straight to try and shake off the black feathers that had settled on me during the conversation. "What happened here?"

Fjola leaned back and glanced at Ulfur. "He saw the light coming from your farmhouse. At first, we thought that there'd been an accident, but something didn't feel right.

"We sent the children off to get help as we dug out our old weapons. It didn't take long for Hildr and Sten to come out and Steinar and Varin soon after that, but by the time we got there the fire was rooted. There was nothing we could do."

Fjola paused. Her gaze rose from her feet and met mine. I could see the hurt in them. The regret that she hadn't been able to save anything.

"It's okay," I said. "You tried."

We shared a sad smile.

"The fight was easily won. You softened them up for us," Ulfur said and slapped me on the shoulder. "We managed to surround two of them and herd them back to the house. Hildr got the last one. Easy kills."

"Are you sure they're dead?" I said. Not all those killed under the Winds' dancing eyes became Windborn, but I wanted to make sure those fuckers hadn't come back.

"I saw Hildr's spear go right through here." Ulfur slapped the centre of his chest. "Trust me, they'll be feeding the crows by now. May the Three Ravens take their eyes."

Fjola and I murmured in agreement.

"I don't understand it," Fjola said. "Why would they do that? Why attack now?"

"They were Wind-hunters," I said. "They were already outlaws, so why would they care when they attacked?"

Fjola's eye widened in surprise, and Ulfur nodded as though I had revealed the last piece of a riddle.

The fire snapped between us and the children came running in, turning the tense quiet into chaotic, joyful noise. When they saw me, Nona and Bersi screamed my name and leapt at me. We toppled back into a heap and they peppered me with questions.

"Where have you been?"

"Why are you wearing that blanket?"

"What happened last night?"

"Are you okay?"

When I had fended off their questions and they realised I didn't have any hidden sweets they ran off. Their shouts and screams trailed them as they found some game to occupy themselves with. I smiled. Fjola shook her head in mock incredulity.

"They're relentless," she said as she pulled me up from the floor and helped me back onto the bench. "Are you sure they were Wind-hunters?"

I nodded.

"They were talking about offerings to the Winds. They only had weapons, no armour, and they had war-paint all over like they thought looking like the Winds would help."

"Gods," Ulfur muttered and took a swig of mead. "Some outlawed bastards fancy their skills and all they've got to show for it is a burned down house. At least they're slowly turning into bird shit."

At the mention of my burnt home, Fjola glanced at me. I felt the familiar press of tears as the memory of the blackened ribs of the house resurfaced and my soul grew heavier. It felt as though the crow in my chest had risen from the ashes and now gripped my heart, its grief-coloured beak poised to puncture me from within.

"It's getting late," Fjola said with forced brightness. "Why don't we turn in? There's nothing to be done now that can't wait until tomorrow. We can go back up to the house then. It should be cool enough to see what we can find."

I nodded and pushed myself up from the bench.

"Come on," she said and took my arm to help me along. "Ulfur's made you up somewhere to sleep."

Fjola helped me to the furs thrown hastily down a little way from the fire. I slumped down on them and my exhaustion surged over me like a wave. I wanted to thank Fjola but as I opened my mouth sleep overcame me.

*

The cold woke me three times.

Each time I found another blanket, but nothing could keep me warm. By the time the sun rose, it felt like I hadn't slept at all.

Fjola presented me with a fresh set of clothes as she came in and then began to tidy the debris from the children's rushed morning.

"Thank you," I said as I pulled on the trousers she'd given me. "I—"

Something in her expression stopped me. The corners of her eyes crinkled and she bit her lip to stifle a laugh. I frowned and then realised what she was laughing at. The tunic was far too big and stretched down to scrape my knees, and the trousers were so short and tight it looked like my shins had turned green. I looked like a small troll-wife wearing white socks. I glanced up at Fjola and we both burst out laughing.

Our laughter echoed around the house and lifted something in me. It felt good to be in a home full of warmth and love and some of the sharp darkness within me smoothed away.

"I'm sorry, Edda, but you look so silly," she said, wiping a tear from her eye. "That's the tunic I wore when I was pregnant with Bersei, but those are Nona's trousers. Ulfur's mother made them much too big. I thought they'd fit you. Come on, I'll find you something else then we can go to your farm."

She got me a different pair of trousers and a belt to keep the tunic from billowing too much and we prepared to leave.

Fjola paused by the door and picked up her shield and axe.

"Just in case," she said. "Do you want to take Ulfur's?"

Ulfur's axe leaned against the wall of their longhouse. The handle was as tall as me and the axe-head was bigger than any other axe I'd ever seen. I would have struggled to use it on my best day and cold exhaustion still glazed my bones.

"No, it's fine."

"You should have something."

She hurried over to the cook-pots and plucked one of the longer knives from where it hung on the wall.

"Thank you," I said and tucked the knife away.

Once Fjola was happy that the house was in order, she led us outside. She shouted goodbye to her family as they took care of the animals and they cried out a farewell in return. We nodded to each other and began the walk to where my home once was.

It was a long walk.

Our usual comfortable silence, smoothed over with years of friendship, was replaced by a quiet anchored with dread and apprehension. Even the birds around us seemed to sense it and stopped their singing. I wanted to forget the last few days as we approached the house. Fjola and I had made this journey hundreds of times together. As we made the final climb up the hill to the house, I wanted it to be the same as it had been. I wanted my home to be there. Then I caught sight of Fjola's shield and the charcoal spires of the house and my heart broke all over again.

Fjola slowed the closer we came, then stopped, letting me circle the house on my own. Ash lay over the charcoal bones like sand covering a shipwreck. Birds fled from their perches on the burnt beams. Their silhouettes looked like pieces of the wreckage flying away, black marks against the sky.

The morning mist still clung to the ground and swirled around the house as though the gods were trying to swallow this reminder of the Wind-hunters who brazenly flouted their laws.

Metal glinted as I walked. What had once been a knife, an axe, or perhaps a shovel was now reduced to a shapeless clump of iron. I realised that I stood near to where our bed had been. I stepped into the wreckage and began rummaging through the damp ash.

"What are you doing?" Fjola called. She walked up to me but didn't step into the house. "Do you want some help?"

"No."

My hand wrapped around something cold, shapeless and I pulled it free. The bag disintegrated as it came into contact with the air leaving only our melted hoard. The metals had swirled together like blood in a stream and it was difficult to see where the gold ended and the silver began.

Fjola's eye widened as the metal shone in the sunlight.

"This is it," I said. "Everything we managed to save."

"It'll be fine." She held out a small sack in front of me. "It's still gold, isn't it?"

I nodded and let the nugget drop into the bag. As the hoard left my hand I felt a weight lift from my heart. Part of me had worried that everything would be destroyed, that the treasure-hoard we had squirrelled away over the years would be gone and with it any hope I had to escape Dagnur.

With the hoard safe, the house looked different to me. Instead of a scar, a patch of razed earth where once there was home, I saw possibility. It was the fertile ground after a wildfire.

After that, the morning was a blur. We sifted through the rest of the house and piled up anything worth saving. We continued in industrious silence for what must have been hours until Fjola called out, but my focus was on the ash-covered trinkets and the memories they sparked. I picked a lump of charcoal from a cup warped by the heat then tossed it onto the grass behind me.

"Edda," Fjola called again.

As I stepped out of the burnt and fallen timbers ash billowed out behind me like a ghost moving in my wake.

"What is it?"

She pointed to a circular patch of flattened grass.

A shield.

Bjolfur's shield was still where I had thrown it. Its preservation may be the only good thing that came from my rage at losing my husband.

It lay in the grass with the shield boss pointed up like a tiny shining barrow. Morning dew had collected in the rough carvings and it looked like the spiralling saga took place underwater.

I fell to my knees and tore it from the ground, smearing ash over the saga as I ran my fingers over it. Tears fell onto the shield.

This was all that was left.

Ash and tears.

Fjola let me weep. She sorted through what we had recovered and when I ran out of tears I joined her. She put a hand on my shoulder and gestured for me to put Bjolfur's shield with the rest of the salvage.

I looked from the pile to her and then to the shield in my hand.

"No." I put one arm through the leather strap and threw it over my shoulder. "I'm not letting this go again."

Fjola nodded and we went back to searching the house.

I tried to focus on the coarse touch of the dust so that I didn't think about what I was sifting through. If I had, I might have wept and not been able to stop. I was focused enough that I didn't notice we had company until I heard a horse snort and stamp.

Spinning around, I tried to pull my borrowed knife free and yank the shield in front of me, but I stumbled on the uneven ground. I threw a hand out to catch myself on one of the burnt beams, which cracked under the impact.

"Easy," Fjola murmured, but she too had her hand on her axe. "It's only Ingvar."

His horse stood on the lip of the hill and he had both hands raised. His heavy cloak fluttered in the cold wind, but I couldn't see any obvious weapons.

"What do you want, Ingvar?" I spat and sheathed the knife.

"Dagnur sent me to check on the house."

He dismounted and tied his horse to one of the few untouched fence posts.

"Tell Dagnur he can fuck off."

Ingvar looked like he wanted to scold me, but then his eyes softened.

"I'm glad you're safe Edda." Ingvar's voice was tired, strained. "We feared the worst."

He came over to us. We must have looked like ash covered ghosts next to him. Ingvar turned to me and then to the wreckage.

"I did survive. Now go and tell Dagnur to leave us alone. We're busy."

His jaw bunched and he looked away.

"I can't go yet. Dagnur's sent me to find out how badly the

farm's damaged, to see if any animals survived."

For a moment the crow stopped stabbing at my heart and exploded in a fury.

"Is that all?" I spat. "To see how much money he's lost? Why don't you take a piece back for him and see if he can sell it as charcoal?"

Without waiting for an answer I grabbed the nearest chunk of wood and wrenched it free. The wood splintered easily. I threw it at Ingvar. He ducked, but the burnt wood sailed far over his head, trailing black dust through the air

I went back to sifting through the ash.

"Edda," Ingvar said softly. He walked a slow circuit around the house, trying to keep himself in my line of sight as I turned. "I'm so sorry about all of this. I can't imagine what this must be like. Come back with me and we'll see Dagnur together. No one knew you were alive. We can talk to Dagnur and rebuild."

He continued around the house and I felt his eyes weighing up what could be salvaged like a wolf sniffing around a corpse. Disgust prickled at the back of my throat. Fjola put a hand on his chest as he approached her. He stopped and looked from her, back to me.

"This is all there is, Ingvar," I said. "Don't you think that Dagnur could at least give me a few days to recover before he starts rummaging through the wreckage of my home?"

Ingvar's shoulders slumped, his gaze went from Fjola to the pile of salvage behind her.

"I wish I could say yes," he said as he played with his silver arm-ring, "but he doesn't know that there is anyone to recover. Come back with me and we'll convince him to give you some time."

I wanted to believe him. My heart ached for a few days to stem the bleeding, a couple of days to wring myself free of tears, but I couldn't trust him. Ingvar might have been a good man once, but years being crushed under Dagnur's avarice and spite left him a puppet.

"Give me five days to mourn, a day for every year of my marriage, and then we can talk about rebuilding. Go and tell your master that."

"Edda, I can't give you that long." Ingvar's posture changed.

His shoulders bunched and fists clenched. "You need to come back with me."

I stomped over to him and pushed my nose against his. Ingvar's eyes widened and he took half a step back. The tip of his nose was coloured with ash where I had brushed against it.

"The way I see it," I said. "I don't owe you or Dagnur shit anymore. This was my home. I swore to work Dagnur's farm and give him his due. In exchange, he promised to protect me and mine. From here, it looks like only one of us has held up their end of the deal. Now you're telling me that I need to ask that piece of shit for permission to grieve?"

Ingvar's eyes looked into mine. I saw fear, but also calculations whirring in his mind, and something else I couldn't figure out.

"You're right."

I narrowed my eyes. I hadn't expected him to agree so readily.

"You both had oaths to one another and you've fulfilled yours. It's only proper that a widow gets her time to mourn. If you come back with me and officially state your case to Dagnur, I can rule in your favour and give you your time, but I can't do that if I go back alone."

Widow.

My fists clenched at my sides. To stop myself from hitting the law-keeper, I walked over to Fjola.

"What do you think?"

"I don't know," she whispered back. "Have you ever known Dagnur to do the right thing?"

"No, but I've never known him to openly break the law before either."

We looked at each other for a long moment. Relying on Dagnur to do the right thing was like relying on a fox to live peacefully in a chicken coop, but if the law forced him to do something without room to wriggle out of it, then he would.

"If I demand five days mourning then Dagnur has to give it to me, legally?" I asked Ingvar.

"He may decline the request for five days but it's the gods' law that you be given at least three days and nights to mourn."

I searched Ingvar's face. He looked nervous, but I couldn't

see any deception.

"Fine," I said. "I'll come with you."

Ingvar's shoulders sagged as the tension left him.

"I'm coming too." Fjola stepped up beside me.

"No, it's okay." I turned to her and took her hand. "Fjola, you've already done so much for me. I won't keep you away from your family anymore."

She put a hand on mine. Her eye looked into mine and then she nodded.

"I'll keep this safe for you," she said and gestured at the pile of scrap and gold.

"Thank you, but I won't leave our hoard again." I scooped up the sack with the heavy metal nugget and tied it to my belt.

Fjola looked like she wanted to protest, but began to collect the rest of our salvage.

Ingvar stepped up again and looked at my hoard. "I need to take that with me as proof of the damage done to the house."

"You can't do that."

"That's theft."

Fjola and I shouted at Ingvar over one another and he held his hands up in supplication.

"I'm sorry, I need to give him proof or he'll come up here himself."

"Your word should be proof enough," I growled.

"It should."

There was such a weight of disappointment and regret in those words that they doused my anger. They were the words of a man broken after years under the boot of a spiteful master.

We stared at each other for a moment longer. Something glinted in the morning sun and I looked over at the pile of tools now reduced to formless lumps.

"If you need proof," I said and scooped up some melted tools and cutlery. "Then take this. I am not giving you my hoard."

Ingvar opened his mouth as though to protest then nodded. "This should be proof enough."

*

73

We shared the horse on the way back. Ingvar rode for a mile or so before offering it to me. Normally, I would have been grateful for the gesture, but I felt restless. I wanted to sprint ahead and get this over with. Instead, we trotted along and enjoyed the scenery.

After what felt like a lifetime, we arrived. People meandered around the square, carrying bundles of cloth or meat. All eyes turned to us.

"They look like they've seen a ghost," I said.

"By all accounts, you were dead. And you certainly look the part."

I glanced down and realised I was still covered in ash which had collected in my tunic and my hair. I shook myself to get rid of the worst of it.

As we made our way across the clearing, I noticed the patch of burnt earth where the ceremonial longship had been. It seemed wherever I went I couldn't escape reminders of my failure to save Bjolfur's soul and do him justice.

The word echoed around my head.

Justice.

Perhaps that was all that was left for me. There was no hope left to build the life we had always dreamed of, but I could seek reparations for what had been taken from me. Bjolfur's soul might take some solace from that.

People moved around the edge of the clearing like driftwood circling a whirlpool. They stared at us as we went by and if we locked eyes, they paused in their whispers to smile with half-hearted sympathy.

"Ignore them," Ingvar said.

"I am. I wish they'd do the same to me."

The whispers followed us like a rising tide, but we were outside Dagnur's hall soon enough. Ingvar passed the reins of his horse to one of the servants and I made to walk straight into the hall, but Ingvar held out his arm to stop me.

I cocked an eyebrow at him.

"Let me do the talking. I know how to deal with Dagnur, okay?"

"I can deal with him," I snorted and made to shove his arm out of the way.

"Please, Edda." He stepped in front of me, showing me his palms in surrender. "Dagnur's temperamental at the moment. He's still upset at how badly the raid went."

I bit my lip to keep myself from screaming. What did Dagnur know of loss? I took a moment to calm myself and forced my face into a neutral expression.

Ingvar took my silence as agreement and went inside. I gritted my teeth and followed.

A fire crackled in the long pit running down the middle of the hall, sending shadows dancing and it took me a moment to adjust to the half-light. Three guards stood along the raised platform where Dagnur lounged on a small throne. He held a cup lazily in one hand and his other arm draped loose over the armrest. He slouched so low that he had almost slipped from the seat. Several people lurked about the hall waiting for gossip like gulls waiting for scraps.

Dagnur's voice slithered from his throne, "I'm sorry, but I can't help you. What could I, a humble farmer, possibly do?"

The question was aimed at the torch-lit stranger a few paces in front of Dagnur. The stranger's cloak looked like it was lined with the thick fur of the white bears that roam the far north.

"Forgive me," the stranger said. Her voice was uncertain, and she looked around as though seeking help. "Is there someone else I should be talking to? Is this not the hall of Dagnur Olafson, who sent out a longship on the summer raids?"

The hall's half-light twisted Dagnur's sour look into a monstrous grimace. A smile tugged at the edges of my mouth. Dagnur had preened like a prize cock when the ship was built and had made sure that everyone knew he had financed it. After a moment Dagnur's grimace smoothed into a sickly smile.

"I am he," Dagnur said, his voice tight.

"Then I must ask again. My king has tasked me to beg any chieftain strong enough to send warriors raiding for their aid."

Flattery.

Dagnur was too wily for that. He could twist between humble or arrogant in a heartbeat if he stood to gain from it. There had once been a new tax levied on large holdings and Dagnur had managed to avoid the worst of it despite having the largest holding for miles.

"I am no chieftain, merely a custodian on behalf of the High King. Perhaps, the tales of the ship we launched did not say how small a venture it was. These things tend to become exaggerated. The longship is barely large enough to carry twenty warriors, and it was a hard raiding season. There were many brave deaths this year."

Ingvar put his hand on my shoulder. Without realising, I had started forward with one hand searching my belt for my knife. Behind the throne, one of Dagnur's guards turned to watch me.

"We cannot help you," Dagnur continued, seemingly oblivious to my aggression. "To send men and women away from their livestock over winter would endanger their farms, and all for some argument between kings I've never heard of? No. We can't."

A tense silence descended. The guards' attention alternated from me to the stranger, unsure which of us they should throw out.

"You should come back in the summer," Dagnur said and waved a limp hand. "The fjords are lovely that time of year."

With their decision made for them, the guards ushered the stranger out of the hall. In the rafters a crow cried out and followed them.

"Dagnur, you fool," the law-keeper whispered to himself.

Surprised, I turned to Ingvar. He blushed and looked away.

"Just because I'm his law-keeper doesn't mean I agree with everything he does. If he wants to be a chieftain and send out raids, then he needs to act like one when strangers come calling for help. He needs to learn that those asking for help now may be the ones that hear his cries for help later. Even if he does not wish to send aid, then he should at least honour the traditions of hospitality."

We waited whilst Dagnur demanded beer, gave his servants orders, and cracked jokes at the stranger's expense. All the while he glanced back to me, taking pleasure in making me wait.

Eventually, he slumped back down in his throne and raised a hand to us.

"Let me do the talking," Ingvar whispered.

We stepped in front of Dagnur. I felt exposed standing in the light of the torches. I had hoped the on-lookers would disperse once the stranger left but they looked pointedly at me and began to whisper amongst themselves.

"Law-Keeper," Dagnur said, trying to put too much gravitas into his voice. "You weren't expected back until tomorrow."

"No, but—"

"Would you so easily shirk your duties to your lord?"

Only a moment ago he was calling himself a farmer, and now he's a lord. I snorted. Dagnur glared at me.

"Of course not, my lord. It is clear that the entire structure needs to be cleared and rebuilt. When I arrived I found Edda Gretasdottir."

Dagnur leaned back into his throne and pursed his lips. He laced his fingers together and rested them on his chin. "Nothing can be salvaged?"

I gritted my teeth at Dagnur's disinterest in my apparent resurrection.

"Only this, my lord."

Ingvar stepped forward and tipped the melted tools onto the floor. Glinting globs of metal tumbled and clattered in front of the throne. Naked avarice flashed in Dagnur's eyes until he realised it was only iron. Dagnur moved forward and nudged each with the tip of his boot.

"And these are...?"

"Tools, my lord, utensils. The only things that have not been burned to a cinder."

"And there was nothing else? No tapestries, food, or anything useful?"

I shifted my weight and the melted gold at my belt thudded against my hip. Panic thrashed in my chest. Please, by the broken eye of the Father, let Ingvar keep it secret.

"No, that's all," he said.

I let out a deep breath and made a mental note to thank Ingvar when this was done.

"Very well." Dagnur slumped back onto his throne. "And you, Edda, how will you pay me back for this?"

The question caught me off guard. I blinked and looked

around, to check that everyone else had heard the question too. Their wide eyes told me they had. My mouth opened and closed. My fists clenched. I had no words, only the desire to throttle Dagnur.

"Well?" he said with a scowl. "You were in charge of the farm, weren't you? It was your responsibility. Don't just stand there and flap your lips like a fish. How will you pay for the damage? Ingvar, why is she not answering me?"

"It has been a trying time for her, my lord," the law-keeper began, stepping between me and the throne. "She has lost so much."

"A trying time for her? Do you know what I've had to go through today? Njal, Mata, search her. She must have something on her."

Two guards out from behind the throne. They wore poorly made chain shirts, old swords hung at their hips, and their helmets had a wolf's head crudely etched into the metal. Dagnur received a stipend from the High King, who truly owned the land we worked, to pay for the defence of the whole community but Dagnur only used it on his personal guards. These weren't true huskalar, the sworn guards of chieftains and lords, but well-outfitted lackeys.

The guards stretched their arms to encircle me and I instinctively protected the most valuable possession I carried: Bjolfur's shield.

As I twisted to keep it away from them, Mata, judging from the stench of beer on her breath, snatched at the bag at my waist. I tried to grab her wrist, but Njal held me back.

"No!" I twisted again to keep them from the bag at my waist, but Njal was there again.

Dagnur leaned forward, his interest piqued by my attempts to fend off his guards. "What is it?"

"Some sort of metal," Mata said as she peered into the bag. "Might be gold."

"Show me."

Mata shoved a sweaty hand into the bag and pulled out my misshapen hoard. Dagnur leapt from the throne, all pretence of nobility and leadership drowned under his greed. He snatched it from Mata and twisted it next to a torch.

"This looks like it will do nicely."

"You can't take that," I snapped.

"Can't I?" Dagnur said in mock surprise. "The way I see it, I now have to rebuild a farm, buy food for winter, and get new livestock next year. All because of you."

I shook off Njal and turned to Ingvar.

"He can't do this. I won't let him do this."

Dagnur chuckled behind me, but I ignored him. Ingvar squirmed and looked from me to Dagnur and back again.

"You are a tenant on his farm. Dagnur can ask for a contribution to repairs for any damage to the farm whilst you are the tenant."

Fury burned in my chest, battling against a cold confusion and despair. I clenched my fists until my knuckles cracked.

"I came here to get time to mourn, Ingvar." I kept my voice quiet, firm. "You're telling me I have to pay this shit for the privilege of having raiders burn down my home? Isn't it his responsibility to protect the people he works so hard to exploit?"

Ingvar wouldn't meet my eyes. His shoulders tensed and he played with the fringes of his cloak. He looked from me to Dagnur as though he didn't know who to side with. Any spine the law-keeper had had melted in Dagnur's presence. My lip curled, I felt a curse rising in my chest.

"You—"

"She has the right to mourn, my lord," Ingvar said and looked up, his eyes shining bright in defiance. "The law allows a grieving family three days away from their responsibilities."

"Fine," Dagnur replied. He examined the gold in the dancing torchlight. We were forgotten, lost to the shining precious metals. "Then you can have your three days. We can start rebuilding the farmhouse. Mata, take this to be melted down into something we can spend."

Dagnur held out the gold for Mata to take and my body moved before I realised what I was doing. My hands shot out to snatch the gold away. Dagnur turned at my primal growl and as his eyes went wide, he squealed and stumbled back.

Something caught the back of my shirt and brought me up short. I spun around, swinging a fist blindly. My hand crunched into Njal's cheap metal faceplate and he toppled back with a yell.

Mata slammed into me and we slid about on the floor. I writhed and threw punch after punch into whatever part of her I could find. In return, Mata kneed me in the ribs and got her arm locked around my throat. Before I could throw her off, Njal leapt on me and they pinned me on the floor.

Three more guards rushed over from behind the throne and pointed their spears at me. I stopped fighting and the hall fell silent except for the crack and snap of the fire and the hiss of the torches.

Dagnur shuffled over and pushed his way through the ring of guards to stand over me.

"I will forgive this outburst, Edda." Dagnur's eyes shone daggers at me. "You are in mourning so I will not have you arrested. I have fulfilled my obligations to you. The raiders were killed and the rest of the community was saved. Your farm was an unfortunate price to pay for it, but thankfully," he raised the gold lump, "we have the means to rebuild."

I strained against Mata then stopped as a spear tip pressed against my side.

"You can't just take my property, Dagnur."

Dagnur rolled his eyes. "I'm not stealing it, Edda. My farm, the one you were responsible for, was damaged outside of the raiding season and you owe me for its repairs. Once we have paid for that, and for whatever damage you've done to my huskalar, then you can have what remains."

He hefted the nugget and examined it, as though weighing it with his eyes. A sly grin wormed onto his face.

"At this time of year labour will be expensive, and materials don't come cheap."

"You fucking—"

A fist slammed into my stomach.

"Calm the fuck down," Njal said and kicked me for good measure.

"Get her out of here."

Dagnur signalled something to a servant and then wandered out of the hall. Mata and Njal dragged me outside and threw me out onto the ground.

I rolled over to take my weight off my sore ribs. At least I had given them a crushed faceplate and a limp.

*

I couldn't face the journey home. When I tried to walk the road back to the farm my nostrils filled with the scent of charcoal. Instead, I found a quiet place out of sight of the hungry sea and slumped down against a tree. I tried to keep my thoughts away from all the things I lost, but could not help but run my fingers over Bjolfur's shield. Already it was smeared with a layer of grime and mud.

"I'm glad I found you before you went home."

I glanced up and watched God-Speaker Sif take a seat next to me.

"What home have I got to go back to?"

I ran tentative fingers across my ribs to check if they were broken. Sif took my hand and wrapped it in both of her own. She looked at me and I saw something flicker in her gaze, something deep and unknowable as the tide. I shuddered and pulled my hand away.

"Did you do it?" she asked.

It took a moment for me to realise what she meant. At first I thought it was an accusation, a mad theory that I had burned down my own farm, then I remembered the smooth pebble she had pressed into my hand. The lost runestone.

"No."

Bjolfur's soul was anchored to the ocean floor until the end of the world. His only relief from wandering the black depths, through the wreckage of a thousand ships, would come when the Winds finally managed to break free of their prison and Bjolfur would be conscripted to fight for them in the prophesied final god-war.

Sounds of people seeped into the world like sunlight breaking through the morning, but none of it broke the silence between us. It was as though my grief and failure had locked me out of the world.

"Where's the runestone? We can go and do it now."

"I don't know. I lost it when the Wind-hunters kicked me

off the cliff."

Sif's eyes widened and a lock of blonde hair fell over her face.

"They kicked you off a cliff?" she said.

I nodded. "I went to throw the runestone and they were there. They overpowered me."

"Thank the gods you're safe." She squeezed my hand. "I'll make you another runestone and we'll do the ritual together, okay?"

Sif smiled and the runes tattooed across her cheekbones stretched and lifted. I couldn't read the gods' words in those black, twisted lines but the compassion in Sif's eyes was clear.

"Okay," I said. "I'm staying with Fjola. Do you know where she is?"

"I've visited a few times when the children have been ill." Sif nodded, then her mouth quirked into another smile. "And a couple of times when Ulfur's sworn to me he's dying of some ailment, but I tell you, every time it's just been a hangover."

I chuckled at the image of the big man lying in bed because he couldn't handle his ale.

We sat together for a time and let the sounds of the world wash over us.

"I'm sorry, Edda, for what happened."

I shrugged. I didn't trust myself to speak without my tongue giving in to grief or rage.

"Bjolfur was a good man and a brave warrior. If anyone deserved to throw their shield onto the pyre at the end of the raiding season, it was him."

"What..." I trailed off as black feathers clogged my throat. "What will happen..."

"First, we pray over the runestone then cast it into the sea. It will draw Bjolfur's soul and the Sea Giants to it, no matter where the tide takes it. Once the Sea Giants meet Bjolfur, they'll offer him sanctuary in their deep palaces. He'll be safe there. He won't be forced to fight when the end of the world comes. He'll never go hungry and never feel pain. He'll be an honoured guest and asked to tell tales from his life."

Sif's voice was gentle. Her words spoken softly to ease their weight. Bjolfur was dead but hearing about his final journey—one that he had to take without me—felt like pouring saltwater over an open wound.

"If he comes to the runestone once we cast it... will we be able to see him? Can I say goodbye?"

"No."

I glanced at Sif. Her face scrunched into a pained expression, and for a moment she wouldn't look at me.

"I'm sorry, Edda. Only powerful, highly skilled god-speakers and rune-weavers can speak with the dead. Even then, all the rituals I know are for ghosts tethered to the earth, not lost to the sea. I'm sorry."

I took a deep breath and nodded. The pain in my ribs ebbed away, lost against the well of loss within my soul. A cold tear rolled down my cheek like thaw from a frozen stream.

"It's fine. Thank you."

I pushed myself up and started to walk away.

Sif clambered up behind me and put her hand on my shoulder.

"Wait, Edda, let me pray for you."

I swallowed down a barbed response. The gods had abandoned me, they let the ocean's deep jaws take my husband, and their laws gave my gold to a greedy stain of a man. Prayers would do nothing, but it might help Sif feel better.

I nodded.

She took my head in her hands and closed her eyes.

"Warrior, Mother, Father. Hear me. Take note of Edda Gretasdottir, who is lost in her grief. Her soul is wounded by love's cruel loss and I beg you to ease her suffering. She needs you, Mother, to be comforted. She needs you, Warrior, to give her strength. And she needs you, Father, to see clearly the path before her."

My jaws bunched at her words. I did not need the gods' pity. It was my convictions that pulled me on. I survived because I fought, not because the gods defended me. I was strong enough alone. But Sif spoke with compassion so I held my tongue.

The runes tattooed across her cheeks flickered and the familiar, dull heat of magic pressed in from her fingertips.

I remembered the last time Sif's magic had touched me. My knife had slipped whilst I butchered a deer and I nearly sliced the meat from my forearm. By the time Sif arrived, I was dizzy from blood loss, but she saved me. Her magic soaked into me with the warmth of summer and my flesh leaned together like flowers towards the sun. Then there was only a scar.

This time was different.

Instead of leaking into me like sunlight, it poured against me then ebbed away. I felt some measure of comfort as the power flowed over me and then it was gone and all I was left with was my cold grief.

Sif frowned at me. She let her hands slowly fall to her sides. Her gaze flickered between my eyes, and with it came a silent question.

"I'll be fine," I said and turned to go. "I'll see you later."

The weight of Sif's gaze dug in between my shoulder blades.

"Take care of yourself, Edda, we don't want to lose you too."

I raised a hand without turning and walked away.

*

It took Dagnur's people a couple of days to start clearing the wreckage of my home.

They surged over it like waves sweeping up driftwood. I sat on a rise overlooking everyone, picking at my scars, and watched Ingvar try to direct the salvagers, but they were largely ignoring him. The sound of axes, saws, and falling branches came from the forest as others collected the materials for the new house.

Ingvar shouted something, waving his arms wildly. When no one responded he took a deep breath, like he was preparing to charge a shield wall, and tried to pick up an enormous piece of burnt timber. His face contorted with effort, but it didn't move. He strained again. His feet slid about in the ashes and he went nowhere. I rolled my eyes and went over to help him.

"You were never going to be able to move this on your own," I said.

"That's the reason I asked Hildr and Sten to give me some assistance." He wiped his ash and sweat covered face on the back of his sleeve. "Will you help me?"

84

"Sure."

I planted my feet wide and lodged my shoulder against the thick wood. Looking down I saw it extended further into the wreckage than I realised and it was bigger and heavier than I first thought.

"Okay," Ingvar said. "On three."

He counted down. I pushed. There was a little resistance. Then, the dust sloughed off like water from a rising shipwreck. The wood growled as we dragged it out of the house then gave a wumph as we let it fall. I slapped the ash from my hands and clothes and turned to compare the timber to the rest of the burnt pieces. Ingvar hadn't moved.

"Why didn't you help?"

"I tried. You moved it before I could."

I shrugged and made my way back over the slope. I sat down with my back to the house, to keep the image of my razed life out of sight. Ingvar came to sit next to me and I went back to picking my scars.

"Edda, how long were you underwater for that night?"

The question hit me like a sucker punch. Suddenly I was falling again, the churning hungry waves devoured me, and my lungs were heavy with saltwater.

I took a few deep breaths to steady myself, to prove there was air to breathe.

"I don't know," I said. "I think I passed out when I hit the water. All I remember is waking up on the beach in the morning. I must have floated over to the cove where I woke up."

Ingvar looked at me like he was searching for something deep in my eyes.

"I think you died out there, Edda," he whispered.

My mind sank again to the sea floor where Bjolfur's soul wandered under the weight of the waves and how badly I had wanted to join him. If only I had drowned.

"I didn't die. I'm still here."

Ingvar shook his head. "Do you know how Windborn are created?"

"Of course, everyone knows the stories."

He raised his eyebrows.

The implications hit me like a tidal wave: the Windborn were resurrected by the Winds and given strength and powers beyond their mortal limitations.

"You think I died and the Winds brought me back? Just because I picked up a piece of burnt wood?"

Ingvar had the grace to blush. He gestured over to the timbers that had been removed from the house.

"It's not just that you moved a piece of wood, Edda. Look at it. It's the biggest piece. It's taken at least two people to move all of the others. There's no way one person could move that on their own, but you did like it was nothing."

"Oh come on." I shook my head. The lengths men go to protect their egos. "Just because you couldn't lift it on your own."

"It's not just that," he said, gently, and put one hand on my arm. "Back in the hall, during your scuffle with Mata and Njal, your eyes lit up. There was a light in them dancing like the Winds."

"That was just the torchlight reflecting off their armour." I shook his hand off. "I'm not Windborn."

Even as I said it I remembered the little details from the last few days. The marrow-deep cold the first night I stayed with Fjola. The hoar frost that collected on my arms overnight. And now I had moved an entire roof beam on my own.

I turned my hands over to examine my scars. Instead of shadows of old wounds they seemed to shine in the sunlight. I looked closer and realised that they were icing over like streams in winter.

"Sif said she noticed something too," Ingvar went on. "She couldn't tell what it was, but she said that something went wrong with her magic. She's not seen that before. I think it all points to you being Windborn."

He glanced at me apologetically, as though this revelation could somehow make my life worse. I looked away from Ingvar and cast my eye over the demolition of my old home and shook my head. I sighed and lay back on the hill.

"So what if I am Windborn? It doesn't change anything."

Ingvar frowned and chewed his lip.

"It might. There are a lot of laws involving Windborn. I was sent here as the law-keeper for a small farming community. My studies focused on property ownership, farming practices, and inheritance laws. I have a basic knowledge of raiding, but Windborn are another matter entirely. I know that it's illegal for them to do whatever they want, but beyond that, I'm not sure what the restrictions on Windborn are. Whatever they might be, I think you know that Dagnur won't let you go back to farming."

I wanted to ask him why, to make him say it, but I knew.

Even with the gold that he had stolen, Dagnur would find some way to put me in his debt whether he charged me for the cost of materials or to replace the dead livestock. If he found out that I was Windborn then I would become another prize to be paraded in front of his peers. He wouldn't waste me herding chickens. I would become a tool to him, nothing more.

I rubbed at my eyes. It seemed that every day my plans cracked and crumbled away. Exhaustion soaked into my bones.

"Then we won't tell him," I said. "Dagnur won't keep me here if he doesn't know. Once the farm's rebuilt I'll take whatever's left and leave."

Ingvar shifted, uneasy at the idea of keeping something from Dagnur. Ingvar had sworn to advise and help the village chief, but he also knew how exploitative Dagnur was.

"The winter Althing will be held soon," he said. "I will be travelling there next week. There will be law-keepers from the halls of the High King. They know the laws regarding Windborn. I will come to you first when I return, and then we can decide what to do."

"We'll decide. You and me, not Dagnur?"

Ingvar cast his eyes down, then shook his head. "Not Dagnur. I'm here to help everyone, Edda. If Dagnur asks a direct question about you being Windborn then I will have to tell him, but I don't have to volunteer the information."

Trust a law-keeper to leap through a loophole so quickly.

I watched the clouds overhead. If I stayed then I may as well help rebuild the house, but my newfound strength would raise questions that Dagnur would want to know the answers to. I steered my thoughts to the Althing. I had heard that local law-keepers' decisions could be overturned at the Althing. If I could appeal to the High King's law-keepers then I could pry my hoard out of Dagnur's hands. I grinned at the prospect and sat up.

"I'm coming with you to the Althing."

"What?" Ingvar twisted to look at me. "Why?"

"You think I'm going to stay here and let Dagnur boss me around?"

"If Dagnur's going to allow you to come with me, then he'll need a good reason."

"Dagnur can go fuck himself if he thinks I'm asking permission. If you need to give him an excuse, tell him that I can't bear to see my home being torn down."

"Okay," Ingvar sighed. "I'll tell him, but he's not going to be happy about it."

"I don't care."

We watched the landscape for a little while. The noise of construction started up behind us; someone yelled, and something crashed to the ground.

Once this hilltop had been full of the smells and sounds of a farmstead. Bjolfur had always said that home smelt like chicken shit and fire smoke. He had been joking, but not wrong. Now that those smells were gone, the hilltop didn't feel like home. It felt empty, barren.

Perhaps once my appeal at the Althing was granted I could start somewhere new, but how long would it be until it felt like home?

"Wait," I said, frowning as I realised something. "Doesn't the Althing start in the third week of winter?"

"It does."

"Shouldn't you be preparing to leave now, then? You'll never get there in time if you leave next week."

"We're going along the river," he said. He sighed the slow deflating breath of the constantly exasperated. "Dagnur wants to show off his longship."

"Show it off?" A bitter laugh boiled out of me. "He's never seen another raiding vessel, has he? That thing was half the size of the longships we saw over the summer."

"I know," he said and shook his head. "Dagnur insists that any ship is a good ship. He won't be talked out of it."

I shook my head. Dagnur's desperate desire to elevate himself only served to make him sound like a child screeching for attention. Next to the longships of the kings and chieftains who would attend the Althing, Dagnur's ship would look like a rowboat.

My mind turned to the journey, to being stuck on the small vessel and the constant peak and trough of the keel. The thought of water beneath me again sent my head spinning. My stomach twisted as I remembered the sound of the waves slapping against the belly of the longship, the water clawing at us as we carved through it.

Ingvar was talking, something about arbitration, recompense and blood-debts but the words were lost under the hiss of the waves in my ears.

My breathing became rapid, shallow. I felt light-headed.

"Edda? Edda."

The sharp concern in Ingvar's voice dragged me out of my mental whirlpool and his firm hand on my shoulder anchored me to the present.

"Edda, are you okay?"

"I'll be fine. I just need a moment."

A few more deep breaths and the world balanced again.

"I'm not going to the Althing on that boat. There are too many bad memories on board."

Ingvar leaned back, taking his hand from my shoulder. He opened his mouth, to protest maybe, but closed it as our eyes met. Whatever he saw there would not be argued with.

"Of course," he said. "Then you will have to stay here. It is too late for us to travel over land. It will take too long for the wagons to navigate the mountain roads."

"No," I said. "I'm not staying here and I'm not taking the boat."

Ingvar frowned at me then offered me a soft smile. "I don't know what else you can do, Edda."

"I'll take the roads and meet you there."

"It's too late, Edda," he said softly. "To make it in time you will need to leave today. Or tomorrow at the latest. It will still take too long."

"Then I need to pack."

I slapped Ingvar on the shoulder then used him to push myself upwards. I brushed the ash from my clothes and walked away from the hill where my house once stood.

CHAPTER FIVE
THE BLESSED DROWNED

"YOU CAN'T GO ALL THAT WAY on your own, Edda."

Fjola was trying to keep one eye on me and another on her children, but as she only had one eye, it was not going well. She whipped her head around as she spoke in an effort to keep everyone in her field of vision.

"Yes, I can."

The door opened and Ulfur ducked through.

"Thank the gods," Fjola whispered to herself. Then, to Ulfur, "can you please put your children to bed?"

The big man puffed out his cheeks and threw his cloak over a roof beam. "Why are they always my children when they're in trouble?"

Fjola's scowled softened as Ulfur kissed her and hopped past her. He chased the children around the house with exaggerated stomps and roared at them whenever they got too close. They screamed and laughed as they vaulted over furniture to get away from their father.

"I'm sorry about this," Fjola said and rolled her eye.

"It's okay," I said, and laughed as Ulfur scooped Nona up and put her on his shoulders.

It was nice to be reminded that amidst the storm of my own sorrows there was still laughter hiding in other people's homes.

Bersi hid behind me as Nona was carried to her bed. I shifted to hide as much of Bersi as possible and gave the boy a wink. He stifled a giggle as Ulfur came back out.

"Where's that sneaky little boy got to?" Ulfur said. "Is he... under here? No. Is he... under here?"

Ulfur stomped about, looking under blankets and bowls, as Bersi stifled his laughter. He peered out from behind me and put one hand on my arm to steady himself. He squeaked in surprise and tumbled away from me.

"There you are!"

Ulfur laughed triumphantly and swept the boy into his arms.

"What's wrong?" he asked when he saw Bersi's worried expression.

"What's wrong with Edda? Her arm feels like ice," he whispered, as though he didn't want me to hear.

"Bersi," Fjola snapped. "Come on, off to bed. Stories won't help you stay up any later."

"I'm not telling—"

"Come on, little man," Ulfur said as he thew a blanket over one of the roof beams to divide the longhouse. "It's bedtime and that means that I have to tell a story, not you."

Ulfur ducked behind the blanket with Bersi and after a moment he began telling a story full of monsters and warriors to the delighted squeals of his children.

"They'll never get to sleep if he goes on like that," Fjola muttered. "I'm sorry about that, Edda, they're just excited you're staying with us and don't want to go to bed."

I looked down at the scars filming over with ice on the back of my arm and covered them with my hand. This was not the moment to tell Fjola I was Windborn. I couldn't ruin her happy home with the news of my resurrection.

"It's fine. I think I've still got the chill of the sea in me."

Fjola pursed her lips and I thought she would press the issue, but she jabbed at the fire instead.

"I'll come with you to the Althing."

"No. I can't let you do that."

"And I can't let you go on your own," she shot back.

"It doesn't matter if I risk the road. I don't have anyone relying on me. Ulfur needs your help working the farm. You have Bersi and Nona."

She glared at me and waved my objections away with the poker. Her red hair shimmered in the fire light as though to reflect her smouldering mood.

"Don't give me that. Ulfur's brother is coming down in a few days to help us get the animals in for the winter, anyway. He can cope until then. Right now, you need me more than they do."

Before I could say anything, Ulfur crashed down on the bench beside me. The wood creaked as he settled his weight on it.

"Gods, they wear me out."

"You don't have to chase them around like that," Fjola said.

"And where would be the fun in that?"

Fjola shook her head and started to pour herself a drink. Ulfur put the back of his fingers against my bare forearm.

"Nine hells, Edda, the boy's right. You really do feel frozen."

Ulfur dodged the cup Fjola threw at his head.

"What?"

Ulfur's expression was so innocent and Fjola's anger so absolute that a chuckle burst unbidden out of me and then we were all laughing.

"So, what are you old shield-maidens conspiring about?" Ulfur asked as he retrieved Fjola's cup then got us all a drink.

Fjola sighed. "Edda wants to walk to the Althing to appeal to the law-keepers, and I'm going with her."

"I see. You know Ingvar's going to the Althing, don't you? You can wait for him and go on the longship. Dagnur's been making enough of a fuss about it."

I looked down and watched the waves in my mead as my hands started to shake.

"I can't get on that longship again."

My voice barely carried over the scratch of the fire.

I looked up and saw their solemn expressions matched my own.

"Fjola doesn't need to come with me," I said. "I know how hard it is this time of year; you'll need all the help you can get."

Ulfur scratched at his beard and narrowed his eyes. "If things were the other way around do you think I could stop you from going with Fjola? You're shield-sisters, Edda. That's all there is to it."

Shield-sisters. It felt like a lifetime ago, but Fjola and I had sworn to stand and fight together until death took us. I moved my hand to cover my iced-over scars. What happened to that oath when a shield-sister dies?

I looked around the room to try and find some support for my argument, but only found Fjola looking at me with her eyebrows raised and an infectious grin on her face.

"Fine," I said, trying not to return the smile. "But I'm not happy about this."

"Please," Ulfur rumbled. "It'll give us a break."

Fjola glared at him, then beamed at me and started fidgeting with excitement.

"It'll be just like old times," she said and lifted her cup to toast the journey.

I raised my cup with her.

"To old times," I said.

We finished our drinks and poured another. After a while, the conversation turned to old raids and adventures shared. The more we drank the wilder the stories became and a few cups broke as the night wore on. By the time we had made it through all the mead in the house, my cheeks ached from laughing. We managed to stop Ulfur from fetching another barrel and I went to sleep happy for the first time in what felt like forever.

*

The next morning my head pounded and my tongue felt too big for my mouth. The familiar price for too much alcohol. I groaned and sat up. The house was empty, but someone had piled some clothes next to me. I put them on and made my way outside.

The morning air blustered around me and I braced for its shiver-inducing chill. It never came. I knew it was cold out, there was still frost clinging to the grass around me, but it didn't reach me. Another sign that I was not what I had been.

"Oh, there you are. I thought we might have to wake you soon."

Fjola waved me over as she threw food out for the chickens. The beasts clucked and cocked their heads around her feet.

"You didn't buy new clothes for me, did you?" I asked and tugged at the tunic.

"No, I dug out some of Ulfur's old clothes," she said. "They've not fit him for years, but they looked to be your size."

"Thank you," I said. "You didn't have to do that, you know, I would have been fine with what I had."

"Oh, come on," Fjola snorted. "If we're going to the Althing you should wear clothes that actually fit."

She threw the last of the chicken feed on the ground and we walked around the house to check on the other animals. Some of the chickens trailed us like a feathered parade.

"Sif dropped by earlier."

"Is she still here?" I looked around before I could stop myself. What if I had missed my chance to get another runestone for Bjolfur?

"No," Fjola said as she nudged a goat out of her path. "She went in to see you but you were dead to the world. I told her we'd meet her by the cliffs."

I felt the tension in the pit of my stomach release and took a deep breath to steady my racing heart.

We finished checking on the animals then prepared for the journey. Ulfur and the children returned as we did a final check of our provisions. When he saw us he raised his walking stick in greeting as the children chased each other around him.

"Ah," he boomed. "The adventurers are ready for their journey."

The children squealed and nearly bowled their mother over as they leapt on her.

"Easy," she said from under the writhing children.

Ulfur looked over our supplies and gave his approval then turned to the pile of bodies that was his family.

"Come on, let your mother get up. I need to say goodbye too."

Giggling, they scrambled off of Fjola. The children shouted a quick farewell to me and then sprinted off to play on the other side of the house. I opened my mouth to comment that their children only ever seemed to sprint anywhere, but I stopped. Ulfur's arms wrapped around Fjola and he'd pulled her tight. His forehead rested on hers and they whispered to one another. Fjola pulled away and kissed him. It was the kind of kiss you give your lover on the eve of a battle, a kiss that tries to encompass all of your feelings within it, but never could.

I turned away to give them their moment alone.

A short time later I heard footsteps and Ulfur appeared beside me.

"Are you sure about this?" he said. "If you wait a couple of days we might be able to get you a horse and speed up the journey. Or we could get you a wagon and hitch the children to it. I'm sure they'd get you there in half the time. Or you could stay."

"I'm ready," I said and offered him a small smile. "I can't stay, Ulfur. Maybe I could have had a farm and a family like this, but that ship has sunk."

"You've got us," he said and put a hand on my shoulder. "You've always got a place here, Edda."

It was a simple gesture and a simple statement. If it had come from anyone else, I would have doubted them, but Ulfur's solemn voice and serious eyes carried complete conviction. Tears welled and I had to turn away.

"Thank you, but I need to do this."

He nodded and then grinned at me.

"Then you take care of my wife, okay?"

He swept me into a tight embrace then, realising that his children were being far too quiet, went in search of Bersi and Nona.

By the time Ulfur corralled them to the front of the house we had collected what we needed for the journey. As well as the heavy bag slung over each of our shoulders, I had my shield and knife, and Fjola had her old spear. We looked at each other. We were ready.

"Stay safe," Ulfur said.

The children paused in their bickering long enough to give their mother another hug and wave at us as we left. Fjola kept looking back and waving until her family was lost to the undulating hills and trees. As we walked down the hill that took away the sight of her family, Fjola's breathing shook out of her in the kind of breath that is the last defence against tears. I wanted to let Fjola have her moment, to let her collect herself, but words pushed at the back of my throat, begging to be said.

"Can we go by the farm?" I asked when I couldn't hold it in

any longer. "It's not too far out of the way, and I want to see it one last time before we go."

Fjola cocked her head at me, her eye shining with tears. She opened her mouth, but then coughed, swallowed, and nodded.

*

After almost an hour of walking the paths became familiar, patterns of rocks and hills that were carved into my soul. And then the house, or where it had been, came into view.

"I wasn't expecting it to be this busy," Fjola said as she came up beside me.

People hurried from one place to another carrying tools or building materials. I could hardly recognise this busy building site as my home. The setting was the same, but the frantic atmosphere was anathema. And there was something else, something that tickled the edges of my mind, but was difficult to put my finger on.

"Something's different," I murmured.

The black earth remained, but it was now scored with trenches and skeletal timber frames dotted the ground. For some reason the building site didn't match up with my memories of the house. I tried to imagine where the door had been against the building's skeleton but it wouldn't fit.

"They're building it bigger," I said.

We wandered down, through the people carrying timber, sawing, or hammering. They nodded to us but said nothing as though to do so might break a spell and I would attack them. It was obvious as we walked, though. This timber post was too far forward, cutting into the space where the chickens had been. That trench extended far beyond the original boundaries of the house.

"Why would they build it bigger?" Fjola murmured. "Surely Dagnur just wants to get it built so that someone can start farming it again?"

"No," I said and shook my head. "The bigger it is, the more it will cost, but for once he's not having to pay for it. He thinks that he can use my hoard for it so he's making the most of it."

"That bastard."

We walked around for a little longer, but even the area around me didn't feel like home. There were too many people, too much sawdust and splinters in the air, too little silence. I tried to find a space that sparked good memories, but I couldn't. Everything was consumed by the new work.

To try and get away from the broken memories of home, I wandered north towards the stream and the edge of the woods. Even this quiet space was tainted with saws, hammers, and axes that littered the tree line. With a sigh, I made to turn back and then something caught my eye. One of the axes, stuck into a spare log, sparked something in my mind and I went over to have a closer look.

A smattering of rust covered the head, except for the very edge which had been recently sharpened. I tugged it free to examine it.

Where the other axe heads had simple, near-square shapes, this one curved like the keel of a longship and there was a pattern hidden under the rust.

My heart skipped a beat.

This was Bjolfur's axe.

He hadn't wanted to take it raiding, as it had cost him far too much and he didn't want to break something so expensive following Dagnur's orders. It looked like Loi had used it to chop wood whilst he had looked over the farm and left it out here to rust.

The oak handle was still smooth to the touch and the head looked like it would shine once the rust was scrubbed off.

Fjola appeared beside me, glancing back at the construction behind us. "It looks like Dagnur's intent on spending all your money, Edda. I heard them talking about all the carvings they're going to do. You know, I think that Dagnur might be making a new home for himself here."

"Look, Fjola," I said and held out the axe.

"An old axe? Great, Edda. Why would you... oh, that's his isn't it?"

I nodded.

Someone had thrown a bag down near the other axes. It had the various sheaths for the axes as well as some oil to be rubbed into the axe handles and some whetstones. I scooped up the rags, oil, and whetstones and straightened.

"Okay, let's go. I don't need to be here. Dagnur's welcome to whatever farmhouse he's building here. Whatever he builds won't be my home."

*

We found Sif at the edge of the world, at the place where I died.

The forest fell away behind us and the ground transformed from root and grass to moss and salt-crusted rocks. The god-speaker stood at the edge of the cliff. A single, knife-thin silhouette stuck through the sharp lines dividing the earth, the sea, and the sky. With every step I took towards the cliff edge, thick dread rose within me like bubbling tar until I was stuck in place.

Fjola nudged me.

"Go on," she whispered.

I tried to take a step forward. A thunderous clap ahead of me. A spray of water exploded up in front of Sif. My muscles seized up. The dread-tar covered me and wouldn't let me move.

"Sif," Fjola called out. "Sif, we're here."

Fjola slipped her hand into mine and squeezed. I looked at her, fear made my eyes wide and my breaths shallow. She smiled.

"Come on. We'll go together."

We walked forward, hand in hand, towards the ocean that drowned me.

Sif turned and we met halfway between the forest and the ocean. She wore a cloak made entirely of raven feathers which was usually reserved for formal rituals and festivals and she had woven leaves into her hair. Oak for the gods. Ash for the Winds. Willow for the Sea Giants. Her expression was solemn and the rune tattoos on her cheeks were underlined by smears of blueberry coloured paint.

"Edda. Fjola."

She extended her hands and we took them. For a moment the three of us stood in a circle and let the weight of the moment settle on us.

Fear spiked within me with every crack of waves against rock. I closed my eyes and focused on the warm skin touching mine. My breathing slowed and returned to a steady rhythm. Sif led us both to the cliff. Fjola protested, saying it was something for me to do alone, but I dragged her along. Waves smashed against the rocks below and saltwater lunged up like the claws of a sea monster. I took half a step back. Fjola squeezed my hand and kept me steady.

"Ready?" Sif asked

Salt in the damp air filled my senses as I took a deep breath.

"I'm ready."

The god-speaker nodded. She pulled out something from the bag at her hip and pressed it into my hand.

A runestone.

It was oval shaped, and larger than the last one. The runes were already carved into it. On one side, scratched into the grey stone, were Bjolfur's initials and on the other the single rune for peace. Where my runes had been ragged, harsh symbols, Sif's were smooth and clear. I was thankful that I could finally give Bjolfur something he deserved, even if only a drowned runestone.

We moved up to the edge of the cliff where the rock fractured and the sea opened up beneath us. Countless waves formed and reformed like an infinite shoal of sharks.

They waited for me.

I had escaped them once and they knew.

Sif raised her hands and began to speak.

"Deep Ones," she called out. "Noble giants who rule the oceans from sun-warmed summer shores to its darkest, coldest depths. We call to you today to beg for your aid. We seek your help to find a soul lost in the reaches of your endless domain."

Something in Sif's voice echoed back to us from the sea, though there was nothing for it to echo from. Power thrummed through her words and I thought I saw the waves begin to move differently. They seemed to surge together like a flock of birds.

"Bjolfur Hugison, brave warrior and loving husband, has fallen into your saltwater embrace. We offer you this runestone so that he will find it, and you will find him and offer him the sanctuary of your palaces."

Sif stepped up to me closed my fingers around the runestone before she wrapped her hands around mine.

"Think of Bjolfur," she whispered. "Then, when I say, throw it as hard as you can into the ocean."

She began to chant.

I squeezed the stone in my palm and let my mind travel back to Bjolfur. I pushed past the memory of his hand slipping through mine and his face disappearing into the storm-churned waves. I lingered on the memory of us lying together after the raid, looking up at the stars and talking about what our lives held. I remembered the way he always picked a bluebell for me if he saw one. I remembered the reassuring weight of him in the bed next to me.

Sif's chanting quickened. The words muddled together and the familiar heat bled out of her hands, through my fingers, and into the runestone. The stone grew warm in my hand until it felt like a hot coal, although it did not burn.

"Now."

She stepped to the side. I pulled my arm back and threw the stone with all the strength I had.

The runestone, shining with some pearlescent light, arced over the waves. The ocean seemed to still as the runestone passed over it, as though each wave watched its passage and hoped it would land with them. The stone kept flying, farther than it should have, before it slammed into the dark water.

For a heartbeat I could see the light of the runestone as it fell, a bright spot in the ceaseless sea. Then it was gone.

I wiped away tears with the back of my hand and looked away. In the distance I saw a half-drowned boat tied up in the chasm below.

The Wind-hunters' boat.

If Sif's words had brought the attention of the gods on us, then I wanted them to make the Wind-hunters' souls suffer. I muttered a dark prayer to the Ever-Rotting Queen that she give their souls to the First Wolf to tear and rend for eternity. They did not deserve peace in death.

"Did you say something, Edda?" Sif asked and put a hand on my shoulder.

"It's nothing. Thank you. I hope Bjolfur will find peace now."

"He will. He's one of the Blessed Drowned."

Fjola came up to us and put a hand on my shoulder. I put my hand on hers and we looked out over the ocean. Sif left us after a little while, telling us she had obligations back in town.

We stayed for an hour longer, watching the waves crack against the rocks and surge against each other, but nothing changed. There was no tug at my heart to tell me if Bjolfur's soul had found the runestone. No dark shape moving beneath the water to sweep him away to the palaces of the Sea Giants. There were only the churning, gnashing waves throwing themselves at the cliffs as though to drag us down too.

CHAPTER SIX
FAFSTOL'S SCAR

WE GATHERED LATE-BLOOMING BERRIES AND HERBS as we travelled. Fjola tried to hunt with her bow, but she was rusty after years on the farm and it was left to me to hunt rabbit to stew or spit over the fire. The roads were safe from bandits in the winter, but we heard wolves sniffing around our camps at night. Most of the time the fire and the scent of iron kept them at bay and when that didn't work, we thumped our shields and screamed at the canine shadows until they disappeared. I was confident my raid-honed instincts would wake me if any wolves came for us whilst we slept, but Fjola insisted we kept an alternating watch overnight.

One evening I leaned back against a split boulder and watched the stars glitter through the forest canopy. We had finished eating and were washing it down with some small beer when a question came to me. It was something that I'd wondered for a long time and if I didn't ask now, I wondered if I would ever have another opportunity.

"Why don't you and Ulfur try to get away from Dagnur?"

Fjola glanced up at me. She seemed to consider the question for a moment then shrugged.

"What do I have to gain from leaving?" she asked.

I kept my gaze focused on the stars and tried to count them, an impossible task as they were too many and the trees weaved on the whims of the wind, eclipsing them as I counted.

"Freedom. Independence. Hells, wouldn't it be worth it just to get away from Dagnur?"

She laughed at that and refilled our cups.

"Do you know why I went on that first raid, all those years

103

ago?" She asked.

"I've never really thought about it," I said. "For the same reason as me, I guess: gold and glory."

Fjola tipped her head in acknowledgement.

"That was part of it, but not the whole reason. It sounds silly now, but another part of why I went out there with you was to impress Ulfur. I'd been watching him go off every summer and come back bloodied, laden with gold, but glowing with fierce energy. You know what I mean."

I did. There was an afterglow that followed the raids. People who came back had a vitality that seemed to shine out of them for weeks. Most said it was the blessing of the gods for showing the world the strength of their followers, but I thought it more likely that when you came so close to death you seized every moment you could when you came home.

"Every time he came back, I would try to talk to him at the Summer's End festival. He might start to have a conversation with me, but he'd always get dragged away to his little group of friends. What did they call themselves? The Sea Wolves, that's it. He'd always end up as part of that little pack. I hated watching him walk away. All year we'd flirt and he'd promise to bring me back some glorious plunder and propose with it, but every time he got dragged away by that damn pack."

I winced into my cup as she spoke. More than once I'd been in the group that had pulled Ulfur away from Fjola during the celebrations. "Sorry."

"It's not your fault," Fjola said with a laugh. "Ulfur's always had a soft spot for a horn of ale with good friends. After a couple of years, I said to Ulfur that if he didn't propose before he went off raiding, I'd make him regret it."

Fjola shook her head. "You know what Ulfur's like. He laughed, told me not to worry, and sure enough, didn't propose. And that's when I decided I'd go out there and become one of the Sea Wolves myself. I remember thinking that if I was part of his little pack then there was no way he could wave me off and ignore me and even if he did, then I'd use my plunder instead of waiting for him."

I refilled our cups and threw another broken branch on the fire.

"I remember that," I said.

The night that Fjola had announced her intention to go raiding had been talked about for months afterwards. It wasn't every day someone stood on the feast table to shout an ultimatum across Dagnur's hall.

"What was it you said to him?"

"Oh, gods, who can remember? We were all pretty drunk at the time. I think it was something like... Ulfur Dvalinson, if you won't use your riches to marry me, then I'll have to get my own and buy you."

In my mind's eye, I was back in the hall on that night.

"And then Ulfur jumped on the table as well," I said. "He said whoever got the most plunder had to pay for the wedding, didn't he?"

"He did."

"Who had to pay for the wedding in the end?"

"I can't remember," Fjola said with a shake of her head. "It's all a bit of a blur. I'm not sure we paid for anything. It all happened so quickly when we got back. Sif was at the jetty and we got married before we got off the longship."

"Oh yes, Ulfur said he didn't want to step back onto land unless you were his wife."

Fjola smiled to herself. "He did."

We sat in contented silence for a while. The trees swayed, sweeping the stars back and forth above us.

"Was it worth it?" I asked quietly. "Do you think you should have waited for Ulfur?"

Fjola snorted. "If I waited for him then I'd still be waiting. That man won't do anything if he's got the opportunity to drink instead."

Her expression softened and became more serious. Her free hand wandered up towards her face and played with her eye patch.

"I paid a price for going out on those raids. There are some days where I get frustrated and wish I hadn't been so rash and never lost my eye, but it's never enough to make me wish I didn't go. Every once in a while one of the kids sneaks up on my blind side and knocks me over with a hug. They always pretend that they forgot I couldn't see them, but their little grins give them away.

"It was worth it. Ulfur and I got married, we raided together, we had two amazing children and I couldn't imagine my life without any of them. And besides, if I hadn't gone raiding we wouldn't be shield-sisters. That's worth it all on its own, right?"

I laughed and offered up my cup in a toast.

"To risks gladly taken," I said.

We finished our drinks and enjoyed the quiet night. The amber glow of the fire danced all around us, drenching us in soft light that kept away the dark.

"Do you think you would have had children?"

A quiet question, barely audible over the spit and hiss of the fire. Fjola's gaze stayed low, as though to let me pretend I hadn't heard. I thought about the question long enough that it must have seemed like I was ignoring it.

"I don't know," I murmured. "Maybe. We were so focused on getting our own farm, getting away from Dagnur, that we never really talked about what we would do after. I guess I always assumed we would, eventually. That seems like the point, doesn't it? Getting some land of our own so we could have a family. I don't know."

I let my voice fall away and Fjola let the silence fill the space between us.

Bjolfur and I had never openly talked about having children. It never needed to be discussed; we were trying to get our own farm and everything else could wait. Thinking about it now reminded me of the chasm in my soul, the cage I'd made of my chest for the grief-crow. Wondering about what could have been only served to show me a bird's eye view of all the roads now closed to me.

"You two were always more independent than me and Ulfur," Fjola said after some time. "We've got the life that we wanted, even if it is on Dagnur's land. We never butted heads with him as much as you did so he's not as hard on us."

"He's never liked that we were so open with our intentions to leave," I said.

"Of course not. Dagnur likes control and you were always trying to slip out of his claws." Fjola picked up a twig and started pulling it apart and throwing the pieces onto the fire. "Ulfur and I have been squirrelling extra money away. A few coins here and there, maybe if we have a really good year we'll keep most of it back. I think Dagnur would start to come down on us if he found out."

"Why? I thought you were happy with what you had?"

"I am, but I'd like to give the children a chance to get away if they want to, without having to go on a raid. I don't want them to lose an eye.

"That's the only thing I regret. Losing this." she tapped her eye patch. "If I hadn't lost it, Ulfur and I could have done another raid and maybe we would have had enough money to go somewhere else where the landowner wasn't such a fuck."

"Or maybe you wouldn't have come back," I said.

"Maybe. We're happy with our little family and if the price is dealing with Dagnur then it's worth it."

I nodded and watched the thrashing flames of our campfire.

Fjola and I had been friends for years, even before she came raiding and we became sworn shield-sisters, but we were so different in this. I tried to imagine what life would have been like if Bjolfur and I hadn't wanted to get away and wondered if we would have been happy under Dagnur's thumb. No, I couldn't imagine it. Our vision of a happy life had always been on our own land, away from anyone who would try and squeeze more than was fair from our yield even though we did the work.

"Get some sleep, Fjola. I'll take first watch."

She nodded and finished her drink.

Once Fjola was bundled up in a blanket, I looked up at the sky and tried to count the stars again. I thought I saw something glint in the night, higher than the trees but lower than the stars. Perhaps now that the Winds had brought me back to life they would watch me every night.

I ran a thumb over the ice-smooth scars on my arm and glanced at Fjola.

She deserved to know. She had a right to know why we were really going to the Althing and why I needed Ingvar to talk to the law-keepers.

I opened my mouth to tell her, but the gentle sound of

snoring cut me off. The words fell away from me and my courage crumpled.

Another time.

I turned to look at the boulder I rested on. It was split almost in two by the slow passage of winters. Water had seeped into a small gap and then frozen and thawed and frozen and thawed. As each sliver of water froze it widened the gap in tiny steps until eventually what had begun as a scratch upon the rock became a chasm that split it in two.

I looked down at my arms and turned them over to examine my scars. They shone in the starlight as though covered in frost and I wondered how long it would take for the power of the Wind to break me.

I went back to staring at the stars and let the crow-coloured night wash over me.

*

We reached the Althing four days later and although we arrived tired and dirty, we had made good time on the journey. As we wound our way up yet another mountain path we heard the indistinct shouts of merchant crowds. The path followed the curve of the mountain and as we rounded the corner the fjord opened up before us, showing us the full discord of a winter Althing.

The mountain's low slopes were packed with people manoeuvring up and down a gargantuan split in the earth that began beneath the fjord and continued all the way to the heart of the mountain. The chasm, named Fafstol's Scar, was a remnant of the final battle of the war between the gods and the Winds. The giant Fafstol had attacked the Father with all his strength to try and end the war in one fell blow. The Father had knocked Fafstol's axe aside with Svelldrepa, the spear woven from glaciers by the Father himself, and Fafstol's axe instead bit deep into the earth. Now we were left with a chasm-scar that cut through the mountain like a log split for firewood.

At its deepest, the chasm could swallow even the High King's mead-hall and was wide enough that three longships could sail abreast without scraping the sides. The Scar stretched from the peak of the mountain and sank down into the fjord at the foot of the Broken Mountain. The water flowed into the Scar a little way which created a natural jetty. Within the chasm of the Scar, beyond the flock of ships berthed at its end, the law-keepers clustered in tents and judged the appeals of the figures that buzzed around them. On the slopes above, bright merchant tents stuffed themselves right up to the edge of Fafstol's Scar and cried out to the crowd that moved around them like shoals of fish around a rocky shore.

We walked down the mountain. The smells and sounds grew stronger the closer we came to the Scar. The crowds thickened, and soon it felt like we were wandering through a city. No one gave us a second glance as we merged with the crowd. We were not the only bedraggled travellers heading to the Althing.

"What do we do now? How do we go and appeal to a law-keeper?" I asked. The sight of the Scar and all the people crying out to one another assaulted my senses and I couldn't see a way through.

Fjola shot me a look. "How should I know?"

"I thought you came to the Althing to sell something once."

"That was a long time ago, Edda, and I came in the summer."

"It's got to be similar, though, hasn't it?"

Fjola shrugged.

All around us people talked in excited tones. The Althing was an event that most people looked forward to all year. Some were keen to get to the wrestling rings and see their favourite fighters, others couldn't wait to get to the skill sports like axe or spear throwing, and even more wanted to find their way to a good barrel of ale and disappear into it. As we pushed our way through merchants and customers, and fended off a few pickpockets, it became clear there was a pattern to the swell of the crowd. A small number of people poured out of Fafstol's Scar, but after a moment the movement ebbed back toward the centre of the Althing like the current pulling the waves back out to sea. We let ourselves be swept up to the edge of the chasm where we saw bridges across the Scar as well as stairs cut into the chasm walls. Standing by each of them was a pair of bored-looking huskalar speaking with people and giving them directions.

"Let's go ask them," I said.

We went to a pair of fighters standing guard at the nearest stairs. They each carried a spear and shield but had nothing else to demonstrate their authority. They paused their conversation as we approached and turned to us.

"We need to speak with the law-keepers," I said.

"So go," the one on the left said. He gestured down the stairs and turned back to his conversation.

I waited for some price that needed to be paid, but there was none. They ignored us and we made our way down. The stairs were uneven and steep, but solid, so we took them with caution and kept one hand on the wall of cool rock next to us as we made our way down.

The atmosphere changed as we descended into Fafstol's Scar. The shadows deepened and it felt as though we were descending into another realm, floating like moths towards the pinprick flames of torches below. The excited chattering and shouting of the crowd were replaced by serious mutterings and low, heated arguments. Fjola began to shiver as the warmth of the sun disappeared and revealed the true chill of the wind.

"Aren't you cold?" she asked through chattering teeth.

"No," I said. I pulled my cloak over my scars. "Come on, let's get this over with."

Fjola frowned but didn't push the issue as we moved towards the law-keepers. The tents and lodgings here ranged in size from small tents that only fit two people and a table, to one as large as Dagnur's hall with banners flapping at its entrance. Law-keepers flitted between the tents carrying small bags or writing tablets and people with worry-creased brows or angry frowns waited by tent entrances for their turn to be heard.

We made our way over to the largest tent, ignoring the smaller ones and the people that peered at us as we passed. They, however, did not ignore us.

"Where are you going?" asked a warrior who stepped into our path. They leaned on a spear and had an elaborately painted shield strapped to their other arm. There was a muffled jangling of metal from under their tunic, likely a mail shirt, and a half-helm fit firmly on their head, obscuring their features.

This was a huskalar, the sworn warriors of a king's household, and given the best weapons and armour. I almost smiled to think of the people Dagnur had given weapons to, and how flimsy they were in comparison to a true huskalar.

"I'm owed a blood-debt," I said but didn't stop walking. Even if this huskalar was doing their duty, they stood between me and justice and I could not wait any longer.

He stuck his spear out to block my path.

"Didn't your law-keeper get your chief to pay it?"

"My... chief," I said through gritted teeth, "is a greedy piece of shit who refuses to pay. Now get out of my way and let me get through to the High King's law-keepers."

He straightened, suddenly on edge, and tightened the grip on his spear.

"We've had a long trip." Fjola stepped in front of me. "And we've not been to the Althing in a long time. Where do we need to go to speak to a law-keeper about this?"

For a moment he looked like he might shove his spear through Fjola to get to me, then he relaxed and shrugged.

"Go and speak to someone over there, but keep your friend in check, okay? I don't want to have to come over there and do something you'll regret."

Fjola smiled and thanked him. I rolled my eyes.

"He thinks he's tough, doesn't he? Big man with a big piece of wood in his hands."

"Shut up," hissed Fjola. "He might be too quick to make threats, but he's still one of the guards down here. Come on, let's go."

The smaller tents the guard waved us towards were obscured by the shadows cast by the craggy chasm walls, but as we passed them I could see that inside each there was a bench and a law-keeper discussing a case with someone. We walked until we saw someone leaning half-through a tent entrance. We moved closer to see if they were leaving and if we would be able to speak with the law-keeper.

"...your continued support, law-keeper," said the man standing at the entrance. He threw something inside and I heard the tell-tale clink of coins.

"Thank you, Lothi," the law-keeper said. "It is unnecessary, but I appreciate it nonetheless. My true reward is justice itself."

The man chuckled. "Of course, law-keeper. My king hopes that your rewards are satisfying enough."

Another clink of coin.

"Very satisfying."

The man turned and walked away from the tent. He was built like a warrior and had a braided beard that hung halfway down his chest. Something about him sparked heat in my chest, but I didn't know what or why. He shot us a grin and stalked away.

We waited a moment longer and then ducked through the tent entrance ourselves.

The law-keeper glanced up from scribbling on parchment and gave an exasperated sigh. "What do you want?"

"I've come to make an appeal."

"And you?" he sneered at Fjola. "Why are you here?"

"Moral support."

He snorted. "I am only able to discuss details with the supplicant, with the exception of witnesses. Are you a witness?"

We looked at each other.

"I don't think so," she said.

"Then you will have to wait outside." He waved Fjola away.

I began to object, but Fjola put her hand on my arm.

"I'll go get us some food. Maybe I can find us somewhere to sleep as well. If you're done before I am, I'll meet you by the top of the stairs."

"Sure," I said.

I bit down on the rest of what I wanted to say. I didn't want the law-keeper to know how badly I wanted Fjola to stay. I was days from a home that had been destroyed and now my only friend was abandoning me on the Scar's shadowed floor. Fjola seemed to sense it anyway; she squeezed my arm, told me I'd be fine, and then she was gone.

I sat on the bench in front of the law-keeper. They had returned to their work and after a moment I wondered if he had forgotten I was there. I cleared my throat.

"In a moment," he said. "I must finish this first."

I waited. In the near silence of the tent, the scratch of the iron stylus ate away at me like a crow pecking at my patience. I thought about what I needed to say, what I needed the law-keeper to do. From what little I knew about the law, I thought that my best chance of getting money out of Dagnur was to claim Bjoflur's share of the raid's plunder, and maybe I could get my hoard back from that greedy bastard as the damage from the Wind-hunters couldn't be blamed on me.

"So." The law-keeper moved his wax tablet to one side and leaned forward on the table. He peered at me over his laced fingers. "I am Einar Vigenson, one of the High King's law-keepers. If you wish to make an appeal against a judgement the law-keeper of your local chief has made you will need to tell me your name, your chieftain's name, the name of your law-keeper..."

The list went on and I rattled off the information as he scratched it down. It felt like hours, though must have only been a small while, and then he actually started listening to me.

"What exactly is the nature of your appeal?"

I told him most of what had happened. Bjolfur died whilst we were out raiding, Dagnur refused to give me his portion. I explained how the Wind-hunters destroyed our home and I was being made to pay for it. The law-keeper watched over his laced fingers, his expression calculating and imperious.

"And which part are you appealing?" His lip curled as he spoke.

"Well, I shouldn't have to pay to rebuild a farm if it was razed by Wind-hunters, and I want my husband's portion of the raid plunder."

Einar shot me a thin press-lipped smile that made him look like a snake. "Edda. It is Edda, isn't it? I am not sure that I am hearing the whole story here. You say that you were not paid for the plunder that your husband rightfully earned with a brave death, but I cannot imagine any law-keeper siding with your chief on this. Refusing to pay a warrior's rightful portion of plunder not only goes against the laws of the High King, but of the gods themselves.

"Let us, for a moment, entertain the notion that your law-keeper is a corrupt, spineless individual who bends to your chief's decisions regardless of the law. Even if that were the case, and I know that it cannot be, then your god-speaker would have stepped in so as to not to incur the wrath of the gods. Something does not add up in your story."

He leaned back and spread his palms out in front of him, inviting me to fill the silence. I stared at my feet as though avoiding the law-keeper's gaze would let me avoid the question, avoid having to relive that moment. The silence stretched on. I tried to swallow the heavy sorrow at the back of my throat, but it resurfaced like driftwood from a shipwreck.

"My husband died whilst we were out raiding," I said, my voice grating against the weight in my throat. I clenched and unclenched my fists under the table.

"How exactly did he die?"

"Does it matter?"

"I wouldn't have asked otherwise."

"There was a storm." I swallowed. The memory still churned inside me, and the thought of telling this stranger twisted my stomach. "There was a storm on the way back and he drowned."

"There we are," he said, as though talking to a difficult child. "Then the decision by your chief and law-keeper was entirely correct. Perhaps a bit callous, all things considered, but I cannot fault their decision from a legal standpoint."

He stood and began gesturing me out of the tent.

"And I can't do anything to help you with the farm burning down either. Tenants are responsible for the upkeep of their chief's property whilst they look after it. If you were unable to protect it from these so-called Wind-hunters then that is down to you."

Einar loomed over me, but I refused to stand up and leave.

"They attacked us outside of the raiding season. There must be someone else I can appeal to?"

"Who? You said they were Wind-hunters. If they were Wind-hunters, they were outlaws, no better than wolves. There is no one else to appeal to. I have heard your case and made my decision, which is final as authorised by the High King."

He took half a step closer, trying to usher me out by moving too close to me, but I still refused to rise. With a sigh, he waved a hand at a guard outside.

"They mentioned someone had sent them," I spoke quickly, trying to change his mind before the guard arrived. "After I killed one of them they talked about someone not caring how many of them died as long as he got his Windborn. They were sent by..." I faltered as I tried to remember who the Wind-hunters had called on. "Hraki. Someone called Hraki."

Einar froze and his eyes went wide, arm still outstretched to call the guard.

"Ridiculous," he spat. He had gone pale and leaned out of the tent to gesture wildly to catch someone's attention. "No one would deal with Wind-hunters like that and risk becoming an outlaw themselves."

"That's what they said," I continued, hating myself for the desperation in my voice. "They said that Hraki wanted Windborn."

Einar stopped waving long enough to fix me with a furious glare. "And who is this Hraki? Do you have any other names for him? No. You have only pulled a name from the air when you've not gotten your way. I have made my verdict and that is final."

People gathered around the tent, having long given up any pretence of subtlety and openly gawked at us.

"No." I stood and the chair toppled over behind me. "I know what I heard. Those Wind-hunters said that someone sent them, someone called Hraki. I swear on my scars."

The law-keeper met my eyes. We stared at each other for what seemed like an eternity. Hot fury burned in my eyes and something cold glittered in his. Sweat beaded on his forehead. His lips parted.

The guard from earlier stomped up to us and broke the spell.

"What's wrong?" the guard said to the law-keeper.

Einar blinked and looked around as though he didn't know where he was.

"What?" He blinked again then straightened and scowled. "I have made my verdict on this woman's appeal and she refuses to accept it and leave."

"You haven't—"

115

The guard grabbed me roughly by the shoulder and started to guide me out.

"Come on," he said. "You don't want to cause any trouble, not here."

I began to retort, but several other huskalar hovered nearby. They seemed eager for something to break the monotony of their day and so I let myself be guided to the stairs out of the chasm.

*

Fjola found me sat on a rock by the top of the stairs. Other people had been wandering past and I had been trying to guess at their success with the law-keepers judging by the look on their faces. Most wore weary, triumphant smiles.

"Sorry," Fjola said as she slumped down next to me. "I couldn't get any food. The only thing I could find was stew, and they wouldn't let me take the bowls away. I did find us somewhere to sleep though. It's... what's wrong?"

I sighed and stood then stretched until my spine cracked.

"They wouldn't listen. I told them what happened, explained what Dagnur did and everything, but they agreed with him."

"What about getting Bjolfur's share of the plunder from the raid? Did they agree to that at least?"

The familiar, crow-sized weight had settled back in my chest and fluttered up my throat. I shook my head, afraid that if I opened my mouth that grief-crow would fly out and bring with it all of my wailing sorrow.

"Shit. I'm sorry, Edda."

She put her arm around my shoulders and pulled me close. I let out a deep breath. The shuddering, shipwreck breath that was a hair's breadth from sobs.

"We can wait for Ingvar," she said. "He knows how all this works, maybe he can think of something to say that will change their mind. He should be here soon and then we'll come back."

We sat like that for a while, watching the surge and pull of the excited crowds. It felt like there was a river coursing next to me, vital and restless but entirely separate.

"Come on." Fjola stood and offered her hand. "I found

where the arena is. Let's go and watch some fighters beat the shit out of each other. It will take your mind off things."

A small smile played on my lips. I nodded and took her hand and we joined the flowing crowd.

It seemed like the arena was on the other side of the world, we had to push our way past so many people. First, we made our way beyond the tents where merchants hawked their goods, we bought some cooked rabbit as we went. As I bit into a juicy leg, Fjola swore to me the stall wasn't there an hour before. After that, there was a smattering of encampments and Fjola pointed out where we would be staying. Then finally, as the clustered tents opened out, we saw the space reserved for games and chief among them was the arena.

A crowd swirled around it where people stood or sat on what looked like a small hill. As we braved the press and got closer, we saw that the arena was a pit dug into the ground and the excavated earth had been used to make a raised circle around it like the dirt walls of a hill fort.

We pushed through the crowd and came in sight of the fighters, two tired men pawing at each other and trying to wrestle their opponent to the ground. Fjola's expression pinched as the tang of blood and the stench of sweat reached us.

There was a roar, smothering some boos and hisses, as one of the fighters gripped his opponent's legs and pulled. The opponent couldn't stop him and their legs twisted out from under them. The pinned fighter struggled to break free, but couldn't. The cheering fell away as the crowd held its breath, but the pinned fighter tapped his opponent and surrendered. Another cacophony of noise. This time the boos and cheers were more evenly mixed.

Once the fighters left the ring an announcer came out. He wore a bright cloak, though it trailed a little in the mud, lined with white feathers at the neck. He raised his arms to greet the crowd and at the same time silence them.

"Friends," he called, once the crowd's noise had lessened to a simmering whisper. "Did you enjoy that?"

A roar from the crowd. He waved them back into relative silence. Behind the announcer a couple more fighters prepared themselves. They stripped down to only tunics and trousers and walked over to something I couldn't quite make out.

"You've seen what these fighters can do with their bare hands. Don't you think it's time we put something in those hands?"

Another cheer.

The fighters behind the announcer stepped into the ring. They had each selected a weapon. One had a wooden stave and the other had picked up a small shield and club. The crowd cheered as the fighters waved, nodded to each other, and then they were on their guard and circling. As soon as the announcer called a start to the fight the crowd cheered and whooped, drowning the sounds of smashing wood.

I looked over the faces surrounding me, watching their reactions. The weight of the crow on my heart muted my enjoyment of the fight.

Some of the people around us looked bored. Perhaps they were waiting for the Windborn to make an appearance. The Althing's fighting arenas were often used by new Windborn to showcase their powers and convince chieftains to offer them a place in their household. It was easy to impress any visiting dignitaries if your household guard was filled with warriors that possessed superhuman strength and supernatural powers.

One of the fighters landed a vicious blow on their opponent and the cheer almost deafened me.

As the crowd settled down I caught a glimpse of someone I thought I recognised. That was hardly a surprise. The Althing attracted people from all over, but there was something about the limp red hair and the ragged moustache that wouldn't let me look away. Whoever he was, he wasn't concerned with the fight. They had a worried expression plastered on their face and their gaze shifted quickly from place to place. He smiled as someone came up to him and began a conversation. Heat surged in my chest as I realised where I had seen him. The grief-crow clawed at the inside of my ribs, trying to rip itself out of me and attack the red-haired man. I had seen his smile before, just before he kicked me off a cliff.

"I'll be right back," I said.

"Be quick. You don't want to miss this," Fjola murmured,

her attention fixed on the fight.

I kept low, trying not to be spotted by the red-haired warrior. As people shifted in their seats I slipped between them, their movement hiding mine. I followed him at a distance, ignoring the annoyed grunts from those I bumped into, until the red-haired warrior found who he was looking for and sat down. I found my own seat far enough away that I would be hidden behind other spectators, but close enough that I could keep him in my sights. I rubbed at the scar, now crusted with ice, where he had scored the flesh from my ribs. I couldn't kill him, not here, but if I got close enough perhaps I could overhear some detail that would let me find him alone and vulnerable. Now that he had greeted whoever he had come to meet, the red-haired warrior looked nervous again. The person Red Hair spoke to had a braided beard and was built like an oak trunk. His clothes were finely made and an elaborate arm-ring glittered in the sunlight.

Judging from the crowd's enthusiasm, the fighters were close to finishing each other off. I glanced over, blood glittered on the ground all around them. Both fighters breathed heavily and the warrior with the club had dropped his shield. There was a final almighty cheer as the stave-fighter smacked their weapon across the club-wielder's face. Club-wielder collapsed. The fight was over.

The cheering died down as the unconscious fighter was dragged away and in the relative calm, I overheard the red-haired warrior and his companion.

"That was never the deal," Red Hair whispered. "You can't go back on it now."

"Easy," his companion said. "No one's going back on anything. You fight and I pick you. You know how it works."

"You said we'd be part of the household once we became Windborn. Well, I'm Windborn. Now make me part of the household."

The stout man put his hand on red-hair's shoulder and leaned in. I shifted a few seats over and strained to listen.

"Look, Soren. I can't just take you in like that. How do you think it'd look if Hraki just offered you a place in his household without any proof of what you can do? You go in there, fight a few people and show us what you're made of. Once we've seen that, I can step up and make you an offer, okay?"

"Okay. Fine."

Red Hair, the Windborn Soren, took a few deep breaths and nodded.

"Just a warning," the other man said and pulled Soren in close by the scruff of his neck. "If anyone else makes you an offer and you even think about accepting it, I will make sure that this is a very swift resurrection."

He let go and Soren reeled back before he slipped through the crowd towards the edge of the arena. I sat back and turned my attention to the fighters slinking out of the arena.

"Some blood at last," the announcer shouted as he stepped back out.

The crowd cried out in agreement.

"Now, I think it's time for something special, don't you?"

Another cheer.

"You want to see a real fighter? You want to see a champion? You want to see a Windborn?"

In answer, the crowd roared and stomped their feet. With each question the cheers grew louder until the ground shook with such force that it knocked snow from the trees.

The announcer took a few steps back and gestured behind him. Soren stepped into the ring looking nervous but growing in confidence as the crowd cheered. He waved. Some of the crowd murmured to one another and shook their heads. Soren was scrawny compared to the other fighters I had seen that day, and it seemed they were not impressed so far.

"Who steps forward?"

"Soren Gunnarson."

"And why are you here, Soren?"

"To prove my worth as a Windborn warrior."

Soren raised his hands, as though in greeting, and they erupted into flames. The ground shook again as the crowd cheered even harder, all doubts forgotten. My teeth ached as I ground them together and my fingernails cut into my palms. The announcer laughed and encouraged Soren to show them what he could do. Tongues of flames shot from his hands like writhing serpents. Embers and sparks floated around him as though he was a walking wildfire. The air around Soren began to shimmer in the heat and the muddy ground beneath him dried and cracked as he circled the arena.

To one side of the arena, four fighters looked on with grim expressions. These were the only fighters prepared to go up against a Windborn and they did not look pleased to see Soren's powers showcased before their fight.

The announcer gestured for Soren to stop and, after a final explosion of blue and red flames, the Windborn stepped back.

"And how many brave fighters will face off against this Windborn? How many do you think would be a good number, Soren? One? A pair? Or more than that?"

"Fighting four at once seems like fun," Soren said and rolled his shoulders.

There was a scripted pause. The crowd whispered excitedly and looked from Soren to those waiting warriors. One of the fighters took a breath and started to step forward, but I leapt up from my seat and stumbled to the edge of the arena.

"I will fight him."

Another brief pause, this one uncomfortable as the announcer looked from me back to the prepared fighters. Then his expression smoothed and he smiled.

"Such courage! We have our first fighter. And who will stand with her?"

He began to turn, but I was already pushing my way past the crowd. I stepped out into the ring and drew his gaze once more.

"No. No one else. Just me and him."

The crowd murmured and a few cheers were heard from the crowd. Fjola burst out of the crowd on the other side of the arena. She rushed over to me and grabbed my arm.

"What are you doing?" she hissed. "Come and sit down. You can't take on a Windborn."

Her objection twisted my insides. I thought back to my conversations with Sif and Ingvar. If there was a time to show her I was Windborn, it was now.

"That's him, Fjola."

"What?" Her face was still contorted into furious confusion. "He's who?"

"He's one of the Wind-hunters. The one that pushed me off the cliff."

I shook her off and there was a tinkling sound. I glanced down and saw that there was ice forming on my arms. Some had stuck to Fjola's fingers as I had shaken her free. The part of me that hoped I wasn't Windborn, that I would be able to go back to a normal life, withered as frost spread across my skin like the slow march of winter.

Fjola looked at her hand and then to my arm.

"It's okay, Fjola."

Her eye widened as her gaze locked on the ice still growing on my arm and then her expression turned grim. She nodded and stepped back into the front of the crowd.

"Perhaps it is not courage, but foolishness?" The announcer asked the crowd. "What is your name, you courageous fool?"

"Edda Gretasdottir."

"And why do you want to fight today, Edda? Are our other fighters not good enough?"

I ground my teeth as I wondered what to say. The axe wound in my side ached, the space where my home used to be burned behind my eyes, and the grief-crow pecked at my heart. Frozen fury seared under my skin. I looked at my hands. Frost spread across them and began to thicken to ice.

"I fight to prove my worth as a Windborn."

Silence washed over the crowd. The announcer frowned. His mouth opened and closed. I turned to the crowd and held up a hand covered in glacier-thick ice.

The crowd exploded into cheers and stomps. I turned to look at Soren. His expression was grim, but he didn't seem to recognize me. Eventually, the announcer managed to wave the crowd into silence.

"What a treat we have for you. It is a rare thing to see a Windborn fight in this arena, and now we have two ready to battle for your pleasure!"

A young man came up to me and handed me a club and a shield. On the other side of the arena, someone else gave Soren the same. The boy explained the rules as I tested the weight of the shield and club.

"The fight goes until someone is knocked unconscious,

122

surrenders, or is knocked out of the arena. When the announcer calls a halt you stop."

I nodded, not taking my eyes from Soren.

The men ran off. The announcer circled the edge of the arena and talked to the crowd. Soren walked along the edge, encouraging the crowd and throwing sparks out from his hand. I shook out the ache from my limbs and watched Soren for any weakness.

"Are you ready, Windborn?"

"Ready," Soren shouted, banging his shield.

I nodded.

"Begin," the announcer cried as he leapt out of the arena.

Soren dashed forward and struck a few blows on my shield, testing my reflexes and reach.

I did the same.

My movements were quicker than they had ever been before and the club whipped through the air like a striking viper. I felt the cold touch of frost on my arm as I struck again and again. Then the hot blast of air as Soren attacked me.

We broke apart and circled each other. Neither of us had given ground, but we both knew this was only a test of our new Windborn speed.

The air shimmered around Soren's shoulders and he came forward.

I lunged to meet him and we fell into an easy rhythm of violence. I smacked at his shield with mine, trying to get an opening, and he brought his club around and under mine to try and trip me. His speed caught me off guard and the club scraped my shin as I pulled my leg away.

Another blow caught me on the arm. There was a mighty snap as the ice there cracked. We jumped apart and the crowd cheered.

I glanced at my arm. It was red and sore, but no blood. Ice reformed over the hole.

"Shouldn't we give them a show?" Soren asked as I came in for another attack. His mouth twisted into a smile. The same smile he wore when he killed me.

I wanted to scream accusations at him, to demand an explanation and reparations for what he had taken from me, but my anger smothered my tongue and all that escaped was a furious growl.

He swung his club in lazy arcs towards me. I kept my ground and parried them easily. Then he started shooting flames.

He pointed his club like a wand and flames gushed out of it, surging towards me. I held up my shield to weather the assault and they surrounded me. The heat bit into me and the cold fury that kept me going waned against it. The ice on my arms glistened, melted, and dripped to the floor. Then the fire sank its searing teeth into me. I cried out and leapt aside.

The crowd whooped as I gasped in the cool air once I was free of the flames.

I knelt on the muddy ground, panting. Soren had turned to the crowd again and was cheering with them, throwing more flames into the air for good measure. I shook my head. I hadn't wanted to accept the powers the Winds had given me, but Soren had, and he was winning.

He turned his attention back to me and twirled his club.

As I put my hand against the wet ground to push myself up, I had an idea. I balled up the cold fury in my chest and pushed it down through my arms. The mud around my hand hardened. I willed the ice to move towards Soren. White veins of frost erupted across the ground like lightning.

I ripped my hand out of the hoar-crusted earth and banged my shield. Soren turned back to me, grinning, and rushed forwards. He hadn't seen the ice. He yelped as his feet slipped from under him.

The overpowering heat from his body melted the ice as he slid over it. By the time he stopped, his entire left side was covered in mud. I swung the wooden club down as hard as I could. Soren twisted and took the brunt of the attack on his shoulder.

I raised my club for another swing, but he kicked at my legs.

We both toppled over as we tried to wrestle each other to the ground. Soren's body felt like hot coals against my winter skin. Soren grunted and kneed me in the ribs. It felt like I had been kicked by a horse. Gasping, I clutched at my side and Soren rolled away.

Cheering drowned out whatever insult Soren mumbled at

me. He spat a hot glob of blood on the ground. We had dropped our weapons in the scramble and now they lay scattered about the arena. The two clubs and one of the shields were within easy reach of Soren. He moved slowly to pick up the shield and tossed it away from us before picking up the two clubs.

His burning eyes never left mine.

I limped over to pick up the shield stuck in the mud nearby. Soren clacked the clubs together and smoke began to rise from beneath his fingers.

"That was a smart move," he growled. All sense of showmanship gone. "It won't work again."

I bared my teeth. Fatigue gnawed at the edges of my fury, but I stoked it with everything that Soren had taken from me. My home, my life, and a peaceful death.

Steam rose from the ground and I glanced down. Darkness leached from the mud around his feet as the dirt dried and cracked.

Soren saw my distraction and leapt to attack. I got the shield up in time to block a vicious right-hand swing from one of the clubs. Another swing from the left, but I was too slow. The club thumped into my shoulder as I tried to avoid it.

The force of the blows shuddered through my bones and with each one I was pushed back a little further. The closer he pushed me to the edge of the arena the louder the crowd roared.

I pushed with my own Windborn power and froze the mud around my feet. I used the frozen earth as an anchor to push against. I exploded forwards and shoved the shield into Soren's face. He dodged, but not quick enough and I sent him stumbling back. I leapt past him and back to the centre of the arena.

Soren grinned and launched himself at me again.

The blows came thick and fast like a rain of boulders against the shield. I spun to deflect as many as I could but couldn't meet all of them. One searing club smashed on the shield from above and the other swooped in from the side and landed hard against my leg. With every blow, I felt the frozen fury in my chest fade, slowly withering with exhaustion.

125

It seemed to go on for hours before Soren relented.

By the time he moved back I had bruises and burn marks all over my legs, arms, and face.

Soren panted, but he only sported scrapes and bruises from the few strikes I had managed to land using the shield.

Some shouts made their way through the noise of the crowd.

"Finish her off!"

"Don't just stand there!"

Soren's clubs smoked, the wood around his clenched fists now charred. I pooled my power into my right hand and felt the growing weight of ice in my fist.

"Is that it?" I called over.

"I thought I'd give you a chance to surrender," he replied.

"I'll kill you," I panted.

He grinned that wicked, clifftop smile and my fury blazed. I edged forwards and Soren raised his weapons to a guard position. We circled one another for a moment before I threw the chunk of ice at his face.

He swatted at it with a club and opened his mouth to make a quip. As he focused on the ice I swept in on his side and jammed the shield into his leg. He went down to one knee with a cry and I smashed the shield into his head.

He dodged the hard iron shield boss at the shield's centre, but I shoved him onto his back. The shield bucked from the force of the blow and it bounced out of my hands. I leapt onto Soren as he tried to rise and pinned him down.

"What the fuck are you doing?" Soren said with eyes wide and an expression flipping between confusion and anger. "We've given them a show. I surrender."

I pulled my hand back, wrapped it in a glove of heavy ice, and punched him as hard as I could.

"You don't remember me, do you?"

Soren groaned. A trickle of blood ran down his face. "What?"

"The cliffs. You kicked me. Into. The. Ocean."

I punctuated each word with another vicious blow. The crowd's cheers had petered out. Soren blinked and gurgled. He tried to look at me, though he had trouble focusing.

My next punch broke the fist of ice. I cried out in frustration and wrapped my fingers around his neck. The skin was hot and growing warmer, but I kept my hands locked around his throat.

The crowd began to cry out with consternation and dismay.

People started to rush towards me.

The air shimmered and the flesh on my fingers blistered with the heat. I pressed harder.

Soren clawed at my hands and spluttering flames burst out all over him. My nostrils filled with the scent of burning. Shouts all around me, but they were lost in the roaring of blood in my ears and the crackle of my blistering hands.

Someone grabbed me and wrenched my arm away from Soren's throat. I threw them off me and whirled back around to Soren, but two more people took hold of me. I struggled. Everything merged into a searing, screaming mess of noise and I was dragged away.

CHAPTER SEVEN
RUNE-MARKED

FJOLA PACED BACK AND FORTH in front of me. My hands were raw and blistered from the heat of holding Soren's neck. I flexed my fingers and the skin cracked. The air around us was hot and tense like the air before a summer storm.

"What the fuck was that?" Fjola hissed.

I kept my eyes down and wrapped wet rags around my blistered fingers. "What?"

"Don't give me that," Fjola said. "First, you're a fucking Windborn and didn't tell me. Second, you could have killed that guy, Edda. I thought we were here to try and get some money so you could get your farm back, not go on a fucking killing spree." She leaned back and rubbed at her eyes. "Gods above, Edda, that crowd wanted to rip you apart."

I squeezed the soaking rag and watched the water cascade over my hands, freezing before it had a chance to drop onto the floor. We sat near the arena, surrounded by guards. They whispered amongst themselves and occasionally shot a worried look in our direction. I waited for some kind of judgement, though from whom, I wasn't sure, and Fjola had refused to leave me. She had brought a loaf of bread which we picked at.

"I told you he was one of them."

"He was what?" Fjola said, in an exasperated tone she probably used a lot with her children.

"One of the Wind-hunters," I whispered. "Didn't you recognise him?"

Fjola's hand froze halfway to her mouth.

"Are you sure?"

I cocked an eyebrow at her. "He was the one that kicked me

off the cliff. He gave me that same shit-eating grin and pushed me over."

"Shit. I didn't realise that's what you meant." She rubbed at her face with her free hand. "Is that why you volunteered to fight him on your own? You thought you'd kill him in there?"

"Maybe," I said with a shrug. "He's already killed me once I thought it was time to return the favour."

She shot me a look that told me she wasn't impressed with the joke.

"And when were you going to tell me you're Windborn?"

"Come on, Fjola, don't be like that."

"Like what? You think it's unreasonable that I want my best friend to tell me when she thinks she's died and come back to life?" Fjola met my gaze and her fury faltered. She covered her face with her hands. "Gods above, Edda, my heart nearly stopped in that fight. I thought he killed you."

I went over and gripped her shoulders.

"I'm tougher than that," I said softly. "It'll take more than that to kill me."

She shook me off and stepped away. "I thought I lost you once, Edda, I don't want to lose you again."

We stood in silence for a while. I sat back on the ground and picked at the bread. Eventually, Fjola came and sat with me.

"I wanted to tell you," I whispered. "The timing was never right. And I thought... I thought if I didn't tell you then maybe it wouldn't be true and I could go back to a normal life."

Fjola glanced over at me and then shook her head. She squeezed my rag-wrapped hands.

"You shouldn't have gone into that arena."

"Maybe."

"Edda," she sighed. "We're at the Althing. We could have gone to find one of the law-keepers and told them about Soren. If they knew he was one of the Wind-hunters, then they could have arrested him."

"If I tell them now it'll just look like I'm trying to weasel my way out of getting punished." I shook my head. "And that law-keeper I spoke to, Einar, didn't want anything to do with me. Why would it be any different after what I did in the arena?"

"We can get Soren to confess. We can talk to a different

law-keeper. Whatever it is, I'm sure we could have come up with something better than charging into the arena to try and kill someone in front of a hundred people."

Fjola rubbed at her eye and sighed. I tore off a chunk of crust and stared at it. Maybe Fjola was right. Away from the roar of the crowd and the iron tang of the arena, it all seemed different. I could have gone to a law-keeper and asked them to arrest Soren, and maybe then I could have gone my own way knowing that justice had been done. But Ingvar had been no help to me, and neither had Einar. Their words hadn't solved anything; only made it more complicated. In the arena it had all seemed so simple. Soren had been asking for someone to fight him. Justice stood in front of me begging to be taken.

"What do you think they'll decide?" Fjola asked. She nodded towards the group of people huddled in intense conversation. I recognised one of them as the announcer from the arena. A witness.

"I don't know." I tore off a hunk of bread and bit into it. "Maybe they're trying to figure out a prize for me. I did win."

Fjola shot me a sour look.

The group stopped their conversation and parted. An ancient woman strode past them. She moved with such fluid grace that it looked like she floated over the ground. She was a head shorter than most of the people around her, but her bearing made everyone else seem small.

"Which one of you is the Windborn?" she demanded.

Her voice was imperious without being condescending. The voice of someone who was obeyed.

"I am." I stood and walked over to her. "I need to speak with—"

"Is your law-keeper here, or have you two come on your own?"

I glanced back at Fjola who shrugged.

"We came ahead of our law-keeper, Ingvar Eirson. He travelled by longship and should arrive soon."

"You did not want to travel in the longship with him?"

"No."

She waited, but I refused to offer any more information. I broke away from the intensity in her eyes and looked her up

131

and down. A wooden arm-ring rested loosely on her right bicep. It was carved from oak, ash, and willow and each plaited piece of wood was carved with intricate symbols and images. Rune tattoos spiralled up from her hands and then disappeared into the sleeves of her tunic. More runes ran up from her neckline in lines so thick her pale skin was almost hidden.

"God-Speaker," Fjola said. She moved up next to me and nodded her head respectfully as she spoke. "Can you please let us know how long this will take? We have had a long day, even without all this happening. We just want to rest."

"You are free to go. It is the Windborn that we require."

Anger flared up inside me "The Windborn? Is that all I am now? I want to speak to—"

The god-speaker raised a hand and cut me off.

"You are Windborn. That is all there is to it. The Winds have stolen you from the gods and so the gods have no place for you. The laws are clear about the status of a Windborn but do not describe punishments for them. Such things are left up to their chieftains, which you no longer have."

I made to protest, to tell her about Dagnur, but then the implications of her words sunk in. Oaths ended when you died. Any oaths I had made before I drowned were now worthless. My mouth dried up and a lump surged at the back of my throat as the grief-crow tried to wriggle out of me. I wanted to shout at the god-speaker, tell her she was wrong, but I knew she wasn't. I was Windborn. All my oaths and promises had been swept away on the tide that killed me. I swallowed and the sorrow at the back of my throat fell and engulfed my heart.

"The law-keepers," she continued, "have decided we shall wait for your old law-keeper, this Ingvar Eirson, and let him speak on your behalf. In the meantime, I will mark you."

"Mark me?"

"The idea of you walking free through the Althing makes the law-keepers uneasy." The god-speaker made no attempt to hide the derision in her voice. "I will mark you with runes to disrupt your Windborn powers as well as runes to keep me apprised of your movements."

She gestured to someone behind her and I instinctively stepped back. Someone broke away from the small crowd gathered behind the god-speaker. He had runes tattooed on his arms and face and wore the same clothes as the god-speaker, though they were not as fine and his arm-ring simple woven wood. Her apprentice. I tensed as he drew near. More people stepped out of the crowd. Fighters this time. Men and women dressed in plenty of armour, wielding spears and axes.

"Do I have a choice about this?" I growled.

"Not really," the god-speaker said with a shrug. "You can choose to struggle, but you will be given the rune-mark one way or another."

Fjola put her hand on my shoulder. Her familiar touch reminded me I was not alone and eased some of the writhing anguish in my chest. "It's okay, Edda. It's not permanent, is it?" She looked to the god-speaker who acknowledged it wasn't. "Once Ingvar gets here he'll help us figure all of this out."

I looked from Fjola, begging me not to resist, to the god-speaker, and then to the guards fanning out behind her.

"Fine," I sighed.

The guards relaxed and the apprentice came forward with a small bag and a bowl. The god-speaker pulled ingredients from the bag and crushed them together in the bowl. Some things I recognised, willow bark and charcoal, but some things were a mystery, a feather that seemed to shimmer and something that could have been a precious stone or a splinter from the heart of a glacier. She mixed them all together and soon had a thick ocean-coloured paste.

"Come forward."

I did and she pulled my left hand out so that the inside of my forearm was exposed to her. She dipped her other hand into the paste and began to scrawl runes along my arm and chant something under her breath. As she finished the first rune, my arm started to feel numb and by the third, I had barely any sensation in my hand. The feeling spread, pulsing up my arm and into my body as though carried by my own heartbeat. The further the feeling travelled, the more dizzy and nauseated I became.

The god-speaker finished her chanting and looked at me.

"Do you feel it?"

The muscles in my neck bunched and I nodded, not trusting

myself to speak. I examined the paste now scrawled over my arm. Each rune glittered with some ethereal light as though they were stars caught in tar. I had learned enough runes to read, write, and make basic charms against misfortune, but these were something else. These were runes that could twist and bend the tapestry of fate. The work of a master rune-weaver.

"Good. The effects will disappear in time, as your friend supposed, but for now it will prevent you from being a nuisance." She turned away from us and looked over to a group huddled behind the guards. "Are you satisfied?"

Something in her voice made me suspect that she had not wanted to do this, but the law-keepers had forced her.

One in the huddled group nodded.

"Good."

The god-speaker whirled around and stormed off, snapping her fingers for her apprentice to follow. A law-keeper approached, dragging one of the guards along with him. Once he was confident I wouldn't attack, he puffed out his chest and spoke with as much authority as he could muster.

"Windborn Edda, we hereby command you to attend a judgement presided by High Law-Keeper Leif Durison for the attempted murder of the Windborn Soren as soon as your law-keeper arrives at the Althing." The law-keeper seemed to have found his stride and he scowled down at me as he continued. "The High Law-Keeper is busy enough as it is without having to deal with you, but with your law-keeper present and able to advise you the judgement will be swift and the High Law-Keeper can get back to his proper duties."

I looked back at Fjola. She glared at the law-keeper but her gaze quickly returned to me and her expression was one of deep concern.

"Fine. As soon as I find him, I'll come and find you, okay?"

The law-keeper nodded. I moved to leave and he hopped half a step back.

"And don't think that you can just run off," one of the others shouted from behind a guard. "We'll find you with that mark."

I glanced down at the glittering runes on my arm but kept walking.

"Come on," I said to Fjola. "I think I could do with a rest."

Fjola nodded. I let her go ahead and take us to our rented beds.

"What's your plan now?" she asked.

"Find Ingvar once he arrives and then go and talk to those law-keepers."

"I mean what are you going to do after that? I'm sure that their punishment won't be too harsh, if Ingvar can't convince them to drop it entirely. Windborn fighters are too valuable."

My mouth twisted at the thought of being used like a piece of plunder heedless of my own desires. "I don't know. I'm not going back to be Dagnur's Windborn. He'd never give me any rest."

Fjola paused to let a wagon pass by. She looked back and shot me a nervous smile.

"Why don't you come back with me? We could use your help on the farm. At least for a little while. Until you decide what you want to do."

My mouth dropped open at the suggestion.

There were no stories about Windborn farming or helping families, they only told of powerful warriors fighting against all odds for their kings, but something unclenched within my chest at Fjola's suggestion. Underneath the ever-present grief, there had been a tension resting on my soul. It had constricted around me when Fjola had found out that I was Windborn and grew tighter when I saw how furious she had been. Now, with this invitation, the tension eased.

"That is," Fjola trailed off and looked away from me, "if you don't mind the children? Bersi and Nona don't stop."

"I think I can handle it," I chuckled. "With all the complaining you do about all the work on the farm, it'll be nice to be able to help for once. I should have a little money left over once Dagnur's taken the cut for rebuilding the farm. It can cover my share of the food and whatever else you need."

Fjola's smile grew and she nodded. "That sounds good. How long would you stay?"

We walked on in silence. I knew I shouldn't impose myself on Fjola for too long. She had two young children and a farm, more than enough for anyone to deal with. But it would be nice to become familiar with the new power throbbing in my veins and to come to terms with my loss.

"Until next summer, maybe? I can probably find a space on a longship somewhere and go on another raid. If it goes well I'll get enough plunder to find a place of my own. Maybe in a couple of years I'll be able to buy myself a small farm."

Fjola nodded along as I spoke. "That would be nice."

We walked until we found where we were sleeping. It was only a tarp hung up over scattered hay, but it was dry and out of the wind. Fjola got our belongings from the steward and we made ourselves comfortable in a corner. People stumbled around us in an effort to find their space under the canvas, but soon Fjola's breathing fell into the heavy, steady rhythm of sleep.

I stared up at the rippling canvas above us. The idea of staying with Fjola went around and around in my mind like a leaf circling a whirlpool. I thought about sitting with them at their fire, watching the children run and play, of being able to help the family with their chores and be a part of something again. But my thoughts always turned back to the burnt husk of the farm I had lived in. Any joy I felt wondering about a new life with Fjola drained away as the life I could have had pulled at me like a black riptide.

*

Our sleep was constantly interrupted by drunks stumbling back to their precious patch of hay. More than once we had to shove at people who were getting too friendly and huddling up to us. In the morning, porridge was slopped into bowls for those that wanted it, which we did. We clambered out of our hay-beds and got ourselves some.

"We should go and see if Ingvar's arrived," Fjola said. She was only halfway through her porridge. The lumpy liquid was the same colour as the overcast sky. She let a spoonful glob back into the bowl.

I shifted my position on my stool and dropped my eyes to avoid Fjola's gaze. "He'll hear about me when he gets here, surely? Then he'll come with the other law-keepers and find me. You heard them yesterday." I waved my rune-covered arm. "They can come and find me whenever they want."

The rune-mark felt sharp against my skin, like a wound exposed to the sea air. I turned my arm and it glittered like a black rainbow. I suppressed a shiver and pulled my sleeve down to cover it.

Fjola frowned. "Maybe, but the quicker we find Ingvar, the quicker we can get that Soren guy arrested. Maybe they'll even reward you for it, too."

It was my turn to frown. I pushed the slop around my bowl without looking up. The image of Ingvar standing at the prow of Dagnur's longship flashed in my mind. Crows circled and the wave's white surf looked like teeth chewing at the hull. Wood creaked like snapping bones.

"I never want to see that ship again, Fjola."

My voice was a whisper and it took Fjola a moment to register what I had said. Her shoulders tensed, then she relaxed and put her bowl down.

"Okay," she said, softly. "I still think that we should see if he's arrived. I can go on my own. We can find you later."

I closed my eyes and nodded. I didn't want to see Fjola's expression. It hurt that I couldn't face the longship and had to rely on her to do this for me. I had never been afraid to be the first to leap from the longship and plunder Ertland, but the thought of seeing that sorrow-soaked ship again twisted something deep inside me.

"Where should I come and find you?" she asked.

"I'll head over to watch the public assembly, see what people have to complain about. Or I will be at the arena."

Fjola gave me a look and stretched. "There's no way you're going to sit still for long watching the public assembly. I'll try the arena first. See you later."

I pushed my porridge around for a little longer before I threw what remained into a bush and handed the empty bowl back.

It was early enough that the mist still clung to the ground, swirling around our feet like an ethereal sea as we kicked through it. Few people walked the paths, everyone else was probably trying to sleep off a hangover.

As I walked to the assembly, I turned over Fjola's offer in my mind like a burning coin. I weighed it against the plans I had had before I died. My thoughts flinched away from my grief and the memory of saltwater in my lungs. Life at Fjola's farm would be happy, but could I latch myself onto someone else's family? I wondered whether staying with Fjola was simply delaying my inevitable move to a lonely place of my own. Each time I tried to imagine myself at Fjola's farm, the picture in my head twisted and stumbled back to the black earth where our farm had been. My breathing came short and heavy and I felt like a raw wound.

I shoved the thoughts away as I reached the stairs to Fafstol's Scar and forced myself to focus on the thin, carved steps. I turned away from the law-keeper tents and made my way towards the rocky shore within Fafstol's Scar. Shadows of longships became visible in the distance as I reached the assembly where steps and seats had been carved into the walls of rock, all facing a carved stone chair opposite a raised platform. A few of the heavily armed guards wandered through the crowds and one pointedly glanced at me as I came in, but they didn't seem to care about me this time. Perhaps it was too early in the day to start trouble. I made my way to a relatively empty section of stone seats and watched.

People came forward with their law-keeper and made their case to Leif Durison, first among the High King's law-keepers, who would then make a judgement. A few were murder cases that the local law-keeper had been unable to resolve, and one ended in a fistfight between the two parties. Most weren't that interesting, appealing decisions about land boundaries or livestock ownership. I watched Leif, the man who would soon hear my case, like a fighter watches their opponent before a brawl. Thick eyebrows shadowed his eyes and a long, wiry beard brushed his chest as he looked down at the supplicants before him. His expression was as carefully carved as his stone chair. I would get nothing from him.

I was about to leave when a woman wearing a law-keeper's silver arm-ring stepped up to the podium. When she was asked to state her case she turned to address the crowd.

"My friends," she said. "The raiding season is now over. By

the laws of the gods and our High King, we must lay down our weapons, bring in our flocks, and reap the harvest. The gods themselves decreed that no one should have to work their farm with the threat of attack hanging over them."

"Stop stating the obvious and get on with it, Katja." This from the High Law-Keeper. "If you wanted someone to marvel at the skill of your tongue, I am sure that there would be plenty of volunteers."

The law-keeper, Katja, opened and closed her mouth. From the flushing of her cheeks, she looked like she was wasn't sure whether to be outraged or embarrassed.

"By your words, High Law-Keeper," she continued after a moment, "you acknowledge these ancient laws." She extended her hand in a gesture that encompassed the assembly as if her next comment had the support of the crowd. "Why, then, does the High King do nothing as King Erling Tormundson is attacked by King Hraki again and again, well into the raiding season and with a blatant disregard for the laws of gods and men?"

I sat up and all around me people began to murmur to one another. I looked around at the crowd. It seemed this was unexpected news to some, but others simply rolled their eyes and looked on with a measure of boredom and irritation. Hraki. The name made me clench my fists and sent a shiver of anticipation up my spine.

The High Law-Keeper leaned back in his stone chair.

"Must we have this conversation again, Katja?"

"We will have this conversation until my king is given aid and Hraki is brought to justice." Katja's voice was tight with anger. Her mimicry of the High Law-Keeper's words brought a scowl from him; the first crack in his granite composure. "At the bare minimum, proper reparations need to be paid for the damage and injury done to King Erling's people and property during these unlawful raids."

"Law-Keeper Katja." High Law-Keeper Leif sighed and pinched the bridge of his nose. "Time and time again we have been over this. There is no proof that any aggressive action has been made by King Hraki outside of the appropriate seasons. I seem to remember that a delegation from the High King's household was sent, at your insistence, to investigate the matter and the emissary ruled against you. If you continue to bring this matter to the assembly, I will be forced to conclude that King Erling holds the decisions of the High King in contempt and does not—"

"The only decisions that King Erling holds in contempt are those made by biased law-keepers," Katja shouted. "The emissary that made that decision was corrupted by offers of riches from Hraki. Any one of Erling's household will swear to you on the gods themselves that what I say is true. Would you hold the word of such noble warriors in such little regard?"

The crowd's muttering grew and the air in the chasm grew heavy with anger. The thought that anyone's word as a warrior would be easily brushed aside raised everyone's hackles.

"Then, where are they?"

Law-Keeper Katja's eyes widened. Her expression flashed from furious righteousness to elation.

"My bodyguard, the only fighter that King Erling could spare, is currently having his wounds bound. As soon as he is fit enough to move we can go to any rune-stone you choose and swear our stories are true."

"Very well," Leif said. "If you and your bodyguard can swear on a rune-stone, then we will reconsider your case."

"Thank you, High Law-Keeper."

Leif inclined his head and opened his mouth to speak when someone stormed out to stand before the crowd. They waved at the High Law-Keeper and shouted across the open space.

"This is ridiculous."

I recognised the voice. Einar, the law-keeper who had refused my appeal.

"I will not have my honour called into question without answer." He stood behind Katja and puffed himself up like a pigeon looking for a mate. "I travelled to King Erling's halls, under the authority of the High King, and interviewed his household and Hraki's. There was nothing at all to suggest that Hraki had initiated any fighting outside of the raiding season. From what I remember, and you may also recall from my official report, Erling initiated a border war with Hraki and then cried foul when he began to lose."

"Lies," Katja screamed. "You were bought and paid for. You—"

"How dare you? I will not be spoken to—"

Their words were lost as they shouted over one another. Katja threw a punch at Einar and then they were wrestling on the ground. The crowd cheered and offered encouragement as guards hurried to pull the law-keepers apart. Einar hastily began to dust off his robes whilst Katja strained against her captors to get to her opponent.

"Enough!"

The High Law-Keeper's voice echoed out over the screaming crowd and their cries died away.

"This is unacceptable. Einar, your integrity is not being debated, despite the venomous words of Law-Keeper Katja, but it has been long enough that another investigation can be called. And Katja, you will not call into question the decisions of the High King nor his agents, and certainly not here.

"You will both consider this matter at rest until I can speak with the injured bodyguard and decide on a course of action. It may be that another investigation is warranted, but that decision will wait. For now, this assembly will take a break and return once everyone has calmed down. Get out of my sight."

Einar bowed to the High Law-Keeper and then let himself be led away, effecting a limp until he was hidden from the High Law-Keeper's sight by the crowd. Katja ripped her arm free of the guards that held her and stormed off.

All around me people started hushed, excited conversations and some decided now was a good time to leave. I watched Katja shove her way through the crowd. The Wind-hunters had whispered Hraki's name. I made to get up and speak with Katja, but she disappeared into the press and I was left in the churning crowd with questions burning behind my lips.

*

By the time I reached the arena, it seemed most people were awake, and they had all crammed around the fighting ring.

The fights got a good response, though they only brought out two fighters at a time. I supposed they would wait for those still sleeping off hangovers to arrive before they brought out the exciting matches. I found my way to an empty seat and the other spectators shifted away from me. Guards with heavier armour and more intense expressions than the guards around the assembly kept a careful eye on me. I saw some of them glance nervously at the runes scrawled over my inner arm.

There was a half-hearted cheer from the crowd. The match was over. The fighters limped out of the arena.

A new announcer stepped forward and said there would be a break before the next bout. People grumbled and most got up and walked out.

I stayed in my seat and watched the milling crowd, then leaned my head back and let the sun warm my cheeks. The winter sunlight felt weak next to the chill that seeped up from my bones, but for a moment I let myself enjoy it. I watched the clouds float by; felt the brush of the wind on my face.

Something moved through the sky, a silhouette-speck against the blue. I frowned, squinted. It was growing larger. No, getting closer. I walked to the edge of the arena to clear the trees from my view. Whatever it was burst through a cloud and kept coming down. The shape was wrong for a bird and there was a strip of red fluttering behind it. Then the stuttering snap of tree branches as it crashed through the canopy before colliding with the wet mud in the arena.

The crashing echoes died away and left a taught silence. Men and women stared at the muddy crater in the centre of the arena. Some moved to stand in front of their companions in the hopes of protecting them from whatever had fallen from the sky, some took a step back then another until they were running and disappeared from view, but most stood in tense anticipation with their hands resting on weapons. I edged over the lip of the crater and my decision rippled out amongst the remaining crowd. Some followed me at a distance, but others took my decisiveness as an opportunity to absolve themselves of responsibility and they fled.

Something in the crater groaned and I froze. I waited, but no other sound came.

In the centre of the mud, sprawled on his front and lolling from side to side, was a man. A tattered red cloak lay crumpled

142

underneath him and cuts littered his limbs. All around me people whispered to one another, unwilling to move closer, and pointed. I rolled my eyes and clambered into the crater. I turned him onto his back and looked him over. Something sparked under my fingertips like a static shock and I felt the cold power within me surge up.

Beneath the mud caking him, I couldn't make out any serious injuries. His face was pale, blotted with blood bright against the streaks of silt, and the light of the Winds danced in his unfocused eyes.

The whispers of the crowd turned to shouted questions as a couple more people joined me.

"Who is he?"

"Is he dead?"

"What do we do?"

"Someone get help!"

Someone brought some water and I tried to feed it to him. He coughed, almost choked, then leaned into the cup and drank.

"Where is Katja?" he croaked then broke down into a spluttering cough

The question echoed through the crowd as people repeated it to one another.

"Law-Keeper Katja," he managed after another sip of water. "I need to speak with her."

That set everyone shouting again and a few people ran off, presumably to find her.

The Windborn tried to push himself onto his elbows. He fell back into the mud. With some help, he managed to sit and stay upright. His breath came deep, laboured and we sat alone like that for some time. Everyone else seemed too nervous to approach the fallen Windborn, or perhaps my exploits in the arena made them wary of me. Eventually, the Windborn gestured for me to help him and I half-carried him out of the crater and to one of the seats surrounding the arena.

"What happened?" I asked.

The Windborn looked down at his bruised, shredded arms and then up to me.

"I—"

143

"Runar!"

The shout echoed across the arena and drowned out whatever the Windborn had been about to say. Law-Keeper Katja appeared in front of us, her curled copper hair bouncing as she fell to her knees and took in the state of the Windborn with wide eyes.

"What happened to you?"

The Windborn, Runar, shot me a rueful smile.

"I must have passed out as I got over the Althing. I started looking for you, then the next thing I know I'm face down in the mud."

He waved a hand at the small crater in the centre of the arena.

"And what about..." Katja frowned and gestured at the cuts and bruises.

"Another attack." Runar glanced at me, uncertain. "Erling sent me to hurry things up down here. Did you get us help?"

Katja's jaw bunched. "Not yet. Einar turned up when I was talking to the High Law-Keeper and we got into a fight. We're meeting with the High Law-Keeper tomorrow so that he can take Muli's testimony on the runestone."

"That's too long. Let's go and see him. He can't put me off."

Runar pushed himself up and swayed. He winced as Katja grabbed his shoulder to steady him.

"Runar," she said gently. "You're in no state to move now. You've got to rest. I'll take you to—"

"People are dying, Katja," he snapped.

He put one arm across Katja's shoulders and they limped a few steps before Katja staggered under the weight of the Windborn. My throat tightened for a heartbeat as I watched my only link to Hraki walk away. Katja stumbled under Runar's weight.

"Here," I said and slipped under Runar's other arm. "Let me help."

They thanked me and we staggered towards the assembly. Something prickled against my skin where it touched Runar's. The hairs on the back of my arms stood on end and a tingling sensation cascaded down from my shoulders.

"You're Windborn too," Runar grunted. "From the look on

your face you've not felt this before, have you? That's the Winds inside us reaching out to each other. It'll fade once you let go of me."

"I've been around other Windborn and didn't feel it then."

Runar grinned, showing blood-stained teeth.

"When they're not trying to kill you? It's a quiet noise you need to look out for. If you've got blood and battle thumping in your ears then it's hard to notice, especially if you don't know to look for it."

"You said there'd been an attack," I said. "Was it another attack by Hraki?"

The way that Runar and Katja's heads snapped around to me told me it was, but they didn't respond.

"I was in the crowd at the assembly this morning. You said it was Hraki attacking your king," I continued. "Just before you got into a fistfight with Einar."

Runar snorted a laugh that turned into a coughing fit.

"Where's your arm-ring? Has anyone sworn you into a household yet?" Katja asked.

I glanced over at Katja's silver arm-ring and then over to Runar and saw a mud-covered iron arm-ring wrapped around his right bicep. I shook my head. "Do I need one?"

They looked at each other for a long moment as we shuffled on, then Katja cocked her head in a gesture that said, why not?

"It was Hraki," Runar said, though his voice was pitched to speak to Katja rather than me. "I think he figured out what Orin has been doing and decided to put a stop to it. Orin had to stop using his powers once Hraki landed. We fought them off, though. They looked like they were going to wait us out on their longships, but Orin will have dealt with them by now."

"Why are you here, then? Couldn't Erling have sent a raven? It sounds like they need you up there."

Runar shook his head. "We tried that. They had hunters to the south. Whenever we sent out a bird or anything else that might take a message they shot it down. We even tried sending out several birds at once, but they always got them. Erling sent some huskalar to flush them out, but that was taking too long. It had to be me. There was no other choice."

Katja grumbled something under her breath.

"When they saw me flying away they tried to attack again, and I couldn't leave them to take the brunt of it. I helped them to fend off the attack but couldn't stop them burning down Magnus' farm."

Runar sighed and shook his head.

"Blood and stone, Runar," Katja breathed. "You flew all that way recovering from a fight?"

"And bleeding," he replied with a lopsided grin.

Katja shook her head and we continued in silence.

I thought we would be stuck when we reached the stairs into Fafstol's Scar. There was no way we could carry Runar down those shallow steps, but he leapt from the edge and floated down slow as a feather. Katja and I had to rush down the stairs to catch up with him. We found him slumped against the wall and waiting for us to help him.

By now everyone had heard about the Windborn falling from the sky. The assembly was crowded, though people parted to let us through, and the seats cut into the chasm's walls were bursting with spectators. Over the excited chatter of the crowd, I heard someone shout my name and turned to see Fjola waving, Ingvar at her side. She tried to push her way through to me, but the crowd was too thick. No one was willing to give up their view of this spectacle.

The High Law-Keeper's guards carved a path through the crowd. Some people called out questions to him, but their detail was lost in the noise and hum of the crowd and he did not answer. Around me more questions, though these were directed to Katja and Runar, asking whether this was Hraki's doing, or if Runar had flown into a tree. Katja waved off the questions and as we made our way toward the High Law-Keeper's throne the crowd thinned. The tension soaked into the hum of voices grew sharper as the noise bounced between the chasm walls, making it seem as though thousands, not hundreds, stood waiting.

High Law-Keeper Leif called for silence as he walked up to his seat. Disquiet clouded his brows and anger flashed like lighting across his features whenever he looked towards Runar. The noise fell away piece by piece as though carried by lapping waves and eventually silence fell when the High Law-Keeper reached his stone throne.

We reached the edge of the crowd and Katja brought us to a stop.

"Thank you," Runar said to me. He grimaced as he took his own weight and limped forward in step with Katja.

Suddenly alone, I felt the weight of a hundred pairs of eyes on me and I hurried back into the crowd. As soon as I disappeared, everyone's attention locked onto Katja and Runar. Above them, the High Law-Keeper's expression was thunderous, his lips pursed.

"Ah, High Law-Keeper," Runar said. He tried to keep his tone light, though he winced and clutched his ribs. "Sorry to keep you waiting."

"I thought that Katja and her bodyguard were the only ones who had come down from Erling's halls."

"At first, yes, but Erling sent me with news. I have—"

Someone shoved past me, into the open space, and shouted over Runar. It was Einar. His cheeks were red from exertion and he paused a few paces behind Runar and Katja to catch his breath.

"High Law-Keeper," he called. "How much longer must this charade go on? You passed judgement on this once before, and today, as a sign of great indulgence, you said you may revisit this issue. Now they send another, bruised delegation to speak with you? Can you not see that this is a desperate cry for attention from a lonely northern king who is desperate to ensure the southern kingdoms still remember him?"

There was some consternation from the crowd, and from Katja and Runar. The High Law-Keeper raised his hand for quiet.

"I appreciate, Einar, that you do not want your decision to be undone. Rest assured, no decision resulting from this discussion nor any new testimony will take away from what you have done."

The High Law-Keeper turned his face away, content that his comment should have been enough for the law-keeper, but Einar's expression twisted and he bunched his fists at his side.

"Runar," Leif said and waved at the Windborn. "Why has Erling sent you here when your law-keeper is already making your case?"

"Because Hraki attacked us two days ago, long after Katja left for the Althing and long after winter began."

Shouts of disbelief, indignation, and fury echoed inside the chasm and made it seem like there were twice as many people crammed between the stone walls.

Runar raised himself unsteadily to float a few paces above the ground and spun in place to address everyone. The noise and shouts tumbled away to a murmur.

"I have come to seek aid for my king," he shouted. "Even now, Hraki's forces are waiting for the right moment to strike at Erling's halls like wolves. The gods decreed that winter be a time to help one another during the harsh, cold months, but Erling's people must hide behind their king's defences."

Einar puffed himself up and pointed an accusatory finger at Runar.

"What proof do you have of this? You come here and make proclamations to the crowd, but where is your proof?"

"Can you not see my injuries, Einar? Are they not proof enough for you?"

"Scratches and bruises," Einar scoffed. "There is no way of knowing how you came by those. Who's to say that you did not fly through a fir tree and now, to save face, you claim something which is impossible to verify?"

Some laughter from the crowd. Runar gritted his teeth.

"Tread lightly, law-keeper," Runar growled. "I will not have my honour besmirched by a bribe-taking fool who runs away at the first sign of danger."

He spun and lifted himself higher into the air.

"Will you hear my case? Is it not the task of this assembly to hear all cases, to judge fairly and protect the innocent? I ask you to protect the innocent people under Erling's care. Outside their walls there is a power-hungry king, no better than a mad wolf howling for blood. Will you send help to Erling and save them?"

"Enough!"

The High Law-Keeper's voice echoed across Fafstol's Scar and silenced everyone. He stood and took a step down from the carved stone throne.

"This is not some drinking hall for you to play the crowd

like a skald," he said through bared teeth. "This is a place of law and reason. You cannot barge in here and ignore all procedure. Do you think that makes you better than anyone who would batter down our doors and do whatever they please?"

"High Law-Keeper, I—"

"Enough, I said. This is not a matter for the public assembly. Runar and Katja, come and see me at my tent."

Without giving anyone a chance to respond, the High Law-Keeper stormed off to his tent. Katja and Runar looked at each other before following him. Einar sucked his teeth and looked around before he disappeared in another direction.

I looked around at the people gathered in the Scar. They did not look happy. Most people were grumbling to one another that they would not find out how this conversation ended. Some of the guards shifted and looked uneasily at the fidgeting crowds. I ducked through the press of bodies towards Fjola and Ingvar.

CHAPTER EIGHT
IN THE SHADOW OF LONGSHIPS

FJOLA SAGGED WITH RELIEF WHEN SHE FOUND ME at the bottom of the carved stairs. She grabbed me by the arm and dragged me away.

"What were you doing with them, Edda?"

"I was at the arena when that Windborn fell out of the sky. I helped carry him over to the assembly."

She nodded, looking relieved.

"When I saw you with those two up there, I thought maybe he'd tried to pick a fight with you and you'd been dragged up there with him."

"Come on," I said with a chuckle. "I wouldn't get into a fight with another Windborn. Not so quickly after the last one anyway."

She didn't look amused. "At least you're safe."

Fjola let go of my arm as we found Ingvar.

"Edda, it's good to see you." He held out his hand and I shook it. "I've been hearing all about your exploits here." He swallowed and looked as though I had declared war on the High King in the middle of the arena.

I shrugged as if to say I didn't know what he was talking about. His nervous expression turned serious and he nodded in the direction of the assembly.

"Do you know if what they're saying is true?" Ingvar asked. "Is someone launching attacks in winter?"

"I didn't get any more proof than you. Runar was all cut up

151

and looked exhausted, but that's all I can say."

"It sounds like that other law-keeper thinks they're just doing it for show," Fjola commented.

"Einar. He seems like a real piece of shit to me," I said.

Ingvar shook his head. "The kings and queens can't let this stand. If what they're saying is true, something will have to be done. The High King might have to step in and overturn the old judgement. The gods' laws cannot be flaunted like this."

He stood on his toes and looked over the crowd at the High Law-Keeper's tent, but the crowd was too thick to see what was happening.

"Come on," he said. "Let's get back to the longship. We've got plenty of food and lots to talk about."

The mention of the longship twisted my stomach and grief-sharp claws squeezed my heart. Perhaps, I reasoned, it would not hurt as much to see the longship in Fafstol's Scar. It would be surrounded by stone and beached between the chasm walls. Nothing like the day I had lost my husband. I swallowed down the memory of saltwater and gestured for Ingvar to lead the way.

We had to shove our way through the throng of people. Most were heading up to the merchant's tents or the arena whilst we were heading down to the fjord at the other end of Fafstol's Scar. The closer we got to the longship the heavier the unease in my belly became. Although I hoped Ingvar would be able to tell me about the laws regarding Windborn, I dreaded what news he must have about the cost of the new farmhouse. I was beginning to suspect all I would get back from our carefully stashed hoard would be a sliver of silver. I found myself straining to try and hear the whisper of the cool water. My heart thudded against my ribs like a prisoner trying to escape execution. I took a deep breath and focused on Fjola and Ingvar's conversation. I let their voices wash over me and my heart slowed. I tried to exhale the tension, but it wouldn't disappear, and I was left with a crow-heavy weight in my chest. As we came up to the edge of the fjord I kept my eyes on the ground, following Fjola's feet, and tried to ignore the memories that threatened to resurface: the open ocean and the loss of a husband.

Looking didn't help. The high walls of Fafstol's Scar continued past us and sank into the fjord like a road leading to the Nine Hells. Longships stuffed themselves between the chasm walls and many had been dragged onto the stony shore to make room behind them. White-crested waves pushed at the sides of the ships and they swayed and bumped together. Some of the hulls creaked as the water slapped and smacked against them. The wet, wooden sound brought that day surging back up to me. The crack of thunder, the pelting rain on my face, the wet fingers slipping through my grasp.

"Edda, are you okay?"

"Yes, I'm fine. I'll be fine. Just... give me a moment."

After a few breaths, I straightened and nodded.

"Let's go."

Fjola kept close as we went on. Her gaze moved from me to the water and then back to me.

"I'm fine, really."

I could tell she didn't believe me.

We finally came into view of Dagnur's longship, dragged half onto the shore, and my heart stopped.

The sight of the longship crashed straight into my soul. Its planks curved forward over the sands like elongated claws reaching out to pluck me from the world like it had with Bjolfur. My breathing came thick and heavy as Ingvar guided us towards the keel's shadow. He gathered up some things for us to sit on and handed out some dried strips of meat. At first, I positioned myself so that the ship was out of sight, but the weight of the unseen wood above my head made me feel uneasy. I felt as though the longship was waiting to tip over and crush me. In the end, I settled for sitting side-on with the ship at the edge of my vision.

Fjola and Ingvar made small talk, unimportant questions and answers bounced between them.

"The house was almost finished when I left," Ingvar said, loud enough to catch my attention.

"What?"

"The farm, your farm. Its walls were done and the roof almost complete when I left. I thought you'd like to know..." he trailed off as he noticed my stormy expression.

"How much money will be left?" I asked.

Ingvar shifted on his crate and avoided my gaze. "Let's not sully this reunion with talk of money. The farmhouse should be ready to see when you return. How have you both been finding your time here?"

I let Fjola reply and frowned as I chewed on a hunk of meat. My mind wandered homeward to the new building that would be waiting if I returned.

Something about it turned my stomach. The place I had known and loved would be replaced. All traces of my home would be gone. The intricate carvings on the front archways, worn smooth where we ran our fingers as we came home, would be replaced by fresh, hard lines. The smell would be different. When we had first gone into the place, it had smelled of sawdust and slowly our scent had soaked into the walls. The smear of charcoal on a wooden beam, or the rotten smell in the corner from when I had thrown an egg at Bjolfur. A hundred scratches and blemishes we never managed to clean, but each added a minuscule weight to the house and together, wrapped us in a home.

Ingvar and Fjola finished their conversation and we watched the passing crowds whilst we finished our food. People moved around Dagnur's longship, carrying supplies on and off.

"I'm glad that Malka came with us," Ingvar said as the big woman stepped off the ship. "She's got a head for figures that just passes me by. If I were in charge of buying all this food, I'm sure we'd have half as much for twice the price."

He laughed nervously and bunched his fists over and over on his lap. His eyes followed the men and women as they loaded the crates onto the ship. Each time there was a gap in the proceedings he opened his mouth as though he wanted to say something. I gave it until the crew wandered off for Ingvar to say whatever he wanted to say. He kept tapping his foot and clenching his fists.

"What is it, Ingvar?" I said, without looking up.

"What?" He jumped as though he had forgotten we were there.

"What are you so scared to tell us?" I picked a sliver of ice from underneath my fingernails. "You know something."

He tapped a knuckle against his knee and looked over to where the parade of people had carried the cargo.

"Whilst Malka was out doing her side of things," he said, slowly as though putting off whatever he wanted to say, "I went to speak with the other law-keepers. To find out about new laws and precedents. I also spoke with them about the laws regarding Windborn."

He trailed off and apprehension saturated the air between us. He clenched his fists again and looked at the empty beach scuffed with footprints.

"And?" I growled.

"Come on, Ingvar," Fjola said, more gently. "Tell us."

He continued to squirm and look away. I clenched my fists white-knuckle tight. Cold mist seeped between my fingers. The rune-mark on my arm fought against my Windborn power. It felt like burning firewood against my skin, but I kept pushing.

Before I could say anything Fjola moved over to Ingvar and took his bunching fists into her gentle hands.

"Ingvar, you're going to have to tell us sooner or later. Take a deep breath and tell us."

He nodded and took a breath. Then another.

"Well," he began, he offered us a half-smile and then looked away. "It doesn't matter how much money Dagnur spends on the farm because you can't have what's left over."

"Why not?" I snapped. Ice blossomed over my fingers. The pain of the rune-mark intensified and tiny tendrils of smoke swirled out from my skin. Ingvar watched the ice solidify and the rune-mark smoke. His face went pale.

He sighed and put his face in his hands then sat up, bracing himself, as though if he didn't do this quickly he would never. "When you became Windborn, you died. The Winds resurrected you, or a stronger, faster version of you."

"And?" I said.

"Don't you see?" he asked quietly. "You died, Edda."

I didn't understand what he was getting at, but something in the desperate tone of his voice unsettled me. He looked at me then to Fjola. He saw the confusion on our faces and went on.

"As far as the law is concerned, you're dead, just as if you died peacefully in your sleep. All of your possessions, your property and debt, has been passed on to your next of kin."

"How can anything be given away? I'm still here."

Dread started to seep through my chest. The fear was somehow deeper and colder than the ice tendrils that snaked through me.

"Yes. I know. You're still here." He looked around, as though for someone to save him from our conversation. He tapped his foot and picked at the fabric of his trousers. "What I'm trying to say is that Windborn cannot own anything. No property, no possessions, no money, nothing. The law says that the person they were before is dead. When a Windborn comes back it is as a new person without anything to their name."

I stretched my fist open and the ice wrapped around my fingers cracked and splintered. The searing pain of the rune-mark against my skin eased and cooled.

"It's a safety measure," he went on, his tone miserable. "Could you imagine if Dagnur became Windborn and kept his position? Think about how much worse he would be."

That was true. If Dagnur had the kind of power that I had seen Soren use in the arena, spouting flame from each hand, then I wouldn't put it past him to set fire to someone's farm to intimidate them into swearing into his protection.

"If she can't own any property now, or any money," Fjola said slowly, "then what about her farm or the money that Dagnur's using to rebuild it with? She can have that money back, right?"

Ingvar's expression answered well enough.

"So now I have nothing? Anything I need now I'm going to have to earn, and I have to build up my hoard again?"

Ingvar looked pained, he rubbed the heels of a palm against his eyes then looked back at me. "I'm sorry, Edda, but no. You can't own anything: property, money, technically not even the things in your pockets. It is illegal for Windborn to have a hoard of their own. That's why Windborn are sworn into a household. That way their lord can give them those things in exchange for their service. Think about it like the huskalar, they're given weapons and armour in exchange for guarding kings and nobles."

The bottom fell out of my stomach. I realised what the cold dread was suffocating inside me. Hope. As Ingvar talked the dread strangled any hope I had of returning to my old life, my old dreams, smothering it like thick mud.

"And if I don't?" I asked.

"What?"

"What if a Windborn refuses to swear into someone's service? What happens to them?"

"A Windborn has to swear into someone's service or they will be considered an outlaw, but with a higher bounty."

"So my choice is to swear into someone's household forever, or try and survive as an outlaw?"

He nodded.

I felt something crack inside me and the black-feathered grief smashed through the barrier I had built around it. The idea that I would one day be able to earn back the money Dagnur had taken from me had been an anchor holding me steady. Now, the grief-crow annihilated that anchor and left me drowning.

A hand on my shoulder. Fjola had come over to sit next to me. I put my hand on hers, but any relief I might have gotten from the gesture was destroyed as she flinched away from my frozen touch.

"I'm sorry, Edda. We'll figure something out," she said. One corner of her mouth twitched into a smile. "You can still come and muck out our pigs for us."

I smiled back, a small thing, and nodded.

I kept my lips pressed tight, afraid that if I opened my mouth there would be nothing to stop the scream of frustration and anguish that raged in my lungs like storm winds. Instead, I patted her hand and stood. Fjola rose with me and met my gaze.

"I'm going for a walk."

"Do you want any company?" Fjola asked.

"No, thank you."

I glanced over at Ingvar who was looking, wide-eyed, from my face to shards of ice littering the sand around me. I gave them both a nod and began to walk away.

Ingvar scrambled up and followed me.

"Edda. I'm sorry. About all this. I—"

I turned to face him. He met my eyes, then dropped his gaze to my feet and fidgeted with his arm-ring.

I wanted to scream at him and demand he do something to change the law. How could I be stripped of my wants and desires like this? Was all that was left for me to be the instrument of someone else's whims? I wanted answers but Ingvar didn't have them. He had done what I asked and told me what I'd wanted to know even if I hadn't wanted to hear it.

"It's okay," I said. "The law is the law. They affect everyone equally, right?"

"Yes, exactly," he said, quickly. Relief flooded his face. "It's nothing against you. It's just how it is."

I nodded. The laws might not be aimed at me, but the gods must be laughing as they watched so many of their edicts tear out little pieces of me at every turn. Ingvar kept his eyes focused on mine as though he were searching for some sign of forgiveness. I tried to smile. It came out as a grimace, just teeth, and Ingvar flinched. He opened his mouth but thought better of it and left.

I wandered away from the ship that had taken my husband and its shadow that had taken everything else from me. The noise and press of people grew as I got closer to the law-keepers' tents and I let myself get lost in the unbiased noise of the crowd.

*

I climbed up the stairs and made my way to the merchant tents. I tried to keep my thoughts distant, focusing on the murmurs all around me, and let myself be pulled along with the surge of the bodies.

Soon it became too much.

The weight of the crowd pressed up against me like a tidal wave ready to smash a boat moored too long. I shoved my way out of the crowd and found a small, worn path that led up into the mountains.

Grateful for some semblance of solitude, I shuffled along the path. I went far enough that the noise of the crowds and merchants shouting for attention was lost under the whistling wind and shuddering trees. I found a rock that looked comfortable enough and sat down.

The Althing sprawled out in the valley below. Longships moved across the water one side and on the other a surge of figures bustled around tents, carts, and the arena. Fafstol's Scar slashed straight through the middle of it all as though to remind us how small our mortal lives were. Above me, two birds circled; their calls like laughter. I threw a rock at them. It missed. Their laughter grew louder.

I leaned back against the rock and let myself sift through the past few weeks. I felt like driftwood that had bounced its way downriver and now, out at sea, waited to be pulled into the fathomless depths. It hurt to think about the journey back from the raid and the feeling of sea-slick fingers slipping through my grasp, but a bad memory never gets any better if you ignore it. I wondered what Bjolfur's soul was doing at that moment. Would he be distracted by the glory and splendour of the Sea Giants' halls beneath the waves? Could he watch the world from his drowned palace? Would he watch me?

Old wounds ached as my thoughts veered back to the fight at the clifftop. My lungs felt heavy as I remembered the waves dragging me into their lightless depths. Perhaps one day I would be able to wrap my fingers around Soren's throat and return the favour.

I played the last few weeks over in my mind and an involuntary growl escaped me. Over and over again one name flickered in the shadows like a shark following a trail of blood. It had been whispered at the cliff edge. It had been muttered at the edge of the arena. It had been shouted in desperation by a law-keeper.

Hraki.

It echoed in my head, around the shipwreck of my marriage, home, and any hope I had of a normal life. Above, the crows laughed again. One of them landed on a low branch and stared at me with one beady eye. I threw a rock at it. It screamed as it flew off. I put my head in my hands and rubbed at my eyes, trying to keep the tears from flowing.

Katja and Runar. They had set themselves against Hraki.

I needed to find out what happened when they spoke with the High Law-Keeper.

Fjola's offer came back to me. My heart ached at the thought of being part of a family again, even if only at its edges, but what good would that do if I could never move on? I wasn't sure I had enough strength to watch my friend have the life I wanted whilst I was reminded of the life and love I lost every day. Dagnur may even force me to swear to him if I went back, and then what? I would be his muscle, bullying poor farmers into servitude and fighting his petty squabbles. I would be a gilded spearhead, something to be paraded around and then stabbed into whatever fool had angered him that week.

I pushed myself to my feet. I needed to talk to Katja and Runar. The law was brutal, uncaring. If it had taken everything from me, then I would see it take everything from Hraki.

I wandered back down to the Althing and threaded my way through the crowds. Some of the people I passed pointed and whispered. It seemed my infamy had grown after I helped Runar. By the time I made my way to the law-keepers' tents, the voices had become a relentless hush that followed me like the ocean. I ducked my head in a vain attempt to hide from the whisperers and chose a route that was not the fastest, but meant I could avoid the busiest parts of the Althing. Eventually, I reached Fafstol's Scar and the law-keeper tents. I breathed a sigh of relief and went to move past the two guards standing at the edge of the tents, but they stepped in front of me.

"Only law-keepers from here."

"What? I was here yesterday."

They looked at each other. The one who had spoken, the younger of the two, seemed unsure of how to deal with this. The other guard nodded with some encouragement.

"Too many people are coming down here and gawking after what happened earlier," the younger said, drawing himself up to his full height. "By decree of the High Law-Keeper, all appeals and legal matters can only be brought forward in the public assembly. This area is strictly for law-keepers only."

He nodded at me as if that settled the matter and stared at a point beyond my shoulder.

"Fuck that," I mumbled.

I pushed through. Their defence was sluggish, as though they hadn't expected any defiance. I took a few paces before the older one grabbed my shoulder and spun me around. The younger guard levelled a shaking spear at my back.

"Now, you listen, just because people are talking about you that don't mean you can ignore the rules."

I narrowed my eyes, judging how seriously he would try to stop me. Something in his eyes told me he didn't want to try, but he was done with people walking over him and I might be the final straw. The Wind in my chest sparked at the threat of the spear and the rune-mark on my arm began to burn.

I sighed. "Why don't you go and get Katja? Erling's law-keeper. That's who I want to see."

The guards looked at each other for a moment before they nodded.

"I'll go," said the older one. "You stay here and make sure she doesn't go anywhere."

He left and the young guard glared at me. He shifted his weight and tried to ready his spear without me noticing. His white knuckles and the wavering spear tip gave it away. I rolled my eyes and walked over to a rock. The guard jumped and followed me.

"Keep calm. I'm just sitting down."

The guard opened his mouth then closed it. He satisfied himself by pointing the spear at me as though he had me prisoner. I picked at my iced-over scars.

Soon, but not soon enough, the older guard returned leading Katja.

"Here you are, Law-Keeper Katja, this is the woman who wanted to see you."

The stormy expression on Katja's face disappeared when she realised who I was.

"Oh, it's you." She thanked the old guard then turned back to me. "He said you looked like you were going to kill him if he didn't let you talk to me. Let's go to my tent and we can chat."

"I wouldn't have killed him," I said with a snort. "Injured, maybe."

Katja threw me a look that said she did not find that funny.

We made our way past the parade of tents. Some were

empty, some had lone law-keepers inside, and others had law-keepers huddled together with their retinues. One of the law-keepers broke off their conversation and made a show of watching us pass.

"Mind your own business, Einar," Katja said. "You're already on thin ice with the High Law-Keeper, do you really want to push it?"

Einar bared his teeth and snarled something wordless at us before going back to his conversation, which now included pointing at us.

"Don't mind him," Katja said once we were out of earshot. "The High Law-Keeper decided that another investigation into the Hraki situation is necessary. Einar led the first investigation and no law-keeper likes to see their verdict questioned."

We came to the end of the tents, but Katja kept us moving until we came to a small camp with a tarp hung across a gnarled tree that was growing into the side of the rock-face. I shot a questioning look at Katja.

"Law-keepers bring their own tents," she said. "We needed to move fast so this is all we brought with us. Usually, the tent would give us some privacy, but seeing as this," she flicked the tarp, "was all we could manage, we set up camp a little way from the rest of the law-keepers."

"I've seen worse camps with more supplies," I replied.

There was a fire off to one side and someone I didn't recognise, presumably the bodyguard, poking at the flames.

"So," Katja said and gestured to a couple of logs they had dragged around the fire. We sat down and she made herself comfortable before she continued. "What do you want?"

"Hraki."

She raised an eyebrow at me.

"You said you need help against Hraki, right? Let me come with you and I'll help."

"No."

The abrupt denial caught me off guard and for a moment I couldn't find the words to argue.

"We need huskalar. We need the High King to step in on our side, not some angry Windborn. Oh yes, I've heard about what you did in the arena. You'd be a liability."

I looked around the camp, at their tattered supplies then glanced pointedly back at the other law-keepers' tents.

"I think you need whatever you can get, and it looks like I'm the only one offering."

Katja sucked a breath through gritted teeth. Something shifted in the tree above us and we looked up to watch a couple of ravens sidestep along a branch until they were directly above us. They looked at each other, then cawed once in unison.

"Where's Runar?"

"He's at the healers' tents," Katja said, absently. She scowled at the ravens and then looked back at me. "Even Windborn need bandages."

"I didn't need as many bandages as we thought."

The voice came from above us and I looked up to see a figure falling towards us. No, not falling, flying down to us.

"Runar," Katja said. Her voice was heavy with concern. "Are you okay? What did the healers say, are you—"

"I'm fine," the Windborn said and waved her away. "Just scrapes and bruises."

Katja didn't look convinced, but to me he looked much better despite the myriad bandages wrapped around him. The colour had returned to his cheeks and his eyes no longer slid in and out of focus. Now that the mud had been cleaned away I saw the stubble covering his jaw and his short, rough-cut blond hair.

"Ah, my saviour," he said as his feet touched the ground. He frowned and scratched his head. "It was you that helped carry me to the assembly, wasn't it?"

"Yes."

"Good. It's all a bit hazy. One moment I was flying and then..."

"You did hit the ground pretty hard. You look much better."

Runar shifted his weight and winced, putting a hand against his side. "Perks of being a Windborn. Pray you don't have to use it very often."

"I doubt the gods would listen," I said. I let my hands stray to the bruises Soren had given me in the arena. The flesh, though still tender to the touch, didn't flare with pain when I pressed my fingers into it.

"They rarely do," he said. "What are we talking about?"

"I want to talk to you about Hraki."

Runar's eyes went cold and he looked over to Katja. The law-keeper's jaw tensed and she shook her head.

"What about him?" Runar asked.

"Let me come with you and fight him."

"Why would you want to do that?" Runar walked to stand by the fire and examine what the bodyguard was cooking. "You're a Windborn, girl," he said without turning. "There's no end of kings and chieftains that want another Windborn in their household. Go and find one of them and let them pamper you. If you come north with us, all I can promise you is blood, but I can't promise whose."

My mind's eye showed me a tapestry of finely decorated halls whilst I, laden with the finest weapons and armour, stood guard behind one throne after another. For an instant the thought filled me with pride, a sense of achievement and then those black feathers closed around my heart. Loss suffocated my imagined pride and a gentle, stirring rage swirled in the depths of my soul.

I stormed over and grabbed Runar by the shoulder, spinning him around to face me. Energy crackled between us, our Windborn power reacting to the other's, and for a moment we stared at each other. Something in his eyes lit up and I wished I had my axe.

"We don't need a bored farmer who thinks they can fight just because they're Windborn," Runar said and shrugged my hand off his shoulder. His voice was quiet, but it resonated with danger like a wolf's whisper.

"A bored farmer?" I spat back. "Hraki sent Wind-hunters to raid my town. They turned my home into a patch of scorched earth. Hraki took everything from me."

"Wait, he's sending out Wind-hunters?" Katja perked up and came over to me. "Are you sure? Would you swear an oath on that?"

"Of course. I overheard them talking about him. Hraki promised them a place in his household if they became Windborn. One of them did become Windborn, and he's here."

Runar's eyes widened and Katja rocked back on her heels as

though I'd shoved her.

"Did you hear that, Katja?"

The law-keeper nodded excitedly. "If we can get him to confess in front of the law-keepers that would solve everything. The High King couldn't ignore that."

Runar slapped a hand down on my shoulder in triumph then whipped it away as the Wind in my chest thrummed. "Do you know where he is? Will you help me drag him to the law-keepers?"

"I fought him in the arena. I can do it again. His name's Soren. Not too big, but packs a punch."

"And what kind of thing can he do?"

"He kept throwing flames at me."

"We can deal with that."

I blinked at his easy dismissal of the power that had bludgeoned me to the floor. How much Windborn blood had been spilled in the north?

"And what about you?" he asked. "What can you do?"

I closed my hand into a fist and concentrated. The rune-mark flared and it felt like I was pushing the Wind's power through tar. Sweat began to form on my forehead, but a film of ice grew over my clenched knuckles. It solidified and transformed into a ragged stretch of glacial shards lining my hand.

"I'm still getting used to it," I said. "But I'm getting better."

"Fire and ice," Runar said with a chuckle. "What a pair you must have made in the arena. That's good, we can use that."

Katja looked at my jagged ice-knuckles and her expression fell. "That won't work. We can't capture a Windborn in the middle of the Althing. As soon as you step inside the Althing you must comply with the god-bound truce. It's that guarantee of peace that makes the Althing possible. If you go grabbing people without sanction then you'll bring the law down on our heads. We need to tell the law-keepers, and they'll bring Soren in. Otherwise, we'll get ourselves arrested and make Erling an outcast."

Runar scowled.

"And how much have the law-keepers helped so far, Katja? No one is willing to help Erling. They mewl about what can be done, but will not act. Maybe we don't bring Soren to the High Law-Keeper. Maybe we take him straight to the High King. That way we skip all the pandering. The High King will denounce Hraki and then Erling will have all the help he needs."

Katja tipped her head back and scowled at the sky.

"And how are you going to bring this Windborn to the High King, Runar? You can't attack him at the Althing. If you break the sacred truce of the Althing, that's all the law-keepers will care about and Erling will pay the consequences. We should talk to the High Law-Keeper. He can get the Windborn to confess. It gets the same result and we don't put ourselves at risk."

I let the argument wash over me. Runar wanted action and Katja wanted to stay on the right side of the law. Neither conceded. I looked between them; one a ragged woman at the end of her endurance, and the other a beaten warrior who refused to go down. On the one hand, the laws should be a safety net, reassurance and protection, but the other hand ached for a weapon and blood and vengeance. I looked down at the rune-mark on my arm and in each of its sharp lines and hidden colours I remembered a time when the laws had failed me.

"I'll bring him in," I said.

Katja and Runar's argument spluttered into silence.

"What?" the law-keeper asked.

"Do you really think that Soren will wait around? If we don't do something now, he's going to slip through your fingers and you will have nothing. I'll bring him to you and make him confess. What you do with the confession is up to you, but I'm not letting him get away from me."

Runar grinned.

"Maybe you're a fighter after all, lass. What do you say, Katja?"

The law-keeper looked between us and then threw her hands up in the air and wandered off.

"I am surrounded by lunatics."

Runar laughed and then slung his arm across my shoulders. The static crack of energy sparked again, and I winced against the writhing Wind in my chest.

"Okay," he said. "You and I will capture Soren and then take him straight to the capital and the High King. If we make enough of a racket when we get there we should be able to see the High King himself."

"Why not bring him back here?"

If I dragged Soren before the law-keepers then I could watch him die within a few hours. If we took him all the way to the capital, it would be days, perhaps weeks, until I saw his blood soak into the earth.

"Katja might be a pain in the arse, but she's also right. The truce of the Althing is sacred and if we bring Soren back here then at best it will look suspicious, and we'll probably end up arrested. No, we go straight to Konvald and make the High King see exactly what we are dealing with."

"It would be quicker to bring him here," I pressed.

"It would, but wouldn't get us what we need. All the senior law-keepers are at the Althing so the High King will have to see us himself. When Soren tells the High King that he was a Wind-hunter sent by Hraki then we'll have the help we need, and the High King will sanction a winter war."

"And," he went on and nudged me with an elbow, "if this goes well I'll put in a good word for you with King Erling. You should have a place in our household. I can't guarantee anything, but I can't see why he wouldn't want you. Can't have you becoming an outlaw, can we?"

I shot Runar a cold smile. I didn't want to be part of anyone's household, but I would become an outlaw if I didn't join a household by the summer; no better than a wolf to be hunted and my pelt traded for gold. As I thought beyond my vengeance, I felt my life crack and crumble beneath my feet once again. Would any chieftain swear a Windborn into their household and let them farm? The parade of thrones and guard duty I had imagined earlier came back to me with full force and each image constricted my lungs.

Runar seemed to take my silence as tacit agreement. He went back to sit on the log by the fire and picked at his bandages. "I'm not going anywhere today. Not if we want to win any fights. Go and say your goodbyes and meet me back here tomorrow."

"Then what?"

Runar's face split into a wolfish grin. "We hunt Windborn."

*

My walk back to the longship was distracted. I bumped into people who hissed angry comments as I barged through, but I ignored them.

Too soon the sound of water reached me. Its angry, swaying hiss sucked away something in the pit of my stomach and I started to feel queasy. Figures moved around the longships like scavengers crawling over beached whales. I saw Dagnur's longship, sending another spasm of unease through me, and made my way over.

I found Fjola loading the ship, moving with several others under Malka's close direction. It seemed that Malka had done her work quickly and had already sold and bought whatever Dagnur had instructed her to buy. A short trip to the Althing, though necessary to make it through the winter. Everyone glanced at me as I approached then went back to carrying their supplies, except for Fjola who dropped the sack she was carrying. She rushed over and threw her arms around me, squeezing hard.

"Edda, I was worried something had happened to you, or you'd run off."

"Not yet," I said, returning her embrace.

"What? What does that mean?"

She pulled herself away and stared at me, a deep frown furrowing her brow.

"Come on," I said with a sigh. "I think we need to borrow some of Ingvar's good wine."

Fjola's shoulders slumped, her bright demeanour dimming, and led me through the men and women loading the longship. We turned and ducked between Dagnur's longship and the one beached next to it. The space between the curving hulls was drenched in shadows. Fjola led me to a couple of abandoned crates and as we sat on them bottles clinked inside.

"One of the crew members set this up to have somewhere to

get away from the bustle." She reached down and pulled out one of the bottles from inside the crate. "Malka knows about it, but she doesn't say anything. You remember how crowded it gets on a longship."

I nodded. Privacy would be only a memory once they got the ship moving, so it made sense that Malka was giving her crew the chance to savour their solitude before they set off in the morning.

Fjola pulled the cork from the bottle and took a swig before passing it to me. I did the same. I let the bitter wine slosh in my mouth before I swallowed.

"Not his best," I said with a grimace.

"So what's going on, Edda?"

Fjola's gaze was fixed intently on my face, her mouth clamped tightly shut. I met her eye but had to look away from the raw emotion I saw there.

"I'm not coming back with you, Fjola."

Behind Fjola the water's edge lapped at the beach as though trying to scratch its way up to me. Fjola let the silence hang between us.

"Ingvar said that I can't own any property or make a new hoard. I won't be able to buy my own farm. If I go back, sooner or later Dagnur will do something that forces me to be one of his bodyguards. There's nothing for me back there, Fjola."

"I'm there."

Her voice was so quiet it was almost lost beneath the whisper of the raking waves. I leaned forward on the crate and took her hands in mine.

"I know. But what if that's the problem?"

Fjola flinched back as though I'd made to strike her.

"No, I mean what if Dagnur makes your life miserable because of me? If I come back and he realises I'm Windborn he might threaten you or Ulfur, or the children."

Fjola's expression softened and then a hard glint flashed in her eye. "He wouldn't do that. He wouldn't stoop that low."

"I don't know," I said, shaking my head. "Sooner or later he won't be able to ignore the fact that I'm Windborn."

She shook off my hands and looked at her feet. "I don't understand, Edda. Dagnur doesn't need to know about any of

169

that. You can come and live with us, help us on our farm. You'll be surrounded by people that love you and you'll be safe."

The tempting image of a life with Fjola played out in my mind. I saw myself herding sheep in for the winter, or playing with the children to give Fjola and Ulfur some rest. My heart ached at the thought of being able to sit with them, warm and safe by the fire, and laugh. Something in all of it didn't feel right, though. I kept watching for another figure, someone else that would make the scene complete. My husband. Bjolfur's absence jarred against my mind like a knife scraping against my teeth. The more I thought about staying with Fjola, the more Bjolfur's absence ate away at me.

"No," I said gently. "I can't do that. If I don't swear to someone's household then I'll become an outlaw. I can't stay with you and put that risk on you. What if someone came to collect the bounty on my head and I was alone with Nona and Bersi? There's too much that could go wrong, Fjola."

She kept her head down and shook her head slowly. "What else is there for you to do?"

I leaned back and picked up the bottle of wine, swinging it in smooth circles to watch the dark movements of the liquid inside.

"Not much. I don't think anyone would turn me away if I went to join their households, but I'm going north."

"What for? Shouldn't you wait until after winter?"

I shook my head. "I need to go now."

When I glanced up, Fjola's good eye darted to meet both of mine. Then her expression widened.

"No. Please don't do it."

"Do what?"

"Edda, I know you. There's only one thing that would pull you away like this."

I dropped my gaze, unable to meet hers, but she knelt in front of me, heedless of the damp sand and encroaching river.

"Please, Edda. Come back with us. There's space for you on the longship and you can live with me. Isn't it better to live with people that love you than to hunt your own destruction? Come back with us and live on the farm. At least through the winter."

"I can't," I said. I dropped the wine into the sand with a wet thud and slid off the crate to kneel with Fjola. "What else is left for me there? I love you, and Ulfur, and Nona and Bersi. If I came back with you, I don't know if I'd ever be able to leave and neither of us needs that. You don't deserve to have an extra mouth to feed, especially over winter, and I can't just live in the shadows of your life."

Fjola's eye shone with tears in our hideaway. She opened her mouth but closed it before she said anything.

"I can't come home."

She nodded slowly and looked away. "What if you don't come back and we never see each other again?"

"Then say a prayer for me and know that I'm with Bjolfur."

We stayed like that for a time, kneeling together in the damp sand as the waves hissed and clawed their way towards us. Eventually, the noises around us stopped and the shouts of the crew faded away, presumably they had wandered off to find drink and entertainment.

"I'm going north," I whispered. "To help fight the king that sent those Wind-hunters."

"Okay," Fjola said with a shake of her head. "Edda, please, please be careful. You've always been stubborn, and the gods know that we've needed that before, but this isn't like chasing a lost lamb or scaring off wolves. You're stepping into a world like the old stories. It's dangerous."

She shifted closer and took my hand in hers. I looked away from the intensity in her gaze.

"You can let this go, Edda. There's no shame in turning away from this. It won't bring him back and I need you safe and alive."

The warmth in my chest that had been dampened and cooling ever since I started talking to Fjola crackled like a campfire and new heat surged into me. Part of me wanted to push her away, to shout and scream at her for reducing the anguish in my cracked, feather-soaked chest to a story of petty revenge. But the raw softness of her words silenced and stilled me. Using her hands, still clasped around mine, I pulled her into an embrace.

"I'm sorry, Fjola," I whispered. "I have to do this."

"You don't," she replied, her voice thick.

I didn't respond.

We pulled apart and held each other for a moment longer before we walked out of the alley between the longships and back onto the beach proper. Where there had been a bustling crowd now there was quiet. One person remained, sitting on a rock a little way up the beach. He looked up as we came towards them. Ingvar. He smiled at us, then his expression dropped when he saw ours. He hopped off the rock and took a few steps towards us, hands half raised as though to open himself up to an embrace.

"Edda. Fjola. Is everything okay?"

"I'm not coming with you, Ingvar. I've got something I need to do."

Ingvar's frown deepened. "What about the judgement? I spoke with the law-keepers and they said that you and I need to discuss what happened at the arena with them. Are you simply going to run away from this?"

"No, of course not." Inwardly, I cursed the fastidiousness of law-keepers. "We'll go and see them early tomorrow, before you leave."

The skin under the rune-mark prickled as though it saw through my lie.

Ingvar narrowed his eyes.

"It's not as if I can run away," I said and showed him the rune-mark.

Ingvar's mouth twisted, whether from distaste at the glittering runes or in disbelief, I wasn't sure. After a moment, he nodded. "Well, there's food and drink here, if you want it tonight. Malka has taken everyone else into the Althing. She said she wanted to buy them all a drink before we leave."

"That's it?" Fjola spluttered. "You're not going to ask her where she's going? Not try to stop her?"

The law-keeper sighed and looked at me, then back to Fjola. "I am sure whatever I have to say about this is a shadow of whatever arguments you have used, Fjola. I could beseech Edda to come with us, but as much as I like her, we are not close, what weight do my words have? The best I could do would be to cite laws and repeat back oaths Edda made before she died.

Oaths which now mean nothing."

Fjola's shoulders slumped with every sentence. Ingvar turned to me and, not unkindly, asked, "Would it help, Edda, if I repeated back to you the oath you made to Dagnur?"

"No," I said through gritted teeth.

"No," he repeated. "I think, then, that the best thing I can do is to offer you a good meal tonight."

He brushed himself free of some imaginary dust and bustled onto the longship.

Fjola sucked in a breath and let it out in a ragged sigh as she rubbed her face.

"You're not going to the judgement, are you?"

"No."

"What if they chase you?"

"I'll survive. I always have. Well, almost."

I offered Fjola a crooked smile, but she looked like she was about to burst into tears.

"Is this it then? Do you think this will be the last time we ever see each other?"

I put my hand out and touched her arm. I wanted to say we would see each other again, that I would only be gone a few months, as though I were running an errand. I wanted her to come with me. The idea of charging north alone sent threads of terror sliding down my spine. My lips parted and I felt the words catch in my throat.

"I don't know," I said at last. I let my head tip forward and I stared at the sand between my feet. "I'm not going up there to die, Fjola, I've already done that once. I just want... I just need someone to answer for what's happened."

She took my hand and squeezed.

Ingvar soon returned with a sack of food and another bottle of wine. He shook the bottle as he came up to us.

"I've got one of the good bottles from Malka's personal store."

We chuckled and then dragged the crates from between the longships out into the open and used these for a table and seats. A tension hung over the meal like a fog despite the jokes and the quality of the wine. The conversation was stilted and deliberately tame. No one wanted to stray too close to topics that would remind us of our impending split and the deathly potential of my chosen path. But as the bottle emptied, our conversation loosened and we were soon sharing old anecdotes, though perhaps we laughed too hard. The night swept over us and the chill forced Fjola and Ingvar to bed.

As my friends slept, I watched the flames and wondered whether I would see Fjola again. Eventually, the fire died with a crack and spit and I let myself sleep.

*

We woke as some of the crew returned in the morning or perhaps we stirred because the crew returned. Our awkward quiet was broken amongst the tipsy merriment of the crew who stumbled between us and offered us slurred greetings. Malka arrived, to another cheer, and the crew were sent scurrying about their tasks. Finally, the big woman made her way to us. Fjola and I rose to meet her as Ingvar rolled over and groaned, clutching his head.

"You coming with us, Edda?"

Her breath was laced with stale beer and though her eyes were shocked through with red, her gaze was still piercing. I bit down on my frustrations with Malka. Whatever she might have said to Dagnur, she had been a staunch companion and friend on our raids together.

"No," I said. "I've got business to take care of."

Out of the corner of my eye, I saw Fjola's shoulders slump as though she had still been holding out some hope that I would come with them.

"Fair enough. May the gods keep you safe."

"May the gods speed your journey."

Malka nodded slowly then disappeared off into the crew, shouting orders. Everyone around her winced and some rubbed at their heads.

We watched the beach within Fafstol's Scar transform from quiet, shadowed sands to a bustling harbour as the longship was prepared for departure. The crew rushed to collect forgotten equipment and more than one curse was aimed at Ingvar as someone tripped over him. Fjola and I pulled him up from the ground.

"How are you two okay?" he groaned as he blinked awake.

"Practice," Fjola said with a wicked grin.

"Ingvar!" Malka's voice boomed out over the noise.

The law-keeper paled even further and, with another groan, began shuffling towards the longship.

"I'll tell her we have to put off our departure," Ingvar shouted back at us. "I'll be back in a moment and we shall head to the law-keepers."

"You'd think he's never had a drink before," I said, shaking my head.

"He probably isn't allowed," Fjola chuckled.

We stood together in the tumult for a moment longer before Fjola turned to face me.

"You should go if you want to be gone before Ingvar gets back."

I nodded, not trusting myself to speak. Fjola wrapped her arms around me and hugged me tightly. I tried to reciprocate but she had locked down my arms.

"Stay safe, Edda, I want you to come back."

Fjola's voice was thick and the words choked.

"I will," I said in a voice just as heavy with sorrow.

The embrace stretched out. I wanted it to last for hours, days, but neither of us could stay. That moment etched itself in my mind and I knew I would remember every part of it: the air being pushed out of my chest, the shouts from the crew as they loaded the longship, the suck and hiss of the water, and underneath it all, the shivering fear in Fjola's chest that was reflected in my own.

Fjola pulled herself free and, wiping away a tear, nodded to me. She was quickly absorbed into the press and lost to me. I stepped away from the longship, but I needn't have worried about Ingvar's return. The crew were too keen to be gone and the cargo was soon loaded and the longship ready to leave. They had sold whatever they needed to sell and bought what supplies were needed over the winter. It was time for them to go home. Beneath the crew's shouts I heard Ingvar's protests, but no one was listening. A few of the crew jumped back down to the shore and put their shoulders to the longship and began pushing it back into the water.

The rest of the beach was beginning to stir now and the cries of Malka's crew were joined by the stirrings and murmurs of the other encampments.

"On my count. One, two, three, heave."

The men and women at the ship's side strained at the longship and it slid a little way down the sand. I stepped up with them and took a place at the stern of the longship. One of the people next to me nodded their thanks then put their shoulder to the wood again.

"One, two, three, heave."

I shoved hard. Memories of sore shoulders and shipmates grumbling that so-and-so didn't put their full weight behind the effort lent me a will. The longship slid down the beach much farther and several people around me toppled forward and from the shouts on board, they weren't the only ones who'd fallen.

The longship was now two thirds into the water. A little more, and the current would coax the longship into the fjord.

Everyone turned to look at me and I managed to keep a straight face, although I was as surprised as anyone.

"Get on the longship," I said. "Go on, I'll handle it from here."

They looked at me as though I had gone mad, but I waved them away and they didn't argue. Once everyone was on board, I gave another almighty heave and the longship slid slowly out. It looked like it would stop and I made to give it another push before the momentum stopped completely, but then it scraped clear of the sand and bobbed out into the fjord.

I stepped back and watched the longship drift into the deeper waters. Oars swung down and the longship began moving with purpose. I searched the faces on the deck, hoping to see Fjola looking back for me, but they were already too far away. The longship wove through the moored vessels and the boats coming to sell their wares. Soon it was lost in the morning haze and I wondered how many more times I would have to watch the water swallow some small part of me. Perhaps one day I might be able to dredge up all the pieces of my soul that were lost, but I could only imagine how twisted and deformed they would be after so long underwater.

I watched the boats and longships jostle for a place to land. Their masts teetered together like spears and I lost myself in the small battles raging over the shallow waters. A longship rushed too quickly onto the beach to shove ahead of a fishing boat and it smashed into the shore sending a wave of sand flying over everyone nearby.

Soon, though, the cold claws of the rune-mark on my arm pushed me to action. I could not stay and would not subject myself to the jurisdiction of these ineffectual law-keepers. I had a king to condemn and a Windborn to hunt.

CHAPTER NINE
THE HUNT BEGINS

FAFSTOL'S SCAR GREW BUSIER AS THE SUN illuminated the day. I shoved past the bodies pressed against me but knew it would only get worse. Every time I spotted a guard or huskalar in the crowd I flinched behind my neighbours. I had no doubt I could fight my way through a few guards, but if they came to drag me to the rune-stone I was sure they could call enough allies to subdue me. With the rune-mark still sucking at my energy I did not want to find out what fresh punishments the law-keepers would devise. There were cautionary tales of Windborn being used for hard labour, in mines or construction projects, until they collapsed. Some called it a waste of good fighters, others saw it as a fitting use for a dangerous resource, and in that moment, I saw it as a death sentence.

I gathered up my things, then pulled my cloak tight around myself and tugged my hood up over my face as I left Fafstol's Scar. The guards at the top of the stairs yawned as I went past and didn't seem to notice me, let alone care who I was. I walked along the edge of the chasm until I passed most of the law-keeper's tents and reached Katja's camp.

The bottom of the Scar was cast in gloom, but I could see a sharp set of shadows next to a dying campfire. There was someone down there.

I found a pebble and tossed it down. It skipped off the cliff face and then got caught between two rocks. I grabbed another, larger pebble and threw that down. This one scrabbled down between the boulders until it bounced from the taught canvas. The figure at the campfire looked up.

"Hey," I called down. "Runar."

For a moment I thought I had found the wrong camp, that the figure below me was staring at me without moving, then I realised that he was getting bigger. Runar was flying straight up to meet me. He reached the top of the cliff in a matter of heartbeats and floated a few paces away from the cliff's edge.

"I was starting to worry you weren't coming. You didn't want to come down to meet me?"

"It's easier for you to fly up here than it is for me to climb down there."

Runar's mouth twisted and he narrowed his eyes, then he shrugged. "Fair enough. You ready to go?"

"I am."

"Great. Wait here."

Runar dropped down away from me like an anchor off the edge of a longship. Whilst I waited I looked over to the nearest staircase. The guards there were huddled together, whispering to each other. I turned away and pulled one side of my hood across to hide my face. There were only two of them. I could throw both of them off the cliff and run before people realised what had happened. When I glanced again one of the guards was making his way over to me. I cursed under my breath and gripped my axe.

"What are you—"

The guard spluttered to silence as he caught sight of Runar rising beyond the edge of the cliff. Runar floated between me and the guard and let his pack slump onto the ground.

"Everything alright?" Runar asked the guard.

"Er, yes, I was just... checking on the situation."

Runar nodded as though the guard was offering sage advice rather than stammering platitudes.

"She was waiting for me, but I've arrived now so I'd say everything is fine. Wouldn't you?"

Runar twisted in the air to look from me to the guard and his feet knocked a pebble. The guard looked down at the clicking stone and nodded quickly.

"Of course, I can't see anything wrong here."

"Good. Then we'll be about our business."

Runar let himself fall to the floor as the guard hurried back to his staircase.

"Bloody guards," he muttered. "Always poking their noses in."

I grunted in agreement as Runar led us away from the cliff edge. We merged with the crowd as Runar aimed us towards a section of grandiose camps that had flags and banners twitching above them. They were closer to the stairs than most camps to give the kings and chieftains easy access to the law-keepers, but they were distant from the main paths to avoid the heavy foot traffic heading to and from the merchants and arenas.

Runar stopped to examine the wares of a small cart selling cooked meats and small beer. He pointed to some rabbit and got himself a drink.

"Do you want anything?" He asked as he fished money from a pouch.

"No."

Runar paid the merchant and we made our way slowly through the crowd. I squeezed my fists and tapped my knuckles against the head of my axe.

"Can you speed it up?" I glanced over to the nearest chieftain's tent, still too far away for my liking. The guards there leaned on their spears. One of them pushed her helm up to scratch her nose. "No one is paying attention to us."

"Patience, lass," Runar said through a mouthful of rabbit. "People always pay attention to Windborn. Better we get there slow and without comment than we stomp off like a bloody raiding party."

I scowled at his back but kept my mouth shut.

The crowd washed up against the edge of the fancy tents and we followed them. Each king and chief had set their camp to stand apart from the others, to claim their patch of the Althing. Some had banners and tapestries hung by their entrances, whilst other camps let their size show their prestige. We moved into the gaps between the camps and away from the rest of the crowd. Some of the guards watched us as we passed, but we moved with purpose and Runar nodded to a few as we went by. It is surprising how far confidence alone will carry you.

"Come on," Runar muttered after we passed the bulk of the camps. "Hraki's camp should be somewhere along here. You go in and see if Soren's alone. If he is, you grab him. If he puts up a fight I'll come help you. You know, help break apart the scuffle. Then, if all goes well, we make for Konvald and the High King."

In front of us, the tents became sporadic and some were in the process of being taken down. Churned mud and grass told me others had recently departed. We may have been too late.

"Shit," I muttered. "Which one is Hraki's?"

"I don't know. Can you see Soren?"

I squinted out at the remaining camps but didn't recognise anyone. I shook my head.

Runar cursed.

"You," Runar called out to a nearby servant carrying a string of smoked fish. "Which camp is King Hraki's?"

The servant's shock at being shouted at flashed into a momentary expression of disgust before dissolving into practised passivity. "I don't know. May the gods have mercy on you, Windborn."

The servant spat the last word and then made to leave, but Runar was already there, lifting the man by the front of his tunic. The man dropped the fish and clawed at Runar's hand. Runar lifted him easily and let the man's legs kick uselessly above the ground.

"I don't need the gods' mercy, son, but you certainly need mine. I'm going to give you another chance to answer my question: which is Hraki's banner?"

Runar let the servant drop and he tumbled to the floor.

"It's not here. They've gone," he said as he scrambled away from Runar. "Early this morning, I think. They were here last night, but when I walked by today they were already gone."

Runar bared his teeth and loomed over the servant. His feet left his shadow and I realised he had floated up off the ground.

"Where did they go?"

"I don't know." The servant looked around, looking for help, but everyone was too busy dismantling their tents. "Hraki's halls are far to the north, maybe they just left to get ahead of the ice."

Runar let himself touch the floor and pulled the servant onto his feet before handing him his skewer of fish.

"There. That wasn't so hard now, was it?"

The servant scrambled back and then ran off. Runar shook his head as he came back to me.

"Sorry about that," Runar said in a nonchalant tone. "It gets to me when people say things like that and I just... well, you saw."

I pressed my mouth shut and nodded. It had not occurred to me that people's prejudice against the Winds and their attempts to overthrow the gods would spill over into their interactions with Windborn.

"Does it happen often? People... talking to you like that?"

Runar shrugged. "Some. Most keep their mouths shut, though. No one wants an angry Windborn bearing down on them." He looked around, the servant's insult seemingly forgotten and cracked his neck. "Let's ask around. If we get lucky, they've told someone what route they're taking, and we can sneak up on them."

We made our way through the nearby camps, seeking out the servants and interrogating them on the whereabouts of Hraki's envoys. No one knew exactly where they had gone, but everyone knew that Soren had left with Hraki's people.

"Shit," Runar said. "We need to find Katja."

"Shouldn't we go after them? They can't have gotten too far. If we're quick we should be able to catch them."

"It's not how far they've gone that's the problem. People know that Soren went with them. If we're seen catching up to them and getting into a fight... It won't look good on Erling. I need to talk to Katja."

As we rushed back to Katja, I had to run to keep up with Runar. His strides were too long, each step taking him as far as five or six of my own, and his feet barely brushed the mud. He was only anchoring himself to the ground for my benefit and I put on a burst of speed, determined not to be left behind. When we reached the edge of Fafstol's Scar, Runar leapt off the edge. I skidded to a halt to stop myself from going straight after him and had to rush down the nearest stairs. Thankfully, the chasm was busy enough now that I didn't draw any attention, even shoving my way through the crowd.

By the time I reached Katja and Runar, they were deep in conversation, though Katja was still rubbing the sleep from her eyes. As I walked up to them and got my breath back, a raucous call brought my attention to the tree branches above me. Two black shapes twitched and unfurled. What I had taken to be patches of shadow at the top of the dying tree were two ravens. They shook themselves awake and hopped to the lowest branch and began screaming at me. Each one cawed like they were trying to ward me away from their territory.

Katja and Runar looked up and noticed me.

Runar gestured me over and then nodded towards the ravens. "Ignore her."

Before I could ask him what he meant, Katja spoke, "We appreciate your help here, Edda, but there's nothing else for you to do. Thank you, but this is for us to deal with."

"I said I would help bring you Soren."

Katja slumped onto a rock then looked up at me with her copper hair curled around her face. "Soren's gone. We can't—"

"Stop telling us what we can't do, Katja," Runar snapped. "If it were up to me, I'd go after them right now and drag them back kicking and bleeding, but we both know what happens if I do that. The gods know that I've paid the price for my rash decisions before, and I know that it won't just be me that suffers this time.

"Tell me... tell us what we can do."

Runar's words became breathless with emotion as he spoke until his voice withered to a whisper. Katja stepped up and placed a hand on his shoulder. That gentle touch seemed to leach something from him and his shoulders slumped like a campfire finally crumbling in a blaze of sparks.

Katja stepped back and rubbed at her eyes with the heels of her palms. She groaned. "This isn't how this was supposed to go, Runar. Maybe if I go and talk to the law-keepers right now they'll send someone to bring him in. He'll be questioned, the truth will come out, and Hraki will be condemned."

"And if they say no? Or want to spend the whole day arguing? We can't let Hraki get another Windborn. We need to act now."

"I know."

The law-keeper started pacing and Runar watched her as intent as a wolf watches its prey. With every step Katja took, each slap of her boots on the mud, I heard Soren's hurried footsteps. She spun and paced in the opposite direction and I gritted my teeth against the feeling that the longer we talked, the further I was from justice. A familiar black-feathered rage unfurled within my chest.

"I'll go."

They both turned, confusion writ on their faces.

"What?"

"You'll do what?"

I stepped between them. "I'll go after Soren. I've said I'll help you and I'm not tied to Erling so it won't come back to you. I'm a decent hunter so it shouldn't be too difficult to catch an arrogant Windborn."

Runar and Katja looked at each other.

"We couldn't ask you to do that," Katja whispered.

"You didn't. I volunteered. I'll capture him and drag him wherever you need him. Here. Konvald. I don't care, but he must be brought to justice."

"But if you fail—" Runar started.

"If I fail," I cut across him, "then what have you lost? You can claim I'm—what did you call me?—a bored farmer who wanted to finish what she started in the arena."

Katja shook her head. "I can't let you do that, Edda, if I let you go, then it would be just the same as it I let Runar go."

"I'm not asking for your permission, Katja. He burned down my home, took everything from me, do you have any idea what that's like?"

Runar's eyes widened and from the concerned glance he shot at Katja I wondered if I'd hit closer to the mark than I'd meant to. Katja's expression hardened and her lips pressed into a thin line.

"If we ignore the laws, then what are we left with?" she said, each word slow and deliberate. "We can go to the High Law-Keeper, I'm sure we can convince them to see us quickly, and once we've explained this surely they'll—"

"No," I barked. "I can't wait, and you can't either. I'll capture

Soren for you, and you help me bring him to justice. Then I'll..." I trailed off and remembered the strangle-hold thought of being joined to a household. I swallowed and took a deep breath. "I'll swear to King Erling. It sounds like you need the fighters."

They faced each other. Katja's cool, impervious gaze locked onto Runar, who floated a finger's width above the ground. After a long moment, Katja let out a deep breath. She shook her head and turned away.

"I don't know if I can agree to that," Katja said.

"This is why you came here, Katja," Runar said. "To get help. This might not be the way we thought this would go, but when do things ever go right? Edda can track down this new Windborn, I'll help her catch up to Soren, then she can do the dirty work. I won't get involved."

Katja's jaw muscles bunched and she shot a savage glare at Runar then at me. "Fine. You track them down and take this new Windborn to the capital. Do not bring him back here or it'll be obvious you went hunting at the Althing, and then whatever this Windborn might have done we'll get thrown out for breaking the peace."

Runar nodded. "What will you do?"

"There's still more I can do here. I can't just disappear. We have friends here, however forgotten we might feel up north. I'll talk to them and see if we can gain their support. Ljot should be here too. She's been travelling around, trying to get support wherever she can. I'll find her and then we will make for the capital. If we're quick enough, and you succeed, I can accompany you when you speak with the High King."

"Thank you," I said.

I stepped up to Katja and offered her my hand. She looked down at my outstretched palm.

"May the gods speed your journey, Edda," she said and shook my hand.

She turned and walked back into her tent. I stood for a moment then looked back at Runar. The floating Windborn was rummaging through some crates and sacks nearby and gestured me over. He handed me an empty bag which he then threw food into. Once the sack was full, Runar collected a couple of bedrolls and we set out.

Runar flew ahead to minimise the risk of anyone seeing us together and assuming that I had been sworn to their king. I walked through the crowds and, despite the supplies and weapons weighing me down, a new sense of purpose lent a lightness to my step.

The grief-crow in my chest lifted its suffocating wings to catch the breeze. The weight of it remained, its knife-sharp talons still gripped my heart, but its attention was focused elsewhere. Its spear-tip beak pointed firmly ahead.

*

The road from the Althing was full. Travelling traders were packed onto the road, both those with nothing left to sell or with nothing left to buy. Farmers herded cattle and sheep through the gaps and left a stinking mess in their wake. A few chieftains' delegations carved through the crowds with their law-keepers declaiming their master's right to the road from the top of their wagons and their huskalar ready to move anyone who didn't listen.

I had posed as one of Hraki's retainers as we left the Althing, pretending I was too hungover to leave with the rest of Hraki's followers, and eventually discovered they had left on the main road straight to the capital.

Now, Runar walked alongside a small herd of goats. He found a branch straight enough to pass as a walking stick, had risked removing his arm-ring, and had pulled his hood up to cover his face. He looked just like any other herder. I travelled a little way behind, hidden in the marching crowd. The Winds in my chest reached out to Runar, so I knew exactly where he was despite the press of bodies all around us. I drew a few stares as I made no attempt to hide the axe at my waist and Bjolfur's carved shield banged against my shoulders with each step.

Every so often, a smaller path or track branched off from the main road and someone would disappear down it leading whatever retinue they had, whether it was poultry, cattle, or people. After a few hours of walking, I sensed Runar move down one of the tracks. I followed him and when we were far enough away from the main road I closed the distance between us.

"What are you doing?" I hissed when I was close enough.

"We need to find out if they're heading for Konvald or if they're heading straight up north. If they were going home right away they'd have turned off about an hour ago."

"Why are we on this bloody path, then? Shouldn't we have turned off back then?"

"Relax." He raised a hand to stop my tirade. "This will take us into the Trolbjolvid. If Lothi and Soren went straight home, their path goes west around the forest before heading north. If they went to the capital, the road goes north-east before curving back around to Konvald. Either way, we can cut through Trolbjolvid forest and catch them."

Trolbjolvid: the forest of broken trolls. I shivered at the thought of entering that dark place. Legends said that at the end of the god-war, many of the trolls who had sided with the Winds fled into the forest to escape the wrath of the gods, but one god followed. The Warrior, furious with the trolls for their part in the plot that had killed his wife, spent a summer and winter hunting them. Now, the forest was littered with cracked boulders and jagged rocks; all that was left of the trolls he found. Some stories said that Warrior did not find all of the trolls and some lived there still. By some accounts, the trolls were biding their time for the end of all things, and in others they regret the part they played in the god-war and wanted to live out their days in peace. I thought of my own warring desires, of the crow pecking and pulling at my heart to bring those who harmed me to justice, and of the tiredness soaked down to the marrow of me that shouted for me to stop and farm.

As the noise and bustle from the road faded away I felt my grief-crow pulling me back, demanding that I run and find Soren.

"What if they turn off the road before they get to the capital?" I asked. "Or we get lost in the forest? Then we'll never catch them."

"We won't get lost. Well, I won't. I can fly. I'll guide you through and once I find our friends I can make sure we get ahead of them. We'll catch them on the other side, don't you worry."

"What about rivers? The road's there for a reason, isn't it? What if we come to a river that can't be forded? We'll lose them."

"I'll carry you over it."

"You'll what?"

Runar turned back to me and cocked an eyebrow. He walked up to a fallen log by the side of the track.

"I will carry you," he repeated each word slowly and then raised himself off the ground and floated over the log, miming carrying something in his arms.

My indignation must have shown on my face. Runar raised his palms defensively and said softly, "Do you want to get there ahead of them or not?"

I glared at him for a moment before I stomped past, cursing Runar under my breath. As I moved off the end of the main path and into the shadow of the forest Runar floated over me.

"Stay on this trail."

He gestured to a track just wide enough for a single person that pushed through the waning winter ferns and wound into the heart of the Trolbjolvid.

"I'll come back and find you," he said and disappeared into the dark foliage.

*

It did not take long for Runar to find Hraki's minions. They were not moving stealthily, and our journey quickly fell into an easy rhythm. Runar flew ahead, checking on our quarry, and then doubled back, appearing like a forest spirit, to correct my course. The first time he came back he guided me off the path and since then my route had been arrow straight, cutting over rivers and through thick patches of moss-covered trees. Now, as the dusky light between the trees turned into thick shadow, Runar floated down to me.

"They've stopped for the night," he said. "We might as well do the same. We've covered enough ground."

189

We found a relatively clear patch of forest and made camp in the lee of an outcrop of trees and rocks. Runar set out the bedrolls behind a small boulder and I pulled out some food. The boulder curved like the crook of an arm and I wondered if this was one of the god-hunted trolls.

"We won't be out of here for a few days yet, but we can't risk a campfire," Runar said between bites of dried meat. "Lothi is clever. He'd probably notice the smoke."

"The cold doesn't bother me."

"Oh, right. Guess it'll just be me freezing my tits off then."

"Why are they going overland, wouldn't it be quicker to take a boat?"

Runar considered this before he tipped his head in half-agreement. "It might be for a while. Hraki's kingdom is downriver from King Erling's lands so they'd have to sail through that first and King Erling won't allow that. This way is more direct and Lothi can carry people over any rivers or whatever might be in their way."

"He can fly too?"

"He can," Runar said darkly. "He's vicious so we should avoid getting into a fight with him if we can."

I nodded and we continued eating in silence. The night was clear and the moon gave us enough light to see by. There was a snap of wood in the distance and I saw a new shadow. Most likely a boulder I hadn't noticed before. Runar's gaze jumped from me to the jumbled pile where I had dropped my things. I caught his eye and raised my eyebrows.

Runar swallowed his mouthful and jutted his jaw at the pile. "What's all that about?"

"What do you mean?"

"Your shield and axe," he said. "They're not what I'd expect a new Windborn to be walking around with. The shield's carved for a funeral pyre for a start. Did you steal them?"

I clutched at the strip of meat in my hands. Runar's tone wasn't accusatory, but the words still jabbed at the black fury inside my chest. I shrugged and waited until I felt like I could unclench my teeth without screaming.

"It was my husband's shield."

Runar frowned as he bit off another chunk of dried meat.

"He drowned on the way home," I whispered. I kept my eyes down and looked at my hands, turning them over to examine the scars. "I carved the shield, but they wouldn't let me put it on the pyre at the Summer's End festival. It's the only thing I have that the Wind-hunters didn't burn."

Runar grunted and I looked up. He was nodding, but his eyes had glazed over and he stared into the middle distance. I shook my head and looked away.

The night settled in and we finished eating and shared some watered down beer.

"You take first watch," Runar said. "Wake me up in a few hours."

He yawned and stretched before lying underneath the boulder's overhang. His snores bounced off the stone within moments. I settled myself for a few hours alone with the moonlight and my scars.

*

The next day was much the same.

Runar remained a distant shadow between the trees leading me through the forest. After the previous night's conversation, I was happy to continue the journey in silence which was broken only by snapping twigs and the cry of distant forest birds.

Most of the trees around me retained their leaves, surrounding me with a thick canopy that let puddles of sunlight dapple the ground. Despite the foreboding twilight, I found myself enjoying the solitude and soon lost myself in the task of clambering over fallen trees, splashing through streams, and watching for low hanging branches.

With my body occupied, my mind began to wander. I shepherded my thoughts away from the sore subject of those I had left behind, and instead played the fight with Soren over in my mind. Looking back, I realised I had been lucky to gain the upper hand. Not only had my anger clouded my judgement, which so often leads to defeat during a raid, but Soren's control over his Windborn powers put mine to shame.

I turned my attention towards the constant cold that stuck

like tar to my insides and tried to force it out. The rune-mark on my arm burned. Nothing happened.

I tried again. The crunch beneath my feet sounded different. I looked down to see the leaves and twigs crusted over with hoarfrost as my feet swept them. Behind me, a shining, frozen trail showed where I had walked. Excitement bubbled up inside me, but I pushed it aside, leaving a trail would not help me. I clenched a fist and imagined it saturated by the frozen power within me. The rune-mark burned again and it felt like pushing my hand through burning coals. Wisps of smoke curled up from my arm, but a weight slowly appeared in my hand like a trickle of melt-water. When I opened my fist there was a rod of ice shaped by the inside of my fingers.

I practised for the rest of the day. The trail of frost-rimed forest behind me made it look like a huge snail followed me. The rune-mark smoked as I worked and I had to stop testing my powers several times as the heat became too much for me, but as the day wore on the rune-mark grew brittle and dry. Every time I pulled ice from within me it seemed to lessen the rune-mark's power. Though it still felt like pushing a thorn through my palm.

Even with the pain, I managed to form a rod of ice in my fist every half an hour or so. I tried to create different shapes as I did, and by the end of the day's travel I could summon a spear-sharp icicle.

Runar was not impressed with my experiments. Once, he came back to check on me and I showed him my latest icicle-knife. He rolled his eyes and told me to get moving.

When we came to a stream in the afternoon I waited by the edge and tried to create an ice-bridge instead of splashing straight across. As the surface of the water frosted over, Runar floated down through the branches ahead.

"Can you wait until we camp before you do that?" he hissed.

"Why?"

"For one, you're making it bloody cold. And those little fucking icicles you're making? You're leaving a really nice trail of them. It's like you want everyone to know exactly where we're going. "

"They'll melt."

"Not soon enough."

I glanced back. My icicles flashed back at me from underneath ferns and laying on tree roots. The glinting ice snaked a trail to my feet.

"Fine."

Runar grunted, a noise halfway between acknowledgement and satisfaction, and then disappeared back above the trees. He corrected my course twice more that day, but when he returned a third time he said it was time to camp. We did and, with no need to hide from prying eyes this deep in the forest, we started a fire in the middle of a clearing.

Once we were fed and watered, I started to clench my fists and make icicles. They came faster now, although I wasn't sure whether that was because I had better control of my powers or because of the waning rune-mark. Clean, sharp edges glinted from the ice-knives and soon several icicles lay next to me in a jumbled heap.

"Do you have to do that?" Runar sighed.

"You said to wait until—"

"I thought you'd forget. It's still making me bloody cold."

He shifted where he sat, turning away from me and pointing himself at the fire. I stretched my hand to shake the numb chill from my fingers and stopped making icicles.

The silence of the forest swept over us in a rising tide. The leaves above us whispered amongst themselves as insects started calling out, and in the distance came the occasional hoot of an owl.

Runar started picking something from his teeth and nodded to where I had piled my things. "You said that stuff was your husband's, right?"

I nodded.

"Can you use it? You said you were out raiding this year, but I've seen people on raids who barely know which end of a spear to hold."

My jaw bunched, but I swallowed down the surge of irritation. I had seen the same thing. Usually, they were young, idealistic fighters who jumped on a longship as soon as they could and didn't take the time to train or consider the risks. They rarely came back.

193

"I've been on enough raids to know how to use it. My equipment was in the house when it burned down, but I'd left Bjolfur's shield outside."

Runar gave a slow nod. He reached out to his own weapons and raised his eyebrows. "Care to show me?"

He paused, his hands not quite touching his shield and sword. Sleep tugged at me, walking the entire day and experimenting with my powers had left me drained, but the image of Soren's control over the flames shooting from his hands wouldn't leave me.

"Fine."

Runar's face split with a wicked grin.

He slipped on his shield and picked up his sword, though he left it in the scabbard. After a few experimental swings that sang in the cold night air, he stepped away from the campfire and beckoned me forward. For a moment I looked down at the carved shield, unwilling to pick it up.

This was all I had left. It told his story. I did not want it to be hacked apart.

I lifted the shield. The spiralling saga stared back at me and for a moment it felt like Bjolfur was with me. If this was all I had left of him then let us make this journey together. We had always faced the dangers of a raid together. This should be no different.

I took up the shield and picked up the axe, hefting both to remember the weight of them, and went to meet Runar.

It started slow.

Runar swung his sword in a lazy arc and my shield rose to meet it. I returned the favour with a slow swing of my own. It sank into Runar's shield with a dull thud, biting further into the wood than I meant. I yanked it out in a panic. Splinters flew out in all directions an eye-blink before Runar twisted his shield in a move that would have disarmed me if the axe had still been stuck in the wood.

I hacked at him with my axe and his sword lashed out at me like a striking viper. Runar moved faster and faster. At first, I kept up with him, blow for blow, my speed far exceeding anything I had before, but soon his sword was a blur in the firelight, and it was all I could do to defend myself.

Runar's sword came at me wide. It carved a long arc at my left and I threw my shield at it, hoping to jar him into a moment's pause for me to attack.

Nothing hit my shield.

I glanced at my left, confused, but Runar was gone.

That moment of confusion was all it took. The flat of Runar's sword slapped me across the face.

I stood there, stunned, and looked up. Runar floated above me, hanging nearly upside down, with his shield pulled tight against his chest and his sword hanging down by my face.

He grunted, then righted himself in the air, and floated back to the campfire.

"You're not bad." He landed and put his equipment away. "But you're not fighting like a Windborn."

"What do you mean?" I panted. "I've never moved that fast before. How can I not be fighting like a Windborn?"

"Oh, you're fighting fast, I'll give you that. Faster than I thought you would." He picked up a waterskin and, after taking a long draught, threw it to me. "But anyone can be fast. You should have seen the look on your face when I floated above you. You completely froze."

He chuckled at his own wit. I stormed over and stood over him, I opened my mouth, ready to let my annoyance fly, but Runar shot me a serious, dangerous look that stopped me in my tracks. He tensed and in that small movement he transformed from a rough-housing friend to a wary foe.

"Put those down."

I paused, not sure what he meant. Runar's eyes never left mine and I realised that I had rushed over, weapons in hand, and loomed over him like a common bully. I took a deep breath then set my shield and axe down next to my belongings.

"What did you expect me to do?" I said. "I've never fought someone who can just float above me before."

Runar's expression eased now that I had dropped my weapons, though he kept a wary eye on me. He slumped down against a tree. "Speed is only part of it. Think about your Wind-given powers. You need to claw every advantage in every fight when you're Windborn. Now more than ever.

"You can't be sure what kind of powers your enemy will

have or how they'll use them. That might have felt like a cheap trick, but that won't matter if it means you get an axe to the face."

I sat down then took another swig from the waterskin and grunted.

"I'll take first watch," Runar said. "Get some sleep."

I let myself fall back to lie on the ground. It wasn't long until sleep overcame me.

*

We went on like this for a few days. Though now when I tested my powers I was careful not to leave a trail. Then, once we had set our camp for the night and eaten, Runar would suggest another fight.

To his credit, Runar let me adjust to his Windborn powers slowly. The second day he raised himself off the ground and attacked me, forcing me down. And on the third, he began circling me from above and darting in to attack like a diving hawk. If he had started using all of these tactics at once I would never have been able to cope, but with each fight he unveiled something new and soon I was able to hold my own against him and even put my own powers into play, hampered as they were by the rune-mark.

Runar's attitude towards me seemed to change each time we fought. Whenever I proved I wasn't some bored farmer playing hero, he respected me a little more. I had seen that kind of thing before, experienced raiders who would not respect fresh warriors until they bloodied their spears. It rankled that he hadn't taken me at my word, but I couldn't blame him. The halls of the gods were filled with overeager young warriors.

As we fought on the fifth day, I pushed the cold within me down and spread it on the ground. The earth frosted over. I retreated from a sword thrust. Runar stepped with me and his foot landed on the patch of ice and slipped out from under him.

Instead of falling underneath me as I intended he paused mid-air, brought his shield up to his chest, and slid away from me. Flew away from me. Then Runar stood outside of my reach with his shield up.

"Good," he said between deep breaths and the tension left his muscles. "You'd have had me then if I couldn't fly. I'm done for tonight. You done?"

"Yeah." I let my shield drop and slipped the axe handle through my belt.

Back at the campsite, once our snared rabbit was cooked and mostly eaten, I shared out the nuts and berries I'd gathered as I walked.

"So, what kind of powers do Hraki's Windborn have?" I asked through a mouthful of berries.

"There's Nal," he began. "He can turn himself invisible, weapons and all. You can be looking right at him and not see anything. Makes him real tough to fight when it comes down to it.

"Jorunn. She's easy enough to deal with, the only thing she can do is turn into a snow bear. It might make her stronger, bigger, meaner, but she's still just a bear.

"Brimir, they call him Stoneskin, but I've not seen him in action yet. He's a big fucker though. There might be others. Soren might not be the only new Windborn that Hraki's recruited recently."

At the thought of facing down so many different Windborn, the berries in my mouth turned sour. I swallowed them, half-chewed as they were, but the sour taste remained.

"What about the one leading Soren, Lothi, you said he can fly?"

"That's right. You leave him to me if it comes down to it."

"How have so many Windborn agreed to serve Hraki? I thought he only had a small kingdom at the edge of the world. What can he offer them that another king can't?"

Runar moved to sit against a boulder. "I don't know. Hraki's always attracted Windborn to him and we've never been able to figure out why. Now that you've heard those outlaws talking about how Hraki promised them a place if they became Windborn, that explains some, but not all of them. Some of them were Windborn before he became king and flocked to him afterwards."

I spat out a seed and threw another berry into my mouth. I rolled it with my tongue, pressing the stretched skin against the roof of my mouth until it burst. As Runar told me about Hraki and his Windborn, his fingers played along his forearms, tracing scars. I wondered if he touched the scars each Windborn gave him as he named them.

Night had truly set in now. Beyond the thick canopy, clouds crowded the sky and the forest was filled with deep shadows.

"I don't know," Runar said with a sigh. "Hraki was the youngest, he was never meant to be king, maybe his Windborn think they can control him."

"What happened?"

"His sister, Solveig, took the throne when their father passed. Old age took him and all seemed well. King Erling was getting on with her but complained of an arrogant prince whenever he returned from their halls. Erling didn't let his distaste for Hraki stop his diplomatic efforts, though. He continued to visit. He even took his son, Dyggvi, along on some trips to try and give Hraki a peer to talk to but still, Hraki grew bolder and more disrespectful. At first, he ignored the king at feasts, then it moved to muttered slights until soon Hraki was being openly contemptuous of Erling when he visited."

"Isn't Erling's kingdom larger than theirs?" I said. "Surely that's reason enough to be civil?"

Runar nodded and raised his hands as if to say he agreed but could not answer. "And they only have access to the ocean through Erling's lands. For what it's worth Erling didn't take Hraki's jibes seriously. He said it was a younger brother's jealousy over his sister taking the throne. Solveig kept the relationship cordial, despite her brother's obstinance, she may have tried harder because of it. She continued to invite Erling to her halls more than was necessary and when we raided together Solveig often gifted some of her spoils to Erling.

"Then, during one of the High King's visits, the High King suggested that the two princes go hunting together. Perhaps someone had mentioned the tension Hraki brought to the relationship and the High King thought a hunting trip was the answer. The princes couldn't say no and Erling and Solveig seemed ready enough to agree.

"They set off the next day, with a small number of their

friends and retainers, but only Hraki came back. He said it was a rockslide. A boar dislodged a stone on a mountainside trying to flee and before they could escape, most of them were already dead. He said he tried to save them, but the rockfall was too thick. They were all trapped. I wasn't there, but Katja was. She says Hraki came back covered in blood and with torn clothes, but when he went to the healer they couldn't find a scratch on him.

"Maybe he got lucky and he only tore his clothes, but I don't put much trust in luck."

Runar shook his head. He picked up a handful of small rocks and started throwing them, one by one, at a tree opposite him. The plunk of stone on wood was the only sound for a time.

"Is that really what happened?" I asked.

"I don't know. They sent for me and I went searching, but I couldn't find Dyggvi. The only body we found was the one Hraki dragged back with him, his personal bodyguard."

"And it was the rocks that killed the bodyguard?"

Runar threw the last of his rocks and rested his outstretched arm on his knee. "His wounds looked like they came from rockfalls and there were enough of them to say for sure that's what killed him. We tried to get Hraki to tell us where the rockslide was, but he couldn't remember. Or so he said."

We sat together in the dappled moonlight. From the way that Runar told it I was surprised that Erling hadn't already declared war on Hraki and taken his son's blood-debt from the prince by force.

"But what about his sister?" I said after a moment. "She was still on the throne, wasn't she?"

Runar nodded slowly. "She died a couple of months later and Hraki took the throne."

"And what killed—"

"Another rockslide."

The look on his face and his bitter tone of voice told me Runar didn't believe that for a second.

"Oh."

"Exactly. Erling could believe the first rock slide, otherwise he would have done something foolish, but two? Erling went to Solveig's funeral, but Hraki hadn't changed. He still made jibes and preened in front of Erling, making himself out to be the stronger king.

"Erling's been at this a long time. He ignored the jibes at the funeral but cut ties after that. He told Hraki that his actions were those of an enemy rather than a friend. Their relationship just got worse from there and Erling told Hraki that if any of his people crossed his borders he would consider it an invasion."

"Hraki did though, didn't he? That's why you flew into the Althing."

"And that wasn't the first time. Erling won't let Hraki's ships have access to the sea, and that's what Hraki wants."

"Why won't the High King do something?"

"The matter is settled as far as he's concerned," Runar sighed. "You saw what happened at the Althing. Einar came up to speak with Erling and Hraki. At first, he seemed sure to rule in our favour but after he spoke to Hraki something had changed and he said it was just a spat between kings. Erling is within his rights to deny Hraki passage until Hraki pays the blood-debt for Dyggvi's death, which Hraki refuses to do because he says he is not at fault. But if we can get Soren to confess about Hraki's deals with outlaws then the High King will have no choice but to help Erling."

We sat in silence for a while and I watched the shadows on the ground as clouds moved across the moon. Runar took a swig from the waterskin and I looked at the boulder he was leaning on. Moss grew up over its rounded side and it had a strange, familiar shape in its curves and hollows. The moon shone bright for a heartbeat and etched the boulder's features in shadow. It was a face. The straight jutting rock there, a nose, and there, the slight curve of an eyebrow. Runar sat up against one of the dead trolls. It had been hunted, broken, killed but it was still here. A cloud covered the moon and I squinted to keep the memory of the troll's face in my mind.

"How did you become Windborn?" I asked before I could stop myself.

Runar looked sharply at me. He frowned and did not say anything for a long moment. I felt the now-familiar thrum of Windborn energy build in my chest for a moment as Runar looked at me, then he picked a twig from the ground and began picking it apart.

"It was years ago. More than I'd like to admit. Outlaws burned down my home with me inside.

"It was just a little farm south of Eylheim and I was drinking with my father. They came up from the river and Da sent me inside. They must have jammed the door because when the fire started I couldn't get out. I tried to climb up to the roof and break out that way, but by then the smoke was too thick and I didn't have the strength. I remember wishing I was higher and stronger, just wishing I had the strength to get out and save my father. And that was it.

"I woke up with Erling's huskalar dragging me out of the wreckage. When he realised I was alive, Erling made sure I had everything I needed, and he vowed to kill the outlaws. And he did. It took him a little while, but he found them. He sent a band of huskalar down there and killed them, took their plunder and gave it out to the families they'd raided. Everyone knew I was Windborn by then, little things giving it away, but there was never any question about me serving anyone but Erling. He's a good man and wants what's right for everyone."

He lapsed into silence and let the dark woods swallow up his story. After a while, he slid down against the boulder until he lay on the floor. He closed his eyes and stuffed his bag behind his head as a pillow.

"I'd be glad to have you fighting with me, Edda," he said. "You could do worse than swearing to Erling."

I slumped against a tree and stared at the ground. The names of Hraki's Windborn bounced around my skull, all the potential enemies that stood in my path. It would be easier to fight knowing I had people like Runar at my side. I shook my head and told myself to focus on the task at hand. Get Soren and take him to the High King. Everything else could wait.

Leaning back, I watched the stars blink through the shifting evergreen canopy and listened to the sounds of the wildlife growing louder as our conversation faded.

A twig snapped to my right and the forest fell silent. I tensed and my hand flew out to grab the haft of my axe.

Out of the dark undergrowth, something appeared.

It crept out along the blanket of twigs and dead leaves towards Runar. A black, snuffling shape twitching its way forward. It moved into one of the patches of moonlight and I saw its back covered in sharp spines. A hedgehog.

I let go of my axe and a giggle almost burst out of me. The hedgehog sniffed its way past Runar and then continued on into the night, searching for grubs and bugs.

"Gods speed your travels, little one," I mumbled.

I looked at Runar, snoring gently. He had left me to take first watch. Again.

CHAPTER TEN
KONVALD

THE FOREST THINNED OVER THE NEXT COUPLE OF DAYS and we moved from a world of twilight to open spaces and clear sky. Runar stopped flying as the tree cover disappeared and the risk of being seen became too great. Once we left the forest proper we followed a jagged river of boulders that grew into mountains. Our path took us north until we crested the mountain's low slopes and the Konvald fjord appeared before us.

Steep, wooded hills surrounded the fjord which flowed south-west, and out towards the sea. Boats and ships swept across it, the fishing boats dwarfed by longships, and all sailing to and from the city perched on the distant shore. I could make out the twig-thin lines of jetties fanned against the edge of the city. The jetties started small, built for one or two fishing boats, and the closer they got to the longhalls in the north of the city, the larger the jetties became until two or three longships could moor themselves at once.

"At last," Runar muttered. "We should make it before Soren and his lot do. I'll go on ahead. I'll stay low. Lothi shouldn't spot me, but it's too late for him to do anything, anyway."

He stepped off the mountain slope, ignoring the fact that the ground fell away under him and began to float away.

"You can't leave me alone."

Runar, already high above the sprawling valley, started to turn away from me. "If you keep to the shore and the edge of the woods then I'll have a clear view of you from here to the city. If I see you in trouble I'll come back and help, but we need to tell our allies in the city what's happening."

I wanted to argue with him, demand that we go together,

but he was already too far away. I would need to shout and that could bring unwanted attention. Instead, I gritted my teeth and checked my weapons before making my way into the valley.

The encroaching winter had sucked the friendliness out of the landscape. Instead of green leaves reaching out to brush my sides, I passed thorny shrubs that raked at my clothes. Rocks moved under my feet where recent rainfall had washed away the topsoil and more than once I nearly slipped down the hillside. I muttered under my breath as I made my way down. Mostly I insulted Runar as much as I could for leaving me behind, but when my feet slipped on the scree I barked out a curse.

As I drew closer to the bottom of the valley something in the air made my hackles rise. Underneath the sound of shifting gravel and the cold waters ahead of me, the woods had fallen silent.

My gaze flicked between the sparse trees around me and back to my feet. I cursed myself for giving myself away. The ground was covered with small rocks and twigs. I took hold of a scraggly tree for balance and made to step forward, but held my foot a finger's breadth above the ground.

Somewhere ahead, a twig snapped.

I put my foot down. Slow, calculated, silent. I strained my ears against the low sound of the forest, trying to pick out what lay hidden under the blanket of natural noise. In between the rustling of leaves, the click of one stone falling on another, something moved. Something heavy and deliberate. Ahead of me on the hillside a blackbird exploded out of a bush. Its undulating song shouted a warning to any who understood it.

I readied my axe and shield.

There was a clearing off to my right. A fir tree had toppled some time ago and there was a small crater where its roots had been. A few shrubs and weeds had grown in the space, but it was clear enough and the worn roots would give me something to put my back against.

I edged over to the clearing. My head whipped to face any small sound. In my agitation, I couldn't distinguish between the sounds of the forest and whatever was following me.

No monster came charging out of the trees as I put my back

against the ripped up roots. No enemy appeared to applaud my vigilance.

And so I waited.

The forest was silent, and the longer I stood in the clearing the deeper my conviction became that something was wrong. I glared at the long, dry grass and ferns with their brown edges, daring something to come forth, and started pushing ice out of me. The rune-mark sank its teeth into my arm. I gritted my teeth against the familiar pain and kept pushing.

I banged my axe on my shield, causing a fresh wave of birds to flee. Let them know their ambush had failed.

Shapes shifted within the bushes at the edge of the clearing. Dark forms I had taken for shadows became men and women with weapons bared like fangs.

On my left came Soren and someone else with a Windborn's arm-ring, most likley Lothi. Now that I could see them, I realised that part of my unease had been the sense of their Windborn souls reaching out to mine like a riptide. On my right, another two fighters appeared from the undergrowth. I couldn't sense any Windborn power from the two on the right, but their shining spears would be no less deadly.

I lifted my shield and bared my teeth. They spread out evenly to trap me against the uprooted tree.

"Well, well," Soren drawled. "Look what we found in the woods. I wanted to run into you again. I think it's time that I evened the score, don't you?"

He kept his eyes locked on mine and the air around him began to shimmer.

"How did you find me?"

"Oh please," Soren scoffed. "It was easy. You think we didn't know you were following us? We were one step ahead of you the whole time."

The other Windborn shot a scowl at Soren before looking back to me. "Your friend isn't so subtle as he thinks, flying about all over the place."

"And now we're here to get revenge," Soren said. He clapped his hands together and sparks erupted from between his fingers.

205

Soren made to take a step forward, but the other Windborn blocked him with an outstretched arm.

"Not yet," Lothi hissed and then turned back to me. "Look, we know that you're going north to swear yourself to Erling. I understand. You can't let yourself become an outlaw, but don't go with the first offer that comes along. Erling's weak, dying, and Hraki's on the rise. Come with us. It's a much better deal for you. Trust me."

"What are you doing?" Soren asked. "You said I could kill her."

"I saw what you did," Lothi went on, oblivious to Soren's pleading. "In the arena. How you put this one down. We could use another fighter like you."

He held out a hand. Waited for me to take it.

I took a couple of steps back, leaving icy footprints over the loose rocks and soil, and pushed myself up against the roots. I looked from Soren to Lothi and the two silent warriors beside them. They stared at me like I was an injured dog, unsure whether I would lash out or submit, and they readied themselves for either. I looked at Soren and realised with a shock that he still didn't remember me. He had that same wary expression on his face, laced with the rage of the revenge-seeker, but nothing more.

He didn't remember that night.

I had fallen away from everything into a cold, surging grave and taken some of his companions with me, but there was nothing in his eyes that acknowledged that.

"You don't remember..."

"What?" Soren's face twisted in confusion. "I remember you humiliated me in the arena. Now it's time that I paid you back."

He lunged at me. Lothi tried to stop him, but Soren was already moving. The other two hesitated then took their cue from Soren and leapt after him.

I braced my shield, but Soren's attack never came. His furious eyes had missed the shining ice covering the ground and his foot slipped from under him. He cried out as he went down and one of the fighters became tangled up in his flailing body.

The other fighter kept his eyes locked on mine, watching

for the first hint of my intentions.

He ducked to my right. I twisted to bring my shield around. The move left me wide open to an attack on my other side, but Soren and the fighter were still tangled together.

My opponent stabbed at me. I batted his spear away with my shield. Half a step forward and I swung my axe. His shield came up to meet it, but I twisted the axe-head over the lip of the shield and pulled as hard as I could. The fighter toppled forward. As he tipped towards me, eyes wide, I head-butted him.

I misjudged the angle and my nose cracked. The pain sent me reeling. I wiped the back of my hand across my face to clear away the blood pouring from my nose.

As I tried to shake the disorientation, something flashed on my left. I stumbled back and twisted away from it faster than I could have before I died and the axe bit into my arm instead of my belly. I cried out in pain and my axe fell from my grip. Soren followed up his swing with a roaring gout of fire that drowned out all other noise.

The smell of burnt hair and singed wood engulfed me.

I screamed again.

I crouched down and got my shield between myself and the endless flames. With my other hand, I reached down and clutched at the earth. I pushed out the cold, trying to send a lightning strike of ice at Soren in an effort to topple him again. The rune-mark strangled my power as I tried to force it out. Soren's hungry flames devoured the ice leaving only melt-water.

I fell to my knees behind the shield. The iron rim creaked in the heat. Everything was flames and whipping shadows.

Beside me, illuminated like a stone around a campfire, the unconscious fighter rolled and groaned. I stumbled across to him, hoping that Soren would ease the conflagration to spare his ally.

The fire kept coming.

Another sound joined the flames' breathless roar: Lothi calling desperately for Soren to stop. The fighter's groans erupted into screams as the flames engulfed him. It seemed that nothing would stop Soren.

I gritted my teeth and concentrated on the ferocious cold at the centre of my chest. I willed it to the edges of myself and kept it there like the surface of a midwinter lake. My skin stopped burning, but the heat came on relentless. The rune-mark's fangs sank into me. I breathed deep against the pain, but the air was too hot. It burned me from the inside.

There was no escape.

I screamed and launched myself forward.

In the split second I leapt into the flaming current, my skin blistered. I rose from the flames like a kraken rises from the waves. Soren's expression flashed from fury to confusion to pain as my fist connected with his jaw.

He stumbled back, unprepared for the blow, and the flames sputtered out. I swung again, my pain and rage matching his, and sent him reeling back another few steps.

I tried to find my axe, but the remaining fighter rammed their spear butt into my leg. I went to my knees again, though I managed to keep my shield up.

Soren wiped the back of his hand across his bleeding mouth. The blood dried and crusted as I watched. The air around him shimmered and he grinned.

I lunged and thrust my shield boss at Soren's head, but the fighter tangled his spear between my legs. I lost my balance and sprawled out on the floor in the centre of my enemies.

"Looks like I'm about to get even."

Soren grinned like a shark swimming towards a shipwreck. His too-white teeth stood in sharp contrast to his smoke-stained face.

"Soren, this isn't why we're here," Lothi growled.

I glanced over to the other Windborn. His feet floated an arm's length off the ground and he moved slowly across to us.

"Why do you think we need her?" Soren snarled back. "You've seen how weak she is. The arena was just a fluke."

Lothi paused and raised his palms as Soren picked up my axe. Bjolfur's axe. Rage surged through my aching muscles and pushed me up, but the sharp point of a spear against the back of my neck shoved me back down.

Soren and Lothi circled each other around me like two hungry wolves around fresh carrion. Soren spun the axe in one hand. His wild eyes ricocheted between Lothi and I. It looked as though he was trying to decide who would be faster if he tried to kill me, him or Lothi.

"I know what happened in the ring," Lothi went on, his voice soft, "and you've proven who's the strongest. Let's do what we came here to do and give her Hraki's offer. If she turns it down, well, we'll take her to the law-keepers and maybe they'll let you be the one to execute her."

Soren circled closer to me.

"There's no way she's going to join Hraki. Let's get it over with."

An untethered shadow passed over the ground in front of me. I glanced up from behind my shield. Runar floated twenty paces above us and slowly descended. He held a finger to his lips and I stifled my cry of relief.

Lothi had moved in as well, matching Soren's movements, but there was a new tension in his frame.

"Now is not the time for this."

"Lothi,..." called the quivering voice of the remaining fighter. The fighter glanced up, pale-faced.

"I know," Lothi growled. "Soren, I need you to put down the axe and step away. If you're going to be part of Hraki's household, you need to put the king's needs above your own. That's the deal. Put. The axe. Down."

Soren glared at Lothi, oblivious to the new tension, and tightened his grip on the weapon. "I've not sworn to Hraki yet."

He yelled and attacked.

It was clumsy. He hadn't readied the blow and had to pull back his arm.

Lothi let off a sharp whistle then drew his sword and flew up to meet Runar. I tried to roll away from Soren, but I was up against the tree roots and couldn't move out of reach.

A woman appeared from nowhere and barrelled into Soren, knocking him down.

As Soren scrambled to his feet the new arrival yanked me up from the ground. She clutched a long knife in one hand, then pulled another from its scabbard and shoved it at me before turning back to Soren. The weight of the knife in my hand anchored me and relief flooded through me now that I was armed once more. I squeezed the knife's grip and set my feet, ready to fight.

"Not another step," she snapped and pointed at the fighter trying to circle us. "This doesn't have to turn nasty."

Soren groaned and rolled on the floor. He had been shoved to the edge of the clearing and he flinched away from a bramble that brushed against his arm.

The newcomer glanced over at Soren as he flinched and the fighter lunged. I tried to intercept the spear thrust, but my legs refused to move fast enough, and I only managed to stumble at the weapon. The newcomer saw the spear coming, but too late.

The tip caught her sleeve and her outline blurred.

She disappeared.

I blinked at the space where she had been. Panic swirled at the pit of my stomach as I tried to see where she had gone. The fighter fell forward with the force of his thrust. Another blur behind him and she reappeared.

"Drop the spear," she said and pressed her long knife against his neck.

The fighter let go of the spear and raised his hands, palms out. "Please, don't—"

"Shut up." She turned to me. "You okay?"

"As good as I can be."

She grinned at me then looked up at the flying Windborn circling each other. She was a little shorter than me and had short cropped hair the colour of fresh-cut wood. She had a Windborn's iron ring wrapped around her right arm.

"Runar," she called out. "We're done down here."

From the looks of it, the Windborn above us hadn't resorted to blows yet. They looked down and both began to descend, keeping a wary distance from each other.

"You can't win this, Lothi," Runar said. "Give us your new Windborn and we'll let you all go."

Lothi looked at the scene below him and his expression darkened. "I can't do that. He's already promised to Hraki. Do you want to send me home empty-handed?"

"Yes," the woman said.

Runar frowned at her before turning back to Lothi. "You're a long way from home, Lothi. What's Hraki going to do? You lost the Windborn on the way home. Tell Hraki that he died in a rock slide."

Their feet brushed our heads now. They continued to circle each other. Now that everyone was occupied, I found my axe and blew some of the ash from the head. I went over to where Soren was still blinking on the ground and I pressed the borrowed long knife against his neck. I wanted to push the sharp iron into his flesh, to feel the life-blood pour out of him, but he was more useful to me alive.

"Do not move," I growled.

Above me, the flying Windborn stopped circling. Lothi's gaze was locked onto me. I bared my teeth.

"Hraki is expecting a fresh Windborn," Lothi called. "I will not disappoint him."

He whistled again and the trees around us rustled. For a moment I thought it was some new Windborn power, then more figures emerged. Two of them had bows with arrows nocked and ready to draw. Three more stepped forward wielding axes or knives.

Lothi floated back a few feet, coming to a stop above the heads of his reinforcements.

"A draw," he said. "You leave without killing Soren or Berik and we let you go without killing you. Sounds even to me."

"You attacked me," I cried. Stories of Windborn heroes fending off countless foes marched through my mind. With three Windborn, surely we would be able to win, no matter how many fighters Lothi called from the trees.

"Rein her in, Runar," Lothi snapped. "I'll do the same to mine. They're just unsworn Windborn who attacked each other. Let's not make this any more complicated than it has to be."

I looked at Soren, his wide eyes moving from me to the blade in my hands. It would be nothing to push down and kill him, to get justice for my own death, then there would only be one Windborn to fight. Blood began to trickle down his neck and I realised that I had been leaning harder against him.

"Fine," Runar said.

I looked over at him, shocked he would agree with a sworn enemy, and saw the thunderous expression etched deep into his face. He lowered himself onto the ground and nodded at me and the newcomer.

She took her knife away from her hostage and shoved him away. He stumbled forward and then fled behind his allies, rubbing his neck as though to check it was still in one piece.

Everyone turned to me.

Soren's breath came quick, shallow. I stared at the edge of the knife. A drop of dark blood ran down his neck, leaving a bright red trail. It was a vicious invitation.

"Edda."

The soft tone of Runar's voice tugged my mind away from the edge of my blade. I blinked and looked up at him as he stepped towards me, hands outstretched.

"Put the knife down, Edda. We're done here, but this isn't over."

I cast a lingering look at Soren's bloodied neck and the knife resting there but lifted it away. I tossed it to the female Windborn. It fell in a puddle of meltwater in front of her. She picked it up and, after wiping it on her trousers, slid it into its scabbard. Runar gestured and I walked over to stand with him.

Tension still smothered the clearing and it almost spilled over into violence again as Lothi floated too close to us on his way to Soren. The fiery Windborn wiped the blood from his neck and stared at me with blazing fury. Lothi put a hand on his chest and pushed him forcibly away from us.

"It's done. We did what we came here to do."

"I didn't," Soren growled, resisting Lothi's touch.

Lothi shoved him a couple of steps back. "I said it's done."

They eyed each other. Soren spat on the ground and stormed off. Lothi's shoulders slumped and he sighed. After a moment, he shook his head and straightened.

"We have injuries to take care of," he said, turning and gesturing to the burnt fighter.

Runar nodded and led us out of the clearing.

"The offer's always open, Edda," Lothi called out after us. "You can handle yourself and Hraki never turns away a capable fighter."

His words seemed to echo around us. It silenced any possibility of conversation.

It took only a few moments before the birds sang in the

trees once more. The only mark that there had been a fight was my still-tingling skin and the cold ache of my injuries. The world had already forgotten the blood spilled across it.

*

We went to the shore so I could wash off my mud and bloodstains. Water soaked into my clothes, making them heavy. The axe wound on my arm had already closed, crusted over by a layer of bloodstained ice. I picked at the edge. A chunk of bloody frost tugged at my skin then snapped off. The wound began seeping thick, semi-clotted blood. Flakes of ice mingled with the wet crimson until the ice-stained scab reformed.

Runar called me back from the water and we continued towards the city. It was the first time any of us had spoken since the fight.

The fjord opened up on our left. The still waters were broken by boats and the ripples they spread on the surface. Out on the other side of the fjord, the ground raised steeply to become mountains. The band of forest by the shore thinned out swiftly, leaving bare mountainside fading to a snow-dusted peak. The slope was shallow on our side of the fjord which let us walk easily along the shoreline. The slope tapered off the closer we came to the capital and the road leading to the city gates, which was hidden by the foot of the mountain, became visible in the distance.

"Edda," Runar said. "I'm sorry that I let that happen." His face was downcast, and he clenched his fist, tapping a knuckle against his pursed lips.

I shrugged, which sent an aching spasm through my chest. "You kept me from getting cooked."

"I shouldn't have left. I was anxious to get to Konvald, I don't usually travel at walking speed, it felt too slow. It was lucky that Valna was still in the city and I could bring her with me."

Valna, the female Windborn, flashed me a smile that was startling white against her muddied cheeks.

"Why did you come back?" I said. "I thought I was on my own."

213

"I had a bad feeling," Runar said, quietly. "You learn to trust these things."

I nodded. I'd seen people call off attacks or choose a longer, more difficult route during raids because someone had a bad feeling. It almost always saved lives.

"Did they wait until I'd gone and then jump you?"

"Not straight away. I managed to set up a bit of a trap: put some ice on the ground, get against that fallen tree so they couldn't flank me. That kind of thing."

"How did you know they were coming?"

"I had a bad feeling."

A smile tugged at Runar's mouth.

Up ahead of us Valna chuckled then called, "I like her, Runar."

The road appeared next to us and we moved over to use it. After too many days travelling through the forest it felt strange to be on the road, with people again. Some rode horses, others led animals bearing bursting bags, and occasionally we were forced to the side as a cart trundled by. Each traveller was met with a nod and a hand raised in greeting, but when they noticed the state of us, they were quick to move on.

The city soon loomed before us. The ramparts seemed to grow out of the ground. They had been made with an earth embankment which had a wooden wall built onto its pinnacle. Beyond the wall, I could see spear tips moving as guards marched one way or another. In front of the walls, they had cut out a ditch to make attacking the city as difficult as possible. The road bridged the ditch and led up to the city's gates.

"Don't worry," Valna said and slapped my shoulder. "It doesn't feel so grim inside."

I grunted, unconvinced. My eyes trailed the line of sharpened tree trunks that had been sunk into the ramparts like the spines of a slumbering monster wrapped around the walls.

As we approached I noticed that the wall above the gates was cut lower than the others and it was there that a man appeared. He was scruffy, his hair stuck out in all directions and he had dirt-covered cheeks, but he cradled a spear on one shoulder and looked imperiously down at us as only a small man with a little power can.

"I'll talk to him," Runar said.

He floated up to talk to the guard at eye level. The guard went wide-eyed and took half a step back.

"We're travelling back from the Althing," Runar called out, loud enough for his voice to carry back to us. "We need to get back to King Erling, though we may stay here for a few days."

The guard, who seemed to have recovered from his initial shock, looked down at us. He narrowed his eyes when he looked at me and then sniffed, wiping the back of a hand across his nose. "You look like you've been in a fight. We don't want any Windborn in here causing trouble. The High King's ordered us to keep you out if we think you'll be a problem."

I snorted. I didn't see how this man would be able to fend off anyone, let alone three Windborn.

"We're not here to cause any trouble," Runar replied, hands up in surrender. "It's dirt from the road. We want to rest, maybe visit the law-keepers, and then be on our way."

The guard narrowed his eyes at Runar and shot us another dirty look, but he gave a slow nod.

"Just don't be causing any trouble, or I'll come lookin' for you."

He turned and called down to let us in and a section of the gates swung open, functioning as a small door within the larger gates. Runar dropped down to walk with us and we ducked through. The guard who had opened the door looked us up and down before turning back to close the door.

Inside, nestled within the walls and away from the nagging thoughts of Soren, I felt a weight lift from me. The High King was here. We could finally seek justice straight from the source.

Tall posts sunk into the ground guided us to the town proper. Someone had hung garlands of mistletoe and bright fabrics on the posts. I was reminded that this was a season of celebration for many, as stores would be full but the harshness of winter not yet upon us. The path guided us past houses, protected by small willow-branch fences, and on to what I assumed was the centre of Konvald as an enormous mead-hall loomed ahead of us.

"Is that where the High King is?" I asked.

"Aye," Runar said. "He holds feasts, and sometimes court, there. The buildings all around it are his too, but they're for

215

servants and his family."

"Let's go and see him then," I said and turned to walk to the mead-hall.

"Whoa there." Runar held me back by the shoulder. I felt the flurry of Windborn energy pass between us at his touch and it left us both with a flush in our cheeks. "We can't just march in there, making a scene. We need the High King on our side, and he might not even be there. We need to rest and wait for Katja. We need a new plan."

"Why can't we just go to the mead-hall and tell them there's someone outside the city that was a Wind-hunter? They'll go and get a confession out of him."

Runar pinched the bridge of his nose. "For one thing, the High King hates Windborn. If we charge in there on our own he might have us thrown out of the city. And you're not sworn to anyone yet. It might have worked to our advantage before, but right now it means that the High King will just have you swear to the nearest king."

"Fine," I said and turned around to follow them.

Under Runar's direction, we made our way past the High King's buildings and through the city. We passed various trading houses looming over the residential housing. I saw a tanner and a blacksmith, a large market place leading to the harbour. Valna and Runar moved with purpose through the marketplace, which was now nearly empty as the day came to an end, and to a small house that was halfway between the harbour and the market.

The house was shoved between two larger buildings with a small area in front cordoned off by willow fencing. It had a thatched roof and wooden walls, a typical home in any town, but there was a post set into the ground in front of it. The post was intricately carved, as were the cross beams on the front of the roof. After a moment, I realised the carvings showed a saga, beginning as its base and spiralling upwards. At the very bottom of the column there were images of ancient warriors fighting hideous monsters, and as the story climbed, the monsters were beaten and killed until they were exiled to the sky. It was the story of the god-war and the exile of the Winds until about halfway up the pillar when the story focused on mythical kings and queens.

Valna came up to stand with me.

"It's the story of Erling's royal line," she said. "Legends say that one of his ancestors was Sif."

"The same Sif who stole the boots from the giant Veidmar? And tamed the First Wolf? That Sif?"

"Yeah. That's her there."

She sidestepped around the column and pointed to a figure carved into the saga soon after the gods banished the Winds. I followed Valna's finger. Compared to the carvings of the gods that preceded her, Sif looked small, but her image was clear and showed the legendary boots taken from the god of the northern forests. Behind her was the silhouette of a wolf large enough to look the gods in the eye.

"I always liked the stories about her when I was younger," I said.

Cast in the warm light of evening, Sif's carved image sent a spark of nostalgia rushing through me. I remembered sitting by the fire, clutching a badly whittled figure of Sif, as my parents told me another story of the mighty warrior. My heart lurched as I realised that the figure I had clutched was gone now, burned away with the rest of my life. I had forgotten about that until now. It had been lost in the magnitude of my grief like the loss of a single, favoured tree in a forest fire. The thought twisted something inside of me, driving another thorn into my heart as I realised I would never be able to tell my children about mighty warriors, or give them their own figures to stave off the imagined terrors of the night.

I straightened and saw Valna had lost interest in the column and was halfway through the door.

"Come on," she said. "It's getting dark."

I took a deep breath and followed her into the house.

Inside, it looked like any other house. It had a single room centred around a fire pit, raised boards lined most of the floor to keep the residents above the cold ground, and tables, pots, and barrels were scattered around the room.

"Whose house is this?"

"Erling's," Runar said as he bent over the hearth to try and light the fire. Each strike of the flint illuminated his frowning face.

I looked around again, but couldn't imagine a king staying here. "Really?"

"It's mostly Katja that stays here," Valna said from across the room. She had wiped most of the dirt from her cheeks and shot me a perky smile despite the rings under her eyes. "She's been staying here to try and talk the High King into sending help for us. I've been here too, to keep her out of trouble."

Valna winked with her last comment.

Before I could ask her what she meant I heard a screech from the rafters. I spun towards the sound and half drew my axe from my belt. A patch of shadow, perched on the rafters, was deeper than the rest of the roof. It hopped along one of the wooden beams and turned its head to examine me before it let out another squawk.

"Easy," Valna said to me. "It's just... just a raven."

I eyed the bird uneasily. It stared at me with an intensity that I had never seen in any animal before. With the weight of the journey still on me, I wasn't in the mood for any more strangeness.

"Where can I wash?"

"There's a well out there," Valna said and jabbed a thumb towards the back of the house.

A wicker wall hid another entrance that led out to an enclosed yard. A few chickens wandered around an outhouse and a well. I pulled up a bucket of fresh water and splashed it on my face. The water must have been cold, though I couldn't feel it, as it crystallised as soon as I touched it. It slid off my hands and cheeks in icy chunks. I scrubbed at my face with the slush and it soon turned dark with dirt.

I let the dirty ice-water fall to the ground. The chickens came over to see if what I had dropped was edible and squawked with indignation as they watched it soak into the soil.

Now that I was away from the eyes of my new companions I felt the weight of the last few weeks press down on me. I leaned against the lip of the well and looked into the darkness. The light disappeared within a few paces, slowly disintegrating until only black remained.

A bird call brought me up and around. The raven from

inside was perched on the edge of the roof. It seemed that there was no escaping the black feathers that still wrapped around my heart. I picked a pebble from the ground and threw it as hard as I could at the bird. It jumped away, cawing viciously, and the thatch splintered where I hit it, but the bird flew right back to the same spot.

Silent now, it regarded me with one eye and then another. I couldn't shake the feeling that it was judging me. After a moment, it ruffled its feathers and fluttered back inside.

I stared after it, scowling at the place it had melded with the shadows. Was I so obviously wounded and dying that even a raven would not bother with me?

Once more I felt a pressing grief within my chest and it started to push its way free. The tears should have felt hot as they welled in my eyes. Instead, they were sharp and cold. When I went to brush them away I felt a prickle of pain. My tears had frozen into minute spearheads.

This Windborn curse had taken everything from me. Soren had killed me and destroyed my life with his lust for Windborn power. Now my own change, which kept me from joining my husband in the depths of the ocean, was slowly taking away my scars, my blood, my tears. It destroyed everything that made me human.

It was a long time until I felt ready to go back inside.

CHAPTER ELEVEN
THE HALLS OF THE HIGH KING

RUNAR FLEW OFF EARLY THE NEXT MORNING to find out how long it would take Katja to reach Konvald. Valna tried to start a conversation, but I couldn't take my eyes from the raven that hopped from beam to beam above our heads.

"Why is that in here?" I asked. "Shouldn't we try and shoo it out of the house?"

Valna's shoulder tensed as she poked at the slowly growing fire. "We can't do that."

"Why not?"

"Oh, we brought it with us." Her voice was saturated with forced cheerfulness. "It's Katja's pet."

"Right."

The raven seemed to sense my glare and it fluttered onto the table and croaked at me. I swatted a hand at it, but it flapped out of the way and squawked again. Valna shook her head and busied herself cleaning her long knives.

"What now?" I asked. "We can't see the High King until Katja gets here, so what are we supposed to do?"

"Wait," she said without looking up and the room filled with the dry rasp of a whetstone being put to use.

I looked around the house. The prospect of being trapped inside until Runar came back made the shadows press in around me.

"I'm going for a walk."

"Oh, that sounds fun," Valna said, pausing the scrape of stone on steel. "Would you like some company?"

"No," I said, then saw Valna's expression crumple. "Thank you, I'd like to be alone."

221

Valna nodded slowly then turned back to her knives. I went over to where I had shoved my possessions and pulled out my weapons.

"What are you doing?" Valna said as I slipped my shield over one shoulder.

"Getting ready to go."

"You don't need any weapons," Valna said and laughed. "You're in Konvald. No one's going to attack you."

I stared at her with disbelief.

"If you wear that, you'll just draw attention to yourself and all the guards will pester you."

My jaw bunched. I disliked the idea of heading out without my axe and shield, but I couldn't afford to be noticed and dragged to the nearest law-keepers.

"Fine," I said and put my things back on the floor. After a moment's hesitation, I picked up a knife from the table and slipped it through my belt.

"Here," Valna said and threw a pouch at me. It landed on the floor with the tell-tale jangle of coin.

"What's this?" I said as I picked it up.

"I'm not using the money, so consider it a gift. Well, a loan." She shot me a shy smile. "You know, in case you want to get anything nice at the market. Just try not to spend it all, okay?"

"Thank you." The weight felt good at my belt as though I had regained some measure of independence, borrowed as it may be.

"And don't piss anyone off," Valna called out in a sing-song voice, "not everyone is as nice as me."

I smiled at her as I left the house.

I retraced our steps from the day before and soon found myself at the market. Morning mist still lay heavy on the ground. It felt like walking through a ghost-world as buildings and people appeared out of the mist like apparitions. The few people who braved the cold this early were wrapped in furs and had cloaks pulled tight against the insistent mist and frost. Most people gave me sideways glances and I realised that I was only wearing a tunic and trousers. Another mark of the bitter Windborn blood now flowing in my veins.

When I examined the stalls of those traders willing to brave the cold I saw that this was not their best stock. I found bruised and half-rotten vegetables, clothes that had holes where the moths had found them, and the mugs and drinking horns I saw had uneven and cracked lips. These were merchants desperate to unload the last of their wares before the journey home. There were only a couple of people wandering through the stalls and they looked disinterested, picking up an item only to put it down once they found its inevitable flaw.

If the market had been more crowded, or if it had been later in the day, I might not have realised I was being followed. I snaked a route back and forth through the stalls, doubling back on myself here and there, but two figures matched me turn for turn. Their heavy cloaks hid their identities, but between the shouts of merchants I heard the unmistakable clink of weapons. I cursed myself for leaving my axe and shield back at the house.

I quickened my pace and ducked through a few more stalls, hoping to lose them in the low hanging cloth canopies, but when I emerged on the road, they were there.

Cursing, I turned down another path. They had cut me off from the house and I wouldn't be able to get back without confronting them. I turned again, hoping that my random movements would throw them off.

The further I went, the more I lost my way. Each time I was about to disappear around a corner they saw me and quickly followed. Eventually, I came to an alley where the sides of three houses pushed together into a dead-end. A few boxes and barrels leaned against one of the buildings. As I went to climb one of the boxes and escape over the houses the two figures swept into view, as sure of themselves as the tide.

They paused when they saw me. I turned and drew my knife.

"What do you want?"

They shifted their feet and they were no longer standing idly at the end of the alleyway but stood battle-ready, blocking my escape. The eager mist curled around our feet. I took a step towards them to give myself room to manoeuvre if it came to it. "This is the one?" asked the one on the right. His voice ground out like it was being dragged over jagged rocks.

The figure on the left nodded and pulled out a stone from

within his cloak. The stone glowed in his palm and he moved his hand from right to left. As the stone pointed towards me the light flared then dimmed as it was turned away from me. I frowned then cursed myself for being so foolish and looked down at the rune-mark on my arm. It was cracked and broken, but the parts that remained glowed in response to the stone. I couldn't let them take me back to the Althing. Soren was here. I needed to be here, not to the south wasting words with law-keepers.

"This is her," the left figure said. His voice was softer, almost friendly.

"You gonna come quietly?" the first said.

"The law-keepers sent us all the way from the Althing to bring you in," said the softly-spoken man. He pocketed the stone and drew his sword with his other hand. "Let's do this the easy way so we can get some rest."

"I'm not going back there," I said and drew myself up to my full height. "Now fuck off."

"It's not a question of where you're going. It's a question of how hard you make it for us." said the friendly one. "You're coming with us one way or the other. Isn't that right, Bardi?"

The other one, Bardi, growled. He took a step towards me and pulled an axe from inside his cloak.

"My ineloquent friend is right. There're two ways to do this. You come with us nice and easy and we take you to the law-keepers, or I let Bardi do it the hard way."

I took my eyes off the two thugs to check the ground between us. The mist still swirled around our feet, but it was thin enough I could see the hard mud underneath.

In the moment that I took my eyes off them, one of them leapt at me. I didn't see who. Their shadow flickered ahead of me. I leaned back, but the blade sliced through the bridge of my nose.

I raised my knife to parry the next blow, but it didn't come. Both men were out of reach. The friendly one flicked his sword. Its tip was speckled red. I gritted my teeth and covered my nose with my hand, letting ice flow out and over my wounded nose.

"Ofri," the gruff one said, reproachful. "You said I could fight this one."

"She took her eyes off us, Bardi, you want me to miss that kind of opportunity?"

Bardi growled again and stalked forward.

"You don't want to do this," I said.

They glanced at each other and I pushed ice out to the floor, hoping they wouldn't notice the slow shining growth.

"We do," the gruff one said with a wicked smile.

"We got paid a lot of money to bring you in. It'll set us up for a long time."

"A year. Maybe more."

They moved apart with cautious steps to encircle me. I jabbed at them with my knife as they reached the sides of the alleyway and managed to keep them both in front of me. As I thrust with my right hand, I covered my left palm in a coating of ice. The rune-mark was splintered, weak. It flared and sank fangs into me, but I forced my Windborn powers through its jaws.

They attacked.

Bardi yelled and swung his axe at my head. The swing was wild, too erratic to be anything but a distraction. I stepped out of reach, knowing it would take me in range of the swift, precise swing of Ofri's sword. I spun around and caught Ofri's attack on my ice-covered hand.

The ice split with a crack and his sword bit into my palm. I gripped the blade, encased it in ice and pulled hard. Ofri tumbled forward. I thrust the knife at his falling chest, but it was knocked wide as Bardi's axe buried itself in my shoulder.

Crying out in pain and anger, I swung around, dragging the sword with me, and punched Bardi as hard as I could. He was thrown off his feet, still gripping the axe, which ripped out of me.

Ofri tugged on his sword and it sliced out of my bloody grip. He slipped on the icy ground before trying to roll onto his feet, but couldn't and slid into his friend.

Blood seeped down my back. It burned hot against my frozen skin.

The two thugs helped each other up and looked at me with fresh determination. I had thrown them about and blocked their first attacks, but I was bloodied and they were only bruised.

"Not bad," Ofri said and gave me an appraising nod. "Now, the way I see it, you've got three options. You can try to run, but we will find you. You could try and win this, but you are outmatched. You might have got a couple of hits in, but you're not the first Windborn we've brought in, and now we know your trick."

The other one grunted and pulled another axe from beneath his cloak.

"Or," Ofri continued, picking shards of ice from his sword, "you can surrender and make this a lot easier for everyone."

He finished picking at his sword, inspected it, and then cocked an eyebrow at me.

I swapped the knife to my uninjured hand and shook my arm to try and get the feeling back. My fingers were too numb to be of much use so I punched a hole in a barrel lid and fused my fist to it with a sheet of ice. I raised the makeshift shield ahead of me and bared my teeth.

"Let's get this over with," I said.

Ofri sighed and pulled out a knife. Bardi grinned and advanced.

They came at me again faster, stronger than before. I managed to ward off the axes with the shield, but the knife and sword were too quick to parry with my small knife. As the blades found my flesh, red sprouted across my arm like leaves in the spring.

I clenched my jaw against the pain and threw my shield into Bardi to push him off balance. As he reeled, I swung the makeshift shield into Ofri's side. Ofri's dagger whipped out viper-fast and stabbed deep into my stomach before the shield crashed into him with a crack of wood and ribs and sent him stumbling.

I kicked away his weapons and pushed my foot down on his chest. Drawing on my pain and fury, I thrust my Windborn power out and fixed Ofri to the floor with a coat of ice. The rune-mark blazed and thrashed against my power, biting into my marrow, but with a yell I forced it through. I turned to face Bardi, breathing heavy and with a chill seeping into my rune-marked arm.

"Only you and me now, Windborn. Just how I wanted it. Ofri only gets in the way."

Bardi wiped the blood from his chin and grinned. He raised his axes and waited. I bared my teeth and tried to breathe through the pain of the wound in my stomach and the thousand slices on my arms, but each breath sent fresh spasms of agony coursing through me.

"Come on, Windborn," Bardi growled. "I thought you were supposed to be tougher than this."

I focused on my frozen, numb core and forced it to spread. Cold found the wound in my stomach. Ice reached my arms. My pain lessened. Then the frost found the rune-mark and a fresh wave of nauseous pain shivered through my bones.

Without taking my eyes from Bardi, I reached down and picked up the sword. It was lighter than the weapons I was used to, but it was better than my knife.

Bardi grinned.

His axes slammed into my barrel-lid shield and I felt it coming apart in my hands. I took another hit on the shield, then stepped back and let the next swing fly wide.

Bardi narrowed his eyes, but couldn't stop his momentum. I swept the sword around, toward his face.

The hafts of the axes met the blade. The edge bit into the heavy wood and for a moment we tugged at each other. He was strong, but not as strong as a Windborn. I twisted the sword and ripped the axes from his hands.

He let go before the force took him with it and threw one, two punches at me. They collided with my stomach, knocking the breath out of me and doubling me over.

I threw my shoulder forward into Bardi's belly and knocked him to the floor. He clawed at my back, trying to throw me off, but I weathered the gouges.

I brought the shield up high, and then smashed it down on his head. The shield splintered and broke. I raised my hands to hit him again, but he was unconscious so I let my arms fall to my sides.

Standing, I sucked in the cool morning air then winced. It felt like I had inhaled a thousand thorns that stabbed at my lungs from the inside.

The ice held Ofri fast and his eyes were unfocused. He wasn't a threat. I paused to lock Bardi to the floor in the same frozen cage. They looked like the corpses dredged from frozen seas that would fight for the Winds in the war that ends the world. I blinked away tears and thanked the Sea Giants that Bjolfur had been saved from that fate.

I moved to the end of the alley and leaned against one of the buildings. I tugged my tunic to unstick it from my bloody wounds and sucked in a breath as it caught on the half-dried blood and pulled my skin. People had begun to leave their houses to start the day, though they did not seem to have heard the fight, or perhaps they simply didn't care. I pushed myself back up and eventually retraced my steps back to the house, thankful now for the lack of crowds to stare at my bloodied, shambling self.

*

I did not leave the house again.

Valna washed my wounds and found me fresh clothes. She kept apologising for letting me go out alone. I waved her off, but her expression was pained for the rest of the day. She dragged some sheepskins into a corner to give me a place to lie down. I eased myself onto the soft furs and drifted in and out of sleep. Each time I woke the pain was less and by the next day there was only a dull ache soaked into my muscles with a spear-shard pain in my stomach.

"How are you feeling? You slept right through the night."

Valna crouched by the fire in the centre of the room, poking a spoon into a pot hanging above the flames.

"Still aching."

"I'm not surprised."

She dipped the spoon into the pot and blew on it before tasting it.

"You woke up just in time for porridge."

I grimaced and stretched my stiff muscles. They felt like they would snap if I pushed them too far. Valna spooned out two steaming bowls.

"Who were they?"

"Who?" I kept the bowl cupped in my hands. The heat felt good against my cold fingers.

Valna rolled her eyes. "The people that attacked you. You never said. You just sort of collapsed."

"Their names were Bardi and Ofri, I think. They said they'd hunted me from the Althing. I was supposed to go and see a law-keeper for attacking Soren in the arena. I... forgot with everything else that was going on. I guess the law-keepers didn't, though."

Valna's spoon stopped halfway to her mouth and her expression had darkened.

"I remember them. They're vicious. The law-keepers must really want to bring you in if that's who they picked."

"I told them I couldn't go with them, but they didn't listen."

"Sounds about right. From what I hear they don't usually let you get your side of the story out. You did well to get away from them."

I shrugged before turning my attention back to the porridge.

Valna seemed to have retreated into thought and my wounds troubled me enough that I was happy with that. The ache was tolerable and small enough that I could ignore it but the scabs plagued me. The myriad wounds on my arms were already healed over with clear ice. They caught the firelight as I lifted the spoon to my mouth and seemed to spark as though flames were trapped inside. When I finished eating, I ran a finger along my stomach to feel the stab wound and though I felt the torn flesh there were patches of smooth, frozen scarring.

Valna took my empty bowl and went outside to pull water from the well. I took the opportunity whilst I was alone to check my old scars.

I rolled up my sleeve and found the mark I was looking for. One of the last wounds I had taken whilst raiding when I had leapt in front of an arrow to protect Bjolfur. It was the last time I had been able to protect my husband. I ran my finger around the scar on my forearm. The skin, which should have been rough to the touch, was cold and smooth. I twisted my arm and the first crystals of ice caught in the firelight. Black-feathered

229

grief tightened around my heart once again. I had always considered my scars earned imperfections that made up the threads of my soul, my very being. But if the Wind inside could take my scars, what else could it take? It seemed that with each step I took as a Windborn part of me was lost, smothered never to return.

The door banged open, sending the fire flinching away from the wind and shadows scurrying across the walls. I pulled my sleeve down. Runar stepped into the room, clapping his hands together to banish the cold from them.

He nodded to me and then peered around the room. "Where's Valna?"

"Fetching water."

He nodded again and moved over to the long table and picked at the bread and nuts.

"Did you find her?"

"Aye," he said, then did a double-take as though noticing me for the first time. He stepped closer, eyes ringed with concern. "What happened?"

Before I could reply Valna appeared at the other end of the room brandishing a spoon, but she relaxed when she saw Runar.

"I thought I heard voices, and after yesterday, I thought I should make sure they were friendly."

"Yesterday?" Runar looked between us, frowning. "What happened yesterday?"

"I had a run-in with some thugs, nothing to worry about."

"Thugs?"

"Bardi and Ofri," Valna supplied in hushed tones. "Edda said they chased her all the way from the Althing."

Runar's eyes went wide. He stopped eating and came over to examine my wounds. I stood and brushed past him to pick at the food on the table.

"You fought them off? And you're okay?"

"Just about."

Runar gave a slow nod. "They're a couple of bastards. Probably best if you let one of us come too if you want to go out into the town, just in case."

I shrugged, indifferent but accepting.

"Why were they after you?" Runar asked.

I tugged up my sleeve and showed him the rune-mark. The letters, which had once been black and thick, were cracked and broken. The skin around them was raw and blistered.

"After I nearly killed Soren in the arena, I was supposed to go and speak with the law-keepers to decide my punishment. One of the god-speakers put this on me to limit my Windborn abilities. They've given Bardi and Ofri something to track me using the rune-mark. They said they were here to bring me in."

Runar scowled at the rune-mark. "Can we get it off?"

I shrugged.

"We'd better try. We can't fight them if they come for you. They'll get law-keepers and huskalar and we will give you up. I don't want to, but we'd have to. It'd set Erling against the High King and we can't afford that."

The thought of facing Ofri and Bardi again made my bones ache but I felt a wave of gratitude that Runar wanted me to stay. To hear that I was needed from another Windborn, from someone who understood what it was like to die and keep walking, felt like I had finally found an ally in this fight. I looked from Runar's thunderous expression and down to the raw skin on my forearm. The rune-mark was shattered, unable to withstand all of the Windborn power that I had been pushing through it. Perhaps its hold on me was weakened and I would be able to remove it entirely.

I grabbed a knife from the table and sat on one of the benches. I pressed the edge of the blade against my skin and scraped across it as though I was shaving a pig ready to butcher. The knife caught on the rune-mark and carved off a little of the dried tar. I tried again and again and each time a small part of the rune-mark came away. It was not a perfect process as I also sliced away a little of myself with some clumsy attempts, but little by little the rune-mark was fading.

"Did you find Katja?" Valna said once I had set myself to the task of carving away the rune-mark.

"I did. She got passage on a longship. It'll put in at Konvald soon. By the time I found her it had gotten dark so I stayed overnight."

Valna nodded and went over to her knives, checking their

shine and sharpness in the light.

"So we wait for her here?" she asked.

"No. We'll meet her by the docks. I'll get myself clean, then we'll go."

He threw his mud-stained cloak into a corner and went out to the well. A moment later we heard the creak of the pulley and splash of water.

I ran my thumb over my forearm to check the skin for any traces of the rune-mark. It was raw and bleeding, but there was nothing left of that rainbow tar. Then, taking inspiration from Valna and learning the lesson from my still aching body, I checked my weapons. The shield had seen better days, its edges charred and with chunks taken out of the carved figures, but it was still usable. My axe needed sharpening and there was some rust starting to encroach the back of it.

"Valna, can I borrow your whetstone?"

"Sure."

She rummaged through her own pile and then tossed me the grained stone. The steady scrape of stone on steel woke up the raven in the rafters and it squawked indignantly at me. Slowly, I put down the whetstone and picked up a pebble from the muddy floor. Without taking my eyes from the bird I hefted the stone and threw it up into the rafters. The bird cried out as the stone clipped its tail feathers. I smiled as it began to hop above me, cawing and crying as though reprimanding me.

Runar came back into the room. "That water is cold," he said. "I almost wish that fiery Windborn was here."

He shot me a grin.

"No?" he said, deflating. "Okay, not ready for jokes. That's fine."

"The only time I want to talk about him is if we're discussing how to kill him," I growled back.

Runar held up his hands in surrender. "Okay. Okay."

We made ourselves ready to leave. Runar and Valna wrapped themselves up in cloaks and furs. I didn't dress for warmth but put on a cloak before I picked up my shield, axe, and two knives from the table.

"Expecting trouble?" Runar said.

"I wasn't expecting it yesterday."

He and Valna shared a look—a silent reminder that even though I travelled with them, I wasn't yet one of them—then led us outside.

The wind whipped at cloaks and pulled down people's hoods. Dark clouds gathered above us and rain began to spit down as we made our way through the city. It seemed that people feared the wind more than they wanted to run their errands as the streets were just as quiet as they were the previous morning. Half of the market stalls had closed and I wasn't surprised to see the rest of the merchants packing up. We soon turned onto the main road from the High King's halls to the docks and I saw a glimmer of blue in the distance.

"Why are people avoiding you, Edda?" Runar said out of the corner of his mouth.

I took my eyes from the end of the road and looked around.

"I don't know. I was bloodied up after the fight yesterday, maybe they recognise me?"

The people bustling past us cast suspicious glances in my direction. I hunched my shoulders and pulled my cloak closed to try and hide in its folds. They kept their heads low and only turned when they thought we weren't watching. As my shield bounced on my shoulder, I began to wish I had left it in the house. Most whispered to each other and then hurried on.

"I don't like it," Runar rumbled. "Have you got a hood on that cloak?"

"No."

"Then try and keep your head down."

Runar and Valna sped up and I fell in behind them, trying to use their bodies as a screen. I unbraided and tussled my hair so that it fell forward and obscured my face. There were still so many people doing their best not to stare at me, I felt as though I were being paraded down the road.

We arrived at the docks and the knots in my shoulders loosened as I anticipated being able to lose myself in the crowds of strangers and sailors. People called out everywhere; confirming how many barrels needed to come off the ship or still needed to go on. Others advertised vacant berths on their ships before they cast off to get ahead of the fjord freezing for the winter.

"What do we do now?" I said, careful to keep my voice low despite the cacophony all around us.

"We wait for Katja."

"No, I mean, after that. I can go back and gather our things."

"What? No. Stay here. This won't take long. Katja said some of the law-keepers agreed to help us, but we need to get proof before they'll do that."

"They want more proof than they got at the Althing?" I scoffed.

"Apparently," Runar said, still distracted. He floated a couple of hand-spans above the ground and craned his neck to look for Katja. The crowd around us murmured and took a few steps away from us. "I didn't get the details out of Katja on the boat. It wasn't exactly private. I don't want you going off on your own if Bardi and Ofri are around and looking for you."

I scowled but took half a step closer to Runar. My hand strayed to the pouch of coins that Valna had given me. Some of the merchants were selling whatever they didn't want to take on the journey back. I craned my neck to find something that would help me hide.

"Ah, there she is."

Runar floated back down to the floor and beckoned us forward. He pushed gently through the crowd and led us to one of the far jetties.

Katja stood on the ship, arguing with an older man. He was jabbing a finger at an outstretched palm. When he noticed us he threw an indignant wave in our direction as though we proved whatever point he was making. Katja shook her head and folded her arms. Her cheeks looked flushed and she responded calmly to the agitated man who gave her a sour look. Money changed hands and Katja walked down to us as the older man counted his coins.

"Katja," Runar said, turning between us. "You remember—"

"The bastard tried to charge me extra because of you. He said we agreed on a price for three passengers and with you stopping off, that made it four. Bloody arse."

"Did you... I..." Runar stuttered.

"Don't worry, I gave him an extra couple of coins, nothing too much."

Katja took a few deep breaths and her burning cheeks dimmed, or at least as much as can be expected in the winter air. She turned around to watch someone holding a piece of slate and some chalk bustle up to the ship's captain and then come over to us.

"You were a passenger on the Wave Cutter?" the woman holding the slate said to Katja, completely ignoring us.

"I was."

"Your name and business in the city."

She hunched over the slate, chalk at the ready, oblivious of Katja's thunderous expression.

"Law-Keeper Katja, for King Erling. Our business is to supply ourselves for the journey home and to seek counsel from the High King's advisors."

The note-taker scribbled along with Katja's words, then nodded and hurried away. Two more figures made their way off the longship, one carrying a sack over one shoulder and the other holding a shield.

"Over here, Muli, Ljot."

The figures glanced over and the shield-bearer tipped his head in acknowledgement. The other, a woman wearing a fur-lined cloak, wrapped Valna in a hug. With a start, I realised that this was the woman I had seen in Dagnur's hall, beseeching him for help.

"Muli, it's good to see you," Runar said and slapped a hand on the man's shoulder.

The man tottered to one side and nearly toppled over. "Good to see you too, Runar. You've saved me some beer, right?"

Runar laughed and took the sack. "Have you ever known me to run out of beer?"

Katja turned back to us, shaking her head. "Come on."

With a gesture, she hurried us on and back towards the house.

"You didn't catch him then?" Katja said back to me. "Runar told me you met him outside the city but things got out of hand."

"He had friends," I growled.

"It doesn't matter now, they're either long gone, or in the

235

city. If they're gone then we might as well head home, and if they're in the city then there's nothing we can do to catch them."

"Edda's still not sworn to anyone," Runar said, then leaned in and whispered: "Wasn't the whole point of this to catch Soren without actually tying it to us?"

"Maybe before, but everyone's seen Edda with us, and now we can't risk sending Edda out alone. There are still people who would try and take an unsworn Windborn for the bounty, and you know how strict the High King is with Windborn walking around the city."

"Where were you yesterday?" I mumbled.

"What?" Katja spun to face me, stopping me in my tracks. "What do you mean?"

"I had a run-in with a couple of thugs. Bardi and Ofri. I fought them off. It's fine."

Katja looked, wide-eyed and intense from me, then to Runar and Valna. The other two Windborn had their heads down to avoid her gaze.

"What's the big deal? They didn't get me."

"Shit. Did you know about this?" she asked Runar.

"I only found out when I got back here. It happened when I was with you."

Katja sighed and looked to the sky, tugging her cheeks in frustration. The noise of the docks died away, I assumed it was because we had started to argue in the middle of the road, but a new sound simmered under the quiet, a steady jingle of moving metal.

"Those two aren't thugs. They hunt Windborn for the law-keepers," Katja said. "I thought they were at the Althing. Why did they come after you?"

I looked away to avoid Katja's gaze.

"I was supposed to meet a law-keeper and they followed me using a rune-mark, but I've got rid of it." I showed her my forearm, complete with frosted scabs. "They won't be able to find me now."

"Ah, shit," Katja said. "They won't be coming for you alone now. You didn't kill them, did you?"

"No, I just knocked them out."

"Fuck. If you'd have killed them then there wouldn't have been any witnesses. We need to get back to the house, now."

The thumping grew louder. I peered through the heads of my companions. Sunlight glinted from a spear tip. The others noticed the tension in the air and turned.

A group of six heavily armoured warriors approached us. Each one was outfitted with a helm, steel shoulder guards, and carried a painted round shield. From the jingling sounds of them as they all came to a stop together, I suspected they wore chain shirts underneath their furs.

Katja swore once more under her breath, then stepped forward, smiling.

"Hail, huskalar, what joyous news brings you to us today?"

The lead huskalar narrowed her eyes at Katja, stepped forward, and gestured with her spear at the rest of us.

"Still your tongue, law-keeper. No joyous news could drag huskalar from defending the High King. We have been told of an unsworn Windborn wandering the city, she matches your companion's description. She nearly killed two honourable citizens as they tried to do their duty to the High King and bring her to justice."

Katja turned, with great exaggeration, and looked Valna up and down and motioned to her iron arm-ring. "I am afraid you have the wrong person. Valna is sworn to King Erling and has been for years. Perhaps these two honourable citizens have been mugged and concocted a story to preserve their dignity?"

"Do not try me, law-keeper," the lead huskalar growled. "You will give us the unsworn Windborn or we will take all of you."

I bristled and let my hand drift towards my axe. A couple of the huskalar saw the movement and shifted the grips on their spears. Runar put his hand on my forearm and gave a minute shake of the head.

Katja's mouth opened and closed. She looked back at me and then to the huskalar. There was no way I was getting out of this without bloodshed, and if I did manage to escape I would be hunted and left with no way to find Soren. I shrugged at Katja. She sighed and stepped out of the way. The lead huskalar nodded to her followers and two of them came forward as though to grab me.

"I'll come along," I said. I pulled my arm away from one of them, causing them to stumble. "But I won't be dragged."

The one that stumbled squared up to me, as though to save face, but the leader cut across whatever he was going to say.

"Let's take her to her prison cell."

The huskalar gestured with their spears and led me away, trapped within their armoured escort.

*

They locked me in a shed. They said it was a prison cell, but someone had forgotten to take out the dried fish hanging from the ceiling and there was old food scattered across the floor. Somewhere along the way one of the huskalar decided that I needed to be tied up and had bound my wrists. It hadn't occurred to them that I could freeze and smash the ropes or simply rip them apart with my Windborn strength. It felt like I had been locked away for hours, although it was hard to tell as the rain-soaked sky cast no shadows. To take my mind off whatever punishments they had in store for me, I examined the fish heads gaping down at me like shocked bystanders.

Could they prove I was the Windborn that Ofri and Bardi wanted now that the rune-mark was gone? If not, could they execute me for assault? Surely they wouldn't, not even if the perpetrator was a Windborn. It occurred to me that the true crime may not be the injuries I inflicted onto the two bounty hunters, they knew the risks of confronting a Windborn, perhaps the real crime was being unsworn.

I shook my head and squinted up again. One of the fish twisted slowly from side to side.

I couldn't remember any stories of Windborn executions. How would they do it, if that was to be my punishment? If they drowned me then maybe it wouldn't matter that I was Windborn, maybe I would still become one of the Blessed Drowned. I could join Bjolfur.

Again, I shook my head. Distracting myself with fish wasn't working. I looked at the floor and examined the leftover food. Rinds of bread with tiny teeth marks littered the edges of the shed. My stomach rumbled. All I had eaten that day was porridge. I knelt on the soft floor and leaned closer to the bread rind. It didn't look too old. It was hard to the touch, but I couldn't see any mould.

Voices from outside.

I tried to stand up, but the door opened before I could manage it and I ended up on one knee before the lead huskalar.

"Good to see you're learning some respect in here," she said with a smirk.

"The fish convinced me."

Her smile disappeared. She looked up, following my gaze, then rolled her eyes.

"Get up. Time to see the High King."

She yanked me up by the elbow and led me towards the High King's mead-hall. She shoved me forwards and I stumbled underneath the overhanging roof at the mead-hall's entrance. We waited before two massive wooden doors covered in intricate carvings detailing various myths and legends. Heavy iron hinges cut across the middle of the doors and were worked into the design so that the hinges became a line drawn across the saga-carvings: below the hinges the carvings told of the god-war and the exile of the Winds, the carvings above told of the first humans and the time of heroes.

"Be quick," the huskalar said, though not to me.

I turned. Katja was standing in the shadows and she nodded at the huskalar.

"Thank you," she said.

The huskalar nodded and disappeared back the way we had come.

"What's going on?"

Katja looked at me and sighed. "We've managed to convince them to hear your case with me as your law-keeper."

"Good. Why are you saying that like it's a bad thing?"

"Because it means that instead of this being a simple execution this is now a full-blown law dispute. It does mean that I get to argue your case, but it also means that Ofri and Bardi get to make a case against you. And they know the laws about Windborn inside and out."

"Against me? Why? They attacked me."

239

"To bring you back to the Althing," Katja sighed again. "Without your rune-mark, it will be difficult to prove you're the Windborn they were sent after. It's their word against yours. In any other court this might even things out, but the High King hates Windborn."

My mouth twisted into a grimace and I nodded.

The High King was an almost fanatical follower of the gods and had always been cautious of Windborn, seeing them as avatars of the gods' ancient enemies, but could not deny their usefulness. Indeed, he had used them to great effect in his war of unification. A decade or so before, when a rebellious Windborn attacked Konvald his mistrust had become hatred. The reasons behind the attack had become muddied over the years. Some skalds said it was to usurp the High King, others said it was an act of revenge for a grave insult, and other stories—the most popular ones—said the Windborn was driven mad by unrequited love. Whatever the reasons, the results were always the same: the Windborn destroyed parts of the city before he could be stopped. In the destruction the High King's wife was killed and his young daughter was crippled. From then on, the High King had used Windborn as tools with brutal efficiency and disgust. I had always understood the High King's hatred of Windborn and having lost my husband I would not begrudge it to him, but I had never thought I would be on the receiving end of it.

"We've got a little time until the High King calls us in." Katja took my shoulders and turned me to face her, looking me dead in the eyes. "Bardi and Ofri have just finished giving their testimony and now we're going to give ours. I need you to tell me exactly what happened, Edda. Don't leave anything out. I've seen it happen hundreds of times, one person leaves out a tiny detail and it loses them the judgement."

"I understand."

I told her as much as I could remember, from when I stepped out of the house until I got back and passed out. Katja's expression stayed grim and intense for the entire story and when I was done she nodded. She opened her mouth, but the door opened and a huskalar beckoned impatiently at us. Katja smoothed her robes and made to step into the mead-hall.

"Katja, wait."

She paused and frowned at me. I bit my lip, reluctant to ask the question that burned in my chest in case Katja decided I would be better on my own.

"Why are you helping me?"

Katja sighed and her expression softened. "Runar asked me to help and, you know, it's not right that Soren gets away when he's the one who broke the law." She smiled and patted my arm. "We'll get through this, just let me do the talking, okay?"

Once again I felt a rush of gratitude for Runar's actions. I had been crumbling like a storm-thrashed cliff face for what felt like forever. To finally be with people, with Windborn, who stood by me kept me from collapsing completely.

I returned Katja's smile and followed her inside. People crowded on either side of the long, dimly lit feast hall. Some sat on benches and more stood behind them. They whispered to each other as soon as we stepped inside. Some of them pointed, looking me up and down as though I were a spectacle brought out for their enjoyment. As we moved further into the hall fewer people were crammed in. Their clothes became less mud-stained, the cloths brighter and embroidered, until the crowds were replaced by armoured huskalar. Then we stood in front of the raised platform of the High King.

Katja stopped a few paces from the platform and I stepped up beside her. The High King sat on a carved throne, draped in a fine purple cloak. He turned to the woman behind him and his crown glinted in the torchlight. The woman, dressed in earthen tones with scrolls and parchments stuffed under her arm, sported the silver arm-ring of a law-keeper. The High King turned back to us and peered down at me. He looked older than I thought he would, even though I couldn't remember when he took the throne, his white hair fell limp over his shoulders. The shining jewels and glittering gold that adorned him, rather than giving him an aura of power and authority, only served to contrast his pallid skin and ragged breathing.

"We have heard the testimony of the witnesses," the High King's frayed voice cut through the murmurings of the hall. He gestured to two men stood to one side, Bardi and Ofri. "We would hear yours."

Katja stepped forward and cleared her throat. The High King narrowed his eyes and waved a hand at her.

"We would hear from the Windborn, law-keeper, she is unsworn and alone. Do not help her."

Panic sparked in my chest and Katja looked back at me wide-eyed. On the opposite side of the hall, Ofri and Bardi whispered amongst themselves, grinning. I would not be able to defend myself if I had to do it alone. My skills were with iron and earth, battle and farming, not words.

The law-keeper behind the High King leaned in and whispered something in his ear. The High King scowled then waved them away.

"Speak, law-keeper," the High King wheezed.

Relief flooded through me and I saw some of the tension leave Katja's frame.

"Thank you, High King. I understand that the two bounty hunters are styling themselves as victims, faultless in this as a tree in a storm, but I would put to you that this is nothing more than self-defence. These two followed Edda through the marketplace and cornered her in an alley, where they pounced on her like common thieves.

"Even if Edda is the Windborn they seek, would it not have been better for these predators to come to you first? Would it not have been better for all—for the inhabitants of the city, for the bounty hunters, and for you—if they had come to tell you first, High King, that they had reason to believe this Windborn is who they sought? The destructive powers of the Windborn are well known. It was lucky for the city that they attacked Edda and not some other Windborn. She left them unconscious rather than dead, and the damage to property was minimal.

"I am sure that your huskalar told you how readily Edda submitted to their authority earlier today. Surely, if these bounty hunters had alerted you to an unsworn Windborn's presence it would have been safer for all and they would still have received the bounty."

The High King narrowed his eyes and stared down at us over his steepled fingers.

"And you, Windborn? Would you have submitted to my

242

huskalar if they had come for you?"

I thought back to that moment on the docks. I had itched to fight, to break through and escape, but the thought of being hunted had stopped me. Would I have been so ready with my axe if I had been on my own? If they had come for me in the marketplace, would I have fought?

"Yes, High King. I know that you are an honourable and just ruler and would have gladly submitted myself to your judgement."

The High King gave a slow nod. I hoped that my pause had been enough to convince him of my sincerity.

On the other side of the hall, Ofri stepped forward. "Whether or not this Windborn acted in self-defence or marched through the streets screaming a war chant is irrelevant. She is unsworn and ran from judgement at the Althing. We were sent to apprehend her. She's no better than an outlaw. The punishment is clear."

The word outlaw reverberated through the assembled crowds and hushed conversations blossomed in the shadows. The word touched on the fears in everyone's hearts: outlaws were remorseless figures that lived in the wilds and only sought civilisation when they were hungry, like wolves. It was a powerful word, one that sent children scurrying to their mothers' skirts, and he had focused it on me.

Fear flashed in my chest, the same fear that I saw in the eyes of those around me, but it was quickly followed by a rush of anger. How dare he compare me to an outlaw? Those hard-hearted villains had chosen to defy the laws and had paid the price. It had not been my choice to become Windborn, but I had been forced to sacrifice everything I loved. My home. My husband. My life.

"It is true, High King," Katja said, almost shouting to be heard over the crowd, "that any new Windborn have until the end of the next Althing to find themselves a new home, or risk becoming outlaws, but Edda has found that. She has agreed to come with us and swear to Erling."

"And what of the fact that this Windborn fled the judgement of the Althing, law-keeper?"

Katja glanced nervously at me and my scabbed forearm.

"I cannot speak to that, High King. These men say that they hunted a Windborn from Althing, but I cannot see a rune-mark on Edda and cannot say that she is the Windborn they sought."

The High King leaned back in his throne.

"Perhaps there is no rune-mark now, law-keeper, but I see plenty of new scars." He turned to the law-keeper standing with him. "What does the law say about unsworn Windborn?"

The woman behind the throne jumped. She stood at attention and recited: "Any person who becomes Windborn has until the end of the next Althing to swear into the household of another. If the Windborn fails to do so, it will be assumed they have succumbed to the urges of the Winds within them and will be considered outlaw, except that the bounty on said Windborn shall be triple the usual outlaw bounty. If—"

"That's enough," the High King wheezed. "The law is clear, law-keeper." The High King bared his teeth on the final word. "She is a Windborn outlaw. I will overlook this issue of who attacked who, whether it was self-defence, and if this Windborn has carved the rune-mark from her skin. She stands before me now and that is all that matters."

"I only became Windborn in the week before the Althing," I said, desperate to find some crack in the arguments. "Surely that isn't enough time for me to find a household to swear into?"

The High King, who had been forcibly ignoring me, turned and sneered down at me.

"You made it to the Althing, did you not? I don't care if you became Windborn the day before the Althing, it goes on long enough that you can make your way there. I will not have unsworn Windborn wandering my lands with their own agendas and taking whatever they like from those who are unable to protect themselves."

"But I wasn't told. My law-keeper didn't know about the laws of the Windborn. We were forced to travel to the Althing to find them out."

"Is she not your law-keeper? You are not from Erling's lands?"

"No, not originally. Before... before I became Windborn, I was a farmer near the coast, under Dagnur Olafson."

"And who is this Dagnur sworn to?"

"You, High King, he manages your holdings in the fjords by the Kjaltonn islands."

The High King pursed his lips. He looked back from the bounty hunters and then to Katja and me.

"Why does one of my own law-keepers not know of the laws concerning Windborn?"

I swallowed, Ingvar had helped me and I did not want him to feel the brunt of the High King's ire. "He was eager to help and to learn all he could once I became Windborn, but he had barely finished his apprenticeship when Dagnur took him on. Dagnur is renowned for his miserly ways and took Ingvar on because he was cheap."

The High King sunk back into his chair and steepled his fingers again. The entire room held its breath as he considered.

"I should pay these men their bounty as their information has brought you into my custody, and then I should have you put to work. I am sure we have some mines that would appreciate a strong body that is unaffected by the cold. However, I have heard your testimony and I am displeased that one of my own people would be so concerned with coin that they hold it above the safety of my people.

"I will send another, experienced law-keeper with you and you will both go back to Dagnur Olafson's hold and investigate this. If my law-keeper is able to verify your claims then you will be allowed to swear to Dagnur Olafson's household. If not, then you will be considered an unsworn outlaw and you will be brought back here and given justice."

"High King," Katja said with a bow, "your judgement is—"

"No." My voice echoed around the hall and all eyes in the room turned to me.

"No?" The High King sat up and raised an eyebrow at me. "I do not accept such statements from kings, why would I allow such from you, Windborn?"

Katja put a hand on my shoulder, shot me a pleading look, then turned back to the High King. "You should not, High King, I think it is just that the potential prospect of punish—"

"No," I said again, ripping my shoulder from Katja's grip. "High King, I urge you to send your law-keeper to investigate Dagnur Olafson. He is a petty man who has used what little power you have granted him to squeeze as much as he can from those he should be protecting. That is also why I cannot go back there.

"If you send me back to him then as soon as he is free of your law-keeper and no longer held to account, he will use my strength to squeeze those around him even harder. All that is left for me there are memories and exploitation."

The High King narrowed his eyes and pressed his lips into a thin line. Katja closed her eyes and muttered a prayer under her breath over and over again.

"You seem to think that this is some kind of negotiation, Windborn. It is not. I do not care what you think is waiting for you in Dagnur Olafson's household. You shall swear to him or you will find your justice, although at this point I think immediate execution would be easiest."

A spark of fear and shock flitted up my spine. The hall had gone deathly quiet. Bardi and Ofri exchanged heated whispers, Bardi seemed to want to say something and Ofri was holding him back.

Katja put a hand on my shoulder again, this time pulling me back gently. "High King, if I might offer another solution?"

He tipped his head ever so slightly, not taking his blazing eyes from me.

"Edda was travelling with us so that we could take her into King Erling's household. Let us take her with us when we leave. She will be out of your way and there will be no risk of her harbouring some grudge against your interests in Dagnur Olafson's household."

"Then why have you not already sworn her into Erling's house?" His eyes moved from Katja and then back to me. "Should I be blaming you that there is an unsworn Windborn wandering my streets and causing fights?"

Katja closed her eyes and swallowed before she replied. "Yes, High King, I should have taken a preliminary oath from this Windborn at the Althing and given her some mark of her intention to swear to Erling. Perhaps this would have avoided the unfortunate incident with the two bounty hunters.

"But my first loyalty, as a law-keeper, is to you and your laws. I sent this Windborn on ahead of me with another of my companions in the hopes that she would reach Erling before the Althing ended and before she became an outlaw. I stayed at the Althing to speak with my fellow law-keepers and learn all I could about your new laws and precedents so that King Erling may rule as you wish. Your huskalar will tell you that Edda was apprehended at the docks because she was welcoming me as I arrived from the Althing."

The High King looked to the law-keeper by his side, who nodded.

"So you would have me believe that it is because you are so diligent a law-keeper, you have failed in your duty?"

"I would not have chosen those words, High King, but yes."

The High King snorted then leaned back in his throne, resting his chin on his chest and looking down on us with disconcerting intensity. As our arguments faded, the conversations in the hall became hushed and a tense finality filled the air.

The word execution echoed in my mind. Each time it bounced off the inside of my skull it seemed to grow louder. In its wake I felt the weight of all the things that I had not yet done. In my mind's eye, Soren's flames washed over my arms again and above me someone loomed, casting darkness over us. Hraki.

As the silence dragged out I became sure that the High King would send me for execution. I seeped cold out into the ropes binding my hands slow and gentle as a morning frost. They stiffened and began to glitter with brittle ice. I had been branded an outlaw, it would not make much difference now if I ran. An intake of breath from behind me. Maybe from Runar or Valna. I didn't turn to look I only braced myself to tear free of the ropes.

"How long do you intend to stay in the city?" the High King asked Katja.

"Only as long as we need to get supplies and to charter our journey north. No longer than two or three days."

"And Erling actually wants this Windborn as part of his household?"

"He has always asked me to look out for strong hands, especially as Hraki now pushes against his borders, and—"

"Quiet," he snapped. "I have made my verdict regarding Hraki and Erling and I do not expect it to be brought up again."

The High King's eyes shifted to mine. Despite his advanced age, I felt the force of that gaze like the midsummer sun. It beat down on me and I felt as though I would burst into flames before he looked away, but I would not be cowed. I stood and stared right back at him. I put a little pressure on the ropes around my wrist and there was a minuscule sound of ice cracking.

"You may take her."

Katja let out a breath and the High King took his gaze from me. I felt a weight lift from me like a boulder moving off my grave. My shoulders slumped in relief.

"Something tells me she would be more trouble than she's worth," he said to Katja. "You will take her from the city by nightfall. I will not have her here any longer than necessary."

"Of course, High King."

"What about us, High King?"

The entire room turned its attention over to Bardi and Ofri. Bardi had thrown off the restraining hand of his companion and had taken a few steps towards the High King's platform.

"Will we still receive our money?"

The High King's mouth twisted into a grimace. "You will receive the bounty, but we will take the cost of damages from it first. See to it."

The law-keeper behind him nodded. Bardi and Ofri began spluttering objections but were silenced with a wave of the High King's hand.

"If you had brought this to my attention without trying to solve the problem yourselves then there would be no damage to pay for. Be grateful that you are receiving anything at all."

Bardi opened his mouth to protest, but Ofri grabbed him back and stepped forward in his place.

"Thank you, High King, you are most generous."

They wandered away, grumbling to each other, and everyone's attention turned back to us.

"To make sure you don't wriggle out of this, Windborn, we

will take your oath here."

The High King whispered something to his law-keeper, who scurried away, and gestured Katja and I forward.

"Law-Keeper..."

"Katja, High King. Katja Sifsdottir."

"Law-Keeper Katja, will you accept this Windborn into the House of Erling on behalf of your king?"

"I will, High King."

"Then," he twisted in his seat, looking for his returning law-keeper. She hurried back into view clutching something tight in her hands. "Is this all you could find? I'm not giving her gold. Give me your arm-ring."

The law-keeper looked taken aback, but she did as she was told and slipped the twisted silver ring down from her arm and passed it over. The High King cleared his throat and sat straight in his throne.

"Then, bestow this arm-ring on the Windborn and consider her part of Erling's household."

Katja took the arm-ring from the High King. The arm-ring's silver was woven in thick cords to form a nearly closed circle. She came back to me, moving slow as though she were trying to instil the moment with some sense of ceremony, and tried to put the silver arm-ring on my arm. She tried, but the arm-ring was too narrow to fit. Katja, after getting one of the huskalar to cut the rope binding my wrists, shoved the arm-ring along my forearm, but it caught on one of my scars.

"Careful," I hissed.

"Runar," she whispered. "Help me with this."

He came over and gripped the metal, pulling it open until it wrapped snug against my right bicep. I flexed my arm back and forth, and Runar adjusted it so that I had full range of movement without letting the arm-ring slip off. When he was done Runar moved away to stand with the rest of the crowd.

"You see how easy that was, law-keeper? Now get out."

*

The house was a flurry of activity. Muli, Ljot, and Valna piled barrels against the wall whilst Runar carried them onto a cart outside. Katja wandered to and fro, counting on her fingers, muttering to herself, and occasionally shouting out instructions.

"Runar, make sure we have enough salt. Valna, do we have any of the mead from the Dennfell? Erling likes that. Edda, help me fold this up. Ljot, don't forget to get the cloak that's being made for Erling."

And so it went.

"Runar, can you fly this note over to King Olvid's law-keeper?"

He let a barrel slip and it thudded onto the floor.

"Fly it over?" he asked, frowning. "You know the huskalar don't like Windborn using their powers in the city. The High King's not pleased with us as it is."

"I'd love to have the time to saunter over there, Runar, really I would, but we're on a deadline and there's a hundred things I needed to do before we went north. Either fly there or run there." She finished scribbling and straightened up to look Runar in the eyes. "Or we can wander nice and slow and see what the huskalar do when we're still here after sundown."

She cocked her head and held out the crumpled note. Runar snatched at it, grumbling, then pulled on his cloak and floated off. She put her hands back on the table and sighed.

I slid the last barrel against the pile we had made and went over to Katja. I put my hand on her hunched shoulders. She flinched away, then, as if realising what she had done, put her hand on mine.

"Sorry," she mumbled. "Your hands are cold. It was a bit of shock."

I slid my hand out from under hers and stepped away. Next to us, Muli panted and then leaned against the wall.

"What's next?" I asked.

Katja looked around, saw Valna reorganising the large pile of crates and barrels so they wouldn't fall, and took a breath to steady herself.

"I still need to go and see the High King's law-keepers," Katja said.

"Why?" Valna piped up from across the room. "We only just spoke to them, didn't we?"

"We need one of them to come with us and verify what we've been saying about Hraki, how he's waging war in the winter."

"He literally just said he didn't want to talk about it," Valna said.

"That was in Edda's hearing. I need to try again, Valna, it's what I'm here for."

"I'll come with you," I said.

"No. After this morning I think it's best if I go with Muli. It's the gods' laws that says there won't be fighting in winter. My request will probably go over better if there aren't any Windborn with me."

She smiled weakly. I glanced over to Valna who just rolled her eyes and shook her head.

"Will they send someone?" I asked. "We're not exactly the High King's favourite right now."

"They'll have to," Katja said. "If I make it an official request for aid they are bound to give it or send a witness to prove we don't need it. By law, the witness is required to be impartial. The easiest way to get someone like that is to get a law-keeper from the High King. At least now Einar is still on his way back from the Althing so they can't send that bastard again."

Katja pushed herself up from the table and came over to where Valna had laid out a selection of furs, coats and cloaks. She picked one up and wrapped herself up in it. Muli, who looked relieved that he didn't have to shift any more boxes, went over to get his cloak and shield.

"Edda, there's a list of things we'll probably need for the journey on the table. Can you head over to the market and get them?"

"Sure."

"Thank you. Most of the High King's law-keepers are at the Althing so who knows who we'll get to come with us."

"I guess that the law-keeper from this morning wasn't their best, then?" Valna asked.

"Couldn't you tell?" Katja replied. "She was so nervous. It's probably the closest she's ever been to the High King, and then to top it all off, he took her arm-ring."

Katja shook her head, moving towards the door, and played

her fingers over her own arm-ring. "Muli, you ready to go? Great. We'll be back as soon as we can. Valna, Ljot, I need you to go and find us a longship to take us home."

They started talking about the ship and I shivered, not wanting to think about any kind of longship. I wandered over to the table, swept up the list and the pouch of coin, and went to the market.

The town felt different. Where before people had avoided trying to catch my attention, now they avoided me altogether. Several people looked askance at me as they tried to figure out why I wasn't wrapped up in furs, then their eyes went wide and they hurried away. Those that didn't try to get away sighed with relief when they noticed the silver ring wrapped around my arm.

The marketplace itself was even more threadbare. Some of the spaces were filled by different merchants, but they were all peddling the last, and worst, of their wares. I stared down at the list—a collection of foods, herbs, and odd bits of clothing—and started searching.

Memories came back to me as I wandered. I thought back to when Bjolfur and I had visited a nearby town to sell our furs ourselves. We managed to sell them to a merchant as we were barely a couple of hour's travel from the market. Not wanting to waste the trip, we had gone into town and found a market much like this one, although much smaller. When I had walked through that market, the merchants had called out to us, asking if my husband wanted to buy me some jewellery or if we wanted to try their mead. The world felt warm, safe, and welcoming. Now, the stalls were empty, the air bitter and cold, and no one would meet my eyes.

It was around the fourth or fifth merchant, as he looked at me wide-eyed and open-mouthed before finding the arm-ring and breathed a sigh of relief, that I realised this was my new life. The easy way that Katja was giving out instructions, the readiness with which all the Windborn agreed to them, and the way that no one looked at me. They all looked for the arm-ring. It felt as though Edda had ceased to be, and now there was only a Windborn. A vicious, deadly fighter who would jump to whatever tune her king and law-keeper played. Perhaps I had drowned and all that was left of me was a Wind-fuelled echo. Perhaps my soul wandered the ocean floor and it would find its way to Bjolfur before the end of the world. The thought was a bleak comfort as I began to follow my orders.

CHAPTER TWELVE
BRAVE THE SEA

RUNAR AND I COMBED THE HOUSE for anything that might be useful on the journey north. Although Katja would be coming back to the house in the summer, she did not want to leave anything valuable behind. We did what tasks we could for Katja, but the least important quickly fell by the wayside and were left undone.

Runar poked his head around a wall and grunted to get my attention. "I think we've got everything. You got anything else to do?"

"No."

"Then let's get moving."

We gathered up our belongings, shield and axe for me, and winter clothing for Runar, grabbed a final few items, and made our way to the docks.

"Come on," Runar said, his tone impatient.

I turned, a barbed response on the tip of my tongue, but he was facing away from me. The raven from the rafters fluttered down and landed on his shoulder.

"We're taking the bird?"

"She's too useful to leave."

"Right."

I shook my head and led the way outside. The raven squawked a laugh behind me.

The sky burned red as the day ended, marking our deadline with charred clouds. The city swelled with people returning from the Althing and we had to elbow our way through the crowds. People turned to reprimand us and then quickly turned away when they saw our arm-rings.

All along the docks, longships groaned into their berths. Crew members leapt onto the jetties as soon as they could, carrying whatever goods they had for inspection. Dockhands followed captains and inspected barrels, hurriedly making notes as they went. Gulls and crows swirled in the air shouting out to each other as they spotted some unguarded food.

"There she is."

Runar pushed ahead and led the way down to a jetty on the northern end of the docks.

The chaotic scene calmed the further we went. The longships seemed unwilling to use the berths furthest from the city and so crammed into the southern end. Katja stood at the last jetty, talking to a group of people, and beside her stood a copper-haired figure I recognised as the woman who had stood next to the High King's throne. Katja turned as we approached.

"Ah, you're here. Oh, and you brought the bird. Good."

Katja introduced the young woman as Alvilda. The young woman kept her head down, which let her shoulder-length hair fall over her face.

"You're the law-keeper who was with the High King," I said.

Her cheeks flushed and she glanced down at the ring on my arm. She nodded. I waited for her to say something, but she kept her eyes down and fiddled with a new silver arm-ring.

"Alvilda was the only law-keeper brave enough to come along with us," Katja said with exaggerated care. "She's only just finished her training, but she's not been assigned a post yet, and this is a great opportunity to see some new places, eh?"

The girl refused to meet my eye and her shoulders were hunched over as though she wanted to disappear into herself.

Before we could say anything else a stout, gruff-looking man stormed up to us.

"This all of you?" he said in a manner that told me he was not used to being challenged. The captain.

"This is everyone," Katja said.

He looked Runar and I up and down. He didn't look pleased with what he saw.

"Right." He twisted and caught a sailor's attention. "Make sure there's enough room for five of them."

The sailor nodded and walked away.

"Okay, you two," the captain said to Runar and I. "I've had Windborn on my ship before. Sometimes they're trouble and sometimes they're not, so consider this fair warning: if someone tells you that Njall's got a job for you, then you better do it sharpish because that's me. I don't care what weird shit you can do. If you don't follow orders then you're off the longship, no matter where we are. The Iron Rib hasn't survived storms, a trip through the Empire of Bones and a shipwreck just so you can fuck this little journey up. Got it?"

He spun on his heel without waiting for a response and made his way onto the longship, shouting at his crew as he went.

"Ignore him," Katja said. "He's just itchy because he knows we're on a deadline. Come on, Alvilda. Let's go check on our little corner of the longship. I don't trust them to give us a comfortable spot otherwise."

The girl followed her without complaint and they moved deftly between barrels and cursing crew.

"I bet you my cloak that girl is the only law-keeper the High King is willing to lose," Runar muttered.

"I don't need a cloak," I said, turning away from the jetty and to the longship.

Runar stepped aside as Valna walked past him carrying a barrel. She passed two men struggling with their own barrel, their faces red with exertion. I smiled as the sailors scowled.

"Why is it called the Iron Rib?" I asked.

Valna set down her barrel and pointed to the water. "They patched her up with iron after they were shipwrecked a few years ago. Njall says it helps them get through the water when the ice is thickening."

The smile playing on my lips died away as I looked into the water. The longship had iron bars fixed onto the hull like ribs of a sea monster. As I watched the water, the hiss and whisper of the waves surged and called to me. The water had a thousand voices and each one made a different promise. Some promised pain, some promised relief, some that I would see my husband again, that I would be warm, safe, that I could not be hurt any more.

Every promise ended in death.

A wave splashed against the side of the longship, spraying water in my face, and for a moment I relived that storm. I flinched away from unheard thunder. My fingers felt slippery with saltwater and they clenched around the ghost of a hand. My heart broke all over again.

"What's wrong?" Runar's voice brought me back.

"I... I can't get on the longship."

He looked at me for a moment before his confused expression transformed into a frown. "You don't have a choice, Edda. You get on the longship or you stay here and die. The High King will not be merciful again."

I took a breath and tried to step down the jetty, but my eyes were drawn inexorably downward. There looked to be shapes under the water, dark shadows moving against the current. I wondered if Bjolfur was there. Did the Sea Giants let the Blessed Drowned travel the waters?

"The last time I got on a longship," I muttered, "my husband drowned."

Runar's eyes lost their hard edge, and for a moment he was lost for words. He reached out a hand towards me and then let it fall.

"I am sorry for that, Edda, but you need to get on the longship. I'll try to stall the captain to give you the time you need, but I won't be able to stall him for long." He looked from me to the waves then floated up and across to the boat.

A barbed response rose in my throat but the water slapped the longship and sucked the anger out of me.

"Come on, Edda," I said to myself. "You've sailed across the Western Sea. You've gone to Ertland. You can take a longship up a few fjords."

The words felt false against my tongue. I took a few deep breaths and looked up and down the docks. The longships and jetties obscured the waves but I heard the whispering waters all the same. I turned northward and watched the fjord. The shoreline curved away from Konvald, transforming slowly from soft sands to jagged rocks. As my eyes darted from rock to rock I saw something glinting between their sharp edges. It floated on the surface, drifting with the waves. Ice. The beginnings of the cold that would cover this entire fjord and lock all the longships in place.

I looked down at my boots. They were lined with hoarfrost that had nothing to do with the weather. It felt like the longer I was Windborn, the more insistent the ice inside me became. At first, it had been like pushing against a current to draw any power, but now it felt more like I needed to dam the flow. I glanced back at the floating ice shards further up the water.

"Edda?" The soft voice came from the longship. Valna leaned against the gunwale and stared at me with curious concern. "Are you okay?"

"I'm fine," I said. "I just need... I'll be there in a moment, okay?"

Her expression softened and she made her way out onto the docks to join me.

"It's okay," she said. "We've all got things we're afraid of. Come on, I'll help you."

She took my hand and, before I could protest, walked us up to the gangplank. My breaths came in short, sharp stabs and I felt the crow scream and thrash in my chest. This was how it all started. The waves had taken everything from me and they hungered beneath me once more.

"There's nothing to worry about. See?" Valna's voice soothed some of the fears inside me. "Just like walking on the docks."

Our feet hit the deck and the firm, steady planks of the jetty were replaced by the undulating movement of the longship. I closed my eyes for a moment and tried not to imagine the water jostling at the keel. When I opened my eyes Valna had led us over to join Runar where he stood near the prow.

"Glad you made it," Runar said. He smiled at me, though his expression was grim. He nodded then turned to focus on the northern horizon with raw intensity.

"There," Valna said. "That wasn't so bad, was it? We can do anything if we work together."

She shot me a blazing smile and then bent down to her pack. I could only nod in response as the rocking of the longship shook any words from me.

The captain appeared on deck and looked around, he leaned over the rail and looked up and down the jetty. "Right, all clear, let's get this hunk of oak and iron up the fjord."

He made his way along the longship, shouting and calling to everyone on board to get on an oar. I sat down at the rowlock behind Valna, my stomach flipping over at the thought of moving out onto the water, but the captain came up to me and dragged me up by my arm.

"No," he said. "We don't sit Windborn together. If you sit behind her we'll just end up going in circles."

He moved me to the oar opposite Valna and gestured for the man sitting there to move. He grumbled but got up. I sat down, gripping the oar as tight as I could. My knuckles went white, ice snaked out from between my fingers, and wood creaked under my grip. I took a deep breath and released some of the tension in my fingers. Valna waved at me from across the deck. I nodded back. Behind me, there were two sailors on each oar. Valna and I were alone on the front two benches.

The captain called out a few last commands, waved to the clerks on the shore, and then took his place at the helm.

Runar, who so far had been ignored as he examined the fjord, lifted himself into the air. He took hold of the longship's figurehead and pulled us gently away from the jetty. Once we were clear, he pivoted us to face north and then the captain called for oars.

The longship lurched as it pulled away. My heart lurched with it and I had to take deep breaths that had nothing to do with the effort of rowing.

Before, whenever I had set off raiding, there would be a crowd waving us off. A small group of family and friends to wish us luck. Not today. The only acknowledgement we were offered was a clerk making another hasty note.

For the first few hours of the journey, I lost myself in the rhythm of rowing. The motions as I lifted, twisted, and pulled were familiar and safe. The mountains looming on either side of us kept me calm as their presence meant there was no room for the waves to grow large enough to swallow us. I closed my eyes, kept pace as it was called out by a crew member, and tried to ignore the fear that spiked in my chest every time a wave slapped the longship.

"Right," the captain shouted some time later, startling me

from my thoughts. "We're coming out of the fjord. This is where it might get messy. The sea ain't forgiving this time of year, and we're going to sail right up her arse. Make sure you're rowing in time and we'll all be fine."

I opened my eyes and looked around frantically. We had reached the god-stones. Those monolithic, rune-carved rocks that were the border between the wild, dangerous realm of spirits and gods and the realm of mortals. The god-stones, one guarding either side of the fjord and one in the centre, were each as tall as the mast of the Iron Rib. Their tops were carved into the shape of ravens. Three stone ravens to match the First Ravens and their never-ending surveillance of the world for the Father, first of the gods. Runes were carved all over the god-stones, each as tall as me. As we sailed past them the runes and the ravens' eyes glowed as though the gods themselves turned their attention to us, for just a moment.

As soon as we moved out into the open sea the water changed. The calm, smooth fjord was replaced with dark, foaming waves moving like sharks. Fear clutched at my heart with its black talons. I saw a shipwreck in every wave. Each white-foam crest on the water was a fanged mouth waiting to swallow me whole. The air tasted like loss and drowning.

Bile and sorrow pushed its way up my throat. I vomited. Warm, thick liquid fell between my knees. I wanted to let go of the oar, wash myself and flee onto the dry land, but I couldn't. If I stopped the whole ship would be thrown off. I closed my eyes and tried to focus only on the motion of the oar, but every time a wave scraped against the keel I flinched. Each roar and clap of the waves brought a fresh surge of terror.

*

For a long time, the steady twist and pull of the oars was all there was. I ignored the cold spray and hiss of the waves. I couldn't think about the lurching longship that was the only thing between me and the black depths. Once or twice, my mind was dragged down by the tidal pull and panic gripped me again, breath coming fast and black spots over my eyes.

Eventually, I was taken off the oars as the sails were

lowered. I stepped carefully as I got off the bench to avoid a patch of vomit that hadn't yet washed away.

Valna stretched her arms out in front of her like a cat and yawned. "That could have been worse. It's been a long time since I've had to row on a longship."

I grunted. My stomach still moved with the rhythm of the rowers and if I opened my mouth I might throw the contents of my stomach up again. I walked back along the ship, past all of the now-empty benches. On the port side were endless shark-fin waves circling us with hungry foaming teeth. On our other side, the shores passed, swift and distant now that the sail had been let out. I leaned against the stern and looked to the shore.

Katja came up to join me, looking out in the other direction.

"Why didn't you want to get on the boat?"

I didn't want to answer. I wanted the waves to catch the question and drag it under, but their insidious hiss grated at me like laughter. I refused to let the ocean have this victory.

"I told Runar."

"And he won't tell me so I'm asking you."

The waves surged around us. The longship dipped and made my stomach lurch. I closed my eyes and tightened my grip on the sternpost.

"It's nothing. Something that happened before I was Windborn."

"You struck me as a raider. You must have been on a longship dozens of times. I mean, we could hardly keep you from getting into fights when we were on land. Now we're out on the water and you're scared?"

She paused, but I didn't respond. The waves roared as the Iron Rib sliced through them. I felt a soft touch on my arm.

"You're not going to drown, Edda," Katja said, her tone gentle now.

"It's how my husband died," I whispered, hoping she wouldn't hear over the waves. "It's how I died."

I felt her stiffen. There was a moment of silence and then she placed a hand on my shoulder.

"Edda... I... I'm sorry. You've got Runar and Valna now. If anything happens, one of them will be able to get you out of the water."

I watched the land sail past. The dark shores and beaches were interspersed with rocky outcrops and within those I saw the occasional set of god-stones guarding fjords. The monumental runes carved into their faces glowed like signal fires, whether to warn us away from the hidden rocks or to warn me to stay out I wasn't sure.

Katja squeezed my shoulder then made her way unsteadily back to the front of the longship. As I listened to Katja's footsteps fade, I wondered what the root of her concern for me was. Before I became Windborn I wouldn't have given it a second thought. It would simply have been concern for a fellow traveller feeling unsteady on the ocean's ever-shifting surface. Now, however, I could sense a different implication behind her worry. Katja needed me to be useful. There was no time for mourning. I was Windborn and I had to be ready.

I let out a long breath to try and steady my stomach.

"I don't like sailing either," a small voice said just behind me. "That's why I didn't want to come."

Alvilda. I didn't know where the young law-keeper had come from and whether she had heard what I'd said to Katja. I wanted to snap at her to leave me be, but I felt relieved that someone else was as miserable as I was. She approached me as an equal, to share in my discomfort and ease it for both of us. In that moment, it didn't matter that I was Windborn, only that I was human.

"Why is the shore so far away?" she whispered.

The longship lurched again and I swallowed some bile that surged to the back of my throat.

"The rocks," I said. "We need to make sure we don't scrape against any rocks hidden under the water."

"Oh."

Alvilda fell silent. She moved until she was beside me and then there was a bump as she leaned against the other side of the carved sternpost.

"A wolf seems like an odd choice," she whispered.

I looked up, examining the images carved into the sternpost. Waves blossomed as the post rose above the keel and from them burst a snarling wolf. The crew had not cleaned properly before we had set off and salt crusted the wolf's features, which made it look like it was made from sea foam.

"This was probably a raiding ship once," I said and turned back to my vigil of the shore. "They call us sea wolves in Ertland and Reimark. They say we cut across the waves like predators and tear into them with axes like teeth in the night."

"A wonderful legacy." Alvilda's tone belied her true feelings.

"You never wanted to go raiding?" I asked, surprised. For as long as I could remember, I had been enchanted with the idea of carving my way across an ocean to prove myself in battle and bathe myself in glory and riches. As I had grown older my dreams had grown smaller but always they had me travelling across the waves and returning laden with gold. Marrying Bjolfur had sparked up my ambitions again, but only in the hunger for our own farm, something we should have easily won through our share of raiding. My mouth twisted into a grimace as my thoughts trod the familiar path of what could have been. It made me wonder if I would ever stop mourning.

"No," Alvilda said, her tone bitter. "I can count enough friends and family that never returned from a raid without counting myself among them."

"Then what did you dream of when you were younger?"

Alvilda shifted behind me. "I always wanted to help people. When I was very young I used to bring home wild animals, try and hide them from my mother, but she always found them and threw them out. I thought they were lost and wanted to give them a home."

The longship surged over a wave and Alvilda's voice sank underneath my fears and the noise of the sea. I swallowed and closed my eyes to focus on Alvilda's words.

"When the time came to decide what I should do, they scraped together enough money to pay my way to the capital. They shoved me on the next longship that came through and sent me off to become a law-keeper. I was upset at the time. I'd always thought that I would just follow them and take over the meadery, you know? I don't blame them now though. If—"

We lurched as the longship's prow dropped. The sea sucked away the wave underneath us and for a moment I thought the longship would pierce straight through the surface and drown us all, then the curved keel crashed into the next wave and we were sailing straight once more.

Alvilda paused, as though to check we weren't drowning, then resumed her life story. I swallowed the bile building up in my throat and focused on her voice.

*

The rest of the journey continued in much the same way. For three days, I clutched at whatever part of the longship was closest and clenched my eyes shut against the sight of the endless sea. I had never suffered from seasickness before, but on that journey my belly tried to tear itself out of me. It was as though it wanted to drag me back to shore. I couldn't have repeated any of Alvilda's life story back to her, but her constant, soft voice gave me something to focus on and helped me through.

After what seemed like an eternity pitching over black waves and crashing through the bared teeth of the sea someone cried out and I looked up.

The longship turned into a fjord bordered by expanding forests on one side and mountains on the other. In the distance, thin plumes of smoke rose into the evening air. Alvilda moved up to stand in front of me, but said nothing. Runar gave his oar to one of the crew and walked up to the edge of the longship.

"Finally," he said. He stretched, cracking his back, and stepped off the gunwale.

The ship drifted as the whole crew stopped to watch.

The Windborn caught himself mid-air then flew towards the plumes of smoke in a swooping curve. I glanced down at the sea and saw Runar's shadow shimmer on the waves. The thought of travelling over the water without so much as a raft to protect me sent a shiver up my spine. The raven perched on the figurehead at the prow of the longship. It seemed to watch Runar's flight for a moment before it turned to look at us. It squawked then followed the flying Windborn.

Around me, the crew began to make preparations to land. The captain stalked amongst them, making sure no step was missed.

The longship slowed as the shark-back waves were replaced with a flat, silent surface. Relief washed over me and I looked to the shore's low slopes. Plumes of smoke unravelled like fraying rope and I traced them back to their houses. The city stretched out on either side of the fjord and in the middle of it all was an island with a huge mead-hall standing proud at its centre. As we got closer to the island, I made out storehouses and homes around the mead hall as well as a small dock built on the island's western side.

A strong wind swept across the deck and a bout of shivering rippled out amongst my companions. Snow-covered the tops of the trees and broken sheets of ice floated across the water. Without thinking I took a step to fetch a cloak in an effort to protect myself against the frozen winds and waters, but as another gust tore across the deck I realised I felt nothing. The wind's force sent my tunic and trousers rippling, but there was no cold. I glanced down at the criss-cross of ice and scars on my forearm and felt a twisting anguish in the pit of my stomach that I had lost another part of me.

Katja walked up to the crew member manning the rudder.

"Take us to the island," she said. "You can drop us off there and King Erling can take stock of your provisions."

The man blinked slowly at Katja and did not change course. He looked past her to where the captain stood and cocked an eyebrow. The captain nodded, the man leaned on the rudder until the longship began an easy turn towards the island's jetty. As we got closer to the shore we met the thin ice sheets on the fjord and smashed through them with thunderous cracks.

Katja rolled her eyes and turned her back on the rudder-man and came over to Alvilda and me.

"Welcome to Eylheim," she said. "The last trading port before you hit the ice sheets of the north."

"That's got a nice ring to it," I said. "Last stop before you freeze to death."

Katja looked me up and down, taking in that I was wearing only a tunic, and pulled her cloak tighter around her. "For some of us."

"What are those things?" I pointed out beyond the king's island. There were dark shapes in the water that seemed to loom against the horizon like wolves in the night.

Katja squinted then scowled at the shadows. "Longships," she said. "For protection. Hraki has tried to send his ships through more than once. Think of them like a shield wall made out of boats."

She moved away to where she had stowed her things. Valna came up beside me and leaned against the railing of the longship. Her short-cropped hair fluttered in the wind. She turned and grinned at me.

"Nearly home," she said, barely able to control her excitement.

"Been away long?" I asked.

"Mm, too long." She kept her eyes locked on the island as it swept closer.

"Does Hraki have a town like this?"

"Not like this," she said and wrinkled her nose. "He's got some nice walls and a few houses inside them, but that's pretty much it. They're farmers and herders mostly. They have to come here if they want to trade anything. Or used to, anyway."

I nodded but didn't ask any of the other questions weighing on me. Valna's attention was locked onto Erling's mead hall and she looked like she was gauging the distance between the longship and the shore. She started tapping her fingers along the gunwale and her outline blurred. Then she was at the other end of the longship, leaning out over the side and looking to see whether the jetty or the shore was closest. She disappeared again and again, shifting all over the ship like a dog waiting to be let out to play.

"Will you stop that?" Katja called.

"We're so close, Kat!"

"Please, you're making everyone nervous. We're nearly at the jetty."

Valna scowled back at her. She stopped using her Windborn powers but hopped from one foot to another.

"Right, I'm going to do it," she said after another few moments.

Katja straightened. "What? We're too far. Just wait, would you?"

"No. I can make it."

I leaned over the side of the ship to see how close the jetty was. There was no way she could make it at a leap, we were still a couple of hundred paces away, but I was curious to see how far her Windborn powers could take her.

"Please, Valna, it's—"

But Valna was already moving. She took a running leap from the prow of the longship. The deck rocked and as she reached the apex of her leap she disappeared. Ahead of us Valna reappeared then fell.

She missed the jetty by about three paces and she crashed down into the water with a yelp and smashed through the thin ice. She clawed at the ice around her but sank to her shoulders.

There was a moment of silence as everyone watched to see if she was hurt, then a whoop of victory from Valna.

"Told you I'd make it," she shouted back at us. She blurred and reappeared on the shore, still dripping wet, before she sprinted off towards the mead-hall.

Katja rolled her eyes and tugged her bag shut. "She'll catch her death of cold if she's not careful."

"Why didn't she wait?" I asked, pulling my own belongings over one shoulder.

Katja hefted her bag and shook her head, looking out at where Valna had disappeared. "Young love."

*

The terror of the sea voyage ended with the deep growl of the longship's iron ribs scraping against the low sloped shore. My heart slowed its war-drum beat for the first time in what felt like a week, although we had only been on the water for a few days. As the longship was tethered to the land, I felt my roiling stomach finally calm and I itched to stand on firm ground once again.

After the formalities were completed and we had started to unload the longship, Katja shouted welcomes and updates to a man on the shore who wore similar robes to hers but had two arm-rings glinting on his arm. It was clear from their shouted conversation that the man, Fainn, was King Erling's hoard-keeper, responsible for the provisions of the palace and the king's treasury. Once our belongings were unloaded, he spoke with the captain to negotiate the sale of the rest of the cargo. After some back and forth the men reached an agreement that neither of them looked entirely happy with.

"Windborn, give us a hand, will you? All your friends seem to have conveniently run off."

The captain leaned against the gunwale and shot me a pained grin. He swept his arm out in a languid gesture that took in all of the cargo on the deck. I looked around and saw Katja walking with purpose towards the hall in front of us. I sighed and made my way back onto the ship to help unload. I did my best not to look down or to think about the waves still clutching at the stern of the longship, but bile rose at the back of my throat nonetheless.

As we finished unloading, Katja returned leading a crowd of people to help transport the barrels, crates, and sacks. Some had pack animals and one drove a cart and took everything up to Erling's halls whilst Fainn counted out payment for Thorin.

I made my way up to Erling's buildings, assuming that I would either find Runar or Valna or that Katja would tell me where to go. As I passed Fainn, he looked me up and down and cocked an eyebrow at me. His plaited beard was grey with slashes of black that still remembered his youth. His eyes lingered on my arm ring and then met my eyes. I looked at the arm-rings he wore and frowned when I saw he wore a copper arm-ring and a woven wooden arm-ring. A hoard-keeper and a god-speaker.

"She brought someone else for Erling to take care of then? Another mouth to feed."

I straightened and looked down at him. "I don't need anyone to look after me," I growled.

"Aye," he said, already turning back to his notes. "So you say, but you'll still eat in his halls, won't you? You'll still drink his ale."

I took a step towards him, but Katja's voice stopped me.

"Leave her be, Fainn. Erling sent me to get help against Hraki and that's what I've brought."

Fainn examined me again, taking in the shield at my back and axe slung through my belt. Our eyes met and I bared my teeth.

269

"And she's all you brought? I think we were all expecting something a little more..."

He let his words hang in the air between us. I stretched out an arm and pushed my Windborn power out from within me. Frost glittered across my hand, then thickened to ice. I clenched my hand into a fist and the ice shattered. I let it fall. It sprinkled onto the sand at my feet. Fainn followed the ice with his eyes, but his expression didn't change.

"We'll see, lass."

He turned away and went to check the loading of the donkey-drawn cart, shouting at one of the attendants about one of the barrels.

Footsteps crunching through the snow and sand. Katja stood next to me.

"Don't mind him. We lost our hoard-keeper a few months ago and Fainn's stepped in to help. He's having to spread our coin more and more to keep us all fed and it's put him on edge. Come on, I'll show you around."

I grunted and made to follow Katja. Glancing back over my shoulder I saw Alvilda standing awkwardly at the edge of a crowd. I watched as she took a step and then changed her mind, shoulders hunched to make herself as small as possible.

"What about Alvilda?"

"Fainn will bring her up with the supplies. It's one of his hoard-keeper duties to decide where she stays. I need to get clean and your new home is on the way."

Shrugging, I turned back to follow Katja up the slope to the buildings and Erling's mead-hall.

We walked in silence for a little while. I stamped as I walked, thankful for the heavy thud of the firm earth that met my feet. The first few buildings we passed were small, no more than sheds and outhouses, with racks of drying fish in between them. The buildings beyond these looked normal enough, lodgings for the servants and animals I guessed, and they spread out to create a pathway that led straight to Erling's mead-hall.

The empty pathway ahead of us dragged my gaze forward and highlighted the ornately carved pillars flanking the path. The curved white pillars stood in pairs and formed a corridor that became smaller as it led up to the mead-hall like jaws closing shut. I stopped by the first pair of bent columns and examined them. They loomed over my head and seemed to disappear into the blanket grey of the overcast sky.

"What're they made of?"

Katja glanced over, following my gaze, before replying. "Whale bones and walrus tusks. Each one leading up to the hall is dedicated to a different god." She pointed to the larger bones lining the entrance to the mead-hall. "The skull is dedicated to the god-war."

I ran my fingers along the rib next to me and traced the carvings in the slow-curving bone. The part of the bone that had been carved away was yellowed with age and looked sickly against the bleached white of the untouched rib. Flames and waves carved into the base of the column looked like they would consume it. Creatures rose from that fire and water, things of shadow with too few limbs and too many mouths, and they all made their way to a figure that stood an arm's length above the ground. She shoved a sword at the creatures and pushed a child behind her. Another figure stood with her and as the carved saga spiralled up the rib they fought off the creatures until the man was shredded by one of the monstrous things and the woman stood alone.

It was the final battle of Herta, an ancient hero from the god-war and now a patron for fighters to call on in times of need. Hers was one of the last battles of the god-war. The Winds had tamed grotesque creatures that lived in the shadowed depths of the sea and in the heart of fire-spewing mountains. In an attempt to break the gods' spirits, they had used them to attack the first humans who were new to the world. Herta and her family fought bravely but their strength was not enough. In exchange for her husband's life, the gods gave her the power to save herself and her child, but the loss broke Herta's spirit. As I traced Herta's last moments and saw her victory I realised someone had snapped the very tip of the rib.

A sharp, broken edge for Herta's broken heart.

"Come on," Katja said. "We're going this way."

Reluctantly, I let her lead me away from the saga-carved ribs and around Erling's mead-hall. Several longhouses had been built around the mead-hall. They all had roofs like inverted keels of a longship and entrances framed by carved pillars, although these were old tree trunks.

"Valna's not with you?"

The voice called from above and we looked up to see Runar floating down towards us. He nodded to me and came to a stop in front of Katja.

"Do you really want to know the answer to that question?" Katja said.

"Oh." Runar's cheeks flushed under his stubble. "I'll find her later, then."

"Probably best."

"I'll see if Fainn needs any help," he mumbled and flew away.

Katja led me into one of the longhouses that circled the mead-hall. The tree trunk pillars at the door were covered in carvings of warriors that stood alone between a layer of clouds above and churning sea below.

"This is where you're staying," she said.

"All of this?"

"No," Katja laughed as she led me inside. "This is where the Windborn stay."

There was a long fire pit dug into the centre of the longhouse, filled with ash and burnt logs. A spit with old meat still clinging to it stood in the middle of the fire pit. Benches and chairs had been stuffed on top of the raised floorboards built around the edges of the longhouse. Heavy blankets hung down from the rafters to divide the long building into separate rooms and give some sense of privacy. They were not enough, though, as one of the barriers at the end of the hall twitched and did little to muffle the excited moans of two people. I smirked as I remembered Katja's comments about young love.

Katja led me up past the fire pit and pulled aside one of the walls to the blanket-rooms.

"Here," she said. "This one's free, I think."

I thanked her and threw my things inside.

"Is she with another Windborn?" I said and nodded to the twitching blanket.

"No. She's with Olek. One of the huskalar. I'll introduce you to everyone tomorrow," Katja said.

"Where are the other Windborn?" I asked, keen to meet my new allies in my hunt for Soren and Hraki.

She yawned and knuckled her eyes. "There's just Gerda and Orin, but they're not as young as they used to be and could use some rest. I'll introduce you tomorrow. For now, I'm going to get cleaned up and get some sleep. I suggest you do the same." She raised her eyebrows and nodded at Valna's room as she left the longhouse. "If you can."

Once Katja had left, I unbraided my hair and ran a few fingers through my stiff locks to break up the worst of the salt still clinging to it. It was clean enough. I looked over at the twitching blankets. It didn't sound like they were going to stop any time soon, but I had barely slept on the longship and my tiredness soaked down to my bones. I stretched out my cloak on the floor, shoved my bag under my head as a pillow, and slept.

CHAPTER THIRTEEN
MEET YOUR KING

SOMETHING KICKED ME. A HARD, SHARP BLOW to my ribs.

I jumped up, grabbed my shield, and held it out with both hands.

Spears of sunlight broke through the roof, illuminating an old woman in front of me. She cocked an eyebrow and shook her head.

"You're in the dog's spot."

"What?"

I straightened and lowered my shield, though I didn't put it down.

"That is where the dog sleeps. Move."

She said each word slowly, as though that would make it easier to understand. I squeezed the shield hard and opened my mouth to curse at her.

Something wet sniffed in my ear.

I yelped and flinched back to see an enormous elkhound with a black muzzle and fine grey fur next to me. It had propped its front paws on a stool next to me so that its face was level with mine. Its tongue lolled out as it panted and I waved away the hot scent of old meat. I took half a step away from the dog and it seemed to take this as some sort of invitation. As soon as I was at the edge of the boards it huffed and lay down where I had slept. I dragged my shield away from the dog with one hand and picked up my bag with the other.

I turned to the glaring old woman. "Who are you?"

"You're the one sleeping in the dog's bed. Who are you?"

The dog's gaze followed the old woman, who sat down on a nearby stool, and then it looked back to me.

"Edda Gretasdottir," I said, slowly. "I came in on the longship yesterday. Katja said this room was free."

"Oh, yes. I didn't recognise you. You're the army that has come to save us, are you?"

I felt her piercing gaze on me, but her face was pointed away, aimed at the wall a few paces to my right. Something about her eyes felt wrong. They were closed but too flat and shallow. I looked over at the dog. Its face pointed straight at mine and the depths of its gaze hinted that something else watched through those round eyes. A shiver ran up my spine and I had to look away. I turned back to the old woman and the Wind in my chest fluttered, reached out to her. She was Windborn.

"You're Gerda, aren't you?"

She grunted. "At least you're not stupid."

"I would have come to see you yesterday," I said, setting my bag and shield down by the fire pit, "but Katja said you were resting."

Gerda snorted. "I may be older than most people here, but I'm still Windborn. That girl seems to forget that."

I felt pinned between the hound's unending gaze and Gerda's disapproval. I couldn't bring myself to move, although I was sure I should. Gerda seemed impervious to any awkwardness and began weaving her iron-coloured hair into two braids, each one resting on a shoulder. My hand went to my salt-crusted hair and I tugged half-heartedly at a couple of knotted strands.

"You look like you've frozen to death overnight, girl. We get true winters up here. I don't know how you'll handle one if you can't sleep inside without breaking out in icicles."

Gerda tapped her cheek to emphasise her point and I put my hands up to my face. My cheeks were too smooth and there was a ridge of ice running along my cheekbone. I picked at it. My fingernail caught the edge and a frozen cast of my cheek fell away with a pop.

"I'll be fine."

Gerda shrugged. "Well, don't say I didn't warn you. Now, go get cleaned up. Erling is getting ready to meet you and this new law-keeper. You can't see him looking like that."

She didn't turn to me, but the dog cocked its head and I realised, now that I was away from the sailors and travellers, how thickly my shirt was covered in dust and salt.

"Fine," I said. "Where do—"

"Go out the back and head straight, you'll find a well and if you're lucky someone might be able to swap those tattered rags for presentable clothes."

I rumbled in wordless thanks and brushed past her out of the longhouse.

"And get some food in your belly. You don't want it to growl like that when you see Erling," Gerda called after me.

I paused and turned back. I opened my mouth to retort but the words died in my throat. A black bird perched on top of the back door. It could have been any raven, but something about the way it hopped told me it was the same raven that had followed us from Konvald. I kicked up a stone and hurled it at the bird. It squawked but flapped away unharmed.

A few people were gathered around the well. Men and women sat with buckets of water and were putting them to use, scrubbing vegetables or clothes. All things that could have been done elsewhere, but based on the hush that descended as I arrived, I suspected they were using the opportunity to gossip about mine and Alvilda's arrival. The quiet, broken only by the crunch of my footsteps, served as a subdued reminder that I was different. I was not only a stranger here, but also Windborn. For a heartbeat, I hesitated, unsure whether I should trespass within their conversation, but then I shook off the thought. I may be a stranger, but I was here to help. I nodded to them when I arrived. They all avoided my gaze and went about their tasks. I pulled a bucket of water and someone lent me some soap. There were a few shocked expressions when I began using the near-frozen water to wash with, but soon I was just another face in the crowd and the conversation resumed. The freshwater felt good as I scrubbed away the layers of dirt and salt from my days of travel. I had to change the water twice more before I was truly clean.

While I did this, I watched the raven out of the corner of my eye. It had followed me. Perhaps waiting for its chance to seek revenge. Every so often it squawked and hopped down onto someone's washing or vegetables. No one batted the raven away. Instead, they stared at it and asked it in an exasperated tone to move.

Once I washed the salt from my hair, one of the men washing vegetables took pity on me as I tugged and grunted with the knots in my hair and brought me a comb. I thanked him and was soon cleaner and more presentable than I had been in weeks. My clothes were still a little stained and wet, but the worst of it was gone. I placed my bucket against the wall of the well before I left, nodding to people as I passed them, and made my way back to the longhouse.

There was no sign of Gerda or the dog and I breathed a sigh of relief that quickly changed to irritation when I saw my cloak. It was still on the floor and there was now a hound-shaped furrow in it. I sighed again as I picked it up and a cloud of grey and black hairs cascaded from it. I batted it with one hand and dog hairs fluttered to the floor, but some refused to be moved. I shook my head and threw the cloak down and picked up my axe and shield. I would not meet Erling covered in dog hair. Neither would I meet him unarmed.

The still air of the longhouse shifted as I bent down. Something silent pushed the air and created a breeze that had nothing to do with the open door. I tightened my grip on my axe and made sure I held my shield properly.

"Edda, you look so lovely!"

Valna's bird-song voice greeted me as I turned. She clapped her hands together and hopped towards me. It took me a moment to connect the figure in front of me with the fighter I had travelled with. She wore a flowing dress the colour of spring leaves and a silver clip pinned up one side of her short hair.

I let the axe slip down in my grasp. "Do all the Windborn just sneak into this longhouse, or is it something about me?"

"What? Oh, sorry, Gerda told me to come and get you. I'm sorry I disappeared as soon as we saw land. I hope you didn't mind. I wanted to show you around, but I really hate being stuck on longships. There's nowhere to go, it felt like I hadn't been able to use my Windborn power in forever." She wandered as she talked, not looking at me and tidying as she went. She folded a blanket over a bench, tied back the hanging room dividers, and piled some cooking utensils on top of one another. "And I especially hate the one we came in on, making us row like that, I'm never going to get on that longship again and that's a promise! Do you know, that—"

"Valna." I slipped the axe shaft through my belt, slung my shield over my shoulder. "Isn't Erling waiting?"

"You're not wearing that." She frowned and put her hands on her hips. "It's filthy. Come on, you can borrow something of mine."

"No, it's—"

Valna shimmered then vanished. A heartbeat later, I heard rummaging at the other end of the longhall. I shook my head and followed.

Tentatively, hoping there would not be a half-naked huskalar lying in the room, I pulled back the hanging curtain. Valna was alone and had already thrown several items of clothing over a table.

"What about any of these?" she said, holding the first one up.

It was an elegant gown with embroidered feathers that cascaded down from the throat, but it was made for Valna's frame and it would have burst if I tried to put it on. I said as much to her. She frowned and held the gown up as though to test the theory, then shrugged and threw it back onto the messy pile behind her.

"What about this one?"

We went through five pieces of clothing until we found one that we were both happy with. I had first pointed to something strewn over a chair, but Valna had refused, saying that it wasn't pretty enough for me and besides it belonged to Olek. We settled on a blue long-sleeved tunic that was too big for Valna.

"I actually inherited this from my mother. She was much taller than me and I could never quite bring myself to throw this one away. Oh, don't give me that look. I want you to have it. I never wear it. It's not really my colour. And my mother was nothing if not a practical woman, she'd hate to see anything go to waste, especially something as nice as this. Go on, try it on."

I took it and ran it through my hands. It was made of finely spun wool, the kind that softened your fingers just by touching it. The cerulean colour reminded me of the sea and my stomach lurched like I was back on a longship. A white thread had been stitched into the neckline and flowed down the length of the arms like the crests of waves. I looked up. Valna had turned around, waiting for me to change. I slipped off my shirt, noticing how rough and stiff it felt, and put on the new tunic. Valna turned around as I straightened the long sleeves and pulled my Windborn arm-ring back on.

She clapped her hands together. "Oh, Edda, it fits perfectly and looks wonderful. Right, come on, we've got to show you off now."

She took me by the hand and led me over to Erling's hall. I ducked and picked my shield up as we passed it.

"You won't need that."

"I know."

Valna's mouth twisted then she shrugged and led me outside.

In the strained light of the winter morning the hall's shadow swept over everything down to the docks. Valna shivered as we got outside. Her dress looked thin, made more for its beauty than for its warmth. Now that we were outside I saw the subtle embroidered leaves spiralling up from the hem to her waist and on up to her neck. One sleeve fell below her wrist and flowed out over the back of her hand, but the other stopped just above her arm-ring. A sharp reminder that despite the beautiful dress, Valna was still a dangerous Windborn.

"What?" she said, frowning at me. "Have I got something on it?"

She twisted her head to try and see the back of her dress.

"No. No. You look different, that's all."

I had meant to say that she looked nice, but the word fell away from me at the last moment.

"I just mean..."

Valna blushed. "I suppose you've only seen me when I was spoiling for a fight, haven't you? I spent a long time embroidering this dress. It might be a silly thing to wear at this time of year, gods know that Gerda tells me that often enough, but I don't usually have to go outside. I can just pop between buildings and it never matters what I wear. It feels so restrictive when I have to put on all that armour. I feel cooped up in it, you know?"

"No."

She scowled at me.

"I mean I've never felt restricted when I put on armour," I said quickly. "The dress is nice. That's a lovely pattern."

Her scowl melted away and a smile spread over her face. She spun and the dress flared out. The embroidery seemed to come alive. The leaves swirled from her neck, all the way down the dress until they burst away on the edge of the skirt. She looked like spring.

"It is lovely, isn't it?"

Valna sighed, but I said nothing more, afraid that I would ruin the moment further.

"I'll see if I can find you a dress," she went on. "You don't have to keep wearing trousers and wander around like you're ready for a brawl all the time."

Her voice was incessant as we stepped into the entrance to the hall. She told me what colours she thought would work best with my eyes, what kinds of styles were her favourite, and who would be best to make the dress. Valna seemed happy to talk with little encouragement and I remembered how I had talked about similar things with Fjola a lifetime ago. The familiar roads of conversation soaked me with a feeling of safety.

I looked up at the carved jawbones flanking the hall's entrance as we approached. Each one was as thick as I was and twice as tall. The spiralling saga carved into them showed the fall of the Giants, their transformation into the Winds, and the end of the god-war. Craning my head back I saw, where the bones almost met above the doorway, the gods feasting before shimmering lines representing the imprisoned Winds. I put my hand on my chest and pressed down until I felt my ribs. Did one of those curved lines that always looked so distant in the night sky now live within me?

The sound of the doors drew my attention back. Valna leaned against the enormous oak panels and pushed them open easily. A small group of huskalar hurried out of the way.

People were crammed into the hall. Everyone turned to face us as Valna stepped into the mead-hall. Some in the crowd were dressed in finery, others with armour and weapons at their sides, and others with the durable, plain clothes of farmers. Whispers surged through all of them as we stepped across the threshold. Valna strode confidently through the parting crowd. Her demeanour changed as we moved through the hall. Her bright smile faded and her mouth turned down into a solemn grimace as she stepped purposefully towards the king. Tapestries and trophies hung across the walls and down from the rafters. Their bright threads shimmered in the dancing torchlight and it seemed that the heroes embroidered on them danced before us. Behind the tapestries and the crowds was the slow clink and shuffle of armour as hidden huskalar matched us step by step. At the opposite end of the hall there was a raised platform where the king sat on his throne. My king. He had a braided beard which fell to his chest and thick locks of silvered hair. His gaze pierced me as though he could weigh my worth with a glance. This was a man that had lost much and knew the cost of it.

He leaned to one side and muttered something to Runar, who stood next to him. Erling's eyes flashed with displeasure as he spoke and he tugged at his beard. He turned back to us as we reached the throne and he waved Runar away.

Runar gestured us over. As we stepped forward he floated off the stage to the king's right. Gerda and her hound stood waiting, and we joined them. I moved to stand on the opposite side of Valna and Runar to keep the dog as far away from me as possible.

"Where's Orin?" Valna whispered to Runar.

"Still resting," Runar replied.

"He needs it and his presence will not be required now." The voice came from the throne, pitched so only the Windborn would hear. "Better that the crowds don't see him. His absence will remind them of how hard he works to protect them."

Erling watched me, his expression serious and his posture spear straight. I stared into his eyes, grey as storm clouds and hard as granite, but refused to look away. The doors opened and everyone else turned to face the newcomers. Erling held my gaze a moment longer before he turned as well.

Fainn came in hissing something to Katja and Alvilda who trailed him. He straightened when he realised everyone was looking at them, nodded to the crowd, and walked up to Erling, his pace measured. Fainn had collected a staff from somewhere and the deep knock of the wood against the boards silenced any muttering.

"Ah, and here they are," Erling said, breaking the silent tension in the room. "The keepers of our gods, our laws, and my coin. Welcome, my friends." He gestured them forward and they came to stand on his left. "It seems that half the city wishes to greet our new arrivals." He looked from Alvilda to me. "Who would like to introduce them?"

Katja stepped forward and waited for Erling to acknowledge her.

"My king," she said and held out a hand towards me. "It pleases me to introduce Edda Gretasdottir, a capable warrior and potent Windborn. She has come here to protect your lands and people."

Runar shoved a hand into my back as Katja spoke and I stumbled forward. Whispers and muttered conversations surged throughout the crowd. Before I could say anything, Katja ushered Alvilda forward. She did not introduce her straight away, instead letting the quiet conversations die out.

"And here may I introduce Alvilda Vorunsdottir, a law-keeper to the High King himself."

More conversations sprang up around the hall, this time their tones hopeful and excited.

"Two very welcome arrivals," Erling said and stood. He picked up a goblet from a nearby table and stepped down from the throne. "Please, Law-Keeper Alvilda, partake of my ale, fill yourself with my food and be a guest-friend in my halls."

Katja ushered Alvilda forward whilst Fainn took the goblet from the king.

"King Erling invites you into his halls and makes you his guest-friend," Fainn said and held up the goblet with two hands. Something glittered under his fingertips that had nothing to do with the goblet's silvered surface. Magic sparked

283

out from his hands and there was a gasp from the crowd. "Drink of King Erling's mead," he continued, "and none shall harm you in his halls."

Fainn passed the goblet to Alvilda. The law-keeper hesitated then took it in shaking fingers and drank. Only a sip, but that was enough for the ritual. Fainn nodded and took back the goblet.

"Eat of King Erling's bread." Fainn picked up a loaf of bread and tore off a chunk. Another fizz of magical energy, larger this time, sparked from between his fingers. "Never shall you go hungry whilst you stay at King Erling's halls."

The law-keeper took the bread and nibbled at it. Fainn nodded again but let her keep what remained.

"Be welcome, guest-friend. Consider yourself a daughter of King Erling and as welcome here as any. Let none harm you or refuse you sustenance lest they be struck down by the gods for breaking this most ancient of traditions and rites."

Alvilda blushed when a cheer went up from the crowd. Erling sat back in his throne and Katja guided her back.

"Now that you are as safe in my halls as my own kin," Erling said. "On to business."

Fainn stepped forward again. He pulled a folded wax tablet from within his robes which had figures scribbled onto it. "We have sold our furs to the longship known as the Iron Rib and have, in turn, purchased from them much-needed supplies such as—"

"My trust that you are keeping us all fed, Fainn, is absolute and I am sure that our gathered friends share my feelings on this, but this is not what we have come to discuss. We will look at that later. Now, we must look to our safety instead of our stores."

Relief washed over Fainn and he nodded and stepped back. Erling tipped his head to Fainn graciously and then summoned Katja forward.

"Law-Keeper, we would all hear of your journey. How were you received at the Althing, and by the High King?"

Katja glanced around at the people crammed into the hall. As she shuffled over to face Erling, she kept her head half-turned to let her voice carry into the hall. "The Althing did not go as well as we had hoped. Due to circumstances we could not account for, the law-keepers at the Althing did not wish to re-open a matter they considered closed. However, I spoke with our friends and allies and, when the High King rules against Hraki, they will gladly stand with us."

"You say that the law-keepers will not look into the matter, and yet you have brought one of the High King's law-keepers to my halls?"

"I have, my king. I was not satisfied with the outcome from the Althing and took the matter to the High King himself."

She turned around and waved Alvilda forward, but Alvilda was hunched over with her hair over her eyes and did not see.

"Law-Keeper Alvilda," Katja continued and pulled the girl alongside her, "has come from the High King's own halls to confirm that war is being waged against us in winter, that Hraki goes against the laws of the gods themselves. She has come to be the High King's eyes and pass his judgement."

Murmuring filled the hall. I glanced around and saw that whilst some of the crowd looked pleased with this, others wore stoic, stormy expressions.

"It is well that you did not give up, law-keeper. Your dedication to me and my people is admirable. We thank you for your diligence."

"Thank you, my king." Katja bowed at the waist then guided Alvilda back to stand with Fainn. She stepped out into the clear space before the throne and faced the crowd head-on. "Please do not be alarmed if you see me leading Alvilda by your homes in the coming days. I will be showing our law-keeper guest the proof of Hraki's attacks. Please do not come to us to give your testimony unless it has been requested. This will give Law-Keeper Alvilda time to properly process the evidence. Once we have produced evidence that is satisfactory to Law-Keeper Alvilda, and, therefore, satisfactory to the High King, we will have the High King's support and that of King Olvid, Queen Sigrid, and King Gamlen."

"I hope," Erling said, low and firm, "that you will be swift in your judgement, guest Alvilda, for all our sakes."

Alvilda kept her head down and nodded, then hid behind Fainn.

"And we have another new face among us, though I have heard much about her already. Please, Katja, introduce us to this fabled warrior."

He waved a hand at me and I strode forward to stand with Katja. The excited chatter from the crowd faltered as my scarred shield, still slung over my back, faced the hall. My shoulder blades itched to have so many people I did not know standing out of sight, but I stood straight and kept my eyes on the throne.

"May I formally present Edda Gretasdottir," Katja said. "A fierce Windborn who would join your household and the fight against Hraki."

Quiet cheers from the crowd.

"Edda has lost much in the face of Hraki's underhanded attacks and tactics. She travelled to the Althing seeking justice, and when she heard of our plight she leapt at the chance to strike a blow against her enemy."

More conversations bubbled in the crowd, although I could not tell whether they were pleased by what they heard. I frowned at Katja and was about to say something when Erling's voice boomed through the mead-hall.

"And you wear an arm-ring already. Though it seems you come before me as a law-keeper instead of a Windborn. Katja have you mistaken a scribe for a warrior because of a battered shield?"

Laughter rippled through the crowd. I bunched my fists and stared up at Erling. I took half a step forward. Katja put a hand against my shoulder and pulled me back.

"This was all I could get," I growled.

"How so?" The good humour in Erling's eyes faltered and I realised that some of this was a show put on for the crowd, but that facade was cracking. "Have you already sworn to me without my knowing?"

"Not through choice," I said, scrambling to find the words to play along. "I would have waited until I arrived at your halls but... I could not due to circumstances I could not account for."

Erling's mouth twisted into a smile as I regurgitated Katja's words, but his eyes hardened.

"They must surely have been wondrous circumstances to

swear to a king without his knowledge."

The good humour in his voice was gone, replaced by something sharp and brittle.

Katja took a step forward and sketched a half-bow to Erling.

"It was my doing and not something that I undertook lightly, my king."

Erling turned his gaze onto Katja and she cringed away from the spear-glint in his eyes.

"Tell me," he rumbled.

Katja told the story of the fight at Konvald and the meeting with the High King, though her version of the story had the bounty hunters as mere muggers. She told the tale better than many skalds I had heard, and the crowd gasped in all the right places.

"I see," Erling said once the tale was done. "It seems that we must thank these petty criminals for sending you north to us, Edda Gretasdottir. As much as I appreciate my law-keeper's quick reactions, you must understand that it can only be the king who invites warriors into his household. I cannot in good conscience give spears to those I do not trust."

Erling pushed himself up from his throne and hopped down from the platform. Whispered conversations surged through the crowd as he walked toward me. My blood pounded in my ears and the crow inside me clutched at my heart. How much of this was an act for the crowd? Was Erling about to turn me away? Would I be sent back to the High King? Would I be forced to serve in Dagnur's household?

I opened my mouth to protest, to argue my case, but Erling held up a hand.

"Tell me, Edda Gretasdottir," he said and pressed his face close up to mine. "Why should I invite you into my household? What rewards do you seek for your service? What is it you want?"

A hush fell over the hall as everyone strained to hear my answer. Erling's storm-cloud eyes pierced mine like knives and I felt Erling weighing every minute movement of my face.

All around us, people leaned close with serious or expectant expressions. Valna clasped her hands together, an eager smile on her lips. Next to her, the dark forms of Runar and Gerda stood statue-still in the shadows. When I looked to Katja she gave me the slightest of nods.

"Well, Windborn?" Erling growled, his voice pitched low so only I could hear. "What do you want?"

I turned back to Erling and paused.

What did I want? I hadn't truly stopped to think about that since I left for the Althing. To be home. To be sat in the familiar warmth of my hearth with my husband and living the life we had planned. For a heart-stopping moment the gods gave me a vision of what could have been. We sat around a fire, our weapons hanging old and dusty on the walls, laughing and drinking with Fjola and Ulfur. Children played all around us. I could not tell if they were Fjola's children or ours. The vision disappeared as suddenly as it had arrived and once more I stood in a mead-hall filled with strangers. Grief clutched at my heart again with sharp, black talons. I wanted to live that life. I wanted my husband and the life we had worked so hard for, but there was nothing left of that dream but ashes on a hillside. My mind reeled back along the path I had travelled to get here. The muddy steps, the aching heartbeats, the bloody knuckles and broken enemies. All of these things flowed through me like an ocean in a storm and on the crest of every wave came that same name.

Hraki.

Rage swelled within me, flaring like a bonfire, and in that moment all I wanted was to bring Hraki to justice. Whatever he had done to these people could serve me, but I would make him pay for his crimes against me. As quickly as it erupted within me my rage died away, as though my bonfire had collapsed in on itself and sputtered to embers and coals. The heat remained but now it was constant and calm.

"I want to fight Hraki," I said. "He has taken so much from me. Give me the chance to fight him and promise me the head of his Windborn, Soren. That is all I ask for."

A few whispers from the crowd, although most seemed to be focused on Erling and his response. The king nodded slowly and then straightened so his voice carried over my head and out into the crowd.

"It seems that I have a new member of my household."

Erling raised his hands and the crowd cheered. "Already she talks of bringing justice to our enemies. I can tell Edda will be a great asset to us all."

Another cheer swept over the crowd. Erling laid his arm across my shoulders and guided me over to where the other Windborn stood.

"I cannot promise you Soren's head. War is chaotic and if another has a chance to kill this new Windborn they should always take it," he whispered. "But I can promise you that as soon as the High King gives his blessing, we will attack Hraki with all the might and justice we can muster. Do you still want to join me?"

I turned and looked into King Erling's eyes, as he had done to me, and tried to gauge him. His expression, now out of sight of the crowd, was tired and stern. It was the expression of a weary man who would not give up. If he wanted to fight Hraki, then I wanted to fight alongside him.

"Yes," I said. "I'm with you."

"Good. Fainn, make sure we have everything we need for Edda to swear herself to my household properly."

Fainn nodded from then left the hall by one of the side doors. Valna squeezed my arm and shot me an excited look. I offered a half-hearted smile in return.

Erling climbed back up to his throne. He waited for the attention in the room to shift back to him before he called out for anyone with petitions or pleas to step forward. Katja moved to stand by the throne as a few people made their way toward the dais and waited to be called upon.

"Come on," Valna said and took my hand. "Let's get out of here."

CHAPTER FOURTEEN
A DRESS MADE OF MIDNIGHT

VALNA DRAGGED ME TO THE WINDBORN'S LONGHOUSE, insisting on finding me something new to wear for when I made my oath to Erling.

"It's a special occasion." She was elbow deep in a pile of clothes. "You need to wear something special."

"You've already given me a new tunic. I don't need anything else."

"Nonsense. We've got a few hours before those old farts stop moaning to Erling about whatever. Plenty of time to find something appropriate."

"If I need something appropriate, shouldn't I be wearing clothes I can fight in?" I asked. "I've got my armour, my shield, and my axe. That will do, won't it?"

"Don't be ridiculous. First, you should never turn down an opportunity to wear something fancy. Second, you can fight just fine in a dress. It doesn't restrict your legs as long as it's not too tight and we'll make sure you can move your arms. I like to wear nice things, Edda, I don't like to be defenceless."

I sighed and resigned myself to the fact that the next few hours would be spent clambering in and out of dresses.

"Oh, I forgot I had this."

Valna straightened, dragging with her a long flowing gown that shimmered as it moved in the air. At a glance, it was the colour of midnight, dark and deep, but whenever the fabric moved colours floated out of the blackness. Shades of green, purple, and blue blossomed at the edges and then faded again.

"This is perfect."

"It's beautiful," I whispered.

Valna whipped the dress to get rid of some of the folds and it seemed to explode with dancing lights as though the Winds had been captured within the dress.

"I can't wear that. It must be worth a fortune."

"It's something that Erling's given me, so it didn't cost me anything, really. It's what I wish I had to wear when I took my oath. I thought that Rollo, that's Gerda's dog, had gotten his teeth into it years ago. Oh Edda, you have to wear this."

I stepped forward and took it. The fabric slid through my fingers with only a whisper of friction.

"Come on, let's see if it fits."

It didn't.

The waist was too small and my chest was too wide. The seams stretched and Valna had to help me pull the dress off. She ran to find some help and after a short while she returned with one of the women I had seen mending clothes at the well.

"Edda, meet Tove. She's a wonder with a needle and thread. She'll let that dress out in no time."

"This seems like a lot of trouble," I said. "I've got things I can wear—"

"Don't be silly, lass," Tove said, waving away my objections. "It's the least I can do if you're coming up here to show that Hraki what for. It will be the work of a moment."

She pulled a small box from somewhere and took out a measuring tape. She wrapped it around me, first measuring my chest then my waist and finally my hips. Valna had slipped on the dress so that Tove could take the dress' measurements before she began her work. The old woman hummed as she unpicked the stitching with a surprising deftness and speed.

"We'll need something to put in the space when we let it out," Tove said.

Valna nodded and went back to the pile of clothes thrown in one corner. She held up a few garments, waiting for Tove's reaction before tossing them back until she got to a black shirt which Tove tipped her head at. Valna brought it over and held it within the dress so that we could see it through the widened seams. The shadow-coloured cloth underneath the midnight dress seemed to bring the shimmering colours to attention even more.

"Perfect," Tove said. "Come on then, girl, let's get this on you so I can do this right."

We tugged the black shirt over my head and then the dress over that. I grimaced in anticipation of a needle scraping my skin as Tove pinned the fabric together, but her old hands were as nimble and gentle as a summer breeze. Once the pins were all in place, we carefully lay the dress down on Valna's table. Tove got out a pair of scissors and pulled a measure of dark thread from the box.

"This will take a little while, girls, you can leave me to it if you like."

Entranced by the dancing swiftness of Tove's fingers, I didn't immediately notice Valna trying to catch my attention and pull me outside. Out of habit, I grabbed my axe as we went. With its handle in hand, I felt some of the anxious weight life from my chest.

We wandered through the buildings by Erling's mead-hall until we came to the fjord's sloped shore and looked out across the water to the town proper. By now it was mid-afternoon and the ground had lost most of its frost.

"I don't know how you do it," Valna said.

"Do what?"

She was hunched over and rubbing her arms. "Just walk around without a cloak or a coat or anything. I've got my furs on and the cold is still finding its way through."

"A perk of being Windborn I guess," I said with a shrug.

Valna narrowed her eyes at me. "As long as you're not trying to impress anyone with only wearing your tunic in this weather. We need you strong and healthy, not sick with cold."

I laughed and let my hands freeze over with ice. "I think I've got enough cold in me."

Valna gave me a half-smile. "You know what I mean."

We followed the crest of the slope, walking parallel to the shore, and watched the boats on the fjord. The wind changed direction and for a moment I could make out the voices of the people shouting and laughing with one another, living a normal life. Beyond them, the town looked much the same as any other with houses and streets stacked haphazardly and filled with the sound of families and animals. We found a sandbar which was spined with rocks and boulders. Valna hopped onto the boulder furthest from the water and patted the spot next to her.

"It's them I feel sorry for," Valna said once I sat down. "All the people down there."

"Sorry for them? Why?"

I couldn't see any reason to pity the townspeople. There were raised voices, laughter. I saw boats carrying goods to and from the town. Eylheim looked to be a normal port.

"They're the ones that bear the brunt of the attacks. That really feel it. Look." She pointed to a patch of dark buildings off to the eastern edge of town, close to the strange wall of longships floating on the water. "That's where Hraki got to. Some of his warriors and Windborn sailed down the fjord and tried to break through. They got to the shore and started burning everything. Another longship came down the fjord, we think it had Hraki on it, and Orin had to call a storm to stop them getting through. We managed to fight them off, but that's not much of a consolation when your home's been burned down, is it?"

I craned my neck to try and see the wreckage more clearly. From this distance, all I could make out were blackened beams sticking out from behind the other buildings like broken ribs. The sight sent a wave of dark emotions through me. I had not seen burnt wood like that since I had left our farmhouse. Suddenly, my chest felt hollow, then weighted with the crow-coloured grief I thought I had outrun.

"No," I whispered. "No, it's not."

We sat like that for a little while longer. The sounds of the townspeople came and went as the winds changed, sometimes overtaken by the lapping water, or the rustling of the trees. My eyes strayed back to the broken ribs of the burned down homes and with each furtive glance more black feathers clogged my chest. As the sun began to brush the horizon, we went back to the Windborn longhouse.

Tove was still working on the dress so we sat together and talked. She and Valna had a great love of gossip and I learnt a lot of small, dangerous details about people I had yet to meet.

"There we are," Tove said during a lull in the conversation.

"Should be ready for you to try on."

I pushed myself up from the chair and took the dress from Tove. This time I didn't need any help to pull the dress on. It slipped over my arms and down to fit snugly against my skin. I tugged it in a few places to make it more comfortable and untwisted the arms. It felt tighter than the clothes I was used to, but I could move easily enough.

"Oh Edda," Valna said and clasped her hands together. "It looks just perfect. How does it feel?"

I stretched and twisted.

"It feels fine," I said. "I don't fancy its chances if I have to swing an axe, though. It'll probably split."

"We'll get you a spear, then," Valna said and flicked a speck of fluff from my shoulder. "You won't need to twist as much if you stab a spear."

Tove snorted. "Listen to you two. I make you a nice dress and all you can talk about is stabbing and hacking. Come here. Let me see how it moves with you when you're not trying to kill someone."

"I'll go and see how long until the ceremony," Valna said and disappeared so suddenly, I jumped.

"I'm still not used to that."

"It takes a while," Tove muttered.

I bent to pick up my arm-ring and slip it back onto my arm, but Tove slapped my hand. "You won't be needing that if you're going to swear to Erling. He'll only be giving you a new one."

"I suppose so."

"Now, come and stand over here."

Under Tove's instructions I held up arms, bent my knees, and twisted my torso. Tove clucked as I moved, whether at the dress or me I couldn't tell. Eventually, Tove was satisfied that the dress wouldn't pop open as I walked and soon after that, Valna reappeared.

"They won't be long now," she said and hopped up to sit on a table pushed against the wall and started to swing her legs back and forth. "Fainn says that it took ages for the king to get through all those petitions and complaints, but we can go whenever we're ready."

"Good," I said then turned back to Tove. "Are we done?"

"Yes, girl, as good as you're going to get in one go."

"Wonderful," Valna squealed and jumped off the table. She leapt forward and gave Tove a kiss on the cheek. "Thank you so much, Tove, you've worked magic with this."

"Just doing what I can, girl," Tove mumbled and waved her off but her cheeks flushed.

"Magic," Valna repeated in a sing-song voice as she skipped out of the longhall.

"Thank you, Tove," I mumbled. "I don't usually wear things like this. I... thank you."

"Not a worry, girl, everyone deserves to look nice, eh? Now, go and do what you're supposed to instead of standing around here and making me look old."

I thought about kissing her on the cheek as well, but she was focused on collecting her things and instead I ducked out of Valna's room. As I walked past my room, my cloak was suspiciously rumpled and covered in a fresh dusting of dog hair, I hesitated. A shaft of light pierced through a gap in the walls and illuminated the metal centre of my shield. For a second I thought the saga carved into the wood was moving, that the pale figures marched around their spiral, but it was only the dust swirling in the air. The iron that ringed the shield's edges was charred and bitten into by blades, some of the figures had been chipped, but it was still whole. It would still serve its purpose. I picked up the shield and slung it over my shoulder and then rummaged through my things for something to fight with.

I stepped out of the longhall with the reassurance of a dagger at my side and the comfort of my shield pressing on my shoulders. Valna rolled her eyes when she saw the iron edges of the shield, but the slight curve of her lips told me it was a joke. She slipped her arm through mine and led me to the king and my final oath.

*

The crowds were gone. The now silent mead-hall filled with the Windborn and Alvilda. Orin had still not risen from wherever he was resting, though Gerda sat by the fire with her hound sat by her side. Alvilda stood by the fire on her own with her shoulders hunched and face downcast. I shifted my weight from foot to foot, feeling self-conscious in my newly-made dress. I looked around as I felt the fluttering power within me respond to the other Windborn in the room. The dead who refused to die.

"There wasn't this much fuss when I took my oath to Erling," Runar grumbled from beside me. "I didn't get any new clothes."

"Be quiet, Runar," Valna said and shot him a withering look. "Things were a bit different when you took your oath, weren't they? Don't listen to him, Edda, he's just jealous."

Runar grunted and turned away.

A crow flew in from somewhere and hopped onto the rafters. No one else spared the bird a glance as it fluttered in and above us, but when it hopped along the beam and started to caw at us, they all stood a little straighter and a tension soaked into the air.

"He's coming," Valna whispered to me.

I nodded and straightened as well. Voices reached us from through the doorway behind the throne moments before Katja came in and rushed over to us.

"Are you ready?" she asked, breathless.

"As ready as I'll ever be," I said.

"And you know what you've got to do?"

"I've seen enough ceremonies like this. I'll be fine."

She nodded but seemed unconvinced.

"Runar, will you be a witness?" she asked.

The Windborn nodded.

"Oh, I'll do it Katja," Valna hopped on the spot and waved to the law-keeper. "Can I be the witness for Edda?"

"Sure, fine," Katja waved distractedly at Valna then turned to Alvilda. "Will you be the witness for Erling? I would do it normally, or ask Fainn, but I have to do the ceremony and Fainn's the god-speaker too."

Alvilda didn't say anything, but I thought I saw her smile through the hair across her face and she nodded.

"Great, the king is coming. Just remember, Edda, you don't know of any reason you can't swear the oath. Okay?"

"I'll be fine."

She nodded again and hurried off to stand by the throne.

Erling stepped through the doorway and strode purposefully to his seat. He carried a spear which he slammed down onto the platform with every step. When he sat down he laid it across his knees.

Fainn trailed slowly after his king as though slowing down his steps would imbue them with gravitas. He had a laurel of twigs entwined in his greying hair and his staff in his right hand. He had rolled up his sleeves and I noticed runes tattooed into swirls across his forearms. He made his way to the right of the throne, whilst Katja stood on the left.

"Good, you're all here," the king said.

He looked different. Without the gentle, sea-whisper noise of a crowd he looked deflated, ragged and his gaze had a sharper edge.

"Let's get on with it, shall we?"

Erling waved Katja on and she bowed to him.

"Edda," she said, gesturing to the space in front of the throne. "Could you come up here, please?"

I walked forward, my heart drummed like thunder in the mountains, and stood silent in front of my soon-to-be king and his law-keeper. I felt a little better noticing that she had changed as well. Instead of the simple robes she wore earlier, she was dressed in robes embroidered with runes and had pinned up her hair. She gave me a small smile and nod, then her posture changed, transforming her from a friend to a king's law-keeper.

"Edda Gretasdottir," she began. Her tone was serious and her voice echoed back to us from the end of the mead-hall. "You stand before King Erling, son of Hakon, to swear yourself to him as a member of his household. Do you know of any lawful oath or bond such as a criminal conviction or debt that would prevent you from performing duties expected of a servant of a royal household?"

She paused and looked at me expectantly.

"I do not."

She nodded and produced an iron arm-ring from within her robes. A simple knot pattern was etched into its surface and the metal glinted in the dim light of the hall.

"Those who would bear witness, step forward."

Valna walked up to stand by me. She grinned and squeezed my hand before turning to face the law-keeper. At the same time Fainn moved to the front of the platform and Alvilda shuffled forward.

"Who stands for the oath-taker?"

"I do," Valna said.

"Who stands for the king?"

"I do," mumbled Alvilda.

"Who stands for the gods?"

"I do," said Fainn.

Katja took the arm-ring in both hands and stepped up to me.

"These few stand for and represent all the realms of gods and mortals and before them may this oath be binding in this life and the next."

She stepped back as Erling pushed himself from the throne and moved to the edge of his platform. He towered over me and stared into my soul. He seemed to accept whatever he saw there, as a few seconds later he extended the spear and pointed its long, flattened spearhead at my chest. I put my hand out and gripped it.

"Swear to me, in front of gods and mortals, that you will serve me in all things. Swear that your actions will bring me glory and power and in return I swear to give you my protection and treasures as compensation for your valour and honourable service."

I felt the spearhead cut into my fingers. Its edges became slick with my blood. Erling's gaze bored into me as though daring me to take away my hand. I gripped tighter. Blood dripped to the floor.

As I opened my mouth to say the words they faltered, as though feathers were caught in my throat.

This was it. This was the moment. Even with all of the scars, grief, and ashes I had collected this was the moment that I couldn't turn back from.

A breeze blew in from behind me and brought with it the scent of salt and soil before leaving me with the iron tang of my blood biting at my nostrils. I watched my blood form bright pools between my fingers and slip through my grip to fall unseen to the floor.

"On my blood, on the life that I might lose, I swear myself to you. I swear to bring you glory and power and protect your house. May the gods strike me down if I break this oath."

The final words were ashes on my tongue. What more could the gods do to me?

"I accept your oath," Erling said. He nodded to me and his eyes softened. I let go of the spearhead. Erling passed the spear off to Fainn whose expression wrinkled in distaste. Fainn held the spear at arm's length as he moved to the side and placed the spear against a wall.

"Take this arm-ring as a mark of your loyalty so that all shall know whom you serve," Erling said. He gestured to Katja who bowed and stepped forward, arm-ring clutched tightly in her hands.

She slid the new arm-ring up my arm. It strained as it reached the end of my forearm, but with some help Katja and I were able to move it up to my bicep. The arm-ring was heavy, but it was reassuring, like the weight of an axe gripped tight in your hand.

I looked around the mead-hall at the people who had seen me swear my life away. Their faces were grim, only Valna's expression had anything approaching joy in it and in typical fashion she looked ready to burst with excitement. Katja gestured that I should step back with the other Windborn. I bowed my head to her and Erling then went to stand by Valna.

"It's official," she whispered and squeezed my arm. She craned her neck around me to get a better look at the arm-ring. I held my arm out for her. "Oh, it's love—"

"Now that we have that out of the way," Erling said as he sat back in his throne, cutting Valna off, "I would speak with Law-Keeper Alvilda."

Erling raised a hand as a summons and the law-keeper moved to stand in front of the throne. She cast furtive looks from left to right as though looking for an escape route.

"Katja told me what happened at the Althing and what happened when she and my Windborn were at Konvald. It seems that you are now my only hope at justice. What is it you need to see to believe that Hraki is fighting a winter war against us?"

She kept her eyes down and paused to consider her response. "To make a judgement against Hraki, I would need evidence that he has organised an attack against you after the Summer's End festival."

The king's expression darkened and his knuckles went white on the arms of throne. "We have plenty of that."

*

Later, long after the sun had set, I wandered the shore of Erling's royal island. The sand crunched and the sea salted the wind. Clouds streaked the sky but the stars and moon were bright enough to give me a clear view of the fjord and the town. To the north-east, towards the mountains and the source of the fjord, dark shapes bobbed on the water. I walked towards them, curious to see the line of vessels that blocked Hraki's passage.

They were not all longships. Some of the boats trapped in that chain were fishing vessels and even a rowboat. Thick coils of rope wrapped around the figureheads of the longships and slipped under the seats of the smaller boats to bind them together. The water knocked the boats together as though the fjord was uncomfortable with the wooden wall woven on it. I scooped a handful of pebbles as I sat on a boulder facing the fjord. I threw the pebbles at the longships. They bounced off with hollow thunks.

Before I had a chance to process the events of the day, I heard footsteps crunch on the cold ground. I turned to see Valna walking along the shoreline. She had a cup clutched in each hand and a wineskin draped around her neck.

"How did you know I'd be out here?"

"You left a trail."

I frowned. The ground was too cold and hard for that. As I opened my mouth to accuse her of following me she gestured with a cup. Sparkling frost seeped out beneath me and a patchy trail of ice led back to the longhouse.

301

"One of the perks of being able to disappear," Valna said. "No one can follow me." She shook an empty cup. "Come on, it's time for a drink."

She poured us each a full cup of mead, the sweet honey and sharp alcohol a welcome break from the salt-tinged air, then hopped onto the boulder with me.

"What are we looking at?"

"Nothing in particular."

Valna nodded.

We sat and drank. I kept silent. After we refilled our cups, Valna surprised me by leaning over and resting her head on my shoulder.

"It's good to have a friend out here," she whispered.

"Don't you have many friends? What about Olek?"

"I have some friends. Olek for sure. Not many though. Katja and I used to talk and eat together, but not anymore. None of the other Windborn have time for it. Runar is always flying off doing this and that; Gerda's a grumpy old woman who likes her solitude, and Orin is usually asleep."

I let the night swallow the bitter grief in her words like a rock falling into the ocean before I said, "You must have friends outside of Erling's Windborn?"

She sat up, shook her head, and took a swig of mead. "Not really. Who would want to spend time with a Windborn? A lot of people are superstitious about us. The huskalar will have a drink with you, but it's always a competition. Who can keep up with the Windborn, you know?"

I winced inwardly as I remembered raids where I had done just that. We had never gotten to know the Windborn, only seen if we could match them drink for drink.

"How'd you get your name, then?" Valna asked between sips of mead. "I've never met anyone called Edda before."

"The same way most people get a name, my parents gave it to me. They wanted me to be a skald, a famous travelling warrior-poet, so they gave me a name to suit. They told me the old stories until I knew them by heart. Whenever we had any visitors they'd ask me to tell them."

Valna's eyes lit up. "You know all the old stories? Are you good? We've not had a good storyteller in so long."

"But," I said, ignoring Valna's interruption, "I never liked telling stories. Something about the way everyone looks at you and makes you the centre of attention makes me squirm. And gods help me if I got a part of the story wrong. My parents would snap at me: 'I think you mean he travelled for three days, Edda' or 'don't you mean Jorgun the Strong, not the Bold?'. I just wanted to get the story over and done with so I could sit down."

"You don't want to tell me a story, then?"

Valna's eyes sparkled over the rim of her cup and I couldn't help but smile at her.

"No, I don't."

"Fine." She puffed out her cheeks in mock outrage. "I guess you'll have to have a drink instead."

She upended the skin and poured the last of the mead into our cups. She dropped the empty skin at her feet and raised her cup.

"To new friends and new beginnings."

I tapped my cup against hers. "To new friends and new beginnings."

The lights had gone out in the buildings across the fjord which left our island floating in a dark chasm between the stars and their reflections. We sat together and the moment pulled close to us, became intimate. The soft light of the moon and stars were the only things that kept us company.

"I'll tell you a story," Valna said and downed her drink. "I don't know many stories, but I can tell you how I became Windborn."

It took me a moment to register what she had said. I gripped my cup in both hands and faced Valna, to better hear the story, then I stopped. The memory of my own resurrection surfaced in my mind. The water pulling me down, the weight of it in my lungs, and the sharp, rending pain of the wounds the Wind-hunters had given me. The thought set my heart racing and made my scars ache.

"No, Valna. You don't have to—"

"No, no." She raised a hand. "I want to tell you. It's not a story I've told many times, it creeps most people out, and if there's any story worth telling, it's how I died, right?"

303

Slowly, I tipped my head in acknowledgement.

"My family had a farm. It was steady and safe, but steady and safe is never fun is it? So I went raiding. I got good at it and made myself a fair bit of money. I had more than enough to get my own farm and settle down, but every time the raiding season came around, I found myself back on a longship and sailing somewhere.

"One year my younger brother came with us. We'd always been competitive, usually just friendly stuff like who could shear the most sheep or feed the animals quickest or something. He always made fun of me because I was still helping out on the farm—a real raider would have enough to buy a farm by now, he said—so when he came on the raid, I wanted to show him just how good I was.

"I got reckless. It started small, just running ahead of the rest of the charge or volunteering to do some scouting or something, but small things add up.

"After we'd raided a few weak-willed places, we finally found somewhere that fought back. Most people fell into a shield wall, but I wanted to show my little brother how it was done. I stayed out as long as I could and I cut down a few people. Then they got smart and got their hunting bows. Even I'm not stupid enough to stand out in the open when that happens. I ran to the shield wall and as I got there I felt something punch into me. I remember wishing I was just that little bit ahead, if only I could just snap myself over there... and then everything went dark.

"I woke up a little while later after we'd won the battle. They said when I died it looked like the Winds cracked and that scared the Ertlanders into submission. We took a few prisoners, got our loot, and got back. My brother had charged out of the shield wall when I went down and taken some prisoners so he came out of the raid well off and he got some of my treasure hoard as well. Most of it went to my parents and I'm happy with that. Now that they're too old to work the farm it means they can afford help."

She paused, trying to take another drink then scowled at the empty cup. I offered her my drink.

"For the storyteller."

We shared a smile as she took the cup. In all the old stories the reward for the storyteller was a drink by a fire and whatever food could be spared. There wasn't much left in the cup, but it seemed fitting.

"Do you visit your family?" I asked.

"No, not anymore. I used to visit a little bit, but it takes a few weeks and Erling can't spare us now. I never realised how lonely being a Windborn would be. I guess no one really thinks about it. You just hear about the battles, don't you? The storytellers talk about kings sending them off to do great things. The victories. The glory. No one tells you about everything you have to leave behind."

Valna tipped her head back, looking to the stars, and shook her head with a humourless chuckle then shook her empty cup. "This was supposed to be a celebration and here we are with empty cups."

"It's celebration enough," I said.

Valna gave me another quick hug. When she leaned back against the boulder her breath plumed in front of her. I couldn't be sure if it was the chill of the night or my own cold that was responsible.

"You know, our farm was close to the Blackwater Lakes, I loved skating on the ice with my friends over the winter." Valna picked up a pebble and threw it as hard as she could at the water. I lost sight of it as it arced over the shoreline into the night. A moment later there came a splash. "I wonder how long until the fjord properly freezes over and we get a good bit of ice. There's hardly any right now."

"Maybe I can help," I said.

I got down from the boulder and went to the fjord. Ice sparkled between the pebbles as the current swept out the water but left its frozen cargo. I watched swirls in the water and for a moment they looked like hungry whirlpools, ready to devour me and drown me again. I stood frozen for a long moment, rooted by the memories of storm-laden seas, but I forced the images from my mind and splashed out into the fjord. Water seeped through my boots and I felt a prickle around my ankles as it froze around me. I took a deep breath and turned my attention inward. I pushed past the layer of grief

305

and anger, past my fears, and down to the core of the roiling Wind woven into my soul. The power recoiled as I tried to ease it out, but then it quivered, eased, and flowed fast and powerful. There was a crackling sound and my legs felt locked in place.

When I opened my eyes it looked like I was a giant stood in the centre of a frozen lake. The ice, translucent and thick, wrapped around my legs like tree roots and stretched out a few hundred paces onto the fjord. After a few attempts, I managed to rip my feet free of the ice. The combined effort of turning the fjord to ice around me and tearing myself free left me panting. Valna appeared next to me, her mouth hanging open.

I stepped onto the ice. It cricked and groaned, but then seemed to settle and I was able to put my full weight on it.

"Come on," I said and stamped my foot. "It'll be fine."

Valna ignored my outstretched hand and a grin split her face.

"Hang on," she said.

She half-turned and then she was gone, leaving me alone with the ice and stars.

The sound of the water was a distant, hushed seething that sent my mind reeling back to the longship where I lost my husband. For the first time, I was glad that my Windborn powers were ice-bound. It allowed me to put something between myself and the hungry waves.

Valna reappeared a handful of heartbeats later. She stumbled as she appeared in the air beside me. Perhaps she had drunk too much mead or had simply misjudged her footing. She had a collection of strange objects clutched to her chest, she dropped them to the floor with a clatter, then picked up something and shoved it at me. It was a pair of bone ice skates. The bones were long enough to slip beneath our feet and had been smoothed to reduce the friction on the ice. There were holes bored through them which held leather thongs to tie the skates to our shoes. I looked back at Valna, who was already tying the skates to her feet, and saw she had some poles with her as well, each with an iron nail jutting from the end.

"Have you done this before?" Valna asked.

"A couple of times," I said. "You might need to help me put

these on."

Once she had hers on, she slid next to me and bent down to tie the skates to my shoes. They were restricting and liberating at the same time as the leather was wrapped tight around my feet but movement over the ice was smooth and easy.

"Use the poles to help with balance. Don't use them to pull yourself forward too much or you'll just get tired."

I nodded and took two of the poles. Valna took the last one and slid out onto the frozen fjord. She pushed forward with one foot then the other and stabbed down into the ice with the pole. She pulled it up as it slid between her feet and after only a couple of dragging motions with the pole she moved as quick as a runner. Laughter burst out of her and she turned, curving with the edge of the ice.

"Come on," she called.

I pushed the poles into the ice with one on either side of me and shoved one foot forward. It was smoother than I anticipated and I almost fell but stabbed the other pole down to balance myself. The brittle ice splintered around the iron nail like a cobweb but I remained on my feet. I soon fell into a rhythm of kicking forward and balancing with the iron-studded poles.

Valna swooped around on the ice, gliding past me as though on a midnight cloud. I kept close to the shore at first but eased my way in wider and wider circles until I skirted the edge of the ice as well. Her laughter echoed around me over and over and soon I was laughing with her.

"How close do you think I can get to the edge?"

"I don't know how thick it is at the edge," I said.

She circled the same patch of ice, spiralling closer and closer to the water. I called out to her not to get too close but she wasn't listening.

The ice squealed, snapped.

With a yelp Valna, disappeared in a cascade of tumbling ice, slush, and foaming water. I tried to rush over, but I couldn't move fast enough even with the skates. The chunk of ice flipped over and floated out into the fjord.

Valna's laughter spluttered out behind me.

I spun towards the shore. Valna sat sprawled on the ice with the pole clutched to her chest and water soaking her bottom half. It took me a moment to register what had happened and then I laughed too.

"I thought I could jump out of there faster than the ice cracked," she said once she could speak again. "Maybe next time."

I moved over and pulled her up. She tried to shake the worst of the water from her legs and then shot me a wicked grin.

"How close do you think I can get this time?"

Before I could answer a voice called out across the beach.

"What happened to you?"

I turned and saw a man wrapped in fur and clutching a waterskin in one hand.

Valna pushed herself to her feet as unsteady as a newborn fawn.

"Olek!" She half-stumbled before she vanished and reappeared next to him. "What are you doing here?"

Olek dropped the wineskin and caught Valna before she fell. He had a wide frame bulked out with muscle and his short-cropped red hair looked the colour of rust in the starlight.

"You woke me up when you came to get the skates and I thought I'd come and bring you some more drink. Did you fall into the water?"

"Only a little bit." She pulled him close and pressed her lips to his.

Olek leaned into the kiss, then flinched away from her. "Gods above, Valna, you're freezing."

"I'm fine. I didn't fall all the way in."

"No, but—"

"Anyway, now that you're here do you want to skate too? We'll take turns. Here you take mine while I dry off and then I can swap with Edda and we'll go round like that. Okay?"

Olek tried to protest but Valna already had her skates off. I watched them struggle to put the skates onto Olek's boots. Their playful bickering was something born of passionate love, tempered by time, but powerful enough to keep you warm in the depths of winter. I smiled as I watched them, but the joy was curbed by my loss and I turned away.

I made my way back to the ice with uneven steps and set

myself to skating. After a few heartbeats of skimming along the frozen water, my sorrow was whipped away by the joy of smooth movement across the ice. Olek joined me and crisscrossed over the lines my skates had scored in the ice. His hunched posture and wavering path showed he was not as confident on the ice as his lover.

Eventually, Valna called out from the shoreline and we swapped positions; she began to spiral on the ice as I guarded the mead and took my due. Soon after Olek came and swapped with me and he took his turn warming himself with mead until Valna came to kiss him and send him back out onto the ice.

Olek and I kept ourselves far from the edge and contented ourselves by skating over the thickest ice, but Valna circled ever closer to the edge. More than once she had to use her Windborn powers to jump away from a collapsing spur, but she always reappeared laughing and used it as an excuse to guard the mead once more.

It went on like this for what felt like hours and we filled the night with the sound of splintering ice and warm laughter.

CHAPTER FIFTEEN
A BURNED HOME

THE NEXT DAY I WAS TOLD to find Runar by the jetty. The docks were busy with people loading and unloading their boats. Out on the water, there was a steady stream of vessels waiting for their berth or travelling between the town and the island. I glanced over towards the stagnant silhouettes of the longships tied at the mouth of the fjord that dipped and twisted in the breeze. They were a silent reminder of the danger waiting upriver and sent a shiver up my spine.

I found Runar next to a small rowing boat at the end of the jetty. Fainn and Alvilda sat inside and the oars had been placed underneath the seats.

"Come on," he said. "We're going to show Alvilda what happened the last time Hraki showed up. Erling thought you'd want to see as well."

I clambered into the boat on the opposite side to the others. Alvilda stared off towards the sea, her back straight as though trying to present a dignified, silent figure. The image was spoiled as I sat down and she flinched at the sudden rock of the boat. For Fainn's part, he seemed disinterested in everything. I nodded to them, but neither responded.

"Hold on to something," Runar called and picked up a rope attached to the front of the boat.

He floated into the air and flew off in the direction of the burnt buildings Valna had pointed out to me the day before. The rope snapped taut and the boat lurched forwards. Alvilda's hands shot out to grip the seat beneath her whilst Fainn and I took hold of the gunwale. Runar looked back to make sure he hadn't lost any passengers then dragged us along behind him.

Water sprayed up as the boat cut across the fjord and the tearing roar of the water killed any hope of conversation. Alvilda squeaked and leaned to one side to try and avoid the worst of it, but her hair was soon dripping. Fainn's face was set in a scowl and hunched himself down as low as he could, but he was slowly soaked as well. I leaned away from the spray but did not bother to avoid it. I took a small measure of comfort that the water froze as soon as it touched me like a skin of icy armour. I kept my eyes forward and took in the town ahead of us. The buildings on this side of the fjord were built a few hundred paces away from the beach and many faced out to make the most of the view. Most were small with some area fenced off to turn the space into a garden or pen for livestock.

Runar twisted the boat's trajectory and we bumped along parallel to the shore until we curved around a jutting sandbar beyond the main town. Passing the sandbar revealed the blackened remains of the razed farm. It had been built away from the other farms and homes, which would have provided the residents with some privacy, but also meant it was the first place Hraki's raiders came to. Runar dragged the boat up onto the beach with the crunch of sand and snap of the thin ice on the fjord's edges. I helped Runar pull the boat further onto the sand and the others clambered out once they could avoid getting wet. Fainn walked straight past us with his hands clasped behind his back and head held high. Alvilda offered a thank you as she walked by, wringing her hair free of water as she went.

I waited for Runar to stow the rope so that I could put some distance between us and the others. He nodded at me as he walked up the beach and I fell in step next to him.

"This was what happened before you came down to the Althing, wasn't it?"

"Aye. We fought them off, but paid the price."

I opened my mouth to ask more but his thunderous expression silenced me. Ahead of us the two keepers reached the wreckage. Fainn turned and glared at us, even from a distance the exhaustion was clear on his face.

"Let's get this over with. You were moving quick enough when you were pulling the boat."

"Seems like I got a right to rest then, doesn't it?" Runar shot back.

"We don't know what's out here. The king instructed you to accompany us for our safety."

"We'll keep you safe," I said, quickly. I wanted to look at the farm, not listen to the tired sniping between Runar and Fainn. "Let's get a move on."

The god-speaker huffed and turned away from us as the sun crept out from the clouds and cast the scene in weak winter shadows.

It had been a big farm once. Parts of the walls remained and showed a fractured outline of the main house and a smaller building off to the side, a shed or smokehouse. The sorrow soaked into the charred skeleton of the farm echoed within me. As I came closer to the wreckage, I noticed the ashen lumps that broke the smooth ground within the house and I prayed to the gods that they were furniture. Some of the blackened wood had a sheen to it as though it was still wet. White congealed fat pooled at the base of those burnt timbers. The sight of it twisted my stomach. I was glad the smell was long gone.

The grief-crow stirred in my chest and gave a spite-filled laugh as this broken, burned home forced me to remember the one I had lost and left behind. My home had been smaller than this farm, judging by the charcoal contours before me, and for an instant I felt guilty. How could I feel so much grief over my own loss when Hraki had caused much more destruction here?

Mournful claws scratched the inside of my ribs and I shook off the guilt. This family's misfortune did not negate my own. My home, regardless of its size, had been saturated with memories and the loss of it still felt as raw as an open wound.

Perhaps if I had been able to sleep that night then I would have died in my bed and taken my grief with me, but who would have thrown Bjolfur's runestone then? No, better to have been thrown from the cliffs. There had been some chance I would have died in the sea's hungry jaws and spent eternity with my husband at the bottom of the ocean. It was not my death that had condemned me, but my Windborn resurrection.

The thought curled within me like leaves caught in a wildfire and inflamed my guilt to rage. There was such suffering to lay at Hraki's feet. My destroyed home, the razed farm before me, and so much else. If I could not rest with my husband beneath the waves, then at least I could use my resurrection to ensure Hraki's destruction.

Fainn paused in front of the farm's wreckage and rubbed at his eyes. Once he had gathered himself, he turned to us and puffed up his chest and made a grand gesture at the burnt wood and snow-covered ash.

"Here, law-keeper, is our evidence." Fainn took a step forward and began pacing as though he were performing at a campfire rather than parading in front of a homestead's corpse. "This is the work of Hraki and his household. They sailed here and burned down this farm to try and punch their way through to the ocean. You will agree, I am sure, that there is no way this could have been done before the Summer's End festival. Therefore, Hraki has broken the laws set down by the gods themselves. I ask you, Law-Keeper Alvilda, to make your judgement against Hraki."

The self-satisfied set of his shoulders made me wonder how much he had practised that speech.

Alvilda moved forward, ignoring Fainn's gaze, and walked up to the edge of the farm. She leaned to peer inside and then circled the wreckage. Fainn followed her, tapping a foot and crossing his arms whenever she stopped to examine something. Runar and I stayed put. He sat on a half-buried barrel and I leaned against a nearby fir tree. We watched them circuit the farm, Alvilda carefully examining the smallest details and Fainn huffing and hurrying her along.

"Well?" Fainn snapped when Alvilda had finished her inspection.

"I can't make the decision—"

"You're the High King's arbiter, aren't you? Making the decision is the only thing you're here for."

Alvilda straightened and she set her jaw. "This evidence is not enough for me to make the judgement. I agree that this happened recently, clearly after the raiding season, but there is nothing to suggest this was Hraki's doing. This could have been an accident or the work of a disgruntled neighbour. I will not condemn Hraki's entire household on this alone."

Fainn's jaw went slack. I glanced over at Runar. His expression had darkened and his eyes narrowed on the law-keeper but kept his silence.

"This is ridiculous," Fainn spluttered. "We present you with an entire farmstead razed to the ground and you tell us it's insufficient? This is—"

"Your arguments are compelling, Fainn, but not conclusive." Now that Alvilda had found her voice she looked to have found her confidence as well. "Would you trust the word of a murderer if, when presented with the body, they denied it was their doing?"

Fainn's eyes looked like they would pop out of his head. His cheeks flushed crimson under his beard and he took a menacing step forward.

"Law-Keeper Alvilda," I said, putting myself between them. "What evidence do you need to verify that Hraki did this?"

Her posture trembled for a moment as I towered over her and her eyes flickered down to the axe at my side. She swallowed. "Testimony from the farm's owners would be sufficient."

"Right," Fainn shouted and stomped off towards the rest of town.

Alvilda moved away from us, putting herself right up to the burnt walls.

"I'm sorry," she said softly. "If I make this decision wrong then the High King will—"

"It's okay," Runar rumbled from his barrel seat. "We need this decision done right. Last time a law-keeper came on the High King's authority they took Hraki's coin and made the wrong call. You keep your integrity and do this right and we won't have a problem. You have my word that this is Hraki's work. If you need to talk to a few people to get that right in your head, then you do it."

The young law-keeper nodded, her cheeks pink, then she took a breath and shook herself. She picked at the wall and let the charcoal flakes fall from her fingers.

After about a quarter of an hour, Fainn returned practically dragging two people with him. One was a woman about my age, her auburn hair snapping in the breeze, and the other was a balding old man.

"Here are your witnesses," Fainn said, triumphantly. He tugged them forward and they stumbled to a halt in front of the law-keeper. "Go on, tell her what happened."

I shook my head as the two witnesses gathered themselves.

"Is he always like this?" I whispered to Runar.

"He is a prickly arsehole, but he's been worse since he's had to be both hoard-keeper and god-speaker. Don't judge him too harshly, Edda. We've all suffered at Hraki's hands and this could save us."

I nodded. That was something I could understand. Something about the way Alvilda had been thrown out of her depth and still managed to help me on the journey, whether she meant to or not, had made me want to take her under my wing. My need for justice against Hraki had only been brewing for weeks. Fainn and the rest of them had months of pain and blood to account for.

The two witnesses looked to Alvilda. The woman straightened and glared at the law-keeper whilst the man looked as though he just wanted it to be over.

"I am Law-Keeper Alvilda, here on behalf of the High King. Can you tell me what happened here?" Alvilda's tone was firm but soothing.

"Hraki," the woman said and spat onto the ground. "He sent a few fighters to burn our farm to the ground so he could sneak his longships by."

Alvilda nodded and turned to the old man. "Is that true?"

"Aye. One of them Windborn came and did this. There was a couple of other fighters with them. We had no hope against them. They started burning everything. Runar came and helped us, but the fire had hold by then."

"When did this happen?"

"A week or two ago," the old man said with a shrug. "It's all been a bit of a blur since then."

"Are you going to help us or not?" the woman snarled. She took half a step forward with bunched fists. Alvilda flinched from the woman's fury, but stood her ground.

"I will if I can," the law-keeper said. "Are you sure it was Hraki's men that did this? Not outlaws or anyone else who had a grudge against you?"

Behind the two farmers, Fainn threw his hands in the air. "Who would possibly—"

"I am asking the witnesses." A hint of iron slipped into Alvilda's demeanour.

"No," the old man said. "It couldn't have been anyone else. I remember the Windborn who did this. He faded in and out so's you couldn't see him. Nal they call him. He's one of Hraki's anyone will tell you."

"And was this Windborn the one that attacked you?" Alvilda asked, looking between the witnesses.

The young woman's gaze flicked back to Fainn who gave a near imperceptible nod. "Yes, that was him."

Alvilda's expression hardened and her mouth compressed into a thin line. Runar and I made our way forward as though getting closer to Alvilda and her judgement would bring Hraki to justice all the sooner.

"Well?" Fainn said, pushing his way to the front. "There's your evidence, law-keeper, now send your birds back to the High King. We can bring Hraki to justice once and for all."

Alvilda looked from Fainn and back to the two witnesses. She picked at one of the pillars and examined the blackened wood underneath her fingernails.

"Not yet," she said. Fainn opened his mouth to protest, and I took half a step forward, but Alvilda cut us both off with a slash of her hand. "I will speak with the witnesses alone. I don't think I can trust the truth of their words with you giving them cues."

"This is outrageous."

"Alvilda," I said, my voice more soothing than Fainn's outburst. "Is that really necessary? These people have told you what happened, and it agrees with Fainn's account. Gods, it agrees with Runar's account too. Is it really necessary to string this out any more? The longer we take to move against Hraki the more people he might hurt."

Uncertainty glimmered in Alvilda's eyes. Fainn's outbursts had done nothing but strengthen the law-keeper's resolve and stubbornness. I hoped that softer words would tilt her thoughts to action, show her what needed to be done.

"Hraki's people might well have done this," Alvilda said after a moment of thought, "but consider the possibilities if they didn't, Edda. What if this was the work of outlaws? I am not working against any of you, but if I make the wrong call then more innocent people will get hurt and it will be my fault. I must hear their testimony alone to be sure of it. I will not risk rushing into this and making the wrong judgement when lives hang in the balance."

I wanted to say more, to take her by the shoulders and shake the words I wanted out of her, but it would do no good. If I forced the judgement I wanted then would we be any better than Hraki bribing the last law-keeper?

Fainn and Runar looked to have come to the same conclusion.

"Fine," Fainn snapped. "Be quick."

Alvilda took the witnesses away so that we couldn't influence the interrogation. She walked them around the ruined farm until they were hidden by the broken, burned ruins. Their long winter shadows were still visible to us and I recognised the formal posture and movements as Alvilda asked them to make an oath. I guessed an oath for truthful testimony. As she questioned them, Alvilda pointed to the house, presumably asking them questions about parts of the building. The only response I could see to her questions were nods or shakes of the head.

"This is a farce," Fainn said. "Who does she think she's dealing with? Some common swindler? I am a god-speaker. I am in charge of King Erling's treasury. My word should be more than enough for her."

"Be quiet, Fainn," Runar said. "The girl is doing what she's been sent here to do. Moaning about it will only piss her off."

The Windborn got up and stretched until his back cracked. I kept my eyes on Alvilda's shadow until a bird fluttered into view and landed on the house. The raven cawed then hopped over to the law-keeper, keeping far enough away not to be a bother but close enough to hear.

"What's with the raven?" I said and wandered over to Runar.

"It's a bird."

"I know that, but there's something else to it, isn't there, like the elkhound? Something to do with Gerda?"

He scowled and scratched at his side. "It's not for me to say."

"I'm sure that raven has been following us ever since I met you at the Althing. I've thrown a stone at it more than once."

Runar laughed. "I like that. Maybe it'll teach her not to spy so often."

"Does she talk to them?" I felt foolish asking, but when talking about Windborn I didn't want to rule anything out.

"Not exactly. It's not my place to talk about another Windborn's powers," he said.

"Why not? You told me about Lothi's."

"That's different. I was telling you about the enemy. I'm not going to spare Lothi's feelings when he's going to try and kill you. I'll tell you that she doesn't talk to those animals. It's deeper than that."

"What happens then?"

Runar shook his head. "Ask Gerda. I won't tell you what it is, but I will tell you not to kill that bird. She won't like it."

I looked up. The bird had hopped its way to the wall closest to me. It squawked at me and fixed me with one beady eye. I felt around on the ground and picked up a pebble without taking my eyes from the bird. It screeched and hopped back over to Alvilda.

"I'll keep that in mind," I said and skimmed the stone across the fjord.

Alvilda returned alone a short while later. Her mouth was twisted into a pensive expression and stared into the middle-distance. She had sent the witnesses off on their own and we watched them trudge back to town.

"Well?" he snapped. "Do you have enough evidence yet, law-keeper?"

"I have their testimonies, but it's not enough for me to make my decision."

"What?" Fainn and I shouted at the same time.

I bit my tongue to keep myself from saying anything I might regret, but Fainn was not so restrained.

"You have a farmhouse that's been immolated after the raiding season. You have testimony from two people that this was Hraki's doing. What more evidence could you possibly want? Do you want a confession from Hraki himself? Heed my words, for they will save you time: Hraki is a sly, conniving bastard and he will kill you if he cannot buy you."

"I want more evidence before I start a war. Take me to Katja."

"Gods help us all," Fainn cried and stormed off towards the boat. "We'll all be dead before we get a decision out of you."

Now that Fainn had gone, Alvilda's expression softened and her posture slipped. She shrank away from the stance of a noble law-keeper and became the scared girl who had comforted me on the longship.

"I'm sorry," she said. "I need to make sure that everything matches up. I can't—"

"It's okay, lass," Runar said. He floated over to her and put a hand on her shoulder. "It's noble that you want to do the right thing, but don't wait too long, eh? Fainn might be a prick, but he's right. We don't have forever to wait for a decision."

Alvilda bit her lip and nodded. Runar slapped her on the back and went over to the boat to get it ready.

"Come on," I said. "Let's get away from this place. It reminds me of things I don't want to remember."

The law-keeper nodded and hurried over to the boat. I sighed and followed. My axe bounced off my leg as I walked and I wondered how long it would be until I could sink it into Hraki.

*

As soon as we got back, Erling summoned Fainn and Runar to discuss Alvilda's decision. From what muffled shouting I could make out through the thick doors of the mead-hall, the king was just as furious and frustrated as Fainn. I had been asked to stay outside, but my indignation quickly faded as another tirade filtered through the doors.

"...dare she call into question ... a child the High King has sent to keep us busy..."

I picked at my teeth. The elkhound sat nearby, its grey eyes staring straight at me. I bared my teeth and it huffed and laid its head down on its paws. Something in its eyes made me shiver so I pushed myself up and walked off. I didn't like the idea of Gerda's minions watching me, or her watching me through the dog, or whatever was happening.

I wandered through the buildings, trying to find someone to talk to and take my mind from the raging discussion in the mead-hall. I heard something from within the Windborn longhall but I soon discovered it was the grunting and moaning from behind Valna's curtained room so I ducked back outside. Next, I thought to find Tove, but all of the servants avoided me. Whenever I managed to get someone to talk to me, they quickly found an excuse to leave. Eventually, I snatched a skin of mead from someone's kitchen and wandered along the shore. I drank straight from the skin. Its sweetness was tempered by a smoky aftertaste and I was glad for its warmth coating my throat.

The chunk of ice we had skated on was still there and I felt a smile tug at my lips. I had never imagined myself to be someone who depended on the company of friends, but I had depended on Bjolfur being by my side. Now I sat alone, hundreds of leagues away from the ashen grave of my homestead with nothing but alcohol for company. I ran my fingers over the scars on one arm. What if Alvilda didn't rule against Hraki? What would I do then? Perhaps I should ask Erling to let me go and start a farm and put this all behind me. Or I could...

A shape on the horizon interrupted my thoughts. It seemed that one of the longships tied across the fjord had gotten loose and was drifting across the water. I stood on the boulder to get a better view of the line of tethered ships. The sound of a beating drum carried on the wind as a hazy shadow drifted into focus.

A sail.

A mast.

A longship.

I leapt down and sprinted back to the mead-hall. People gawked as I whipped past them. The doors were still closed when I reached the mead-hall and the sound of raging voices still came from inside. I turned to the elkhound. It sprawled in a patch of sun, breathing slow and deep.

"Hey," I called out to it.

No response. I stomped over and knelt next to it.

"Wake up," I repeated and shook its side.

It jerked awake and yawned.

"Gerda, you're in there, aren't you?" I waved my hand in front of the dog's eyes. "There's a longship coming to the barricade."

The dog started to lick my outstretched hand. I pulled it back.

"From upstream," I said, in case the dog didn't understand me. "It—"

A bird called from above, cutting me off, and I saw the raven perched on the edge of the roof. I stood, ignoring the dog, and turned to the bird.

"Okay, I don't know if you can hear me, Gerda, or if I'm making a fool of myself, but there's a longship coming. You—"

The bird swooped down off the roof straight towards me. I ducked, cried out, and put my arms over my face. I felt its wings brush against my arms, but no sharp talons. Its laughter cawed out as it disappeared in the direction of the barricade and I swore under my breath.

"You're not making this easy, you know," I said to the dog.

He snorted in response, then pushed himself up and wandered over to the mead-hall's door before looking back pointedly at me.

"Are you serious?"

Bark.

I sighed and pushed open the doors. The air inside was still hot from the argument and weighted with a sharp tension. Everyone except Gerda turned to me, or the dog, as we entered.

"There's a—"

"We know," Fainn snapped.

The king leaned forward in the throne with his gaze locked onto Gerda. Fainn and Runar stood to the left, staring at Gerda with the same intensity. The dog padded straight past them to Gerda and she slid her fingers through the fur of its shoulders.

"We can see the longship," she said to the room. Her tone was distracted and her empty eyes pointed towards the floor.

"It is small. We can only see six people aboard, just enough to pilot the craft it seems."

"Could there be more?" Erling asked.

"Possibly. I can't see anywhere they could hide."

Erling began pacing in front of the throne. "Can you see anything else? Any other ships in the distance?"

"No other ships. I could send Sjofn to scout the trees."

"No, that would take our eyes off the longship. Who is on board?"

Gerda shrugged. "No one I recognise, but one had an iron arm-ring. Ah, he's calling out, asking for someone to talk to him."

"What does this one look like?" Runar asked.

"He has fiery red hair and a plaited beard, but I cannot see more from here. He moves with arrogance and keeps leaning out from the figurehead as a child would."

"Soren," I growled.

"Who?" Erling said, his head snapping round to look at me.

"Hraki's newest Windborn," I said. "I fought him at the Althing. He can summon flames from nothing. Seems like an odd choice to send on a wooden ship."

"He seems like an excellent choice to me," Erling muttered. "How close are they to the barrier?"

"Close enough to leap onto it," Gerda said. "They have weighed anchor and seem to be waiting. He still calls for talks."

"There can be no harm in talking to them," Fainn said. "Send me out with a boat. Gerda can keep her raven above us and hear what we have to say. Perhaps talking with a god-speaker will remind them of the gods' laws and keep them in line. If not, then Runar will be able to help."

I clenched and unclenched my fists. Soren's face flashed in my mind: at the cliff edge where I died; in our fight in the Althing.

"I will go with you," I said.

"You?" Fainn sneered.

"Why should I send you, Edda, when Runar would be better suited to this?" Erling asked and sat back down in his throne.

"I have beaten Soren before, but he doesn't know I'm here. Send me out with him and see if my presence unnerves him."

Fainn scoffed and shook his head. "That is ludicrous. What good will goading him do? If they come to wash away the bad blood then let me go alone, or if I must be accompanied, then let Runar do it."

"No," Erling said with a wave of his hand. "Let Edda go. Runar will be ready to help if they move to violence. Let them see Edda has joined us and wonder who else we have brought to our cause."

Fainn scowled and folded his arms but didn't dare contradict his king.

"Go. Find a boat and see what they want. Runar, go and fetch Alvilda. This should help sway her judgement."

Gerda eased herself into a seat and the elkhound looked expectantly at us from the doorway. Runar nodded at Erling and swooped out of the hall. Fainn picked up his staff and gestured for me to lead. As we walked the only sound that bounced between us was the dog's panting and our own footsteps. I would have liked to head back and retrieve my axe and shield, but when I made to deviate from our path Fainn barked at me that there was no time and commandeered both from a nearby huskalar.

News of Hraki's longship had spread and all the longships and rowboats that had been out on the water now stuffed themselves into the jetty. We got into the same boat we had used to get to the farm earlier and I readied the oars.

An old man rushed up to Fainn as he made to get on the rowboat, wringing his hands and with worry writ large on his face.

"Is it another attack? My children are alone at home and—"

"It's not another attack," Fainn said in a surprisingly soft tone. "Hraki has sent a representative to speak with us and that is what I am going to do. There is only one fighter on the longship and the rest are simply crew. They have only come to talk. Don't worry about your children. Head home if you wish."

The man nodded, relief washed over his face, and the tension in his shoulders eased. "Thank you, god-speaker, if it's as you say then I'll keep up my work here. The children will keep themselves busy."

Fainn put a hand on the man's shoulder and offered him a

smile. "They will be fine, friend."

As soon Fainn clambered into the rowboat his expression soured. "Let's get on with this."

We cut through the water, bumping into the small lumps of ice floating on the fjord, and as we closed in on the line of tethered longships Fainn held up a hand.

"That's far enough."

We drifted between two of the longships and Fainn caught the rope tying them together to keep us from drifting further. Hraki's longship waited about twenty paces beyond the tethered longships. Fainn stood, stumbling as another chunk of ice collided with the boat, then primped himself up to his full height and looked over my head.

"Hail, stranger, you wish to talk?"

A pause, then a shout from a deathly familiar voice.

"Aye. Who's come to do the talking?"

"Fainn Bjornson, god-speaker for King Erling. Who has come to talk for Hraki?"

"Me. Take your first look at Windborn Soren Gunnarson. Make note of this, holy man, people will ask you of the day you first met me."

I turned about on the bench so that I could see what was happening. I couldn't help it. Soren leaned against the figurehead with his arms crossed and a smirk on his lips.

"What do you want?" Fainn called out.

Soren pushed himself off the figurehead with a shrug. "We want what Hraki's always wanted: passage past Erling's little town and out into the sea. I have come to make it happen. These kingdoms have worked together for years, if not as allies, then as trading partners at least. Do not let this single unfortunate episode cause a rift between people with such deep history."

The stilted way he reeled off the words and his disinterested tone made it clear he had been instructed to spout the speech. He didn't seem to care.

Fainn glanced down at me. "What?" he hissed.

I wasn't sure what Fainn meant then I realised I was growling. "I don't trust him," I said.

"You think I do?" he whispered to me, then raised his voice

325

again. "And we want what Erling has always wanted: the body of his son and the blood-debt for the damage you have done to us. Do you have the prince's body? Or the gold for the lives you have taken?"

"The prince's body is gone. Fallen down a mountainside or something," Soren said and picked at the figurehead. "If you want the body then go and ask the moles and the rats, or whatever else lives under the mountains."

"Why won't you tell us where it is?" Fainn persisted. "We have a Windborn who can fly. If you will not risk your Windborn to retrieve the body, then let us."

Soren looked over at us, one hand stroking his plaited beard, thinking about how to respond, but then he shrugged. "I can't tell you where it is, holy man. Hraki hasn't told me. So either you agree to give us passage or—"

His eyes went wide and I felt his hot glare on me. He threw his head back and laughed.

"It's the ice bitch. You just can't keep away from me, can you? If you want to fuck me, that's all you've got to say. I'm right here. No need to chase me all the way up north."

My hand moved to my axe. Rage churned at the pit of my belly. My fighting muscles itched.

"Why don't you come on over and we'll see what happens?" I called out.

"Oh, well I'd love to, but there's this big chain of boats in the way. How about you get your friends to move them? We'll get some ale, have a little food, and see where things go?"

My stomach turned at the thought and bile tickled the back of my throat.

"The longships will remain where they are until we get the blood-debt," Fainn shrieked. His eyes bulged from their sockets as he looked from me to Soren and back. "This is not an opportunity for you to find a new partner."

"I need him close to kill him," I growled.

"Well, Hraki sent me to get rid of the longships one way or another," Soren called. "One last chance, holy man, are you going to move them?"

"Not without the prince."

Soren nodded as though he hadn't expected anything else.

He grinned at us, wide and sharp, then turned back to his crew. We couldn't hear what he said to them, but it looked like Soren was at odds with them. One man folded his arms and shook his head. Soren took the man by the neck and lifted him clear off the deck. Smoke crept out between Soren's fingertips. The man nodded frantically and Soren dropped him. He scrambled away and the rest of the crew fell into place at their benches. After a moment, oars slipped out from the sides of the longship like the slender legs of a beetle. They dipped into the water and pushed the longship gently forwards until it butted up against the chain of boats.

Gerda's raven swooped down and landed one of our rowlocks.

"I don't like this," Fainn said. His eyes, filled a moment ago with anger, were now rimmed with fear.

"Me neither. Gerda, if you can hear me, get Runar out here."

The raven croaked and hopped.

"Is that a yes?" I said, unsure whether I should ask the bird in front of me or the man beside me.

Fainn's attention was locked onto Soren's longship. I glanced over to see the Windborn stretching to the empty ships blocking his path.

"What is he doing?" The god-speaker scrambled to the back of the boat as though Soren was coming straight for him.

The air around the Windborn started to shimmer like the air above a campfire. The weight of my Windborn arm-ring pressed against my arm. It was a promise, an obligation, my first oath after my resurrection. I couldn't let Erling's longships be destroyed. They were the only thing keeping Hraki penned in. I glanced at Fainn. Fear shone in the god-speaker's eyes, but there wasn't time to get him to safety and stop Soren. I cursed and slammed our oars back into the rowlocks, earning a furious squawk from the raven, and pedalled us towards Soren as fast as I could.

Fainn stumbled and fell back into the boat, hitting his shoulder on the keel as he went. "What are you doing?"

"He's going to burn down the ships."

"With what? Don't..."

Soren jumped aboard the empty longship and burst into

flame. He held his arms out wide as though receiving praise from an adoring audience and flung blazing gouts of fire onto the neighbouring longships. The flames caught, their jagged red edges rising and falling like gnashing teeth.

"We have to get away," Fainn cried.

He grabbed my arm and tried to rip the oar out of my grip. I threw him off and gave the oars a final heave, hoping it would put us close enough.

"Get Runar," Fainn screamed at the raven. "Get Orin. Get Valna. Gods above, help us!"

The bird screeched and flapped. It looked utterly confused. I took the axe from my belt and waited. The boat, still moving on the final surge from the oars, slowed and then bumped up against the longship Soren stood on.

I leapt.

Behind me, the boat rocked dangerously and Fainn yelped. The splashing of water incongruous as I entered the dry, intense heat on the burning longship.

Soren hadn't noticed me. He stood at the deck's edge shooting flames out along the line of tethered ships, setting one after another ablaze.

I readied the axe in a white-knuckle grip and shifted the weight of my borrowed shield. I crept forward as quietly as I could in the growing blaze. A single swing. One good swing and I would have justice. Out of the corner of my eye I saw a silhouette appear on the horizon.

"Edda," Runar called. He hovered above the deck of the burning longship, one arm outstretched. "I'll get you off there, just—"

Soren spun around at the sound of Runar's voice and saw me. He snarled and shot a spout of flames at me. I raised my shield, caught its red teeth on the cold wood.

"Get Fainn out of here," I shouted. "I'll deal with him."

"You should—"

"I'll be fine."

I kept my attention on Soren. Embers fell from his fingers.

"There's no one to stop me killing you this time." His words dripped with gleeful bloodlust and the grin slashed across his face was the kind of smile reserved for wolves and madmen.

I said nothing. I watched his eyes, waiting for that split second tell that would show me his next move. The Windborn powers within us called out to each other, trying to pull us together. Soren circled the edge of the deck. I matched him step for step.

All around us was fire. The longship bucked beneath our feet as one of the timbers cracked and snapped and then a great hiss as part of the burning ship fell into the water.

Soren threw a burst of flames at me, and then another. Each one bounced off the shield and dull heat seeped through, singeing my arm.

I pulled on my Windborn powers and tried to cover myself in some protective ice, but it slipped. The power felt slick and wet, warm almost. I gritted my teeth and tried again, harder.

A film of frost crept up my arm and onto the shield. It wasn't much, but it was enough. The frost's cool touch on my skin gave me respite from the blazing heat.

I lunged forward, shield out to catch another blast of flames and then swung hard with my axe.

Soren ducked out of the way. The axe caught the edge of his shirt and tore away a chunk of fabric.

He snarled.

A flame-wreathed hand came at me. No time to move the shield. I grunted as his fist slammed into my ribs with a flare of pain and then a deeper, wilder pain as the heat and flames clawed at my skin. I gritted my teeth and tried to ignore the sizzling, the smell.

Soren made to hit me again and I slammed the shield edge into his shoulder. He stumbled back a step.

I brought the axe round again. My arm jerked as the axe bit into his shoulder. Soren's eyes went wide and he screamed.

He twisted and the axe-head tore free. Hot blood spurted from the wound. It sprayed onto me, hissing and steaming as it came into contact with my hoarfrost protection.

Soren used his momentum to shove me away. I stumbled back and tripped over a plank warped by the heat. As I fell, the longship bounced dangerously, the wood all around me splintered and spat embers.

I dragged myself upright with teeth bared and prepared to

rush forward in another attack. There was another shuddering crack and the longship canted, bringing with it a surge of water. I stumbled as I tried to keep my balance and splashed through the hungry shallows creeping up the deck.

Panic thundered through me.

As I tried to pull myself free of the rising water I glanced up. Clouds moved over the pale winter sun and a sudden gust of wind whipped the flames all around us. Shadows surged for a heartbeat as though the fingers of the gods came to claim us. The cold water crept up to my knees and I was transported back to the cliff-edge where I died. Again the water rose to meet me, but this time there would be no coming back.

A groan from Soren brought my attention round. He leaned against the gunwale on the other side of the deck and had one hand over his wound. Smoke snaked through his fingers and flesh sizzled. The acrid scent of his cooking skin swept over to me as the wind picked up again, making my stomach turn.

"You can't win," he panted and pushed himself up. "One way or another you're going to die here. I'll take you. The flames will take you. The water will take you. It's over for you."

He winced then slipped a knife out of his belt.

"I'll kill you before I let the water take me again," I yelled.

He grinned and held the knife up, ready. He tested his arm and I saw the scrapes along his forearm closing, his Windborn powers healing him even as I tried to kill him.

I edged forward.

The sound of my splashing footsteps competed with the roar of the flames and was joined by the sound of rainfall. I circled, finding my way onto planks of wood that looked like they could take my weight.

Soren slashed at me with his empty hand and a line of fire whipped towards me. I ran into it, shield raised, and pushed through the searing pain. I swung the axe low, aiming for a kneecap, but Soren was faster. He spun out of the way and brought his knife up to slash across my face. Its razor edge slit open my cheek, caught on the bone, and then sliced through my nose.

My shield blocked his next swipe and I stumbled back. I tried to wipe away the blood, but it had already frozen on my cheeks.

"Edda." Valna's voice called out from beyond the flames.

Soren's furious gaze moved from me to something behind me. He snarled a wordless curse and sprinted away from me. I leapt after him. One of the planks, weakened by the flames, snapped under my foot and I fell, my leg caught. Soren vanished from sight.

I waited until I heard him hit the water, to be sure it was not a trick, then turned. I saw another vessel through the flames, tinted with the burning red. Too small to be a longship, or too far away to be any use.

Another gust of wind dampened the flames long enough for me to see Valna and Runar, her standing in the boat and him floating above it.

"Edda, are you still there?" Valna cried out, panicked.

"I'm here," I screamed back.

I tried to pull myself free of the splintered wood. Ice clutched at me where my leg hit the water and it was too wide to pull up through the gap in the wood.

Once, twice I yanked myself up before the wood splintered and I could stand again.

The flames were the only light now. Black clouds rolled above me like waves and smoke suffocated everything else. The rain, now a torrent, hissed like a horde of snakes as it hit the water and flaming ships.

I moved down the longship to its sinking side as carefully as I could.

"I'm—"

The figurehead, its bottom half-submerged and top half aflame, snapped as I leaned on it. I cried out and stumbled back to stop myself falling into the water. I dropped my axe and fell onto the burning deck. In the blink of an eye, the heat ate through the frost I wore and burned me.

Valna appeared, a wordless shout of pain and fear escaping her. She stumbled, bouncing from the burning mast, embers catching her clothes, then she saw me.

"Edda," she cried.

We fumbled towards each other. Thick smoke turned Valna into a deep shadow. I swiped through the air, trying to find her hand, but the sinking longship and the swirling smoke kept us apart. Sparks and flames erupted from beneath us as the fire closed its jaws on the planks beneath our feet.

The steaming waves reached up to drag me under.

Something caught me under my arm and then the world turned inside out. Everything went dark. I felt weightless and as though my stomach was being forced up through my mouth.

The world reappeared and Valna let go of my arm.

We were on the boat.

We fell apart and I wretched, trying to cough up the ash coating my throat. The smokeless air felt smooth and cool in my lungs. I fell back and lay on the deck. Runar stood at the stern and Valna was bent over, on her knees, spluttering.

"Valna, you mad fool," Runar growled once he was sure we were alive.

He took hold of the prow and pulled us away from the burning line of longships. I fell as the boat jerked, tripping over Valna. Her breathing was shallow, the skin of her cheeks was cracked and dry and her clothing singed. I called her name but she couldn't hear me.

Lightning split the sky. Thunder shook my bones.

"We need to get out of here," Runar shouted over the rising storm. "Get on the oars."

There was nothing I could do for Valna now. I moved her from the bench then put the oars in their place.

I felt my hackles rise. As I turned to face the burning longships and put the oars to the water another spear of lightning struck. The mast of the longship I had been on exploded. Burning splinters stabbed into us.

The lightning severed whatever held the longship together and it collapsed in on itself. Each end rose as though in salute and then sank, glowing red as it disappeared beneath the waves.

Runar grunted and the boat moved faster. I ignored the thousand searing splinters in my arms and rowed. My breathing, fast from fear, changed to the deep, smooth breathing of hard labour.

I watched the storm as we moved away from its fury. The clouds swirled and twitched with lightning, the rain thundered.

Something about it made my heart pummel the inside of my ribs. This was not the first time I had seen a storm like this. The way the lightning stabbed through the air like the sky was breaking; the wind whipping the waves into barrows; the movement of the dark clouds above like wolves as large as the horizon. All of it sent my mind reeling back to another storm when a hand, slick with seawater, had slipped through mine.

After a handful of heartbeats, we passed the storm's border and it died away. The rain and wind were gentle around us, but they still raged all around the longships under the shadows of the storm clouds.

Runar lowered himself back into the boat and we let our momentum carry us forward.

"What could make such a storm?" I muttered.

"That," Runar panted and gestured to the shore, "would be Orin. The Storm Weaver."

A crowd had gathered on the beach to witness the destruction. A gaunt old man stood on the shore in front of them, ankle-deep in the shallows. He had his arms outstretched and the wind whipped at his clothes, though the crowd behind him was unaffected. Sparks danced between his fingertips and a moment later a flash came from behind us. Another crash as lightning struck the longships.

"Has he done this before?"

"A few times. The worst one was a few weeks back, just before the end of the raiding season. Hraki tried to push to the sea and Orin made a storm to stop him. It was like nothing I've ever seen before. It stopped Hraki's longships, but Orin had to push the storm out to sea before it destroyed any of our ships." Runar shook his head. "Thank the gods you weren't in that storm's path. It would have torn your ship apart."

Runar kept his eyes on Orin. He didn't see my expression change, harden. I couldn't thank the gods for anything. They had not stopped Orin's storm before it took my husband, and now his storm had saved me from the flames. I could almost hear the Trickster laughing. I clenched my jaw and looked at Orin, the Storm Weaver. He stumbled, flicked his lightning-wreathed hands out once more, but the storm was made, the damage done.

ALEX S. BRADSHAW

My heart cracked. Out poured my black-feathered grief, fury and vengeance in its wake, and aimed its sword-sharp beak at the old man with a storm between his fingertips.

334

CHAPTER SIXTEEN
THE BROKEN CHAIN

ORIN COLLAPSED AS WE CAME UP TO THE SHORE. People rushed up and caught him before he hit the sands, then carried him away on a stretcher.

I want to say that I pushed through the press of people to reach him, to hold him accountable, but the adrenaline had left me. I felt only the hot scratch of my wounds and the dull ache of my bruises. My hands shook.

People rushed over as we stepped out of the boat. I batted away their fussing hands. My wounds had already frozen over and there was nothing they could do for me that time would not do on its own. We directed them to Valna's quiet form.

Someone elbowed their way through the crowd.

"Valna!"

Olek. The huskalar wore only a chain shirt, as though he had rushed to join the fight but had only managed to half-dress himself before it ended.

"Oh, Valna, what happened?"

"She jumped into the flames to save me," I said as gently as I could. "She's still breathing."

Olek knelt in the sand next to the boat and put a hand in front of Valna's mouth to feel the gentle proof.

"She'll be okay, son," Runar said and put a hand on Olek's shoulder. "She's tougher than most of us. Just give her some time to rest and she'll be fine."

Tears welled in Olek's eyes and he nodded. Runar and I lifted Valna onto the stretcher. Olek clutched Valna's hand tightly in both of his and rushed away beside her.

Now that the injured had been taken away all eyes turned to

the ebbing storm and the makeshift longship barricade. At the centre of the chain, the fire burned unchecked and had turned five of the longships into immolated anchors. Beyond those, the storm washed away the flames before they took root. Charred driftwood began to collect on the shore. A couple of children pushed their way free of the crowd, grabbed some driftwood, and started fighting with them. Somewhere in the distance, the heavy silhouette of Soren's storm-drenched longship disappeared upstream.

Another opportunity for justice, gone.

I sat down heavily on the ground. Water soaked my legs, making my clothes heavy against my exhausted limbs. I tried to push the Windborn power from my soul, freeze my clothes and at least stop the fabric sticking to my skin.

Nothing.

The power that had thrummed within me now only twitched, exhausted. My eyelids drooped and I yawned. The skin of my face felt taut. I reached up and ran my fingers lightly over the wound on my face. A frozen splash of blood covered the cut, from my jawline up and along to slice through my nose just beneath the bone. I picked a chunk of frozen blood from my cheek then let my hand fall limp and closed my eyes.

The murmur of the crowd quietened and was overtaken by quick footsteps over the sands. Two voices, one furious and the other placating, grew closer.

"...someone out there to fix the gap in the defences. This is exactly what Hraki wants. A pathway. And we've just given it to him on a fucking platter."

Erling.

"There was nothing we could do, my king. The Windborn set the longships aflame before we could—"

Fainn.

"We could have bought some time if you had invited him to speak with me directly."

"But, we could not—"

"You should have forced him. If we had invited him over the barricade maybe we could have saved it."

I opened my eyes and sat up. The king and his god-speaker were alone at the edge of the shore. Fainn stood still, wringing his hands and trying to appease the furious king whilst Erling paced back and forth, staring out to the burning wreckage.

"Runar," Erling called. "Go and tell Gerda to send out her birds. I don't want a fucking thing to move out there without me knowing about it. We can't let Hraki get through."

"Yes, my king," Runar said whilst lifting himself into the air. "She won't be able to yet. I can't even fly through those winds. It will—"

"I know," Erling snapped. "Just get them out there as soon as she can."

Runar nodded and flew away.

"And you," Erling spun to face me. "What the fuck happened? You only went to talk and now you've burned five of my longships?"

"He didn't want to talk," I said.

"It doesn't sound like you tried to keep him talking. You should have kept him distracted."

"He stepped onto the longship," I said, voice churning into a growl. "He started to burn it down. I tried to stop him."

"It doesn't matter now," he said. He moved past me down the shore and watched the storm. "Orin at least managed to save some of the longships." His voice was quiet, something about the sight of the burning storm dampened his fury.

I looked at him. The tired slump of his shoulders and the deep-set shadows under his eyes. He stared out at the crooked, charred line of longships. I felt my own sorrow, fury, and grief echoed in those tired shoulders. Within me, the black-feathered grief lost some of its edge. He had lost a son and was doing everything he could to bring him back. Was he so different to me? Was that not why I found myself sat on a distant shore, staring at burnt ships with my face cut open?

I sighed and pushed myself to my feet.

"We'll find him, or we'll kill Hraki," I said, slapping a hand down on Erling's shoulder.

He stiffened. "You would talk so easily of taking a king's life?"

"When he's taken so much from me? Yes."

I let my hand slip down to my side and left Erling to watch his ships burn.

*

The air all around Erling's island was thick with worry and adrenaline. The first that most people had known of Soren's arrival had been watching Fainn and I rowing out to see them. For everyone else, their first warning was the flames. People huddled together and talked in hushed tones. They clung to one another, their eyes flickered about nervously as though waiting for an attack to spring out of the shadows at any moment. Some sagged with relief when the birds left; a black cloud blossoming over the island, twisting as it rose. Tendrils reached out then broke into crows, blackbirds, starlings, gulls and others I didn't recognise. The birds flew around the fjord like guards at a fort. Some circled in small circuits, others perched in trees, and more flew back and forth over the fjord. I watched them leave, then stumbled to the Windborn's longhouse.

It was empty.

The blanket walls billowed in the cold breeze from the door. I collapsed onto the floor that served as my bed without bothering to remove my sodden clothes. My eyes fluttered closed, I was ready for my exhaustion to finally overtake me and drag me to sleep.

But it didn't.

The longhouse filled as I lay there. Valna shuffled in with Olek and they murmured to one another for a little while until falling to silence. Some time after that, the elkhound came in. I didn't hear Gerda, just the padding and panting of the dog as it sniffed its way past me and then slumped onto the floor. All the while the storm played over and over in my mind. The lightning between Orin's hands sparked underneath my eyelids.

After what felt like hours, I pulled myself out of bed and left the longhouse. Other than a phantom wag of the dog's tail, no one seemed to notice and I stepped out into the night.

Orin's storm had dragged all of the clouds with it and now the stars looked down, bright and infinite. In the distance I thought I saw the flicker of green across the sky from the Winds but it was gone as soon as it appeared.

I made my way between the buildings around the mead-hall.

The water frozen into my clothes shattered and sloughed off as I walked. Thunder still echoed within me and my fists clenched and unclenched. Several rodents skittered across my path, rushing from one piece of rotten food to the other, and I heard an owl call in the distance. No one but the rats and their hunters were awake.

I wandered until I found a stretcher resting against a house. I stopped and pulled the knife from my belt. The door opened without a sound and I leaned my head through the doorway. In the room, outlined in the starlight, a frail figure lay opposite the door.

I stepped through and closed the door, then fumbled around until I found a lantern, lit it and pointed it towards Orin.

He was blanketed in several thick furs and his breath came shallow, though his wheezing enveloped the midnight quiet. Sweat glittered on his forehead. The image of a frail old man was almost enough to stop me. Then the thunder echoed in my bones and I felt sea-slicked fingers slip through my fingers. I tightened the grip of the knife in my hand and tested the weight of it against my palm.

"If you're going to kill him you'll have to kill me too."

I spun around, knife forward and hunching to a crouch.

Gerda sat in the shadows behind the door. Her head lolled against her chest and her breathing was laboured. She was in no state to move against me, but I didn't know what creatures she had with her.

"Would you stop me?"

Gerda's face was as sallow as Orin's. Her bones stark, sharp lines against her skin.

"I would try, but I doubt I could."

I straightened, relaxing a little without moving the knife away from her.

"I've looked through a thousand eyes today, but I didn't expect to see anyone come at Orin with a knife."

"Why are you here, then?"

A rat skittered along the bench and sat on Gerda's shoulder. I looked from the rat's shining eyes to the shallow pits where Gerda's eyes should have been.

"Orin and I have known each other a long time, girl, and it's nice to see a friendly face when you wake up, isn't it?"

Her words prickled as they struck.

"It is," I murmured. "He took that from me. The storm he threw out into the ocean before the raiding season ended..."

Gerda gave a slow nod, beginning to understand. The rat twitched its nose and clambered across to her other shoulder.

"Why don't you come and sit by me and we can talk about it? No need to do something that can't be undone." She shifted along the bench to make room for me to sit. "While we're at it, I can clean some of that blood off your face."

I squeezed the knife. The leather-wrapped around the handle creaked. The rat's ears twitched. I had come here to do something sharp and full of wrath, but Gerda's simple offer of kindness softened my intentions. I sighed and slipped the knife back into its sheath.

Gerda nodded again.

"Bring me that bucket. Don't worry, it's clean."

I brought over the half-empty bucket by the foot of Orin's bed and placed it between us on the bench. Gerda felt around behind her and pulled out a cloth which she dipped into the water.

"Tell me if it's too cold," she said and dabbed it against my cheek.

"Cold isn't a problem."

Gerda snorted a laugh. "I suppose not."

She worked the cloth gently over the cold, dry blood on my face. After a few swirls, she held the cloth up for the rat to inspect. It sniffed and at some signal I couldn't see Gerda rinsed the cloth then dabbed at my face again.

"How do you speak to them?" I asked.

She shrugged, the rat hunched down as she did to avoid falling. "How do you summon ice? There's something inside me now, and I can see through their eyes—which is handy since I lost mine—and get them to help me."

"You control them?"

"Not really." She dipped the cloth in the bucket. "I encourage them to help me. If I tried to control them, they'd fight and then neither of us get what we want. That was a hard lesson. No, I make suggestions and they follow them. They know that

I'll feed them or pet them or whatever they want so they don't mind."

I nodded, which made her miss with the cloth and she got my eye.

"Don't move, you stupid girl. It's hard enough to do this with rat eyes."

I grunted an apology and we fell into a companionable silence. The only sounds in the room were Orin's wheezing, the squeak of the rat and bench, and the occasional splash of the water.

"There we are," she said at last. "There's something in the wound, I can't see what, and it doesn't want to be cleaned."

My heart sank. I glanced down at the scars over my arm, now shining in the lantern light.

"It's ice. Seems to be happening to me a lot lately."

"We're all broken in our own ways," she said and threw the cloth into the now murky water.

"Do you want to tell me why you came in here with a knife for a sleeping old man?"

I looked from her to Orin and then pulled the bucket over. It was too dark to make out much in the reflection, just the dark silhouette of my head. I ran my thumb gingerly over the new scar. My skin, rough from years of sea air, became frictionless ice just below my cheekbone. I felt my nose and the frozen scars there. It was as though my skin didn't hold back blood, muscle, and bone, but instead I contained cold waters waiting to freeze at the first touch of air.

"I lost someone because of him," I said and put the bucket down. "He's the reason I'm here."

"Did you come north to kill Orin?"

"No. I came for Hraki."

"Can you wait to deal with Orin until we've put this mess with Hraki behind us?"

The crow gripping my heart ruffled its hateful feathers, but the deathly old man before me did not conjure the same rage I had felt when I saw the storm. My hand went to my stomach and the ice covering the wound Soren gave me on the cliffs. "I guess Orin can wait."

"Probably for the best, girl."

She fished a small piece of bread out of a pocket and fed it to the rat. It snatched the bread then jumped down from her shoulder and disappeared in the shadows. A low thump came from the door. My hand went to my knife.

"Easy with that," Gerda said as the door bumped open and the elkhound padded in. "You're welcome to stay here with us, girl."

"No."

I stowed the knife again and made to leave. The elkhound sniffed at me as I passed and I scratched its ears, a reflex. I pulled my hand away and saw Gerda smiling at me.

"He's still a dog. He still likes his ears scratched."

The hound sniffed at my hand again but I pulled back and left.

When sleep finally came, it was fitful and full of dreams. I found myself alone on a longship travelling through endless fjords with ever-splitting paths and I never knew which one was the right one.

*

I woke up alone. I gathered my axe and shield as I left the longhouse and made my way to the mead-hall. Though the sky was clear, the air was still heavy with the weight of the storm. People scurried about their tasks with quick footsteps and none of them looked up. All took pains to avoid the mead-hall.

I heard the voices before I entered the hall. The words were muffled from outside, but the fury in them was clear. I pushed the door open enough to let me slip through and ducked straight into the shadowed corner of the room.

Erling sat, face flushed and hands gripping the carved arms of his throne. A naked sword lay across his knees, flashing in the flickering light. The law-keepers and god-speaker stood in front of him. Alvilda stood a few paces away from the others as though wanting to keep herself safe. Katja and Fainn stood on the throne's other side. Fainn's hands clenched into fists and Katja had her arms crossed. Valna sat slouched against Gerda on a bench ahead of me. Her cheeks were still raw and red from the fire's touch and I was thankful that my ice-wrapped soul had saved me from the fire's heat. She offered me a weak smile. I sat down next to her and squeezed her hand. She shifted her head from Gerda's shoulder to mine.

"And why not?" Erling growled. "Are you not here to decide for the High King whether war can be waged on Hraki?"

"The High King was clear," Alvilda replied, "that I am to collect all information that I can and offer advice on a judgement. It is not my place, nor has the power been granted to me, to declare war."

Fainn threw his arms in the air. "Can't you see that war has already been declared? What would you call the burning of our ships, if not an act of war?"

"Perhaps a retaliation. I don't know what happened out there."

"We have told you what happened," Fainn said, taking a step towards the law-keeper.

"I understand your concerns, law-keeper," Erling interjected. His sharp words stopped Fainn in his tracks. "But we must move quickly. The longships were chained to deny Hraki access to my lands. It is my right to decide who I let cross my lands, and now that defence is destroyed. Do you want someone out there who would so easily flaunt the laws of the gods?"

Alvilda looked from the king to his keepers and took half a step back.

"I have sent word to the High King and asked for his judgement with all haste."

"A bird is not fast enough," Erling said and slammed his fist down on the throne's arm. "This is ludicrous, we—"

"These are the stipulations you put on the High King when you submitted to him," Alvilda shot back. Her cheeks flushed and her fists clenched. "A key part of the treaty that your father signed states that war cannot be declared, no raids can be launched, no blood can be spilled in winter. It is only with the express approval of the High King himself that such actions can be taken. No law-keeper could do it on his behalf. It is very clear."

Erling's jaw muscles bunched and he turned to Katja who nodded.

"If you are so worried about speed," Alvilda went on, "then send Runar with the message. You say you sent him to the Althing before, why not do so now?"

"We were not at such a disadvantage before. He is too valuable."

In the eaves, I shrugged a gentle warning to Valna that I was about to move. She murmured and shifted her head back to Gerda's shoulder. Valna looked much better already, her puckered, dry skin had resolved to an angry red, but the healing process clearly left her with little energy.

"What about what Soren did?" I asked, stepping from the shadows.

"What do you mean?" Erling rumbled.

"He was the one that broke the parley. Surely there is some recompense that we can take there? If Hraki cannot be held accountable without waiting for word from the High King, then we should go to Hraki and take Soren prisoner."

"Take him prisoner?" Fainn said, incredulous. "He's just burned our longships and tried to kill you. He needs to be executed."

Everyone frowned at me. Katja's eyes widened and she stepped up to stand beside me.

"Yes," she said. "Surely we can go to Hraki now and ask him to give us the Windborn who burned the ships? We can put aside the issue of the actual attack for now and wait for the High King to make the judgement, but Hraki can give us Soren."

"If Hraki hasn't given me my son's body or the blood-debt he owes me, then why would he do this?"

"Because we have a law-keeper from the High King," I said. "Alvilda, you would agree that Soren was the one that burned down the longships. That much, surely, is beyond contention?"

She narrowed her eyes at me, wary of a trap. "Yes, if he can be proven to wield fire as you say, or if he could have otherwise set the fire on the longships."

"Then it would follow," Katja chimed in, "that the one who set the fire can be brought to King Erling's halls to face justice for the crime of destruction of property. The greater crime and the question of war can be left until we have heard from the

High King. The only obstacle would be if Hraki refused to hand over a member of his household, but as you are one of the High King's law-keepers then you can force him to hand over Soren. Is that not also written in the treaty?"

"It is," Alvilda said.

"Then let's go," I said. "We will take Soren for burning the longships, starving Hraki of one of his Windborn."

"And if he refuses to give up the Windborn?" Fainn said.

"He must," Alvilda said. Her words more confident now. She had caught on to the fact that doing this would dampen Erling's fury long enough to hear back from the High King. "I can judge on this and Hraki will be forced to abide by my decision."

"Good," Erling growled. "I was beginning to forget why I swore to abide by the High King's laws."

Alvilda bristled at the comment and straightened to her full height, though she was still a head shorter than the rest of us.

"I will sanction this only as a diplomatic endeavour," she said. "Its purpose is to decide whether the Windborn Soren did break the laws of guest protection that is automatically afforded both parties in a parley. If I am able to judge in your favour, then King Hraki must give up the Windborn as a hostage and to be transported here for your judgement, or else pay for the damages you have sustained either with gold or with longships in kind. I trust that this will be a suitable course of action to keep your hand from your sword, King Erling?"

Erling cocked his head to the side, surprised at her firm tone, but he tipped his head and Alvilda nodded back.

"You will not find fault with me sending my Windborn with you, I trust?" Erling said. "These are dangerous times and I would not wish to lose one of the High King's personal law-keepers on such a trip."

Alvilda looked over us, at the scarred people watching from the shadows, and nodded.

"Good. Edda will go, of course, to identify the Windborn that burned my ships. And I will send Fainn and Valna to accompany you too."

"Very well. I will make my preparations," Alvilda said with a bow then turned to Katja. "Law-Keeper, if you could please watch for a message from the High King I would appreciate it."

345

Katja nodded her acquiescence. Once Erling waved a dismissal, Alvilda left the mead-hall. No one spoke until the law-keeper was well out of earshot.

"Runar, you will stay here. We can't leave ourselves totally unprotected and your speed is better put to use here than tethered to the speed of your companions."

"Aye, my king, as you command."

"Katja," Erling went on. "What do you think of this? Is it worth us chasing after minor victories when Hraki may well be bearing down on us as we speak?"

"What else can we do?" she said with a shrug. "Alvilda won't completely denounce Hraki without the approval of the High King. The kings insisted on that part of the treaty to stop corrupt law-keepers declaring war on their own whims. At least this way, as Edda says, we can strip Hraki of some part of his power—whether that's a Windborn or gold or ships—until we get the decision from the High King."

"Fine," Erling said. He sank back into his throne and tapped the arms of the throne. "Edda, Valna, Fainn. Get yourselves ready. I want you to leave as soon as possible."

CHAPTER SEVENTEEN
THE BEAUTY OF THE WINDS

WE PACKED ONE OF ERLING'S LONGSHIPS with provisions and warriors and made ready to leave. My nerves surged as I walked up to the longship. The freshwater of the fjord didn't instil the same gut-wrenching fear as the deep, ravenous sea but something about travelling on a longship sent a shiver through my soul. Perhaps the salt in the oceans had burrowed into me and carved the fear deep into my bones. I took a breath and walked out along the jetty.

"You okay?"

I turned and saw Runar drifting towards me above the water.

"I'll be fine."

He landed on the jetty next to me and slapped a hand down on my shoulder. The Windborn energy within us sparked.

"It'll be okay, Edda," he said. "You're going upstream so there's no way you're going to sink, no waves to throw you overboard. And besides, Valna's going with you and if she's willing to jump onto a burning longship to save you, you think she'll think twice about jumping in the water?"

My insides writhed at the mention of going overboard, but I nodded and tried to smile at him. What Runar said made sense, but there was no logic to the terror burrowing through my marrow.

"Thanks. I'll be fine."

He didn't look like he believed me, but he nodded and picked up a barrel to fly it to the longship.

"You're part of Erling's household now, Edda," he said then went back to loading the ship. "We'll keep you safe."

I shifted my bag and shield over my shoulders and stepped onto the deck. My stomach dropped as the longship lurched with my weight. It bobbed in the water and I took a deep breath. I nodded to the other people readying the longship for our journey, stowed my belongings, and then went about helping them move supplies.

Valna arrived after about half an hour. She had her arm slung through Olek's and she leaned against him as they walked. She still looked pale with dark rings under her eyes but she wore her weapons and armour. It felt odd to see Valna ready for battle again, though she wore the armour so naturally. I had become used to the sight of her in dresses as they so easily fitted with her free-flowing smile.

"Don't even think about it," I said when she tried to begin helping with the barrels. "Go and rest. There's furs there for you to lie down."

"I'm fine, Edda," she mumbled.

"You're well enough. You need your rest. I can handle this."

She shot me a half-hearted glare which was undermined by her smile.

Katja arrived shortly after with Alvilda by her side. She gave a perfunctory inspection of the longship and declared us ready to depart. The crew threw off the ropes mooring us as I raised the anchor. Runar pulled us out into the fjord, occasionally flying ahead to move debris or ice out of our way. Progress was swift and we soon reached the broken chain of ships.

We looked over the edge of the longship to see charred skeletons of the boats we couldn't save staring from beneath the cold waters. Through the shimmering waves those black, curved timbers looked like the bones of some monster rotting under the water. Some people shook their heads, a waste they called it, and cursed Hraki.

The atmosphere changed as our prow moved beyond those drowned corpses. It felt as though the line of longships, broken as it was, marked the edge of safety. The shores pressed in on either side of us as the fjord narrowed. The shoreline grew from low slopes and hillocks into crags and mountains that rose to steal the sunlight from us. Everyone's gaze darted around, looking for anything that might attack from the shore or from above.

"This is as far as I go," Runar said. "Good luck."

Runar kept pace for a moment before letting us float by. Valna rushed to the figurehead at our stern and waved frantically. Runar smiled and returned the wave before he flew back to Erling.

"You look better than you did this morning," I said to Valna as the crew deployed the oars and sail.

Valna turned, still leaning on the gunwale. "I'm tougher than I look, you know."

"You look tough enough to me."

I leaned on the gunwale next to her and looked ahead. The fjord was now a river that curved around a rocky outcrop. Underneath the shouts of our companions and the splash of the oars, the wind rustled the firs sprouting from the high slopes on either side. Birds called to one another and a raven swooped so close I felt a feather brush my nose.

"I hate that bird," I grumbled.

"Oh don't let her get to you. Gerda likes to wind people up. And from what I hear you've been throwing stones at that bird for ages."

My mouth twisted into a grimace. The raven landed on a nearby barrel and flapped its wings. We watched it preen its feathers and call out nonsense to the crew. I glanced at Valna, her eyes were closed and she took deep breaths.

"Thank you," I said. "For saving me from the longship. I don't think I could have made it out on my own."

"I'm sure you would have managed. You look pretty tough." She grinned, then looked down and picked at her arm-ring. "It's what friends do, isn't it? They help each other and make sure they're okay."

I watched her for a moment and edged next to her. She looked up as our shoulders bumped together and the Winds within us flashed like a surging bonfire.

"It is," I said. "I'm glad I've got you to keep me safe."

Valna's face split into a broad grin and she leaned her head on my shoulder, letting the flicking power crackle within us. She pulled a strip of meat from her pocket, held her arm straight and offered it to the raven, who promptly hopped onto her forearm and began picking at the food. I shifted away from the bird and turned my attention back to the fjord. Someone at the prow was shoving the sheets of broken ice out of our way with a pole. After some time the captain called out for Valna and me to take up oars. We set to our task and for the next few hours the longship carved through the water like a knife through cloth.

At sunset, we beached the longship at a bend in the river and made camp. The crew fell into an easy rhythm borne of repetition and familiarity. They set up the tents, pulled the supplies from the longship, and had a campfire set up in short order. Valna and I carried the heavier supplies from the longship. We dragged some boulders and fallen trees around the fire and soon everyone was sitting comfortably with a cup of mead and a bowl of stew.

I sat on a log with Alvilda and Olek, chatting with Olek about his life as a huskalar. I imagined his days working as a household guard could tell me much about my new life as Erling's Windborn had in store. Valna came over to sit between me and Alvilda.

"So," she said, "what was it like to grow up in the capital? It must have been amazing."

Alivlda kept her shoulders hunched and took a drink before answering. "I loved to watch the boats come in. They'd come from all over and you never knew what they'd bring with them or who would get off."

"That sounds fantastic," Valna said and sounded like she meant it. "You must have so many friends there." She refilled Alvilda's cup and lowered her voice to a conspiratorial whisper. "Did you leave someone special behind?"

"What?" Alvilda's cheeks flushed.

She glanced at Valna to see if she was being serious. Valna's mischievous grin was answer enough.

"You can tell me. There must have been someone?"

Olek pushed himself up from the log.

"I think I'll go and talk to Snorri," he said. He tipped his cup in farewell and wandered to the other side of the fire.

"Oh, good, now it's just us girls," Valna said as she refilled all of our cups.

"It wasn't that interesting," Alvilda mumbled. "I had to stay with the other law-keepers, mostly. We got to wander around the city maybe once every month or so. Not very exciting."

"Trust me, Alvilda, as a farm girl, that sounds plenty exciting to me."

Alvilda straightened and turned, frowning, her eyes shining from the mead. "A farm girl? You're Windborn. You can do incredible things."

"You get used to it," Valna said with a shrug. "I'd rather have grown up in the capital, if I'm honest."

Alvilda shook her head in disbelief.

The fire danced and spluttered as the night was filled with conversation and laughter. I sighed. The memory of my last raid dredged itself up in my mind. The campfire had been much the same. My husband had been next to me then and my heart had been full of courage and love. Now it was saturated with rage.

"Will you show me?" Alvilda said quickly.

"Show you what?" I said, wondering if I'd missed anything.

"Your powers," she said. "I've never seen a Windborn use their powers up close before. The High King is very strict about it."

"I remember," I muttered into my cup.

"Of course," Valna squealed.

She downed her drink and picked up a fist-sized stone from the floor. "I'll play catch," she said.

Alvilda made to get up from her seat. Valna pushed her back down and threw the pebble out towards the fire. Alvilda watched the stone arc out towards no one and turned to Valna, a question forming on her lips. Valna disappeared and reappeared in time to catch the stone. Alvilda's jaw dropped. Valna tossed the stone back and shifted back to her seat on the log, catching the stone easily. She did this a few more times, Alvilda's wide eyes followed the stone and Valna's flickering form with disbelief.

"Edda, can I see you use yours?" Alvilda said, shaking with excitement.

Valna reappeared on the bench between us, tossing the stone up and catching it with one hand. I offered them a small smile and moved my hand to cover up the scars on my forearm.

"Mine isn't really that impressive," I said. "It—"

"Is this really how you should be spending the evening?" Fainn yelled. He'd had enough mead that a slur tainted the edges of his words. He put his hands on his hips and swayed a little. "Wasting your energy showing off? We need you rested and ready."

Everyone turned to watch. It wasn't every day that someone shouted at a Windborn. Alvilda had hunched back over, staring at her feet. Valna scowled and went to say something, but I got in first.

"Sorry, Fainn." I refilled my cup and offered it to him. "We'll stop."

As he reached out to take it I pushed my power into it. Frost flared underneath my fingertips. He nodded and took the cup. He was too drunk to notice what I'd done, how cold the cup was.

"Quite right."

As he tried to take a drink a look of confusion spread on his face. He glared into the cup and tipped it until a chunk of frozen mead fell out and hit him right between the eyes. Fainn spluttered and looked up, trying to figure out what hit him. Laughter broke out around the campfire. Fainn turned around, confused, then looked back in the cup with a scowl.

"Very funny," he said. He threw the cup at me and stomped back to join the others.

"You shouldn't have done that, Edda," Valna said. She tried to throw me a stern look but couldn't hide her smirk. "He'll be grumpy about that for days."

I shrugged and gave myself a healthy refill.

We sat in the glow of the fire and let the murmuring of friendly conversations wash over us. At some point a raven swooped down and landed in front of Valna. She started talking to it, asking if it was Gerda or a real bird, and ended up feeding it strips of dried meat.

"How does it happen?" Alvilda asked in a whisper.

My stomach twisted at the question. Alvilda's eyes washed in and out of focus and I wondered how much she'd had to drink and how well she handled it.

"How does what happen?" Valna said.

"Becoming Windborn," the law-keeper replied.

Valna froze with one empty hand outstretched. The bird squawked at her and flew away. For a heartbeat, I smelled salt and felt like I was falling. My breath quickened. The cliff-edge in front of me rising, too far away to latch onto, and the hungry waves below me roaring in anticipation.

"Oh, that's not a story you want to hear," Valna said with forced cheerfulness. "It's not a story for tonight. Why don't you tell us more about growing up in the capital? Did you ever get to eat any exotic foods?"

Alvilda was deep enough into her mead that either she didn't notice Valna's tone or didn't care.

"No, no, I want to hear about you and—"

"It's not really something we like to talk about," Valna said, squirming. "We don't—"

My mind played out the smothering touch of ice-cold saltwater. I shivered and shifted closer to the fire. Then I remembered the night Valna and I spent on the shore of Erling's island, the weight that seemed to lift from her shoulders once she'd told me how she became Windborn.

"I'll tell you," I cut in.

Alvilda's face lit up, no longer a nervous law-keeper, but a teenager waiting to hear a gory tale.

Valna's expression darkened. "No, Edda, you don't have to. We can talk about something else."

"It's okay." I put my hand on hers and squeezed. "I want to tell you."

Valna didn't look convinced. I downed the rest of my drink and poured myself another.

"I'd just come back from a raid. My husband didn't make it home."

The words pulled a lump up into my throat and I took another drink before I could continue.

"Why didn't he make it back?" Alvilda asked with all the tact of a drunk.

Valna shoved her to try and shut her up, but I waved her down. I wanted to tell them, to see if Valna would recognise the storm that had killed my husband and realise who had sent it.

"It's okay," I said. "He didn't die on the raid, nothing so lucky. It was on the way back. We were weighed down with our plunder and a storm hit us."

I described it as best I could. Some of the descriptions were too much for me and the sentences fell away. Piece by piece I described the storm. Valna kept her gaze down and avoided looking at me.

"That sounds terrifying," Alvilda said.

"It was."

"Edda, I'm so sorry," Valna whispered. I wondered if she was sorry for the storm, the loss of Bjolfur, or the loss of his share of the plunder.

"That's why I was out on the cliffs. I wanted to make him one of the Blessed Drowned. I stood on the edge of the cliff, ready to throw his runestone into the ocean, and then I saw the boat."

"What boat?" Alvilda said, she had moved to the edge of the log and leaned forward, hands clasped together.

"Wind-hunters," I said. "I put up a good fight but not good enough. They threw me from the cliff and I drowned."

"How many did you fight off?"

"Some," I said with a shrug. "It's not important. They turned me into a Windborn and by the time I found my way back, my house was gone. They'd burned it down. All I've got left is my husband's shield."

Neither of them said anything. I glanced at Valna out of the corner of my eye. She looked miserable and stared into her cup. I poured some more mead for each of us.

"Maybe we could have fought them off if we'd avoided the storm." I watched Valna for a reaction. Nothing. "Maybe two of us would have been enough."

"You can't play that game," Valna whispered.

"What game?"

"What if?" She looked up at me and I flinched at the tears and raw hurt in them. "Wounds can't heal if you keep picking at them. You can't wonder at what could have been. I've done that for so long. It just means you keep bleeding. You can't heal if you don't accept what's happened."

I looked away from the ferocity of her gaze and down at my

arms. The scars scattered across them glittered in the firelight and then with an eerie green light. The clouds had cleared and through the barren branches of the trees I saw the flickering lights of the Winds.

"I don't think I heal properly anymore," I said.

Alvilda, seemingly ignorant of the tension, looked up and pointed to the dancing Winds in the sky. "Aren't they beautiful?"

We watched the Winds, but they were only beautiful for Alvilda. For Valna and I, the Winds were a reminder of everything we'd lost and everything that could have been. I looked at Valna and our eyes met. Even in the dim illumination of that night I saw the skin still red from her burns. She tried to smile but it turned into a grimace. The light from the Winds painted every worried line in sickly green.

*

The weight of that first night's conversation pressed heavy against my chest. I had hoped that telling the story of my death would lift some weight from me, but it had only dragged my feelings back to the surface. I spent the rest of our time on the longship sullen, trying to keep my black-feathered grief from suffocating me entirely. Thankfully, I spent most of my time on the oars and there was little time for talking.

The captain told me we were travelling to a waterfall at the bottom of the Norskug mountains to avoid risking sailing past his villages and other longships. It would be a longer walk for us once we got there but overall it would be better, he said, to journey through the forest and avoid the risk of open confrontation. I understood his logic but thought he would have risked more if he were the one to do the walking. Eventually, the longship came up to the waterfall which fell into a small lake. Ahead of us the mountains rose out of the forest canopy and stabbed into the overcast sky. We landed and the few of us who would be making the onward journey began to prepare, whilst the rest of the crew set up camp.

Before we started our trek, Valna offered me a cup of mead. "Before we leave the rest of it behind," she said with a smile and

355

toasted me with her own cup.

It didn't fix my low mood, but it helped.

Fainn and Alvilda readied themselves in a few moments. All eyes turned to Valna and I. Next to the god-speaker and law-keeper we looked like wolves beside cubs. I carried Bjolfur's axe and shield with several knives at my belt whilst Valna had a sword and shield, her long knives and a spear. For a moment, I could have been back on those foreign shores preparing to take whatever we could with our strength alone.

"Ready," I said.

Valna nodded. Before we left Valna ran up to Olek and said goodbye. I turned away. This was a tender moment of parting and it belonged to them alone.

The snow under our feet was unreliable and more than once someone slipped on some unseen obstacle. After a while I pushed ahead to walk in front. I solidified the snow as I went, turning each footstep from a slippery gamble to a stomping surety. Our route took us up the mountain paths and the evergreen trees, dusted with snow, grew thinner the higher we climbed, though once in a while a bird fluttered out from the branches to swoop over us.

"We're still being watched then?" I asked as Valna came up to walk with me.

"Of course." She had her arms wrapped around herself and was rubbing her arms. "Gerda's always watching out for us, even so far from home. It's reassuring, isn't it?"

I pressed my mouth into a thin line. "It doesn't matter how far we get from her?"

"I don't think so. She's never told me if it makes a difference, anyway."

Our path took us through low valleys where the mountain blocked the sun and the snow lay deep around us. The others hunched over and shivered in the harsh cold, but they agreed that travelling over snow was easier than trying to clamber over icy rocks. As we trekked across the mountain surrounded by nothing but snow and shadow, it felt like we trespassed on the realm of the Lofmyrk trolls. They were vicious spellcasters employed by both the gods and the Giants during the god-war. It was their magic that had forged the Líkrifa, the executioner's axe forged from shadow so sharp it had sliced the Giants souls from their bodies, turning them into the Winds.

The next day we came upon footprints in the snow and smooth sledge tracks. These markers of civilisation felt out of place after our time in the wilderness surrounded by unbroken snow and shadow. As we rounded the next outcrop of rock we saw twisting tendrils of smoke in the distance.

"That should be it," Valna said.

"Everyone stay wary," Fainn called from behind. "We don't want any surprises. And keep your weapons sheathed. Let's not give Hraki's people a reason to get aggressive."

Valna slid a knife back into her belt and offered a half-smile by way of apology. When Fainn's back was turned she stuck her tongue out at him.

Our pace slowed as the trees thinned and the snow was replaced by the muddy swirls of winter roads.

"What if they mistake us for a war party anyway?" I said.

"Why would they do that?" Alvilda said.

"We've got two war-ready Windborn leading the way. It would be an easy thing to do."

"There's no way we would be attacked." Alvilda sniffed. "We are now deep into winter and there is no ambiguity as to whether an unprovoked attack would be legal."

"Unprovoked?" Fainn asked. "What if burning down the ships is provocation enough?"

Alvilda strode forwards, ignoring the question, but I heard her mumbling about precedents and winter warfare. Now that we were out of the wilderness it seemed that Alvilda was settling back into her role as law-keeper.

We crested a rise and found ourselves looking at a fortress perched at the edge of the forest. Gated earth walls, much like those that surrounded Konvald, curved around a town built at the bottom of a cliff. A gate stood in the middle of the walls, and the walls themselves encircled the town so any attack on Hraki would either need to breach the palisades or deal with the steep, sharp mountainside.

"Valna, you go out first," I said. "You'll be able to get out of there if there's any trouble."

She nodded. Her eyes, locked onto the fortress gates, had

lost all levity. The girl full of laughter was gone, and here was the vicious, efficient warrior I first met.

"I'll see if I can get someone's attention," she said.

"I should be the one to open a dialogue," Alvilda said and took a step forward. "I am the reason we're here."

I grabbed her arm.

"Let's get the gates open first," I said. "Once we're inside, you can do the talking. Let Valna go ahead for now. It's safer, in case they think we're here for retribution."

"But—"

"This far from the High King's throne the laws aren't as powerful as you think," I growled.

Alvilda glared at me without heat. I let go of her arm. She didn't move.

We moved down through the edge of the forest, keeping a safe distance behind Valna. Figures appeared along the walls, calling out to people behind them although we couldn't make out what they said. The space around the walls had been sheared clean of vegetation and a few boulders had been pushed away from the fortifications. It had not been maintained, however, as saplings and shrubs dotted the killing field, though none were large enough to provide any real cover. Valna put out a hand to stop us as we got to the edge of the trees. A raven landed in one of the branches near my head and cawed at me.

"Wait there," Valna said.

She passed me her spear then walked out into the open space, hands held above her head. The guards on the walls started to move and shouted amongst themselves. One of them nocked an arrow and moved to a gap in the wooden wall.

"We've come to talk," Valna called out. "We bring a law-keeper from the house of the High King. She seeks an audience with Hraki and the Windborn Soren."

More guards appeared, spears ready to throw at Valna. One of them stepped onto a small platform behind the walls as his head and shoulders bobbed up above the height of the wooden planks.

"Who are you sworn to?" he said. "The High King?"

"I'm sworn to King Erling," Valna said, her arms still up. "Law-Keeper Alvilda is sworn to the High King and has come to discuss what happened at the parley."

"Oh aye?" He rolled his shoulders. "Why should I believe you? Seems you might want revenge."

Alvilda snorted and mumbled, "This is ridiculous." She made to storm forwards. I grabbed her again and hissed at her to stay.

"Law-Keeper Alvilda just wants to talk," Valna called out. "We only came to keep her safe."

"You don't want to talk," someone called. "You're never interested in talking."

A spear flew out from behind the wall and went straight for Valna. She sighed and disappeared a breath before it would have pierced her then reappeared a few paces to her right. The guards shouted and cried out. Someone launched another spear without conviction and it landed far too short.

"We're just here to accompany the law-keeper. Do you think we'd march up to the gates if we were here to do anything else?"

The guards' spokesperson seemed to consider Valna's argument, but the rest looked unconvinced.

"I couldn't say why ye's coming up and talking to us like this. Could be a trap. We's got orders not to let anyone in. So yer not getting in, much less yer friends over there."

He started to step down.

"No, wait, the law-keeper is here to—"

"So you say," the guard called as he disappeared behind the palisade wall.

"Let me go," Alvilda whispered. "This clearly isn't working."

A fierce energy burned in her eyes. Valna seemed to be at a loss. Her hands had dropped to her sides and she craned her neck to look for someone else to talk to.

"Fine," I said. "But I'm coming with you. Stick close unless you want to be skewered by one of their spears. Come on, Fainn."

"What? Where are we going? Are you going to storm the gate?" he hissed.

I readied my shield. We made our way out of the trees to a fresh rippling of attention from the guards. Alvilda marched over the open space like she owned it. I kept close, alert for any projectiles. Fainn scurried along in our wake.

"I am Law-Keeper Alvilda from the house of the High King. I am here to talk with King Hraki. Open the gates."

More faces appeared at gaps in the walls. They eyed us, sizing us up. I took half a pace forward so I was between Alvilda and whatever weapons were hidden behind the walls. The law-keeper scowled at the walls and clenched her fists.

"I am here to discuss a matter of utmost importance with your king on behalf of the High King. By the laws of—"

"We're no opening the gates, lass," the guard called out over the walls.

"They won't listen," I said.

"They have to," Alvilda replied, incredulous. "It's part of the treaty..."

I shrugged.

"Come on," Fainn said. He tugged on Valna's sleeve and took half a step back towards the trees. "We're exposed out here."

Valna nodded and I was about to agree when there was a commotion at the walls. Shouting. Valna whipped out her shield. I tossed Valna her spear and pulled out my axe.

"Go, get back. Carefully," I said.

Alvilda fell into my shadow and Fainn fell into Valna's. We inched towards the tree line, our shields up and weapons drawn.

Someone else popped up in the same place the guards' spokesman had. This one looked different. He was wrapped tight in furs and had no weapons I could see.

"I hear that someone out here is claiming to be from the house of the High King?" His voice, high and whining, cut through the winter air.

Alvilda shoved past me. "I am from the house of High King."

"Do you have anything to prove that?"

"My arm-ring," she called back. She held her arm forward, though her thick cloak hung over her arm-ring.

The man sighed. "Very well. You alone may enter."

"You would leave my companions out here? In winter?"

"One of your companions has demonstrated her Windborn abilities. Another of your companions seems to be dressed for a summer stroll, leading me to believe she is the Windborn Edda that I have heard so much about. Tensions are high. I would be a fool to invite those two within our walls. What if they decide to start killing everyone? We could stop them, yes, but at what cost?"

"What?" Fainn cried. "We would never—"

"Easy," Valna whispered. "He's trying to get a rise out of you."

He stopped shouting and scowled up at this new messenger.

"You see?" the man on the gate said, gesturing to Fainn. "Even their god-speaker is aggressive. How can we trust such creatures? The High King would agree with me, I am sure."

I glanced back at Alvilda. She frowned and chewed her lip, then took half a step forward. She looked from the gate to me and then back to the gate as though she was moments away from agreeing to enter the fortress on her own.

"We're not being left out here," I whispered. "There's no telling what they'll do to you in there. What if they kill you and then rush out and kill us? With your authority we cannot be turned away, but when we stand apart we are all fleas to be caught and crushed."

She looked from me and back to the gates.

"Where else will they go if they do not accompany me? They have brought me this far, to turn them away now would be a disservice."

The man shrugged. "They can look after themselves I'm sure."

A moment of tense silence passed. Valna and I scanned the guards on the walls, waiting for one of them to reach for an arrow or ready a spear.

"What about guest-friends?" Fainn shouted up. "The gods decreed that if we are all guests of the household no harm shall come to us and none shall be dealt out. Surely you can agree to that?"

The figure at the gate cocked an eyebrow as though Fainn had shouted at him in a foreign language.

"Guest-friends?" the man repeated. "That would require some faith between the parties involved and you have proven you cannot be trusted."

"I will be there to witness the oath," Alvilda shouted. "It will be as if the High King himself is witness."

The man scowled and disappeared from view. I made out the sounds of an argument over the rustling of the evergreen leaves and bare branches. Eventually, the fur-clad spokesman reappeared over the gates.

"We will open the gates," he said with a sickly smile. "We would not want to insult the guardians of the High King's law-keeper. I hope you will not think unkindly of me for my caution. Safety is not known to follow foreign Windborn, after all."

Alvilda sighed with relief as the spokesman's head disappeared once more. Valna and I glanced at each other. Neither of us eased our grip on our weapons.

A great scraping and groaning sounded from the gate and it swung out and open. Alvilda strode forward into the growing gap, leaving us to trail her like hounds.

"I don't like this," Fainn said.

"Neither do we," Valna said. "All we can do is make sure the law-keeper is safe and makes the right decision without being strong-armed."

Two guards, one for each side of the gates, eyed us as we walked through and then began straining and pulling the gates shut behind us. We caught up with Alvilda, who had stopped a few paces inside the courtyard. She pulled herself up to her full height, which was not as impressive as she thought, and smoothed her clothes.

The spokesman appeared ahead of us trailing several ragged, clinking guards. He was tall, a head taller than any of us, with long, lank hair falling to his shoulders and a gaunt frame visible even beneath his layers of elk furs.

"Welcome, Law-Keeper Alvilda. I am Law-Keeper Reynir," he said, and sketched a half-bow. "Welcome to the home of King Hraki. Apologies that we cannot offer a grander welcome than this, but times are hard and winter is upon us."

"Of course, Reynir. I thank you for the welcome that you can offer us. I have come on the High King's behalf to speak with the Windborn Soren. He was involved in an incident a few days ago and I would hear his side of things."

I let their conversation wash over me, their words were too

smooth to be genuine, and they made me shiver as they slithered through my ears.

White dusted the courtyard's muddy ground where the snow had been improperly cleared and shoved into white slopes against the walls. The rustling of the trees and scratch of the wind was dimmed inside the walls and, except for the droning of the law-keepers, there was little sound. The few people that wandered around, clutching bundles to their chests, had the same ragged look as the guards and their faces were gaunt. At the edge of one house, a woman watched us. She never took her eyes from our party, but her hands moved deftly fletching arrows, one after another. A single repeating noise broke through all other whispered sounds of the courtyard: the rhythmic clang of a hammer striking an anvil.

"These people look desperate," Valna whispered to me. "I can't see any food or beer or anything."

I nodded, not wanting to speak with so many sallow eyes staring at me.

The houses, too, seemed like decaying shadows from another place. Debris, perhaps once caught up in a breeze and now trapped against itself, pressed up against the buildings or had become locked within frozen puddles. Barrels and crates lay cracked open like the carcass of a forest spirit.

"Yes, please, Reynir," Alvilda said. "I, for one, am excited to meet King Hraki."

Reynir led the way out of the courtyard. The guards circled us and put themselves between us and the gate.

"Will it be you that makes us guest-friends?" I asked, making sure my voice carried. "Or does the king need to do that?"

Reynir paused and turned. His eyes glared daggers at me.

"Alas," he said with a forced smile, "I am unable to perform that particular rite myself. Once we see Hraki, you will have your guest rights."

Reynir led us on an uphill path that wound through the buildings until we came to the mead-hall. The stench of desperation grew heavier the further we walked. Some of the houses, with broken roofs or doors clogged open with snow, looked abandoned. My Windborn energy swirled within me, recoiling and reacting to Windborn I couldn't see. The hairs on the back of my neck rose. Valna slowed her pace and we fell a few steps behind our companions.

"Do you feel that?" I whispered.

She nodded and she squeezed her spear tight.

We arrived at the mead-hall. It matched Erling's hall in size, but that was where the similarities ended. Where Erling's approach was full of carefully maintained columns dedicated to the gods only four short columns led to Hraki's halls. The columns were canted as though tipped in a storm and no one bothered to right them again. One of them was snapped in half. Mud and snow caked them so that whatever images the heartwood held were hidden beneath a layer of much and snow. The mead-hall's doors stood ajar and Reynir pushed through without preamble.

Once I adjusted to the darkness, I saw it was much the same as the outside. Banners hung from the rafters, tattered and aged, their images long lost to grime. Rubbish was scattered across the wooden floor and much had collected in the corners and underneath the dust-covered benches. There was a fire pit carved into the centre of the floor and within it coals smouldered, the first sign I'd seen that this town was not simply a corpse waiting for the maggots to die.

The only sound was the hiss of the fire and the rattle of weapons as people shifted in the shadows. It was difficult to tell which of the figures watching from the shadows were townsfolk, retainers, or what passed for huskalar. All of them wore something to protect themselves and had weapons cradled in hand.

Beyond them, on a raised platform, a shadowed figure sat. He pushed himself from his throne and stepped forward into the dim light of the fire.

Hraki.

He was broad-shouldered and well-muscled, with shoulder-length blond hair tied back and a trimmed beard. His clothes were clean and finely made, in stark contrast to everyone around him, and a golden brooch tinkled in the firelight. For a heartbeat, I was taken aback that the font of so much of my pain was not deformed or hate-twisted, but instead walked with a dignified grace.

Then I remembered the weight of saltwater in my lungs.

My heart stuttered and my hand strayed to the axe at my belt. My black-feathered grief thrashed against its bone cage. Its razor-beak rammed at my chest as though trying to force me forwards to kill the king.

Hraki smiled down at us, easy and welcoming, and I wondered how quickly the guards would reach me if I leapt for him.

"Welcome," he said. His deep voice boomed out into the hall. "Be welcome, my friends. It is not often that we receive winter visitors so far north."

He stepped towards us and threw his arms out wide in greeting. The motion drew my attention to a bench behind the throne. For the first time since I had drowned, I felt a chill run up my spine.

The bench was shoved right up against the back wall and was packed full of people. As I looked down the line of hunched figures, the Wind within me writhed, either trying to escape from these strange, powerful shadows or to join them, I didn't know. They were all Windborn. One of them had red hair, bright even in the gloom of the hall, and he shot me a shit-eating grin. I pulled my hand away from my axe and took a deep breath to steady my heartbeat and calm my fury. Beside me, Valna shifted her feet ready to run or fight, I wasn't sure.

"I have been told you have come to discuss our parley. From what Soren recounted, it seems it did not go well. I hope that if we have been sent a law-keeper from the High King it is so that we can untangle this disagreement? I presume this means Erling will finally allow us to pass through his waters?"

His tone was fatherly, as though we were errant children returned from teasing his livestock and now was our gentle reckoning. The words flowed over me like grease on water.

"You are right that we come to discuss the recent parley, King Hraki," Alvilda said, oblivious to the tension in the room. "I have come to discover what really happened. The testimony of the Windborn Edda is that your Windborn, Soren, attacked without provocation and burned the ships of King Erling. If I determine that this is the truth, then I propose that reparations are made to King Erling. The value of the ships can be paid to him or the Windborn Soren can be handed over for justice."

I ground my teeth when Alvilda referred to me as though I were an object, but managed to stay my tongue. Throughout Alvilda's speech, Hraki's expression was a picture of rapt attention and as she made her pronouncement for punishment it transformed into a perfect blend of shock and astonishment.

"I must thank you for bringing this to my attention, law-keeper. It is clear that we must get to the bottom of this. There can be no ambiguity when lives are in danger. Soren's account gave no indication that he might be the perpetrator that the burned ships, in fact, he had said that the ships were burned by the Windborn that attended the parley to stop him from speaking with King Erling's representative."

"Why would I do that?" I sneered.

Hraki cocked an eyebrow at me. "Clearly, you are impulsive. You demonstrate that even now when you speak without leave. Soren also tells me that you and he have clashed before. Perhaps you acted under some misguided belief that burning him along with the ships would undo the defeats Soren pressed upon you?"

Hraki's expression never changed. His tone never changed.

Alvilda twisted to face me. "Is this true?" She hissed.

Fury rose in my belly. I bared my teeth and opened my mouth to let the tirade free. Valna put her hand on my arm, gentle pressure to hold me back. I swallowed the ball of anger bubbling up inside me and took a breath.

"Soren and I have met before. A few times. But it is not true that I burned the ships. Don't you think that he's more likely to set something on fire?"

Alvilda frowned and turned back to interrogate Hraki.

"Perhaps," Hraki said before Alvilda could say anything. "But once again, you cannot hold your tongue. If it was Soren's fault the longships were burned, which again is not the account I was given, then surely it was simply because you goaded him until he broke the parley? Whatever happened I suspect that your abrasiveness was the reason for the breakdown. It seems that you have much to untangle, law-keeper. Let me invite you to be guests in my house for your stay."

He raised an arm and a servant scurried out from behind the

throne and passed a cup and some bread to Hraki.

"Apologies," he said. "We have only water to offer you, but I hope it will suffice for the purpose?"

"It will," Alvilda said with a bow.

"Excellent. Please, my friends, partake of my water, fill yourselves with my bread and be guest-friends in my halls."

He stepped forward and we did the same. One by one he offered us each the cup and bread. Fainn was first, his face soured as he looked into the cup and took the chunk of bread. When I was passed the cup I saw why. It was clear that someone had held a cupful of snow by a flame for a heartbeat. There was still snow on the rim and the water was only half-melted with a broken twig floating in it. I looked up at Hraki, his expression was serene, as though the cup contained only the purest spring water.

I sipped.

The taste of the twig had soaked into the water and the stale bread did nothing to take it away.

I moved away and let Alvilda take her drink. She spluttered on the water and sucked on her piece of bread to try and take away the taste of twig. Once Valna had taken hers, Hraki threw the cup and what was left of the bread off into the empty mead-hall.

"It is done," he announced. "I now guarantee no harm will come to you in my halls. Please make yourselves at home and refresh yourselves, then we can discuss this matter properly."

He brought his hands together and clasped them tightly. His tattered guards rounded us up and tried to herd us out of the mead-hall.

"Wait," Fainn said. "We haven't—"

A few of the Windborn behind the throne stood and another two reached for weapons at their belts. Soren stalked towards us. His eyes were locked onto mine and his fingertips brushed the hilt of a knife.

"I am sure," Hraki said with a sharp edge to his voice, "that you are tired, friends. Take some time to rest and we can discuss this when you are refreshed."

The Wind inside me worked itself up to a gale and from the look of Valna's face, she felt the same.

"Come on," I mumbled. "It'll be good to rest."

Hraki nodded and turned away. His Windborn flinched back from him as he pushed through them and strode out of the hall. We let the guards, too badly equipped to be true huskalar, lead us to a dilapidated longhouse.

It had no door and one end of its roof had collapsed. Sharp winds gusted through the gaps in the roof and some of the walls. We found the driest spot in the room and cleared it as best we could. Fainn and Valna bent over the saturated fire pit and tried to light a fire as I tore open old sacks to cover the door. Alvilda sat on an old crate, her knees pulled up into her chest, and she scowled at nothing.

We worked in silence. No one willing to speak out against the oppressive weight of Hraki's broken home.

There were none of the usual celebrations to welcome strangers. Hraki had no skalds to warm our hearts with tales of ancient heroes, and the food we had was barely enough to share between us. As we settled in for the night, we heard shouts then someone screamed.

Our hands went to weapons.

The screaming stopped.

Something clattered above us. All eyes snapped up. Two ravens guarded the hole in the roof. Valna offered up a sliver of dried meat and one of them swooped down to take it. The other cawed again and hunched down against the cold wind, keeping its beady eyes trained out like a guard dog. For once I found myself glad of Gerda's ever-present birds.

Unease soaked into our bones as we tried to sleep. The sounds of arguments broke out from Hraki's longhouse and we all shuffled closer together. It was a long night underscored by the brittle, lonely echo of hammer on anvil.

*

Someone banged on the wall of the longhouse, rousing us awake. We turned, bleary-eyed, to see the same guard from the night before glaring at us.

"Get up," he said. "Time to see the king."

The wind rolling through the abandoned longhouse had not

been enough to disperse the tension that drenched us. Alvilda looked despondent and the rest of us shared worried looks. I had clutched my axe all night and I flexed my fist to try and get rid of the cramp in my hand. We had all found a flat space to sleep within the debris of the abandoned house, but from the looks on everyone else's faces, they had been just as uncomfortable as me.

The guard grumbled for us to hurry and we followed him. The streets were as empty as they had been the day before and now we attracted even less attention as though we were ghosts wandering through the corpse-town. Law-Keeper Reynir met us outside the mead-hall with a forced smile and hands clasped too tightly together.

"Good morning, friends. I trust you slept well. Please come inside." He led us through the doors and a few figures hurried out of the hall, leaving it empty. "King Hraki prefers that servants are out of sight. I am sure you understand."

"Where is the king? Where is Soren?" Alvilda asked. "I must discuss the parley with them to resolve this. Will they be joining us soon?"

Hraki's law-keeper bobbed his head. "I am afraid that neither the king nor his Windborn are in a position to meet with you this morning, but he has authorised me to offer you these reparations."

Alvilda frowned. He walked up to the throne's raised platform and picked up two sacks that lay against its base. One of the bags made the music of coin.

"Should the High King's law-keeper not decide the amount of the reparations?" Fainn said, his brows knotted together in a scowl.

"I am sure you have all seen that Hraki's household is not as it once was," Reynir said. The bags swayed, both heavy, as Reynir stepped forward. "We discussed our course of action at great length and these gifts are all that we can offer. Any more, and we would be destitute."

"He won't come out and say this himself?" Valna said.

"Alas, my king is a kind and sensitive soul. Once his Windborn's treachery became known to him, as well as the damage Soren had done to his beloved neighbour, he was wracked with guilt and has been inconsolable since."

I shook my head and turned away from Reynir to hide my disbelief. Valna and Fainn wore similar expressions. Alvilda frowned, though not as deeply as the rest of us. She looked between us and Reynir as though trying to decide whose lead to follow.

"Regardless of King Hraki's current state," Alvilda said after a moment's hesitation. "I must insist that I speak with him. The High King must know as much as possible about this incident. I am the High King's representative and I am requesting an audience with King Hraki."

Reynir paused, the sacks still swinging, and offered Alvilda a strained smile. "With apologies, Law-keeper, I cannot stress enough the turmoil that King Hraki finds himself in. He is so upset that I fear it would take the gods themselves to wring anything close to a conversation from him."

Alvilda opened her mouth as Hraki's law-keeper stepped towards us again.

"I appreciate," Reynir continued, cutting off another protest from Alvilda, "that the situation is not ideal, but I hope that you will take these offerings as a gesture of good faith and as a promise that King Hraki has the best interests of the High King at heart."

I looked to Alvilda, hoping that she would force Reynir to fetch his king, but she looked as though she was trying to calculate the amount of coin in the sacks. As Reynir stopped in front of Fainn and passed the bag over to him, Fainn's disbelief melted as he felt the weight of the reparations. This small signal from Fain was enough to sway Alvilda and she nodded to herself.

"I hope that you will consider this to be enough," Reynir said and offered Fainn a half-bow.

Fainn opened the bag and looked inside. His eyes widened.

"I am sure this will go some way to repairing the damage already done," he said. "However, we still need to discuss the matter of King Erling's son. Tell—"

Reynir held up his free hand. "Let us not sully this triumph of diplomacy with old, thorny issues."

"We won't let this issue go, Reynir," Valna said through

gritted teeth. "Tell your king that."

"Of course," he said. "After all this time, we have come to expect that King Erling will not accept any decision on this that isn't the one he wants."

"What he wants," Fainn said, stepping forward, "is to put his son's body to rest. Tell us which ravine the body fell into. Take us there. Runar can fetch the body."

"Please," Reynir said. His expression crinkled into embarrassed disdain. "Now is not the time. King Hraki has tried to resolve this with you and the High King's law-keeper ruled in our favour. We will not talk of this today. King Hraki cannot meet with you to apologise for Soren's behaviour himself, and for that you have his further apologies. Take these reparations for your longships and return home. Tell King Erling of Hraki's willingness to reopen discussions at a later date. Perhaps Law-Keeper Alvilda would be willing to stay on and help adjudicate that another time."

"I am here now. Why must we wait to resolve the issue?" Alvilda said. She had stepped away from the conversation as the voices became tense, but she spoke firmly. "If this matter is still in contention then let me settle it."

Reynir offered her a smile as though she were an errant child asking why rivers flow downhill.

"The king is indisposed. It would be an insult to both you and the High King to entertain you when we are unable to give you the proper respect. King Hraki would beg your indulgence in this and ask that you return to King Erling's halls. Once he has recovered, which should take no more than a day or so, he will make haste to King Erling's halls and this matter can be decided once and for all."

"Could we not stay here whilst Hraki recovers?" Alvilda pressed.

Reynir's smile became strained and he took a breath. "You can see, Law-Keeper Alvilda, how our halls are not in the best repair. We would gladly entertain you in summer, but we are unable to grant you—as the representative of the High King—the proper respect that you deserve. We could not, in good conscience, host you in a manner inappropriate for your office."

Alvilda narrowed her eyes but was not yet content. She

drew herself up and nodded.

"This matter is clearly important to King Erling and to my companions. It is important enough for them to have travelled to the Althing and also to have brought it up again now. I will now consider the matter reopened and will discuss this with King Erling upon my return to his halls. If you are unable to continue to entertain myself and my companions now then so be it, but King Hraki must arrive at King Erling's halls within five days to make his statement. If he has not arrived by then, judgement shall be made in his absence."

I found myself nodding along to Alvilda's speech. I knew that if a judgement was made without your presence then it was all but guaranteed to be a judgement made against you.

"Thank you, Law-Keeper Alvilda," Reynir said and bowed stiffly to her. "I assure you, we shall not be so long as that."

The law-keeper went over to Fainn and asked to check the amount of coin that had been offered. Reynir turned to face me.

"Windborn Edda, we know that there is little we can do to restore the honour you lost in Soren's victories against you, but we hope that this gesture will ease your ill-will toward the household Soren was a part of."

He threw the other sack to me. It was heavier than I thought and the rough cotton slipped through my fingers as I tried to catch it. It thumped onto the floor and something rolled out. Something drained white and stained crimson. Soren's head.

Soren's face looked furious, his mouth still wide in an angry scream and his brows locked into an everlasting scowl. His hair, limp over his face and matted with blood, was still bright and shining.

Alvilda wretched and took a step backwards. Air hissed through Valna's teeth and her hand went to a knife.

"What am I supposed to do with this?" I said.

"That is entirely up to you," Reynir said sweetly. "It will make a fearsome addition to your battle raiment I am sure. There are plenty of birds who will gladly accept a meal of carrion, especially in winter. There are two ravens with you, are there not? Perhaps they would appreciate it."

"I didn't want you to give me his head."

Reynir shrugged. "King Hraki is a generous man. It is a gift for you as a guest-friend."

I looked up. Reynir's smile still slit his face, but his eyes were hard, hungry. A gift to a guest-friend. Stories of heroes surged in my mind and I remembered the fate of Kvindal. He had survived a thousand battles but was killed when he stayed with a wolf and refused its gift, the head of a freshly killed deer, thus breaking the pact of the guest-friend and leaving the wolf free to feast on him as he slept. The sound of Alvilda retching again snapped my attention back to the mead-hall.

"Pass on my thanks to Hraki for his generosity," I said through gritted teeth.

Anger flickered across Reynir's face, gone in an instant, then he was back to his slimy self and bowed to me.

"You will forgive me, my friends," he said. "But I cannot stay with you any longer. I must see to my king and make sure that he has not lost himself to grief."

He graced us with a final thin smile before walking by the throne and exiting the mead-hall. As he disappeared through the door it sounded as though people moved out of his way.

"We should go," Valna said, her voice pitched low. "We're not safe."

"Agreed," Fainn said.

Alvilda stumbled away from us and threw up onto a pile of rubbish.

I looked down at the head and grabbed it by the hair. Congealed blood dripped from the ragged stump where his neck had once been. The skin was bleached white, but a bruise had been left on his cheekbone. His eyes were wide open, glazed over and sightless. My grip squeezed tighter. Some of the hairs ripped free and the head tilted.

Three deaths had been stolen from me and each of them had fractured my life. Orin had stolen my husband from me. Soren had taken my own life from me. Now Hraki took Soren's death from me.

I wanted to scream. I wanted to throw the head to the floor. I wanted to charge at Hraki and take what was owed to me from his flesh.

I let Soren's head drop from my fingers and brought out my

axe. The head rolled onto its cheek. I turned it and shoved it into the ground so I could watch those sightless eyes. I readied my axe to split Soren's face like a cord of firewood.

"Edda, come on." Valna put her hand on my shoulder. "It's done. We need to go."

I cursed then shoved the head in the bag and followed my friends out of the mead-hall. The ravens would eat his eyes, I could take comfort from that at least. Alvilda was still bent over the rubbish, spitting out the last of the bile. I grabbed her by the arm and steered her out the door.

Outside, Valna stood in front of Fainn protectively and I shoved Alvilda behind me when I saw why.

Men and women, more than I had thought could live in Hraki's broken town, watched us. Some leaned against the crumpled houses, others loomed in the shadows within the buildings, and still more moved in the alleys and pathways. Spears rested against shoulders, knives and axes rasped against whetstones. All eyes were locked on us.

"Come on," I said. "We're still guests. They can't hurt us, can they? And the gates are open."

Valna nodded and began to make her slow way forward.

No one moved as we walked by. Valna and I kept Alvilda and Fainn between us, herding them out, step by step. The sun, now risen above the cliffs and was overpowering the shadows in the fortress, glinting from weapons. I counted three iron arm-rings amongst the huskalar. Three Windborn, hidden and waiting for us to break the rite of guest-friends.

We kept our pace until we reached the treeline, then we ran.

CHAPTER EIGHTEEN
DANGERS UNSEEN

WE RAN FOR AS LONG AS WE COULD. Our pace slowed as one of us faltered and the others paused to let them catch up, then we set off running again. Eventually, we had to stop for Fainn. The old god-speaker slowed and then bent over, panting.

"Come on," Valna said. "We need to go."

"I can't run anymore," he said, waving her off.

"I don't think they're following us," I said.

A raven croaked and we saw two birds sat above us. Black feathers against the thin, snow-drenched fir trees.

"Here," I called and up-ended the sack. Soren's head tumbled out, painting a dark red line through the snow as it rolled, and came to a halt at the bottom of a tree. The ravens shouted at me, hopping excitedly from one branch to another. "All yours."

One of them fluttered down and started stabbing at the cold flesh. When the other flew down, they fought to get to the eyes, wings beating and voices shrieking. Alvilda turned away and gagged.

"I think we can walk from here," I said.

Valna bit her lip, then nodded. She went over to Alvilda and rubbed her back as the young law-keeper retched.

"Are you going to be okay?" she said.

Fainn gulped down more air then stood. "Yes, just give me a moment."

Valna rolled her eyes at him and bent back to check on Alvilda.

I dropped the sack and looked around. The forest was busy with small movements. Every snapping twig and gust of wind sent my hands to my axe, but nothing jumped out at us. One of the ravens thrashed its wings and lifted itself into the air and cawed, its beak glistening red.

"Come on," I said. "We've rested long enough."

Fainn, who was still panting heavily, shot me an incredulous look. "We've only just stopped."

Before I could respond, the gore-slick ravens squawked and flapped at his back, then flew off ahead of us.

"I don't think we have a choice," Valna said.

We ran. We were no longer driven by spine-chilling fear and so our pace was slower, but we didn't stop. The journey was a wretched, relentless dash. We stumbled over logs and through streams. I stayed at the front and kept the snow compact enough to walk on. Valna ran along with the others and ushered them on when they thought they couldn't continue.

Not long after the sun dipped below the mountains, the sound of familiar voices and crashing water broke through the forest. We had reached the waterfall and the beached longship. Alvilda sobbed with relief and Fainn swore a thankful prayer. Valna and I let them run ahead and turned to watch the trees behind us, mindful of anyone who might have somehow followed us, but the only movement was the swaying of leaves and the whirl of snow.

At the sight of our exhausted panic the crew grabbed whatever weapon they could. Olek rushed over to us and pulled Valna into a tight embrace. I trudged past them and found myself a drink as Fainn called for the captain.

"We need to leave. Now," Fainn said.

The captain nodded and began shouting orders at his crew. They scrambled up and dashed around, grabbing whatever was closest and packing it away. Fainn rushed in and, together with the captain, swiftly coordinated the chaotic crewmembers.

I threw my empty cup onto the longship then rushed back to the treeline with Valna, keeping watch as the crew packed the camp. A sense of danger still prickled at the back of my neck. I twitched at any small movement, bringing my shield up every time the wind jostled the leaves or a bird burst from the low branches. Valna shimmered and disappeared as she patrolled the edge of the camp using her Windborn powers, whilst I moved to keep myself between the forest and the crew closest to it.

After what felt like an age, the captain called out, "That's it. Everyone on."

I paused with Valna for a moment longer to make sure the crew were safe as they clambered onto the longship, then dashed to the shore. Once everyone was on board Valna pushed us off, using her Windborn tricks to hop onto the longship once its keel scraped clear of the sand.

"What happened?" the captain asked once we were making our way downstream.

Fainn sighed. "We got some money for the longships and Alvilda's forced them to open discussions again about Dyggvi's body. But they also gave us the head of one of his Windborn."

"How much money did they give us?" Valna asked.

"A considerable sum. Enough to pay for a longship, but not enough to pay for everything."

"It was all they could spare," Alvilda said. Her tone suggested she was trying to convince herself, as much as any of us. "You saw the state of them. They are destitute."

"They've got enough money for weapons," I said.

"Aye," Fainn agreed. "That blacksmith didn't stop all night."

I let the conversation fade to noise as Alvilda offered weak protestations. I kept my eyes on the trees and rocks that passed us as we sailed downriver. The current lent us speed that would be hard to match on land, but I did not want to be caught out.

"When they meet us for the talks," Alvilda said, "I will make sure that King Hraki makes up the rest of the money. We can take this as a token of good faith and work out how he will pay for the rest of them."

I turned to Alvilda, incredulous that she still had faith in Hraki's intentions. She sat on a bench by the rudder, biting her fingernails and staring into nothing. Hraki, directly and indirectly, had been the reason I was killed, my home had been destroyed, and my husband taken from me. The laws were the reason I hadn't been able to reclaim my life. They were why my resurrection left me nothing but a tool. The laws were stacked in favour of kings and chieftains. For anyone else, to live by the letter of the law was to die by a thousand weeping cuts. It was not enough to know the laws, then. You had to know when to ignore them and when to bring them down like the Warrior's hammer at those that abused them.

"Hraki is not going to pay for those ships," I said. I tried to keep my voice soft but she flinched from its intensity all the same. "What about all those warriors that chased us out of there? We need to tell Erling to get ready for a fight. Maybe if Runar destroys Hraki's longships before they leave we can—"

"No. I can't let you do that," Alvilda said and her voice echoed out across the deck. Tears welled in her eyes and underneath the force of her words I thought I heard something crack. "It is the gods' law that none may take violent action against another in winter. Let all lay down their weapons as the ground grows cold and the night grows long."

I moved over and sat next to her. "There are some people who don't care about the law. They do what they want, Alvilda," I said, gently this time. "Hraki is one of those people."

"He wouldn't just ignore the law. He paid for the boats in good faith."

"He gave us the gold to buy himself time, Alvilda, not to pay for any damages." I put my hand on her shoulder. Frost blossomed under my fingertips. "Sometimes people think they are above the laws, whether set by gods or mortals, and they cross lines they shouldn't."

"If the laws don't work then what am I supposed to do?"

"Try and make them work," I said. "The laws might not work all the time, but that's only because people ignore them because they think they're powerful enough to get away with it. But they can't get away with it forever. You are powerful and you can make sure the laws apply to everyone equally. You did well to reopen the judgement about Dyggvi's body. It will force Hraki to come to us. He'll either come for a fight and then you can rule against him or he'll come to make his case and we'll finally be able to catch him out in his lies. Whatever happens, we'll stop him."

Alvilda offered me a weak smile. "I can't think like that, Edda. I have to be impartial. I can't go into this with the assumption I'm going rule against Hraki. I'm sorry." She met my gaze and I saw a glint of steel in her eyes. "I will stand by the law and make sure it's followed."

I nodded and bunched my jaw before I replied. "And what if Hraki does come with an army? Will you force us to wait until he is charging across the battlefield?"

Alvilda's brow furrowed and I could almost see the thoughts swirling in her head. Everyone on the longship stared. Even the ravens paused on the figurehead to face Alvilda.

"If it is clear that Hraki has no intentions to abide by the law and there is no time for us to wait for the High King's response," she paused. "Then I will rule against him, but if you or anyone else tries to deal the first blow before that judgement is made, then King Erling will face the wrath of the High King and all the gods."

"Fine," I said, "but we won't stand around and do nothing." I looked up at the ravens. "Gerda, tell Erling what Alvilda said, but you make damn sure he's ready to fight if we need to."

I stormed over to the oars and shoved someone out of the way. I set myself to the oar, pushing all of my frustrations out on the creaking wood. At my first stroke the longship veered off course and Valna had to jump to take another oar on the other side.

Between the fast-flowing current and the Windborn rowers, we sped down the fjord twice as fast as we had clawed our way upriver. Eventually, the night's darkness became too deep and we were forced to stop. We found a safe place to beach the longship and the crew poured out of the longship like beetles from a rotten log. This time there was no laughter around the campfire. The fire spat and hissed at us as we cooked a stew. Everyone wordlessly collected their share. I took mine and sat on a rock at the edge of the firelight, once again next to Alvilda. I wolfed the meal down to try and feel some warmth in my body, but by my fourth mouthful the bowl was cold in my hands.

Valna wandered over to me and passed me a cupful of mead. I thanked her and took it.

"Why would he kill him?" Valna said into the quiet night. "I don't understand why he wouldn't give us Soren. Alvilda, didn't Hraki murder Soren? Shouldn't we be arresting him or something?"

There was an edge of desperation to Valna's words.

The law-keeper thought for a moment, staring into a now-empty cup, then shrugged. "There's nothing we can do. We don't know how Soren died, maybe he volunteered to die, but it doesn't matter."

"No?" I asked, curious how the death of a man could so easily be swept aside.

"No. He is... was one of King Hraki's Windborn. If King Hraki did kill him then he was well within his rights to do so."

My jaw dropped. Valna's desperate stare turned into something hard, sharp. The people around us shifted away and found reasons to be busy. Olek sat next to Valna and put his hand on the small of her back. The gentle touch seemed to still something in Valna's eyes.

"Are you telling me that because Soren is Windborn it doesn't matter if he is murdered?" Valna whispered.

"No, no," Alvilda said quickly. "If anyone else kills a Windborn except the person they're sworn to, then it must be investigated, but a Windborn's master must be able to act if they need to. It's a safeguard."

"Like we're some kind of dog that needs to be put down if it turns rabid?" Valna growled.

I thought back to my fight in Konvald. No one had stepped in to help me, not that I needed it, but someone must have seen two people follow someone into an alley and known something was wrong. The words of the High King rang in my ears. I thought of how easily he made threats and how small I seemed to him. In his eyes I was Windborn and nothing more, something to be set to work or put down. Something owned.

"The law's always been against the Windborn," I said. Valna turned to me. There was hunger in her expression, for something more than I could give her in that moment. A hunger to be valued, and to be part of something bigger than herself.

"We're just swords to them," I said, trying to keep my words soft. "Sure, we can fly and we're strong, but we're still weapons to be pointed and loosed. Without a patron, a king to swear to, if we're lucky, we're nothing better than wolves to be hunted."

My bladder pressed for my attention and I stood.

380

"Is that all we are?" Valna asked. "Weapons?"

I walked over and took her hands in mine. "Not to everyone. When I look at you I see a friend. And Olek doesn't see you as a weapon, does he? He sees you. He sees the beautiful, exciting person that you are."

The hunger in her eyes faded a little. Her desperation lost its edge. She glanced behind her to where Olek sat. He smiled and nodded.

"Right," she said and turned back to me. I saw tears in her eyes. "It's just a bit shit, isn't it?"

"Very shit," I said, "but there's not a lot we can do. Now, I need a piss."

Valna gave me a weak smile and patted my hand. I squeezed her hand and walked out of the camp.

I walked far enough that the sound of the river faded. I moved to the other side of a snowdrift that had collected against a copse of trees and crouched to add the sound of my own running water to the forest. I sighed, wishing that my breath would plume ahead of me, but there was nothing. I was frozen inside and out. I wondered how Erling would have reacted if a law-keeper demanded recompense for something I had done. Would he have paid the money, argued on my behalf, or have me killed to be done with it?

I finished pissing and stood, sorting out my clothes. The silence of the forest pressed in against me. Unease stirred in my chest. The only sound was the gentle hiss of fir branches rubbing against each other. I felt the echo of Windborn power somewhere nearby, too close to be Valna. The rustling of small creatures had stopped, even the ravens had ceased their incessant squawking.

My hand moved to my axe but before I could touch it I felt the cold, sharp iron press against my skin. I tried to look around and see who had their blade to my throat, but I couldn't see anyone.

"Keep still," a rough voice said. His voice was so close that he could only be Hraki's invisible Windborn. "Take your hands away from the axe, nice and slow."

As he spoke his figure appeared next to me. His silhouette appeared first then the details of his face and limbs then the colours of his clothes and hair. It was as though he stepped forward through shadow and the further he moved the more was revealed. He pressed the edge of a long knife against my throat. I kept my hand by my axe. I felt the Wind inside and teased it downward, hardening the snow around my feet and trying to snake ice around my assailant's feet.

"Don't be stupid," he sneered and pressed the knife harder to my neck. "You make a move, I slice your throat. You make a sound, I slice your throat. You do anything I don't like, I slice your throat. Your only way out of this is to come with me, nice and easy, so stop doing whatever the fuck it is you're doing with your ice power and get your hand off your fucking axe."

I swallowed and the edge of the knife cut into me. A drop of blood slid down my neck and soaked into my shirt. I leaned back. The knife edge followed.

"What do you want?" I said, trying to give myself some time.

"I want you to get your hand away from the fucking axe," he growled. The pressure against my neck increased and there was a burning pain as the knife began to slide across my throat. I raised my hands and focused on the ice at my feet.

"I said to stop that, you think I can't feel you doing that, you stupid bitch?"

He pressed harder. More blood tracked down my neck. I stopped pushing at the Wind inside me.

My captor narrowed his eyes at me, examining my expression for any potential trickery, then relaxed. "That's better."

He pulled the axe from my belt and tossed it carelessly into the snow-covered undergrowth.

"Come on, Jorunn," he called behind him. "She's alone."

A shape lifted through the trees ahead of me and I realised what I had taken for a snowdrift was actually an enormous snow bear. It shook frost and pine needles from its coat and padded silently over to us. It sniffed at me and bared its teeth. Each glistening fang was as long as my head and I shuddered away from the stench of rotten meat. My heartbeat faltered when I saw black feathers stuck between its teeth. Raven feathers. Any hope I had that Gerda would bring help disappeared as the feathers fell from the snow bear's jaws.

"Leave off," my captor said and batted the bear on its flank.

The bear turned and snorted again before sitting behind me.

"Right," the invisible Windborn said. "Here's what's going to happen. I'm going to take the knife away, and you come with us. You make any noise, or try to make a run for it, then we kill you. No one's going to care. Jorunn will mess you up a bit and everyone will think a snow bear found you. Got it?"

I tensed, wondering how fast a snow bear could move and how well it would balance if I could leave a trail of ice behind me. Maybe I—

A deep, bone-shuddering growl came from behind me.

"Fine," I grated.

"Good," the man said. He took the knife away slowly, like someone who had set a trap and did not want it to go off. When he saw I wasn't going anywhere he relaxed. "Good," he said again. "Now, off we go."

He grabbed my arm roughly, steered me to the north and then shoved me forward.

"We've got a lot of ground to cover so let's move."

I tore my arm from his grip and began to walk. The man kept the knife out and followed behind me. After a moment, the bear lurched to its feet and trailed us too.

We marched through the snow and up the mountainside, heading straight back for Hraki's stronghold. Once we had walked for about an hour the snow bear shivered, fur and flesh sloughed off of it like snowdrifts, and a woman walked alongside us. She was almost as enormous as the snow bear. She was a head taller than me and seemed twice as wide in the shoulders. She kept her gaze straight ahead and her expression was sour as my captor handed her some clothes.

"What's wrong with her?" I asked.

She cuffed me, a casual blow that was enough to send me stumbling and set my ears ringing.

"She didn't get to eat you," the man said. "It's not too late, though."

I scowled at them both and kept walking.

After a few more hours, the one who would make himself invisible, Nal, called us to a halt in a clearing. He looked up through the gap in the trees, then put his fingers to his mouth and sent out a piercing whistle. As he did that, Jorunn dug around in the small snowdrifts and pulled free a coil of rope.

"Hands," she grunted.

The boredom in her voice sent shivers of anger up my spine. Had I come all this way, lost everything, just to be tied up like some hunter's quarry? I clenched my fists, filling them with shards of ice and frost, and held out my hands to be tied up. Jorunn shuffled forward, her eyes half-glazed and disinterested. As she reached out I flung the ice and frost into her eyes.

She reeled back with a yell. The other Windborn turned, but I was already running.

I ducked under branches and swerved through the trees. Jorunn's yell turned into a bestial roar and the earth began to shake under the weight of enormous footsteps.

I summoned a spike of ice and got ready to defend myself in a last stand against Hraki's Windborn.

Something slammed into me like a falling star. It hit me hard enough that it carried me forward, carving a deep furrow into the earth.

Rough fingers scratched my head and yanked back a fistful of hair.

"Hello, Edda," a familiar voice wheezed. "Good to see you again."

Lothi, Hraki's flying Windborn.

"Is she alive?" called Nal from somewhere nearby.

Lothi twisted my neck to get a look at my face. I spat a bloody glob onto his cheek.

"She's alive," he shouted back, without wiping the blood off. "Got a broken nose, but she'll live."

My face was scraped raw from the impact with the ground, but my nose wasn't broken. I snarled at him to get off and he punched me square in the face. I felt the cartilage in my nose snap and crunch. Pain shattered my vision and I blinked away stars.

"Give me the rope."

Lothi pushed my face back into the ground. Dirt and snow forced its way into my mouth and nose, causing more spasms of pain. Someone grabbed my arms and legs and tied them tightly together. He looked over me like a hunter over their catch and then kicked me. More pain exploded in my side and I cried out as something snapped in my chest.

"Get me a gag," he said. "Then I'll take her back."

My breath came in short bursts as anything more would have rekindled the pain in my chest like a lightning strike. Within a few heartbeats, my breath became soaked through with the rank, stale sweat of whoever they'd torn the cloth from.

"How long will you be?"

"Should be back by early morning. Jorunn can carry me again."

"Make sure of it. He won't wait for you."

Someone lifted me up as easily as a sack of grain, and then the ground fell away beneath me. I bucked, ignoring the stabbing in my side.

"I wouldn't do that," Lothi drawled. "Or I'll have to drop you into a river or something."

I stiffened and watched as the trees became like ferns beneath us and blurred together. Rivers carved paths through the carpeted green and branches. The high winds whipped at my face, making tears stream down my face, and we flew north back to Hraki's halls.

*

I fell in and out of consciousness as Lothi carried me across rivers and over mountains. I caught glimpses of the world below, breathtaking in a way I'd never seen before. Strong flowing rivers were reduced to quivering silver lines carving through blankets of white. Crags and boulders nothing more than specks of piled pebbles. Eventually, Hraki's stone-cradled halls came into view. Lothi swooped easily over the walls, some of the guards cheered as he passed over, and then we were inside one of the buildings that looked to be an abandoned barn. A couple of people helped Lothi bind me with ropes to the thick wooden beams running along the length and breadth of the barn. Their rough hands shoved and prodded me, and I cried out at the ripping pain in my sides. I fell to my knees as soon as they stopped supporting me. My muscles shivered with exhaustion. I had been tensed against being dropped for the whole journey which took everything out of me. My eyelids fluttered closed.

"She's no good to us like this," Lothi said.

He grabbed my head and twisted it from side to side. I tried to snarl, bite, or wrench myself away but I had nothing left.

"Let's give her a few hours then see if she's still alive. You, make sure she doesn't try anything."

I heard some murmured acknowledgements. I tried to lift my head, but it was too heavy. I let my chin rest on my chest.

Consciousness left me again.

Someone threw water over me. I spluttered and flinched as it froze to my cheeks.

"See, told you she's not dead."

"Fine, go tell him."

I blinked to clear the water and frost from my eyes. One of Hraki's guards stood a few paces away, clutching a spear and eyeing me with a mixture of contempt and fear. Her grip tightened on her weapon when she noticed me watching her.

Sacks lined the walls of the storeroom, one of them was torn and grain spilled out onto the floor. Rubbish collected in the corners: rotting food, sodden piles of rags. I let my head slip down again and noticed, on the hard ground in front of me, streaks of frozen blood and chunks of cold meat. I tensed my arms, testing my bonds, and the guard stepped forward with a growl. She shoved the tip of her spear at me.

"Don't try anything," she snarled, but there was a quiver in her voice and the spear-tip wavered at the base of my throat.

"Okay," I said. The words were muffled by the gag, but I hoped the tone of my voice would soothe her. "I'm not doing anything."

After a moment the guard relaxed and stepped back.

We waited.

The walls and roof of the storeroom creaked as the wind picked up outside. I pushed a little power into the ropes around my wrists, they were too tight to break without the guard noticing, but for now I could soak them with brittle ice. The rough texture of the rope slowly smoothed as ice seeped through the fibres. My Windborn powers burned against the inside of my bruised ribs. The guard kept her eyes on me, but couldn't sense when I was using my powers. I tensed my arms enough to be ready but not so much the ropes attaching me to the beams would go taught and give away my plan.

Footsteps outside. I stopped pushing ice into my bonds and looked to the door.

Hraki ducked into the room followed by Lothi and two other people I didn't recognise, but neither of them wore the iron arm-ring of a Windborn.

"She still tried to get away," Lothi said, "even with Jorunn and Nal there."

Hraki stepped up to me, hands behind his back, and smiled. Even with ropes binding me like cattle ready for slaughter his cheery demeanour hadn't changed.

"You've got a warrior's spirit," he said. "You came from the Kjaltonn coast, didn't you? That's where Soren said he became Windborn."

I bared my teeth around my gag.

"I'll take that as a yes."

He leaned forward to look at the ice on my cheek. He picked a piece of it off then removed my gag.

I spat at him.

His face creased with distaste and he wiped away the spittle. The backhanded slap hit me before I saw it and it was so strong it rocked me to the side. I managed to balance myself before I toppled and snapped the frozen ropes around my wrists.

"There comes a time when a good warrior knows to put down their weapons," he said, eyes sharp as flint. He waited for me to blink away the pain. "You can't fight your way out of this. Your friends are a couple of days travel away and my people will kill you at a word from me.

"You're strong, Edda. I respect strength. A strong enemy can be a strong ally."

"Ally?" I snorted and nodded towards the streaks of crimson soaked into the floor. "I've seen what you do to your allies."

"Soren was a fool," Hraki said. "Too impetuous. He disobeyed Lothi numerous times. I sent him to parley with Erling to provide him with an opportunity for redemption, but what did he do? He burned down enough ships to bankrupt me and forced me to accelerate my plans. No, Soren was a liability. But you... you have tracked Soren with a singular will. Your tenacity is something few people possess.

"You've been sold a lie, Edda. The High King and Erling made themselves seem like the only option, but they're wrong. There's another way. I can offer you another path that leads to whatever your heart desires."

"What other way?" I said.

"The High King is blinded by his own prejudice. His strength once united countless kings, queens, and clans under his banner, but ever since his daughter was crippled by a rogue Windborn he has been stuck following outdated laws and customs.

"I offer all my followers, even my Windborn, the same thing: if you help me fight, then you can have a share of the spoils. I don't care what the laws say about Windborn and ownership. Those laws stifle those who have been blessed with Windborn powers because of old superstitions about where those powers come from. If you were part of my household you would be rich, powerful. Not just a tool for an old man too long on his throne. Fight by my side, with me and my Windborn, and no one will be able to stop us."

"Why should I listen to you?" I said. "You sent the Windhunters that burned down my home."

"And think about how much stronger you are now," Hraki said, his voice crackling with passion.

The guards behind Hraki stared at me, fists gripped whiteknuckle tight around their spears, but I wasn't worried about them. Lothi's disinterested gaze flicked from me to the dirt under his fingernails. If I was quick I could throw Hraki in Lothi's way and give myself enough time to get away.

"Before you became Windborn you were what?" Hraki went on. "Some farmer's daughter? Maybe a half-decent raider. Now look at you. You're a god."

He leaned in close enough that his breath, thick with mead and meat, brushed against my face.

"You fought Soren at the Althing and spoke out against me to the law-keepers gathered there, didn't you?"

Gods above, it seemed so long ago that I fought in that

muddy ring. I took too long to answer. Another backhanded slap sent me rocking before I saw it coming.

"How did you know I was making deals with Wind-hunters?"

I spat a tooth onto the floor. The Wind within me began to squirm and writhe. I looked over at Lothi who was still picking at the dirt in his nails.

"Soren used your name," I said. "When he was talking with the other Wind-hunters. He said you sent them."

"You see," Hraki said over his shoulder to Lothi. "I told you Soren would have ruined us sooner or later."

He leaned back in to speak with me, close enough that I saw my bloody reflection in his eyes.

"Break your oath to Erling and we can—"

I snapped the rope. My right hand swung around, a shard of ice forming between my fingers, to slam deep into Hraki's throat. I twisted to shove him at Lothi.

He was too fast.

The shard of ice I intended for his neck instead sliced a line from his cheekbone to his mouth as he pulled away. He grabbed my other hand, pulled me around and slammed me onto the floor. His knee crashed into my chest and shoved all the air out from me.

I gasped then bucked to throw him off with all my Windborn strength.

He didn't move.

Lothi rushed to help, but there was no need. Hraki had me pinned. His knee pushed into my chest and his hands locked my arms to the floor. I squirmed and tried to throw him off, but couldn't. The Wind inside me roiled as I froze the ground beneath me to try and give myself some advantage.

Hraki scowled down at me, working his jaw against the healing wound in his face.

I stopped and stared up at him.

The skin, sliced through by my shard of ice, knitted itself back together. It healed faster than any Windborn wound I'd seen before. Bruised skin faded and, as I watched, the vicious wound disappeared and became nothing more than an old scar.

"You're..."

Words failed me. This man was the catalyst for everything I had lost like the pebble that starts a landslide. He had dealt with Wind-hunters, lied to and bribed law-keepers, and murdered a prince. I bared my teeth and struggled against Hraki as the crow in my chest cried out with indignant rage, but he forced me back down. This man was the reason I was Windborn and because of him I would never get to grow old with my husband or even own anything ever again. All of it, every blood-stained act, was to hide the fact that he was resurrected. He was Windborn and he refused to be bound by the same laws as everyone else.

Hraki's expression soured. All the cautious warmth that had been in his eyes when he had been trying to recruit me was gone and now his gaze was filled with hostile irritation.

"Help me," he said to Lothi.

Lothi grabbed one of my arms and Hraki took the other. Between them, they forced me up and onto my knees and twisted my arms behind my back so I couldn't struggle against them without breaking a bone.

"Bring that stool," Hraki ordered.

One of the guards set it down in front of us. Hraki and Lothi forced me down, pressing my cheek against the smooth wood. Out of the corner of my eye I saw the other guard pull an axe from somewhere. Not a slim woodcutter. A big, broad killer. He hefted the axe and walked over.

I bucked.

Lothi and Hraki held firm.

I wrenched myself again and broke myself. My left arm popped out of its socket in a blinding flare of pain. The muscles in my right arm tore as I stretched too far to escape. I screamed and twisted away. My hands, slick with melted frost, slipped out of their grasp. I smashed an elbow against one of them and stumbled towards the door.

The axe-wielding guard swiped at me. I was already beside him. His blade nicked my shoulder as I ducked under the axe and the shaft thudded into my collarbone. I made to punch him. My arm screamed in painful protest and refused to move.

I yelled and headbutted him. There was a wet crunch and he crumpled.

I sidestepped the body and darted for the door, desperately reaching for the cold wind outside.

Something slammed into me.

Lothi.

"You can't run away," he growled. "I thought you'd have learned that by now."

I snarled, started to spit something back at him, but a hot eruption of pain cut me short. It came again and again. Agony lanced into my stomach, scraped across my ribs, and stabbed into my neck. Lothi stood. His hand, clutching a knife, now dripping dark with my blood.

I tried to get away, but my body refused to move. My mind became a litany of desperate, impossible instructions. Roll away. Drag yourself away. Get out. Live.

My fingers scraped at the hard dirt beneath me. Hot stains seeped through my clothes. My vision blurred and someone joined Lothi to stand over me. They rubbed at their red-stained face.

"Throw her with the rest of the rubbish," Hraki's cold voice said.

Someone grabbed my arms and pulled me out of the barn. My world became an avalanche of pain. The agony in my arms and shoulders reignited for a split second, eclipsing the pain racking my body. They dragged me around the side of the building, then, in a final rending effort, I was tossed away.

My vision faded to shades of grey and the world disappeared. I prayed, if the gods still listened, that this time I would die and whatever was left of my soul could finally rest.

CHAPTER NINETEEN
SNOW AND BLOOD

I WAS NOT LUCKY ENOUGH TO DIE A SECOND TIME.

The world came back into focus in shades of heat and pain. The first thing I felt was the stunted, burning ache of puncture wounds all over my chest. Then came the twisted, tearing pain in my arms and shoulders. Last came the final, frozen stiffness of the dead.

I suppressed a groan and looked around.

Whoever had tossed me out had not gone far. The smell of rot and shit suffused the air around me. I lay in a back alley, the rest of Hraki's mead-hall visible through a slim gap between the buildings. The other end of the alley was cut off by the cliff side. A dead end.

After a long moment, I gathered enough strength to move and leaned against the rock wall. I gritted my teeth against the pain and shoved my arm back in its socket. I ran my hands over the burning wounds in my chest. I blinked, panted, and grit my teeth. The raw, rough skin around the wounds gave way to smooth ice. I looked under what was left of my bloodstained tunic. My skin was smeared with crimson frost and peppered with spots of ruby ice. The ice had clotted the wounds sooner than they should have and so they weren't fatal. My Windborn powers had saved me. Something else to hate them for. First, it took away my scars, earned and beloved, and now it would not let me die. I tipped my head back and looked up, past the rough rock wall and to the overcast sky.

"Have I not earned my scars? When do I get to rest?"

The words were barely a whisper, but that didn't matter. The gods weren't listening.

Shouts came from the buildings, calls for preparations, and I heard the clatter of wood with the clink of metal. The sound of weapons being gathered. The sharp snap of a whip, then the rumbling of a cart moving off.

I wanted to move. Get away. My body refused.

All my muscles screamed with pain. I closed my eyes.

Sleep came and went briefly, lightly. Every so often another crash would come from beyond the alleyway and jerk me awake. Someone threw some old food out onto me. Luckily, they did not see me flinch.

Some hours later, the noises beyond the alley died down and I became used to my pain. My world had become an overcast sky, aching limbs, and the weight of regrets. I wondered if I could lie there and die. Would starvation or dehydration kill a Windborn? I could find out.

I closed my eyes.

Unbidden, the image of Hraki surfaced in my mind. The bleeding slash across his cheek. The unnatural speed with which it sewed itself back together. Who else knew that this distant king was Windborn? Outside of his household, I suspected I was the only one. The hot ache in my limbs was joined by a new fire in my soul. Hraki was why I had lost everything. He was the reason Orin's storm had killed my husband. He was the reason that Soren had killed me. He was the reason I was Windborn and lost my home, my hoard, my dreams. He had even taken my revenge from me when he gave me Soren's head. And now he was marching on Erling's pitiful blockade with a household full of Windborn. No one else knew his secret. No one knew what he really was. To them he was still a rightful king, a bastard of a king, but still a king. I couldn't kill him, not like this, and not with all his Windborn around him, but I could reveal his secret. Then Alvilda could finally rule against him and the weight of the law could work its justice.

My arms were tight with pain and felt like they might snap if I moved too quickly or too far, but they moved. I scraped the rotten food and scraps off of me and pushed myself up, blinking hard as lightheadedness washed over me. Once it passed, I took a shaking step towards the end of the alley. The small movement sent shuddering gasps of pain through me. I took another. Then another. One more, and I reached the end of the alleyway.

I fell against the corner of one of the buildings, panting. I stood at the edge of a small square, too big to be an accident, too small to be anything useful. Homes and storerooms were built up against the cliff and a wide path led into the town proper. Myriad footprints and cart-paths churned the snow-covered ground before me. The shouts I had heard earlier were distant now. I tipped my head, as though that would help me listen, and couldn't hear anyone nearby.

None of this helped. Not really. I was stuck inside the fort of a king who wanted me dead, with no one to guide me out. It was full of weapons, enemies to wield them, and Windborn all prepared for war.

I looked back into the alley and let my gaze climb the rough cliff.

If I was at the cliff, that meant I was stuck within the fort at its deepest point, but with the cliff at my back I would not have to worry about enemies surrounding me. The cliff ran all the way to the walls. If I followed it then maybe I could find my way out. The cliff, its boulder-strewn face now bloated with a fresh covering of snow, didn't tell me how close I was to either wall so either direction would do.

I slipped out, gritting my teeth against the ice scraping within my skin, and ducked into the nearest building. It turned out to be my short-lived prison. A splintered rope lay by the back wall and a streak of deep crimson stained the floor. I rummaged through the room, ignoring the bloodstain I had left, in the hope I would find a forgotten spear, an axe, a knife, anything.

Nothing.

I picked up a splintered shard of wood from an old barrel. If I covered it in sharp ice, it should cut as well as a knife. I reached for the Wind inside me to use its frozen power. It felt like trying to drag shards of iron up my throat. It lashed out against the underside of my ribs and I doubled over, gasping in pain.

"Fine," I said through gritted teeth.

I listened for the noise of Hraki's followers then moved off in the other direction. The pain in my limbs eased the further I moved from my alleyway resurrection, though I didn't know if it was because my muscles remembered how to move, or if my Windborn power was healing me. Snowfall drifted, threatening to turn into a blizzard, and I hoped it would drive anyone in my path scurrying for cover.

The snow absorbed the sound of my passage and I slipped silently between the buildings. The endless snowflakes falling on me made it feel as though I was being slowly buried and would be entombed under the soft, frozen rain. The thought made me shiver.

I neared a well in the centre of a clearing and a wide shadow appeared through the raging snowfall, looming in the distance.

The outer walls.

I pressed myself against the nearest building and stared into the clearing. Three houses had been built along the cliff and two others stood opposite. I hid between the first and second cliff-houses. The snow lay thick on the ground, a clean slate that would mark my passage. The cliff pressed up against the end of the houses, leaving no gap for me to squeeze through. If I ran around the edge of the clearing, it may keep my footsteps inconspicuous and I would only need to pass three houses to reach the other side.

I squinted through the growing blizzard. No sound other than distant shouts. No movement except the falling snow.

I ran out, ignoring the blaze of pain across my chest and shoulders, sprinting in a tight circuit next to the houses.

A few paces and I passed the first house. Five more strides took me beyond the second.

Movement in the blizzard. I skidded to a halt and pushed my splinter before me.

A woman stood in the doorway of the final house. She stared at me, eyes wide and mouth open, a bucket lying forgotten at her feet.

She raised a hand to point at the blood-covered stranger before her. Snow glittered all around us as we stared at each other. She started to turn. Her chest rose as she inhaled.

I was already moving. I pressed my hand over her mouth

and stabbed the splinter into her neck. Hot blood pulsed against my hand and began to bubble down her throat. She struggled against me and my muscles burned as I held her still. Blood dripped onto my clothes. I pulled the splinter free and covered the wound with my hand, afraid that the blood would stain the snow and reveal me. This time my Windborn power came easily as I pushed it onto the spurting wound. Her blood froze.

I tipped her back as the life left her and caught her in my arms. I carried her out of the clearing and propped her corpse against the side of her home.

Snow landed on her eyes, melting against the sightless pupils. A lock of chestnut hair caught in the sticky blood on her neck. I brushed it away. A bruise blossomed around the wound.

I wanted to explain everything. Tell her what was at stake, but the dead don't care for explanations.

"Frida?" a voice called from inside the house. "Is everything okay out there? We need to get moving."

"I'm sorry," I whispered to her.

I ran.

*

The rest of the way to the wall was clear. The buildings around me were deserted and I managed to scrounge some stale bread from one of the houses along the way. My stomach had already begun to growl and, if I made it out, I would not let myself collapse from hunger.

The wall solidified as I made my way through the snow. There were no guards. Perhaps they refused to face the blizzard, or perhaps Hraki was using all his forces for one last attack.

From within the fort the earthen slope used to create the wall was gentle and easy enough to clamber up. I scrambled up the slanted wall and to the walkway without issue. My feet crunched into the tiny drifts of snow that had collected against the wooden palisade. I looked out towards freedom. The world was a churning torrent of white between the wall and the tree line. The ground was a perfect, unbroken sheet of snow. My footsteps would cut a clear signal for anyone who wanted to follow me.

I heard an anguished cry from somewhere behind me. It echoed and left a heavy, empty silence. I hadn't had a choice, but that didn't stop the guilt and regret from stabbing at me like a crow's taloned foot squeezing my heart.

I had to go. I grabbed the lip of the palisade and was about to jump over when someone appeared next to me.

They were covered in a heavy dusting of snow which obscured their features. They whipped around and threw a punch at me. I jerked back, but not enough. The attack lost its edge but it still snapped my head back. I bit my lip to muffle a cry of pain and leapt at them. I grabbed their arms and pinned them to the ground.

"Edda?"

I froze at the soft, surprised voice. I leaned back, though I didn't get off them entirely. The woman underneath me pulled back a hood and scarf to reveal Valna's soft face.

"Edda, I'm so sorry, I thought you were a guard. I didn't mean to—"

"It's okay," I said in a shaking voice. I slid off her and slumped against the wall. Relief surged inside me like water from a hot spring. It smothered the cold terror I'd felt since I had seen the crow's feathers in Jorunn's teeth.

Her eyes were wide, her hands cupped over her mouth. "Edda, I... we..."

She threw herself at me again, this time wrapping me in a breath-squeezing, rib-creaking embrace. I hissed as my still sore wounds stabbed at me in protest.

"What are you doing here?" I whispered.

"You disappeared. Fainn said you'd abandoned us, but I didn't believe that. Then I found the blood. I told them to sail back and I'd come and get you. I've run the whole way here. Oh, Edda, I'm so pleased you're okay. I was worried you were dead."

"I almost was," I said, the words squeezed through gritted teeth.

Valna looked me up and down. "Are you okay? What happened?"

"Let's get out of here," I said. "I'll tell you everything once we're safe."

"Right," she gathered herself. She brushed some of the snow from her clothes, as futile a gesture as that was, and looked around. Bags weighed heavy under her eyes and her skin looked pale.

"Do you have any food?" she asked.

"A little." I held up the bag.

Relief flooded Valna's expression. "It's more than I have," she said. "Okay, I think I can take us both across the gap to the trees."

I thought back to Valna's leap from the Iron Rib and how she had misjudged the distance.

"Are you sure you can make it all that way?"

"Yes," she said and rubbed her eyes with the heels of her palms. "It's a stretch, but I can do it."

"Valna, you're exhausted. I'm exhausted. Let's just climb out of here so we can rest."

She looked at me, determination writ plain on her face, but it dissolved when she realised I wasn't questioning her abilities, just trying to save her energy.

"Fine. I—"

Shouts from within the fort.

We squinted through the snow. Shapes with glinting weapons moved between the houses.

"Shit. They must have found the body. I had to murder someone, I didn't want to. It was just that..."

The guilt must have been writ on my face because Valna's hand squeezed my shoulder and her stern eyes locked onto mine. "Whoever they were, they were helping Hraki plan a war, Edda, there's no time to feel sorry for them."

The image of the woman's chestnut hair, caught in her blood, flashed into my mind. I broke away from Valna's gaze.

Doors slammed out in the fort. The hazy silhouettes of the warriors with pointed spears swept forward through the streets.

Valna put her hand on my arm and closed her eyes. The hairs on the back of my neck stood on end. I felt the power in her grow and the Wind in my chest writhed.

"Valna, no, you're exhausted. We should jump over and run."

"We'd need some rope or something. It's a longer drop than it looks."

"The snow will break the fall."

"The fall will break us, Edda. We—"

A thunk cut Valna short. An arrow shuddered from the palisade by my head. The calls of the hunters turned triumphant, energetic.

Another arrow slammed into the palisade. Then a spear.

"Fuck this," Valna said.

She grabbed my shoulder with her other hand and before I could do anything, we were gone. Her power erupted like a geyser. Everything went black and it felt like I was being crushed from all directions at once. There was an immense pressure on my head and I thought my eyes would pop out of my skull. I screamed, but there was no noise, no air, no mouth.

Then we were back.

We hadn't made it all the way. The trees stood sentinel ahead of us, looking down like disappointed giants. I turned back. Our hunters' shouts were now lost in the screaming wind of the blizzard. Valna let me go, her fingers slipped from my arm and she fell in the snow.

"Valna," I called.

Her eyelids fluttered. She was barely conscious.

I grabbed her under the arms and dragged her to the trees, carving a deep furrow through the snow. I stopped some way into the trees. I hoped that the blizzard and the trees would hide us well enough. The storm seemed to be blowing up from the south towards the cliff face. All of the trees had a covering of snow on one side like white moss. I dragged Valna to the dry side of a tree and propped her against it.

"Valna?"

Her eyes moved beneath closed eyelids. Her breathing was steady. A tiny groan escaped her.

"Wh... what happened?" She opened her eyes and looked around. Her bleary confusion evaporated as she realised where we were. "We made it?"

"Almost," I said. "Can you walk?"

She pushed herself up with a hiss and then nodded.

We stumbled away from the fort as quickly as we could. The

blizzard seemed to take our escape as an insult and became a howling, tearing thing. Valna took us on a slow, curving path away from the fort until we faced south-west. After a short while Valna stumbled, falling into the snow up to her waist. I helped her up, but she couldn't thank me. Whatever breath wasn't whipped away by the blizzard was needed to keep moving.

The snowstorm followed us through the forest. The next hour was a blur of white razor wind, pain stabbing at my chest as breath came hard against my wounded ribs, and stumbling over ground we couldn't see.

We had to slow. We couldn't run anymore.

Valna bent over with her hands on her knees and gasped in air. I fell against a tree and did the same. For a brief moment, I thought the gods were smiling on us as the blizzard calmed to gentle snowfall.

"Valna," I said once I could speak. "Hraki is Windborn."

She spluttered then coughed before she looked up.

"What?"

"I cut his face. It healed right there. The cut closed up and disappeared."

"He can't be Windborn. He's king. Are you sure you weren't dreaming or anything?"

"No, Valna, I'll swear to it. He's Windborn and once I found out, they tried to kill me."

She gave me a long, hard stare as though trying to decide whether what I said was true, or the product of some fever dream of exhaustion and fear. A few heartbeats then she nodded.

"Shit. We need to tell Erling and the High King."

I nodded. "Which way now?"

Valna looked up. The sky was still a swirling mass of white, but there was a pinprick of light where the sun hid behind the clouds.

"We keep heading south. Fainn said they'd send Runar out to look for me. For us. We should hit the river eventually then we follow it until Runar finds us."

"Then let's find the river."

I pushed off the tree and helped Valna stand.

As we started walking, something caught my eye. Something was moving through the distant trees fast enough to throw up cascades of snow, like a longship coursing through the ocean.

"What's—" I started.

A figure sprinted towards us, limbs blurred with speed, and the Wind inside me flared. Valna felt it too. She spun, pulling a knife from her belt, and they were on us.

The first punch hit me in the gut. The blow carried all the momentum of a battering ram and I was thrown back, smashed into a tree. The tree cracked and shook, covering me in a small avalanche as I hit the ground.

I gasped against fresh shock waves of pain and tried to stand. My heart thundered and the Wind whirred within me as it hardened the snow covering me in makeshift armour.

Valna faced off against a long-haired man. He grinned as he darted forward to stab at her with a knife in each hand. Valna batted them away, but he was toying with her. It was clear in the set of his feet, the languid circle he walked around her, and how he kept his knives down.

I struggled to my feet. Snow, now ice, stuck to my back and I summoned a deadly icicle in each hand. He looked back at me as I waded through the snow and back into the fight. He smiled, easily dodging a slash from Valna.

"You don't go down easy," he said and pointed at me with the tip of a knife. "I thought Lothi was being paranoid when he said you got out."

His dark hair fell limp over his face, down to the shoulders, and his grin was full of crooked, broken teeth.

"Still," he went on. "You've given me a chance to stretch my legs properly, so for that I should—"

Valna snarled and lunged with her knife. The new Windborn turned, lazily but still too fast to stop, and knocked the knife away. Valna stumbled back and his other hand whipped out to stab her in the chest. She blinked away and reappeared a few paces away, panting and pressing her hand to her chest.

"Did I get you?" he asked. "Felt like I got you."

Valna took her hand away, I didn't see any blood, just a tear in her clothes. "Fuck you."

"I'm only here to fight." He flipped the knife in his hand and looked between us. "You want to do this one at a time or..."

Valna bared her teeth and drew her other knife. I stepped with my ice-knives up in a guard position.

"Okay, I can take you both."

He blurred.

A knife came at me, stabbing and striking at my belly. I knocked it aside with an ice-knife. The blade scraped a patch of frozen snow on my side. I swung my other ice-knife to stab into his neck. He was already gone.

Valna cried out as he attacked her. There was a blur of motion as he thrust, cut, slashed and she parried, batted aside the knives and blinked away again.

He rushed after her, on her almost as soon as she reappeared. She stumbled back, deflected his too-quick knives, and disappeared. She reappeared. He attacked.

I ran forward as fast as I could on the treacherous snow and tried to anticipate where the fight would be once I got there.

Valna cried out. Blotches of red blossomed on her clothes. I threw one of my ice-knives at the too-fast Windborn. It bounced off him harmlessly. He snarled, spun, and leapt at me. His knives glinted as he stabbed, like deadly sunlight.

With only one knife to defend myself, I had to stumble away from his onslaught.

Chunks of ice splintered from me as his knives connected. Bright red slashes appeared on my arms. I tried to stab at him, but it was easily batted away. His other knife scored a deep gouge across my other arm. I couldn't attack, only defend.

Valna leapt back into the fight. She appeared next to me already stabbing with her knife as our enemy attacked me. He moved back and stumbled on the uneven ground. Valna's knife sunk into him. A spot of crimson soaked into his shirt.

"Draw him away," I whispered. "Just for a heartbeat, then lure him back to me."

Valna's gaze never left the Windborn. She was breathing heavy, all colour drained from her face, but she nodded.

We circled the Windborn. He bared his teeth and held a hand pressed to his chest, trying to staunch the blood.

"Come on, Drafli, is that all you've got?" Valna snarled.

She threw herself forward. He brought his knives up to block her, but mid-stride she disappeared and reappeared on the other side of him. For anyone else the trick would have been enough, but with his supernatural speed Drafli was able to twist and catch Valna's twin knives with his own.

They began a blurring, blinking dance of iron and blood between the trees. The snow whorled around them as though eager to be part of the deadly spectacle.

I took a few slow steps away. Careful not to draw Drafli's attention. I reached out to the Wind within me, still gusting in my chest and pushed its power down. I felt the rough earth freeze into slick ice around me.

Valna cried out again. Sweat shone on her brow and her arms were covered in fresh wounds.

"I thought Hraki wanted me dead," I called out.

The Windborn made a vicious attack at Valna. Her outline blurred, but she didn't go anywhere, too exhausted to use her power anymore. Her hand came up to deflect the knife. She was too slow. The angle wasn't right. The Windborn's knife cut into her hand and she screamed as two fingers fell to the floor. Life-dark blood spurted onto the white forest and Valna dropped her other knife to clutch at her injured hand.

Our enemy smiled and turned to me.

"See," he said between laboured breaths, "I can take both of you."

He ignored Valna. She fell to her knees and clutched her hand to her chest. Shuddering sobs fell out of her.

Drafli stalked towards me. I pushed against the Winds in me one final time, and a fresh cold whispered through me. The deathly chill of exhaustion.

My body screamed at me to give up.

Lie down.

Die.

I looked over at the red snow growing around Valna. I couldn't. Not yet.

I widened my stance and bared my teeth. As Drafli circled me I pushed my ice-knives together and melded them into a short spear of sharpened ice.

"Come on," I growled.

His smile widened, showing me the bright sharpness of his teeth, but it faltered as he put a finger to the growing patch of blood on his chest.

Once more he blurred, rushing to meet me with impossible speed. I braced, hunching down to make myself a small target, and brought up my weapons. The snow exploded out of the way of the Windborn's pumping legs and then he found the edge of the ice beneath.

His feet went out from under him and he yelped. The momentum of his sprint kept him moving forward and he slid towards me. I stabbed down.

It met Drafli's chest, but his momentum was too great. The spear snapped and was ripped from my hands, but half of it was already deep in his chest.

He slid to a stop, gasping and clutching at the shard of ice stabbed through him. Blood welled from the jagged hole in his chest and his fingers clawed at the icicle spear. His hands, glistening with blood, couldn't find a grip.

I walked toward him. He made to roll away, but he was sluggish now. The snow underneath him darkened with crimson.

"You bitch," he hissed between bloody breaths.

I tried to summon another ice-knife, but could only manage a covering of frost across my palms. I looked around to see where his knives had fallen and saw Valna stumbling towards us. Each slow step seemed to be a burden. One hand clutched a knife. The other arm hung limp, the hand at the end of it dripped gore onto the snow.

She fell to her knees beside the Windborn. He tried to squirm away but he had no strength left.

"Hraki will come for you," he said. "It's too late. You can't..."

Valna pressed her ruined hand down on his chest, slipping a little in her own blood, then raised her knife and tore out his throat. The Windborn convulsed. Hot blood sprayed onto us, onto the snow. Where it fell, steam rose gently into the air.

I went over to Valna and she fell onto me. I held her until she stopped shaking and then helped her sit upright on her own.

I used some of Drafli's clothes to bandage Valna's hand. The blood quickly seeped through the cloth and I had to redress it. I managed to ice over the wound to help with the clotting and tied the bandage tight. The two smallest fingers on her right hand were gone. Sliced off before the first knuckle. After I bandaged her hand, Valna kicked through the bloody snow, trying to find her fingers.

I took her gently by the shoulders and guided her away from our battlefield.

"Come on," I said. "We need to get back to Erling. We need to tell them what's coming."

Valna turned her glassy gaze onto me and nodded.

We left the body and the blood-stained snow behind.

*

The snowfall eased, as though disinterested now the fight was over. We marked our route south by the moss on the trees. I had given up trying to cover our tracks. There was no way I would be able to hide our path as we ploughed through the snow, especially as some part of Valna's hand refused to clot and she left a rusty trail.

"Valna."

No response. Only the crunch of footsteps in the snow.

"Valna," I said again, louder.

She stopped, turned to face me. Her face was so pale it was almost lost in the snowfall.

"We should eat."

She blinked slowly, shrugged acquiescence and slumped to the floor. I crunched over to sit with her and pulled out the food I had taken from Hraki's fort. The bread inside had been squashed at some point during the fight, the round buns now flat. I rippled one of them in two and shared it out. I gave most to Valna, despite my churning belly. Her hand had stopped bleeding but I needed her moving. I didn't have the strength to carry her.

"I don't know if I'm going to make it, Edda," Valna murmured as if hearing my thoughts. "Leave me. Go south."

I looked at her sallow cheeks and watched shallow plumes of

her breath in the winter air. I could move quicker on my own, get help. I chewed a chunk of bread and thought back to the night we spent skating at the edge of the fjord. Valna had been so kind to me from the moment I met her, and all she asked for in return was a friend.

"I'm not going to leave you." I pulled her back up onto her feet. "You can't stop. We need to get you back to Olek."

A smile twitched at the edge of her lips. She tried to say something, but it was lost under the rustling trees.

We took a step then another and another. Valna stumbled and I pulled her up. When I stumbled Valna tugged me along without breaking her stride. If we stopped, I was not sure we would be able to begin again.

"Runar will find us," I said, although I didn't know who I was trying to reassure.

Valna grunted, nodded.

We kept on like that for an age, crossing streams and clambering over hills and rocky outcrops. Always south. Each step was a challenge, a fight, and our pace slowed until we barely shuffled forward at all. My eyes itched for sleep and my body cried out for rest, but I wouldn't give in. I couldn't. I saw Hraki's face every time I closed my eyes. Over and over again I saw the bright wound close, fade to a purple bruise, and then disappear completely. Every step brought me closer to justice. Slash, heal, step. Slash, heal, step.

A bird called out, snapping my attention back to the present.

I put a hand on Valna's shoulder. She stopped.

It called out again. A gull. Its obnoxious laughter echoed around the forest.

I sagged as I watched the sea bird's silhouette slice over the trees. How far had we walked? Time was lost in a haze of snowfall and exhaustion. Had we gone so far off course that we had reached the coast?

A smaller silhouette joined the gull. It laughed with the gull, this one a grating raven's cackle. More shapes flowed above the treetops. Each a bird, but none the same. A starling. A wood pigeon. And even an eagle.

"Do you think..." Valna started. "Hey, down here!"

Before I could react the eagle screamed and the birds dived. I ducked, but none of them attacked. They swooped around us. Each one called out until we were surrounded by a whirlwind of feathers and beaks. More birds filled the sky above us until the clouds were blotted out. A raven flew out of the whirlwind and squawked into my face. I flinched back.

"Gerda," I muttered. "You playful bitch."

A few moments after the birds found us, Runar descended through the branches and stumbled to a stop in front of us.

"You're alive. Thank the gods."

He snatched us both up into a tight embrace. I grunted in pain and Valna cried out. Runar let go and hopped back with a horrified expression on his face.

"Are you hurt?"

"Valna," I said. "Valna needs help."

She clutched her broken hand to her chest and began to shake with relieved sobs.

"I'll take her back now. I'll come back for you."

I nodded, unable to say anything more.

Valna put her arms around Runar's neck and he took her weight. Runar made a slow ascent above the treeline and then accelerated south. I slumped against a tree and watched them disappear through the evergreen leaves.

The raven swooped down beside me and cawed. I pulled some bread from a pocket. The bird hopped back. It spread its wings and opened its beak in a silent, violent promise.

"Thank you," I said and offered the raven the rind of bread.

The bird cawed and ruffled its feathers before jumping forward and stabbing at the offering. I watched it feast and waited for Runar. The shadows of the birds above made a black whirlpool around me.

"Thank you," I whispered, quiet enough that I barely heard it myself.

Chapter Twenty
A Raven and a Longship

I woke the next day with Gerda's hound next to me. His warm, reassuring weight pressed against me as he slept. I pulled away and his fur, stuck to me with a coating of frost, snapped with a crinkle. I sat up and winced. The wounds in my chest and the beating I had taken from Hraki's lightning-fast Windborn still scraped against my bones.

The memory of my journey came back to me in patches. It had taken Runar a few hours to return. I remembered being lifted into the sky, the leaves grazing my skin as we broke through the canopy, and the cutting air as we flew back to the safety of Erling's kingdom. The king had wanted to see us as soon as we got back, but neither I nor Valna were in a position to answer questions. We were waved off, given food and water and sent to rest.

The elkhound grunted as I struggled to my feet, annoyed that his cushion had moved. He stretched and shook himself. Frost flew from his fur like sea spray.

Further up the longhouse, Valna snored. I walked to her and the hound came with me. Valna's corner was as messy as ever. She lay sprawled across several piles of clothing. Her right hand, now properly bandaged with clean cloth, stuck out towards us. The hound wandered over and licked at it as though that would heal it. Valna frowned and rolled over. The hound, undeterred, licked her face instead.

"Wh— Get off," she mumbled.

The dog gave a muted woof and Valna started awake.

"Did Gerda ask the dog to lick you, or does he do that all on his own?" I asked, trying to contain a smile.

"I don't know," Valna said. She went to rub her eyes and then stopped and stared at the blood-tinged bandages on her right hand. "Oh. Right."

The dog nuzzled her, licking her face and almost pushing her over. Valna smiled and shoved the dog playfully away. I leaned on her table. The colour had returned to her cheeks and the bags under her eyes were gone, though she still looked weak.

"Valna..." I paused, grasping for the right words. "I... Thank you. You saved me. Again. I don't know what to—"

"It's fine." Her eyes flicked back to her bandaged hand. "You'd do the same for me, right?"

I watched Valna fuss the elkhound. She giggled as it licked her cheeks.

"In a heartbeat," I said.

Valna scratched Rollo's chin then pushed him away. "Oh, good, Fainn brought the axe back."

"What?"

Valna pointed to the wall behind me and I saw an axe resting against the wall. Bjolfur's axe. Tears blurred my vision.

"I... how?"

"I found it when I came to find you. Before I came after you I gave it to Fainn for safekeeping, asked him to put it in your room."

"Valna, I..."

I didn't have the words. The thought of Bjolfur's axe rusting and rotting in the forest was a slow-bleeding wound, but it was still with me and that dulled the pain. I let out a slow, shuddering breath and some of the tension left my chest.

Footsteps sounded at the door and Runar stepped into view, bowls in hand and bread balanced between them.

"Gerda said you'd be awake," he said and handed us each a bowl of stew and split the loaf between us. "Erling's going to be along soon. He wanted me to drag you over to the mead-hall, but I convinced him to let you have a little more rest."

"Thanks," Valna said through a mouthful of bread, spraying breadcrumbs everywhere.

"Any sign of Hraki?" I asked.

"Gerda's seen his longships moving, but she can see Lothi

flying over them, and after what happened to those ravens she sent with you, she's not getting too close."

I nodded then turned my attention to the food. I dipped the warm bread into the stew and bit off a chunk covered in strings of meat and specks of vegetables. After wandering through the frozen forest and days eating cold food, the warmth of the meal spread through my chest like sunlight. For a time, the only sounds in the longhouse were the slurp and chomp of Valna and I eating and the low scritch as Runar ruffled the dog's ears.

Footsteps stomped into the longhouse as we finished our food. Runar and I helped Valna to her feet. She winced and stumbled but managed to right herself without help.

"Are you finished?" came Erling's stern voice.

We left Valna's room and stepped into the longhouse proper to find a small crowd making themselves comfortable. Erling had taken a seat, staring out from the wobbling stool as though he sat on his throne. Alvilda, Katja, Fainn and a couple of huskalar moved some of the benches and chairs into a rough semicircle to face Erling. The huskalar stood guard at the doors and everyone else found a space in the circle, including the dog who flopped down next to Valna.

"I sent you to weaken Hraki and it seems you've brought a war down on me," Erling said. His voice tremored with barely restrained fury. "Gerda told me that you wandered away from the campsite and then her birds died. What happened after that?"

I told him.

The expressions around the circle moved from surprise as I described my capture, to outrage as I revealed Hraki's secret, to grim determination when I told how they tried to kill me, and finally to consternation when I mentioned Hraki's plan to ignore the laws regarding Windborn and his talk of men too long on their thrones.

"I found Edda at the walls," Valna chimed in. "We got out of the fort, but one of his Windborn caught up to us." She held up her hand as if she needed proof. "Then Gerda and Runar found us."

Erling hunched forward and scowled. He brought his clasped hands away from his face. "Is there any way you could be mistaken about King Hraki being a Windborn?"

He emphasised the title, as though reminding me of Hraki's crown would spark some confession.

"The wound disappeared as I watched. He had been trying to recruit me. He said if I joined him no one would be able to stop him and his Windborn. Once I saw his Windborn power, though, he tried to kill me instead."

"Then shouldn't you be dead?" Erling asked. There was an undercurrent of accusation in his tone and the huskalar by the door seemed to straighten.

I lifted my tunic and pointed to the myriad rose coloured ice-scars across my midriff. "Ice clots quicker than blood," I said. "They thought they'd stabbed me enough and threw me out to die. It didn't take."

I let my tunic fall and Erling nodded. He sat silent for a moment and tugged on his braided beard before he turned to Alvilda and Katja.

"What does this mean, law-keepers?" Erling asked. "Hraki must surely forfeit his crown?"

"Yes—"

"No—"

Katja and Alvilda started together. They frowned at one another.

"Once one becomes Windborn they must forfeit all of their property and previous ties, surely this applies to kingship as well?" Katja said.

"Well, yes," Alvilda said, avoiding the intensity of the gazes around her. "But at the moment we have only–I'm sorry, Edda–only the word of a Windborn who has a known motive to see Hraki fall. If Hraki is indeed Windborn, then we need proof, and the High King will strip him of his title and lands."

"It should be easy enough to prove," Fainn said. "Even a small cut across the palm would be proof either way."

"And would that be enough for you, Law-Keeper Alvilda?" Erling rumbled.

Alvilda nodded, and to her credit did not back down from the king's furious gaze. "It would be conclusive, but if we are in a position to submit Hraki to such a test, then we can wait for the High King. The treaty forbids any law-keeper, even one serving the High King directly, from making such an judgement."

"But how would we get such proof? I can see no reason why King Hraki would submit to this test," Erling said. "He stands to gain nothing but lose everything."

"We should capture him," Runar said. "Strike him first for once. I am tired of sitting and waiting. Send out your Windborn, my king. I can distract them. Valna can sneak in and capture Hraki. And Edda can help us to bring him back. Then—"

"You can't do that."

We all turned to Alvilda. The law-keeper's expression was stern and she held her chin up.

"If you attack King Hraki before the High King has made his judgement then you will be the aggressor and earn all the penalties that come with that."

She stared at us but could not weather all of the anger in our eyes and dropped her gaze.

"Are you telling me," Erling growled, "that I must sit here and wait for an army of Windborn to kill the people under my protection before I can move against them?"

"You cannot know that they are on their way to attack. I requested they come to talk, and that is likely why they are coming."

"There's no one left at his halls," I said. "They are all on his longships, weighed down with weapons."

Katja put her hand on Alvilda's shoulder. The girl turned her head away.

"Alvilda, you must see the need for action?" Katja asked gently. "We cannot wait for the High King to send a message to us for this decision. Hraki's people have shown their disrespect for the laws of parley already. Lives hang in the balance."

The young law-keeper looked around the assembled people and then to me.

"You have to believe me, Alvilda. Hraki is Windborn. He is ignoring the laws of gods and mortals so that he can hold on to his power. We have to act first."

She bit her lip and stared into me. For a moment it felt like we were back on a longship, travelling from Konvald and were the only two people hating the journey.

"I believe you, Edda," she said. "But that's not enough."

Alvilda looked around the room without shying away from the intensity in everyone's eyes. She looked back at me and seemed to reach a decision then stood.

"I will send a message to the High King and inform him of developments here. I will notify him of the allegations that King Hraki is Windborn and advise him to make his way to Eylheim in all haste. If the gods are with us the High King will arrive in a few days and he will be able to hear Hraki's testimony personally."

Relieved murmurs echoed around the longhouse.

"Thank you, law-keeper," Erling said. "I trust you have no objection to us preparing to defend our homes in the meantime?"

Alvilda chewed her lip then shook her head. "Of course not, King Erling, although I cannot let you attack unless Hraki leaves no other choice. Prepare your forces, but do not instigate a war."

Erling's jaw bunched but he nodded thanks to Alvilda. She bowed to him and swept out of the room, clearly relieved to have an excuse to leave.

All eyes turned to Erling once Alvilda left the longhouse. The king's jaw clenched and unclenched.

"I don't care what that law-keeper says," he growled through gritted teeth. "We must prepare for war."

Grim faces looked back at him, but none baulked. We knew that the river brought death on its currents and, one way or another, the crows would feast.

*

Alvilda stood alone on the southern shore of Erling's island and threw a raven into the air. It squawked with indignation then found its bearings and disappeared into the overcast sky. The black-feathered bird carried a message to the High King, and with it our last hopes.

Erling worked us hard to prepare for the worst. He sacrificed all but a few of his boats and longships to reconnect the chain of vessels that cut across the fjord to block Hraki's passage. The rest of the boats, small vessels used for transport between the island and the town proper, were put to use moving warriors and weapons. The huskalar handed spears, axes, and shields to anyone that could wield them. Most had some experience raiding and those that didn't were quickly shown the rudiments of blood-letting. Runar was put to work flying supplies one way or another and helping with the reconstruction of the chain of ships. Valna and I were given our tasks, but our recovery was at the forefront of Erling's mind and we were told to rest as often as we were put to work.

"Edda, would you mind going to look after Orin?" Katja asked me on the second day of preparations. "He's still not recovered properly. I want to make sure he eats enough, but I've got so much to do."

I stopped and set down the barrel I was carrying. I had been ignoring the weight of Orin in my mind, pushing it away in favour of action against the impending threat. Now, I felt the familiar rise of grief and rage aimed at the storm-fingered Windborn.

"Sure," I said, slowly.

"Thanks, Edda, just grab something from the kitchen and make sure he eats all of it." She patted me on the shoulder then rushed off, calling over her shoulder, "I really appreciate it."

I went to the kitchen in a daze. The hot air inside felt like the tension before a storm. I took a bowl of soup, a hunk of cheese and some bread. People rushed all around me, but they had their own tasks to occupy them. I took a knife from a scrap-covered table, wiped off the slivers of vegetables, and slipped it through my belt.

"Where you going with that?" A gruff old man asked me, pointing at my haul.

"To Orin."

"Oh. Right you are. Tell him that Magnus is praying for him. Oh, and here." He shoved a bottle of mead into my hands. "Don't tell anyone though, eh?"

I nodded.

Outside was filled with bustling activity that bordered on frenzy. People shouted instructions or yelled at someone for getting in their way. I moved through them like a ghost. Silent. Unnoticed.

As I approached the longhouse, the same one I had found Orin in some nights ago, I wondered if Gerda would be waiting for me. I looked up. The sky, though clear of clouds, was half-obscured by the silhouettes of countless circling birds. She couldn't focus on all of those birds and Orin at once, could she?

Inside was dark. Orin was alone. I set the food down on the bench and looked at him. His shallow, wheezing breaths barely lifted his chest. The tangled mess of hair seemed to be thinner and his skin was so tight I thought his bones might punch through. I sat on the bench where Gerda had once reprimanded me and pulled the knife free from my belt.

This man, made of tight skin and withered limbs, was the source of the most intense storm I had ever seen. For all I knew, each of his shallow, pained breaths could still summon a mast-shattering gale. I tapped the tip of the knife against one of my iced-over scars.

"You're new." The voice rasped from Orin's bed. His heavy-lidded eyes looked over at me, though the rest of him hadn't moved. "The girl from the longship."

I tightened my grip on the knife. "From the longship?"

"The burning longship."

"Oh. Yes, that's me."

"I hope you were worth it," Orin said, then broke out into a fit of coughs. "So? What do you want?"

"Katja sent me. She asked me to make sure you eat something."

Orin nodded, or at least his head dipped for a moment. "She's good to me, but don't waste your time."

"What do you mean?"

"Look at me, girl, I'm wasting away." He raised a skeletal arm. "I'm just a jumble of bones waiting to fall apart. You eat it."

I looked at the food and broke off two pieces from the loaf, I kept one piece and handed the other to Orin. He frowned at me, but sat up and bit into it.

"How long have you been sworn to Erling?" I asked.

"Long enough. I was one of his father's huskalar. Helped

him carve out this little patch of earth."

"You stayed with them once you became Windborn?" I said through a mouthful of bread, spraying crumbs all over Orin.

"Watch it," he said. "I didn't see much point trying to find some other bugger to take me. They sent me raiding and I had a good time, got them a lot of plunder. You ever hear about the lone longship that sailed against forty ships sent by the Emperor of Sheketh?"

"You're that Storm Weaver?"

Most people didn't believe the stories. It went that the raiders travelled too far through the Empire of Bones and had to try and outrun the first fleet of the Sheketh. Some versions said they only survived because their god-speaker had obtained the help of the Sea Giants. Other versions said a single fighter, favoured by the Warrior, patron of thunder, had saved them, and some told of a single Windborn that stood on the prow of the longship and destroyed all arrayed against them. Whatever version you heard, the storm clouds that saved them were so thick they blocked out the sun for three days.

"Aye, that was me. It was only about a dozen ships I got, though. Blasted them right out of the water. Have you got anything to wash this down? It's too dry."

Orin waved away the soup so I poured out a cup of mead and passed it over.

"Magnus sent this and said he's praying for you."

Orin wheezed a laugh after he had taken a sip. "He's wasting his time, but he does make good mead."

As he chewed on the bread the muscles of his jaw stood out like cords of rope. I turned away and picked up the knife.

"You've been staring daggers at me ever since you came in. What's your problem?"

"You..." I trailed off.

"Me? Got any reason, or just jealous I got a nicer bed than you?"

I meant to tell him what happened, what he had done to me. I thought I wanted him to squirm under my grief and anger and all the choices he'd taken away from me, but I couldn't. The way I played this moment in my mind, when I was finally placed before my husband's murderer, it wasn't like this. I didn't loom over a man who was more bone than flesh as he sipped his last drink. He hadn't been old enough to be my grandfather. We had faced each other with weapons in hand as enemies should.

"No, no, I mean..." I sighed and broke the cheese into two pieces. "I don't know. I lost my husband in a storm this year coming back from a raid."

"When was that?" Orin asked, only mildly interested as he half-gnawed, half-slurped on his cheese. "Was it one of mine?"

I paused, surprised. I wondered if I would get an admission of guilt from this withered man who was focused only on his scrap of food or if he would just ignore the deep scars he had given me.

"It was right at the end of summer. I... I think it was one of yours."

He tutted but didn't look up from his food. Old teeth and wet gums worried away at the hunk of cheese. "Shame. I told Erling he's going to get other people killed if I kept throwing storms about, but did he listen? No. Didn't want Hraki getting any more money, he said. That was good cheese, no one gives me stuff like that anymore. Is there any more?"

"You mean," I said as I passed him my untouched cheese, "you threw that storm out into the seas to keep Hraki from getting money?"

"Well that's not exactly what Erling said, is it?" Orin pulled his face into an exaggerated expression of concern and affected a deep voice to imitate Erling's. "Orin, throw out a storm. Make it a big one. Orin, we can't give Hraki's men safe passage if he won't give me my son back. Blah blah blah. We're just tools to them, you know. Only as useful as long as we're killing."

I opened my mouth, closed it, and waited for the acknowledgement of what he'd done. The only sound in the house was the wet smacks of gums and lips on cheese.

Erling, in his grief, had ordered Orin to make a storm of such power that even half-way to Ertland we were not safe from it. But if Erling was to blame for the storm, then Hraki was to blame for its summoning. The Windborn king had hidden his resurrection from the world so he could cling to his throne and as the two kings had come to blows it was everyone else that suffered. I could not blame Erling for his obstinance in standing against Hraki. Erling had lost a son and his righteous anger was magnified because he could not give his son the burial rights he deserved. I wondered if my sorrow and anger would have been sharpened if I had not been able to cast Bjolfur's runestone.

At the thought of the runestone, my mind came back to the storm that had drowned my husband. I turned my attention back to the old man before me. It was Orin's storm that had nearly sunk our longship. Orin was the one that washed my husband into the ocean. He had killed Bjolfur as surely as a spear through the chest. Could you blame the spear for the injuries it inflicted, or should you blame its wielder?

"Aren't you sorry?" I asked eventually, unable to stop myself. "Bjolfur wasn't the only one we lost and there must have been other ships."

"Who's Bjolfur? Oh, right. Why should I be sorry? Any raider worth their salt should be able to sail in a storm. It's not my fault you couldn't handle it."

Fury and grief warred in my chest. My anger had long since turned to a cold thing of singular purpose, like a sword quenched in its making. Orin's flippant remarks, his apathy, meant that singular sharp edge brayed for him. It reached out from the place where my heart had been, the thumping centre of myself where I once kept all my plans, my dreams, my loves. Empty now, but it could be filled with blood. The knife twitched in my hands. Its wooden handle creaked in my grip and I pointed it at the font of storms lying before me. Ice crept out between my fingers, locking the knife onto my palm.

Orin lay oblivious to my changing mood. There was no guilt, no remorse for what he had done. There was no flicker of Wind within him like I sensed in Valna, Runar, or even Hraki.

This was the moment. This was what I wanted. My reckoning. The moment I confronted the digger of my husband's grave, but Orin wasn't the murderer I thought he was. He was a grumpy old man who had served his king and hurt innocent people in the process. I remembered the woman I had left with a hole in her neck, cold blood on her clothes, and the anguished scream that followed. I thought of Soren's head, likely picked clean by scavengers by now, and the role he'd played in my descent. Soren's death had done nothing to fill the hole within me. Blood could not drown my grief, nor bring back my lost dreams and family. What price would Orin pay if I killed him? He wanted to die. It would be a mercy.

I could take nothing from Orin, the Storm Weaver, whose blood was thunder. We needed whatever strength he had left for the fight. Salvation from my grief wouldn't come from his death. I needed to bring Hraki to justice, to force him to submit to the laws that had almost broken me. Then, I could rest.

I snapped the knife out of my hand and placed it on the bench.

"Do you need anything else?" I said, suddenly wanting to be alone.

"What? No. I can feed myself. Leave the food and drink and leave me alone."

I nodded. I pushed the bench closer to Orin so that he could reach the rest of his food. There was a clatter as I walked out of the room, cups falling from old, fumbling hands, and then cursing.

I left.

*

A rogue silhouette swooped through Gerda's thousand swirling eyes. It landed on one of the carved ribs marking the path into Erling's mead-hall and squawked.

"Not one of mine," Gerda grunted when we confronted her about it.

Valna, Katja and I stood around it. The bird, a raven, twisted on top of the rib and cocked its eye at each of us in turn. When one of us tried to grab it the raven hopped, wings akimbo, onto the next rib-column. Valna appeared next to it and snatched it before it hopped away. As she held it, Katja picked off the message from its leg. The scroll was small and tightly bound with a bright purple ribbon.

"It's from the High King," she said, her face pale. "I can't open this. Where's Alvilda?"

Someone was sent running to find her. Valna cried out as the raven pecked at her and she let it go. It flapped its great wings, catching itself as it fell, and screeched at us. With its purpose fulfilled, it climbed into the sky, seeming to sway lazily from side to side as it got higher and higher.

"She wasn't very nice," Valna said, sucking the blood from her finger.

I watched its slow ascent and thought back to my flight with Runar a couple of days before. The blurred treetops beneath me belied a speed to our journey that I couldn't imagine a bird matching. So much had happened in the past few days, but surely the High King hadn't received our message that Hraki was Windborn yet.

Alvilda arrived, puffing and cheeks red, and took the message from Katja.

"Thank you. Where is the raven?"

"It's already gone," I said and pointed off into the southern sky.

"Damn it. Couldn't someone have held on to it? My two birds have gone with messages already."

Valna stuck her finger out at the law-keeper, a fresh red welt bulged out from her fingertip. "I tried."

"Oh, sorry."

"Come on," Katja grabbed at her arm. "King Erling is going to want to know what that says. Valna, can you find the king, please?"

Alvilda was about to object then she noticed the people craning their necks to see what brought the law-keepers and Windborn together. She seemed willing to wait for a private space to open the message so she nodded and let herself be led inside the mead-hall.

By the time Erling had been found and made his way to his throne, a small crowd had amassed in the mead-hall, rendering Alvilda's worries pointless. Some were servants, brushing the spotless floor or stoking the long fire. Others were well-dressed and well-armed; the wealthy come to see if they would be saved.

"Well?" Erling said as soon as he was in the room.

Alvilda looked nervously between the king as he sat on his throne and then looked to the assembled crowd.

"Perhaps this is something better discussed in private, King Erling."

"We have a mad king bearing down on us with all the strength he possesses. I think my people deserve to know how the High King intends to help us."

Alvilda swallowed and nodded.

"The High King is on his way here. He talks about the Windborn Soren burning the longships and says he will judge this case himself. I am instructed to collect information only and wait for his arrival."

"It's a bit late for that," I snorted.

Alvilda shot me an annoyed look and Runar punched me playfully in the arm by way of reprimand.

"He makes no mention of the Windborn king?" Erling asked.

"No, King Erling. I think it likely he has not received that message. The tone of the High King's words suggests he left immediately after sending the raven."

"And how long ago did he send the bird?" Erling asked.

"It is difficult to tell. Two or perhaps three days ago."

"And you left Hraki's fortress two days ago," Erling said, nodding at me. "Katja, how long did it take the Iron Rib to sail here from Konvald?"

"Three days, my king."

Erling sucked on his teeth. "It may be that we can tell the High King of Hraki's deceit in person. Perhaps then his law-keeper will let us attack this Windborn army on our own terms rather than waiting for the wolves to surround us."

Alvilda squirmed as Erling denounced her, but said nothing.

"Did you hear that, friends?" Erling said. He stood up from the throne and raised his hands to address the crowd crammed into the mead-hall. "The High King himself comes to bear judgement on Hraki. Go now and set yourselves to your preparations. Sharpen your weapons and rest your bodies. We will stop Hraki here and make sure he cannot burn any more homes or take more lives."

A small cheer went up from the crowd and everyone rushed out. Erling held his Windborn back and gave us fresh instructions on how we would attack Hraki if we were allowed to take the offensive.

"Go," he said. "I pray that the High King arrives in time, but ready yourselves for battle without him, nonetheless.

Word spread quickly and preparation efforts redoubled. The possibility of active engagement stoked the heart-fires of Erling's warriors. Runar, Valna, and I rushed from one place to another, wherever the strength of a Windborn was most needed, and soon weapons and shields were stored in every available space and supplies hoarded into almost every house.

The next day, when Erling had summoned his Windborn to the mead-hall to check on our progress, one of the huskalar rushed in.

"Longships, your majesty, sighted on the horizon," he said, between gasping breaths.

"The gods do listen," Erling rumbled. "The High King has come."

Confusion rippled over the huskalar's face. "No, my king, it is Hraki. He has arrived with full ships."

Valna disappeared from the hall and Runar flew out the door, leaving Erling and I to catch up with them. We followed them to the beach. Valna's footsteps started halfway down the low sand, and Runar floated above the wet ground, leaving no trace.

In the water, beyond the chained line of empty boats, longships waited. Four. Maybe five. It was difficult to count them through the other ships. Each one was low in the water, full of warriors and lined with shields. Behind those longships was another boat lying heavy in the water. No shields lined this vessel and it was too bulky to be a raiding ship. The people that weighed it down all looked to have grey hair or were too young to hold a shield. The small fleet drifted to a stop in the belly of the fjord.

"This can't be a diplomatic mission," Runar said.

"It's too much for a raid," Valna muttered. "There must be hundreds of warriors out there."

"Look behind them," I said. "It's not an invasion. It's a migration, and we're in the way."

Erling looked out at the longships, his fists clenching and unclenching, his brows brought together like thunderclouds. His eyes darted from ship to ship and I suspected that even after everything that had happened Erling still hoped that somewhere on those ships was the body of his son. But hoping for something does not make it so and we all knew that Hraki's longships carried only axes, spears, and the promise of blood.

Erling sighed, then straightened and turned to us.

"Ready your weapons."

*

A figure rose from Hraki's convoy. Lothi. He came forward until he was directly above the chain of longships and waited. We stood on the beach with the king, all dressed to fend off an invasion. Even Katja wore a helmet and had an axe at her side, though she clutched it like a child would clutch at their parents' clothes.

"See what he has to say," Erling said.

Runar nodded and flew to meet the floating ambassador.

The two flying shadows came together. Against Gerda's swirling flocks they looked like giants. Lothi inched forward and for a moment Runar moved to block him until something was said and they came back to us together. Runar put his spear across Lothi's path to stop him before he got too close. I tightened my grip on my axe and Valna took a step closer to Erling.

"He will only speak with you, my king," Runar called over to us.

"Your king has brought an army to my shores," Erling shouted back. "If you do not take your longships back to your own lands I will be forced to consider this an act of war."

Lothi held up his hands in mock surrender. "Please, King Erling, this is an act of desperation, not war. My king begs that you break the chain you have so cruelly made of your longships and allow him passage beyond your lands and waters. He seeks only the horizon."

"You expect me to believe you after that Windborn burned my ships?"

"That was an error in judgement, King Erling. We have made reparations for that and had hoped you would be able to overlook it."

"An error in whose judgement?

424

"Hraki's." Lothi clasped his hands together over his belly and bowed his shaking head. He was the picture of regret, though none of us believed him. "Had he known how... volatile Soren's reaction to failure would be, another would have been sent in his place. You have already been given the gold for those ships, have you not?"

I spat on the beach at that and others shook their heads or scoffed under their breath.

"Gold is poor comfort when you press steel against my throat. The gold for the longships was due, the High King's law-keeper saw to that, but that does not free your king of his past crimes. Bring me my son's bones and I will consider your request. Otherwise, go home."

Lothi's easy smile became strained and his shoulders had begun to hunch. "We cannot turn back."

"It seems easy enough to me."

"The ice upriver is too thick to allow passage; King Hraki's lands are barren and his stores empty; the warriors were promised plunder, and King Hraki keeps his promises; King Hraki will not back down," Lothi said and shrugged. "Pick a reason, King Erling, they all end the same. One way or another, we will pass."

"Is that a threat?" Erling's eyes seemed to spark with anger.

"It is what it is, King Erling," Lothi said, though his eyes wandered as though he grew bored with the conversation. "I have been sent to ask passage for the sake of peace. King Hraki does not wish for anyone to die today, but sometimes even his regal hands are tied."

"I've had enough of this," I murmured.

"We know what Hraki is, you fuck," I shouted up to Lothi. "All this posturing is pointless. Hand Hraki over to us so the law-keepers can do what's right."

"Who...?"

He squinted at me, trying to get a look at the face beneath the helm, then he laughed.

"I will say one thing for you: you are fucking hard to kill. But I always liked a challenge." His expression hardened and he twisted in the air to face Erling again. "Is this your answer then, Erling? You are refusing to let us pass?"

"You leave us with no choice, Windborn. Either leave this place or bring your king to us for judgement," Erling said. "The gods will not stand for a Windborn king nor one that brings war in winter. I will not stand for it."

"What of you law-keeper?" Lothi said and drifted along the shore until he floated in front of Alvilda. Runar kept pace with him, shoving his spear in Lothi's path. "Is our request not reasonable? We only ask for passage and yet King Erling threatens war. Will you not step in and defend us as the High King's subjects?"

Alvilda broke away from the Windborn's gaze and stared at the beach. We all turned to her, breath held, and she squirmed under the intensity of our eyes. Fear uncoiled beneath my ribs as the silence stretched on. Within her silence I heard the echo of all the judgements made against me.

"No," she said, too quiet to carry, then again, almost screaming it at him. "No. King Erling has the right to refuse passage, and this many longships can only be an act of aggression. Tell your king that I demand he come alone to meet me so I can confirm or dismiss the claim that he is Windborn. If he is not, then I will do what I can to mediate a peaceful solution. If King Hraki is Windborn, then... then he will be brought before the High King for judgement."

Lothi's expression crumpled. His arrogant smirk deflated and for a moment we saw the sharp edge in his eyes before his mask resurfaced.

"Your answer pains me, law-keeper. We had hoped that at least one of you would see reason." He floated back, keeping his eyes on us as he went. "In the hours to come, remember that this is not what King Hraki wanted. All of the pain could have been avoided."

Runar started to move with Lothi to escort back to Hraki's longships, but Lothi accelerated ahead. The speed of his retreat cut a line through the water beneath him as though an invisible longship sped under him.

"Did he just declare war on us?" Valna asked.

"Not in so many words, but I imagine the effect will be the same," Erling rumbled. "I trust, Law-Keeper Alvilda, you have no objection to us treating that as an act of war?"

426

Alvilda paused and bit her lip. Then the sound of a horn came from Hraki's longships and they began to move on the water. Alvilda sighed.

"No, it seems that war is now inevitable."

Erling nodded.

"To your places, then, everyone. Do not let them through. I don't know what Hraki wants with the horizon, but we must refuse it to him."

Erling spun, sweeping his spear from where it was stuck in the sand, and stormed off. The huskalar followed along with the law-keepers, but the Windborn remained. We looked out across the calm waters and watched.

The shields hanging over the longships' sides were pulled up one by one like the retreating legs of a monstrous, waterborne insect. Low chants began, then the sound of hundreds of shields beating in time. The chanting and thumping grew louder, and I thought I saw the water ripple alongside them. Underneath the noise and movement came windswept anticipation like a lover's lips brushing against your skin, or the cold press of a knife against your throat.

I looked at Valna and Runar. Their expressions mirrored my own. The pressure built in my chest, calling out to the warriors in the longships, to the Windborn preparing for the fight.

The chant became a roar and the clash of shields was as thunder. Above us, Gerda's birds swarmed and called out in return, a screeching cacophony of piercing cries. The oars slid out from the longships and they advanced.

CHAPTER TWENTY-ONE
A BATTLE IN WINTER

RUNAR TOWED VALNA AND I ACROSS THE FJORD in a small fishing boat. I had spent the last few days growing miniature icebergs that now floated across the fjord in the hopes that they would sink Hraki's longship before they reached the ocean. Runar pulled the boat along slowly, weaving us through the field of icebergs as we used poles to push them out of our way. The ice floated away from us easily enough and I wondered what good they would do against a longship. Two of them collided with a shuddering crunch. We felt the aftershocks through the water. Though they looked small on the surface, these chunks of ice had deep roots.

Almost all of the warriors from Erling's palatial island had been moved onto the mainland. It was unlikely Hraki would land there, as it was easily defensible and the chunks of ice were thick around the island, but these were not things to leave to chance and so a few huskalar remained around Erling's mead-hall to protect the vulnerable who hid there.

The Windborn were only a small part of the defences. There were many farmers and merchants from the town who volunteered to fight alongside the huskalar and refused to be transported over to Erling's island. As we arrived on the mainland, huskalar with grim expressions nodded to us and handed us spears. They couldn't sense the weight of the Windborn in Hraki's longships, but they felt the war-beat of thumping shields. Armoured huskalar and nervous warriors were scattered throughout the town, hidden and waiting for whatever might come their way. Each of them had a rune drawn on their forehead, a gift from Fainn. The god-speaker had burned branches of oak, willow, and ash and used the thrice-blessed ashes to draw runes of courage on any that wanted them. Everyone wanted them.

The sky was overcast and thousands of sharp, black silhouettes circled beneath the grey clouds. It seemed that Gerda had found all of the birds in the world to defend us.

We reached the burned farmhouse and Valna and I took our places with the waiting warriors. This blackened beach was the most likely landing spot and the familiar skeletal home lent iron to our spirits. The rest of Erling's forces, and the king himself, were scattered along the fjord to hinder the longships from pushing through. The king had wanted to be on the front line but had been shouted down by those that would protect him. He had agreed, with gritted teeth. He could do more as a symbol and commanding from afar.

A thunderous crack sounded from across the fjord as Hraki's foremost longship smacked into one of the chained ships. A wave surged out over the water. The longships tipped and tugged the chain taught. Someone jumped to the empty boat and began to hack at the rope wrapped around the figurehead.

Runar flew over to try and stop the axe-wielder, but a volley of arrows rushed up to meet him like a flock of iron-beaked birds. He threw a spear but banked away. Gerda's birds screamed, as though to drown out the rhythmic chopping, but we heard it all the same. Some of the people around me flinched with each thunk of the axe. Each swing brought Hraki's spears and fury closer.

Soon the figurehead toppled and crashed into the water. The figure jumped back onto the spear-bristling longship and they were through. The longships pushed aside the broken chain like a guest pushing past an open door. At a distance, the movement of the longships looked slow, serene. It was the gentle pace of predator closing in on wounded prey. One of the ships broke away from the others and lined its prow up to face us. The rest kept their course, though they had to break apart to try and sail through the iceberg teeth unscathed.

"We're not going to be able to stop them," one of the huskalar, holding a cerulean-painted shield, said. "They're not coming this way."

I turned and was startled to see Olek standing next to me. His skin was bone white, which made the ash-rune clear and stark on his forehead. His eyes darted from the lone longship bearing down on us, then to the other five ships making straight for the sea. Lothi rose from the leading longship and began to push the icebergs out of the way. A spear flew out towards him, easily dodged, and then another flying figure was next to him, slashing and stabbing. Birds joined Runar in his assault on the flying Windborn, coursing down from their maelstrom like a taloned waterfall.

"We'll stop them," I said, loudly to draw everyone's attention back to us.

Some of the huskalar glanced at us and Valna leaned forward to see around me. She grinned.

"They're sending one ship. As if that'll be enough." She disappeared and reappeared next to her lover. She grabbed the back of his neck and pulled him in for a fierce kiss. "There's nothing we can't do together. We—"

Her attention snapped back to the longship as the enemy began chanting once more.

"Get ready," Valna called out. "We rush them as soon as their feet touch the sand. Don't let them make a shield wall."

Shadows on the longship became figures, became shields, became faces. Shields thumped, voices screamed war cries. It felt like my own thundering heartbeat reflected back at me from across the waves. It was the arrival of blood.

The longship crunched into the sands. Warriors leapt from the deck. We charged forward, adding our screams to the surging sound of battle.

They tried to form a wall, to lock their shields together and keep us out. We sprinted to stop them, but Valna was already there.

She smashed into them from the other side, throwing her Windborn strength behind her shield, sending warriors stumbling, falling.

I met the tumbling warriors with iron-sharp teeth. My spear sank into the neck of one. My shield's iron heart crunched into the skull of another. All around me men and women smashed together with shields and screams.

Something wild exploded within me and I stumbled with the force of it. I turned and saw an enormous, muscled woman jumping down from the longship. She didn't have any weapons or armour. Her white hair, ruffling in the wind, flowed down her neck further than it should have. Jorunn. She stalked forward, moving slowly across the boot-churned sand.

One of the huskalar leapt forward with her shield raised and swung her axe at Jorunn's chest. The Windborn roared. Truly roared. I have heard shouts and screams loosed in the midst of battle-fury, but they were weak mewls compared to the bestial sound that came from Jorunn. The shock of it sent the huskalar stumbling back. That saved her life. As Jorunn swiped at the huskalar she transformed into a hulking, white-furred bear and her hand—now a clawed paw—sliced the air where the huskalar's head had been a moment before.

I sprinted towards them as Jorunn advanced on the huskalar scrambling backwards on the wet ground.

Too late.

Bear teeth sank into a flailing leg. Jorunn slammed a barrel-sized paw down on the huskalar's ribs. White-furred shoulders tensed. She pulled. A scream tore through the air along with a wet, jumbled snap and the huskalar's leg was ripped from her body. Red splattered across the frost tinged sand and Jorunn tossed the leg into the water. She roared again and hunched down to snap at the huskalar again.

I gripped my shield with both hands, put it to my shoulder, and leapt.

The shield boss collided with the snow bear's head and shoved the jaws away from the huskalar. The bear stumbled. I dropped down and put my hand against the warm, spurting stump of the huskalar's leg. The wounded warrior cried out as ice spread into the wound and froze the bleeding. I glanced up at the rest of the fighters, still trying to fend off Valna's whirling strikes.

"I'll stop this one," I said. "Tell Valna to get help."

The huskalar, wide-eyed and ghost-cheeked, nodded. I gave her my spear to use as a crutch and she limped along the beach.

I drew my axe and turned back to the snow bear Windborn who was pawing at her open muzzle as though to check if it still had all its teeth.

"Come on," I shouted and banged my axe against my shield.

The bear snarled at me. She bounded forward, each paw carved a pit in the sand deep enough to drown in, and pounced. I dove to my right and slipped under her. I swung my axe up as I moved. It caught deep enough that it was an effort to yank it out, painting the bear's white fur with her own blood, but it didn't slow her down.

She twisted. A paw collided with my shoulder and sent me flying.

Other huskalar rushed around me as I skidded to a halt in the sand. Two helped the injured warrior find safety, and the rest, five shield-bearing fighters, closed in around the Windborn.

The bear stood to face us. She was double the height of any of us. Her arms, each as long as a spear, hung loose by her side. She looked at the wavering warriors before her and roared.

Everyone stepped back.

I pushed myself to my feet and walked back up to the huskalar. They looked from me to the bear-formed Windborn and shifted their feet. I kept my eyes on the bear and stretched my arms out. Ice built up on my shoulders, cooling the bruises on my chest, and giving me an extra layer of frozen armour. The bear slumped to all fours and snorted as though amused we had chosen to fight her.

I charged.

The huskalar followed. A spear flew from the hand of one and buried its head deep in the bear's shoulder. She roared again.

The next moment was lost in a haze of white fur, spraying blood, crunching bones, and flashing steel. I struck out. Once. Twice. The Wind inside me raged like a trapped animal and lent me strength. On the third strike, my axe was caught in the bear's flinching flesh and was torn out of my grasp.

I leapt away from the hulk of red-stained fur.

Two of the huskalar lay broken beneath the monstrous Windborn. The three that remained fought on, trying to keep twisting the Windborn's attention away from one another. As well as my axe, two spears jutted from her side and there were red tears in her fur.

She roared in frustration as a huskalar leapt out of the way of her jaws and another attacked from behind. She ignored the slash and stab from the huskalar to lunge at the one in front. Her jaws closed over his head. The huskalar's scream was silenced in the crunch of metal and bone. The bear stood and threw the warrior over us.

I took a spear from one of the dead and ran at the bear before she had a chance to drop back to all fours.

The spear sank into her chest. My arm reverberated with the force of it. I pushed. The spear scraped and skittered along the ribcage.

Jorunn batted the spear shaft, which shattered like straw, and snapped her jaws. Hot, blood-scented breath washed over me. I threw myself to the side. Too late. Her teeth grazed my cheek, cracked my icy armour, then sank into my shoulder. Serrated pain blazed and my Windborn power leapt up against it. Cold smothered my shoulder to dull the agony.

The bear twisted, lurched upright to throw me too. The ice covering my shoulder splintered and her teeth slid over it. What should have been a tearing, rending of my flesh became a deep, spurting slash.

I landed some way down the beach. Freshwater lapped against my elbows. I tried to push myself up and the waves turned to frost as they touched me. My injured shoulder gave out with a spasm and I splashed down into the shallows.

Jorunn batted distractedly at the two remaining huskalar. They were knocked down but squirmed on the ground, still alive. The bear cantered at me. Her maw stretched open to engulf me once more.

I shuffled back, trying to get away as the hulking snow bear closed on me, but my shoulder couldn't take my weight. The shallow water froze, keeping me in place.

I groped for a piece of ice and snapped it into a sharp point ready to slice her from the inside if I had to.

Shadows swept from the sky and battered the snow bear. It whined and pulled away. Gerda's birds streamed down like a landslide. Screeches, screams, and squawks drowned out the sound of the bear.

Valna appeared beside me and grabbed onto my shoulder. I tried to scream. The world turned inside out, went black, then we were up along the beach, away from the fighting. My stomach twisted and I vomited.

"Erling's coming," Valna panted.

I sat up in time to watch the first of our reinforcements round the corner of the beach, then more crested the hill where the farm had been razed. Erling ran with them, adding his voice to the battle-cry. When the huskalar saw him they cheered and fought with renewed intensity. Erling led some of the new fighters away from the main group to charge at Jorunn. The bear roared, then was lost to a writhing mass of steel and teeth. I wondered how many of those brave, foolish fighters had been tending their livestock a few days ago.

"We need to help them," I said and looked around for a weapon.

Before I could find one, Valna caught my attention and pointed down the beach. We watched another longship slide ashore. Warriors leapt from it as though a terrible sea-beast birthed a clutch of deadly children.

These new fighters formed a shield wall next to their ship and began chanting. Arrows rained down on them. Judging from the screams, some arrows slipped through the gaps, but not enough. A figure jumped onto the beach behind them. The cold power in my chest, already agitated, now writhed. The figure, a head taller than his fellows, pushed through the shield wall. The arrows continued but he was unfazed. He raised his arms and his skin turned the colour of a pale mountain. An arrow found its mark, striking him in the chest, and bounced off. He grinned.

"Brimir Stoneskin," Valna muttered.

I turned back to look at Erling and his fighters who were trying to herd the enormous bear back to her longship. Erling stumbled away from a blow that caught his shield and noticed the new Windborn.

"Go," the king shouted. "Deal with Brimir."

Jorunn swiped for him as he shouted. The king leapt nimbly out of reach. Jorunn roared as another fighter stabbed their sharp spear-tooth into her underbelly. I nodded and turned my

435

attention back to Brimir, but Valna's expression was pained as she looked between the two enemy Windborn on our shore.

"It's fine," a warrior shouted as he ran to help the king. Olek's stern face rushed past us and to Erling's side. "We can handle this. She's wounded."

Valna shouted something after him. I couldn't make it out over the sound of battle and banging shields.

The shield wall behind Brimir began chanting his name. The boulder-tough warrior moved forward. The shield wall shuffled along behind him as arrows and spears clattered harmlessly off the Windborn. Our fighters fanned out and retreated before him, unsure of how to fight this man-mountain.

Valna disappeared and reappeared a moment later holding two old timber frames she'd ripped into clubs.

"Stabbing him won't work," she said and handed me one of the clubs.

I nodded and gripped my club with both hands. My muscles ached with the memory of enemies already fought, warriors already slain, but I couldn't stop. Brimir spread his arms wide. An invitation. I stepped forward.

A couple of clumsy swings with my club kept Brimir's eyes focused on me. He leaned easily out of the way of one swing and deflected the other with an open hand. The wood scraped harmlessly against his granite palm. Then he stumbled as Valna attacked him from behind. One of the warriors broke out of the shield wall to try and attack Valna, but our allies were waiting for that opportunity and an arrow found his throat before he took two steps.

Brimir growled, a deep earth-scraping sound that shook our bones, and swung around at Valna. She had already disappeared and was by my side.

"You are quick," Brimir rumbled.

Valna shrugged. Brimir advanced.

He leapt forward, reaching with grasping hands toward Valna. She ducked out of the way. I swung my club down, twisting to put the full force of my body into the swing, and slammed the club into his knee. A snapping sound and the end of the club splintered open. Brimir grunted and went down on one knee. White glittering cold crept up his leg as it connected with the frost-ridden sand. Ice glinted as it filled a crack in his stony-flesh like the scars on my arms.

The memory of the boulder seen so long ago, on the road to the Althing, flashed in my mind. It had been slowly torn apart by ice expanding over many winters. I looked at the ice-filled crack in Brimir's knee. I was sure I could speed up the process.

I threw myself towards his bent knee and pulled on my Windborn power. The cold poured out of me and cascaded onto the floor. I felt the ice sink its fangs into Brimir's broken knee. I pushed as deep as I could and felt the splitting, heard the crack. Brimir roared and pushed himself to his feet, swinging his hands wildly.

Valna appeared in front of me, blocking the fist destined for my head with her club. The force of the blow sent her tumbling backwards. Brimir took shaky steps toward her and raised both hands high, fists clenched and ready to slam down on her.

I sent a spray of frost and slush at his face. Brimir cried out as it hardened over his face. The icy fog blocked my view and his enormous fist slammed into my chest. My club slipped from my grasp as I tumbled across the cold sand. I came to a stop lying on my back and gasping for breath.

My shoulder burned despite the cold armour covering it. I tried to push myself up, bones ground against each other and my arm gave way. Sand and snow pressed against my face, muffling my agony-drenched scream.

Brimir loomed over me as I tried again to stand.

"Enough now," he said, voice vibrating low like a wolf made of stone and shadows.

I looked around, trying to find Valna, to call out for her help.

Brimir grinned, each tooth like a shattered pebble, and raised his arms to strike.

Valna appeared, already moving and with a rock held in her hands. She grunted as she smashed the head-sized stone into Brimir's arm with a deep clap that echoed around the fjord. A fresh crack appeared in his upper arm like a miniature ravine.

Brimir roared and flailed back at Valna, but she wasn't there.

437

I sent a wave of freezing air and frost at Brimir. It crinkled to ice as soon as it touched him. The ice spread out and slid down like tree roots, keeping him locked in place on the sand. Brimir shouted again, so loud I thought my eardrums would burst, and tugged at his icy bonds. The sands shifted with the force of it, and underneath the sound of battle I felt, more than heard, the shattering of ice.

Valna had found a spear and danced to and fro in front of Brimir, dodging his clumsy hands and stabbing at him. The spear scraped ineffectively against his skin, but it was enough to distract him. I grabbed his cracked arm from behind, put my knee against the back of his elbow, and pulled as hard as I could. Brimir tried to throw me off, but couldn't.

I put all my weight against his arm. I strained until it felt like my eyes would burst.

Brimir screamed. His other arm battered against my back like the kiss of a mountain. Something snapped within me then there was a crack of colliding glaciers. His arm broke. I tumbled back and his forearm fell onto the sand.

He staggered away from me, clutching at the stump of his arm, and roared with fury and pain. I leapt back, moving out of his range, and followed his gaze.

The first of Hraki's longships was almost through the icy obstacle course. The crack hadn't been from Brimir's arm, but the ship carrying the old and infirm as it smashed into a miniature iceberg.

Ice fell in clumps as the foremost longship scraped past the final frozen hurdle to freedom. The warriors on board, who had been holding their shields high to protect against the birds swooping down at them, lowered the sail. Even at this distance, I could see red streaks on their arms from the birds' attacks. Above them, Runar and Lothi continued to fight, though now Lothi tried to disengage.

A cheer rose from our enemy and they began pouring back onto their longships.

Sand crunched. I jumped back. Air buffeted me as Brimir's stone knuckles scraped the space where I had been. He broke away from me and ran to his longship. His skin began to soften in blotches and return to supple flesh. The stump of his arm dripped blood, but not enough to slow him down. He moved faster as a man than a mountain and I was too tired to sprint after him.

A broken spear lay on the ground near me. I picked it up and threw it at Brimir's chest. The throw was uneven. The broken spear-shaft wavered in the air and gouged into his back, rather than running him through.

Brimir yelled, stumbled and clutched the lip of the longship. Before he could pull himself up Valna appeared behind him, club already swinging down to crunch into his back. Brimir caught the club with his hand and tried to fend Valna off and clamber up into the longship.

A bone-shuddering roar joined the cheers. I turned to see Jorunn swiping and gnashing at her opponents with renewed fury.

I started to move. Jorunn matched my steps with her gouging claws. It seemed as though each time my feet hit the ground, another fighter took a vicious wound. I scraped up debris as I ran, my shoulder screaming at me to stop, and threw rocks, knives, axes at her to try and distract her.

Halfway to Jorunn, Erling was thrown back. He tried to drag himself along the beach, but his strength gave out. Erling lay, panting, watching as Jorunn bore down on him.

I wouldn't make it.

Someone else leapt in the way. A huskalar with a cerulean shield. Olek.

His shield battered away the snow bear's claws inches away from Erling's chest. His knife sliced into the bear and carved a bloody line through the white fur.

Jorunn howled and reared back on her hind legs.

A few steps more and I would be there. I tried to throw a spray of ice at her, but nothing came. I was spent.

Olek stood, shield up, in front of his king.

Jorunn attacked.

Massive paws smashed the shield to kindling. Hungry jaws closed on Olek's chest and squeezed with a snapping, popping sound. Olek collapsed and Jorunn stamped down on Erling.

I leapt, throwing my shoulder into her head. Jorunn stumbled away, lost her footing, and fell onto the sand. The once white snow bear was now covered in life-red stains. Her chest heaved and her shape changed. A naked woman, bleeding from dozens of wounds, smiled at me.

"We're through," she growled. "It's too late."

She began to shuffle back to her longship. I picked up a spear from the ground and threw it with all of the hatred and fury Hraki had earned since I came back from my final raid.

The spear flew straight and stabbed through her shoulder. She stumbled and fell to her knees, but shuffled on. Her longship was filling with warriors, but they ignored her as they rushed to escape this deadly shore. I tried to force myself to rush over and finish her off, but I had nothing left.

I stumbled back over to Olek and Erling and fell to my knees.

Too late. They were too still.

Erling's chest had caved in with the force of Jorunn's final blow. His tunic and armour rested too low on his chest, as though he had let out all the breath in the world. Olek's skull had been lacerated and broken by Jorunn's jaws. His handsome face now turned to bright red strips.

People rushed around me. Friends. Enemies. Warriors still killing in a battle we had already lost. The sand around me soaked themselves with a growing red that frosted and glittered the nearer it came to me.

Valna appeared beside me. Sweat glittered across her face.

"They're sailing straight through. We need to try and sink them. If—"

Her gaze skimmed over the bodies in front of me and her voice stuttered to a stop. Her mouth fell open. Suddenly she was by Olek's body. She lifted his head and it flopped back against her arm. Valna put her hand to Olek's bloodied cheek as though trying to comfort him. The lacerated skin twitched and wavered in the cold wind.

"Who?" she rasped.

She turned to face me. The tears in her eyes seemed to magnify their sorrow and hate. I pointed to Jorunn's bloodied form as she limped away.

Valna blinked away, Olek's head fell to the floor, sending a spray of fresh red across the sand. She kicked and screamed at a woman who, until moments ago, had been a fearsome snow bear. A bear who had crushed Valna's heart between merciless jaws. Jorunn's movements stopped. Her breathing stopped. She went still.

I pushed myself up and walked slowly over to Valna. I saw my own grief mirrored in her frantic kicks, heard the echoes of my own loss in her ragged, wordless screams. Jorunn's body jolted along the sands, rolling and tumbling with every blow.

"Valna," I whispered and reached out to touch her shoulder.

She spun. Teeth bared in a rictus grin of fear and rage. Her breathing came hard and fast and I took half a step back. I knew that rage and what it demanded. It did not care who paid. Her shoulders slumped, her fists unclenched, and she fell into me.

I wrapped my arms around her, careful not to touch her bare skin in case my frozen soul stuck us together.

She took a deep breath that shuddered out of her.

"He promised he wouldn't leave me," she whispered.

I said nothing. It wasn't said for me and nothing I could say would help.

"Why must I lose everyone?" she said between her tears.

I opened my mouth, but had no answer. As her sobs reverberated in my chest, I felt her swelling loneliness. I remembered what Valna had told me of her life. When she became Windborn she had lost her family and ever since she had been an outsider. Erling's huskalar only spent time with her to try to prove themselves against a Windborn, whether in training or at the drinking table. The only one who had seen beyond that had been Olek and it had grounded Valna, made her feel wanted and included. Now he had been ripped from her with bloodied teeth. I squeezed her tighter.

"I have to go," she said into my chest and started to pull away. "This is Hraki's fault. I can still get to him."

"He's on the water, Valna," I said as gently as I could, but I let her go. "It's too late."

Valna took a step away and pulled out her knives before wiping her tears away with the backs of her hands. She straightened and met my gaze, a defiant question in her eyes. I wanted to stop her. I stood, bloodied and bruised, as my only chance at justice sailed towards the horizon, but I couldn't stand to lose anyone else. I didn't want to lose Valna. Beneath the question in her eyes, I saw the sharp edge of her sorrow. It was the same sharpness that still clutched at my heart with black talons. I said nothing and stepped out of her way.

She flickered and disappeared.

*

All but one of Hraki's longships escaped.

They scraped and ground against the icebergs scattered on the fjord, but they made it. The ship with the children and elderly was not so lucky. Its prow bumped against one iceberg and canted in the water until its stern caught on another and it became stuck.

Jorunn's longship did not have enough warriors to launch without their Windborn's strength. Our warriors pulled them from their benches and slaughtered them. This close to the corpses of their friends and family there would be no mercy.

What other fighters we had sent spears, stones, and flaming arrows at the fleeing ships. Some connected, prickling the keels like wooden hedgehogs skimming across the water. Nothing stopped them. Lothi pushed each longship in turn, lending it speed and rushing them out of range of our ineffectual attacks. He tried to come back for the boat that held the children and elderly but the arrows and spears flew too thick and he retreated.

I watched from my place between the bodies. Clumps of birds continued to dive at our enemies. They darted in to attack the flying Windborn and to peck at the warriors on the longships, but Gerda must have been exhausted as their swooping clumps became smaller and smaller. Runar was too wounded to fly after them. He sat on the shore opposite with his clothes saturated with crimson battle-stains.

Some of our huskalar cheered when they saw Valna hopping from one chunk of ice to another, but they didn't notice the sluggish way she moved. To them, she was still a lightning-fast Windborn, dancing across the ice. I saw the way her feet slipped on the tiny icebergs, the way she only just made it to the next one, and there was nothing I could do.

Lothi noticed her too. He paused in pushing the longships and floated above the water, putting himself between his king and this grief-stricken Windborn.

Valna threw something at him. A knife, perhaps. Lothi didn't move. The attack sailed by with inches to spare. Lothi flew away and shouted something at Valna. I couldn't make out the words but I heard her scream of rage. As Lothi moved back to the ship the clouds above him rippled and the birds all disappeared. For a brief moment I thought Lothi was getting bigger, then realised it was his hair standing on end.

He realised what was happening and sped through the air, past the final longship and landed on the next. As his feet touched the deck, a bright arc of lightning broke free from the clouds and shot towards him. It whipped down, following Lothi's path, and struck the rear longship.

The mast exploded. The keel cracked. People screamed.

The longship descended into a mess of flames and panic. Figures threw themselves into the icy waters and swam towards the other longships.

I glanced back to the shore of the king's island. Orin stood with his arms outstretched and hair standing on end. His arms dropped and he collapsed onto the floor. Two nearby huskalar rushed over to him and carried him out of sight.

By the time I looked back all I could see of the flaming longship was the tip of the mast and the edges of the prow.

The rest of Hraki's longships were long out of reach. They had reached the open waters and, now that they were free of the dangerous floating ice, their oars slithered out. They cut through the stained, swirling waters too swiftly for us to follow. We could only watch. All of our strength was spent, used to kill a snow bear Windborn, and heart-fires were doused as news of Erling's death spread amongst the survivors.

Step by slick step Valna tried to make her way to Lothi. The floating Windborn lifted his drowning allies over to Hraki's surviving longships. Once he had saved everyone that he could, he called out to Valna, the words lost in the wind. She screamed something back. Lothi's exhausted, arrogant posture was clear, even at a distance, and Valna leapt at him with a swiping knife. Lothi was too far away and she fell into the water. Lothi called something down to Valna and flew away.

Windborn or not, Valna wouldn't last long in those cold waters. I forced myself to move.

Everyone had seen her fall and a crowd formed along the shoreline, calling out to her and some of them had started to take off their armour.

I ducked through the gaps in buildings telling them not to go in the water. It was too cold. They might be able to reach her, but the cold would kill them before they returned to shore. When they realised who I was, the onlookers called for the crowd ahead to make a space for me. I shoved my way through, dropping my shield and armour on the sand before I sprinted out into the fjord.

The water froze as I moved through it and I had to fight for every step. I began to shake. My battle-sparked adrenaline was gone and my limbs screamed at me to stop, lie down, rest. Ahead of me Valna made one of her Windborn jumps and went from splashing and drowning to slowly slipping off a slice of ice.

"Valna."

Her head turned to me. She took one hand from the ice and reached out to me. She fell and disappeared.

A splash to my right.

I spun and saw her in a cascade of white foaming water, drowning. I waded through the shallows, fighting my own frost and the fjord's ice, and pulled her free. A few heartbeats of struggle and we both lay panting on the cold beach.

"We have to go after them," Valna whispered between shivers.

"With what?" I said as gently as I could.

"With everything," she whispered.

I looked around. A crowd gathered. Each and every figure was bloodied. Gashes glistened on every limb and every set of shoulders drooped, exhausted.

"We've already given everything."

Chapter Twenty-Two
The High King's Verdict

It felt like the battle had taken no time at all but long shadows now stretched out across the fjord like the claws of great night-beasts. The shore was littered with corpses. The living moved through them, dragged them together, collecting these once-warriors into grim piles like fishing hauls. We had cleared a path in the glacial obstacles across the water, shepherding the ship with the elderly and children to Erling's island at the same time, and now there was a constant stream of boats sailing to and from the island carrying food, water, and supplies for the survivors.

"Valna is swearing up a storm," Katja said as she walked up to me.

I grunted. I was focused on unclasping a helmet from one of Hraki's huskalar. It was armour we couldn't afford to spare.

"She's talking about taking a longship out to hunt Hraki," she continued. "She doesn't see the point in all this." Katja waved at the activity around us.

People sifted through the dead to collect whatever was useful; armour, warm clothes, money. For my part, I had first gone over to Jorunn's mangled body and retrieved Bjolfur's axe before helping with the rest of the bodies. Hraki's fighters were thrown into piles once they were stripped, but those we had lost were laid reverently beside one another with their arms crossed and eyes gently closed.

"She's in no state to go hunting," I said. I grunted again as I freed the clasp and slipped the helmet from a dead woman. "Here. Hold this. I'll start moving the body."

"Valna doesn't seem to think so." Katja took the helmet and

stepped out of my way.

"She wouldn't." I grabbed the dead warrior by both feet and started dragging. "She's lost someone close to her and it's Hraki's fault. Gods above, I know what that's like. She wants action."

"I can't let her charge off like a one-woman army. She'll get herself killed. Or worse."

"Then ask her to help with the dead. It'll give her something to focus on and we need to get them ready for their funeral."

We arrived at a collection of bodies. Katja's mouth twisted as she looked at the macabre mound.

"Do we need to?" she asked quietly. "These people were all trying to kill us, Edda."

I stopped and stretched.

"Do you want to leave them on the beach for Gerda's birds? Shove them all together on a longship and send them out into the sea? I don't think you have the heart to let them rot, Katja. No, we need to stick them on a pyre and let the gods decide what to do with them."

Katja chewed her lip and turned over the helmet in her hands. We stood next to the dead for a long moment and let the hushed whisper of the waves fill the silence.

"What do we do now?" I asked.

She looked up, her eyes full of uncertainty.

"I don't know. I'll need to talk to Alvilda. Without a king, I suspect the High King will have to decide what to do. Normally, the neighbouring rulers might get some stake on the land, but with Hraki gone that only leaves Queen Sigrid. Would the High King want to give that much land to one person?"

I shrugged, unsure if Katja was talking to me or thinking aloud. "The High King will still rule. I doubt he'll care who's looking after it for him."

"Perhaps."

Katja was only half-listening. I recognised her expression. It was the look of someone lost, unsure and unable to find their own footing. I remembered that feeling. Often, it was only mindless, physical work that could get you out of it.

"Come on," I said, and started walking back to the unlooted

dead. "There's work to be done."

Katja followed and we spent the next hour taking the armour and weapons from the fallen warriors before dragging them to their respective comrades.

It was close to midnight by the time we were done. Torches and lanterns had been set up along the beach to give us light to work with. The pale light dragged my eyes to the bodies and made it seem like all the world was corpses. I shivered. We threw whatever cloth we could find over the dead then called a halt for the night, but it was a short-lived reprieve.

As soon as the sun's rays tipped over the mountains, we began our work again.

The day was given over to mournful carpentry for the funeral pyre. Some people gathered driftwood from the destroyed longships. Alvilda was among them, trying to ease the burden of the survivors by sharing in it. Despite that many glowered at her as she worked and it was clear that they placed at least some blame at the law-keeper's feet for their loss. Others went to the forests to collect fresh timber under Fainn's watchful eye. There were few circumstances when a god-speaker allowed the god's grove to be used for a funeral pyre, but this massacre was one of them. Fainn walked out of the woods with his workforce pulling a felled oak behind them, then a willow, and then an ash. The three trees would form the base of the funeral pyre and call the attention of the gods, the Sea Giants, and the Winds in turn. The immortals would witness the passage of these souls to the afterlife. By the time we finished making the pyre, it stretched longer than any of Erling's longships. It lay, pointing at the horizon, like a holy sacrifice ready to carry its passengers where no mortal could follow.

The sun touched the horizon as we began to move the bodies, as though it were respectfully leaving us to mourn.

One by one the bodies were lifted onto the pyre. First, we placed the bodies of those Hraki had abandoned here. Then came the volunteer fighters that we had lost, those farmers and sailors who had not been familiar with war, but who had been willing to protect what was theirs. Next came the huskalar; these brave, fearsome warriors were the final support before the last body was placed like a keystone. The huskalar would support their king one final time.

Olek was among those huskalar. Valna wept and would not let anyone else touch the body of her beloved. She looked like she had not slept since the attack and her wild hair and dirt-stained cheeks were soon soaked in tears. After she placed his body on the pyre, one more death to lay at Hraki's feet, she collapsed to her knees.

I knelt with her. I didn't say anything. I let her feel her grief. It was a pain I knew and, despite the agony it still caused me, I would not have traded it for all of the treasure in the gods' halls. Her pain was the black-feathered shadow to the love she had for Olek. Once her tears ran dry and her shaking sobs could pry no more sorrow from her, I offered Valna my hand. She looked at me with red-stained eyes. She knew I wouldn't offer practised sympathies or dull platitudes. To try and ease any of her sorrow would be to cheat her of the proof that her love had been deep, real, powerful. I promised that I would be there when she was ready.

She took my hand and let me lead her from the pyre.

There was only one body left.

Runar took Erling in his arms and lifted him onto the pinnacle of the pyre. He stayed aloft for a few moments after he let go of the body. Perhaps he had some final words for his king before the gods took him.

The beach was crowded with people. Most had fought in the battle and their bone-soaked exhaustion was obvious in the set of their shoulders and the shadows in their faces. Those few who had not fought, mostly children and the infirm, had worked tirelessly to fetch food, water, and medicine for the survivors and they too looked ready to collapse. Those Hraki had abandoned had been brought over and kept under guard. We would not deny them their mourning, but we could not let them free.

Runar drifted to the ground and silence spread out across the crowd.

He walked over to join Valna and I where we stood at the edge of the crowd. We watched the pyre as though something would change. A pile of broken wood, unmoving bodies, and a king. It was a hesitation, a silent acknowledgement that whatever the next step was, there was no going back. Erling was gone. Hraki was gone. Olek was gone. Whatever anyone had wanted yesterday had either disappeared over the horizon or was about to go up in smoke.

"Someone should say something," I said.

Reluctant faces turned to me, their expressions taut with grief, apprehension, and loss.

I met their eyes one by one. Runar and Valna were moments from collapsing from fatigue. I turned to Katja. She opened her mouth, closed it, then covered her tear-stained eyes with one hand. To Alvilda's credit she met my gaze, but she shook her head. We both knew it was not her place to speak. Fainn's usually stormy expression was for once clear and calm, which was somehow worse. His eyes were a window and through them I saw grief for every person we had laid on the pyre. He was the god-speaker for these people and he knew each and every one of them. He knew their hopes and their dreams. He knew every family that had lost a father, mother, brother, or sister. Even those who had fought against us were lamented in his eyes. Each person on the pyre was a child of the gods and Fainn mourned them all. He nodded.

He walked up to the pyre and stepped on to a piece of driftwood jutting out from the bottom so that he could see everyone in the crowd.

"My friends," he began. His voice wavered and he let out a shuddering sigh before he continued.

"Friends, today we stand in the battle-shadow. We fought bravely, but not everyone made it through. Today, we give the fallen to the gods so that they can be rewarded. We celebrate their lives, their sacrifice. No matter how dark the battle-shadow seems, we must hold on to the fact that we have survived. We survived and we will continue to survive.

"I don't know what will happen to us now, but Katja and I will protect you as best we can. All of you. We will make sure we are not forgotten at the edge of the world. That, however, is not something to address tonight. For now, we honour our dead."

Someone stepped forward and offered him a flint. Fainn nodded his thanks and began setting fires all along the pyre.

"I call upon the gods to welcome these brave souls into their halls. I call upon the Warrior to welcome them as brothers and sisters in battle and grant them glory everlasting. I call upon the Mother to welcome them as sons and daughters and give them whatever they most desire. I call upon the Father to welcome them as long absent travellers who have finally found their way home."

Fitful sparks glowed within the dark spaces between the wood like angry spirits. After a moment their anger spluttered into flames that licked the shards of wood and the pyre seethed with smoke a heartbeat before flames clawed their way free.

I watched the smoke. It caught the wind and drifted away like a longship sailing towards the horizon. Three enormous ravens silently circled the smoke. Gerda had either set the rest of her birds free or grounded them. No other birds would dare taint the passage of the dead with their flight.

When Erling finally disappeared beneath the fire's red talons and the soul-thin wisps of smoke poured from his body, someone started to sing.

The song rang out deep and slow. The Final Ballad, a mournful song that asked the gods to give safe passage to those we had lost, and to let them watch over it. It was the last song these warrior-souls would hear before the gods took them forever. More voices joined the first and scattered songs echoed across the beach until the shore shook with the swaying, sombre sound. Others rolled barrels out from their homes and pressed cups into the hands of anyone nearby. I took a cup from someone who disappeared before I could thank them. After a few moments, everyone watching the pyre was singing or drinking and many were doing both.

This would go on for hours.

The song would die away as more people turned to drink and then we would tell stories of the dead. Stories that would become exaggerated as we drank. No doubt, the song would swell when one merry mourner or another hummed a verse or two and it spurred on another chorus. Then the drink would overtake them and the song would fade until someone else sobered up enough to remember the words or until the sun came up.

It was a long ritual I had taken part in many times. A life of raiding between winters gave plenty of opportunities to drink around a funeral pyre, but something about this one ate away at me.

This was all to make sure the gods welcomed the dead into their halls, to prove they had died a good death, with blood in their lungs instead of saltwater.

My drink turned sour in my mouth.

What funeral had I given Bjolfur? A rune-marked stone sitting at the bottom of the sea was not enough. He deserved flames and smoke and songs. He deserved this.

I downed my drink and shoved my cup at someone. They stumbled back at the force of it. They looked down at the cup and then to me, surprise clear on their face. I turned away from the pyre and elbowed my way through the crowd until I reached the other side of the beach. As I looked up and down the shore, I saw Alvilda clambering into a rowboat and making her way back to Erling's island. She was still a stranger here and was astute enough to know she should leave the funeral to those who truly knew the fallen.

I turned back to the sea.

Large waves, painted by the light of the pyre, foamed up in the twilight distance. Within this endless, incessant body I could chart my entire life. I'd grown up by the sea, splashing through the shallows with my parents and watching them disappear over the waves as they fished. I'd travelled across the sea; weighed down with weapons as I left and weighed down with plunder as I returned. I'd lost my heart in the sea. I clenched my fists at the memory of Bjolfur's slick fingers slipping from my grip. Fingers that should still be woven into mine. I had drowned in those roiling waves.

Everything I was and everything I had had been buried in those waters.

And what now? Hraki was gone and with him, any chance I had at justice. There was no way to catch him. No way to know his destination.

I sighed. What else did I have? What else could I have as a Windborn? Did I have any obligation to stay? My oath was to Erling who was now nothing more than memory and smoke.

451

I let the water's undulating whisper seep into me and played out the different scenarios in my mind. Bjolfur always found this infuriating, that I would sit and think rather than just take action, the thought brought a smile to my lips.

Something moved over the ocean's distant white edges.

A mast. A sail. A longship.

My heartbeat fumbled.

I spun, watching the smoke trail up into the darkening sky and the amber light spreading out on the beach from the bonfire. No longer a bonfire, but a signal-fire.

I squinted back out to sea to try and see if there were any other longships, to see if Hraki had brought his warriors back. In the fading sunlight I could only see one, its blue and white striped sail fluttering as it caught the breeze.

Panic scrambled up my chest and I sprinted back to the crowd.

"A longship! There's a longship coming!"

The approaching warriors would be fresh, having waited safely on their ship. The best of us had been slaughtered and the rest of us were exhausted and drunk.

Heads turned. People began to hurry to and fro, their jovial expressions crushed under stern practicality as they picked up weapons and armour. However exhausted these people were, it did not change their warrior spirit and soon it seemed that everyone had taken up a weapon or a shield. Even those abandoned by Hraki, shown how much he truly valued them as he disappeared across the sea, stood with us.

I found Valna and Katja. They stood at the edge of the crowd, eyes fixed forward. Both had weapons clutched in their hands and Katja passed me an axe.

"Did you see Hraki?" Valna asked. She thrummed with tense eagerness. This was her chance for revenge and for that she would push herself beyond breaking.

I shook my head. "I don't know who's on board."

Katja took in the grim faces around us, the sloughed shoulders, the laboured breathing. "I'm not sure we'll survive another attack."

"We'll have to," I mumbled back.

The longship came slow, weaving through the scattered

icebergs, and slid onto shore with a creaking finality. People moved on deck, but no one leapt off to lead the charge. We paused, tense, and even the wind seemed to be holding its breath to see who or what would leap from the longship.

"Come on," Katja said and gestured for me to follow. "Let's see what they want. Valna, if it goes wrong, you can help us."

They nodded. Valna started bobbing on the balls of her feet, eager to fight. Katja twisted the long-shafted axe in her hands.

We edged forward, our cheeks red with drink and black with ash until we were halfway between the crowd and the longship. Now that we were closer details on the sail became clear. Images were woven into the fabric. Sea serpents swam on the blue stripes with their eyes pointed straight at me as though waiting for me to get close enough to catch me in their teeth.

"Name yourself, strangers," Katja called out.

After a moment of silence someone clambered out of the longship in slow, awkward movements. They tried to use the keel as a step-ladder, but the smooth planks were not made for that and they slipped down into the wet sand with a yelp.

As they righted themselves and brushed the sand from their clothes I had a flash of recognition. The disdain on the sharp-featured face was etched into my memory. He had once refused my appeal and ushered me out of his tent. He had argued against us at the Althing. It was Einar Vigensson.

"What happened here?" Einar said, still brushing sand from himself and smoothing creases in his tunic as he walked up to us.

"Law-Keeper Einar," Katja said, her surprise obvious in her voice. "Forgive me, I was not expecting to see you here."

"Oh yes, I remember you," he said, as though he were speaking to a child brought to a schoolmaster for punishment. His watery eyes slid from Katja and across to me. "And I remember you."

The tension in the air behind us eased as the possibility of another fight bled away.

"Well, give me an answer. What happened here?"

Katja shoved her axe behind her back and stood straight like a soldier for inspection.

"There was a battle, Law-Keeper Einar."

"I can see that," Einar said through gritted teeth. "Give me some information I can actually use. Who were you fighting and why? You are aware it is illegal to fight in winter, surely? Are you so piteous a law-keeper you are unaware of this?"

Katja tried to answer each question Einar spat out, but as she began to speak Einar cut her off with another question. Each time he cut her off I felt an old fury stoking. This man worked against us at the Althing and now, whilst the funeral pyre still burned, he dared to interrogate us. I took half a step forward and raised the hand holding the axe to poke a finger into Einar's chest. He reeled back from my axe-heavy hand with terror-wide eyes.

Before I could speak someone else got off the longship.

I glanced back in time to see them hop over the gunwale and land on the sand in one fluid movement. They bent to take the weight of the fall but did not straighten. By the time the hunched figure made their way to us, he was wheezing.

"High King," Katja said and kneeled. She tugged my arm and pulled me onto one knee as well. "It is an honour to receive you."

"Get up," he grunted.

"My apologies, High King," Katja went on as she clambered back up, "for meeting you in this state. We have recently had to defend ourselves and have not yet been able to wash. Had we known you were coming, we would—"

The High King waved Katja's objections away.

"Einar, you were supposed to be telling them to fetch their king. Where is King Erling, law-keeper? Would he not come to greet his lord?"

The crackle and hiss of the funeral pyre was the only response.

"I see."

The High King's expression softened. He looked at the pyre and then cast his eyes across the sullen crowd, who had dropped their weapons.

"There is clearly much to talk about, but we can talk in the morning. Tonight, give the dead their due."

"Thank you, my king," Katja said and bowed.

The High King brushed aside her thanks and walked past us. He made his way straight toward the pyre with patient, deliberate steps. The crowd parted before him, silent awe keeping any greeting from escaping their lips. He stopped close enough to the pyre that the image of him wavered in the heated air.

Hot air billowed out from the fire and caught his cloak. The flames cast his shadow tall and broad and in that moment it was easy to look past the frail old man and see the king that had conquered countless clans and forged a nation.

*

The night passed in a haze of song and ale. When the sun rose it found footprints, trails of a hundred dances, and empty cups that had poured a thousand drinks. Everyone had found their way to safe lodging. Some had gone with friends so they did not have to face their empty houses. Some even offered Hraki's abandoned people places in their homes. The alcohol and their shared hatred for the fled king having thawed any enmity between them. All that was left of the once sun-strong funeral pyre was a patch of charred wood and blackened sand. I stood on the shore of the king's island, watching the shadows retreat across the waters and listening for the slow growth of birdsong in the sunlight.

"He's ready."

I turned to see Fainn gesturing me to follow him. He had a black eye from the battle but had otherwise come out unscathed.

"Valna could have come to get me and saved you a trip," I said as we started walking.

Fainn shook his head. "It's better if I do it. The High King mistrusts Windborn. He trusts in the gods and so, in me."

"What have the gods ever done for us," I snorted.

"Careful."

Most had stayed on the mainland overnight and it felt like the small island had been made into a silent monument to Erling. The columns leading up to the mead-hall, which had once held the weight of legends and the promise of hope, now felt like the bony fingers of death stretching for me.

"Katja's explaining everything," Fainn said as he pushed open the doors to the mead-hall.

Inside, the High King had taken up Erling's throne. He leaned forward to listen to Katja. She had been retelling the events of the day before but came to the end of her tale as we entered. Valna and Runar stood to one side whilst Katja stood directly in front of the High King. Alvilda was beside the High King and looked like a weight had been lifted from her now that he had arrived.

"Ah, the Windborn," he said. "Thank you, god-speaker. This is the one who saw it?"

A bow from Fainn and a nod from Katja.

"Come forward."

The High King waved a hand at me and I strode up to take a place next to Katja.

"Tell me," he said, leaning forward as though proximity would mean he could better sniff out a lie, "is what your law-keeper says true? Did you see King Hraki exhibit Windborn powers?"

"I did. He had a cut on his face that healed as I watched. It healed faster than anything I've ever seen. It became a scar in a few heartbeats."

The High King straightened in the throne and rubbed at his eyes.

"I see."

He looked from me to Katja and back. The pained expression on his face made it clear he did not want to believe me.

"Did you see this happen also?" he asked, turning back to Katja, Valna and Runar.

A chorus of negatives.

Einar sidled out from the shadows by the throne and cleared his throat.

"High King, how can we trust the word of this Windborn? I remember her from the Althing. She had issue with Hraki even then. Some fabricated issue about Wind-hunters and her homestead. Surely her testimony cannot be trusted?"

I stepped forward and Einar flinched away, hiding himself

behind the throne. The High King squinted and scratched the underside of his chin.

"Regardless, Hraki has attacked during winter. That much cannot be denied. He must pay for the lives he has taken here, if nothing else. Hraki's lands shall be forfeit and sold, the sale will be used to pay the blood-debt."

"And what about Hraki himself?" I asked. "He's still out there. Send us out to find him. Gerda can send her birds and—"

"Yes, we can—" Valna began.

The clink of armour and creak of leather stopped us short. Figures, who, until now, had been too still to catch my notice, shifted against the walls of the mead-hall. The High King's personal huskalar, armed with the best weapons and armour that could be crafted by mortal hands. The High King turned his sharp eyes onto us and I felt the stab of his undiluted hatred.

"Do not presume to question me, Windborn," he hissed. "You live by my grace and you will die by it if you are not careful."

He stood and walked to the edge of the throne's platform. He pointed at Valna, Runar and I and gestured us forward.

"You are without a king. By law, you cannot swear to another before the next Althing. I will decide your fates until then. You are too valuable to waste, but we cannot put you to work properly until the thaws start. I will have to discuss this with my law-keepers. For now, help the people to rebuild and I will send for you when I am ready."

"Are you serious?" I spluttered.

I turned to look at my fellow Windborn. Anger rumbled across their brows and their fists were clenched with white-knuckle tension, but they said nothing.

"Send us to hunt Hraki," I said. "Gerda can see through the eyes of birds. Runar can fly. For fuck's sake, I'll freeze the water and walk over it if I have to. We can't let that fucker get away with this."

The air in the room turned cold. Cold enough for me to notice. The High King's eyes looked black in the shadows beneath his brows and he swiped his fingers in a gesture I didn't recognise. Then two sets of hands gripped my shoulders from either side and began to drag me out of the hall.

"If you cannot be trusted to hold your tongue," the High King's voice called out after me, "then I cannot trust you to stay your hand. Confine her somewhere until she has learned patience."

I tried to wrench myself free of the two huskalar dragging me. The force of it threw one of them off their feet and they tumbled into Runar.

"Easy," he said to me. "You'll only make it worse, Edda."

Two more huskalar jumped onto me and forced me back. I gritted my teeth against the buffeting power rising in my chest, not wanting it to burst out of me and get me killed. Even so, frost glittered over their fingers and their breaths came in hot plumes.

I looked past them. I wanted some sign of support from the other Windborn, from the people I'd considered my allies and my friends. Runar's expression had softened and he shook his head; the quiet disappointment of a teacher who had lost his student. Valna's face flashed between anger and sorrow and her eyes looked from me to Runar, taking her cue from whomever she looked at. She appeared to be on the edge of action, but something was broken in her. She had already lost so much, I couldn't blame her for not wanting to lose more. On the raised platform the High King gripped the throne's arms so hard I thought they might splinter. Behind him, Einar stepped back and ducked away from the confrontation and out of the hall.

"You're making a mistake," I yelled as they shoved open the doors and dragged me through.

"Enough," the High King yelled. "I will not—"

The doors slammed shut.

Chapter Twenty-Three
To Face the Open Sea

Once again I found myself locked in a shed with dried fish. I couldn't help but wonder if the High King deliberately imprisoned his enemies in storerooms to humiliate them. The voices of my huskalar guards drifted under the walls. Their words were lost somewhere in the dirt between us, leaving only a muffled mumbling.

Everything I had done over the last few weeks had been to get justice for Bjolfur. If I couldn't have that, then what was I doing? I tried to wring some meaning out of everything that had happened, but, like driftwood circling a whirlpool, my thoughts always came back to Hraki. All of this—losing my husband, losing my home, my death and the deaths of so many others—stemmed from Hraki's actions. From his selfishness and disregard for rules that didn't suit him. It wasn't right that he was given freedom through the High King's apathy, whilst I was forced to sit here, trapped by thin wooden walls, huskalar, and ignorance.

The High King was waiting for an excuse to get rid of me, of all of Erling's Windborn, but if I could find Hraki and bring him back, at least then we might get justice. If I died in the attempt, that would solve a few problems at once. I would need a raven's eye view to find Hraki and I wouldn't find that trapped here.

I examined my store-room prison. The soil was cold, sparkling with frost that blossomed out from me like a bloodstain. Too hard to scrape away and slip under the walls. The walls themselves were thinly cut planks, easy enough to break through, and there was a flimsy wooden latch on the door.

Laughter from outside. The cadence of the voices changed and then the crunch of footsteps on the frosted ground as one of the huskalar left. I waited, long enough for the huskalar who'd left to be out of earshot. I focused on the power within me, let it slide out to my fingertips, and kicked the door out.

The latch exploded into splinters and the door flew open. It bounced back with the force of the blow, but I was already outside.

The huskalar turned to me, spear gripped in both hands, ready to strike.

I shoved my hand over his face and pushed ice out over his mouth, careful to leave his nose free so he could breathe. He tried to scream, shout, but it was muffled against the skin of my palm, then muffled against ice.

"Don't worry," I said. "It'll melt."

Fury and fear warred in his eyes. I dragged him into the fish-laden room then tied his hands and feet with some old rope hanging from one of the roof timbers.

"Someone will find you eventually," I said.

The muffled cries of the huskalar dimmed as soon as I closed the door. I hoped it would give me enough time to get away.

I got my bearings then darted into an alley. I had hoped that the gaps between the buildings would provide a hidden path to the Windborn's longhouse, but twice I was forced to duck behind some barrels and wait for a huskalar to pass before I dove across a street. The third group of huskalar I stumbled across were stood around talking in the middle of a crossroads and I was forced to double-back and find a different route. Eventually, the familiar shape of the Windborn's longhouse loomed ahead of me. I sighed with relief and my heart slowed its dancing beat.

After a final sprint across the open ground, I was inside. In the moment it took for my eyes to adjust to the darkness, something huffed from across the room.

"You smell like ice and rage, girl."

A long shadow picked itself up from the floor next to me and wandered into one of the curtained rooms before slumping back to the floor. Gerda sat at a table, put down a cup, and leaned down to scratch the elkhound's ears.

"Don't you want some light?" I asked her and rummaged for something to light the fire.

She shrugged. "If the dog can see well enough then so can I."

I found what I needed and, once I had thrown some kindling and bark strips into the hearth, started to scrape sparks with a flint and tinder.

"I need you to help me."

"I'm done, girl. Go find yourself someone else."

The hot sparks fell into the hearth, seared the wood then faded away.

"I just need your eyes, your birds."

I looked at Gerda. Her hollow eyes, outlined in the rhythmic sparks, looked like pits of grief and she shook her head. "Let me be."

She shifted around and the chair scraped against the wooden floor as she turned away from me.

"If you send out your birds we can find Hraki. I'll go after him. I'll bring him back. I'll—"

"I'm done, Edda. Let my eyes close. Please."

"Gerda, I know it looks bad, but we can fix this. If we bring Hraki back here, then the High King will have to—"

"I've already taken the hemlock."

"I... what?"

I fumbled the flint. It scraped across my knuckles and tumbled from my hand. I leaned back on the soot-covered floor and looked from Gerda to the cup in front of her.

Something in me splintered.

It felt like the floor I'd built for myself was crumbling. Another attempt to move forward scuppered by another death. At least this time I could talk to the deceased.

"Why?"

"I'm done, Edda," Gerda repeated and her shoulders slumped. "Erling was the only reason that I kept going and now he's gone. I damn near raised that boy while his family was doing whatever it is kings and queens do and I did the same for his son, but now they're gone. I couldn't protect Dyggvi and I couldn't protect Erling. Two boys dead."

"But the culprit is still out there," I said, still on my knees. "Hraki is the one who should be put down for this. You did everything you could. Use your birds to show me where Hraki is and—"

"And what? You kill Hraki? Then his children or his sworn warriors will take their vengeance. When does it end, Edda? Revenge is a serpent biting its own tail. Let go and slither away. It's the only way you'll survive."

"I'm not—"

Hurried footsteps at the door. I leapt to my feet, an ice dagger forming in my hand. The dog lifted its head and sniffed. Gerda settled into her chair.

A slim woman ran into the longhouse, Valna. Her usual pristine appearance was lost underneath a ragged dress and armour that hadn't been tightened properly so it banged against her shins and arms.

"Gerda? I can't find... Edda!"

She saw me and pulled me into a tight embrace.

"I thought you'd run off."

"Not yet. Are you going to tell the High King that I've broken out?"

Confusion then anger rippled over her face.

"Fuck them. I was going to break you out so we can go after Hraki. Who cares what the High King says? That bastard owes me a blood-debt and I will take it. Are you coming?"

Fury smouldered within her eyes, trying to hide a deeper hurt within. The intensity of it echoed in the sparks of my own familiar anger. I couldn't help but smile.

"What? Are you coming or not?"

Beside us, Gerda shook her head. "Thank the gods you have good hearts, smothered as they are in sorrow and fury. I think, if you had a mind, you could burn the world." She sighed so deeply it seemed to rattle her bones. "Edda was already trying to get me to find Hraki for her when you walked in, girl."

Valna jumped up and clapped her hands together. "Wonderful. Then what's the plan?"

I stood and looked from Valna to Gerda and then to the empty cup on the table, still glistening with the memory of its deadly contents.

"Find the boat with two ravens on its mast," Gerda said before I could say anything. "It belonged to Mimir, but he died in the fight so he won't mind if we borrow it. The birds will lead you to Hraki."

"You know where he is?" Valna said.

"I will find him."

"Oh Gerda, thank you." Valna leapt forward and wrapped her hands around the old woman's neck. "I will make you such a wonderful necklace for this, I promise."

"Just come back safe, girl. That's all I want."

"I will. Edda, I'll get the boat ready."

Valna disappeared.

The longhouse seemed darker without her. The weight of our decisions saturated the shadows and pressed in against us.

"You didn't tell her about the hemlock."

"She will be happier not knowing for now. I should have enough time to show you where Hraki is and then... then, I will find out what is next for an old Windborn."

I glanced over to the dog beside her. "What will happen to your animals?"

"They'll be fine," Gerda said with a shrug. "They'll go back to whatever it is they do and be just as happy without me. My death won't affect them at all."

The dog huffed without raising its head.

"Except maybe this one." She leaned down and ruffled the dog's ears. "Keep an eye on this one."

I nodded.

"Now, get to the boat, girl. Don't waste whatever time I have left."

*

The harbour was busier than I would have liked as people carried barrels on and off the High King's longship. I wore a cloak with the hood pulled up to hide my face, hoping that the blustering wind was cold enough to warrant it and I wouldn't arouse suspicion. Gulls squawked above, waiting for some unguarded food, and at the other end of the jetty two shadow-coloured birds hunched on a small boat. Beneath them, Valna's silhouette waved me over.

"I've got us some supplies and borrowed some of the

huskalar's gear," she said. "A couple of shields, chain shirts, a couple of axes and spears, and some knives."

She pointed to each one as she named them. My eyes flickered back to one of the battered shields and an axe with familiar curves. My heart sang. They were Bjolfur's. The shield had my hastily scarred saga circling on its face and the axe had the now-ice-warped handle. My breath caught in the back of my throat and I threw my arms around Valna and squeezed. She returned the embrace, squeezing me tight enough to think we would never see each other again. When we broke apart, I saw that one of the chain shirts had a bloody streak by the neck and holes in the chest. Olek's armour. It seemed that we would both have one final chance to march into battle with those we had lost. As soon as I settled into the boat we made ready to leave; checking the ropes, the sail, the small amount of food and water.

Valna dropped a bag and as she leapt to catch it something beneath the boat clapped.

I froze.

Another clap. The sound of the water slapping against the keel of the boat like the clamping jaws of a ravenous beast. I looked at the water. It was clear. I took a deep breath. Not the murky, hungry depths of the ocean, but the clear, smooth surface of a fjord.

"Let's go," Valna said.

Above us, the ravens cawed their agreement.

I glared up at them but leaned down to pick up the oars. The boat rocked and for a moment I feared it would tip over and we would drown. My hand shot out and steadied myself on the jetty, gripping so tight the wood creaked.

"Are you okay?" Valna said, shields still in her hands and eyes ringed with worry.

Not trusting myself to speak, I nodded.

"Good, do you want to push us off?"

Reluctantly, I let go of the jetty and shoved against it as hard as I could. The boat jerked through the water with a surging whoosh. The ravens leapt from their perch at the top of the small mast and cried out their indignation. As soon as we were safely away from the rest of the boats, I passed the oars to

Valna and she slipped them into their rests. A few heads turned in our direction as we pulled into the open water, but no one tried to stop us. The ravens circled ahead of us and I directed Valna so that we kept on course.

The boat rocked with each tug of the oars and soon the waves had grown large enough that we rose and fell with the swell on each stroke. Once we reached the edge of the ocean, the waves grew still larger. The boat crashed down into the water and sent a spray of seawater over both of us. I wiped my eyes with the back of my hand and looked out over the sea.

Dark clouds, darker waves, the white-foam surf smashing them together like gnashing teeth. The death that took my husband was out there, waiting. A thousand mouths forming and reforming ahead of me and the only thing between us was the keel of an old boat. My breath came fast, too shallow and all I could taste was the wet salt.

"Edda, are you okay?"

The voice pulled my gaze away from the endless hungry waves. Valna, oars resting against her knees, stared at me with her brow furrowed.

"I—"

My voice was lost as we hit a wave and surged up another. My mouth went dry as the vista of dark waves came back into view.

I wrenched my gaze from them and looked back at Valna. The furious light in her eyes gave way to something softer, kinder.

"Why don't you row for a bit. My arms are getting sore."

We switched places, with Valna at the stern of the boat as I sat on the bench in the middle. I took a swig from our waterskin to soak my dry mouth, then I took up the oars.

"You'll need to turn us a bit," she said. "The ravens are due east and we've twisted around."

"Okay. Tell me when to stop."

It felt good to plunge the oars into the water and pull against the sea's weight. It was a reminder that even though we travelled over those hungry waves, we decided our route with our own strength, not reliant upon the uncaring currents.

"That's good," Valna said.

I nodded, leaned forward, and began to row. I kept my eyes fixed on Valna or the wood beneath me. My world was reduced to the solid planks between my feet or the focused expression on my friend's face.

Other birds joined us on our journey. Gulls, and cormorants, and a sea eagle soared above us for a short time. They swooped close, calling out with piercing shrieks before they flapped away. Every time one of the birds came close I felt its eyes on me and through them the un-eyes of Gerda. It was comforting to know that she still looked after us even though the shore was a distant speck.

Valna unfurled the sail. It caught the wind with a crack dry as thunder. The boat surged forward as though to mirror with our eagerness and, with the oars clawing through the water as well as the sail pulling us onwards, we sped across the open sea.

I kept my attention locked on the boat's bottom. Lean forward. Dip the oars. Pull. Lift. Lean forward. Dip the oars. Pull. Lift.

CHAPTER TWENTY-FOUR
NO WAY BACK

IT TOOK HOURS, UNTIL SUNDOWN, but Valna finally spotted land. We climbed another wave and I saw the edge of the small island. Its edge was lined with boulders and shards of rocks seemingly without end. It was one of the myriad, nameless islets that lined our shores which were, more often than not, too rocky or sea swept to be of any use. As I looked to the north side of the island, I saw masts standing like spears above the rocks.

Hraki's longships.

"Let's head over there," I said and pointed to the masts before putting my weight back to the oars. "Hopefully there's somewhere nearby we can find to land."

Valna nodded and renewed her grip on the rudder.

The waves calmed the closer we got to the island, but not by much. Every time we were caught on a wave's upswell my heart shuddered with the fear of being thrown against the island's sharp edge.

"Wait," Valna said over the crash of the waves. "I saw a rock go underwater there."

I tried my best to stop the boat from moving with the tide and I did well enough that we didn't crash, though we came too close to some rocks for comfort. Valna gave me directions and wave by wave we edged around the island and into a cove. Three beached longships waited for us. All looked empty.

"Keep the course steady and you'll hit the beach," Valna said. "I'll go and make sure there's no one guarding the longships."

She picked up a shield and spear and disappeared.

I wanted to call after her and demand she keep me safe on

the water, but she was gone and we had come too far for me to give our position away now.

Instead, I gritted my teeth and did my best to make my way to the shore alone. Without Valna's guiding voice I had to steer and keep watch at the same time. I kept my gaze on the sharp rocks beside me and twisted around to watch the beach, but the vast dark waters called to me. Each wave's foamy edge lit up in the winter twilight like pale teeth. Between the dark edges of the rocks waiting to wreck me and the bright teeth of the ocean, I felt trapped and my breathing became too short. I tried to focus on the oars, on the stroke, but too many breaths came between each one.

I felt lightheaded.

The waves were coming for me.

I twisted to see the shore. It must be close. The rocks lurched next to me like claws. I cried out and let go of the oar. Two birds dived past me. I lashed out with a fist, catching the edge of the boat and punching a hole into the gunwale.

Something grabbed the boat and pulled it forward.

I spun, determined not to miss this time, and shot a chunk of ice out from an outstretched palm.

"What the fuck, Edda?" Valna hissed. "I told you to just go straight."

Valna yanked on the prow, scraping the boat against the sand to beach it. I looked to my right. The rocks were perilously close. Close enough to touch.

"I'm sorry," I said between deep breaths. "The water... It... I... I'm sorry."

"Don't worry about it." Once again the anger in her eyes dimmed behind a kinder light. "At least the birds caught the oar."

Two gulls paddled forward, pushing an oar between them. I took it and threw it into the boat.

"Thank you," I said, unsure if I was aiming it at the birds or Valna.

"Did you find anyone?" I asked as we hid the boat between the rocks up the beach.

Valna nodded towards the longships and I saw scuffed sand and still figures on the ground.

"Only a couple of people. They weren't expecting me and didn't make much noise."

We got our supplies from the boat and made our way over to the beached longships. The two dead guards, lying in the alley between two longships, wore furs to protect against the cold but had not bothered to wear anything to protect against a blade.

"Thank the gods for arrogance," I said.

The ravens had followed us, flitting from one perch to another in our shadows, and they watched us from the edge of the nearest longship. One of them bent forward and cawed urgently.

We watched the other raven fly up and away from us, calling down as it disappeared into the dark sky.

All around us the other birds began to pull themselves into the air, call out, and peck at each other. After a moment it seemed like hundreds of birds circled above us, wheeling in random patterns before breaking off and flying away.

The raven on the longship spread its wings wide and cawed at us again. It held the stance, then something in it changed. It moved in short bursts. It hopped along the longship until it was above the bodies then swooped down to rest on one of their chests. It looked at us with one beady eye then started to peck at the guard, now carrion.

I watched the motley flock of birds above us dissolve until only a few gulls remained. The tether that had held them all was broken. The poison had done its work.

"She's gone, isn't she?" Valna asked. Her eyes shone with tears.

My silence was answer enough. We had another death to lay at Hraki's feet.

"She was a cranky old woman, but she was always good to me. Well, most of the time." Valna wiped away a tear with the back of a hand that held a bloody knife she'd pulled from one of the bodies.

"May the gods embrace her," I said.

"May the gods embrace her," Valna echoed and then added, in a voice as quiet as the night, "please."

For a moment we watched the birds. The sky bruised to a

deep, glittering purple as the stars became visible. The birds flew above. Patches of shadow obscuring the night as they circled. A weight of sorrow stuck in the back of my throat, which warred with the curious practicality wondering how we would get back without the birds to guide us. Valna looked lost in her own grief. I walked up to her and put a hand on her shoulder. She turned to me and I squeezed gently.

"Let's burn the longships," I said. "I don't want any of these fuckers to get away."

Valna slapped her bloody hand on mine and nodded. The grief in her eyes was overwhelmed and replaced with familiar fury.

The small bushes and scrub that lined the shoreline were soaked with the sea air and too damp to be used as kindling so we clambered into the longships and found what we needed there. We scattered wood and fuel across the decks and once we were satisfied a fire would envelop the entire longship, I pulled out my flint from my bag.

"Here," I said and pushed it at Valna. "You set the fires and I'll keep watch. It'll go quicker if you jump between the longships."

"I'm not sure." She looked from the flint and back to me. "I've never been any good at it."

"You'll be fine. Look, wipe the blood off your knife and give it here."

She did and I showed her the best way to scrape the sparks from the metal. She didn't look utterly convinced but still disappeared and I soon heard muffled curses coming from behind one of the longships. Smothering a smile, I picked my spear up from beside the longship to save it from the oncoming conflagration.

The cursing slowly moved from one longship to another and a low light illuminated the curve of the wood from the inside. I walked along the beach, keeping myself halfway between the prows of the longships and the rocky cliffs. I kept my eyes on the deep shadows between the rocks, any one of them could hide a pathway and an enemy waiting for me to drop my guard. The sigh of the waves washed over the small sounds and I wouldn't have been able to hear careful footsteps.

The man who appeared from between the rocks was not careful.

"Oi," he called out as he stumbled free of the shadows. "I brought you something to drink to warm you up."

He had a waterskin thrown across his shoulders that sloshed with each uneven step, presumably full of ale or mead. The curses and the scrape of the flint stopped. I twisted my grip on my spear and readied to throw.

"Fuck," he said. "It's cold out here."

He stumbled to a halt and let the skin fall from his shoulders. His drunken eyes found me. A slow blink. A frown.

"Where's Aethel and Gorm?"

As he looked past me, his gaze reflected the glowing longships. His eyes hardened. He fumbled for a knife.

My spear hit him as Valna appeared beside him. He spun from the impact of the spear in his shoulder and Valna slashed her knife across his throat. The drunkard crumpled to the ground.

I ran up to Valna and ripped the spear out of the body. Viscous blood soaked into the sands. Each drop illuminated by the burning ships.

"Is there anyone else coming?" I whispered.

We both squinted at the gap in the rocks where the drunk had come from. I couldn't make out anyone else in the shadows, but with night's jaws clamped down on us it was hard to tell.

"I don't think so," Valna replied.

"I can't see anything," I said. "Did you set the last fire?"

"No, I thought it was more important to do something about him," Valna said and kicked the body.

"I had it covered."

She opened her mouth to say something but I waved her down with my spear-wielding hand.

"We don't have time for this. Someone might come looking for this one. Go and set the last fire and then we'll make a move."

"Can't you do it?" Valna huffed, an echo of her old playful self. "It takes me ages."

I shot her a look and she rolled her eyes before she

disappeared. The scrape of flint and muttered curses began again.

Whilst Valna set the final fire, I picked up the fresh corpse and carried him over to his two friends. I was sure that the night would conceal any tracks we made on the beach, at least until the flames took hold, but I didn't want to make it any easier than I had to for Hraki to figure out what had happened.

"Done."

Valna appeared beside me. She handed me back the flint and then readied herself for battle.

A glow grew within each longship. The flame-cast shadows gave life to the figureheads, all carved into vicious dragons, as their eyes stared balefully down at us. I met their gaze for as long as I could, but after a moment I had to look away from the brightness.

"Well, I hope you've not got any second thoughts. There's no turning back now," Valna said as she moved up next to me to watch the flames engulf the longships.

"There's been no way back for me for a long time."

We stayed long enough to be sure that the flames were rooted and then followed the drunkard's footsteps on the dark pathway between the rocks, hoping we would find Hraki at the other end.

*

The rocks became steep walls as we crept forward. We moved slowly with our shields held high and our spears low. I took each step with care so as not to slip on any unseen scree and Valna followed a few paces behind. As we travelled further into the chasm, the clouded sky began to clear as though the stars were keen to witness the coming slaughter.

"I don't like this," I hissed at Valna. "I can't see anything."

"That drunk came this way. There's nowhere else to go."

I paused to look at the walls. They were rough, as if the island had been ripped in two and this pathway was little more than a jagged tear in the earth. Salt stained the sharp edges of the stone all the way up. The thought of climbing the walls and slicing my palms on those salt-crusted rocks made me wince. I murmured a curse. There was nothing else to do but push on.

After another hundred heartbeats and half as many paces, warm firelight caressed the contours of the rocks ahead. The corridor widened and the ground sloped up a small distance before disappearing. As we came to the edge of the path we heard the gentle sound of a distant crowd. We found a boulder, perhaps broken off when the island was split, and hid behind it. The boulder was halfway between the top of the slope and the end of the path, too far from the path to be safe, and too low for us to be able to see our enemies. The amber firelight passed over our heads, only illuminating the tip of the passage. For the moment we were hidden. We were safe.

I peered around one side of the boulder and then the other.

"It's no good," I said. "I can't see anything."

Valna pursed her lips and looked around.

"I'll jump on top of the rocks." She pointed back the way we had come. "From up there I should be able to see everything."

She set down her shield and spear and edged away from the boulder. Now that we had stopped, I felt the distant pull of a volatile energy. It was a quiet mirror to the vibrating power of the Wind I felt inside me and reflected in Valna.

"No, wait." I grabbed her arm before she could disappear. "Do you feel that?"

Valna frowned at me then her eyes went wide and she nodded. The feeling was strong, but blurred. Trying to say how many Windborn were ahead of us would have been like trying to count the nicks on a sword as it swings towards your head.

"If you start jumping it might give us away. What if they feel you do it and I have to deal with a whole army on my own?"

Valna's jaw tensed and she shook me off her arm.

"Fine. What do we do then? Do you want to go back to the boat and sail around the island? Try and find somewhere else to land and come at them from the other side?"

"No."

I rubbed at my eyes and tipped my head back against the boulder. We couldn't charge in and try and take everyone on. There would be too many people between us and Hraki and, Windborn or not, the two of us would be cut down before we reached him. I looked around at the salt-rimed rocks, hoping that something would come to me, but nothing did.

"What about—"

Valna went silent as someone shouted.

A wordless cry of alarm from beyond the slope. The gentle hum of the crowd was replaced by shouted orders and the clatter of things hastily shoved out of the way.

We looked around, desperate to discover if we had been seen, but I couldn't see any sign that our hideaway had been discovered. Valna's wide, confused eyes showed me that she didn't know what was going on either.

Then I saw it: a faint, burning amber staining the night. The burning longships. I tapped Valna and pointed. We had not been able to see the fire as the rock walls obstructed our view, but now that the flames wrapped themselves around the masts like burning ivy, the flame-engulfed longships were visible from all over the island.

The shouts became more organised as they realised what was happening. Footsteps. A group headed to the longships. They would need to go straight by us.

There was no time to go anywhere.

"Wrap the spearheads," I hissed at Valna.

She nodded. I flipped our shields so that the bosses wouldn't give away our position and Valna twisted the spearheads in her tunic to hide the shining metal. We pressed ourselves against the boulder, trying to hide in the rock's rough edges just in time for a group of warriors to rush past us.

They held torches, knives, axes.

We pressed hard against the boulder. We would survive a fight, but it would be a short lived victory that brought the rest of the fighters down on us.

The first warrior sprinted past without noticing us or our tracks. It was as though he set the standard for the others. None of them glanced in our direction, their attention focused solely on the burning longships. I tried to count them as they went, but they disappeared into the rock-path too quickly. A dozen, maybe. Our distraction had not thinned their numbers by much, but I was thankful for each warrior we had drawn away, for now.

"What now?" Valna whispered.

It was possible they would send someone back for help to fight the fires. We couldn't wait for that. Whoever came back would see us right away and our only tactical advantage would be lost. I chewed my lip, trying to think of something we could do to get Hraki away from his small army.

Something moved behind Valna.

I looked around her but saw only footsteps across the sand and rocks. Almost all of them pointed to the burning ships but some moved toward the boulder, and us. Three sets let to the boulder. One for me and one for Valna. Whose was the third?

I spun in time to see a rock lifting behind Valna's head. I yanked her forward as the rock smashed down where her head had been.

Valna's eyes went wide as I grabbed her, but she was a fighter to her bones, and faster than I could follow she pulled a knife and slashed behind her.

A grunt and a red gash appeared from nowhere.

I pulled my axe from my belt and swung it at the space where I felt a Windborn's echo. The axe met something solid.

Valna scrambled to her feet and threw a handful of dust and sand at whoever was attacking us. They grunted and spat, but the dust had done its job.

A figure stood before us outlined with a fine coating of sand like a man made from dirty stars. A red line marred the dusty warrior-echo and he slowly bled into view from the wound.

"You bitch," he grunted.

He launched himself forward to swipe at me with whatever weapon he had in his hand. I blocked with an ice-covered forearm. The ice cracked against the force of it and the invisible weapon bounced off to stab my leg.

I stifled a cry and took another swing with my axe. He blocked it easily and slashed at me again. I flinched back, feeling the air from the weapon brush my cheek, and tripped over the shields on the floor.

The warrior, his blood-soaked tunic now visible up to his shoulders, loomed over me. A shield appeared in the air and he raised it to smash down at me.

"I knew whoever set those fires wouldn't be stupid enough

to stay with the longships. You—"

Valna crashed into him. He crunched into the boulder and bounced off. Valna didn't let up. She sprinted after him and stabbed at him again and again. Crimson blossomed all over his chest and then he brought the shield around and knocked Valna off her stride.

She fell back, dizzy from the blow, dropping one of her knives.

I jumped in and used the hook of my axe to pull his shield towards me. The movement caught him off guard and he stumbled forward.

By now I could see one of his legs, his arms, and his blood-spittled lips.

I lifted the axe with both hands to bring down on his head, and as I did his weapon slashed against my arm. I kept my grip on my axe and swung hard. The axe connected with his skull with a wet crack. I yanked the weapon free and swung again and again and again and again.

On the fourth swing, his invisibility faded. His body, now in full view, lay still. I let my axe drop to my side.

Valna walked up to me, wiping blood away from her nose with the back of one hand.

"Help me drag him out of sight," I said. "They might not have spotted us."

When I tried to grab him, pain shivered through my left arm. I gritted my teeth against the pain and we shoved the body against the boulder.

"Are you okay?" I asked.

"I'm fine, he only shoved me. What about you?"

I glanced down at my arm, hidden in the boulder-shadow, only a scratch and already iced over. The wound in my leg still bled and I pressed my hand against it.

"Let me see," Valna said.

My muscles burned as I stretched out my leg for Valna to inspect the wound. I felt like a haunch of meat on a butcher's table.

"It's fine," I said. "It's already freezing over."

It was, but not fast enough. Nal's knife had stabbed deep into me and black-red ichor, thick with ice crystals, ran down my leg like deadly warpaint.

"We've got to get that bandaged up," Valna said and started to tear strips from her tunic.

"No, wait." I panted.

I placed my hand over the wound and a fresh wave of pain flared. Blue light shone between my fingertips. I bit down so hard my tongue bled, and pushed as much cold out of me as I could. When I took my hand away, there was a cocoon of ice over the wound, but blood still glistened beneath.

"See," I said. "Good as new."

"Bullshit." She rubbed at her face and looked from me to the body beside us and then to the glowing longships. "This wasn't how this was supposed to go."

"It wasn't a great plan," I conceded.

Valna offered me a sad smile. She came to sit on my good side and leaned her head on my shoulder.

"Can I go and jump up on the rocks now, then? If they didn't notice the fight I don't think they'll notice me do that."

I tried to straighten my arm and winced at the blaze of pain. Beyond the slope, the sounds of the crowd had fallen back to a murmur. Although it was a low, tense sound rather than the easy quiet of a hundred conversations.

"I don't—"

The sharp sound of a kicked stone. A muffled curse. I nodded to the path and picked up my axe. Valna took up her knives and crept to one side of the path's entrance and I made my way to the other.

Whoever was making their way towards us was doing a piss poor job of masking their movements. Their feet scraped the pebbled floor and there was the intermittent scratch of cloth on stone as they bumped into the walls.

I looked to Valna. Our eyes met. We raised our weapons and nodded.

Two men stepped off the path. One old, the other younger with a bright blond beard, both strong. I swung my axe at the older one.

Runar and Orin.

I saw Valna's eyes widen and she dropped her knives. Runar spun towards her and flinched back. Orin turned towards me and I felt the hairs on the back of my neck stand upright. There was a flash of recognition in his eyes. He smiled as though he expected me to stop the axe, drop it maybe, and he straightened.

I felt myself standing on the threshold of a mistake that could bring me justice. The axe kept moving.

All my reasons for wanting Orin dead rumbled through my head with all the excuses I could give merging with them: it was too dark to see who it was; I didn't recognise him; he owed me a life.

Every step I had taken since my husband drowned echoed in my feet. Each denial of justice clawed its way free of my memory and screamed into the face of the man who took my husband from me, but through my primal fury I scented the true source of my misery.

Hraki.

I had gone too far to jeopardise bringing the Windborn king to justice.

The axe stopped moving. Valna appeared between us and held up her hands to stop me. I pulled the axe close and slipped it into my belt.

"It's okay, Edda," she hissed. "It's Runar and Orin."

The boulder couldn't hide all of us so we crouched down at the entrance to the pathway. Blood splatters shone on their clothes and Runar had crimson smears on his arms.

"Why are you here?" Valna asked.

"To get you, you bloody fools," Runar whispered. "The High King sent us to bring you back. We would have lost you, though, if you hadn't set light to the longships."

"We're not going back without Hraki," I said.

Valna spun to look at me. "Until we kill him."

"Valna, now that Runar's come, we could take Hraki back with us and give him to the High King. He might just let us go if we do that."

"I don't want to go back." She frowned at me. "There's nothing for me back there, Edda, it's just pain and memories. We came here to kill Hraki. Fuck the High King. Fuck his justice. Fuck the consequences."

Her eyes hardened as she talked. Her anger was the kind of

rage that can only be stoked by the death of a loved one. I knew that rage. How could I turn Valna away from it, when it had carried me this far?

"Valna." I spoke softly and took her hands. "I understand. My husband died because of Hraki. I lost everything because of him. My home, my family, my friends, but I found you. There's still things to live for even if it doesn't feel like it right now. I'm not saying that we let Hraki go, I'm just saying we should try and bring him to justice. If we can't do that... then we kill him."

Her fury fluctuated as I spoke. It seemed like she tried to hold her anger like a shield, but some part of what I said got through. She nodded.

"Fine."

"We're not here for Hraki," Runar said. He pinched the bridge of his nose. "We're here to take you back."

"What if you brought Hraki back too?" I said. "You'll deliver the renegade Windborn king to the High King for his justice. You'll be heroes."

"Or we could die."

"That's always a risk." I shrugged. "We're going to try and we could use your help. Once we get him then we'll come with you. Right, Valna?"

There was a pause. Valna shrugged.

Runar looked from me to Valna and back again. His shoulders slumped and he sighed.

"Fine, but if it goes badly then I'm grabbing who I can and leaving."

Valna beamed and clapped her hands together. Everyone turned to her and we all hunched a little lower.

"Sorry," she whispered.

For a tense moment, we listened to the camped warriors over the slope. Nothing seemed to have changed and we relaxed.

"What about you, old man?" Valna asked, with a hint of her old, playful self.

Orin looked around the group. His white hair stood at odd angles and his cheeks had more colour to them than when I had last seen him. His face split into a wide grin.

"It's been a long time since I've had a proper fight."

Valna threw herself at Orin and hugged him. There was a spark and a crack when she touched him and her hair stood straight up. Valna pulled away, saw where I was staring, and tried to smother her hair back down. It didn't budge. I stifled a laugh.

"What's the plan, then?" Runar said.

"Did you kill the people who went to the longships?" I asked.

"We did. We got some of their weapons too."

"Good, then we don't need to worry about someone sneaking up behind us."

"Let me see what's over the ridge," Valna said. "I'll crawl up there and if anyone sees me I can jump back here."

"Okay, just be careful."

She shot me a grin and started to move up to the top of the slope. She kept to the side of the walls, trying to hide her shape in the rough texture of the rock. Once she got close to the crest of the slope, she dropped onto her belly and squirmed forward.

"What do you see?" I whispered.

She ignored me and came back down a moment later.

"There's at least a hundred of them. They've set up tents and there's a few campfires down there, but all the fighters look on edge. A load of them have their weapons out and none of them look happy."

"I wouldn't look happy if I was stuck on this shithole rock," Orin muttered.

I shot him a look to silence him. "Did you see Hraki?"

Valna shook her head.

"There's a bigger tent at the back. I'd say he's in there."

I looked around our small group. Four fighters wouldn't be enough to take on one hundred, even if those four were Windborn, and we didn't know how many Windborn Hraki had left.

"There's too many," I said. "We can't charge in there. We need to draw them out."

"I can take care of that," Orin said with a grin.

A shadow passed over his eyes and I felt the echo of his power building in his chest. Above us the stars started to disappear. Clouds blanketed the sky, forming from nothing but thought. Thunder in the distance.

"We can't just make it rain on them," I snorted, trying to cover the fear that snaked around my throat at the memory of that first, deadly storm. "We need something to make them come to us."

"I'll make us a target," Runar said. He slapped a hand down on Orin's shoulder and a tiny streak of lightning jumped at Runar's hand. "How far are they from the crest of the slope, Valna?"

"Maybe two hundred paces."

"They'll be confident with their numbers and should charge straight for us," I said. "We'll make a shield wall and—"

"Edda, there's no way you can stand in a shield wall with your leg," Valna said, gently.

"I'll be fine—"

"What's wrong with your leg?" Runar butted in.

I showed him.

"Shit, you can't be in a shield wall with that."

"I can try. A shield wall is the best option. Let them come to us. They'll tire on the charge and then we cut them down."

"You'll not be able to push back in a shield wall with your leg like that. Then you'll die. Then we'll all die." Runar shook his head. "You're thinking like a fighter, Edda, but not like a Windborn. We don't want to defend. We need to attack.

"We make a line on that ridge. Orin gets their attention. We can throw these rocks at them as they come running over, a good throw will be lethal, then we take the fight to them. Valna, you fight at the edges and don't stay in one place too long. The usual. Edda and Valna can go and get Hraki once we've thinned out the numbers. Sound good?"

Runar looked at each of us in turn and we all nodded.

A knife-thin grin sliced across Orin's face. "Let's show them what it means to be Windborn."

CHAPTER TWENTY-FIVE
FIGHT LIKE A WINDBORN

FAT GLOBS OF RAIN FELL AS WE READIED ourselves, slow at first, then building to a battle roar. As irritating as the rain was, I was glad that its noise and haze concealed our movements. Valna rushed to the longships to fetch a shield for Runar, taking it from the dead guards. When she returned she told me how well the longships were burning like a proud mother espousing the virtues of her children.

Valna kept watch, in case they sent any more to help with the longships, as we armed ourselves and collected rocks to rain down on the enemy. I strapped my husband's shield onto my arm and double-checked his axe at my belt. In this small way, it felt as if Bjolfur was with me and would protect me, attack alongside me one last time.

I looked over at my companions. One looked too old to swing an axe. Another looked like he would rather be anywhere else, and the last was already panting from her efforts. Despite that, we were Windborn and would be more than a match for any fighter out there.

"Ready?" I said.

Nods.

Another couple of deep breaths and we made the short march to the top of the slope.

We stood so that our silhouettes were clearly outlined by the flames from the longships. Some people turned and straightened in their seats, but clearly thought we were their returning friends. They could not feel the crackling, convulsing energy that whirred in our chests and echoed back from the Windborn hidden before us. For once, I felt strong, not

483

exhausted from creating icebergs to float across a fjord, not drained from using my power to keep me from burning on a longship, and not recovering from stab wounds that would have killed anyone else. Though my leg ached, it took my weight and would carry me to my enemies. I stood ready for battle. I squeezed my spear and looked at the warriors watching us and glared at the tent beyond. Hraki waited there. Justice waited there. I could wait no longer.

"Hraki," I cried. "We've come to claim you. Give yourself up and your warriors can go free."

No one said anything.

Some of them got up, clutching knives, but they looked to the large tent behind them, waiting.

"They need some encouragement," Orin said and took a step forward.

My hair stood on end as a sudden tension filled the air. Orin threw an arm out and light twitched in the clouds. Another flash. Lightning crashed down into the middle of their camp. Burning. Screams. Thunder.

Orin stepped back in line with us.

"Tell 'em again, lass."

My mouth fell open, but words failed me. The still echoing thunder brought that storm back. With each rumble that bounced back and forth I felt my husband's hand slip away.

"Hraki, you cowardly fuck!" Valna screamed, beside me. "Come out or we will come and get you."

Valna's voice filled the space between echoes of thunder and for a moment it was all you could hear. Thunder and rage. None of the people below looked sure of what to do. Some still looked back to the tent for their orders whilst others looked to their fellows as though they didn't want to be the first to charge.

The entrance to the tent twitched and someone stepped through. A ripple of relief ran through the fighters. Lothi. The Windborn moved to the edge of the crowd then began to fly over them. He twisted in the air to take in the whole scene.

I picked up one of the rocks by my feet and threw it. It whistled through the air, but Lothi moved lazily out of the way. The rock hit Hraki's tent with enough momentum to tear a hole and send it shuddering.

"What are you waiting for?" Lothi shouted over the rain. "Fucking kill them."

I gripped my shield and shifted my stance, pain twinged in my leg, and gratitude surged through me again that I stood with some part of my husband. His presence had always eased the nerves that came before a fight.

A yell reached us from between the campfires. Someone else joined their voice to it, then another and another. With each battle-cry, another warrior charged towards us.

Lothi floated above the mass of charging warriors, his eyes firmly fixed on us. He waited until they had almost reached us then surged forward with them, his speed putting theirs to shame.

"I've waited a long time for this," Runar muttered.

He threw his spear with such strength that it seemed to tear the air as it flew. As soon as it was out of his fingers he flew after it in an explosion of dirt and rocks.

Lothi swooped to the side to avoid the spear but he couldn't avoid Runar. The Windborn smashed together with such ferocity that Runar's shield shattered. The flying Windborn swirled around each other like eagles stabbing and slashing with iron talons.

"Edda, throw some fucking rocks," Valna cried. Her voice snapped my attention back to our enemies.

I picked up a handful of rocks and threw them into the enemy as hard as I could. Valna launched hers almost too fast to see and each one found its mark with a wet, empty crunch. Mine and Orin's rocks flew slower and whistled past our enemies as often as they hit.

The charge lost speed as they dodged our missiles and clambered over their dead. They spread out but then someone called for a shield wall and they huddled together. With their shields raised, they came on again with slow, deliberate steps. Our rocks bounced off wood, though the force of it gave them pause.

"Fuck this," Orin grumbled.

He stepped forward, dropping the rocks, and clenched his fists. Light shone from within him, outlining his dark bones through his flesh, and he threw out both hands. Again the sky lit up with a lightning-mirror before a column of crackling fury burst from the clouds. It struck the centre of the shield wall and the force of it threw the warriors into the air.

Valna and I managed to hit a few of the fighters with our stones before they closed the shield wall again. It was difficult to judge, but perhaps thirty fighters lay still, never to rise. The shield wall curved in the middle as they climbed over the dead, but their pace never slowed.

"We can take them, right?" Valna said, her voice wavering.

"Of course we can. They're not Windborn," Orin growled then laughed. "Yet."

He pointed up to the sky. Between the thick layer of clouds came the faint, dancing glow of the Winds.

"The gods have got a shit sense of humour," Valna said.

"I guess the Winds have come to see what we can do," I said and took up my spear.

"Or see if there's anyone here worth saving," Orin muttered.

Then the shield wall met us and there was no time for conversation, for uncertainty, for anything but death.

They tried to keep their formation and jab at us with spears, but they quickly fell apart as Orin tossed lightning into them and Valna slashed at them from behind.

As soon as the shields in front of me fell away, I thrust my spear into the gap. It hit something. I felt the familiar tug and scrape as the spear-tip cut through flesh and scored deep into bone.

One of the shields fell away from corpse-limp hands before another fighter at the back took it up.

Again and again, I thrust the spear into whatever spaces I could find. Again and again, I felt the tear and scrape. Soon, the spear looked like a bloodied fang.

A blinding strike of lightning.

The shield wall fractured.

Valna leapt forward with her knives, slicing anyone that came too close. Axes and spears came for her. Whenever their sharp edges were close enough to kiss her skin, she disappeared.

A warrior surged towards me with her shield raised high.

I met it with my own and we smashed together like rutting rams. I yelled against the pain in my wounded arm. Her ragged breathing was heavy with adrenalin and panic. Its scent thick with honey and blood.

I shoved her back.

She recovered and came at me, swinging wildly with her axe.

I caught the first swing on the shield then ducked beneath the second swing. I thrust my spear up. It bit through the side of her neck.

Desperate fury boiled in her eyes and she pulled away. Blood spurted like a geyser, but she wasn't done.

Her shield came up again and she barged into me. I tried to push against her but the pain in my leg forced me to take a step back. My feet hit the pile of stones and I fell.

The ground slammed the air out of me. As I sucked in a breath, my opponent loomed over me and raised her axe. Blood poured down her chest like a river. She brought the axe down.

I rolled to one side and the axe chopped through my hair, cutting into the ground where my head had been.

As she tugged at the earth-trapped weapon, I leapt up and smashed my shield into her head. The shield boss crunched into her skull and she collapsed.

I looked out over the battlefield.

Orin kept the fighters at bay with lightning strikes. Whenever someone managed to dodge close to Orin, he struck out with a fist covered in sparks that seared their skin. Runar and Lothi still swirled together above everything. Whenever lightning illuminated them, I saw how splattered with red they were, how shredded their clothes. Valna hopped between lone warriors, slicing at them and dancing away before they could turn to attack her. She made her way along the back edge of the battle and left a thousand wounds in her wake.

I gripped my axe tight. Orin needed help. The surge of enemies showed no sign of stopping and I doubted even he could stand against them forever.

He glanced at me as I approached, and nodded. The air around him was heavy with a static tension and bright white energy crackled over him.

The tide of enemies paused. Even though they outnumbered us, they seemed unhappy to attack two Windborn at once.

"It looks like they need some encouragement," I said.

Orin shot me a vicious grin.

"Let's see if I can convince them," he said.

He bent down and picked up a couple of axes. As soon as he touched them, the wood blackened underneath his hands and tiny columns of lightning leapt from his fingers to the metal axe heads.

"Come on," Orin shouted at them. "You scared of an old man?"

Someone roared back at us. A deep, mountain-shaking roar.

The crowd parted for a giant one-armed man. As he walked towards us, his skin turned granite pale and stone-tough.

"It's been a while, Brimir," Orin said calmly and took a few steps towards the Windborn.

"I'm going to kill both of you. You," he pointed to Orin, "for keeping us in that fucking hall. And you," he pointed at me, "for taking my fucking arm."

He stomped up the slope. Each step sent a shudder through the earth. I took a breath, then strengthened my shield with a covering of ice and wrapped my shoulders in a layer of frozen armour.

Brimir roared and charged.

His fist slammed down at us. We dove to either side as the ground exploded under the force of the attack.

I stabbed my spear at Brimir's back, but the weapon bounced off the stone skin. Orin did the same on Brimir's other side. I heard the crack of miniature lightning, but Brimir didn't react.

The stone Windborn swiped at Orin, who ducked out of the way, then he swivelled and threw a punch at me.

I leaned back but the edge of his knuckles caught my shoulder and sent me spinning to the floor. My spear snapped as I fell and spun out of my hand.

Brimir followed up with a swift strike down, aimed at my face.

He stumbled midway through the blow and Orin came into view, righting himself after barging into Brimir with his shoulder. Orin followed it up with three quick slashes, each attack popped with a tiny lightning burst. Brimir held up his arm as a shield and each blow bounced harmlessly off his granite skin.

Orin backed away from Brimir who chased after him, swiping and punching with his remaining arm.

The two of them traded blows. Orin's axes ricocheted from the stone Windborn, whilst Brimir's heavy fist was too slow to catch the old warrior.

I marvelled at Orin's speed. The Windborn before me was so different from the gaunt old man I had seen struggling to breathe in his bed. Even from this short distance, I could see the battle-joy sparking in Orin's eyes. This was a man made to fight. It wasn't old age that had been killing Orin; it was boredom.

I glanced over to the rest of the battlefield. Hraki's warriors looked unwilling to get any closer to the Windborn fight than they had to. Valna still carved her way through our enemies, but there were too many for her to do much more than keep them busy. As I watched, it looked like Valna might be overwhelmed by several warriors at once but Runar swooped down and picked up one of Valna's opponents. He whipped around in the air and sent the warrior at Lothi like a slingshot looses a stone. The warrior collided with the Windborn and they went down in a tangle of limbs and weapons.

I looked back to Orin. No matter how good he was, Orin could not carve out any of the stone flesh from his opponent.

I knelt and pressed my hands against the earth, pushing my fingers as deep as I could into the hard, rocky ground. Frost coated the rocks around me in a shining white and I drew as much of my power as I could. The cold flowed easily out of me and covered the ground next to the battling Windborn. The frost thickened to ice, like winter in miniature. Brimir stepped onto a patch of frozen earth and the ice latched onto him, clawed its way up his leg and held him in place.

Brimir roared and spun around. His fists clenched and stretched out to crush me, but I was well out of reach. Orin reached out and called down a column of lightning which hit the trapped Windborn. The force of it pushed me flat on the floor and I covered my face against the intense heat. Brimir's cry of pain was lost underneath the storm-screech of the lightning and the low shake of the thunder.

The lightning stopped.

Brimir stood. Panting and scorched, but alive. The ice around him turned to a steaming puddle.

"Is that it?" Brimir said, trying to sound confident but his strained voice belied his pain. "Ice and lightning. That's all you've got?"

Brimir leapt for Orin. The old Windborn ducked beneath Brimir's grasping fingers, though not without earning a deep scrape across his back from Brimir's fingertips.

Brimir panted as he followed up with another attack and another. Something in the cadence of his step was off. His right leg, the one that had been coated in ice, was riven with cracks. The instant change in temperature had splintered Brimir's rock-like skin.

Two huskalar stepped up to me, courage and fear writ in their eyes in equal measure. I glanced behind them at Orin and Brimir's duel. There was no time for this. The huskalar raised their shields. I drew Bjolfur's axe. I screamed a war cry and charged.

They moved apart to try and pincer me between them. I caught a spear thrust on my shield and the spearhead caught on the carved saga. I pushed, and the spear snapped. The other huskalar swung for my face with a sword. I ducked and hooked their leg with my axe. They fell and I strode forward and stamped down. My boot crunched through their skull and sank deep into the mud. The first huskalar, now with a knife, came at me with short, flashing stabs. I leapt back, then forward, swinging my axe for their neck. They raised their shield just in time and the axe sank into the wood, too deep for me to tug out. I let the axe go and covered my fist with a gauntlet of ice. The huskalar lowered their shield, expecting me to move back and ready another weapon. Perhaps forgetting they fought Windborn. I was the weapon. I punched them with my glacier-wrapped fist. Their skull crunched, their head snapped round too far, and they fell limp. I put my foot on their shield and wrenched my axe free.

490

I moved over to the edge of the Windborn duelling with stone and iron and pushed my fingers into the soil again. The frost spread out over the muddy ground, creating minuscule mountain ranges out of ice and wet earth. I tried to aim for Brimir's injured leg, but he took an unexpected sidestep to avoid one of Orin's axes and I trapped his other leg.

Brimir tugged at the small winter locking him in place. Cracks appeared in the ice-trap and I gritted my teeth against the effort of pushing more power, more ice around it.

"Hit him again," I yelled.

"What do you think I'm doing?" Orin growled and advanced on Brimir with his axes raised.

"Not with your axes."

Realisation lit up Orin's face and he held out his hands again. Lightning poured from the sky like a blazing waterfall. Brimir screamed.

The world became blinding light and midnight dark. The campfires, the Winds, and muffled stars were as nothing compared to the searing brightness of Orin's power.

This time I heard the brittle splinter a heartbeat before the lightning stopped.

Brimir fell to his knees, one of his legs blackened and riddled with the open cracks we'd caused. He tried to stand but the broken leg snapped, sending a puff of hot stone-dust from his leg, and he tumbled to the floor.

I pushed the ice back over him. It crept across his chest and face like a deadly cocoon. Brimir pushed himself away from the ice, scrambling across the floor, but it caught his hand then his arm and locked him in place.

Another blast of lightning. Another crack.

Brimir's stone body which had seemed immutable moments before, now glowed with a fierce heat and glittered with deep gouges.

He flailed away from us, scraping his way across the rocky ground with one leg and only one working arm. He screamed at his allies to help him, to kill us, to do something. Most of them looked on, mouths agape at their Windborn brought low. Some steeled themselves and charged us.

Orin faced them, a lightning bolt shot out to cook the first charging fighter. He met the others with storm-covered axes.

Another three charged me. I batted away the first warrior's spear and swept my axe into their chest. He sucked in a wet breath as I wrenched the axe free before I slammed the axe into his head and kicked him away. The other two hesitated for a few heartbeats. Too long. I sent a shockwave of Windborn power across the ground and the mud froze, locking their feet in place. As they both tried to tug their legs free I strode over and in two easy motions, they were dead.

I walked towards Brimir like the goddess of winter herself. Frost followed in my wake and death waited at the tips of my fingers. I let the ice within me pour over Brimir. The frost overtook him and covered his remaining leg, his chest, his arm, his head. The ice drowned his screams under a white-shining prison.

"Orin!"

I turned, trying to get his attention for the final strike, but he had disappeared into a whirlpool of crackling energy, knives, and spears. Orin's white hair, now stained with mud and crimson, flashed through the gaps of limbs. I called out for him again, this time fear tinged the edge of my words.

I charged into the maelstrom. I swung my axe and hacked into arms, legs, chests. A few fighters turned to face me. I barged into them and when they fell I slammed my shield down into their heads and necks until they stopped moving.

Two more fighters fanned out before me and in the darkness it seemed like I had returned to the clifftop where I died. It felt like years ago that I had fallen into those ravenous waves, but the same pulse-stopping flash of fear gripped me. Then came the rage. This time I was Windborn and justice lay beyond this battle. I refused to die a second time.

My heartbeat hesitation was enough for them. They lunged. A knife slashing for my face. An axe swinging for my chest.

I caught the axe on my shield. The force knocked me back half a step. A small movement. Enough to watch the knife, not enough to dodge it.

The iron blade skittered across the edge of my shield and then punched through the ice-armour on my shoulder and bit deep into my chest.

I roared as the knife caught on my clavicle. I shoved axe-wielder back and sank my axe into knife-wielder's neck. I left the axe there and spun to face axe-wielder. They swung again and I blocked. I covered my fist in ice and slammed it into their face as hard as I could. Their skull crumpled in a spray of hot red and cold white.

I shook the ice off my fist and retrieved my axe. Another two fighters came up to face me. Ice cracked beyond them as the Windborn struggled to get free.

"Orin," I called behind me. "Hit him again."

My opponents came forward slowly, caution beaten into them with the death of their friends.

I edged towards them, shield up and axe ready. They fanned out to make sure I couldn't swing at both of them at the same time. I watched as their hair began to stand on end and the now-familiar static tension flowed through the air.

I screamed a war-cry and charged. I made for the one on my right who readied their shield. The other watched, waiting for their chance. A heartbeat before I attacked, I switched targets and sent a flash of ice out along the ground. My shield boss crunched into the face of the left fighter and knocked them dead. The other tried to move but their feet were locked in ice. I turned to the ice-locked warrior and brought my axe down on them.

The axe and lightning struck in the same moment, illuminating my opponent's confusion and terror as the iron cracked their skull.

I jumped over the corpses, letting the axe fall with the warrior, and ran towards Brimir.

Lightning still fell from the sky, forcing me to stop as its heat and power shook the marrow from my bones. The fractured ice-armour on my chest began to weep and then sloughed away. Lightning kept blazing down, and I felt my skin begin to blister. I raised my shield and took another step towards the incandescent pillar. I took another step and it stopped.

I stumbled forward. Brimir glowed the muted red of a sword fresh from the forge. His stone skin was covered in hairline cracks. He groaned as he tried to get away from me, but he was too weak, the mud too slick. I raised my shield. I slammed it down into Brimir's face. The superheated stone splintered with a hollow pop. I did it again. And again. Each time the rock became a little softer and bloody spots glimmered on the edge of the shield. As I brought my shield down for the final time, his body thawed from stone to flesh. The shield pushed deep and slammed into the ground beneath.

I pulled back for another attack, but he wasn't breathing. He was barely recognisable as a corpse. I wiped dark blood from my face. It was the kind of red that showed you how dark you were inside. I turned to see if Orin needed help.

A spear flew through the air straight at me.

I brought my shield up to stop it. Too slow with my wounded arm.

Valna appeared beside me and threw me to the floor.

The spear sailed past her, cut through her tunic, and tore a line across her back.

We rolled across the ground. Valna growled through clenched teeth and disappeared again.

As I looked up she was already behind the spear-thrower, her knives punching through their chest. She ripped the knives out and slashed them across their throat.

"Are you okay?" I asked and pushed myself to my feet.

"I'll be fine," Valna said as she walked over to me.

Bodies lay all around us, not all of them were still but none of them were a threat. More fighters were coming up from the camp. It looked like they had gone back to retrieve their helms, shields, and whatever else they thought would protect them from Windborn.

We looked over at Orin who had left a trail of singed and mutilated bodies behind him as he was forced to retreat. His wiry limbs were covered in scratches and all of his clothes were soaked with crimson. Those fighters left ahead of him had backed away, waiting for their armoured allies to arrive.

Orin nodded at us and we walked over.

"Oh, that felt good, girl," he said and stretched his back until it cracked. "Ah, Valna, you're back. Good. Take Edda and get to Hraki."

He glanced over his shoulder and threw lances of lightning at the waiting warriors.

"I'll keep them busy."

"What?" Valna said. "There's too many. You can't—"

"I've got a lot to make up for, lass. I've done a lot of bad things and... and I've caused a lot of pain. This is the first time in a long time that I've chosen to fight for the right reasons. Let me do this and maybe the gods will look kindly on me."

I thought Orin glanced at me as he said it.

A body fell from the sky and into the waiting warriors ahead, then someone slammed into the ground beside us. We all tensed, weapons raised and powers ready.

"I've wanted to kill that pig fucker for a long, long time," Runar said.

He stumbled forward and Valna caught him.

"You still up for a fight, boy?"

Runar stretched as though that would close the wounds and suck in the bruises covering him. "I'm not done yet."

"Good. These shield-maidens are going to get to Hraki and we're going to keep our friends busy. You remember how this works?"

Runar took a deep breath then picked up a shield and axe from the ground. "Aye. Keep out of your way."

Orin grinned.

"Go on," Runar said. "I'll make sure no one follows you."

I looked from the two exhausted Windborn to the ten warriors waiting to charge and the thirty others coming to reinforce them. My gaze was drawn past them and to the tent at the other edge of the island. It seemed like all of Hraki's warriors had come to face us and left the tent unguarded. The tent canvas bucked in the strong winds and something illuminated it from within. We had turned this small island into a battlefield, slaughtered his warriors, and still Hraki did not come to us. Perhaps he knew to fear us and was content to hide behind those he saw as expendable. More likely he did not think we were worth his own sweat and blood. I squeezed my axe until the wood creaked. He could not hide from me. I would make him bleed.

Valna bounced on the balls of her feet, torn between helping her friends and chasing down the murderer of her beloved.

"Come on, Valna," I said. "The sooner we get Hraki, the sooner we get away from here."

She turned away from Runar and Orin to look at me. The worry in her eyes hardened into the same cold anger I knew was in my own eyes.

"Okay."

She took half a step then spun and hugged Orin and Runar. They both tried to return the gesture as best they could with weapons in hand.

"Don't die," she said and walked over to me.

"And you," Runar replied with a sad smile.

Valna took my hand. We watched Orin and Runar nod to each other before they charged screaming down the slope. Orin shot lightning bolts out before him and Runar leapt into the air before he crashed down and smashed his shield into the enemy.

I looked at Valna. She squeezed my hand. Then the world turned inside out.

*

We tumbled back into existence between abandoned campfires and discarded food.

After standing shoulder to shoulder with Orin's lightning-soaked hands the world seemed dark and silent. Some way behind us Orin's white sparking spears needled our enemies like a tiny thunderstorm, but the world around us was lit only by dappled starlight, the Winds, and the decaying campfires.

I helped Valna up. She hissed and flinched from the wound in her back.

"Are you going to be okay?" I asked.

"Yeah. What about your shoulder?"

I put a hand on my bloody shoulder and winced at the spiking pain. The blood was dry. The wound was cold.

"It's frozen solid. I'll be fine."

Valna didn't look convinced, but I gestured at her wounds and she showed a weak smile.

We picked our way through the abandoned campsites, stepping around detritus and cold firewood. A dangerous, muted glow came from Hraki's tent like a wolf's eyes reflecting firelight. For a moment I wondered if Soren would be waiting for us, arms aflame but I shook off the thought.

"What's the plan?" she asked.

"We go in hard and fast. We put him down as quick as we can and make sure he can't get away."

Valna nodded, her jaw tensed.

I looked back to the tent and tried to make out who was inside. I felt a glimmer of hair-raising energy, but nothing stronger than I felt from Valna. The tent flap fluttered open and firelight flooded into the night. It flickered as someone moved inside.

"Ready?" I said.

Valna nodded again. I pushed out a fresh layer of ice over my chest. The power within me felt calmer as though the glacial tidal wave within me had crashed against a cliff-face and would soon be spent. Valna came up to me and rested her forehead against mine.

"Don't die, Edda," Valna whispered. "I couldn't take it."

"Neither could I," I said.

We stayed like that for a moment. My mouth quirked up in a smile when I saw the circle of frost on her forehead as we pulled away from each other. Valna offered a small smile in return, blunted by the danger ahead of us.

Frost blossomed under my feet as we crept over to the tent. I glanced back and saw the trail of ice I had left through the storm-soaked night. It felt like I stood at the threshold of the underworld. Another deep, steadying breath.

I gripped my axe tight, nodded to Valna, and we burst through the tent's entrance.

A shield smashed into my face and I tumbled to the floor. A blur beside me as someone tried to do the same to Valna.

They tried to kick away my axe and shield, but the Wind inside me seemed to understand what was happening. It danced in my chest and power flowed over my hands to make gloves as hard as glaciers, locking my axe and shield in my grip.

I brought my shield up to block a downward sword swing. It hacked into the shield and the force of it shoved the air from me. The huskalar above me lifted a heavy boot to ready to stamp down on me. I hooked his other foot with my axe and yanked hard. He fell with a grunt.

I looked around to see Valna facing off against another armoured huskalar. She darted around them as they slashed at her with a sword. Her knives bounced off the huskalar's helm and scraped across the chain, but she couldn't find a place to sink her iron fangs.

I shoved my shield at the huskalar on the ground next to me and used it as leverage to push myself up as I kept them pinned.

Beside me, Valna's opponent stabbed at her. They overextended and Valna batted the sword easily aside. She grabbed onto their arm and used their momentum to throw them from the tent.

She glanced at me.

"Go," I said. "I'll be fine."

She disappeared and the sound of clashing iron came from outside.

My huskalar opponent had clambered to his feet. He bared crooked teeth at me beneath the rim of his helm.

"Come on," I said. "What are you waiting for?"

He growled and attacked.

He kept his shield up and slashed at me with the sword once, twice. The shining edge sang as it swept past me. I dodged out of the way then hooked his shield down with my axe. He stumbled and I whipped the axe up to sink into his neck.

Something caught my arm mid-swing. I tried to bash my shield into his head, but whoever had hold of me threw me aside. I crashed into a table which splintered under my weight, then rolled to a stop next to a crackling fire.

Two figures stood over me now. One was heavily armoured and breathing heavy. The other stood with a regal bearing and an easy smile. Hraki.

"Go and help Arvid," Hraki said with a lazy wave of his hand. "I'll handle this one."

The huskalar looked between us and then hurried out the tent. Hraki walked around the tent, circling me as I clambered to my feet, and righted what furniture I had not destroyed.

Now that I wasn't dodging a sword-wielding huskalar, I was able to take in my surroundings. There was a small fire pit in the centre of the tent, filled with crackling driftwood, and the smoke caught at the top of the tent, staining it before it seeped out. There had been four chairs in the room, two were now broken and a third lay on the floor as though someone had leapt out of it. The chairs faced a table laden with half-eaten food and drink. I turned back to Hraki, who seemed unconcerned that two Windborn had just burst into his tent. He placed one of the chairs at the head of the table and sat down, then waved his hand, offering me a seat.

I stared at him. Wood creaked as he leaned back in his chair.

"Your tenacity continues to impress me, Edda." He picked up a handful of dried fruit from the table. "I admit, I didn't think you would chase me so far across a winter sea, at night no less, just to see out Erling's petty vengeance."

Hraki's sword was at his waist and his shield lay behind him. Metal shone between the gaps of his clothes, a chain shirt, and he had placed a helm on the table before him.

I let the power of the Winds flow through me, freezing the ground and making the fire stutter.

"I haven't come for Erling's vengeance. I've come for mine."

"You're still angry I tried to kill you? I expected better from you. You've been raiding. Would you hold a grudge against a warrior who stood against you in battle? We do what we need to survive."

"Survive?" I stepped forward. The fire flinched away from my ferocious cold and the dying flames drenched the room in quivering shadows. "You were a king. You would have survived just fine."

"Not forever." Hraki shook his head. "Erling would have found out eventually. His son knew. Dyggvi and I had been told to go hunting by the High King and I was killed, pushing myself too hard to prove my mettle in another prince's company. Everyone was heading back, to give me a suitable funeral, when I was reborn, became this. My retainers probably could have kept it secret, but certainly not Dyggvi and his lackeys. So I killed them all. It was supposed to make everything easier. I simply swapped one prince's death for another, killed anyone who would know any different. I told Erling it was a rock slide, something to explain away all the deaths, but he wanted his son's body. I suppose I can't blame him for that, but the problem was, Dyggvi had fought back. He was covered in axe bites and spear wounds.

"The old fool wouldn't drop the issue and I knew that sooner or later he would find out the truth. My people would keep my secret, those who I let find out, but the guilt of Dyggvi's death weighed on them. Sooner or later, word would have gotten out."

"Why are you telling me this?"

My attention swung from Hraki to the world outside the tent. With every word Hraki spoke I wondered how many knives stabbed at Runar and Orin, how much longer they could go on. Valna should have been able to handle the two huskalar but we had already fought so many. I couldn't hear anything beyond the howling wind and rain.

"Because we find ourselves here." Hraki gestured to the tent which twitched violently against the wind. Each gust that made its way into the tent stripped a layer of frost from me like snowfall. "On a tiny island in the middle of the sea, on the cusp of a decision that will change the world."

"Surrender," I said. That single word, spoken with clarity and conviction, carried more weight than any of Hraki's tirade. "I am taking you back to the High King."

He cocked an eyebrow.

"Look at yourself, Edda. You're in no state to do anything. You're covered in blood, your shoulder looks injured, and you have had to fight your way here." He pushed himself up, picked up his shield, and put on his helm. "I, on the other hand," he said as he examined his reflection in his sword's blade, "am fresh to the fight, and without injury." He grinned. "I am always without injury."

"This will go easier on you if you surrender," I said and turned side-on, shield raised. "The High King will be merciful if he knows you cooperated."

Hraki shook his head and took a few steps towards me, walking around the fire pit. I stepped back and kept my shield up.

"You are a poor liar. I thought you might be different. You hunted Soren for weeks until you chased him to my halls."

He punctuated each sentence with a lazy swing of his sword. They were easily blocked with my shield. He was testing me, looking for weakness. Then the sword was too fast. It caught the bottom of my shield and scraped my leg.

Something changed in Hraki's eyes as he circled me. I stepped with him, keeping him in front of me, and when his back was to the entrance, I attacked. He blocked my axe easily. Once, twice, then a third time. My eyes darted to the tent's entrance. Valna was out there. Had she beaten the huskalar yet?

"Do you know what it's like to have everything ripped away from you, Edda?"

The question almost stopped me in my tracks. Something exploded in my chest. It felt like an erupting geyser showering everything with scalding water. How dare he ask me that? This man, who had lied and killed to keep his position of power and privilege, had taken so much from me. I was left with nothing but ashes, memories, and frozen scars. A hot, furious wash of emotions scrubbed some of the exhaustions from my bones and I swung my axe at him again.

"What would you know about losing anything?" I spat, trying to keep him still. "You're still a king. You could have gone on just like before."

He tried to keep circling and I moved to block him. We were two wolves with our teeth bared.

"For how long, Edda?" Another lazy swing of the sword. "You know what it's like, don't you? Once you're Windborn, that's the end. Any plans you had, any hopes; all destroyed. Why do you think I've been trying to sail past Erling? To get to a place where none of that matters."

He paused and let his sword and shield fall a little. I shifted my stance, readying myself, and waited. Hraki was too fast. I was already spent. My flush of anger had subsided and my exhaustion echoed back up from my bones. My only hope was to stall until Valna arrived.

"Do you know what Ertlanders do with Windborn?" There was a new note to his speech. An earnest desperation as if he truly wanted to convince me. "They flee before them. They know that Windborn are faster, stronger, better than them. Think about that, Edda. You've been raiding, haven't you?"

I nodded before I could stop myself. I ran my tongue over my teeth, found the gap where Hraki had knocked out a tooth. I let my tongue press against the soft gums as a reminder of what this man was: a vicious bully, not a king.

"Think about what we could take from them as Windborn with no masters, without the petty prejudice of our High King. We could build a kingdom to put the Empire of Bones to shame. You're strong. You're tenacious. If you stood with me you could take whatever you want."

He took half a step back and lowered his sword until it pointed at the floor.

"What do you want?"

Something changed in his voice.

These weren't the words of a pontificating king. These were the words of someone who had lost everything speaking to someone who might understand.

Without meaning to, I thought about my answer. I thought about the world after this moment. What did I want? The answer was buried deep in my soul but had been torn away from me in pieces since that storm. All I ever wanted was a farm, a home, a place that lifted your soul whenever you stepped inside. The image played out in my mind as it always had: A small home, built with wood and with turf covering its triangular roof. As I held the picture, a familiar, shadowed figure stood at the door, beckoning me home.

"A farm." I whispered my answer, hoping the hissing fire would smother it.

"A farm?" Hraki asked, incredulous. "Easily done. Come with me and you can have a farm. Have nine. Have as many as we can take from them."

Could it be that easy? Could Hraki give me everything that I had lost as a Windborn?

I thought back to my farm, to that picture that twisted my heart and thrummed at my soul. The sun moved from behind a cloud, illuminating the figure at the door. Bjolfur. He smiled at me, said something I couldn't hear. From inside the house, someone laughed. I couldn't see them, couldn't be sure who they were, but they were young. Young enough to be ours.

My arms felt leaden. Bjolfur's carved saga tugged at the

shield like a riptide. The saga was chipped, each image wounded by iron like punctuation. The central picture was somehow unscathed. The moment we met. The moment we knew that together we could take on the gods themselves and live to tell the tale.

"Come with me, Edda. We'll travel west and be as gods."

Naked avarice shone in his eyes. The moment was lost.

"I want a farm with my husband," I said, louder, and brought my shield back up. "You took him from me, and you took our home. You took everything."

Hraki's expression hardened as he realised his grip on me was gone.

"I didn't take anything from you," he said, fury rasped in his voice like a blade scraping from its sheath. "You're Windborn now, Edda, and the High King won't stand for it. If I don't kill you, then they will once you've outlived your usefulness. You'll think of me when you lie broken and bleeding on the floor and you'll wish you'd made the right choice."

His sword flashed. My shield caught the blow, splinters exploded. The force of it made me step back. His other attacks had been nothing like this.

Hraki grinned at me from beneath his helm and attacked again.

I grunted in pain and swung my axe to cut his legs, but his shield batted the axe aside.

Hraki attacked again and again. I blocked over and over and hacked at him when I could.

His attacks were slow for a Windborn. Too easy to catch on my shield, but far too strong. Each one sent shock waves through my arm. With each shudder, my wounded shoulder sapped my strength. The only thing keeping my shield in my hand was the ice-glove wrapped around the handle.

I moved away. Step by agonising step.

My foot caught the edge of the fire pit. I tried to dodge out of the way, but my wounded leg twitched and gave way. As I fell, I used the lower angle to chop my axe into Hraki's leg. He couldn't move fast enough to stop it.

He roared with pain and blood spurted from the wound.

I tried to roll away but Hraki slammed his shield down into

my chest. Something within me cracked. I panted, each breath lancing pain through me.

"I should have seen your weakness before. You are too weak minded, blindly following outdated laws and stuck in the past. Don't you realise you're in a trap you could easily escape?" Hraki said. He kept the pressure on my chest and raised his sword over my face, ready to plunge down.

Valna appeared two paces to my right. She roared and lunged forward with both knives extended like fangs.

She disappeared, mid-lunge, just as her knives began to eat into his shield. She reappeared on Hraki's other side. One knife skittered across the chain shirt, carving out a few of the rings, then slipped out of her three-fingered grip. The other bit through the chain and sank into Hraki's back.

He cried out and spun to face her. The knife jutted from his back like a broken bone.

Valna reeled as Hraki's sword whistled past her. Its tip scratched her forehead. She leaned too far to avoid the blow and fell. Hraki stomped towards her, readying his sword to stab down. I tried to pull myself up. There would be no gloating this time.

The sword came down.

I barged into him.

Hraki smashed into the chairs and rolled toward the fire.

I turned back to Valna, hoping there was something I could do, that somehow I could save her, but she wasn't there. The sword quivered in the ground.

A few paces behind me Valna groaned and pulled herself to her feet. She pulled the sword free of the ground, swapping the knife into her other hand as she did so.

"I don't have many of those left," she whispered to me.

I nodded. My body ached from the enemies killed outside of the tent. I thought of the fight still to come. Valna did not look any better. Blood dripped down from her forehead, one of her cheeks was bruised and scratched and her armour was torn. She slouched with exhaustion but stood to face Hraki with me nonetheless.

"We can finish this," I whispered back. "If we can trip him up, I can catch him."

She wiped the blood from her eyes and nodded.

Hraki got up, pieces of broken chair tumbled off him with a clatter. He looked at the sword in Valna's hand and his mouth twisted. Reaching behind him, he pulled the knife from his back. The chain shirt rang like falling coin and we heard a wet, hungry sucking as the blade left the wound.

As he came towards us, he flicked the knife. A splatter of black blood flew to the floor.

We came together again. A clash of axe and shield, sword and knives.

Hraki twisted and spun to catch our attacks on his shield or parry them with the knife. Whatever attacks made it through bounced from the chain shirt.

Valna overextended with a sword lunge and sucked in a breath as the knife sliced across her forearm. I threw my shield at Hraki, but he met it with his own, putting enough force behind it to make my shoulder scream with pain.

We moved apart. All of us panting, only Valna and I cradling wounds.

"I thought you were better than this," Hraki said. He waved the bloody knife at Valna and shook his head. "Where's your little disappearing trick? And you call yourself Windborn."

He stretched, wincing at some tightness in his back.

I tapped Valna's foot with mine. She nodded but didn't take her eyes off Hraki.

I spread frost across the ground, then ice, but it came too slow to catch Hraki like it had caught Brimir. I needed time.

"This has gone on for long enough," Hraki said. "Either get out of my way or let me kill you."

He waited a heartbeat, but when we didn't move he growled and rushed forward with his shield raised.

Valna moved to block him then disappeared. Hraki jerked forward and lost his balance as his shield didn't meet the resistance he had expected, and I knocked his shield aside with my axe.

Hraki swiped at me with his knife. I ducked and it skittered over my shield.

Behind him, Valna swung the sword at his ribs. Hraki cried out and twisted. Chain rings fell to the floor, rusty with blood, as Valna pulled the sword free. Hraki stepped back, breathing heavy, and bent to take the weight away from his wound. The blood pouring from him slowed even as we watched, and after his third laboured breath, it stopped entirely.

I moved away from the fighting and froze the ground around me, pushing hard to make sure that the floor became slick with ice.

Valna angled herself to drive Hraki towards me and renewed her attack. She stabbed at him, again and again, until her attacks became a blur as she frantically tried to find a gap in his defences. Step by bleeding step she pushed him back until he found the ice.

Hraki put his foot down and swiped at Valna. His foot went out from under him, his attack went wide. Valna yelled as his knife found her belly and ripped through her.

Hraki fell to his knees and used his shield to catch himself. I hooked his foot with my axe and yanked it out from under him. Hraki grunted as he fell face-first onto the floor. I leapt onto him, throwing my shield and axe away, but as I leapt, he managed to twist onto his back. His shield caught my chin. My head rang with the force of the blow and I blinked away spots of light, but I couldn't stop.

I knelt with one knee to either side of his chest and wrapped my hands around his throat. Ice rippled out from me and rooted him to the floor.

He writhed underneath me, heedless of the crunch of his neck underneath my fingers.

At first the ice splintered under the force of his movements, but whenever he touched it, it wrapped him in its glacier embrace. Every time he fought, it grew thicker. In a few heartbeats, the ice covered his body and was too strong for him. His writhing slowed. His skin paled. His eyes burned with hatred. I let go of his throat and let the ice creep over his raw neck and up to his mouth, leaving the nose free so he could breathe.

I leaned back, but didn't get up, and looked over to Valna.

Her face was set in a grimace and one hand pressed against her ribs. Blood seeped through her fingertips. Too much blood.

"Valna," I called over. "Are you—"

A crack. A hand around my throat. I tried to breathe but the hand squeezed too tight.

I tried to pry the fingers off my skin. My icy fingers couldn't find purchase on his thick, calloused hand.

The dying fire had melted the ice locking Hraki's left arm in place, making it weak enough for him to rip his arm free and now his fingers crushed the life from me.

I felt around for my axe. It was too far away. Hraki's grip locked me in place and my hands pawed at the ice.

Fire burned in my chest as my lungs emptied. Every part of me, down to the marrow, screamed for air, for relief. I clawed at Hraki's hand, but my fingers kept slipping. I couldn't breathe. I was drowning on land. My vision blurred. Black swallowed the edges of the world as my eyes fluttered closed. Would I become one of the Blessed Drowned if I drowned this way? Maybe that was all it took. All you needed to do was to suffocate and it didn't matter if you did it above or below the water. I prayed that was the case. I prayed I could see my husband again.

A weight lifted, but no air came.

I opened my eyes.

Valna stood next to me, teeth bared. Blood spurted from an open wound. An arm hung from my neck, still gripping tight but no longer attached to a body.

Valna stumbled over and got her knife between the fingers, cutting them free. After the burning need for air, the small slices she made to my neck felt like relief.

Hraki's dismembered arm fell from my throat and I tumbled off the Windborn king. I sucked in air thick with woodsmoke and the iron tang of blood. Nothing had ever tasted so sweet.

I rubbed at my sore and bloody neck. Hraki's dismembered arm twitched and slid down the ice covering its former master. Valna had sliced through his arm above the elbow and the wound had already stopped bleeding. Scabs covered it and as I watched, it turned to puckered, pink flesh.

"Thank you," I panted.

Valna grimaced at me and nodded before she slumped into the last surviving chair, still clutching her wounded side.

"What do we do with him now?" she said.

507

I looked over at the imprisoned king. The ice keeping him in place was thick and covered with white scars where we had scuffed it. Through the translucent cage Hraki's body looked distorted, bulging in all the wrong places. Anger seethed in his eyes and condensation formed in short bursts on the ice underneath his nostrils.

Valna looked on from his throne, her eyes full of hatred when she glared at him. I pushed myself up and walked over to her. I took her hand in mine, it was slick with grime and sweat, and I squeezed it.

"We bring him to justice for what he's taken from us."

CHAPTER TWENTY-SIX
THE END OF THE WORLD

I LEFT VALNA GUARDING HRAKI, although she could barely sit upright, and went to see what had happened to our friends.

The rain and clouds were gone, replaced by brightly shining stars and the slow, persistent Winds. Their strange colours shivered over the ground like sunlight through waves: the green at the heart of a glacier; the blue of a still fjord; and at its edges a hungry red.

Runar and Orin nodded to me as I approached them. Orin's lean form was covered in countless cuts and it looked like some of his hair had been burned away. Runar dripped blood from myriad injuries, fresh wounds to overwrite old scars, and one eye was swollen shut.

"We won," I said. The words felt hollow. Two words to sing of victory, but here we were bleeding, with barely the strength to stand and surrounded by the dead.

Runar's shoulders slumped with relief. "We didn't get all of them," he said. "They couldn't handle us and they ran. They're around, but they won't want to see us again."

Orin smiled, but it twisted into a grimace and he sat on one of the bodies.

"We need to go," I said, looking to the dead then up to the Winds. "I don't want to be here if the Winds are bringing any of these people back."

"Too right, lass," Orin said. "I don't want to have to kill them again."

"Valna?" Runar asked.

"She's alive. Wounded, but alive."

"Aren't we all?"

509

As I moved back to the tent Runar fell in step behind me. Orin stayed seated, his eyelids fluttering open and closed.

"Guard the pass, Orin," Runar said. "We'll get Hraki. We can rest when we're on the boat."

"Right you are, lad. I'll be here."

Orin's eyes closed and his breathing fell into the slow, even rhythm of sleep.

"Do you think he'll make it?" I asked.

"I don't know," Runar sighed. "He's taken a beating, but he's surprised me before."

I glanced back at Orin. He was surrounded by earth that had been scarred by the lightning thrown from his fingertips, and the remains of his enemies. Now that the fighting was over, the spark in Orin had faded and he once again looked like that old man on the cusp of the afterlife.

We picked our way through the bodies. Some had tumbled down the slope once the life had left them and collected in a heap. Runar floated over the corpse-barricade as I shoved the bodies aside.

"Do you want help?" Runar said as he watched me.

I shook my head. The bodies thinned and the campfires grew in number. The empty spaces, illuminated by the dying flames, seemed to highlight the deathly silence, that no one would ever sit there again. It felt like I had walked to the end of the world.

Thaw covered the tent. The dripping water froze as I stepped through the entrance.

Hraki twitched underneath his ice prison. There were new cracks along its length. Valna was still slumped in the chair with her hand clutched to her side. The bleeding seemed to have stopped. Runar looked around, taking in the debris-ridden tent, and then his gaze fell on Valna. He took a step forward but she held up a bloodied hand.

"I'm fine," she said.

Runar didn't look convinced. He frowned at her, mouth twisting, but didn't say anything. He turned his attention to the imprisoned king.

"How do we get him out?" he asked.

"Either we cut him into pieces," I said and pointed to the

arm lying still on the floor. "Or we thaw him out piece by piece and tie him up."

Runar crouched down and picked up the sword. He turned it in his hand, letting the light from the dying embers of the fire reflect in Hraki's eyes.

"I'd love to cut this bastard up, but we'd better bring him back whole." Runar's gaze wandered to the arm. "Mostly."

I nodded, not sure which part of Runar's statement I was agreeing to.

As I gathered some rope from the campsites Runar took up the splintered wreckage of the chairs and set them smouldering like torches within the fire pit. Once everything was in place we thawed out Hraki's legs. Valna came over to help hold them down and we wrapped them in thick coils of rope, tying them with the kind of knots that saved lives at sea. I knelt, ready to cover Hraki in a fresh coating of ice if it looked like he would break free.

Hraki's chest and arms presented more of a problem.

Valna picked up a spear and thrust it through Hraki's left shoulder. It exploded through the ice and crunched through Hraki's chain shirt, pinning him to the floor. Hraki's eyes flashed with pain and fury. Valna leaned down and met his eyes with a steady gaze.

"I should do worse than this," she hissed. "Be grateful for mercy you do not deserve."

He still struggled as we thawed out the rest of him. His body bucked up and down the spear, covering it in his dark blood, but it was stuck deep and kept him in place.

Eventually, the king was bound, his body outlined in thick rope and gagged with a strip of cloth. We dragged him out and past the campfires, past the cadavers of his followers, and up the slope. Orin's eyes fluttered open as we approached. His breathing was shallow, and his bones pushed against his skin like gaunt shadows.

"Time to go?"

"Aye," Runar said. "You must be stiff after that fight. Let me help you."

Orin offered a thin smile through dry lips. He let himself be lifted from the floor and half-carried as we walked. Valna went first into the chasm path, holding the burning remnants of a chair as a torch. Orin and Runar followed her like some injured, four-legged monster and I came last, dragging Hraki behind me.

The longships had fallen in on themselves whilst we fought. The fire still stretched up like a beast trapped in mud but did not roar so furiously. Perhaps now their passengers were dead the longships had lost the will to fight. I dragged Hraki along the beach, carving a furrow through the sand as though the bound king was nothing more than a plough. A tool to be put to use.

We fetched the boat and began to clean our wounds. I found a bowl and a bit of cloth that was, if not clean, at least not as dirty as we were. I filled the bowl with ice, then walked over to the burning longships and melted it to freshwater which we used to gently wipe the grime and blood from ourselves. Whilst Runar cleaned Orin's wounds, Valna and I checked our supplies and lifted Hraki into the boat. We grabbed him as you would grab a heavy sack and he writhed in our grip, but he was bound well and wasn't going anywhere.

I had to fetch another two bowls of water as Runar cleaned Orin's wounds, then I began on Valna's. Both of them were covered in countless scratches, too many deep wounds, and Valna's side still wept with blood if she moved too quickly.

"Let's take a look at it," Runar said and pointed to Valna's side.

She did as she was told. I took one look at the torn flesh, sticking together like honeyed fingers, and got a fresh bowl of water.

Runar washed as much blood as he could from the wound. Every time he finished wiping away the worst of it would bleed again. Exhaustion was writ deep under Valna's eyes and eventually Runar was forced to rip part of our sail off and wrap it around her chest. She sucked in air through her teeth but didn't complain.

"That will have to do until we get back," he said. "Edda, do you need me to clean yours?" Runar asked when we were done.

I glanced down at the scars covering my arms, the wounds had healed and were written in ice. Frozen strands of blood quivered within my deep wounds like the Winds themselves. "No."

We wandered back over to the boat, ready to shove it into the sea and head back, but as we leaned against the cold wood none of us could summon the energy.

"We should rest," I said. "We'll leave when the sun comes up. I'll take first watch on him."

Everyone nodded, but no one said anything. They wandered over to the longships and lay in the sand, close enough to feel the warmth from the fires but not so close they would burn.

I sat on the edge of the boat and looked at Hraki. He must have sensed it as he looked back at me and narrowed his eyes, twitching as though he could break free from his bonds and kill me.

I tried to recapture the fury that had dragged me so far away from home, that same passion that sent me forward with my hand clutching an axe, but it wouldn't come. Before me was the man whose actions had taken everything away from me and when I looked at his twitching, uneven figure it only served to remind me that nothing would bring back the pieces of me that were now lost to ice and death.

Hraki renewed his writhing within the rope and started shouting beneath the gag. I looked him up and down, to be sure he couldn't break free of his bonds, then threw a cloth over his face.

"Go to sleep," I said. "I have nothing else to say to you."

He kept moving and shouting for a moment longer but when I didn't react he fell silent.

The Winds danced in front of the stars, though the stars were still visible through them. It was as though the bright, pulsing lights were interlopers and the tolerant, steady stars waited for their turn to watch uninterrupted. One of the curves of light broke as I watched. A web of cracks rippled across it and the Wind swept down like blood sinking in water. A single, glowing strand of light snaked to the quiet battlefield behind us and drained out of the sky. The other strands of dancing light flowed into the space the falling Wind had left between them and after a few heartbeats, it was as though nothing had happened.

The entire, sky-wide spectacle was utterly silent. Too quiet for a resurrection.

I looked back to the passage and wondered how long it would take the new Windborn to wake.

*

I woke to the call of gulls. There were hundreds of them, and for a moment I thought that Gerda had returned, but the gulls swirled and swooped over the battlefield. They laughed with joy at the feast of flesh that we had given them.

Valna sat on the edge of the boat, just as I had the night before, and Runar lay next to me on the sand. He blinked in the dim light and pulled himself up. I didn't tell them about the birth of a new Windborn. It would only lead to more blood and pain and we had soaked the earth with enough of that.

Runar stretched until his back clicked. "I needed that," he said with a yawn.

"I think we all did," I replied.

Valna still moved gingerly, trying to avoid pulling at the wound in her side, but the colour had come back to her cheeks and the familiar spark had returned to her eyes. Orin slept by the remnants of the longship bonfires, his breathing shallow, and looked like he might sleep there forever.

Valna came over to where Runar and I sat on the sand. She passed us a bag of nuts and berries and took a swig from a waterskin before passing that over as well. We thanked her and I was amazed at her forethought. I remembered the furious haze that descended on me when I first wanted Hraki dead. I wasn't sure I would have remembered to pack food and water.

"Let's get the boat ready," Runar said. "If Orin needs help I can carry him."

We all agreed and began to prepare ourselves for the journey home.

"How did you find your way here?" Runar asked as we dragged the boat to the water.

"Gerda helped us," I said. "She sent birds ahead."

"Well, where are they now?" He shifted around, looking for some pattern in the gulls above us.

"She's gone," Orin said as he shuffled over. His left side was covered in sand that fell away in waves with each step he took. "Didn't you feel it?"

Runar shook his head and looked to us.

"Feel what? No, she can't be. She always said she'd outlive us all."

"None of us will go on forever," Orin said, and put a hand on Runar's shoulder. "We've lost a lot of people recently, lad. It takes a toll."

"I..." Runar wiped away a tear with the back of his hand. "I didn't get to say goodbye."

"Sometimes we don't," Valna said, her gaze lost in the middle-distance. "But we have to trust that they knew how much we cared."

Runar opened and closed his mouth. I let them soak in the sorrow alone. They had known Gerda much longer than I, and they deserved to share this without me.

"She knew, lad. Don't worry about that." Orin patted him on the shoulder and walked unsteadily over to the boat. He said something to Hraki and spat on the king before he clambered into the boat and slumped onto a seat. The small journey into the boat seemed to have exhausted him and he panted as though he had just fought for his life.

"Which way do we go, then?" Runar said in a wavering voice.

"East," Valna said. "We'll hit land sooner or later."

Runar cocked an eyebrow. A smile tugged at the corners of his mouth. Valna smiled back, a sad curve of her lips, but a small mark of joy in the centre of a storm of sorrow and blood.

"Once we've been travelling for a few hours, you can fly up and make sure we're going in the right direction, right?" I offered.

Runar rubbed at his eyes again and nodded. One by one we gathered our things and went to the boat. Orin slumped down against the mast, dozing. At some sign of silent agreement, we made Orin a bed from blankets and cloaks and lifted him into it. He snored and twitched but didn't wake up.

Once we were certain everything was ready, Runar pushed us into the water. Valna and I used the oars to help steer the boat around the island's sharp edges.

It was a good day for sailing. The waters were smooth, the sky was clear, and the wind was strong. The even surface of the sea calmed the tension that rose within me as we got further and further from land and the close presence of my friends comforted me, especially considering one could fly and save me from drowning. Once we were beyond the hidden dangers of the island's rocky talons, we set the sail and let the wind do the work. Runar set himself down and took up the rudder.

We sailed into the ever-expanding horizon. The island fell away and all we were left with was sky and sea.

"I've not seen a sky like this in a long time," Orin said. His voice barely carried over the gentle shush of the water and the crackle of the sail. "There have been storms for so long. They bring me out and make me fight someone, summon a storm to sink someone, it's always too much. I'd forgotten what the colour blue looks like."

Orin leaned his head back and sighed.

"It's easy to miss the beauty around us when you're Windborn," he said.

His words sank into me, made me realise the lengths I had gone to fuel my own pain and rage. I thought of the path that had brought me to a small boat in the middle of the sea, without sight of land, escorting a king bound like wrapped meat, and I wondered if I would have done it all over again if I had the chance. I rested my arms on the gunwale and looked at the waves. White surf reeled off the keel and folded back into the sea behind us. The water was clear beneath us. I stuck a hand into it. My hand carved through the sea as easily as our boat, and a trail of ice swirled in my fingers' wake. My hand was visible through the water, but beneath them, the fathomless, pine-coloured depths were impenetrable. Somewhere within those impassable depths my husband waited.

I looked back at the coils of rope that hid Hraki.

I would do it all again.

Runar made to get up and fly ahead, to check where we were going, but I put a hand on his arm. He cocked his head and I gestured to Orin.

"Let him enjoy a clear sky for a while longer," I whispered.

He nodded and settled back onto the rudder.

We kept pace for another hour until Runar began to fidget.

"Go on," Valna said and waved towards the sky. "Better make sure we're heading in the right direction."

Runar let out a breath and grinned at me before he leapt out of the boat. Valna and I grabbed on to our seats to steady ourselves as Runar circled higher and higher until he was a silhouette no bigger than a fingernail.

I looked to the prow to check on Orin. He hadn't moved. One of his hands slid off his belly and fell limp by his side. He stared up at the clear sky, sightless, serene.

Valna caught my eye and looked over to Orin as well. Her face fell and she put one hand over her eyes, her lip began to tremble. I shifted in my seat and put an arm around her. Frost crept along her tunic where it touched me, but she leaned into the embrace.

Runar landed. The boat tipped with the weight of him and his words died when he saw us. He looked to Orin and his shoulders slumped. He moved back to the rudder and adjusted our course.

It was one of the shortest sea journeys I had ever made, but justice waited beyond the horizon and so it felt like the longest.

Chapter Twenty-Seven
A Funeral and an Execution

People called out as we sailed into the bay. Some shouted and waved whilst others rushed off to fetch friends to usher us home. By the time we swept up to Erling's island, a crowd gathered on the jetty.

Katja and Fainn elbowed their way to the front as we moored the boat. Valna and I threw Hraki out onto the jetty, Runar caught him with a foot to stop him from rolling into the water, then we wrapped Orin in blankets and carried him carefully onto the shore. Orin's face still wore the same serene smile and the crowd parted for us as we walked. Muttered prayers followed Orin and we lay him down on a patch of frost-hardened grass near the mead-hall. Runar appeared a moment later dragging Hraki behind him. The Windborn king writhed and bucked in an effort to free himself, but all eyes were on Orin. There was whispered discussion of funeral arrangements and I wondered if anyone would mourn my passing.

I returned to the boat to gather what I needed. I left the spears, the torn armour, and the food on the boat and pulled Bjolfur's axe and shield from under a discarded pile of blankets. The saga I had lovingly carved into the shield was decimated. Each image of Bjolfur and I was chipped and scarred. Wherever we appeared something scarred the wood between us. I ran my fingers over our first meeting. Frost spread out from my fingertips, covering us in a glittering sheen. I smiled. If only I could have frozen us then and kept us in that moment. I looked over the axe. It was whole, though the handle was warped and frost-bitten where I had gripped it.

I sighed, stood, and slung the shield over my shoulder as I walked back toward Hraki.

The crowd around Orin's body had grown, but I circled it. The mournful quiet was not for me to join, and not for me to break. Instead, I walked to Hraki and righted an abandoned stool to sit by him. I snatched up a handful of grass and started to chain it together but it froze too quickly and I ended up snapping each blade. It seemed as though Hraki and I had been forgotten.

Someone walked down from the mead-hall flanked by two huskalar. Alvilda. The young law-keeper clasped her hands in front of her and her eyes were ringed with a cautious sadness. She stopped a few paces away from the crowd and stood between me and them.

"The High King summons you," Alvilda said. She kept her head bowed and her voice low. It was clear she didn't want to break the solemn silence, but knew she had no choice.

Everyone fell silent and turned to her.

"Who is he summoning?" Katja said.

"The Windborn. They're to bring the prisoner along with them."

"May we accompany them?" Katja asked, gesturing to herself and Fainn.

Alvilda offered a half-bow as a response before turning on her heel and walking back to the mead-hall. The huskalar lingered a moment before they followed.

"I will stay here," Fainn said. "I can do more good here."

Katja nodded and then approached me.

"Do you need help with him?" she asked and pointed to the imprisoned king.

"No, I can manage." I grabbed the looped rope that Runar had used to drag Hraki and fell into step behind the law-keeper and my fellow Windborn. Some of the crowd followed us, but they quickly fell back and returned to Orin when they saw the huskalar standing guard at the mead-hall's entrance.

It took my eyes a moment to adjust to the dim light inside the mead-hall after the sharp brightness of the winter sun. Torches spluttered on pillars and the fire spat along the hall's centre. A few huskalar stood around the room and the ones following Alvilda broke off as we entered to go to their allotted spaces. The High King leaned back in Erling's throne, picking at some half-eaten meal on his lap.

"Thank you, law-keeper," he said as we made our way across the room.

Alvilda bowed and took her place beside the High King. We walked around the fire and stopped before the raised throne. Katja mirrored Alvilda's position and moved to the other side. Runar, Valna and I stood in front of the throne and Hraki ground to a stop behind us.

"Where is the old Windborn? The Storm Weaver?" The High King handed his plate to an attendant and wiped his fingers on his tunic. "Is that him bound behind you?"

"No, my king," Runar said. "Orin did not survive the journey back. He—"

"Fine. That's one less thing to deal with." The High King waved a hand dismissively, then turned it into a gesture to encompass Valna and I. "You were instructed to find these two Windborn and bring them back to me as prisoners. I cannot help but notice they are free and still holding their weapons."

His words rang out through the mead-hall. The huskalar tightened their grips on their weapons. These huskalar were ornately armoured. Each helm was forged to look like snarling wolf, and their chain shirts hung down to their knees. As the High King pointed to us they tipped their spears down in our direction.

"My king, you sent me to bring back the Windborn who fled, but Valna and Edda did not flee. They went to find Hraki and bring him back for your justice."

The High King tipped his head to peer around us and examine the bound figure behind us.

"That's him? Bring him forward."

I bent down to pick up the rope.

"Not you."

The High King gestured and one of his huskalar came to drag Hraki forward. The huskalar tried to shove me aside with a shoulder, but he bounced off. He grabbed the rope, ignoring me to save face, and strained to move Hraki in front of the High King. Hraki renewed his attempts to escape. Muffled shouts made their way through Hraki's gag. The huskalar leapt away and the others pointed their spears at him.

"Remove his gag."

The huskalar who had flinched away inched back again and carefully reached for the dirty cloth wrapped around Hraki's mouth. I stomped forward and ripped off the gag before anyone could stop me.

"—off me. This is outrageous. I'm a king. I demand you untie me and give me the respect that I deserve."

Hraki's voice rang out in the mead-hall and bounced around the room. He writhed on the floor to stare at each of his captors in turn. The huskalar looked away, eyes suddenly focused on their feet or the tips of their spears. The law-keepers turned their heads to the High King. Only the Windborn and the High King met Hraki's gaze and he found no mercy there.

"Be silent," the High King cut across Hraki's echoing voice. "It seems these Windborn have retrieved you so you may answer for your crimes, Hraki Jolafson. Firstly, you have been accused of attacking King Erling's land and people during winter. I have seen this for myself and I have given judgement on it. Secondly, your captors say that you are Windborn and you have tried to hide this. Given your status, I will give you leave to explain yourself, but we will not untie you until I am satisfied. How do you answer these accusations?"

Hraki twisted on the floor again, trying to keep the High King in his line of sight. The raised floor where the throne stood made it awkward, and he had to squirm back a few paces to see the High King properly.

I gritted my teeth as I watched Hraki roll on the floor. Would the High King's hatred for me and my Windborn friends win out against the truth? We may have brought Hraki back only to see him set free.

"By the gods, someone help him to his feet," the High King said. "It is bad enough he is bound, but it's pitiful to watch him flop about like a worm."

Two of the guards came forward to cut Hraki's legs free and help him to his feet.

"Thank you, High King," Hraki said and bowed. He shook himself to try and rid the worst of the dirt and grime from his shoulders.

"You have passed judgement on the first of my so-called crimes and so I will, of course, respect and accept your decision, but I hope you will listen to the reasons I was forced to take such drastic action. I may have attacked King Erling's land in winter, but only because he would not let my longships pass.

"I did not wish to sail through Erling's lands because I am Windborn, if that is the ridiculous idea these fools are peddling to you, but because my halls were filled with sorrow. My mother and father died a few short years ago and before we had truly recovered from our grief, my sister also passed away. Hers was a particularly tragic loss as she had many more years of service to give to you and the gods.

"I could not bear to live in those empty halls without the faces I loved, so I gave my people a choice. They could stay and continue to work and live in the homes they had known, or they could come with me and we would colonise one of the islands to the west. A new beginning for all of us. A fresh start that could bring only joy."

"This is the first I have heard of this," the High King said. His voice tight and the words clipped. "You intended to abandon your lands and obligations without consulting your king?"

Hraki bowed his head and I saw a sheen of sweat shining on his forehead.

"Of course not, my king, it is only that in my grief I forgot the proper procedures and for that I am truly sorry." Hraki kept his head low as he talked, eyes focused on the ground between his feet. "If you deem it necessary, I will accept whatever punishment you decide for my accidental omission. In fact, when law-keeper Einar visited my halls I did mention my plans to him, but only as idle musings over a cup of mead, and I asked him to keep it secret until firm plans were made. He will testify to this, I am sure."

"Einar is gone."

Uncertainty and anger flickered over Hraki's face. I wondered what other secrets Einar had sworn to keep and how much gold it had cost.

"Einar's position as an arbiter of disputes was in question," the High King went on. "He should have been able to predict your foolish desire to attack Erling in winter and warned me of it. For now, I have sent him with a team of law-keepers to inspect my holdings around the Kjaltonn islands to ensure that the laws are being properly followed, beginning with Dagnur Olafson."

I started at the mention of my old chief and muffled a smile that he would be subject to a vicious inspection by the High King's law-keepers.

"A fair and just decision, my king. Let me reassure you, it was not out of any sense of secrecy that I did not tell you, but only because of my grief. I beg your forgiveness and accept your judgement."

There was a moment where the High King looked as though he was reminded of something in his past and the hard light in the High King's eyes softened. The tension in his shoulders eased and he nodded at Hraki.

I took half a step forward and cried out, "Cut him."

The High King narrowed his eyes and loomed forward in the throne, leaning his chin on interlocked fingers. He levelled a stare at me that would have stopped an avalanche.

"Tread carefully, Windborn. Your fate is still to be decided and yet you continue to talk to me without respect and without leave."

"Yes, High King. Apologies, High King." I tried to lace my words with as much respect as I could muster, which wasn't much, but I could not let Hraki get away. "I swear to you that Hraki is Windborn. He has the power to heal wounds quicker than anything I have ever seen. In our fight to capture Hraki prisoner, we cut off his arm and you can see that already it has healed.

"If he has already been punished for the crime of waging war in winter, then let him be tested for the crime of continuing to hold property and his crown as a Windborn. Make a small cut, across his cheek or his palm, and see if it heals. If it does not heal before your eyes then you will know me to be a liar and you can kill me. But, before you do, please cut him."

The High King and I stared at each other for a long

moment. Everyone else in the hall had gone silent. The High King looked to Hraki and examined his stub of an arm.

"King Hraki, would you submit to such a test?"

Hraki swallowed, looked around the room, then bowed. "If it is what you desire, my king," Hraki said. "Though I give you my word that I am not Windborn. I hope that will be enough for you, as my father's word would have been enough."

"Perhaps." The High King tapped a finger against his pursed lips. "But you do not become the High King by taking everyone at their word. You, make the cut."

One of the huskalar nodded and stepped forward. He pulled a knife from his belt and advanced towards Hraki.

"I'm sorry," he said as he extended the knife out ready to slice Hraki's cheek.

Hraki smiled warmly and turned his face, as though presenting his cheek for the blade. Then Hraki threw his shoulder into the guard, sending him flying into a pillar. Dust and snow rained down through the roof and Hraki sprinted towards the door.

He was quick, too quick for a mortal man, but so were we. I sprinted after him and kicked his feet out from under him as Runar dove on top of him and pinned him to the floor. Valna appeared by the door, knives drawn, but relaxed when she saw us dragging Hraki back to the throne.

"Innocent men do not run, Hraki." The High King snapped. "Cut him."

Another guard stepped forward, a knife in his hands. Hraki twisted and bucked in our grip, but with two Windborn holding him, he wasn't going anywhere. The knife sliced a long, bright line across his cheek. Runar forced Hraki's head to one side to show the cheek to the High King.

Murmuring built up in the hall as blood welled on Hraki's cheek. Then silence fell as the blood flow slowed, stopped, and the red welt paled and disappeared.

"Chain him and lock him up," the High King said. He slumped back in his chair and looked to Alvilda. "Make preparations for the execution."

Alvilda bowed and left the room.

"Follow me." This from the huskalar that cut Hraki, his face was pale and I saw his jaw bunching underneath the helm.

"No, you can use me," Hraki screamed. He twisted beneath our grip but couldn't break free. "You need strong Windborn. You can use me."

"I have no use for liars and traitors."

Hraki's screaming continued as we dragged him away. Everyone inside the mead-hall looked away as we passed them, but once we were a safe distance away they watched him go. Once we were outside, Hraki stopped calling for clemency and started spitting hateful words. He told us of all the things he would do to us once he was free. He threatened us in the way the powerful do when they are brought low. We ignored him.

The huskalar led us to a place behind the mead-hall ready for prisoners, likely prepared for Valna and I. We left Hraki in the custody of too many guards. They wrapped an iron collar around his neck which was connected to a thick chain. Runar, Valna and I heaved a boulder onto the chain and I froze it in place. More heavy iron chain wrapped his chest and cuffs held his feet together.

We walked away. Hraki's cries, reduced to wordless fury, followed us until someone stuffed a gag in his mouth.

I glanced back at the circle of huskalar, wondering if the High King would still use those chains to hold me.

"Come on," Runar said. He slapped a hand down on my shoulder, turning me towards the Windborn longhouse. "I'd say you've earned a drink."

*

Runar was already gone when Valna and I woke the next morning. Our footsteps echoed in the Windborn longhouse as though to remind us of those we had lost. Word of Orin's death and Hraki's capture had spread and it seemed that everyone from the town had arrived and crammed themselves into the space between the hall and Hraki's boulder-prison where the huskalar had built a small scaffold and dug some smaller fire pits.

"They're not giving him a funeral pyre, are they?" I asked as we came to the edge of the crowd. People parted before us and we made it to the front with ease.

"They better not be," Valna muttered. "That fucker deserves to be eaten alive by wolves, not given a proper funeral."

Although the crowd ended some way away from the pyre and fire pits, there was a smaller group moving through the scaffolds, Katja and Fainn among them.

"Let's go and see what's going on," I said and pulled Valna along with me.

"Edda. Valna." Katja came up to us and threw her arms around us. "I'm so glad you made it. We didn't want to wake you. You deserved your rest."

She examined each of us with sorrowful eyes. The kind of sadness mixed with pity that you might offer an injured animal that won't recover.

"We're fine," I said, brushing off her hand.

"What about him?" Valna pointed up to Runar as he flew past us, low in the air and carrying a log. "You woke him up?"

"I couldn't sleep," Runar said as he lowered the log onto the pyre. "Thought I might as well do something useful."

"I reckon that's enough," Fainn said. "Thank you."

Runar landed by us and rubbed his palms together to get rid of the wood and sawdust.

"Who's this for?" I asked.

"Orin and Gerda," Fainn said. "We convinced the High King to give them a proper funeral. He wanted to throw them into the fjord, but we told him how much they meant to the people here and how hard they fought Hraki and eventually he relented."

"I thought the gods didn't accept Windborn souls?" I asked, my head snapping up. "That's the point of a funeral pyre, isn't it?"

Fainn nodded and leaned on his staff. His exhaustion was clear in the deep lines across his face. He must have read something in the speed of my question or the way my eyes sparked. He sighed, shook his head, and offered me the same sad pity Katja had.

"By all accounts, once you're Windborn then your soul is lost to the gods, it is too closely entwined with the Wind inside you. Not even the gods can untangle your mortal soul from the

Wind any more than we can retrieve the iron from a steel knife. No, to accept a Windborn soul into the halls of the gods could give the Winds the key to break out of their prison. The High King has given Orin and Gerda the honour of a funeral pyre but I cannot officiate. He will give a speech, but that is all. It is more than we hoped for."

Heavy footsteps and the brittle sound of chain. The High King approached with a contingent of huskalar dragging Hraki, bound and gagged, behind them.

"Are they ready?" asked the High King.

Katja and Fainn confirmed they were.

"Get out of the way, then."

The huskalar shepherded us to stand with those guarding Hraki.

"People of Eylheim." The High King's voice echoed from his gaunt frame and silenced all conversations. "I stand before you humbled. I was told that a renegade king had sent an army to your shores in winter. When I came north I expected to find nothing but bodies and ruins. Yet, when I arrived I found a community who came together to defend one another and still stood together, despite their wounds, when my longship came into view and you thought I was an enemy. Don't worry, I won't hold it against you." Some nervous laughter broke out in the crowd and the High King offered everyone a smile. As his speech went on, his posture changed and he stood a little straighter, moved a little easier. "You stood before me, still bleeding, prepared to defend your home once more. For that, you have my respect and admiration."

The High King nodded to Runar. The Windborn stepped forward and, one by one, lifted the bodies of his friends onto the pyre.

"These two Windborn," the High King went on, "Gerda Freyasdottir and Orin Ragnarson, stood with you then, as they have been at your side for years. They've defended you, helped you build your homes, and I've been told they even bought a drink once in a while. And so we gather here, in the light of a winter morning, to give them the funeral they deserve; a funeral pyre to match any warrior's and hope that it is enough to say thank you."

The crowd cheered as the High King walked over to one of the fire pits and pulled out a burning torch. His movements looked awkward and slow after his easy speech, but he hobbled to the pyre without assistance and shoved the torch deep inside.

Everyone held their breath as thin tendrils of smoke leaked through the wood and branches. I wondered if the winter morning was too cold to let the flames find their teeth in the pyre and it looked as though many in the crowd wondered the same thing. The High King waved at his followers and three huskalar took up torches and thrust them into the pyre.

After a heartbeat, a single tongue of flame licked at the wood underneath Orin's body. There was a collective sigh of relief as another flame clawed its way free of the firewood. More tongues of fire sprouted from the pyre and obscured Gerda and Orin's outlines. Black smoke billowed into the air, carrying their ashes and souls skyward, but without the words of a god-speaker to carry them to the gods' halls, the moment felt hollow.

I looked at Valna. Her eyes shone as she watched the flames. I took her hand and squeezed. She looked at me, smiled, and tightened her three-fingered grip on my hand.

Most people wandered off once the flames obscured Gerda and Orin's bodies. Mothers held their children close to them as they left. Friends supported one another as they wiped away tears. They did not care about what happened to Hraki. Their interest lay in paying respect to their friends, not in the execution of a criminal.

I stayed.

Valna stayed too.

Whilst the High King had been making his speech, his retainers had secured Hraki to the ground with his limbs splayed. Two huskalar waited with heavy axes. Each axe blade was as long as my forearm and the shaft came up to the huskalar's shoulders. At a nod from the High King they began.

Both huskalar moved up to Hraki's neck, but as they began to raise their axes the High King raised a hand.

"Leave the head. I want him to feel this."

All the warmth the High King had shown in his speech was

gone, replaced with a sword-sharp edge.

The huskalar set to their work like butchers. There was no mercy in their movements, they sought only the most efficient way to undo him. Hraki screamed, issuing muffled threats for longer than anyone has a right to when they're being picked apart. Soon, all that was left was the chest, heaving and slick with bloodstains. The stumps of his arms and legs began to scab over.

One huskalar moved up to stand by Hraki's shoulders. She lifted the enormous axe high and, with a grunt, brought it down. The axe head bit through Hraki's neck and the head parted from the body with a wet thud. Even then, Hraki's eyes glared out at everyone until one of the huskalar kicked it away. It stopped, eyes down, in a puddle of mud.

The huskalar collected the body parts from the blood-soaked ground and threw the pieces of him into the fire pit with less care than they would throw logs onto a fire.

The High King, flanked by his huskalar shadows, wandered up to the fire pits and peered inside. He took one of the axes from the huskalar and used the shaft as a poker. The smooth wood blackened as the High King used it to rummage through the flames until he was satisfied with what he saw.

"Check again when the fires die down a little. Make sure he is not coming back," the High King said as he shoved the axe back at the huskalar.

I walked over to the three smaller fire pits. Each hissed and spat as they burned their parcels of flesh. Small plumes of smoke rose from each of them and spiralled together into a miniature mirror of the pyre's pillar of smoke.

Hraki was gone, absorbed into the flames never to return. It was done.

I turned back to the funeral pyre. The once dark wood glowed white with the heat and sparks exploded skyward as something inside it collapsed. The column of smoke flinched away from the explosion. Its heat reached out to me, began to burn my cheeks, but I didn't move. The sensation was hollow and didn't sink beneath my skin. Underneath, I was still frozen. I ran a thumb over a scar on my forearm. It glinted in the dancing firelight but didn't melt.

I looked up and let my gaze follow the smoke columns. First Hraki's, then Gerda and Orin's. I wondered if the gods would know the difference. How could they tell which of the souls rising to meet them deserved their attention? Could they sense that two of the Windborn souls had worked to protect those around them when the other had sought only to exploit the weak? Would they even care?

The High King shuffled up beside me.

"You are still here," he said.

I glanced around to see I was the last one left staring at the fires.

"I'm watching the pyre. It—"

"You haven't fled. I ordered you imprisoned, you break out, but then you return. I would have expected you to run, to get away before I decide what to do with you."

I shrugged. "We brought you the Windborn king. I am not naive enough to think we would be rewarded, but I hoped that you would offer us some clemency for that."

"I am grateful that you brought Hraki back. To let such a man loose on the world would be a terrible thing. You trusted the law enough to bring him back to face justice."

The High King tapped his teeth with a fingernail. He squinted at the fires and looked deep in thought.

I wanted to shove my arm in his face and show him the crescents of ice sunk into me, to tell him of everything the law had taken away from me for those glacier scars. My home, my wealth, my husband. How many of those were lost to me because Hraki felt trapped by the laws that were meant to protect him?

"I have taken the flying one into my service," the High King said after a moment.

"Runar?"

"Yes, that's his name. A flying messenger that can also give me a bird's view of a battlefield. He will be a great asset to me."

Gerda's dog appeared from behind the mead-hall and walked over to us. He loped up to me and pushed his nose into my hand as though looking for a treat. I wondered if he had been drawn by the smell of the burning bodies. The thought turned my stomach.

"I will make you the same offer: that you swear yourself to my throne. Your oath will carry over to my successor and you will never have to worry about being an outlaw again. There is your clemency."

I watched the High King as he spoke. His face pulled into a pinched, sanctimonious expression. He seemed to believe his offer was salvation as sure as a boat to a drowning woman. He kept his eyes firmly fixed ahead and under the roaring crackle of the pyre came the clink of iron. Huskalar shifted uncomfortably around us.

"Is it better to be sworn to a throne than a single person?" I asked. "You say that I'd never be an outlaw again as though that's a good thing, but all I feel when you say that is the yoke that will be forever around my shoulders."

I examined the scars on my arms. Ice ran through me. Its roots brushed against my bones. The pain of Bjolfur's death had numbed somewhere between that first storm and this funeral pyre. My heart was still broken, ripped apart by black-feathered grief, but it no longer bled. The grief-crow had left its perch inside my chest, dissipating feather by feather into the black, corpse-fuelled smoke. I wondered if the ice in me would reach my shredded heart. When ice fills cracks in stone it leaves it more broken than before. Had my ice-scars done the same to me? For every wound that froze upon me, I had taken one more step on a path of revenge. I had lost more for each step, but I had not been able to stop.

"My steps have felt forced for a long time. I don't think I can do that again."

The High King pursed his lips then picked a string of meat from between his teeth.

"I can't let you walk away, Windborn, even if you did bring me Hraki. What is it you want?"

I broke away from his gaze and thought. Gerda's dog, realising it would not be receiving a treat from me, began to sniff around the fire pits. The heat of them pushed it away and it came back to lay in front of us.

"A home," I said at last. "I've only ever wanted to have a little pocket of somewhere to call mine, to live with my husband. A place for us to live."

The king snorted and shook his head. "You can't have land. Windborn can't own land."

I gritted my teeth against a response. Despite the brightness of the morning, the fires cast long shadows that swept over us. I crouched down to ruffle the hound's ears. They twitched, but he didn't wake.

"You can look after some of my lands."

"What do you mean?" I stood slowly and turned to face him. The possibility of owning something fluttered in my chest like butterflies in the sun. "You would break the law and gift me lands because I brought Hraki back?"

"Don't be stupid, girl. Even if I wanted to do that, which I don't, what would become of all the other Windborn? They'd all be clamouring for possessions and then where would we be?" He shook his head again. "No, I can't let you own any land, but I can give you a parcel to farm on my behalf."

The butterflies in my chest slowed but did not die. Our eyes met. He looked at me with the assurance of a man who has never been questioned and I looked back at him with the hard eyes of a dead woman.

"I know that you have some power over ice and given that you're not wearing a cloak or any furs I'm assuming you don't feel the cold?"

"Not since I drowned."

The High King shivered, perhaps something in my gaze had shown the horror of that moment.

"Yes, well," he stammered and offered me a pained smile. "The path to the Althing is a small one and I cannot, in good conscience, ask anyone to guard it through winter. The mountain passages clog with snow and I waste too much time and money clearing and maintaining them each spring. There is space for a home somewhere near those passages, but the winds are too cold. They feel like teeth sinking into the skin and will eat anyone who stays there too long. Something that is not a problem for you.

"Guard the pass of the Althing over winter, maintain the passages and I will not ask more of you. You will have your... pocket of somewhere, and I will have clear roads throughout the year. Perhaps I will have you keep goats or sheep there so that we can have fresh meat when we come to the Althing."

I watched the High King, trying to find hints of mockery or treachery in his words, but his expression was impenetrable. He looked to the pyres with squinting eyes and looked just as serious as I had ever seen him. I had always ignored political games in favour of an axe swing and this felt no different.

"And if I decline?"

"If a Windborn is not sworn to someone, they will be killed," he said and gave a slow shrug. There was a brittle edge to his words.

I ground my teeth at the thought of that. The High King's offer came with chains, but I suspected the chains that came with any other offer would be thicker, heavier. I could run. The chains of a fugitive would at least be those of my own making, but they would be heavy chains that would drown me if I ever stopped. And yet I could refuse. After all of this, was death such a punishment?

A gust of wind whipped the smoke from the funeral pyre in our direction. For a moment, the world fell to shadow and I used a hand to cover my eyes.

"Let me know your decision, Windborn." He brushed the soot from his robes. "But consider this: the fires before you contain those I choose to reward, as well as those I must punish. Choose your side wisely."

"It seems like an easy choice from here," I said.

"It should be, but it is yours to make. You always have a choice, Windborn," he said, staring at Gerda's dog.

The hound sniffed after the High King as he left, but did not get up. I sat next to it. One eye opened and acknowledged me and then the dog was asleep again. I rubbed the dog's belly as the fires burned themselves out.

*

I found Valna on the same boulder where we had danced at midnight. She had her knees pulled up under her chin and her eyes were locked onto the ice and debris floating out on the water. Long, twilight shadows reached out all around us like talons ready to pull us into some dark underworld.

This far away from the buildings and people, the only sounds were the thud of my footsteps and the lapping water. Valna was the only living thing I could see and something in that image made me realise that I would never be scratched by Gerda's ravens again. The thought made the world seem hollow and sharp. Any birds I saw would be just that, birds, and I could never rely on their eyes again.

Valna looked over as I approached, her eyes still brimming with raw emotion. It softened when she realised I was alone, she stared back out at the nearly-frozen fjord.

"What are you going to do?" I asked and leaned against her boulder-seat.

"I can't stay here," she said. "There's too many memories, too much grief."

I nodded and watched the water with her, keeping my silence and letting Valna choose the speed of the conversation. A chunk of ice out on the fjord cracked as it floated into a jutting rock.

"I don't want to swear to another king," she went on. "Who knows what they'll ask me to do? You heard Orin and how much he regretted being merely a game piece. I can't let that happen to me."

We watched the water. The shadows lengthened. I squinted at the sun as it sank into the sea. It was a subdued sunset, not an evening lit with blazing, glorious amber rays, but one that gently covered the world in shadow until darkness settled.

"I'm sailing west," she said.

I turned back to Valna. Her shadow-wreathed expression was now one of utter determination.

"Will the High King let you go?"

She shrugged. "What's he going to do if I never come back? He didn't want to go after Hraki, so why would he come after me?"

I thought back to the funeral pyre and the small fire pits that had burned away the last of my friends and the last of my enemies.

"He might send someone else."

"I can handle someone else."

Clumps of clouds swept across the sky and the stars began to make themselves known. There was a fresh tension in Valna's shoulders. Her fingertips were white as she gripped her knees and the sharp edges of her apprehension stabbed at me.

"I've not been sent to bring you in," I said.

The easing of her muscles was like pulling a knife free from my back. It eased the pain but some vital part of me bled away and more of me was lost to ice.

"I'm going to live by the Althing," I went on. "The High King wants someone to guard the mountain passages over winter."

She looked at me.

"No one else is going to survive up there over winter, are they?" I said with a crooked smile.

Valna nodded and watched as I pulled myself free of the frost that had stuck me to the boulder. It broke with a crackle.

"What's the High King going to do with Erling and Hraki's lands?" she asked.

"Katja says they're sending Runar to look at Hraki's town, but they're expecting it to be deserted. If it is, I think they'll just give all of it to Queen Vigdis. For now, though, Alvilda is going to stay here and run things with Katja and Fainn."

Valna let her legs stretch down along the boulder's slope. She leaned back on her elbows and shook her head.

"She doesn't need this. The High King should give it to King Olvid. He's only a few day's travel and I hear he's been struggling the past couple of years, having this place could really help him. If King Olvid's smart, he'll petition the High King for it."

"Maybe he will."

A sharp wind blew in over from the fjord. Without the light of the sun to keep her warm, Valna's breath came in misty plumes. She shivered and pulled her cloak around her.

I moved my hand over hers. She sucked in a breath at the cold touch but kept her hand in place.

"If you ever need a place to stay, find me," I said. "I was so far away from home, and almost lost, and you gave me a friend. You saved me. If you ever need someone to do the same you come to me."

She smiled, a sad smile, and looked down at our hands. She

shifted her position, put her other hand on top of mine and squeezed.

"Maybe one day, Edda. I'm still angry, still mourning. I'm not ready to let it go. I need to do something with it."

"I understand."

We stayed together, watching the silver shimmering fjord, until the cold forced Valna inside. We embraced for one last time. It was a tight, brief embrace as we tried to show our affection before the chill of my skin became too much for her. I watched her hurry away. I would not see her in the morning or perhaps ever again. I offered a silent prayer that the gods would keep her safe, but I did not expect them to listen to a Windborn.

I stayed for another hour to give Valna enough time to make her escape, then wandered back to the Windborn longhouse.

It was dark and empty.

I lit one of the braziers to give myself some light and went to my bed.

I looked into each room as I passed. The cloth walls that used to twitch and billow with the life of the people within, now only caught in the wind as I walked by it was as if they reached out to me, begging me to stay. Valna's room was empty. An overturned cup remained on the table, but all of Valna's clothes and weapons were gone. Runar's room was still full of his things. A half-eaten bowl of porridge lay next to his bed, staining the floor with wet oats.

I went to my own room. It looked empty and forgotten compared to the other rooms. What few clothes I had were strewn across the bed I had barely slept in and the furniture was too neatly packed away. It was a room for someone who was passing through, not for someone who belonged there.

Bjolfur's shield leaned against the table. I picked it up.

The round edges were, like the rest of the shield, beaten and bruised. One hundred dented markers for the times it had saved a life, or taken one. I touched the start of the carved saga, Bjolfur and I meeting for the first time, and followed its story with my fingers so I could feel every scratch and tear in the wood.

I heard the click of claws on floorboards and a sniff. The dog came into view and began snuffling around my room as though checking to see if it met his standards. It did and he moved over to the bed, circled in place, and then lay on top of my clothes. He looked up at me. The bright intensity in his eyes was burned out with the death of Gerda. Where they had once been filled with ferocity and certainty, now they were filled with isolation and sorrow.

I sighed and retrieved the half-eaten bowl of porridge from Runar's table.

"Are you hungry, Rollo?"

I sat next to him and offered him the bowl. A cautious sniff. He lifted his head and looked at me for approval before he lapped up the leftovers. I ruffled his ears with my free hand.

"It's lonely in here, isn't it?"

The dog kept slurping and his tail started wagging. It thumped into the wall as he repositioned himself to get to the last of the porridge. He looked up at me and this time his eyes were filled with hope, though I suspected it was hope for another meal.

"I'm not staying here." It felt good to say it aloud, even if he couldn't respond. "There's a place near the Althing. I'm going to start a farm. I don't know if anything will grow, or what I can keep, but I'll figure it out."

He cocked his ears and tipped his head to one side.

"You can come with me if you want to. Do you mind the cold?"

He licked my palm and I chuckled as the rough tongue tickled my skin. I ran my fingers through his long, ragged fur. I expected him to yelp or try and move away from the frost in my fingers, but he didn't. He rolled to one side to show me where to scratch. I smiled and obliged. A low, contented growl escaped him.

"You don't mind the cold, do you?" I gave a final pat to his belly and slumped down into bed. "We'll leave in the morning."

The dog huffed at me as I lay down and got myself comfortable. He sniffed at my face for a moment before moving up to me and falling asleep.

*

Runar swept me up in a bone-creaking hug when he found out I was leaving, promising to come and visit me. Fainn gave me food for the journey plus a little more to be safe, and Katja gave me one of her favourite cloaks. I tried to protest, to tell her I didn't need it, but she waved me away. I swore an oath to the High King, which was as brusque as the man himself, and he gave me a curt goodbye that was mostly instruction. Throughout all this Rollo, Gerda's dog, trotted along beside me. He sniffed at the food Fainn gave me and shot me a hurt look when I wouldn't give him any. Once I was ready, and I had given the dog more treats than I should have, we made our way to the jetty.

Mimir's boat, that had carried us to Hraki and back, was gone. I suspected that if I found that boat, I would find Valna.

I soon found someone willing to carry Rollo and I across the fjord and as we loaded the boat a shadow fell over me. I turned to see a red-haired woman with a green cloak.

"He's going with you?" Katja asked and nodded to the dog. Despite her furs and cloak, she rubbed her hands together to warm them up.

"Seems like it," I said. "It'll do us both good to have a fresh start."

Katja nodded. She smiled at the dog but it was strained.

"Edda, I need to... Do you know where Valna's gone?"

I faltered as I handed a bag to the boatman. Katja kept her head down when I turned to look at her but met my gaze nonetheless.

"Who's asking? Her friend or her law-keeper?"

"Does it matter, Edda? If you know where she is then I—"

"I don't know where she is."

I grabbed the last bag by my feet and threw it into the boat. It rocked with the impact and my guide stumbled as he made his way to the moorings. The dog sniffed at Katja's feet then bent down and reached out a paw as though trying to pull the edge of the boat close and clamber in. Katja's neutral expression cracked and tears shone in her eyes.

"I don't know where she is," I said, gently this time. "I saw her last night, but she wasn't in the longhouse when I went to sleep, and she wasn't there this morning. None of her things are there. Wherever she's gone... I don't think she's coming back."

Katja chewed her lip and looked around. The only other people on the jetty were townsfolk moving supplies to and from the town to the king's island. There were no huskalar to overhear us.

"Edda," Katja whispered and leaned in close. "If she told you where she was going, would you tell me?"

Her voice was scraped raw from holding back sobs. I pulled her close to me and embraced her. She leaned into me and let out a shuddering breath that misted in the cold around me.

"She didn't tell me, Katja."

I scooped up the dog under one arm and clambered awkwardly into the boat. It rocked from side to side, but this time our guide steadied himself against the jetty. The dog let out a huff and squirmed out of my grip.

"I need to go, Katja." I turned and offered her a sad smile. "I've got a long way to travel."

She nodded, gave a small wave and I returned it.

I pushed the boat away from the jetty and the water hissed as we carved a path through it. As we slowed, the boat-owner looked at me and gestured to the seat in the middle of the boat.

"Well, you going to put that Windborn strength to use or are you going to watch an old man break himself carrying you across the water?"

I grunted and set myself to the oars. Katja watched us from the jetty. White mist plumed from her mouth and she crossed her arms over her stomach. After a moment, she was a green smudge in my vision, but two figures with shields and spears appeared beside her. Huskalar. I watched the law-keeper for another moment then turned my attention to steering through the ice-clogged fjord.

When we reached the shore I helped the boatman load his wares onto a cart. The dog jumped out as soon as the hull scraped land and started sniffing around the mud and sand.

"Thank you," I said. I started to say more, but he had already waved away my words and moved off with his cart.

I shrugged, whistled for the dog, and began my journey south. Bjolfur's shield bounced against my back, his axe tugged at my belt and I took comfort that I still carried a piece of him with me. The dog ran around me, never straying far but keen to smell everything around us. He disappeared in the thin forest that encroached the road and barked at some hidden creature in the trees above him.

Soon, we came to a sharp bend that carried the road around the edge of the mountains. I paused and looked back at Eylheim before the jutting rocks hid it from sight. Hatred had dragged me to that town, and it had almost killed me a second time.

Rollo barked at something hiding in a bush. He shoved his nose through the leaves, then yelped as thorns caught his muzzle. He shook his head then looked to me. I smiled and picked out a treat from my pouch.

"Come on," I said and ushered him on, eager to go before the way was lost to ice. "Let's go home."

EPILOGUE

AUDEN HAD BEEN TRAVELLING THROUGH THE WILDERNESS for several days, but he didn't mind. The summer had just begun so the midges were few and the weather was cool enough to warrant his cloak, but not so cold that he needed furs. He felt like a dashing explorer traipsing through forest and over fjords with nothing but his own wits to guide him. As he climbed up into the low valleys south of Konvald, he found a muddy path leading up into the mountains that, if you followed it far enough, would take you to the valley of Fafstol's Scar where they held the Althing. He smiled, pleased that his explorer instincts had steered him true, and followed the upward path.

There were stories of a woman who lived high in the mountains all year long with hair the colour of fresh snow and a temperament as sharp as shattered ice. Some said she was in exile for her part in the winter war rumoured to have taken place decades ago, whilst others simply muttered that using a Windborn to guard goats and rocks was a waste. Had she been part of a winter war or was she another broken warrior waiting to die? All the skalds that had travelled to find the truth of the tale had been put off by the weather or, as was usually the case, by the Windborn's demeanour. Auden would not be deterred. He was determined to be the first skald to discover the truth, and if he got a good tale to tell in mead-halls across the land, then all the better.

Rocks crunched beneath his feet, then they splintered. Auden looked down to find frost glittering over the path. He frowned. Summer snows were known, but much further north, and only in valleys cradled between mountains so high the sun's warmth was but a rumour. The frost beneath his feet glittered in the sun, winding across the stone and up the mountain like a shining trail.

His smirk became a toothy grin and he pressed on.

As he climbed, the forest was replaced by crooked, moss-covered rocks. The winds became fierce with cold and he had to pull his cloak tight about him. After an hour's trudging, Auden paused to get his breath back. The mountain still loomed above him. Its broken peak cut into the bright blue sky like a split spear stabbing at the gods.

Auden puffed out his cheeks. He rallied himself to continue up the rubble-strewn slopes when a bark echoed above him. A dog came trotting down the track. It stopped twenty or so paces away from him and barked again.

"Hello there, boy," Auden said. He reached out one hand in front of him and with the other pulled a strip of dried meat from his bag. "I'm not here to hurt anyone. Do you want a treat?"

The dog barked again and came forward slowly. It sniffed at Auden's hand, then at the dried meat. Auden turned his hand to let the meat lie on his palm and the dog licked it up.

"Are you going to be a good dog and show me where she is?"

The dog sniffed, trying to decide if Auden had any more treats, and then scrambled back up the path.

"I'll take that as a yes."

He followed the dog, moving quickly to keep his new friend in his sights and was soon panting and sweating again.

The rocks on either side of the path grew thicker, larger. Stones turned to boulders, and boulders to cliff faces. For a little while, the warmth of the world was lost as he walked through a broken shelf of rock, but soon the passage widened and cleared. The stone covered ground gave way to mud, scored with deep lines as though a monster had clawed their way free of a rocky prison. Auden shivered, hesitating for a heartbeat before he followed the dog around the corner.

The path opened onto a clearing that looked out over the fjords and forests, reduced to broad strokes of colour below him. To his right, nestled against the hard edge of the mountain, was a house like any other. Its steep roof, which had dark moss and grass growing on it, extended to the ground. There were tools stacked against the front of the house, though a mud-caked shovel and pick-axe lay on the ground, and there was a fenced vegetable patch to one side. Auden moved up to the edge of the yard and peered through the open door, which had an old battered shield hanging above it, to see a figure moving about inside.

"Hello," he called out.

Chickens scurried out of the way of the dog as it barrelled past them and into the house. The figure inside went still, disappeared, then came out clutching a knife. Her hair, tied back though some strands fell loose over her face, was the colour of steel and snow. She was lean, the kind of muscle that was won through years of hard labour, and moved with the surety of an old warrior. Auden was surprised she did not bother to put on a cloak as she came into the cold mountain air. Frost glittered out from her feet with each step like ripples in water.

Auden put his hands up and grinned.

"Apologies, I didn't mean to startle you. I'm looking for Edda Gretasdottir, Windborn of the High Queen. Do you know where I can find her?"

The woman's spear-sharp gaze narrowed. She kept the knife between them and took a few steps forward. The blade glinted in the dim light as did her arms. Somehow her scars caught the sunlight like the surface of the sea.

"Why are you looking for her?"

Auden grinned again and bowed.

"I am Auden Leifson, a skald, and I have come to hear her tale."

"Why?"

His smile faltered. The laws demanded that travellers not be harmed as there was no telling when a stranger wandering through a town might be a god in disguise, but this was the worst reception he had ever received.

"Well... Her tale is only told when it crosses paths with another, even though it took much to impress the old High King. I would wager that hers must be a story worth telling and

I would hear it from her own lips so I may spread her story and let her be the hero she deserves."

Flattery opened doors that suspicion often closed and he waited for it to work its magic.

The woman came forward again, the knife still pointing at Auden. He matched her movements with backward steps of his own. Frost glittered on the blade.

"Do I look like I want to relive these scars?" the woman, Edda Gretasdottir, said and waved her arm. The scars along her forearm glittered in the pale sunlight.

She looked at him with glacier coloured eyes. Auden kept his gaze locked on the tip of the knife, ready to dive out of the way if she came at him. Both of them jumped when the dog barked. It came out of the house and sniffed at Auden. It barked again and sat down in front of him and tilted its head expectantly.

The knife tip lowered. Auden reached into his bag and gave the dog another strip of meat.

"How far have you come, skald?"

The question caught Auden off guard and he had to think about it.

"I'm originally from the Lovouy islands. But I have come to you from the halls of Queen Sigrid, whom I left two weeks past."

"You've been hunting me for a while, then?"

Auden spread his hands as if offering an apology. "Stories are my lifeblood and fresh tales are like honey to me. Yours is a tale no one has heard, and I suspect it's well worth the time."

"If I throw you out on your arse and kick you down the mountain? What then?"

Auden swallowed. The knife glinted in Edda's hands and he prayed that the gods would help him choose the right words.

"I would respect your wishes, Edda Gretasdottir, but I would most likely return once the bruises on my arse healed and the memory of the pain was distant."

The Windborn narrowed her eyes, weighing Auden in her mind. "You would, wouldn't you? Most would take the hint."

"I can be painfully slow on the uptake," Auden said and offered her a crooked smile.

Edda huffed and the tension in her shoulders eased.

"I'll tell you." She whistled and the dog came bounding back to her. "Come on, Frida. Good girl." She ruffled its ears and put her knife in her belt. "Lucky for you, skald, the jobs are done for the day."

"Thank you, Edda, it is most generous of you—"

"Come on, let's get this over with."

She led him into the house. Auden glanced up at the shield above the door as he passed it and noticed that its bottom was covered in icicles as though it felt winter's touch every time someone entered the house.

The cabin had a single room with a hearth in the centre, and, compared to most other houses, it looked barren, with only a table, two chairs, and a bed. A single lantern set on a table illuminated the inside of the house in blocky shadows. Where the furniture was dusty, austere, Auden noticed a well-kept axe and sword leaning against the wall opposite. He swallowed as Edda gestured for him to sit down.

"Shall we—"

Edda stomped off to a dark corner and pulled something out from under a pile of clothes and ornaments. They tumbled to the floor and Edda dragged a sloshing barrel over to the table. She dipped two wooden cups into it before passing one to Auden. He took it, thanking her as he did so, and was surprised to find the cup cold to the touch. He tipped it to look inside and saw shards of ice swirling in the beer.

She looked at him with those glacial eyes and Auden felt the weight of a Windborn's attention. For the first time, he realised how far he had come, how far away help would be, and how quickly Edda could reach her weapons.

"Where do you want to start?" Auden asked, his voice strained and barely above a whisper.

Edda leaned back and stared at the axe then looked to the shield above her door.

After a moment she nodded and took a long draught to wet her throat.

"The longship was too small."

Author's Note

Thank you so much for reading Windborn.

I hope you liked it and that you'll consider leaving a review.

If you'd like to be the first to find out about my future books and get occasional freebies then please subscribe to my newsletter by heading over to my website.

You can also find out more about me and what else I'm up to.

www.alexsbradshaw.com

ACKNOWLEDGEMENTS

No book is ever finished alone and Windborn is no exception.

It's been a long road, but we've gotten to the end of it and there's a whole raft of people I am incalculably grateful to for helping me finish this book.

Firstly, I'd like to thank Rachel, who has kept me going through my ups and downs over the years and supported me as I've run off to dig the right words out of the word mines.

Thanks also to my parents and family who have always encouraged me to follow my passions, beginning with endlessly talking about dinosaurs as a child and now resulting in a whole book.

Thank you to Timy and Benedict for beta reading Windborn and their excellent advice that helped to forge this book into a stronger story. And thank you also for being supportive friends. Thanks also to Matt (both my brother and Matt Duke) for your early readings and catching the errors I'd missed.

I am also grateful for the groups Writer's Refuge and the British Irish Writing Community which are both filled with excellent people who can provide motivation, answers, or whatever else you might need on the writing journey.

I must also thank my editor: the incomparable Sarah Chorn. Sarah's an inspiration and if you haven't already looked at her books go check them out. She's done an absolutely wonderful job squeezing every last bit out of this story and fixing the errors in the text. If there are mistakes left over then they're mine alone.

And to Raph and Shawn: thank you for making the phenomenal cover. I am absolutley overjoyed with how it's turned out! You have been extremely, unendingly patient with me as I have asked for tweaks and your hard work has really brought Edda to life and given Windborn a truly epic look.

And finally, of course, my thanks to you the reader. Thanks for joining me on this journey.

CREDITS

Beta Readers: Timy Takas
                           Benedict Patrick
                           Rachel Sheldon
                           Matt Duke
                           Matthew Bradshaw

Editor: Sarah Chorn
                           www.sarahchornedits.com

Cover Artist: Raph Herrera Lomotan
                           www.artstation.com/raphlomotan

Cover Designer: STK Kreations
                           www.stkkreations.com